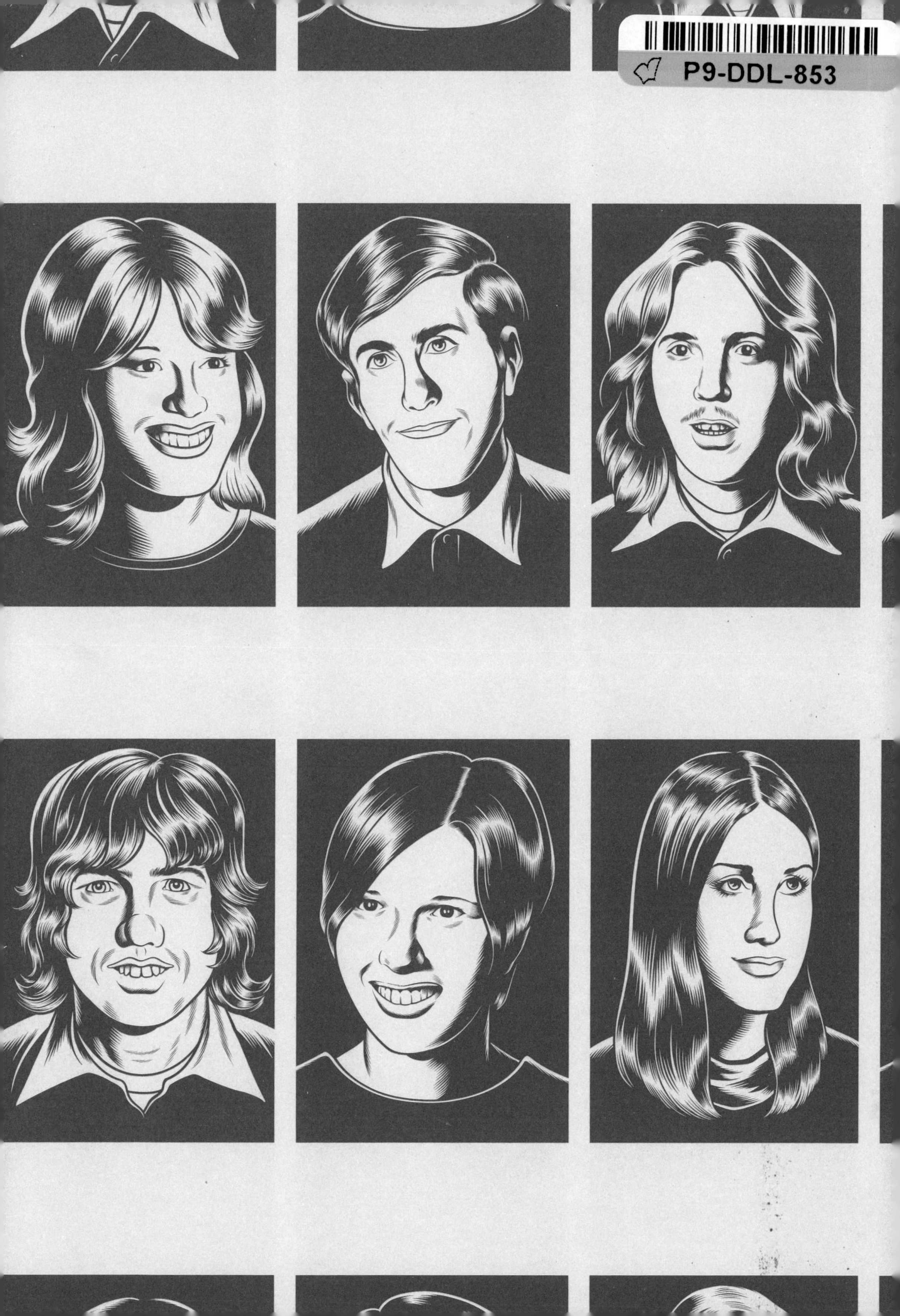

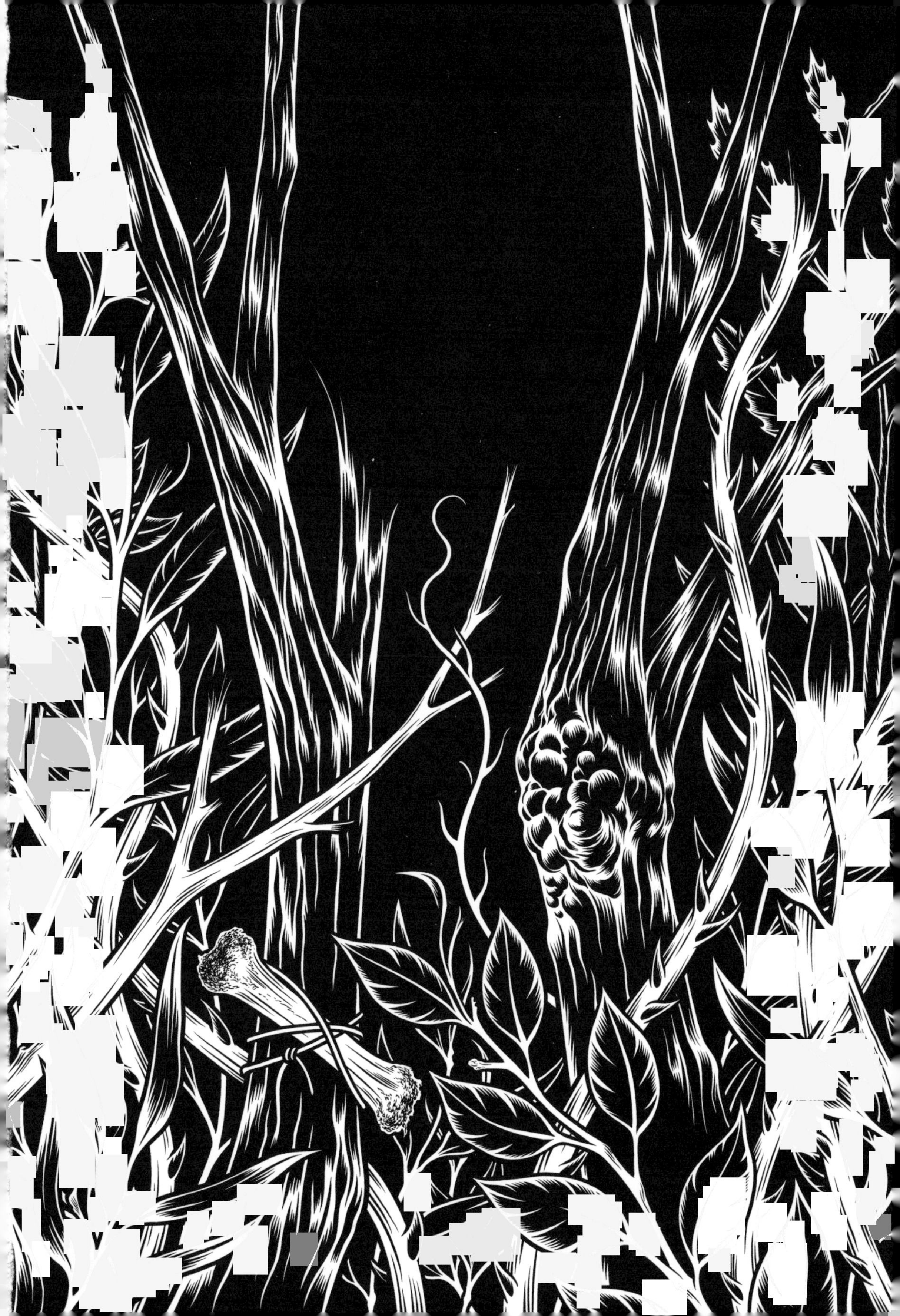

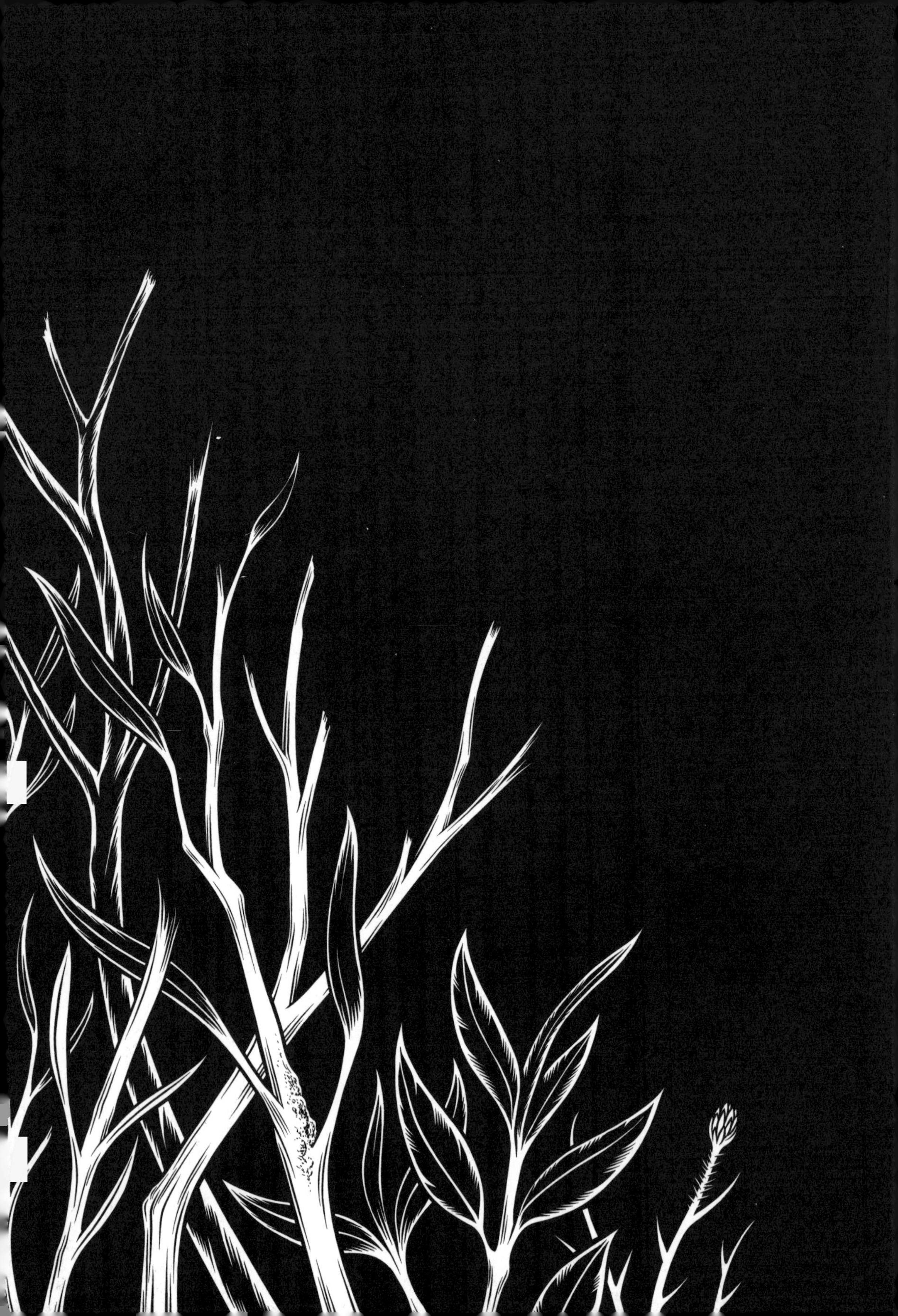

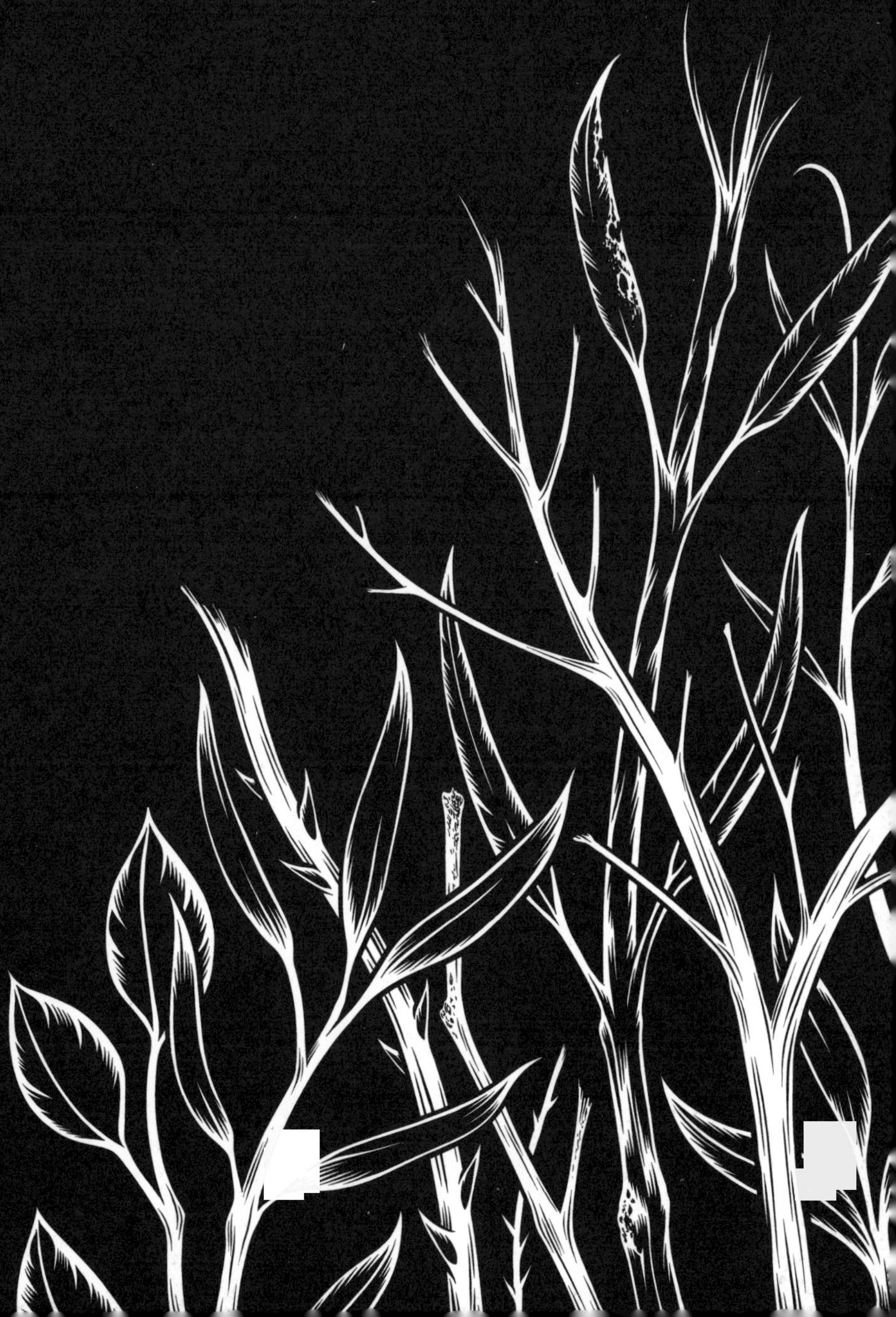

BLACK HOLE

CHARLES BURNS

THIS BOOK IS DEDICATED TO DEAN, MARK, J., PHIL, CASEY, COLLEEN, VICKIE, MIKE, PATTY, JANET, PENNY, LISA, JERI, JOHN, KAREN, KATHY, RETA, CLAUDIA, TED, TERRI, DOUG, PAUL, JAN, TOM, SCOTT, KURT, ANN, KIM, DIANE, SALLY, KATHLEEN, MARI, LIBBY, JON, JIM, PAT AND PETE. I NEVER FORGOT YOU.

THANKS TO JOHN KURAMOTO FOR HIS TECHNICAL ASSISTANCE AND TO SUSAN MOORE WHO LETTERED THIS ENTIRE BOOK.

 PUBLISHED IN THE UNITED STATES BY PANTHEON BOOKS, A DIVISION OF RANDOM HOUSE, INC., NEW YORK, AND IN CANADA BY RANDOM HOUSE OF CANADA LIMITED, TORONTO.

THIS WORK WAS ORIGINALLY PUBLISHED AS 12 SEPARATE COMIC BOOKS BY FANTAGRAPHICS BOOKS, SEATTLE, FROM 1995-2004.

PANTHEON AND COLOPHON ARE REGISTERED TRADEMARKS OF RANDOM HOUSE, INC.

LIBRARY OF CONGRESS CATALOGING-IN-PUBLICATION DATA
BURNS, CHARLES
BLACK HOLE / CHARLES BURNS.
P. CM.
ISBN 0-375-42380-X
I. GRAPHIC NOVEL. I. TITLE.
PN6727. B87B53 2005 641.5'973--DC22
2005046431

WWW.PANTHEONBOOKS.COM
PRINTED IN SINGAPORE
FIRST EDITION
9 8 7 6 5 4 3 2 1

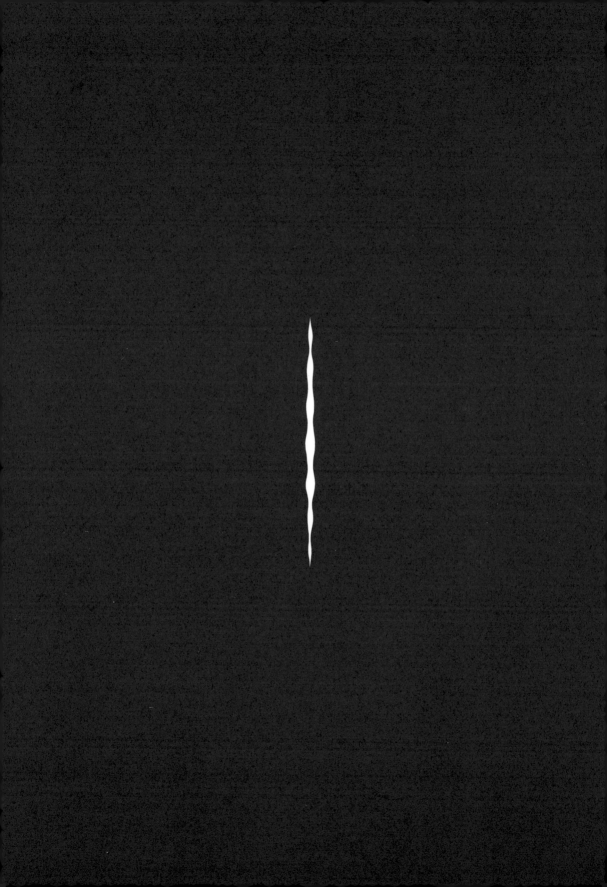

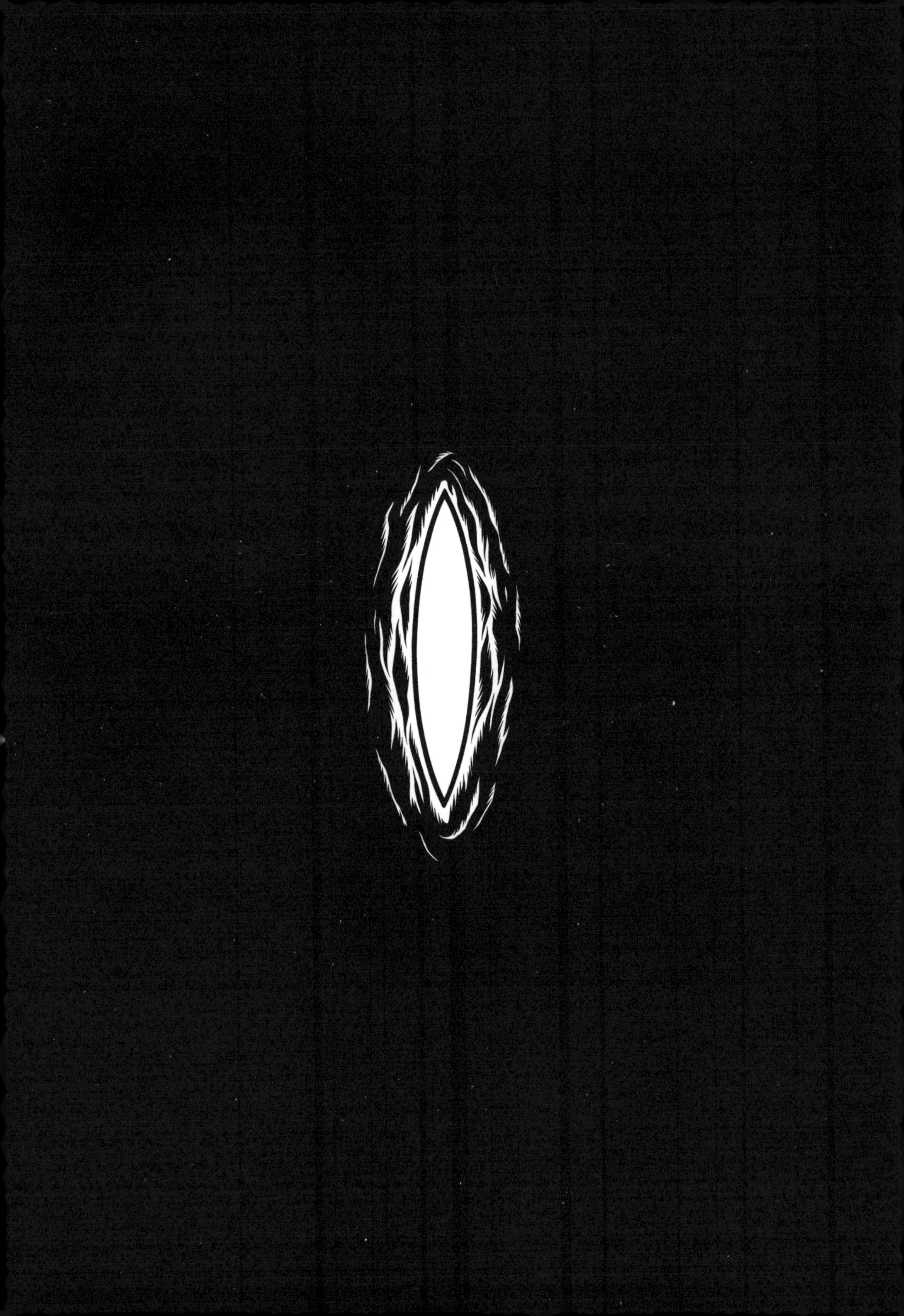

BIOLOGY 101

parts a⬚
breathi⬚
live on ⬚
lay egg⬚
North ⬚
or in m⬚
  Frog⬚
illustr⬚
Frogs ⬚
nam ⬚
latter⬚
Texas⬚
are t⬚
of e⬚
131⬚
ing,⬚
Fro⬚
ilie⬚
⬚
int⬚
St⬚
an⬚
Th⬚
o⬚

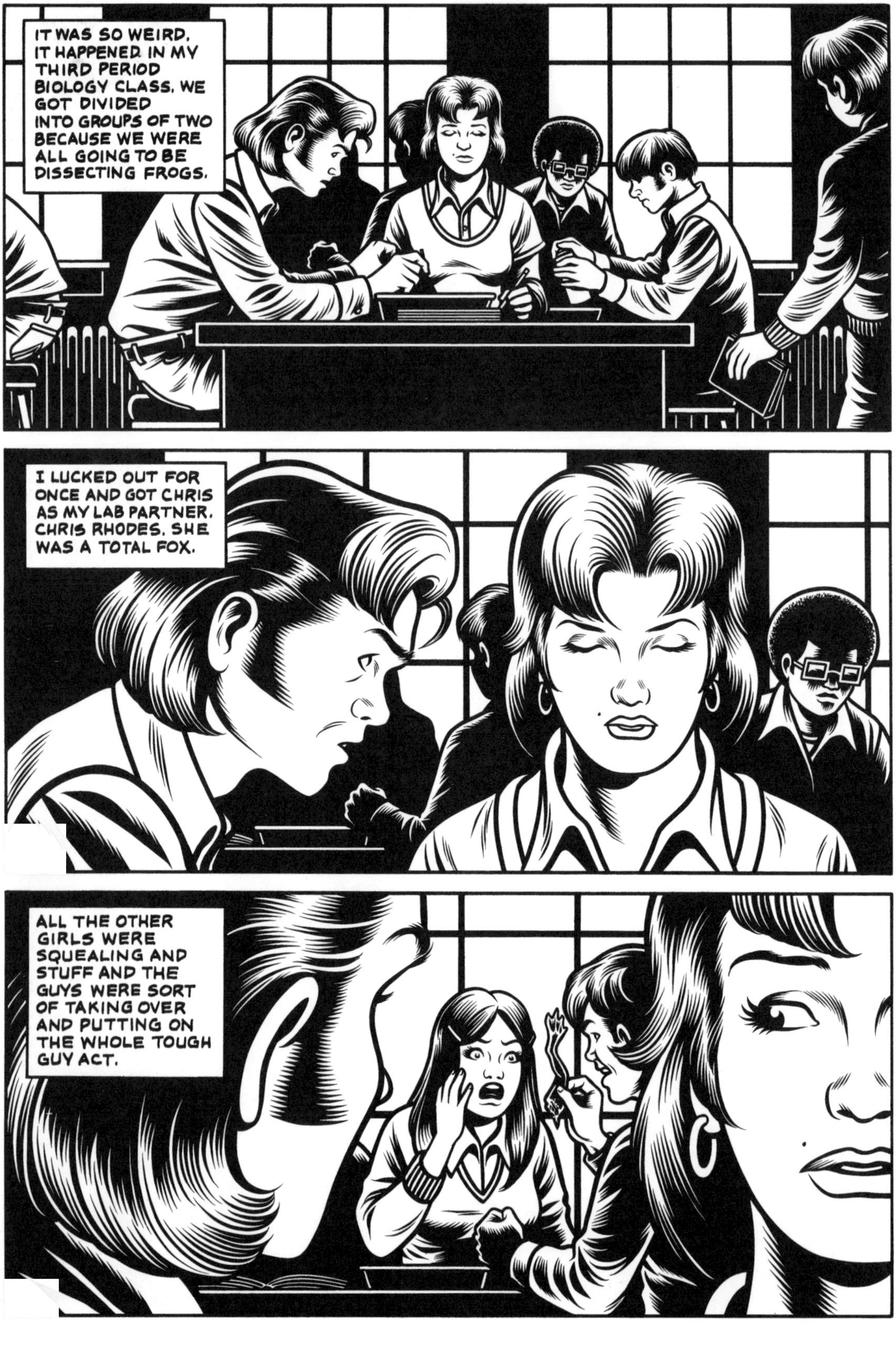
IT WAS SO WEIRD. IT HAPPENED IN MY THIRD PERIOD BIOLOGY CLASS. WE GOT DIVIDED INTO GROUPS OF TWO BECAUSE WE WERE ALL GOING TO BE DISSECTING FROGS.
I LUCKED OUT FOR ONCE AND GOT CHRIS AS MY LAB PARTNER. CHRIS RHODES. SHE WAS A TOTAL FOX.
ALL THE OTHER GIRLS WERE SQUEALING AND STUFF AND THE GUYS WERE SORT OF TAKING OVER AND PUTTING ON THE WHOLE TOUGH GUY ACT.

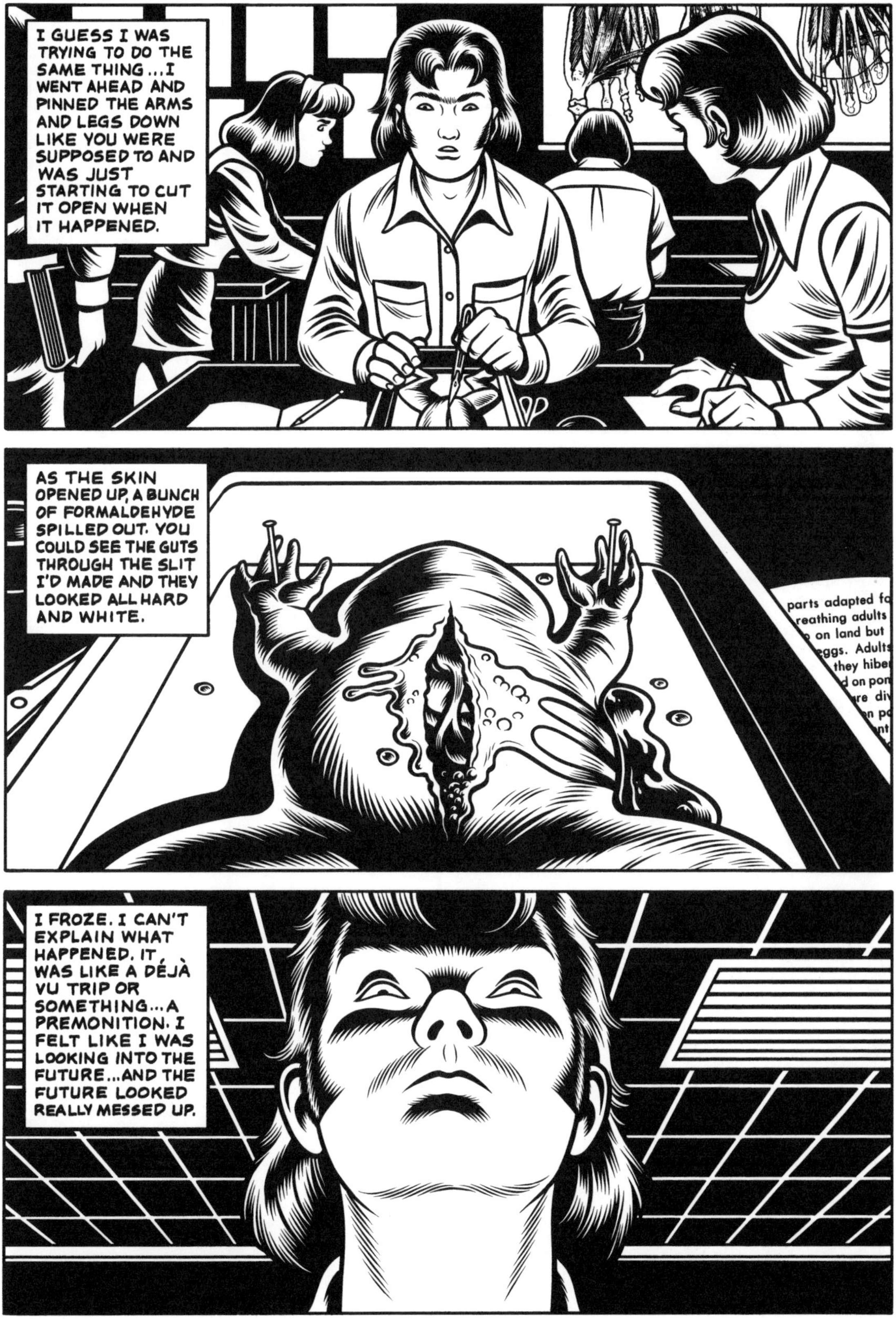
I GUESS I WAS TRYING TO DO THE SAME THING...I WENT AHEAD AND PINNED THE ARMS AND LEGS DOWN LIKE YOU WERE SUPPOSED TO AND WAS JUST STARTING TO CUT IT OPEN WHEN IT HAPPENED.
AS THE SKIN OPENED UP, A BUNCH OF FORMALDEHYDE SPILLED OUT. YOU COULD SEE THE GUTS THROUGH THE SLIT I'D MADE AND THEY LOOKED ALL HARD AND WHITE.
I FROZE. I CAN'T EXPLAIN WHAT HAPPENED. IT WAS LIKE A DÉJÀ VU TRIP OR SOMETHING...A PREMONITION. I FELT LIKE I WAS LOOKING INTO THE FUTURE...AND THE FUTURE LOOKED REALLY MESSED UP.

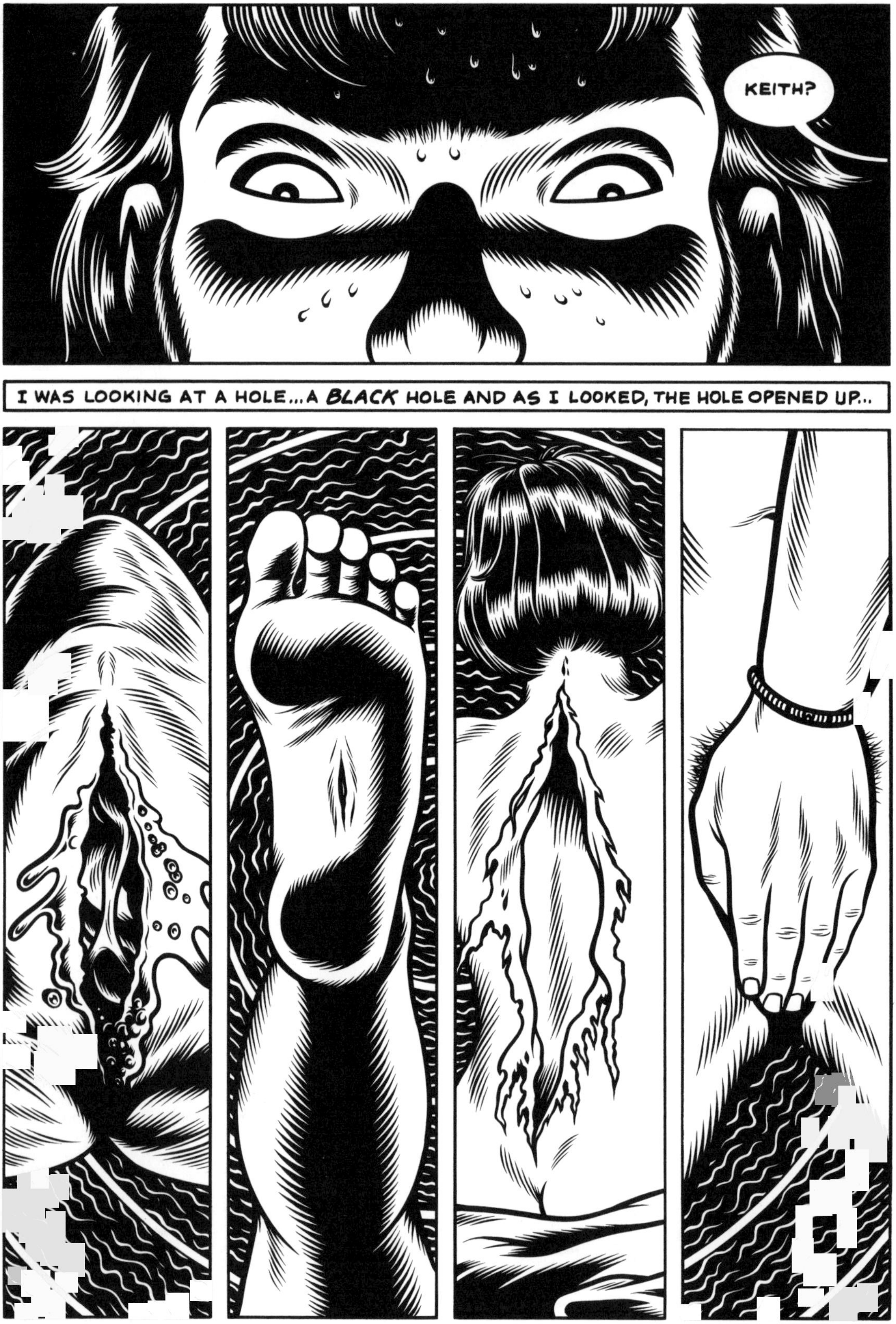
KEITH?
I WAS LOOKING AT A HOLE... A BLACK HOLE AND AS I LOOKED, THE HOLE OPENED UP...

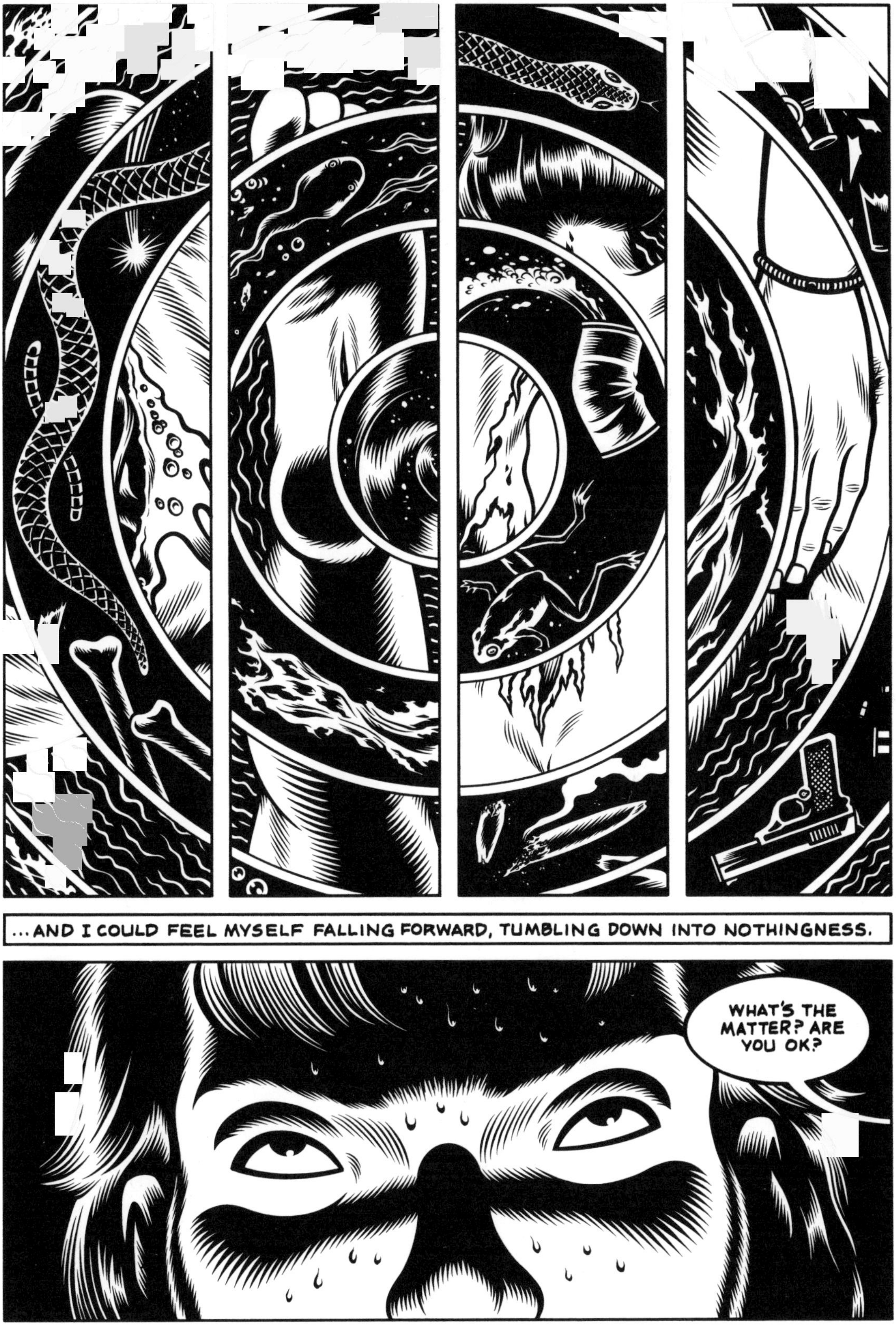
...AND I COULD FEEL MYSELF FALLING FORWARD, TUMBLING DOWN INTO NOTHINGNESS.
WHAT'S THE MATTER? ARE YOU OK?

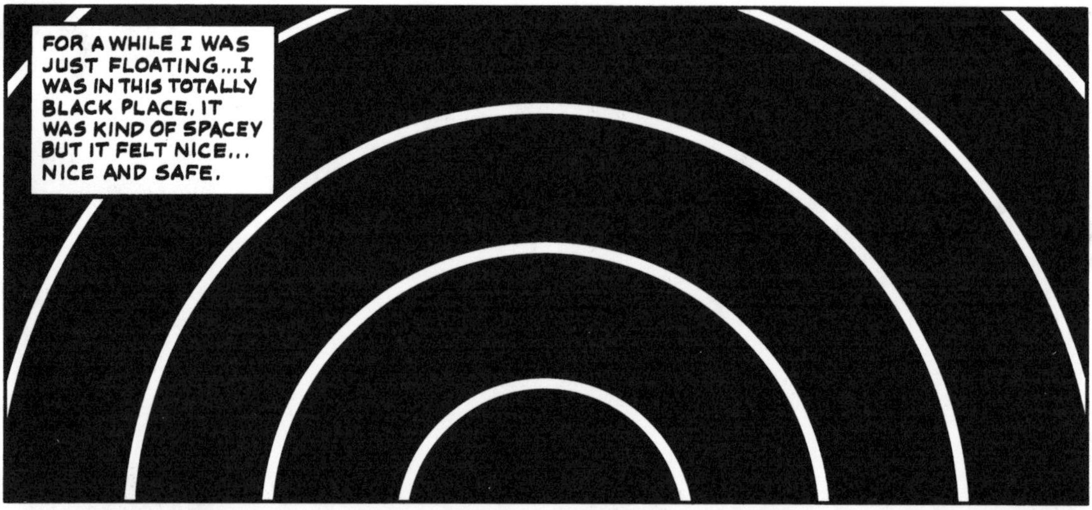
FOR A WHILE I WAS JUST FLOATING...I WAS IN THIS TOTALLY BLACK PLACE, IT WAS KIND OF SPACEY BUT IT FELT NICE... NICE AND SAFE.

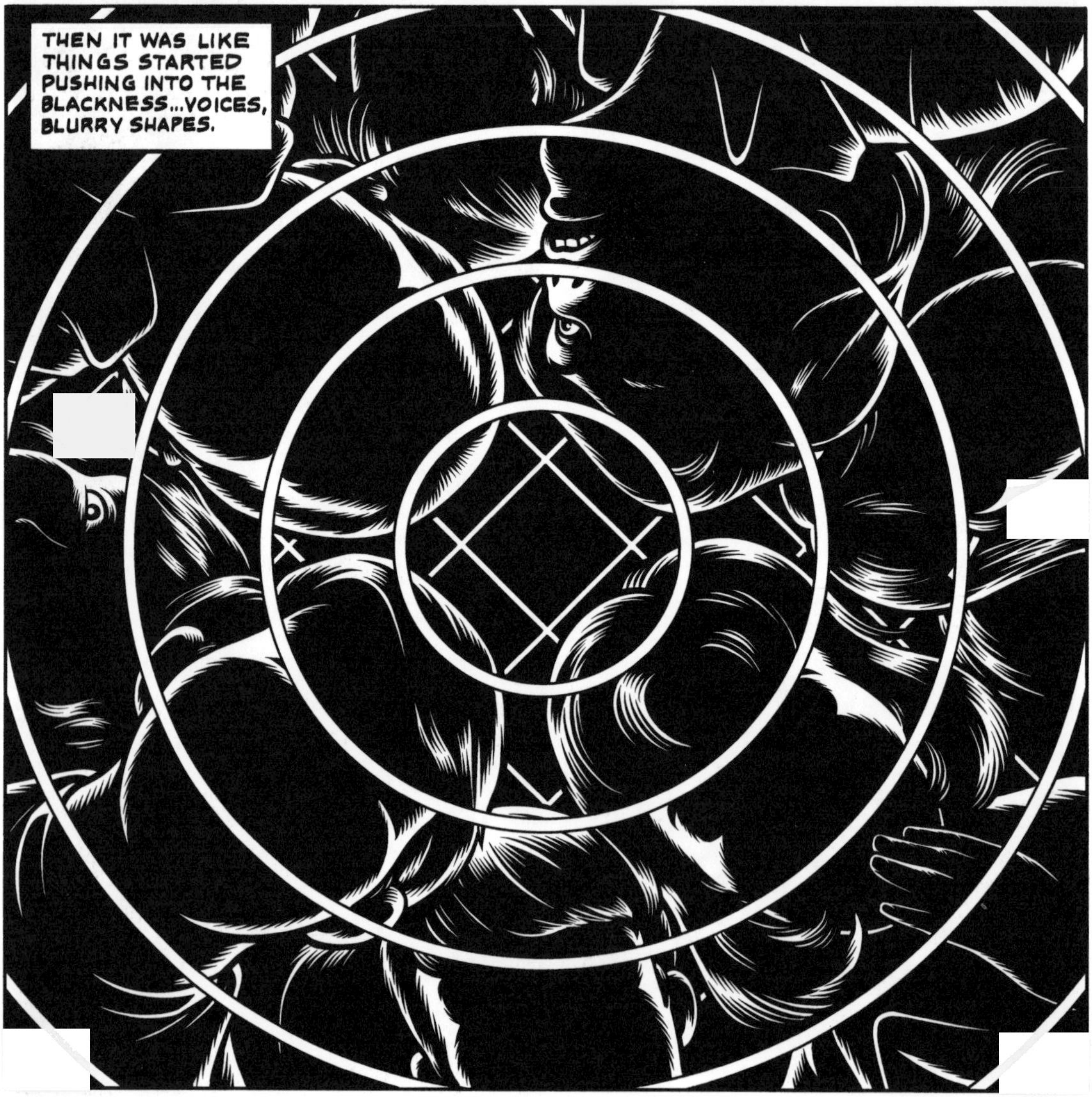
THEN IT WAS LIKE THINGS STARTED PUSHING INTO THE BLACKNESS...VOICES, BLURRY SHAPES.

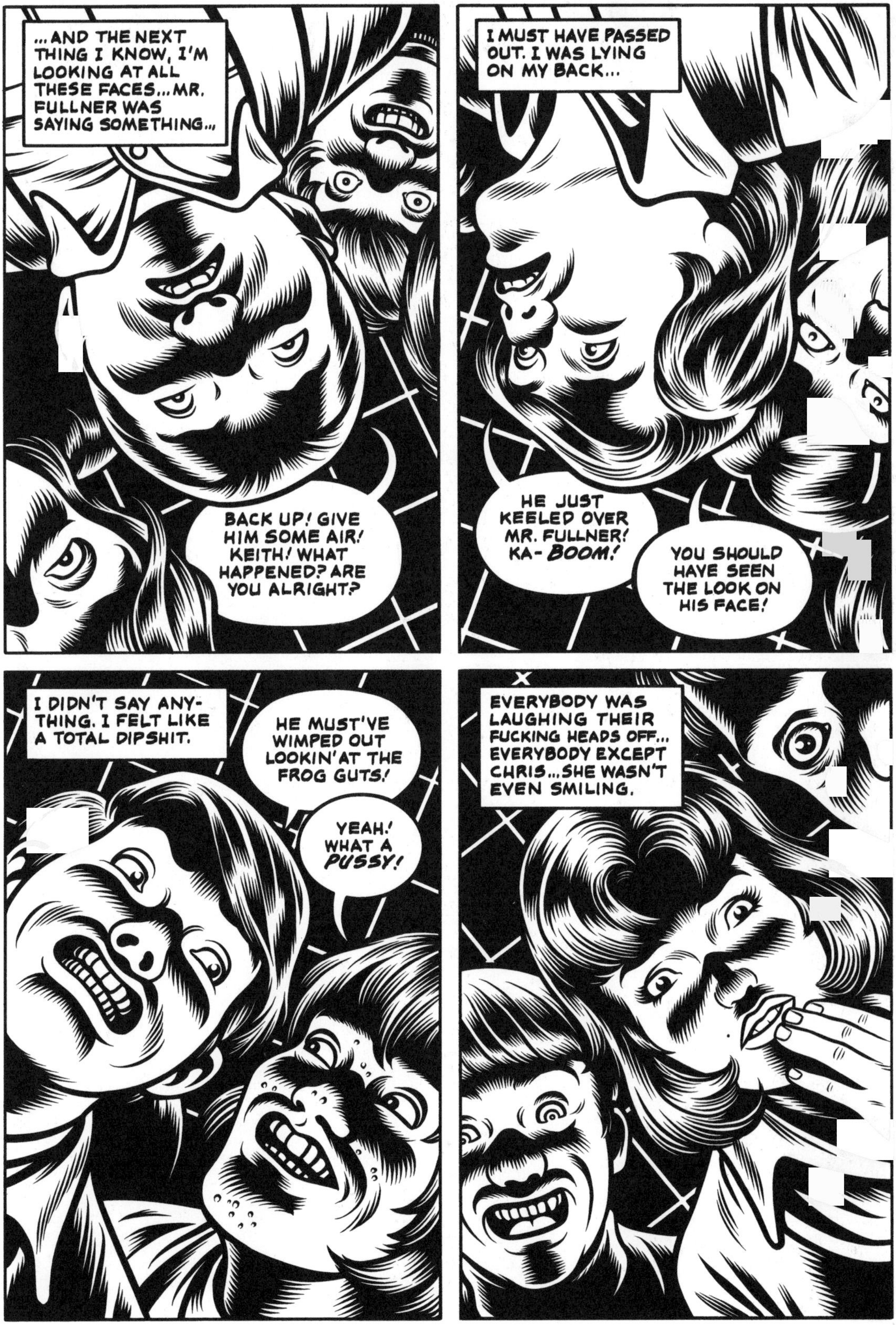
...AND THE NEXT THING I KNOW, I'M LOOKING AT ALL THESE FACES...MR. FULLNER WAS SAYING SOMETHING...
BACK UP! GIVE HIM SOME AIR! KEITH! WHAT HAPPENED? ARE YOU ALRIGHT?
I MUST HAVE PASSED OUT. I WAS LYING ON MY BACK...
HE JUST KEELED OVER MR. FULLNER! KA-BOOM!
YOU SHOULD HAVE SEEN THE LOOK ON HIS FACE!
I DIDN'T SAY ANYTHING. I FELT LIKE A TOTAL DIPSHIT.
HE MUST'VE WIMPED OUT LOOKIN' AT THE FROG GUTS!
YEAH! WHAT A PUSSY!
EVERYBODY WAS LAUGHING THEIR FUCKING HEADS OFF... EVERYBODY EXCEPT CHRIS...SHE WASN'T EVEN SMILING.

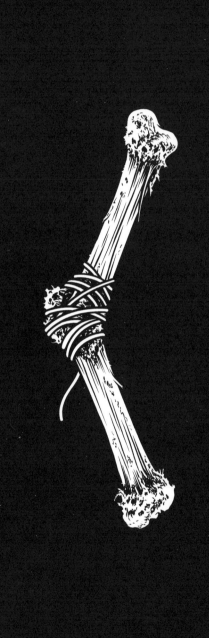

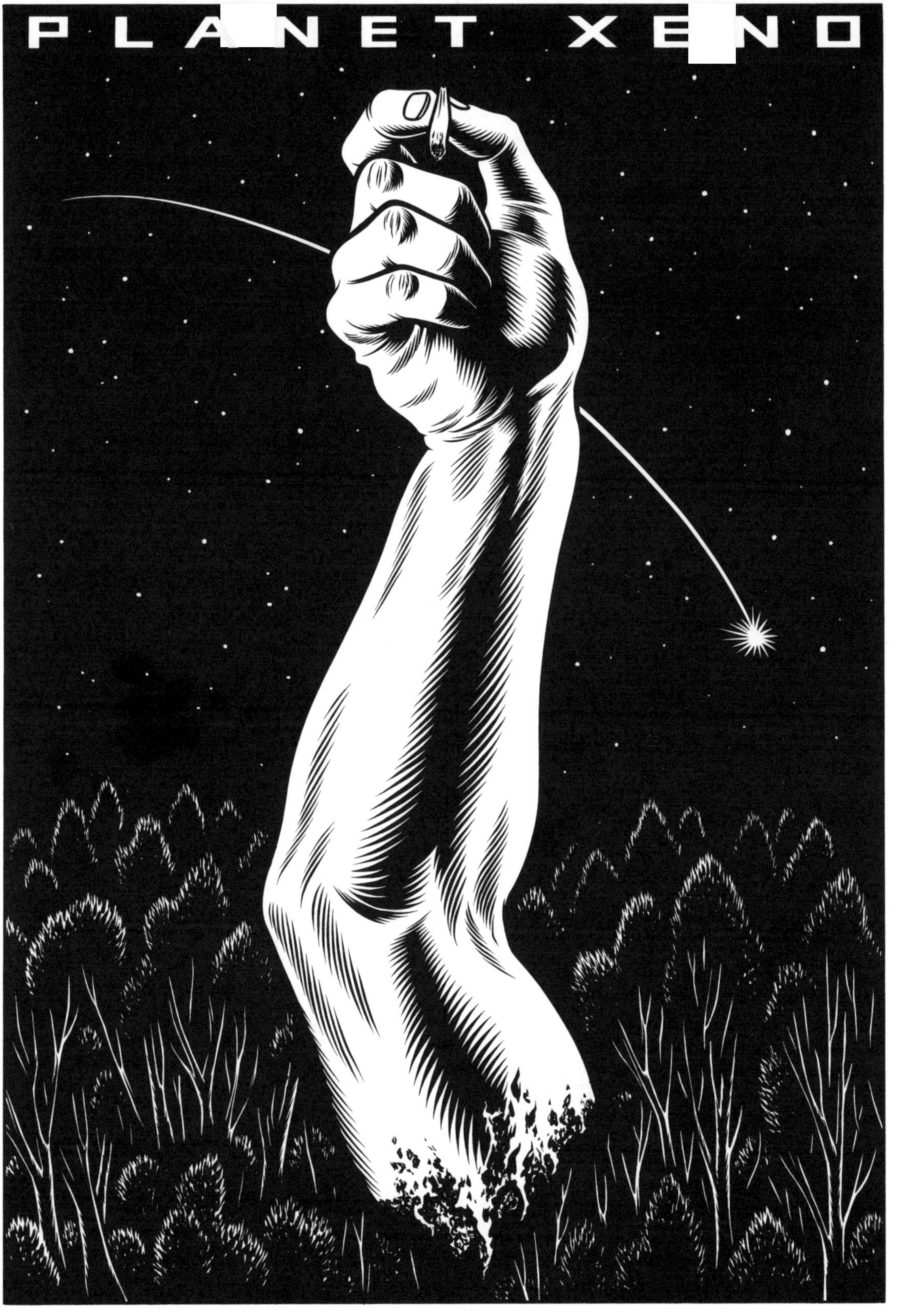
PLANET XENO

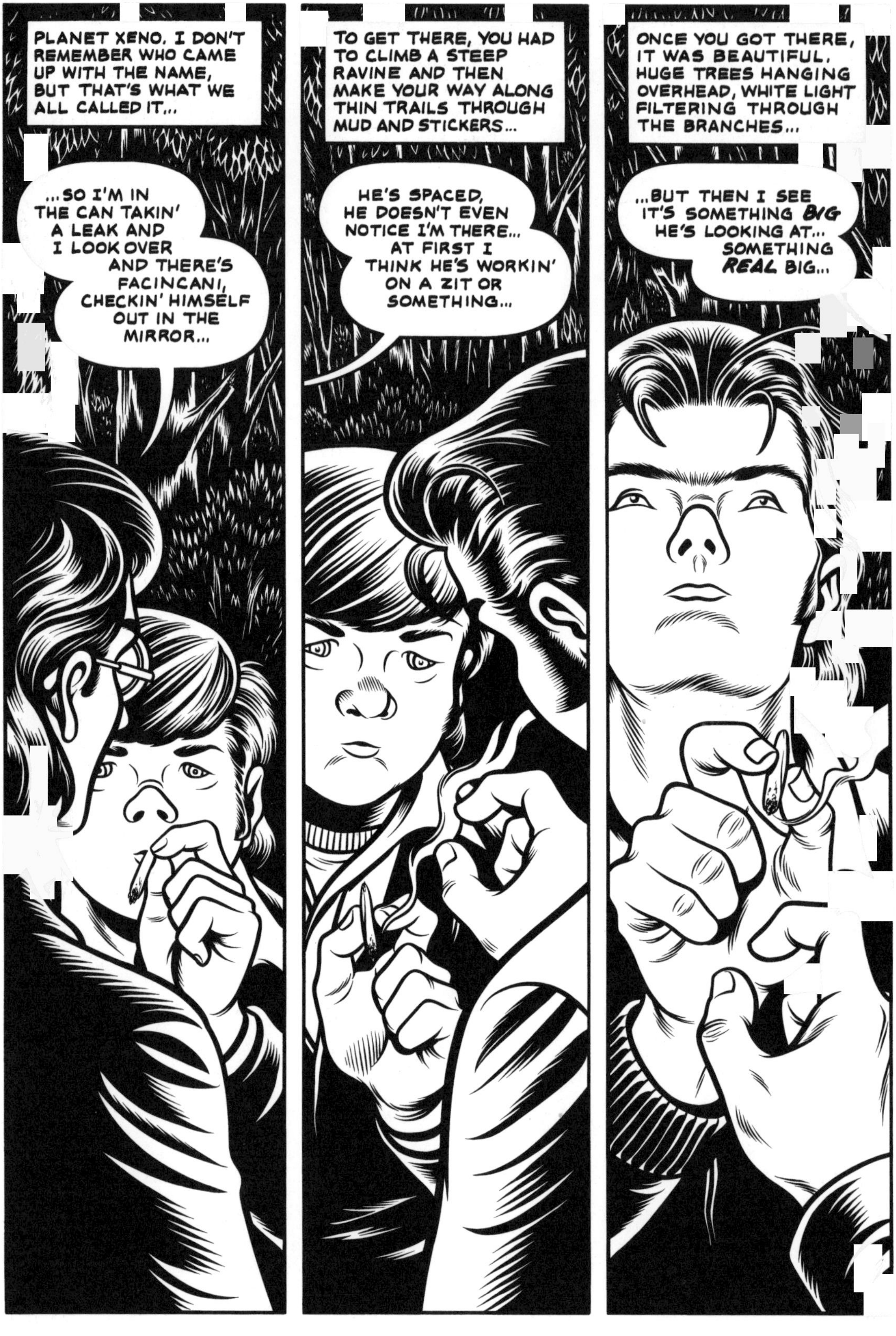
PLANET XENO. I DON'T REMEMBER WHO CAME UP WITH THE NAME, BUT THAT'S WHAT WE ALL CALLED IT...
...SO I'M IN THE CAN TAKIN' A LEAK AND I LOOK OVER AND THERE'S FACINCANI, CHECKIN' HIMSELF OUT IN THE MIRROR...
TO GET THERE, YOU HAD TO CLIMB A STEEP RAVINE AND THEN MAKE YOUR WAY ALONG THIN TRAILS THROUGH MUD AND STICKERS...
HE'S SPACED, HE DOESN'T EVEN NOTICE I'M THERE... AT FIRST I THINK HE'S WORKIN' ON A ZIT OR SOMETHING...
ONCE YOU GOT THERE, IT WAS BEAUTIFUL, HUGE TREES HANGING OVERHEAD, WHITE LIGHT FILTERING THROUGH THE BRANCHES...
...BUT THEN I SEE IT'S SOMETHING BIG HE'S LOOKING AT... SOMETHING REAL BIG...

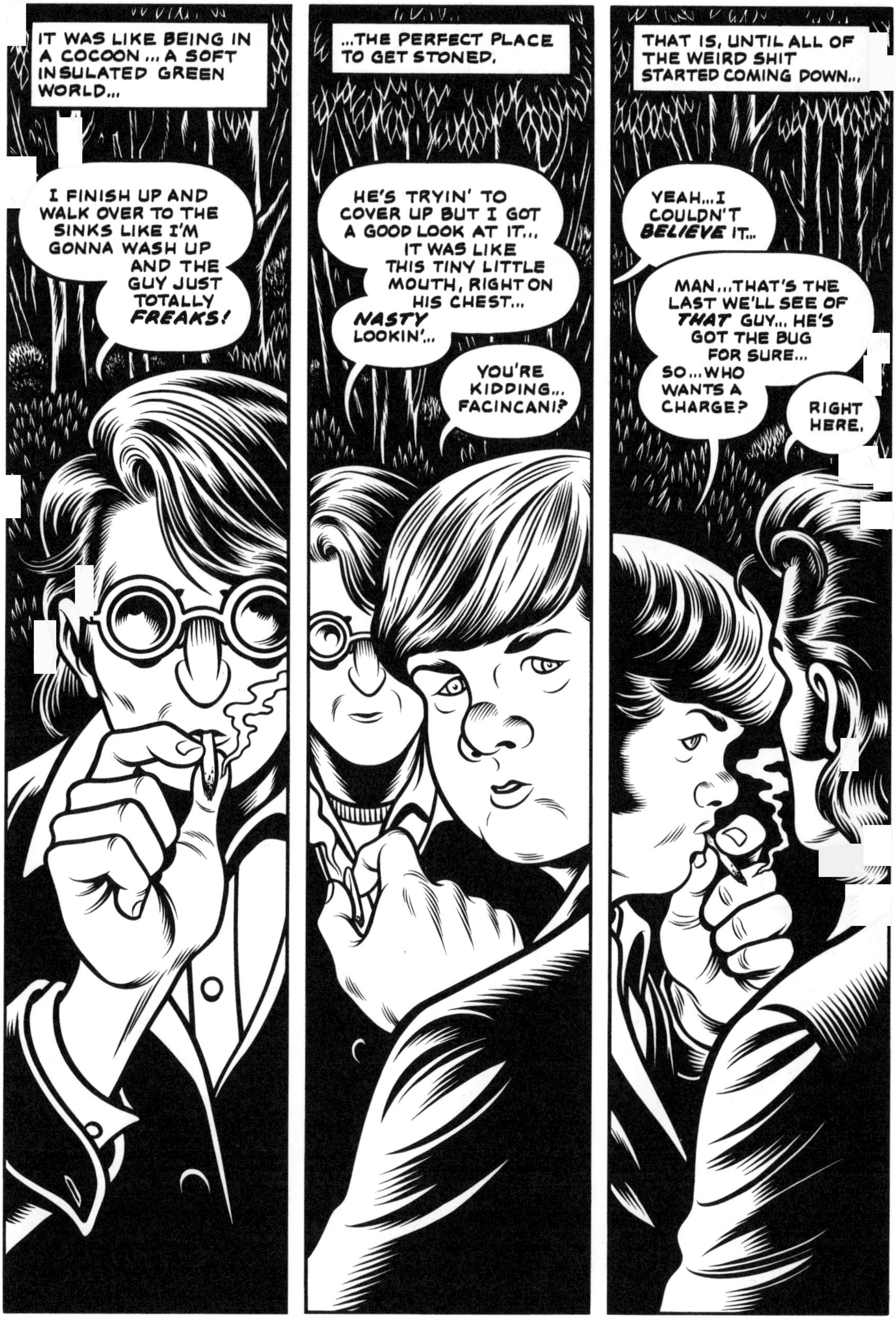
IT WAS LIKE BEING IN A COCOON ... A SOFT INSULATED GREEN WORLD...
I FINISH UP AND WALK OVER TO THE SINKS LIKE I'M GONNA WASH UP AND THE GUY JUST TOTALLY FREAKS!
...THE PERFECT PLACE TO GET STONED.
HE'S TRYIN' TO COVER UP BUT I GOT A GOOD LOOK AT IT... IT WAS LIKE THIS TINY LITTLE MOUTH, RIGHT ON HIS CHEST... NASTY LOOKIN'...
YOU'RE KIDDING... FACINCANI?
THAT IS, UNTIL ALL OF THE WEIRD SHIT STARTED COMING DOWN...
YEAH...I COULDN'T BELIEVE IT...
MAN...THAT'S THE LAST WE'LL SEE OF THAT GUY... HE'S GOT THE BUG FOR SURE... SO...WHO WANTS A CHARGE?
RIGHT HERE.

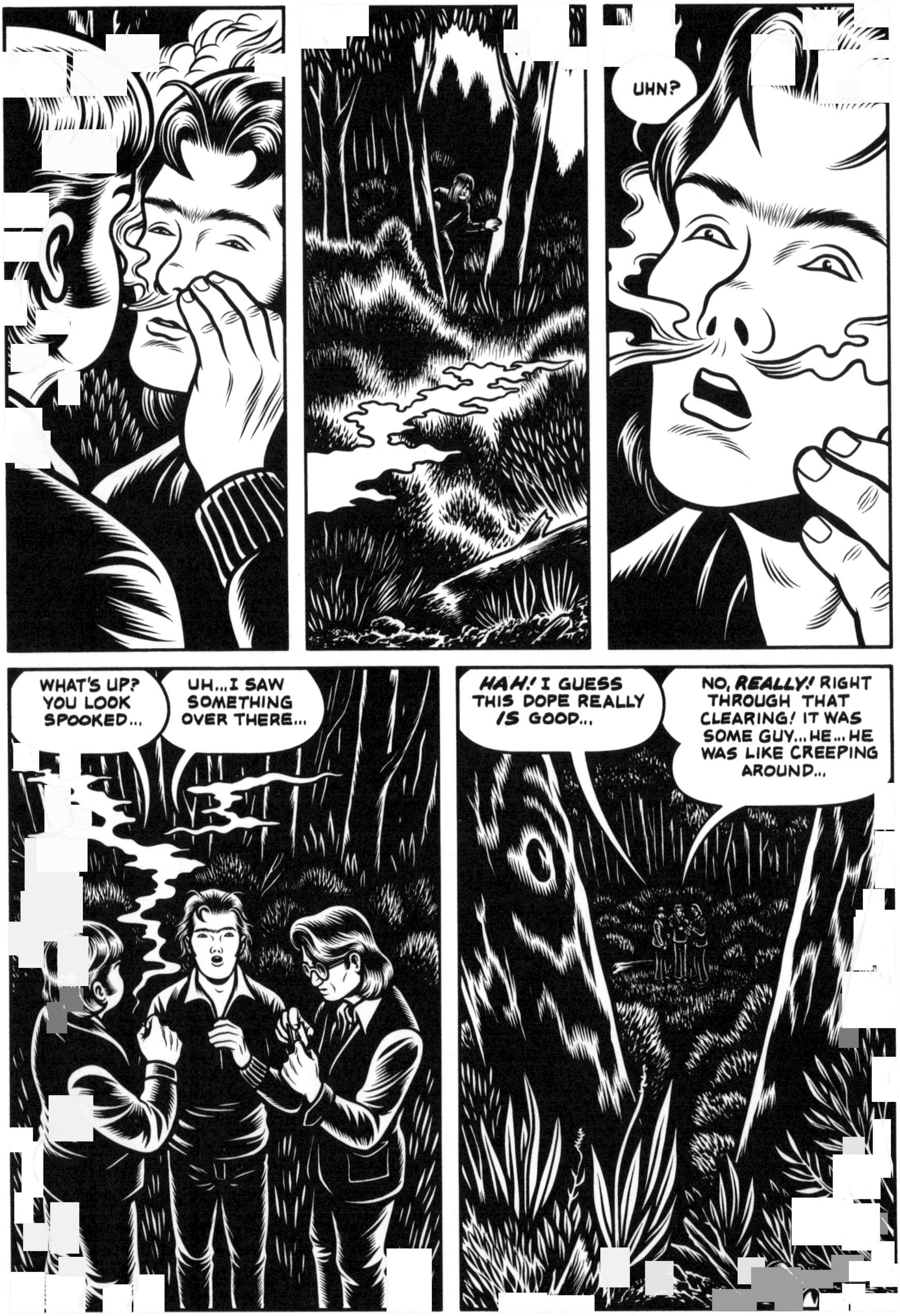
UHN?
WHAT'S UP? YOU LOOK SPOOKED...
UH...I SAW SOMETHING OVER THERE...
HAH! I GUESS THIS DOPE REALLY IS GOOD...
NO, REALLY! RIGHT THROUGH THAT CLEARING! IT WAS SOME GUY... HE... HE WAS LIKE CREEPING AROUND...

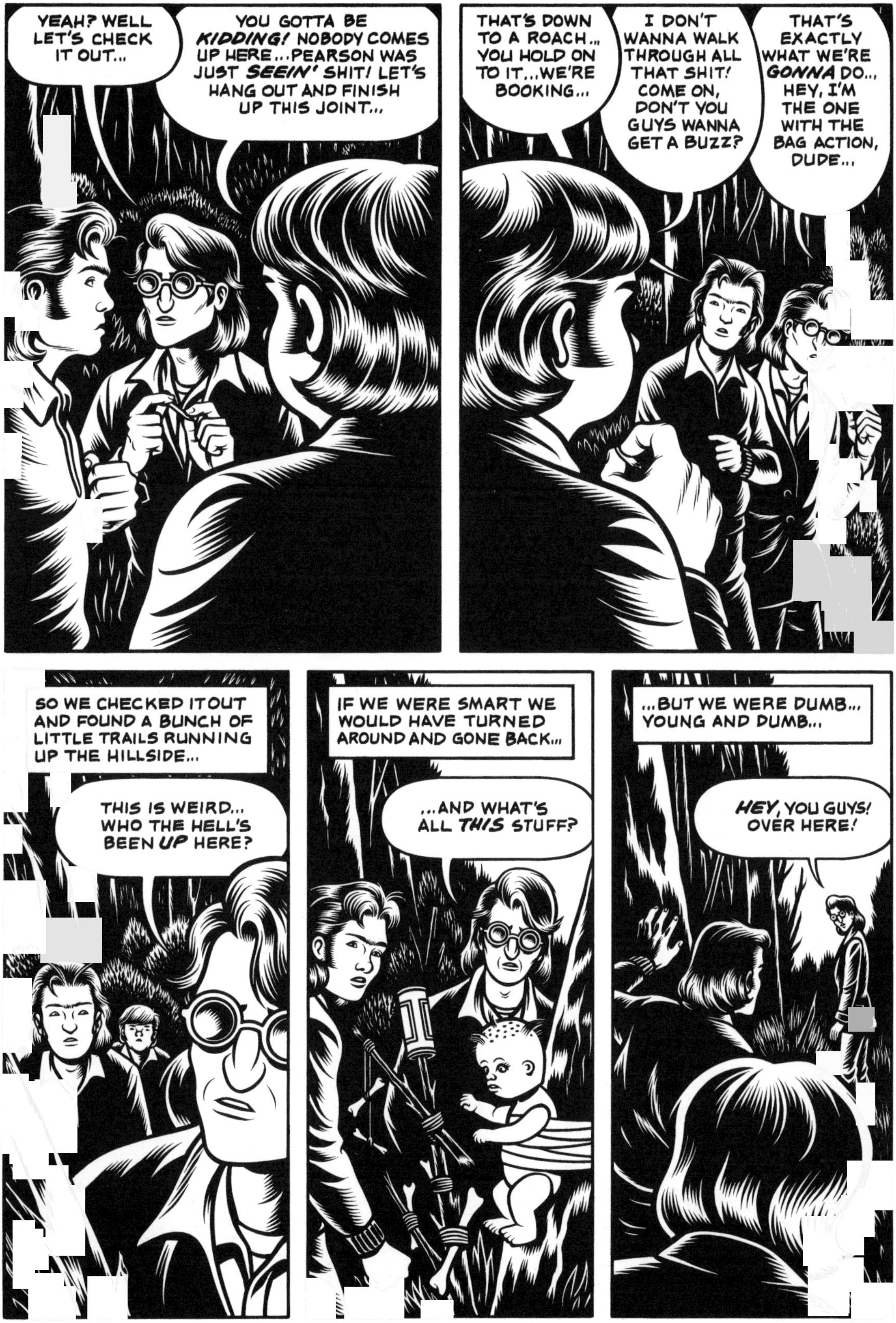
YEAH? WELL LET'S CHECK IT OUT...
YOU GOTTA BE KIDDING! NOBODY COMES UP HERE... PEARSON WAS JUST SEEIN' SHIT! LET'S HANG OUT AND FINISH UP THIS JOINT...
THAT'S DOWN TO A ROACH... YOU HOLD ON TO IT... WE'RE BOOKING...
I DON'T WANNA WALK THROUGH ALL THAT SHIT! COME ON, DON'T YOU GUYS WANNA GET A BUZZ?
THAT'S EXACTLY WHAT WE'RE GONNA DO... HEY, I'M THE ONE WITH THE BAG ACTION, DUDE...
SO WE CHECKED IT OUT AND FOUND A BUNCH OF LITTLE TRAILS RUNNING UP THE HILLSIDE...
THIS IS WEIRD... WHO THE HELL'S BEEN UP HERE?
IF WE WERE SMART WE WOULD HAVE TURNED AROUND AND GONE BACK...
...AND WHAT'S ALL THIS STUFF?
...BUT WE WERE DUMB... YOUNG AND DUMB...
HEY, YOU GUYS! OVER HERE!

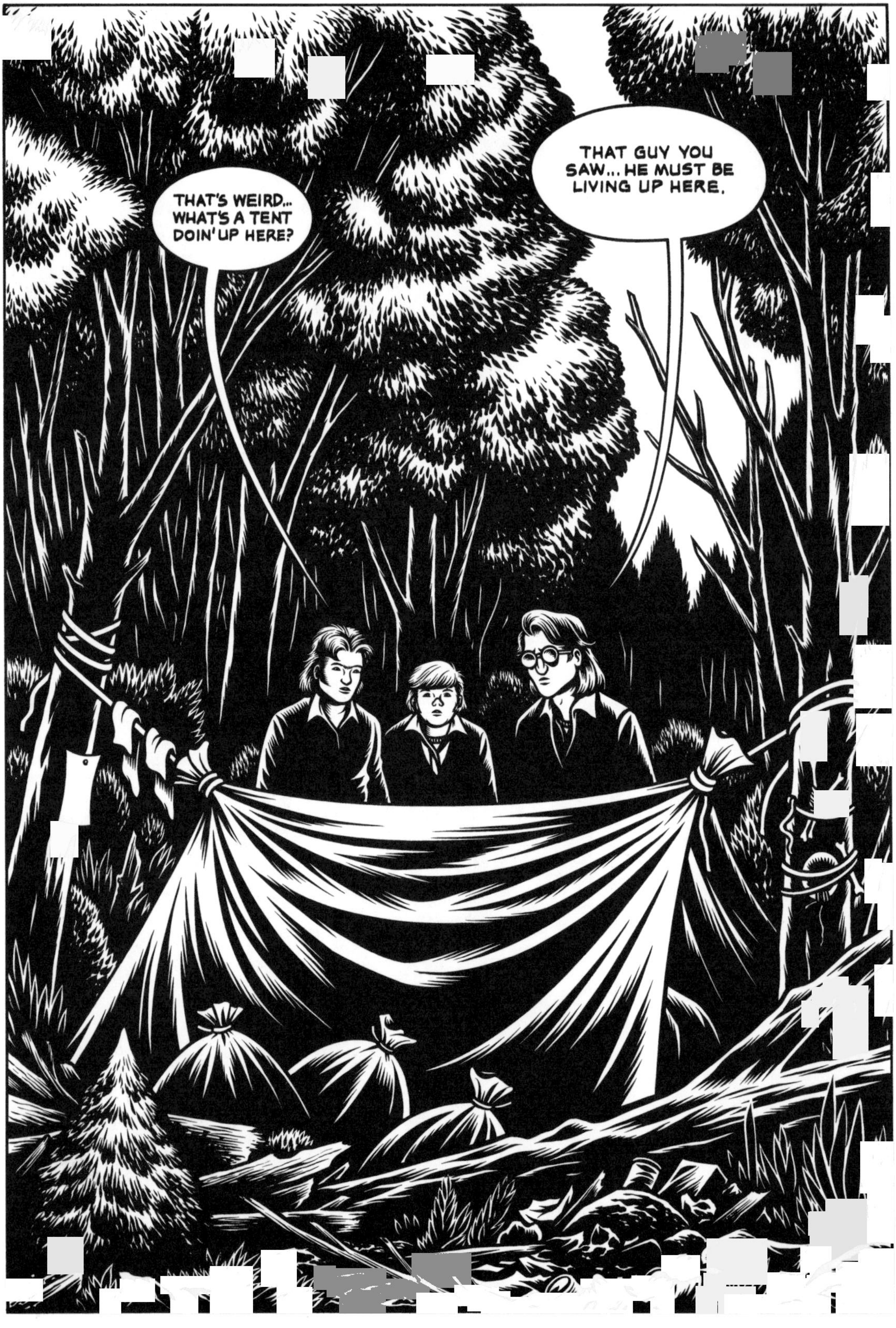
THAT'S WEIRD... WHAT'S A TENT DOIN' UP HERE?
THAT GUY YOU SAW... HE MUST BE LIVING UP HERE.

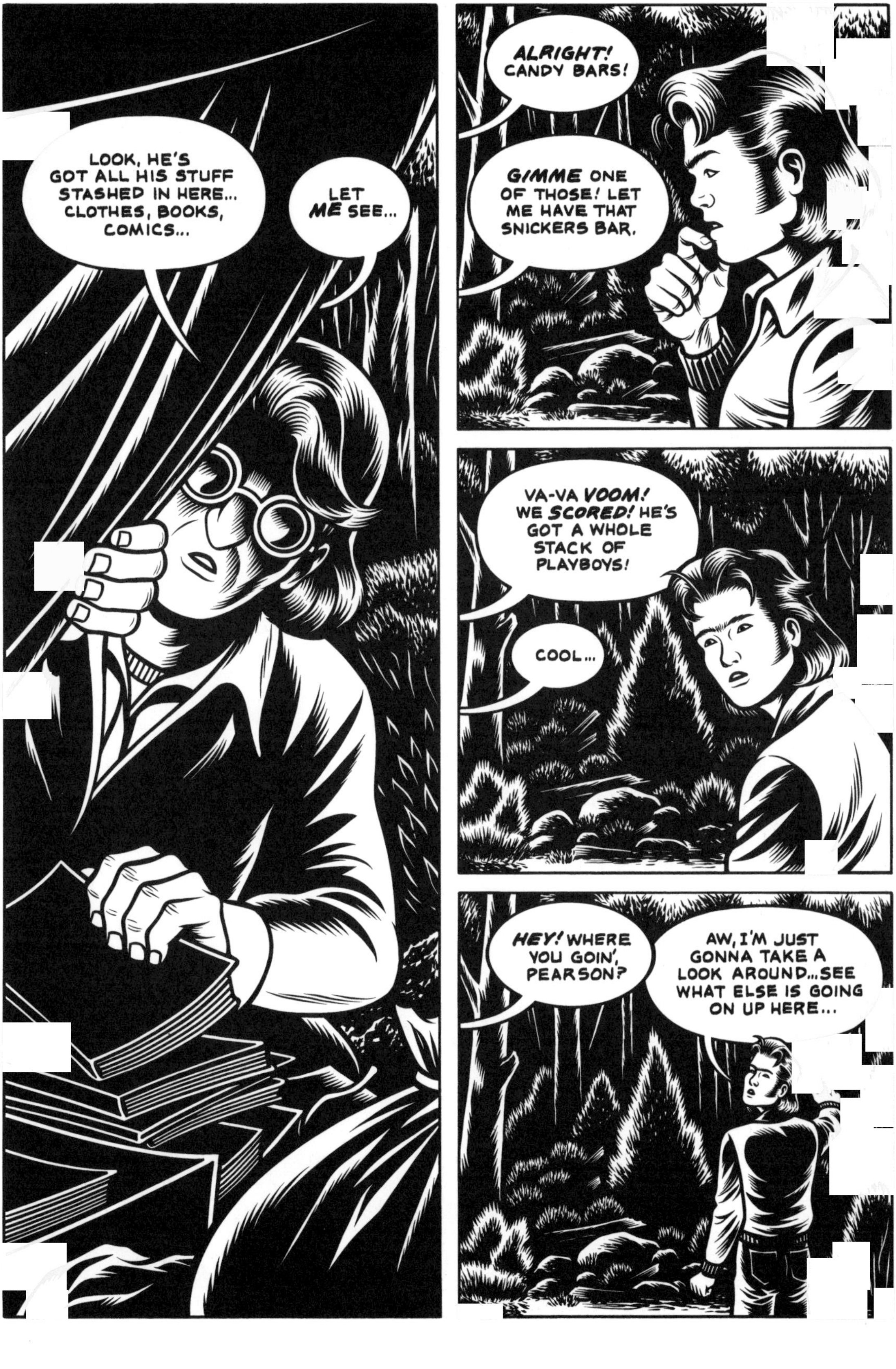
LOOK, HE'S GOT ALL HIS STUFF STASHED IN HERE... CLOTHES, BOOKS, COMICS...
LET *ME* SEE...
ALRIGHT! CANDY BARS!
GIMME ONE OF THOSE! LET ME HAVE THAT SNICKERS BAR.
VA-VA *VOOM!* WE *SCORED!* HE'S GOT A WHOLE STACK OF PLAYBOYS!
COOL...
HEY! WHERE YOU GOIN', PEARSON?
AW, I'M JUST GONNA TAKE A LOOK AROUND...SEE WHAT ELSE IS GOING ON UP HERE...

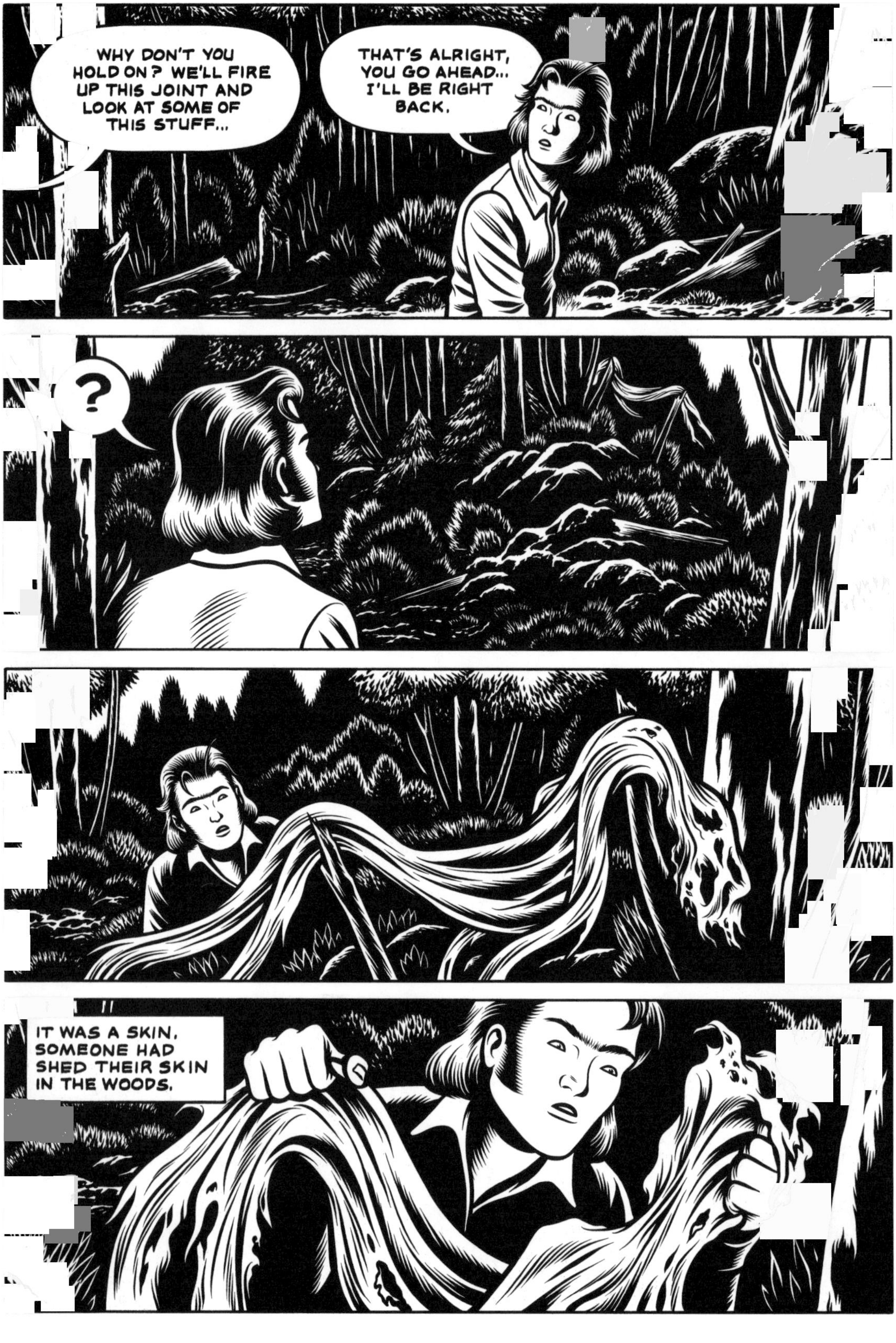
WHY DON'T YOU HOLD ON? WE'LL FIRE UP THIS JOINT AND LOOK AT SOME OF THIS STUFF...
THAT'S ALRIGHT, YOU GO AHEAD... I'LL BE RIGHT BACK.
?
IT WAS A SKIN. SOMEONE HAD SHED THEIR SKIN IN THE WOODS.

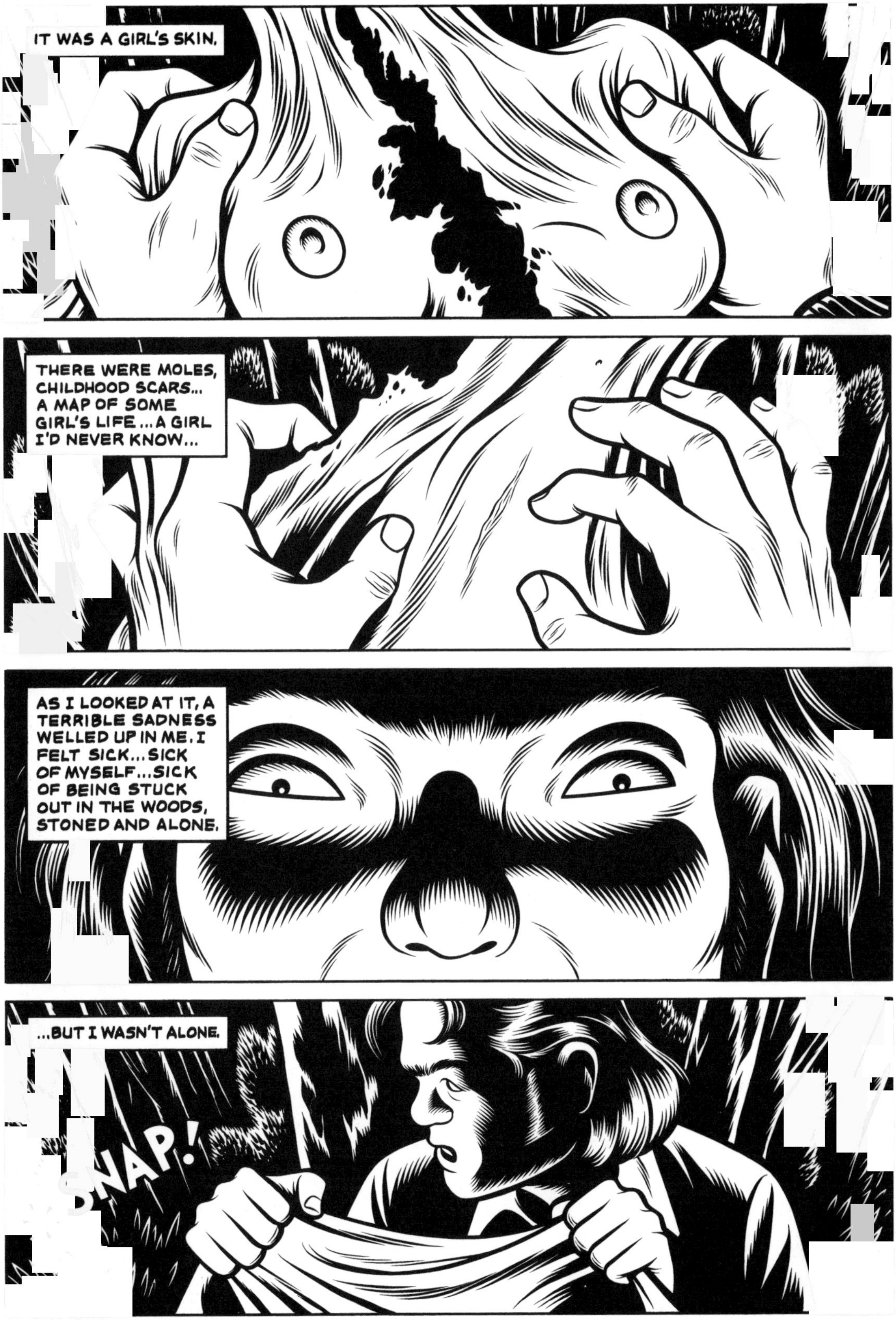
IT WAS A GIRL'S SKIN.
THERE WERE MOLES, CHILDHOOD SCARS... A MAP OF SOME GIRL'S LIFE... A GIRL I'D NEVER KNOW...
AS I LOOKED AT IT, A TERRIBLE SADNESS WELLED UP IN ME. I FELT SICK... SICK OF MYSELF... SICK OF BEING STUCK OUT IN THE WOODS, STONED AND ALONE.
...BUT I WASN'T ALONE.
SNAP!

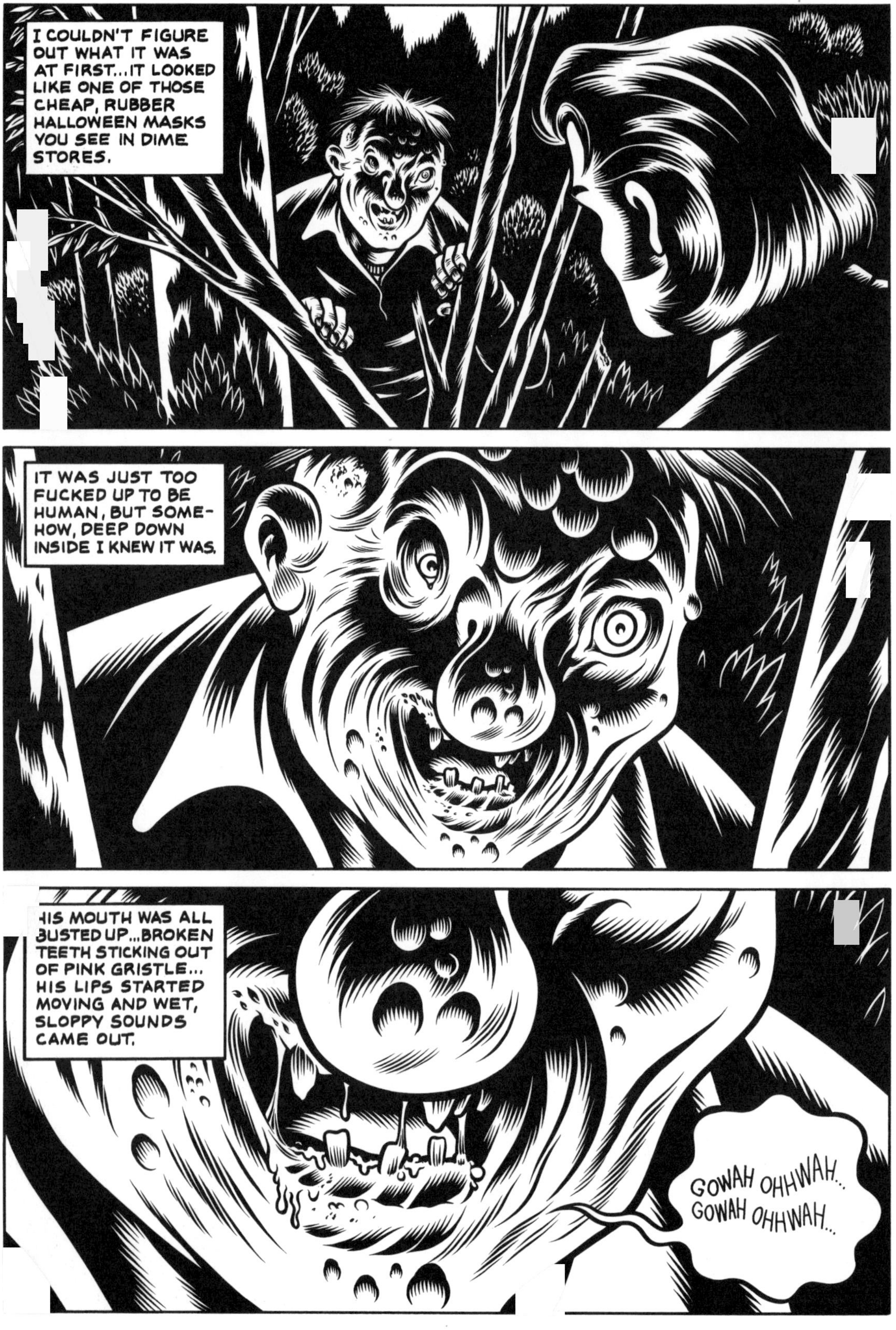
I COULDN'T FIGURE OUT WHAT IT WAS AT FIRST...IT LOOKED LIKE ONE OF THOSE CHEAP, RUBBER HALLOWEEN MASKS YOU SEE IN DIME STORES.
IT WAS JUST TOO FUCKED UP TO BE HUMAN, BUT SOME-HOW, DEEP DOWN INSIDE I KNEW IT WAS.
HIS MOUTH WAS ALL BUSTED UP...BROKEN TEETH STICKING OUT OF PINK GRISTLE... HIS LIPS STARTED MOVING AND WET, SLOPPY SOUNDS CAME OUT.
GOWAH OHHWAH... GOWAH OHHWAH...

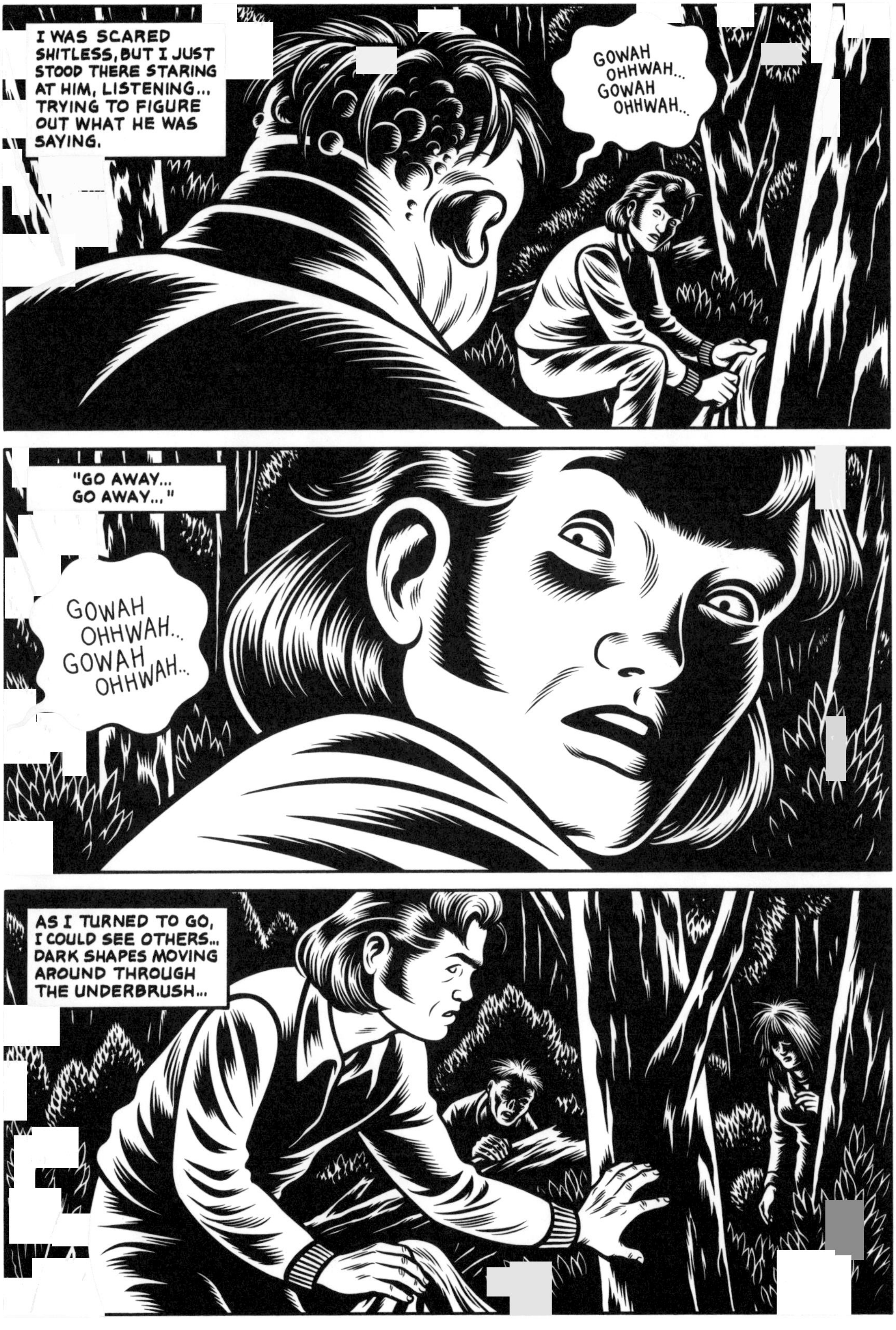
I WAS SCARED SHITLESS, BUT I JUST STOOD THERE STARING AT HIM, LISTENING... TRYING TO FIGURE OUT WHAT HE WAS SAYING.
GOWAH OHHWAH... GOWAH OHHWAH...
"GO AWAY... GO AWAY..."
GOWAH OHHWAH... GOWAH OHHWAH...
AS I TURNED TO GO, I COULD SEE OTHERS... DARK SHAPES MOVING AROUND THROUGH THE UNDERBRUSH...

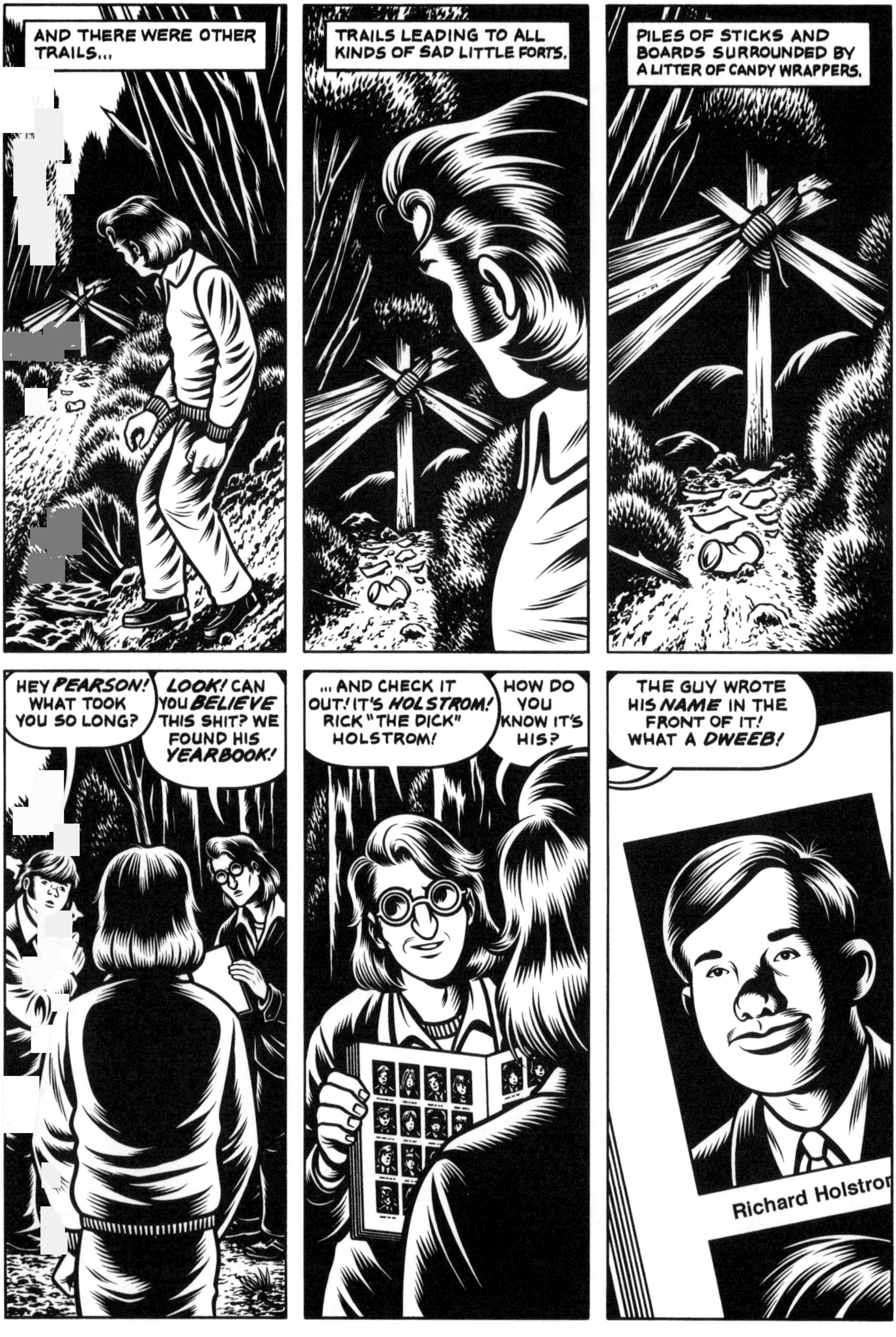
AND THERE WERE OTHER TRAILS...
TRAILS LEADING TO ALL KINDS OF SAD LITTLE FORTS.
PILES OF STICKS AND BOARDS SURROUNDED BY A LITTER OF CANDY WRAPPERS.
HEY PEARSON! WHAT TOOK YOU SO LONG?
LOOK! CAN YOU BELIEVE THIS SHIT? WE FOUND HIS YEARBOOK!
...AND CHECK IT OUT! IT'S HOLSTROM! RICK "THE DICK" HOLSTROM!
HOW DO YOU KNOW IT'S HIS?
THE GUY WROTE HIS NAME IN THE FRONT OF IT! WHAT A DWEEB!
Richard Holstrom

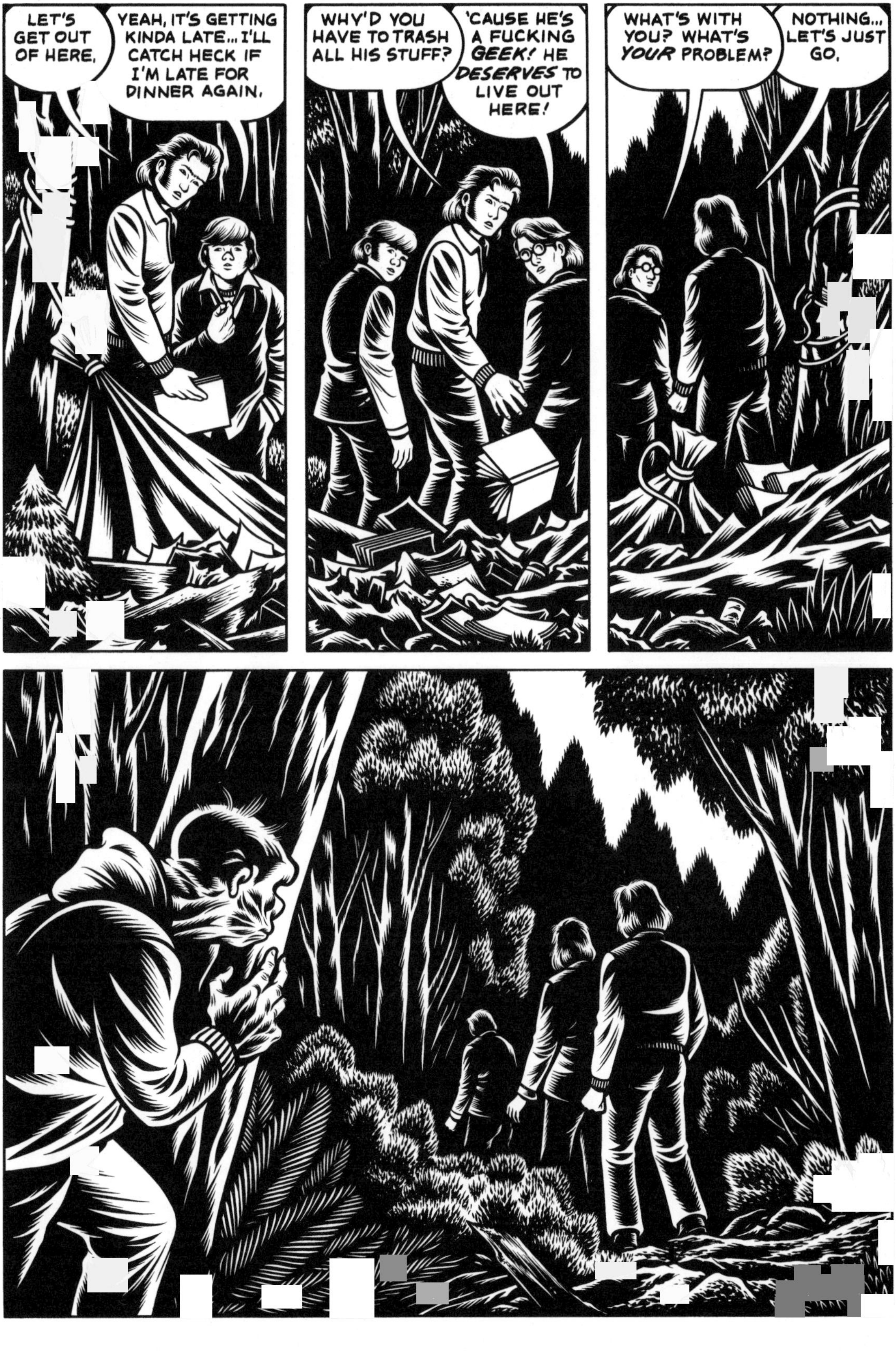
LET'S GET OUT OF HERE.
YEAH, IT'S GETTING KINDA LATE... I'LL CATCH HECK IF I'M LATE FOR DINNER AGAIN.
WHY'D YOU HAVE TO TRASH ALL HIS STUFF?
'CAUSE HE'S A FUCKING GEEK! HE DESERVES TO LIVE OUT HERE!
WHAT'S WITH YOU? WHAT'S YOUR PROBLEM?
NOTHING... LET'S JUST GO.

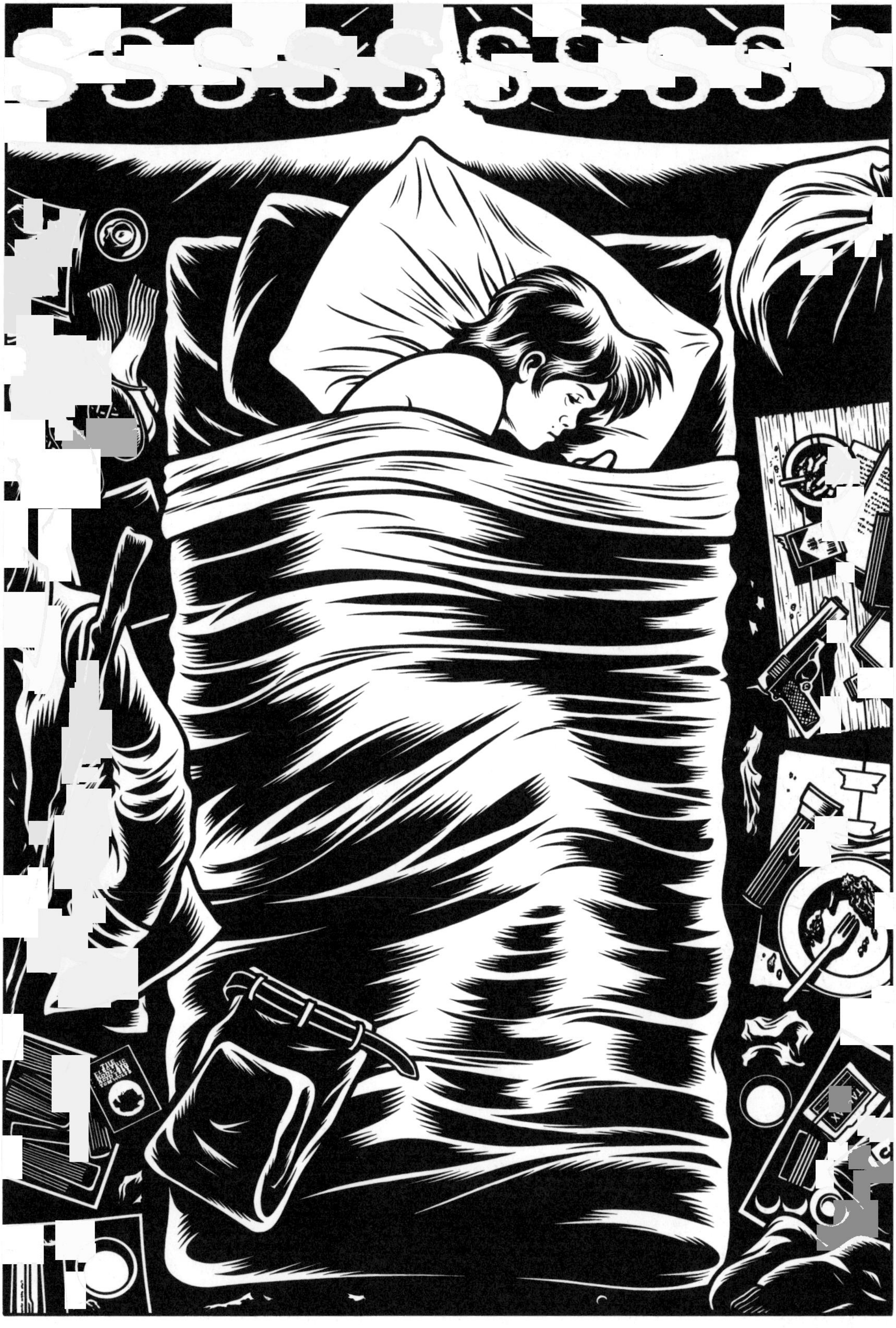

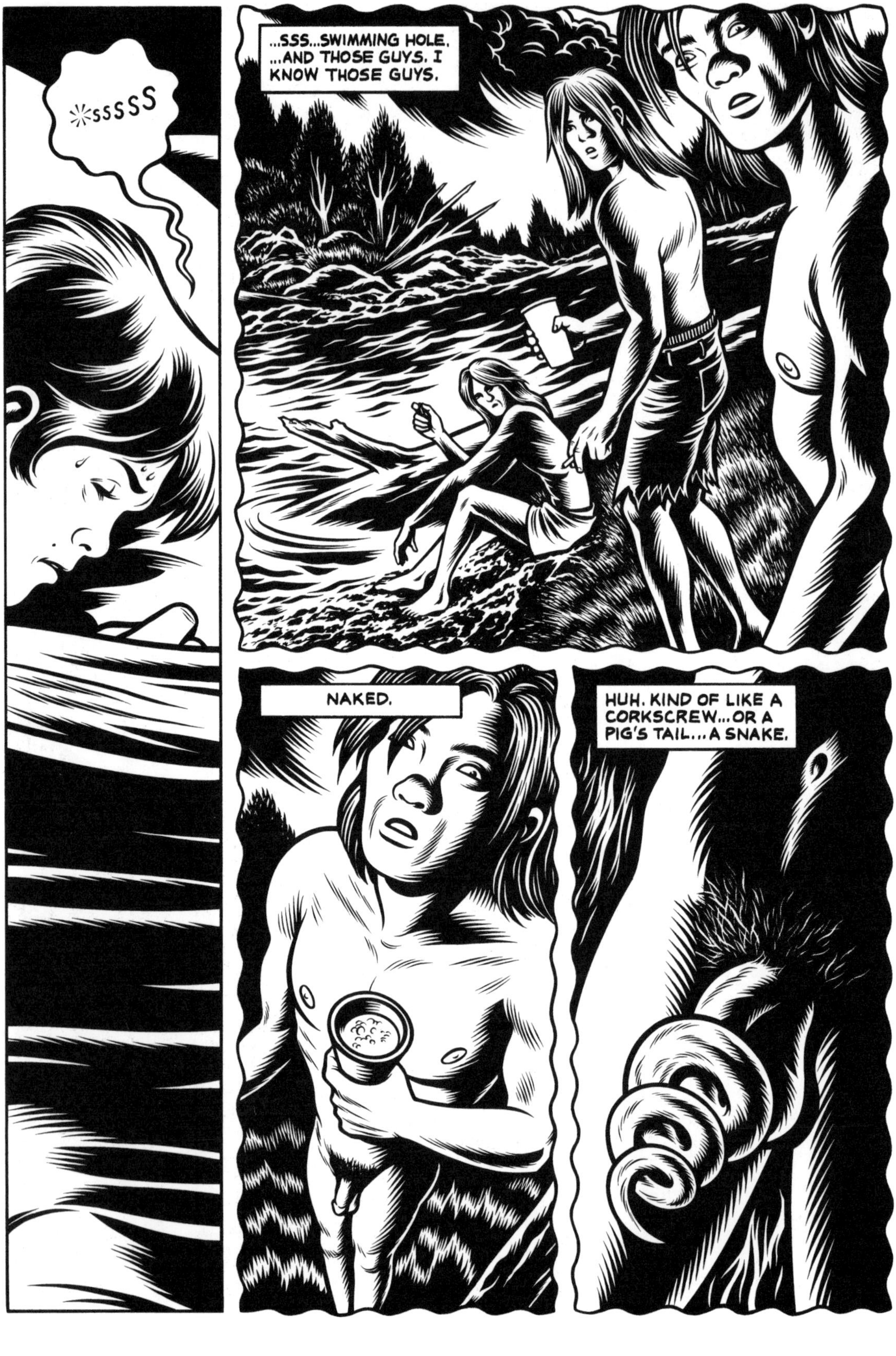

*sssSS
...SSS...SWIMMING HOLE. ...AND THOSE GUYS. I KNOW THOSE GUYS.
NAKED.
HUH. KIND OF LIKE A CORKSCREW...OR A PIG'S TAIL...A SNAKE.

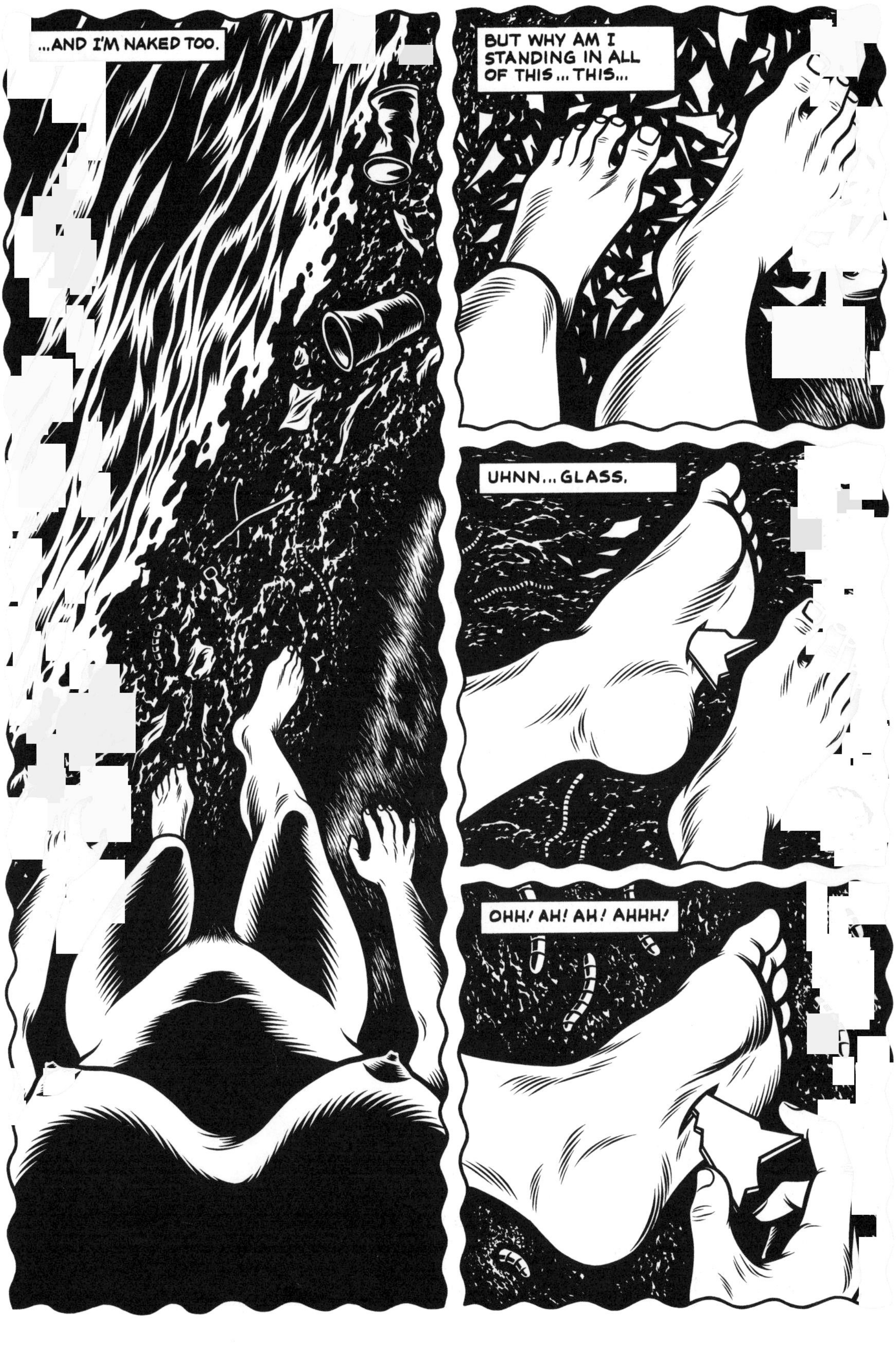
...AND I'M NAKED TOO.
BUT WHY AM I STANDING IN ALL OF THIS... THIS...
UHNN... GLASS.
OHH! AH! AH! AHHH!

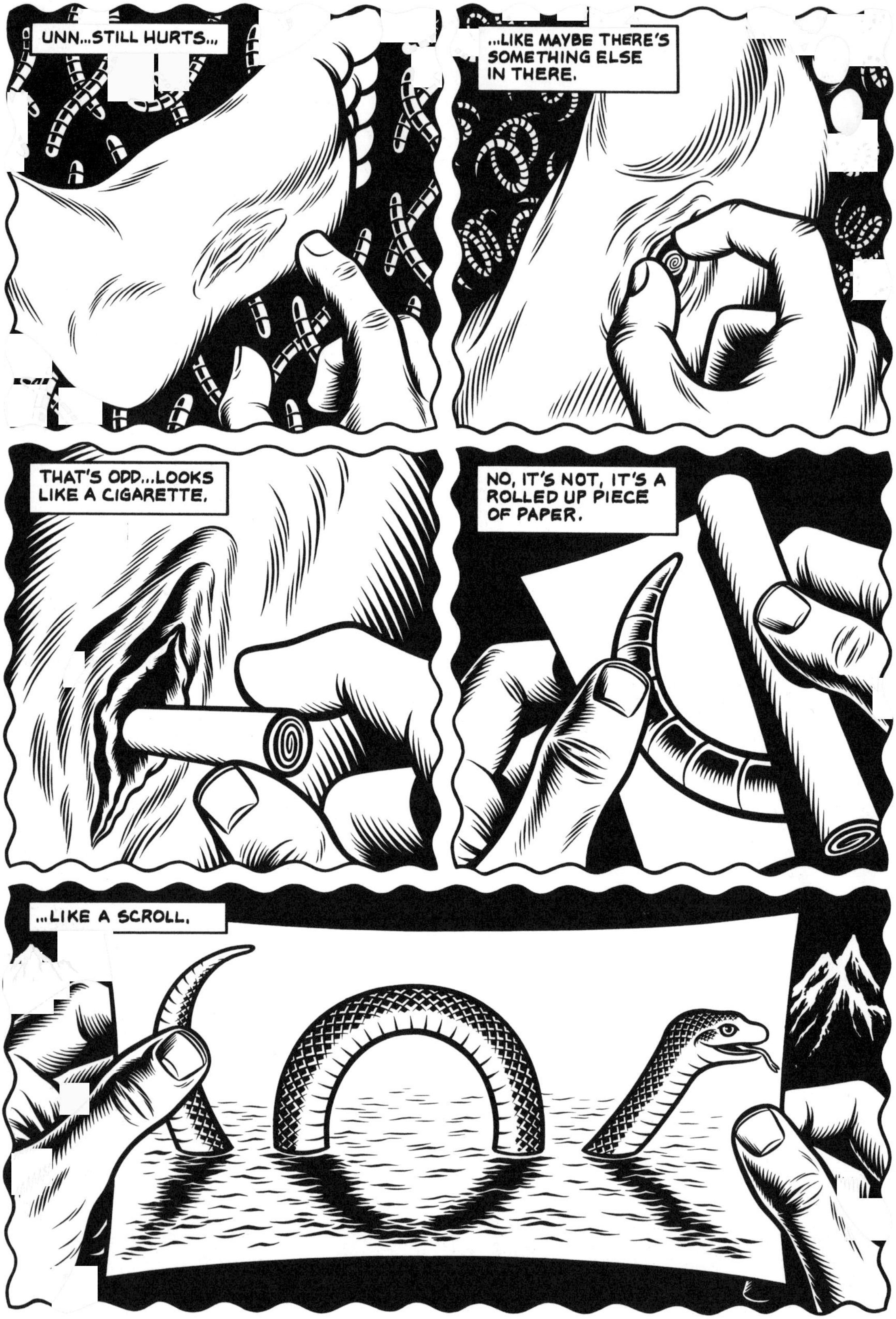
UNN...STILL HURTS...
...LIKE MAYBE THERE'S SOMETHING ELSE IN THERE.
THAT'S ODD...LOOKS LIKE A CIGARETTE.
NO, IT'S NOT, IT'S A ROLLED UP PIECE OF PAPER.
...LIKE A SCROLL.

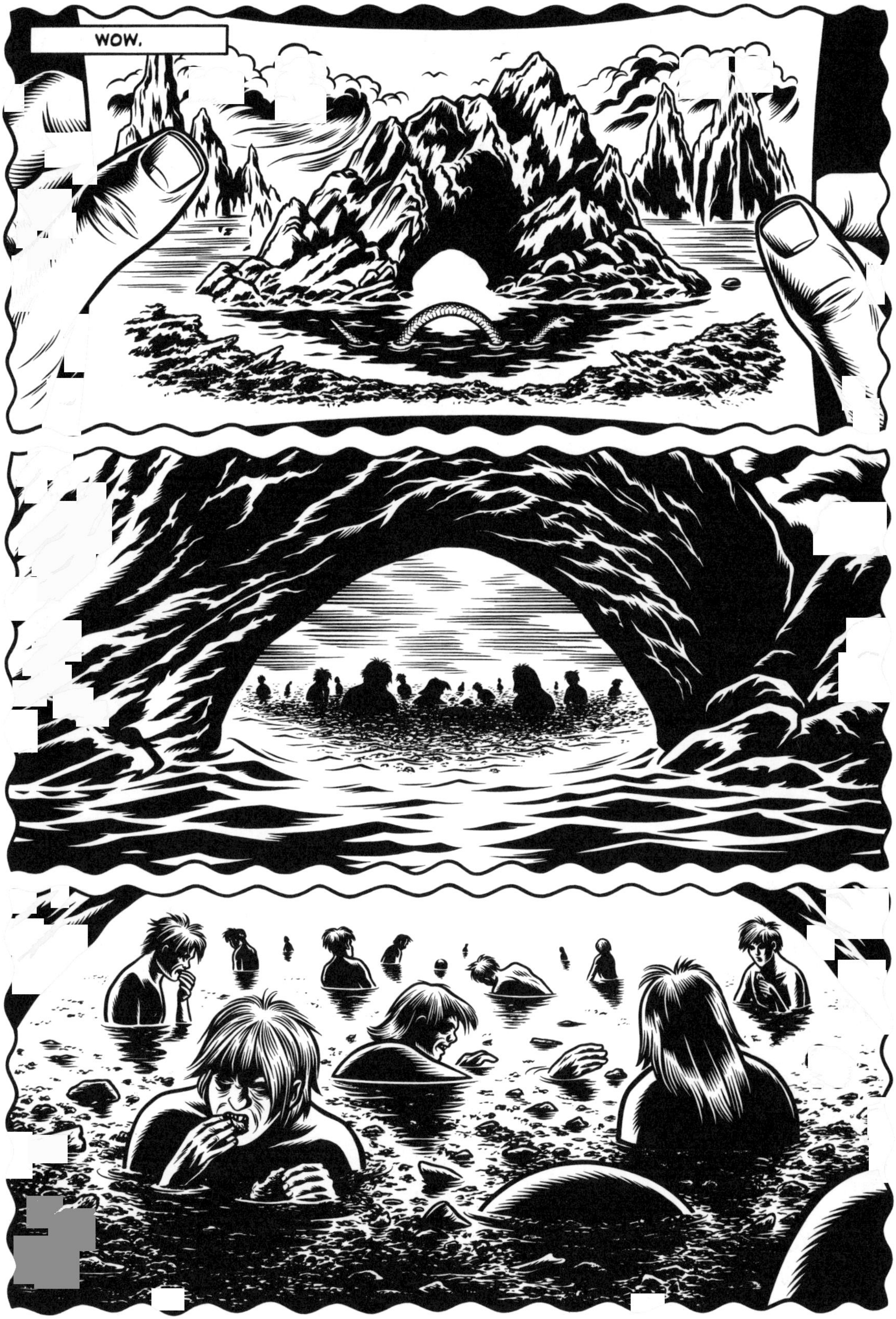
WOW.

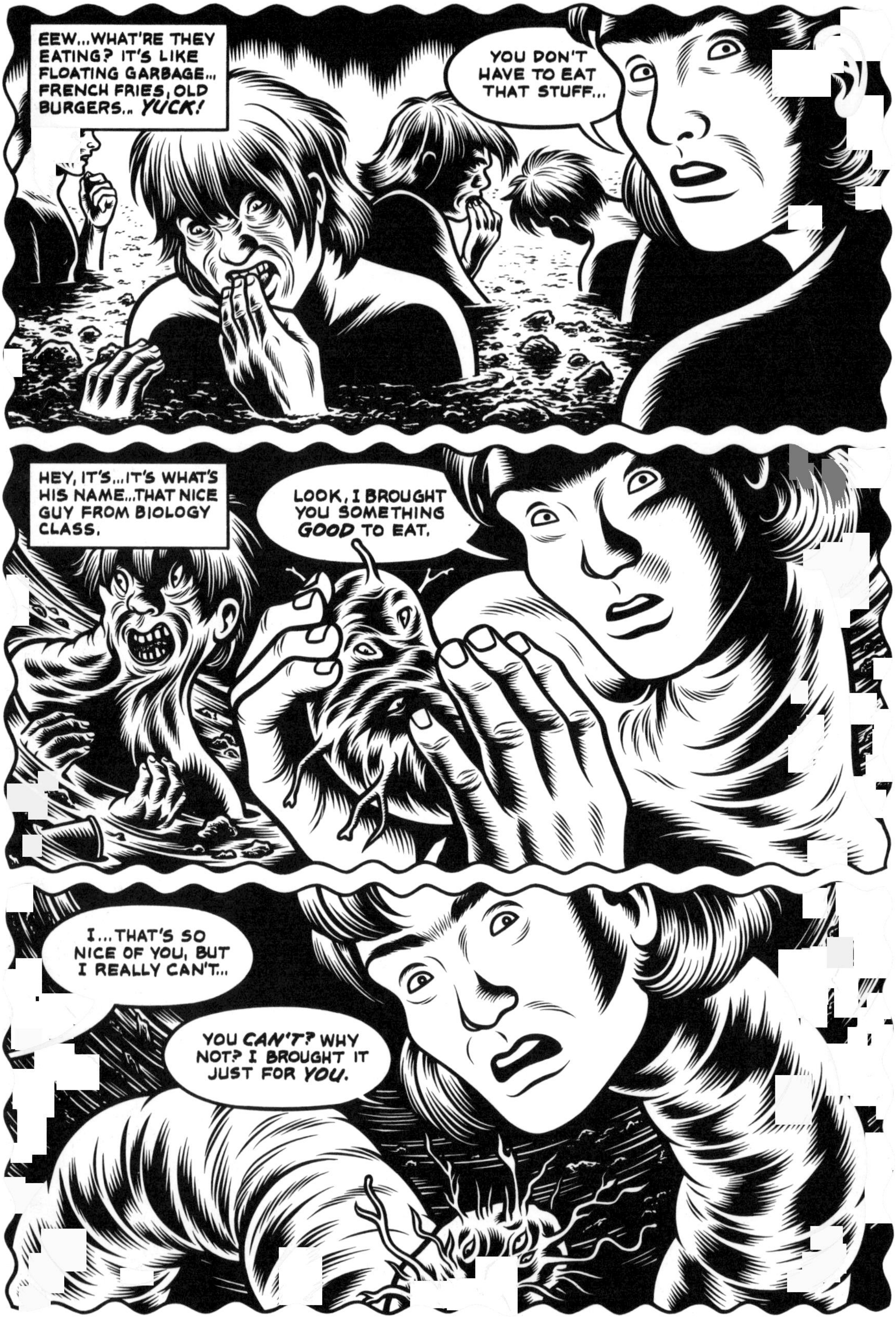
EEW...WHAT'RE THEY EATING? IT'S LIKE FLOATING GARBAGE... FRENCH FRIES, OLD BURGERS... YUCK!
YOU DON'T HAVE TO EAT THAT STUFF...
HEY, IT'S...IT'S WHAT'S HIS NAME...THAT NICE GUY FROM BIOLOGY CLASS.
LOOK, I BROUGHT YOU SOMETHING GOOD TO EAT.
I... THAT'S SO NICE OF YOU, BUT I REALLY CAN'T...
YOU CAN'T? WHY NOT? I BROUGHT IT JUST FOR YOU.

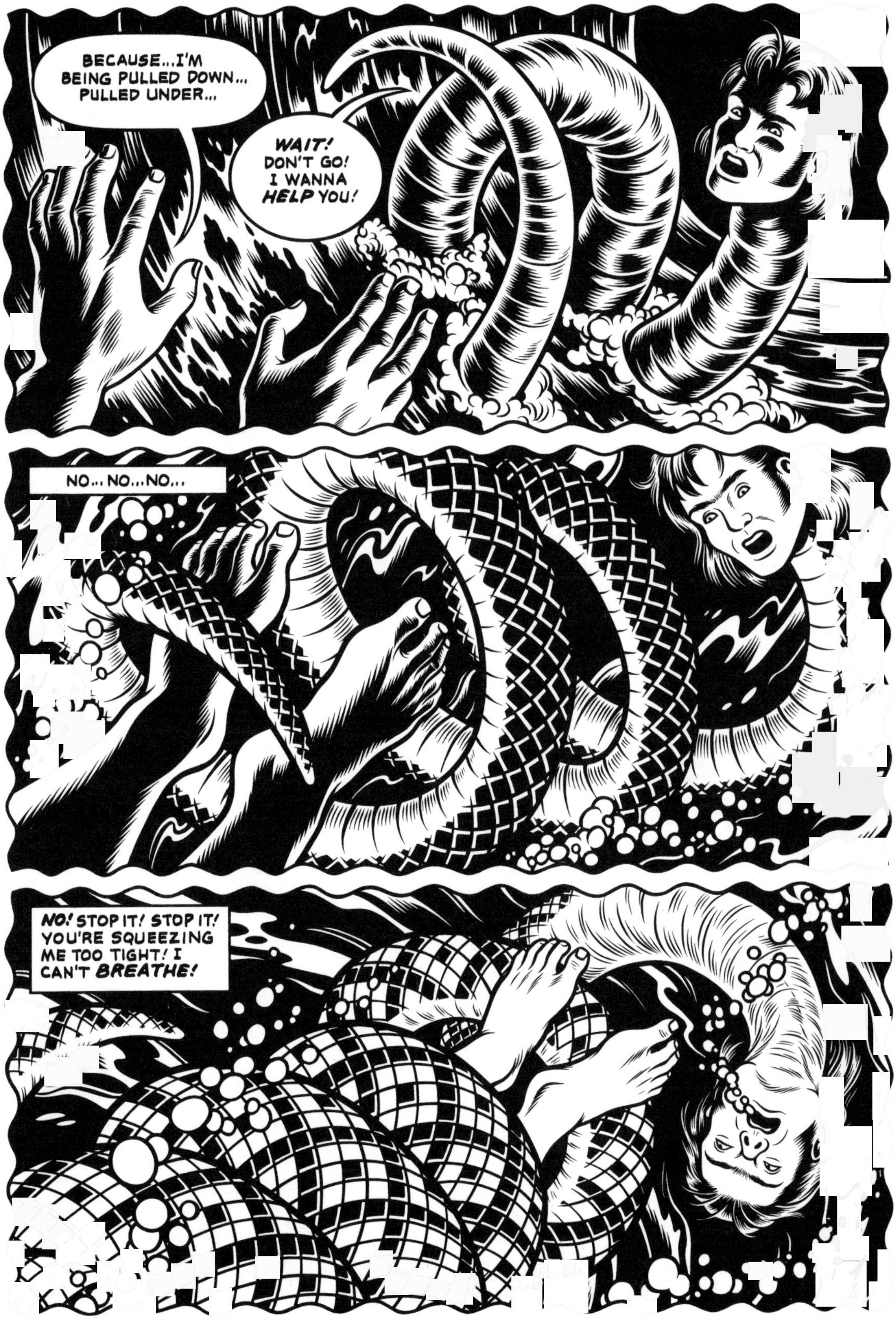
BECAUSE...I'M BEING PULLED DOWN... PULLED UNDER...
WAIT! DON'T GO! I WANNA HELP YOU!
NO... NO... NO...
NO! STOP IT! STOP IT! YOU'RE SQUEEZING ME TOO TIGHT! I CAN'T BREATHE!

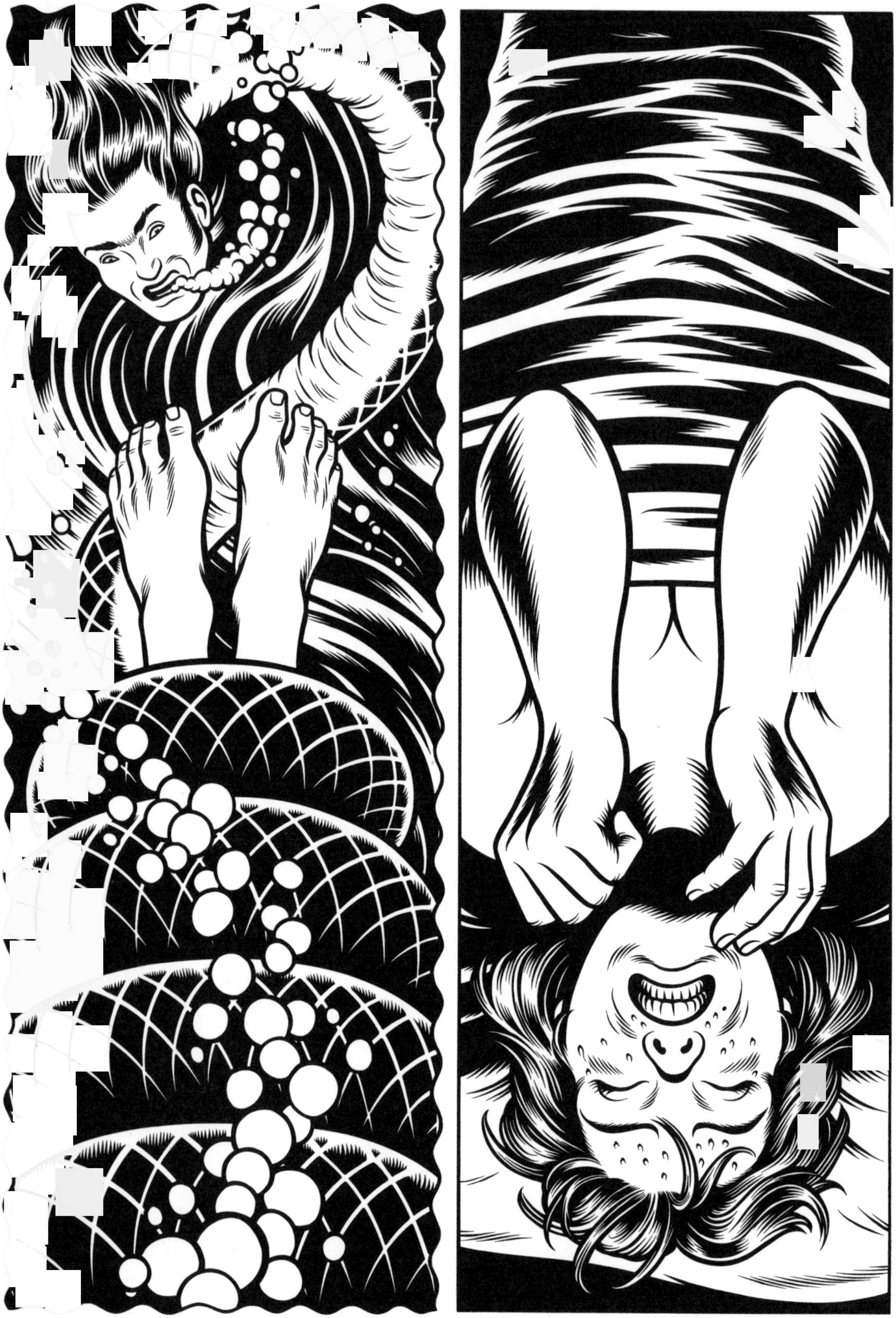

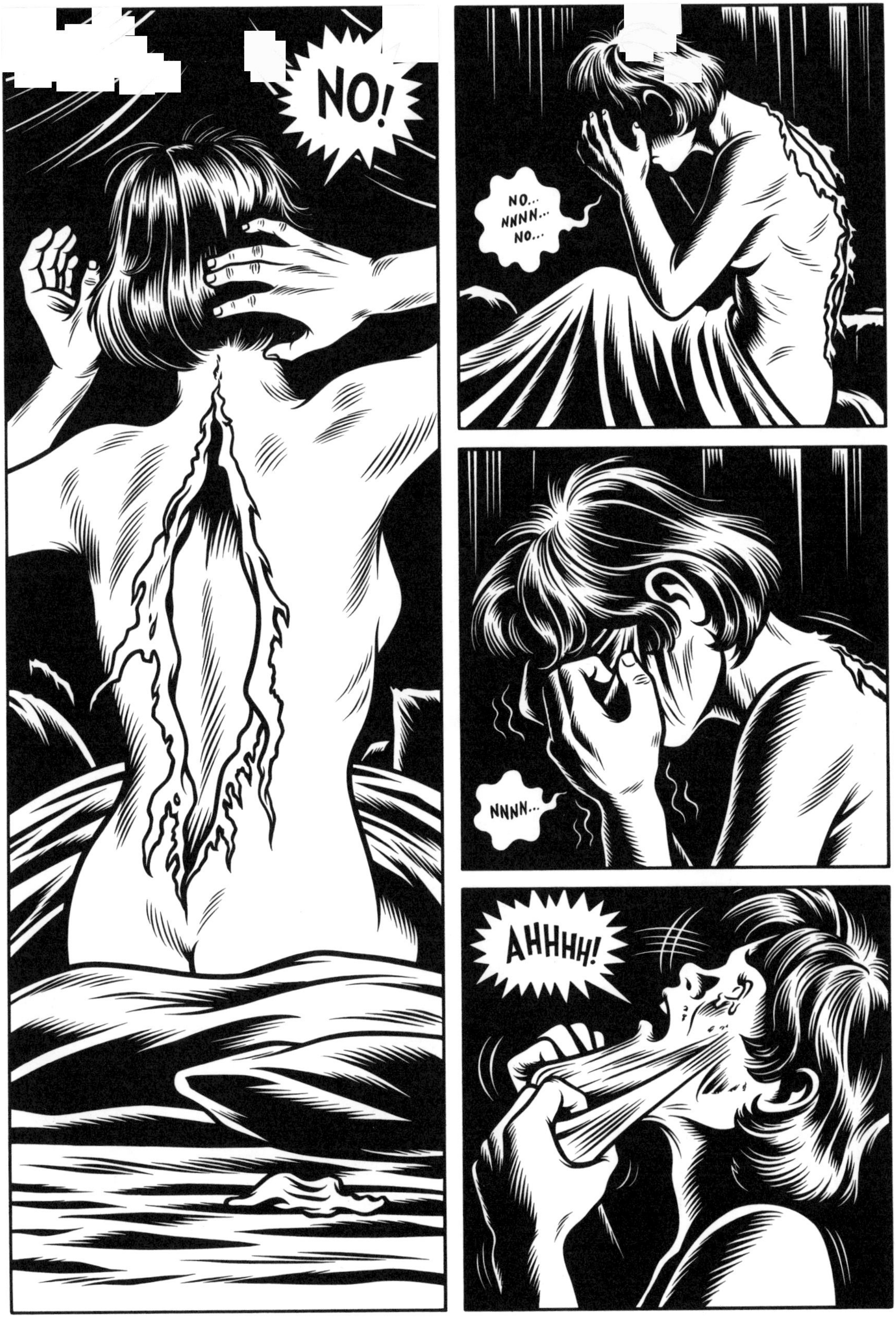
NO!
NO... NNNN... NO...
NNNN...
AHHHH!

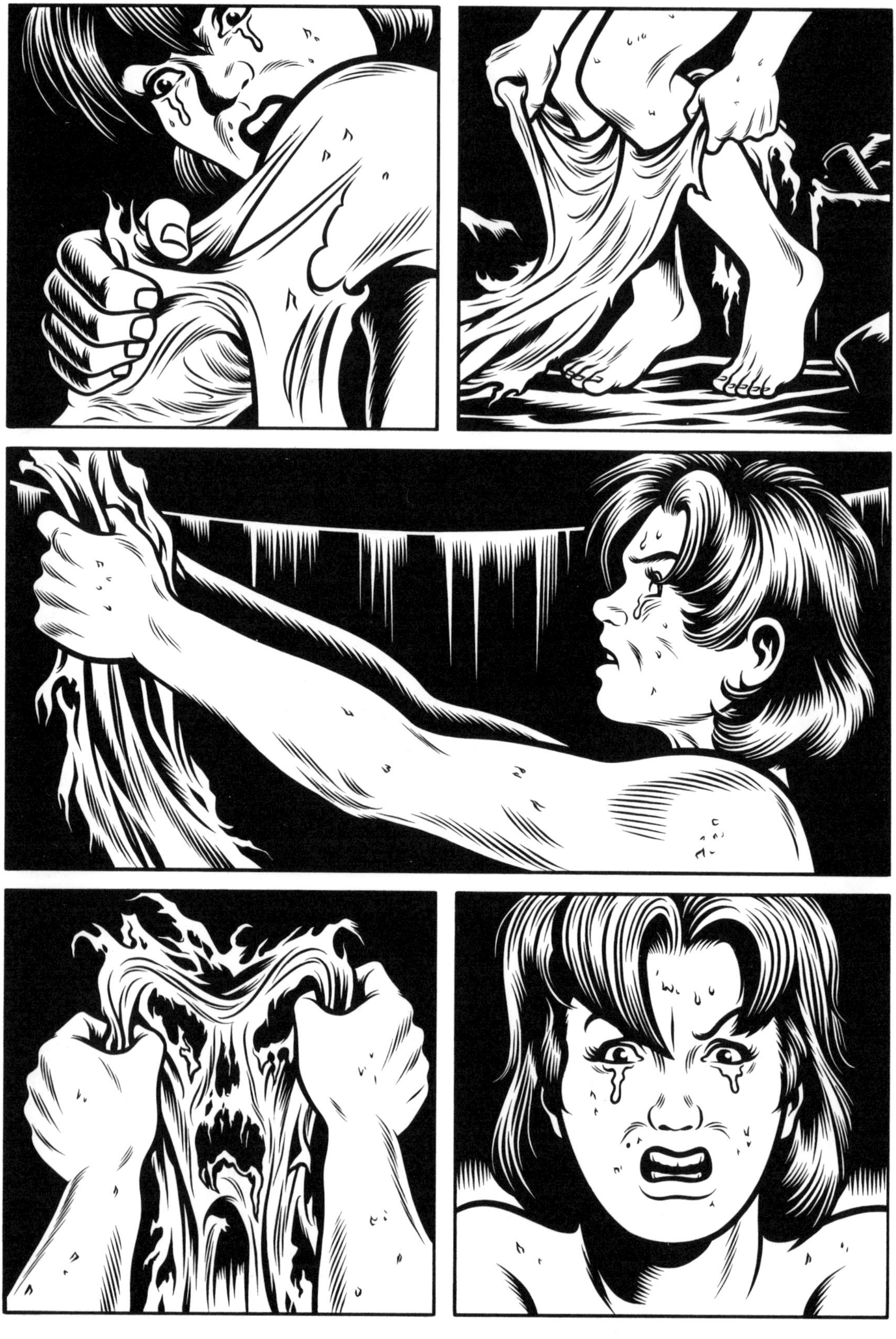

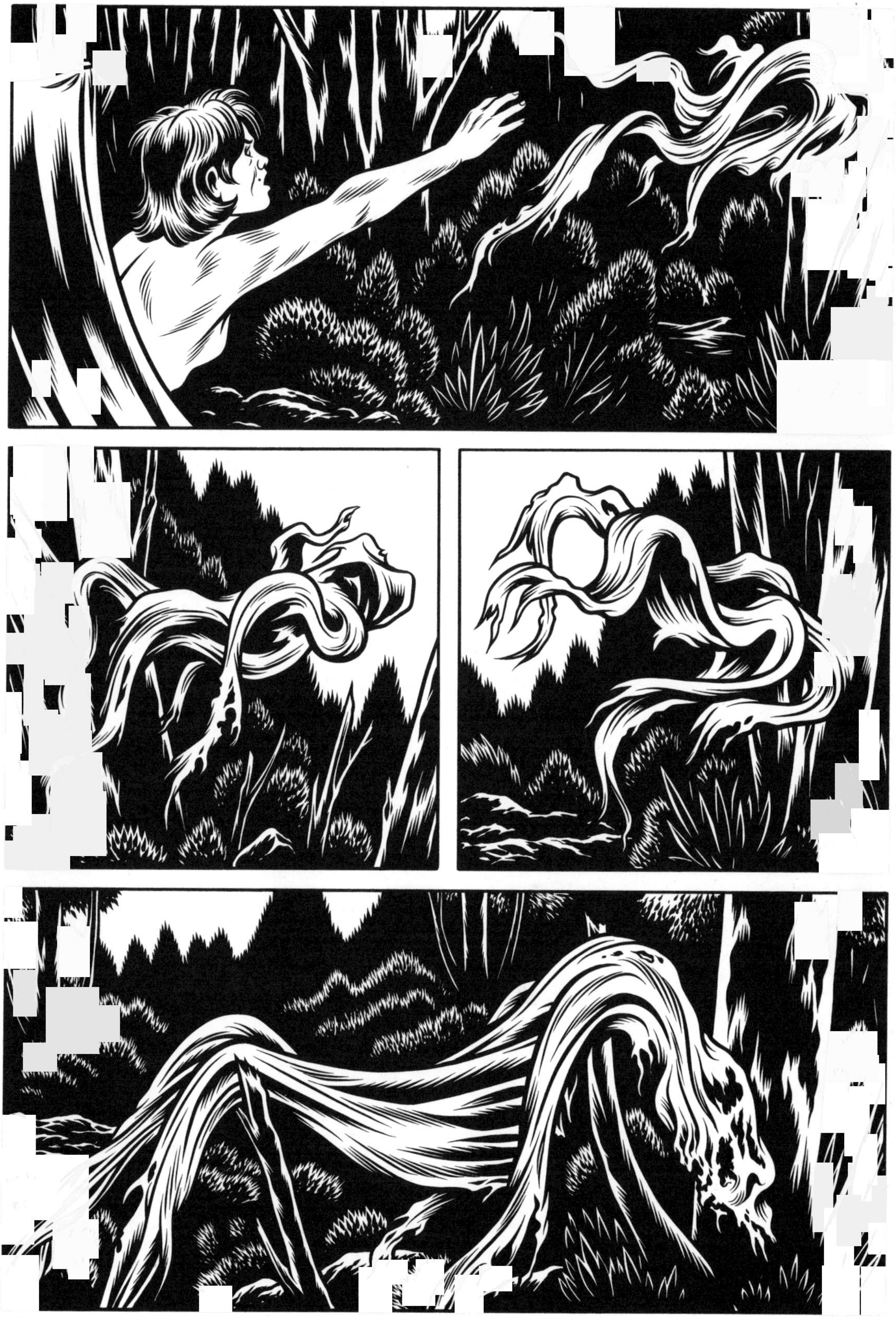

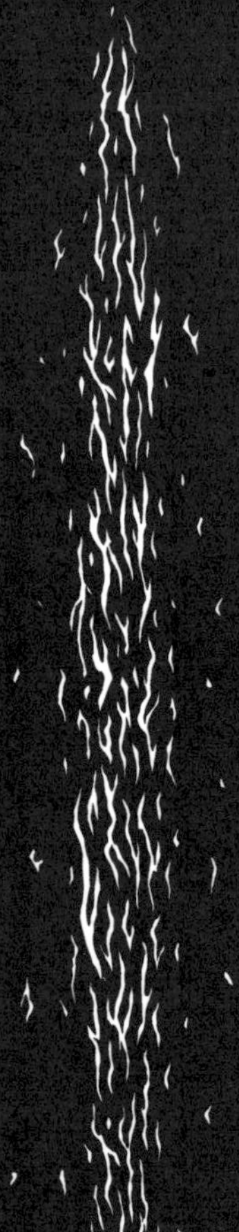

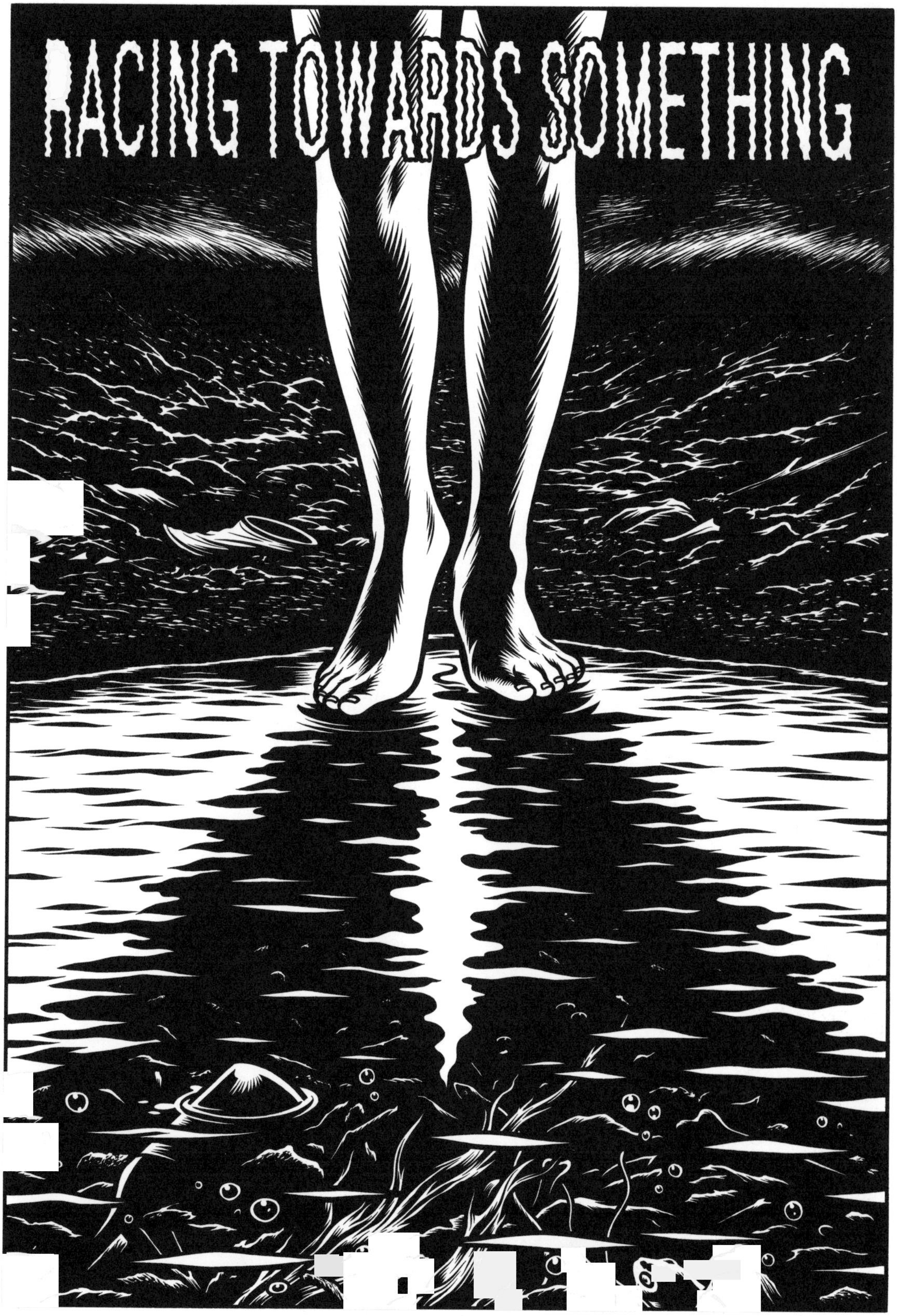
RACING TOWARDS SOMETHING

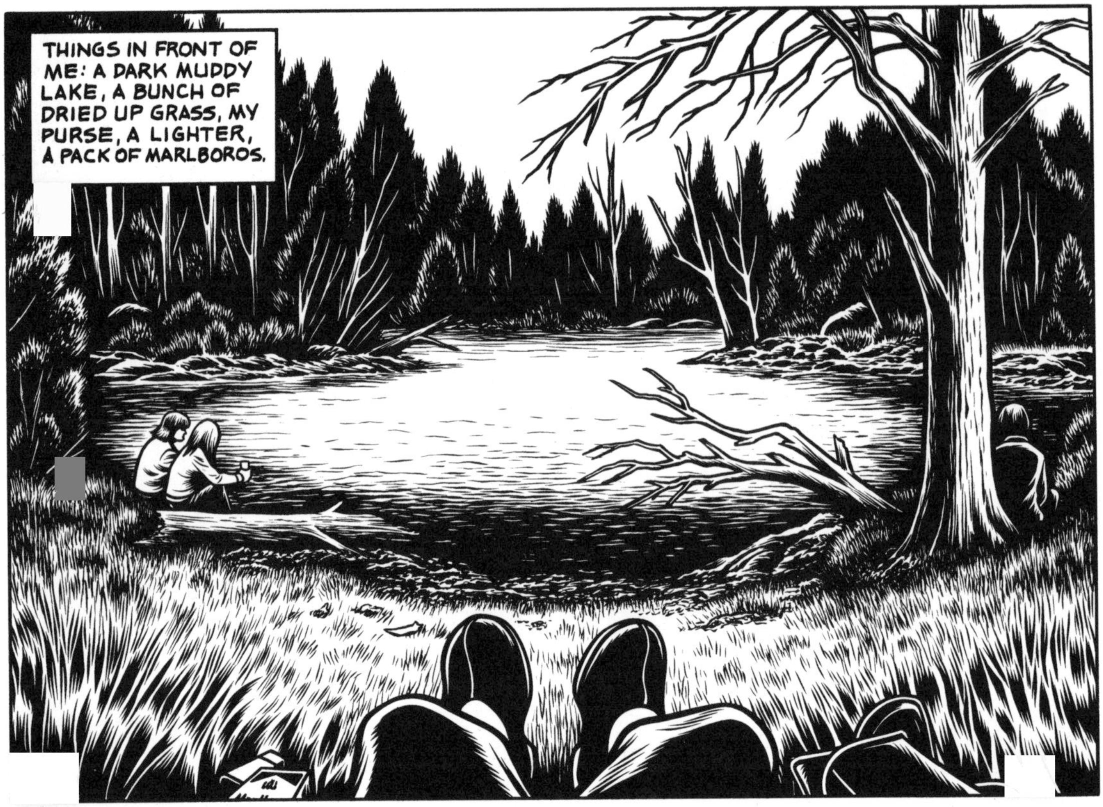
THINGS IN FRONT OF ME: A DARK MUDDY LAKE, A BUNCH OF DRIED UP GRASS, MY PURSE, A LIGHTER, A PACK OF MARLBOROS.

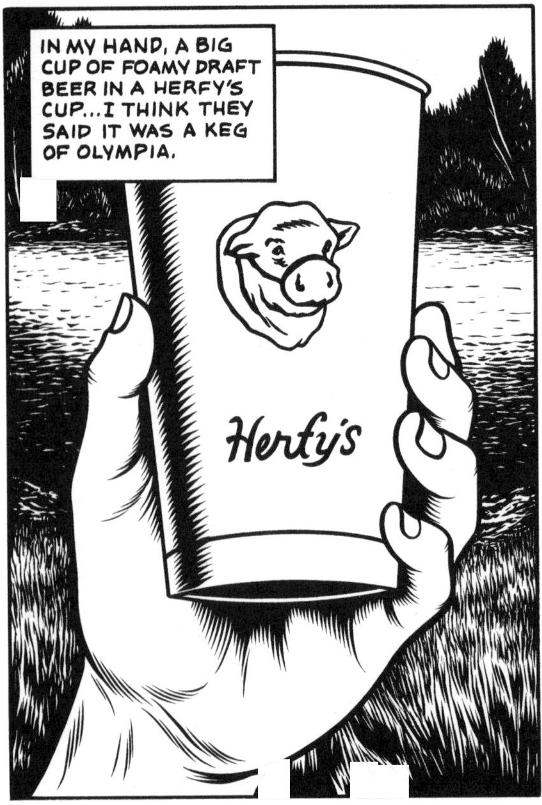
IN MY HAND, A BIG CUP OF FOAMY DRAFT BEER IN A HERFY'S CUP... I THINK THEY SAID IT WAS A KEG OF OLYMPIA.
Herfy's

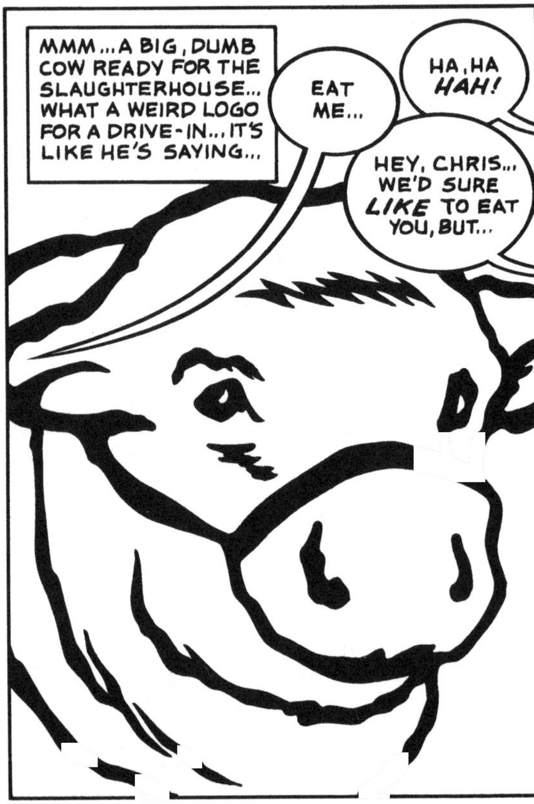
MMM... A BIG, DUMB COW READY FOR THE SLAUGHTERHOUSE... WHAT A WEIRD LOGO FOR A DRIVE-IN... IT'S LIKE HE'S SAYING...
EAT ME...
HA, HA *HAH!*
HEY, CHRIS... WE'D SURE *LIKE* TO EAT YOU, BUT...

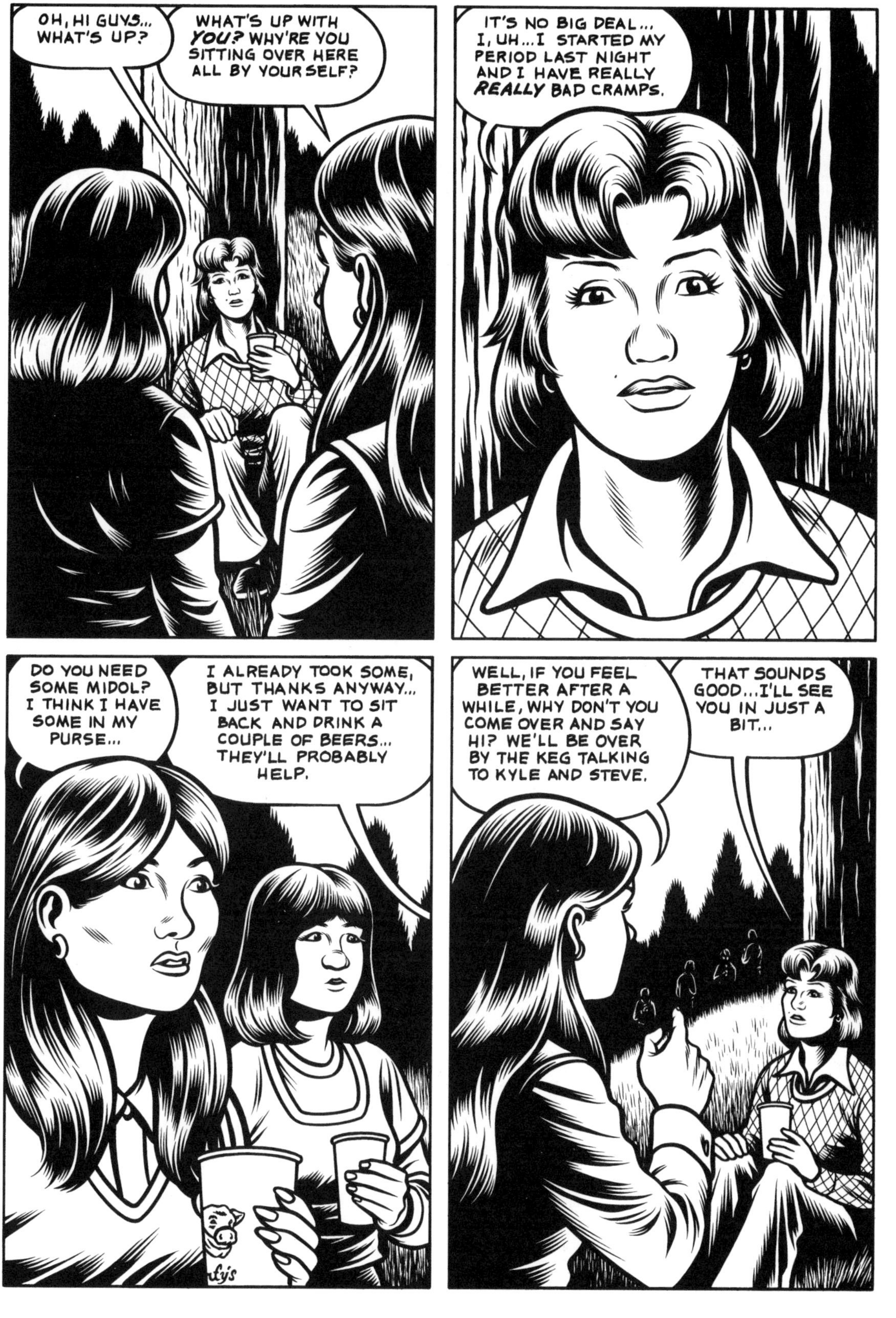
OH, HI GUYS... WHAT'S UP?
WHAT'S UP WITH *YOU?* WHY'RE YOU SITTING OVER HERE ALL BY YOURSELF?
IT'S NO BIG DEAL... I, UH... I STARTED MY PERIOD LAST NIGHT AND I HAVE REALLY *REALLY* BAD CRAMPS.
DO YOU NEED SOME MIDOL? I THINK I HAVE SOME IN MY PURSE...
I ALREADY TOOK SOME, BUT THANKS ANYWAY... I JUST WANT TO SIT BACK AND DRINK A COUPLE OF BEERS... THEY'LL PROBABLY HELP.
WELL, IF YOU FEEL BETTER AFTER A WHILE, WHY DON'T YOU COME OVER AND SAY HI? WE'LL BE OVER BY THE KEG TALKING TO KYLE AND STEVE.
THAT SOUNDS GOOD... I'LL SEE YOU IN JUST A BIT...

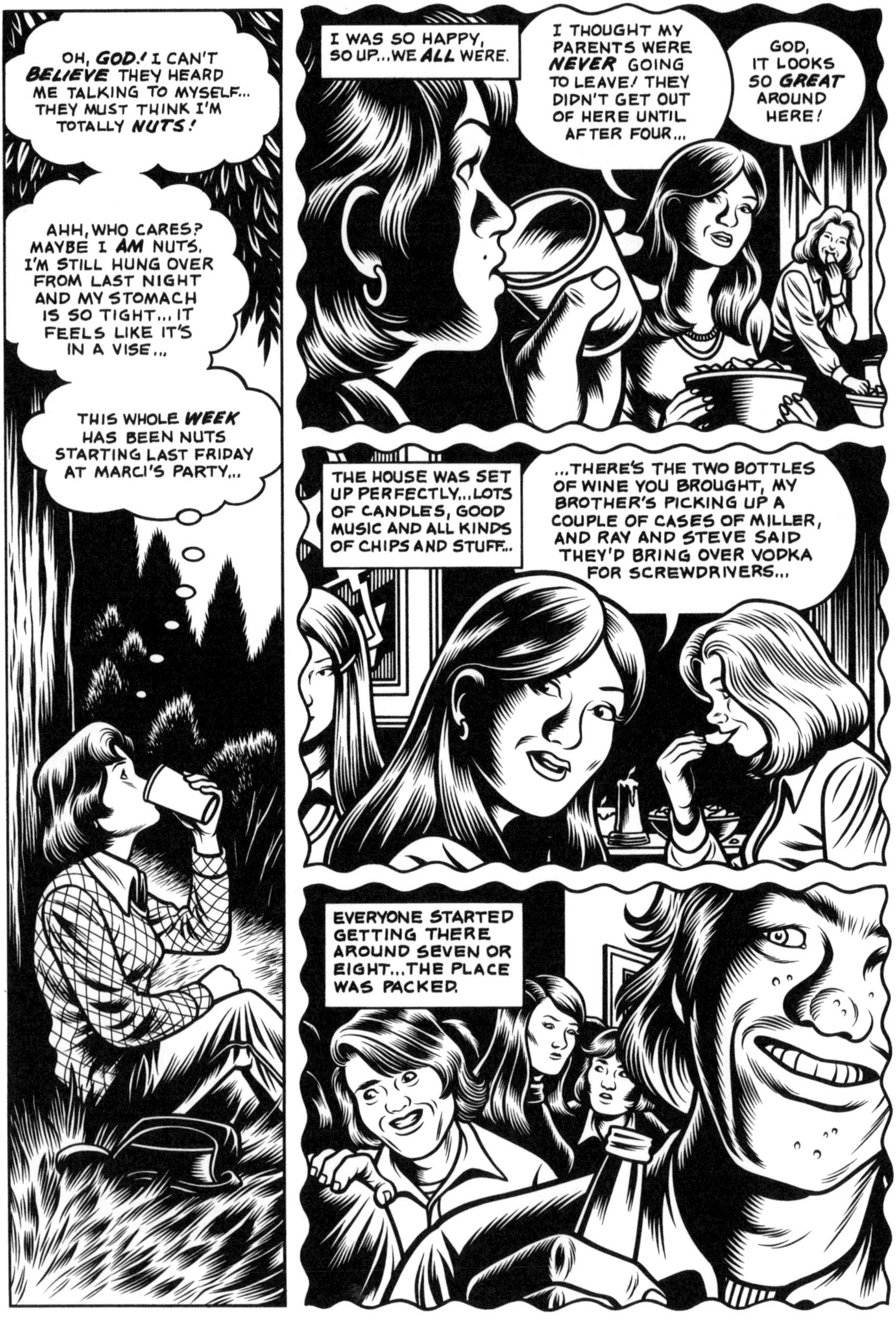
OH, GOD! I CAN'T BELIEVE THEY HEARD ME TALKING TO MYSELF... THEY MUST THINK I'M TOTALLY NUTS!
AHH, WHO CARES? MAYBE I AM NUTS. I'M STILL HUNG OVER FROM LAST NIGHT AND MY STOMACH IS SO TIGHT... IT FEELS LIKE IT'S IN A VISE...
THIS WHOLE WEEK HAS BEEN NUTS STARTING LAST FRIDAY AT MARCI'S PARTY...
I WAS SO HAPPY, SO UP... WE ALL WERE.
I THOUGHT MY PARENTS WERE NEVER GOING TO LEAVE! THEY DIDN'T GET OUT OF HERE UNTIL AFTER FOUR...
GOD, IT LOOKS SO GREAT AROUND HERE!
THE HOUSE WAS SET UP PERFECTLY... LOTS OF CANDLES, GOOD MUSIC AND ALL KINDS OF CHIPS AND STUFF...
...THERE'S THE TWO BOTTLES OF WINE YOU BROUGHT, MY BROTHER'S PICKING UP A COUPLE OF CASES OF MILLER, AND RAY AND STEVE SAID THEY'D BRING OVER VODKA FOR SCREWDRIVERS...
EVERYONE STARTED GETTING THERE AROUND SEVEN OR EIGHT... THE PLACE WAS PACKED.

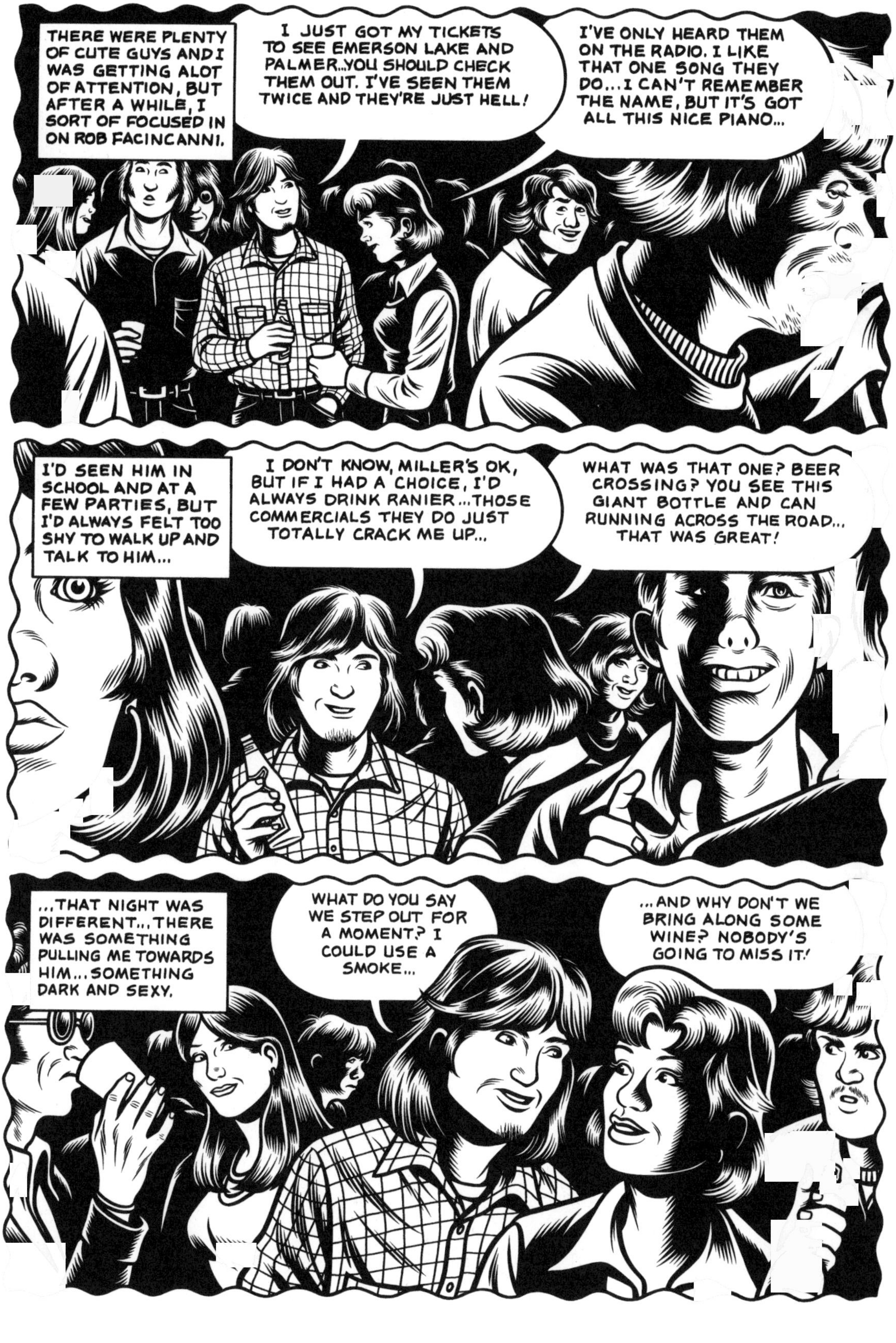
THERE WERE PLENTY OF CUTE GUYS AND I WAS GETTING ALOT OF ATTENTION, BUT AFTER A WHILE, I SORT OF FOCUSED IN ON ROB FACINCANNI.
I JUST GOT MY TICKETS TO SEE EMERSON LAKE AND PALMER...YOU SHOULD CHECK THEM OUT. I'VE SEEN THEM TWICE AND THEY'RE JUST HELL!
I'VE ONLY HEARD THEM ON THE RADIO. I LIKE THAT ONE SONG THEY DO... I CAN'T REMEMBER THE NAME, BUT IT'S GOT ALL THIS NICE PIANO...
I'D SEEN HIM IN SCHOOL AND AT A FEW PARTIES, BUT I'D ALWAYS FELT TOO SHY TO WALK UP AND TALK TO HIM...
I DON'T KNOW, MILLER'S OK, BUT IF I HAD A CHOICE, I'D ALWAYS DRINK RANIER... THOSE COMMERCIALS THEY DO JUST TOTALLY CRACK ME UP...
WHAT WAS THAT ONE? BEER CROSSING? YOU SEE THIS GIANT BOTTLE AND CAN RUNNING ACROSS THE ROAD... THAT WAS GREAT!
...THAT NIGHT WAS DIFFERENT... THERE WAS SOMETHING PULLING ME TOWARDS HIM... SOMETHING DARK AND SEXY.
WHAT DO YOU SAY WE STEP OUT FOR A MOMENT? I COULD USE A SMOKE...
...AND WHY DON'T WE BRING ALONG SOME WINE? NOBODY'S GOING TO MISS IT!

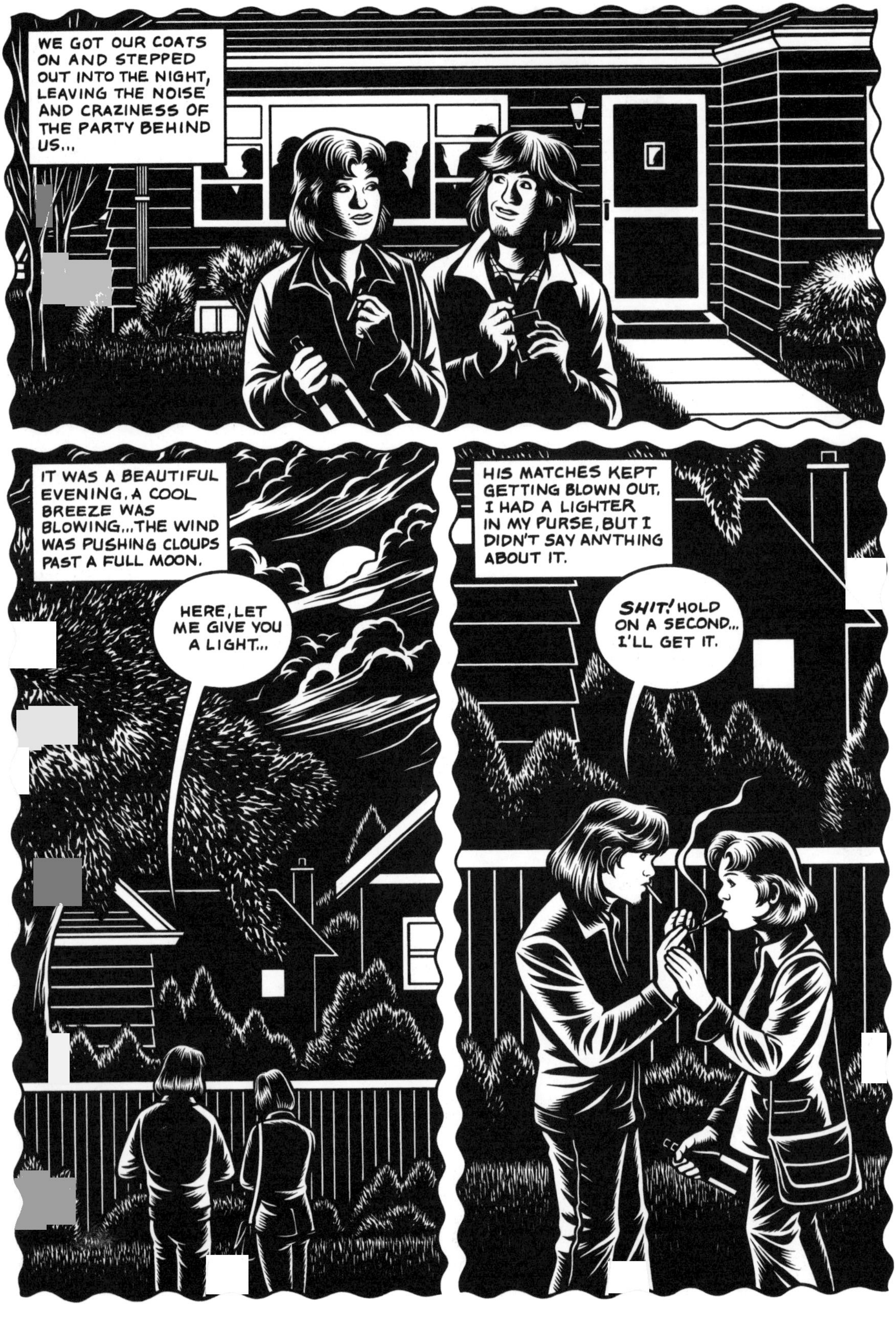
WE GOT OUR COATS ON AND STEPPED OUT INTO THE NIGHT, LEAVING THE NOISE AND CRAZINESS OF THE PARTY BEHIND US...
IT WAS A BEAUTIFUL EVENING. A COOL BREEZE WAS BLOWING...THE WIND WAS PUSHING CLOUDS PAST A FULL MOON.
HERE, LET ME GIVE YOU A LIGHT...
HIS MATCHES KEPT GETTING BLOWN OUT. I HAD A LIGHTER IN MY PURSE, BUT I DIDN'T SAY ANYTHING ABOUT IT.
SHIT! HOLD ON A SECOND... I'LL GET IT.

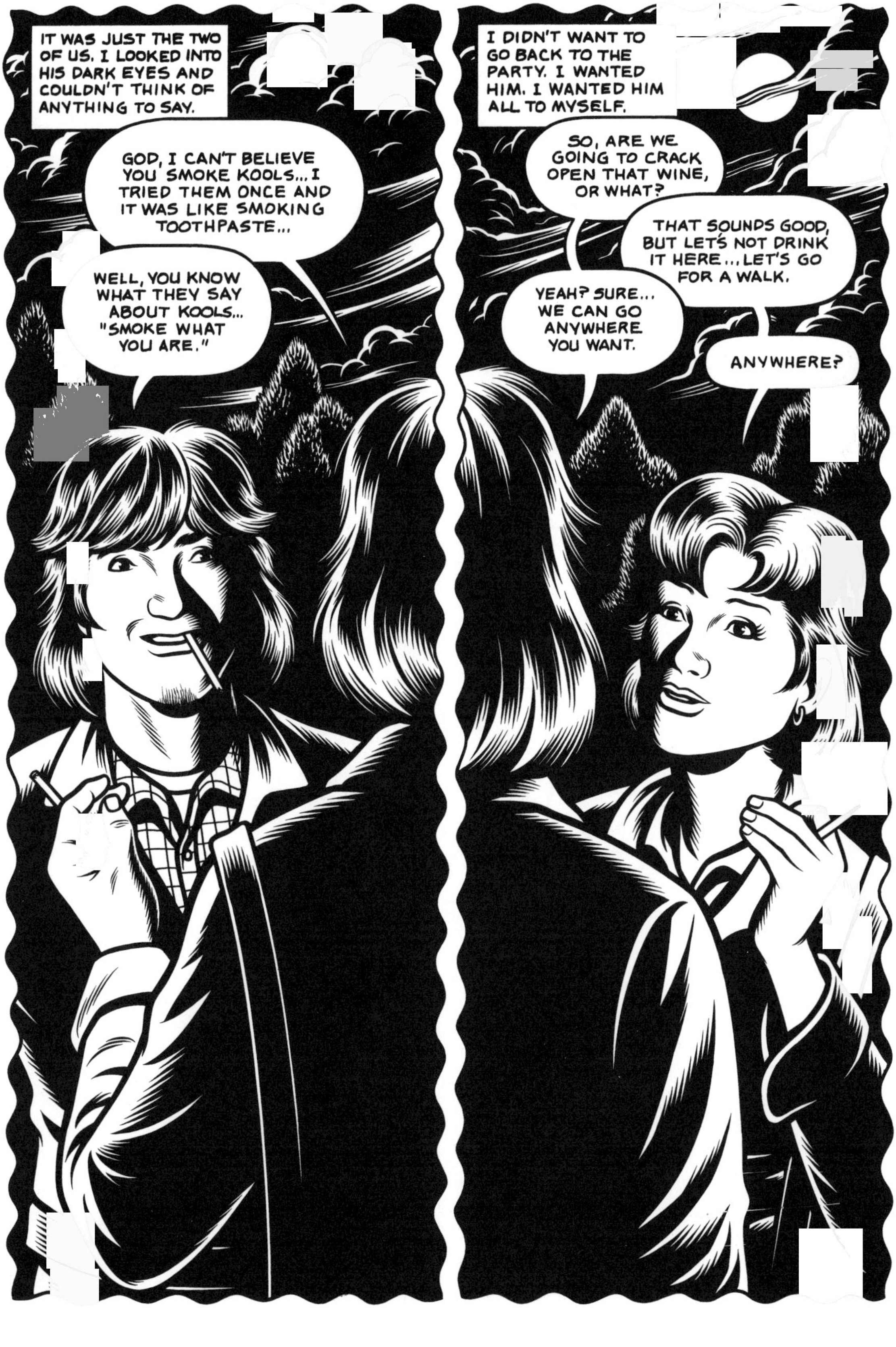
IT WAS JUST THE TWO OF US. I LOOKED INTO HIS DARK EYES AND COULDN'T THINK OF ANYTHING TO SAY.
GOD, I CAN'T BELIEVE YOU SMOKE KOOLS... I TRIED THEM ONCE AND IT WAS LIKE SMOKING TOOTHPASTE...
WELL, YOU KNOW WHAT THEY SAY ABOUT KOOLS... "SMOKE WHAT YOU ARE."
I DIDN'T WANT TO GO BACK TO THE PARTY. I WANTED HIM. I WANTED HIM ALL TO MYSELF.
SO, ARE WE GOING TO CRACK OPEN THAT WINE, OR WHAT?
THAT SOUNDS GOOD, BUT LET'S NOT DRINK IT HERE... LET'S GO FOR A WALK.
YEAH? SURE... WE CAN GO ANYWHERE YOU WANT.
ANYWHERE?

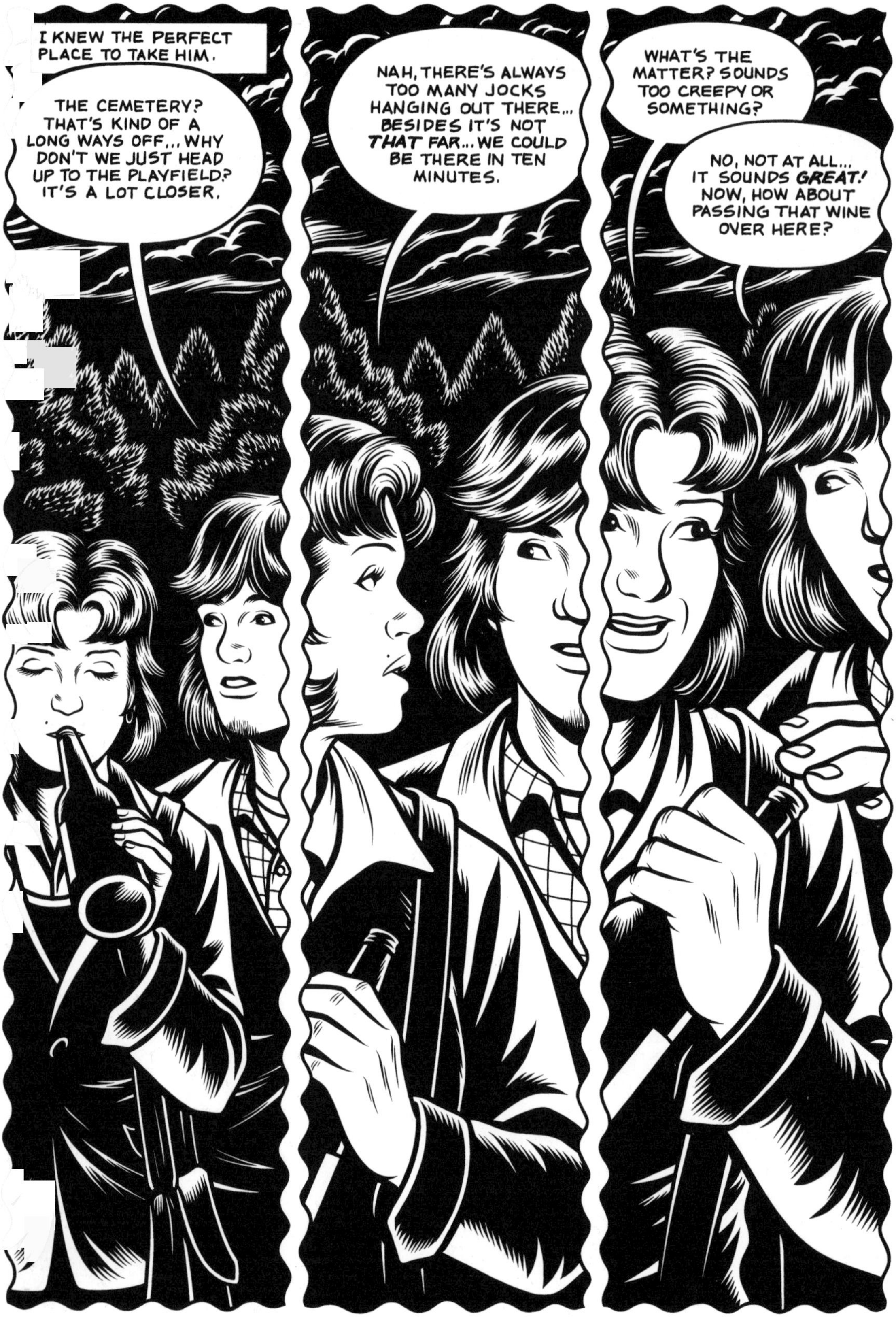

I KNEW THE PERFECT PLACE TO TAKE HIM.
THE CEMETERY? THAT'S KIND OF A LONG WAYS OFF... WHY DON'T WE JUST HEAD UP TO THE PLAYFIELD? IT'S A LOT CLOSER.
NAH, THERE'S ALWAYS TOO MANY JOCKS HANGING OUT THERE... BESIDES IT'S NOT *THAT* FAR... WE COULD BE THERE IN TEN MINUTES.
WHAT'S THE MATTER? SOUNDS TOO CREEPY OR SOMETHING?
NO, NOT AT ALL... IT SOUNDS **GREAT!** NOW, HOW ABOUT PASSING THAT WINE OVER HERE?

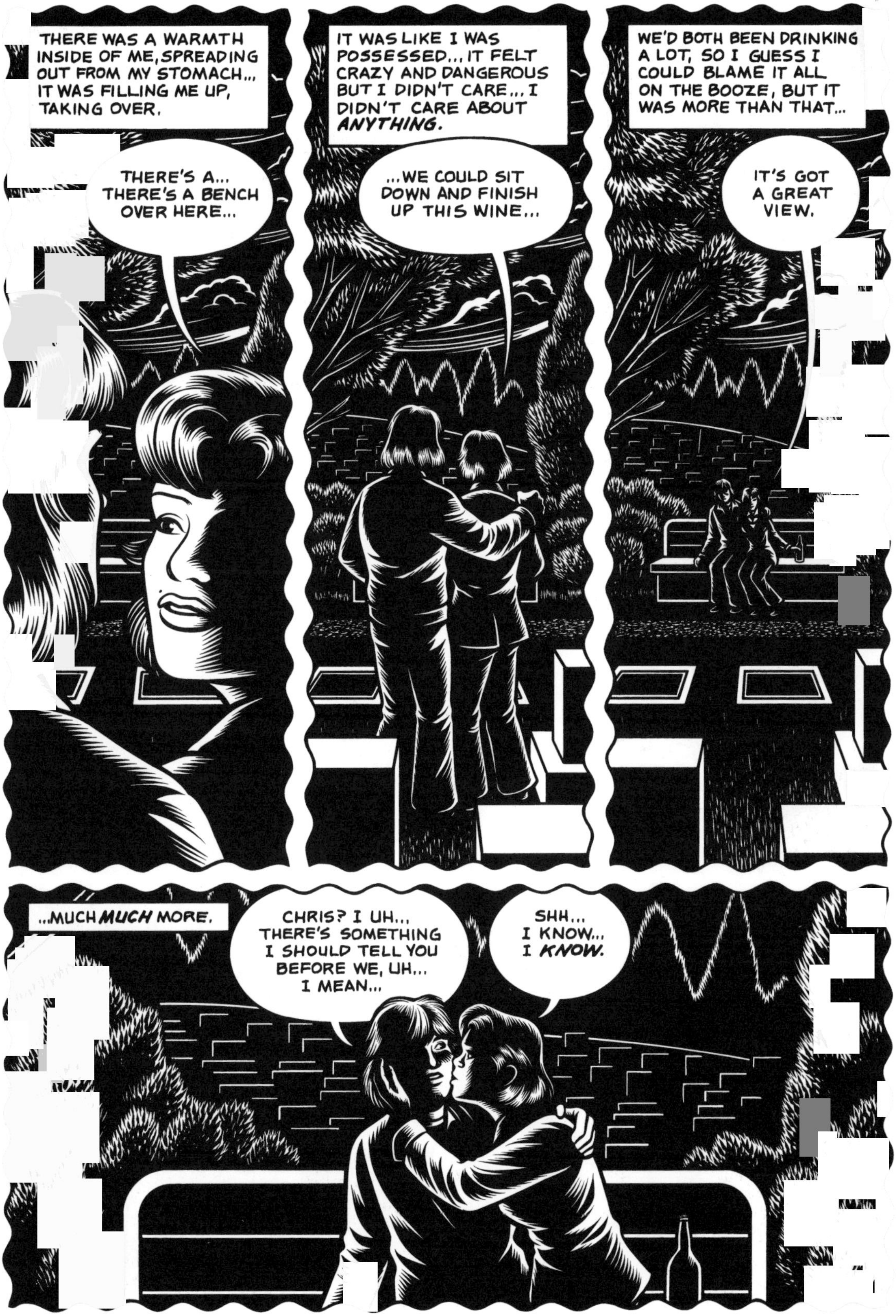
THERE WAS A WARMTH INSIDE OF ME, SPREADING OUT FROM MY STOMACH... IT WAS FILLING ME UP, TAKING OVER.
THERE'S A... THERE'S A BENCH OVER HERE...
IT WAS LIKE I WAS POSSESSED... IT FELT CRAZY AND DANGEROUS BUT I DIDN'T CARE... I DIDN'T CARE ABOUT ANYTHING.
...WE COULD SIT DOWN AND FINISH UP THIS WINE...
WE'D BOTH BEEN DRINKING A LOT, SO I GUESS I COULD BLAME IT ALL ON THE BOOZE, BUT IT WAS MORE THAN THAT...
IT'S GOT A GREAT VIEW.
...MUCH MUCH MORE.
CHRIS? I UH... THERE'S SOMETHING I SHOULD TELL YOU BEFORE WE, UH... I MEAN...
SHH... I KNOW... I KNOW.

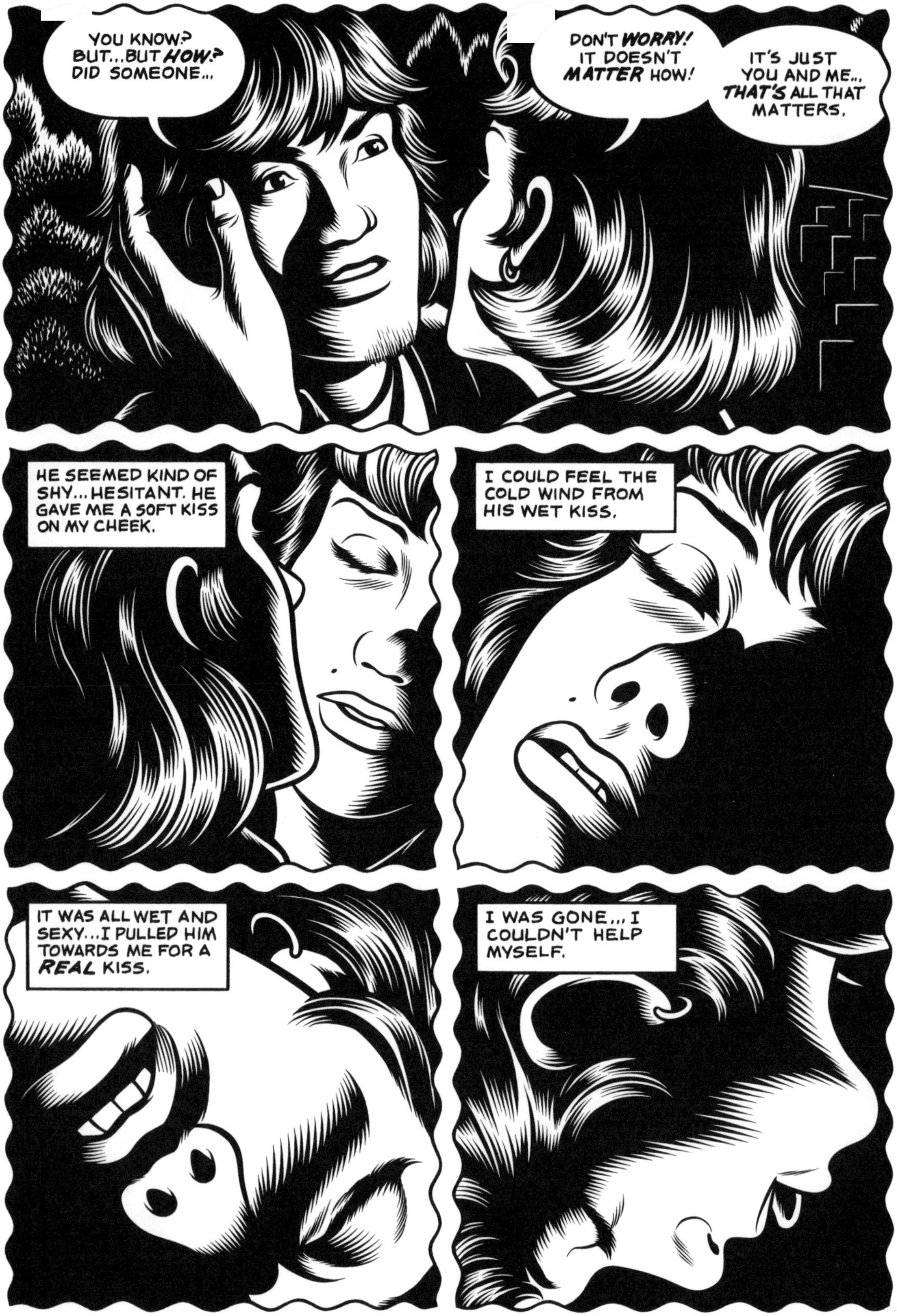
YOU KNOW? BUT...BUT HOW? DID SOMEONE...
DON'T WORRY! IT DOESN'T MATTER HOW!
IT'S JUST YOU AND ME... THAT'S ALL THAT MATTERS.
HE SEEMED KIND OF SHY... HESITANT. HE GAVE ME A SOFT KISS ON MY CHEEK.
I COULD FEEL THE COLD WIND FROM HIS WET KISS.
IT WAS ALL WET AND SEXY...I PULLED HIM TOWARDS ME FOR A REAL KISS.
I WAS GONE... I COULDN'T HELP MYSELF.

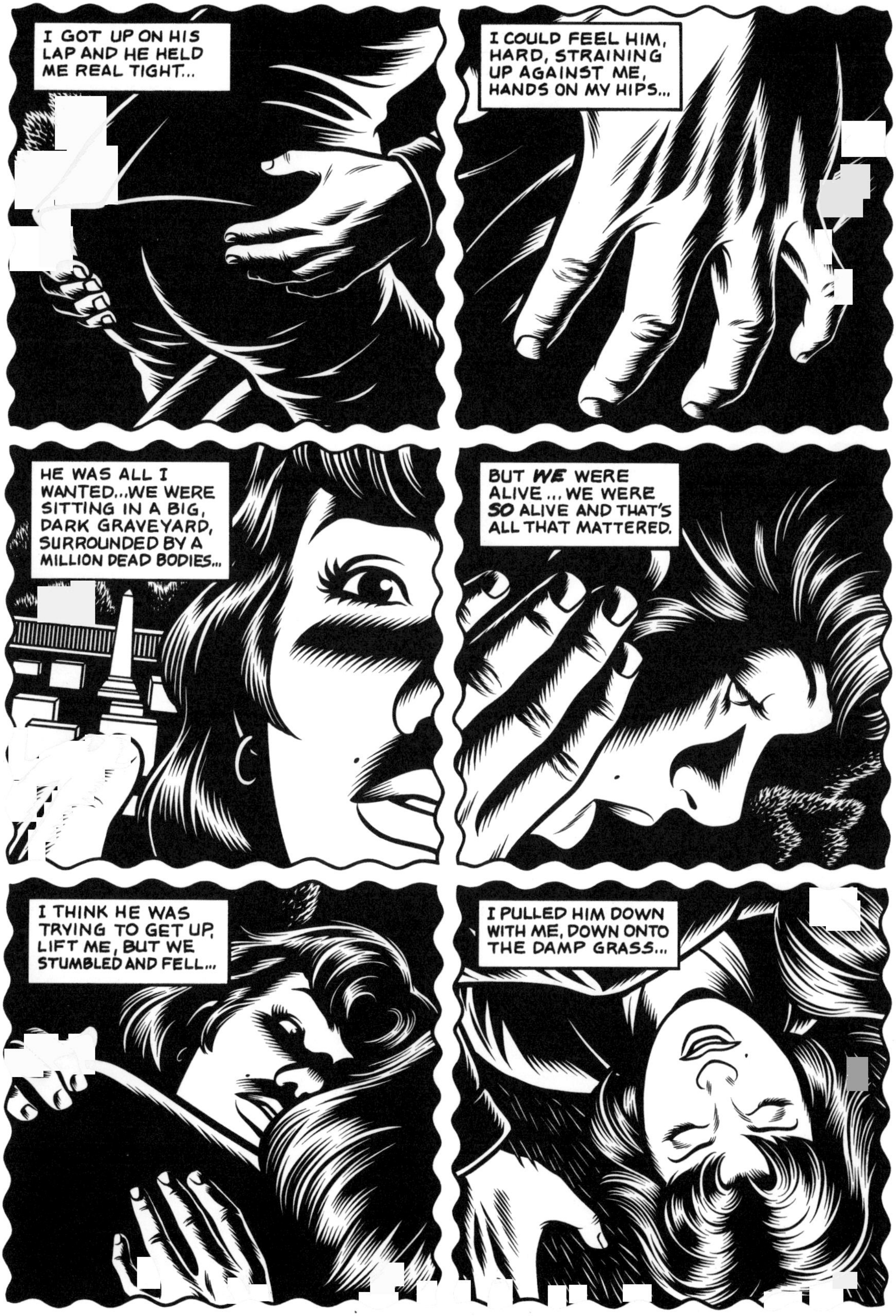
I GOT UP ON HIS LAP AND HE HELD ME REAL TIGHT...
I COULD FEEL HIM, HARD, STRAINING UP AGAINST ME, HANDS ON MY HIPS...
HE WAS ALL I WANTED...WE WERE SITTING IN A BIG, DARK GRAVEYARD, SURROUNDED BY A MILLION DEAD BODIES...
BUT WE WERE ALIVE... WE WERE SO ALIVE AND THAT'S ALL THAT MATTERED.
I THINK HE WAS TRYING TO GET UP, LIFT ME, BUT WE STUMBLED AND FELL...
I PULLED HIM DOWN WITH ME, DOWN ONTO THE DAMP GRASS...

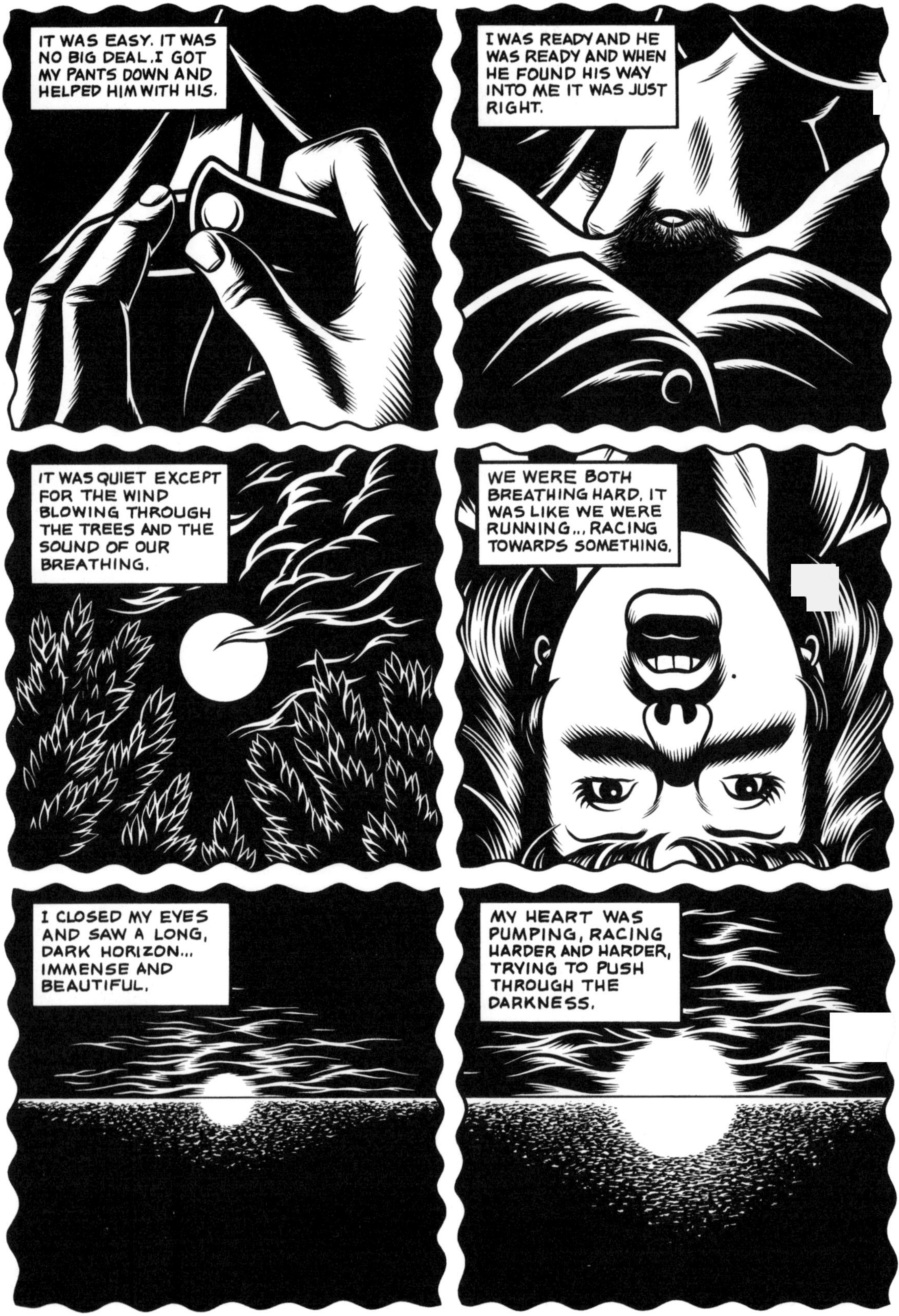
IT WAS EASY. IT WAS NO BIG DEAL. I GOT MY PANTS DOWN AND HELPED HIM WITH HIS.
I WAS READY AND HE WAS READY AND WHEN HE FOUND HIS WAY INTO ME IT WAS JUST RIGHT.
IT WAS QUIET EXCEPT FOR THE WIND BLOWING THROUGH THE TREES AND THE SOUND OF OUR BREATHING.
WE WERE BOTH BREATHING HARD. IT WAS LIKE WE WERE RUNNING... RACING TOWARDS SOMETHING.
I CLOSED MY EYES AND SAW A LONG, DARK HORIZON... IMMENSE AND BEAUTIFUL.
MY HEART WAS PUMPING, RACING HARDER AND HARDER, TRYING TO PUSH THROUGH THE DARKNESS.

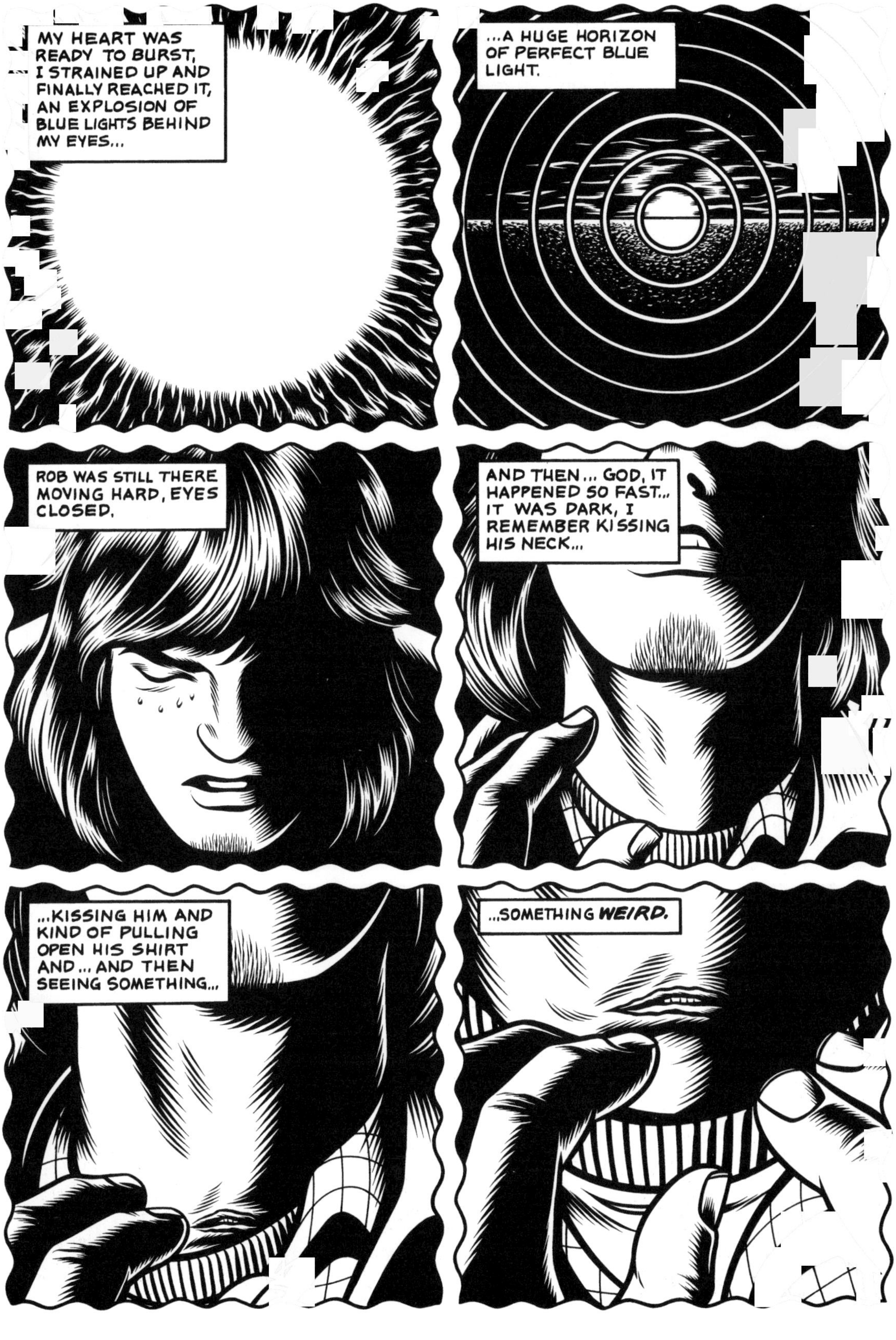
MY HEART WAS READY TO BURST, I STRAINED UP AND FINALLY REACHED IT, AN EXPLOSION OF BLUE LIGHTS BEHIND MY EYES...
...A HUGE HORIZON OF PERFECT BLUE LIGHT.
ROB WAS STILL THERE MOVING HARD, EYES CLOSED.
AND THEN... GOD, IT HAPPENED SO FAST... IT WAS DARK, I REMEMBER KISSING HIS NECK...
...KISSING HIM AND KIND OF PULLING OPEN HIS SHIRT AND... AND THEN SEEING SOMETHING...
...SOMETHING *WEIRD.*

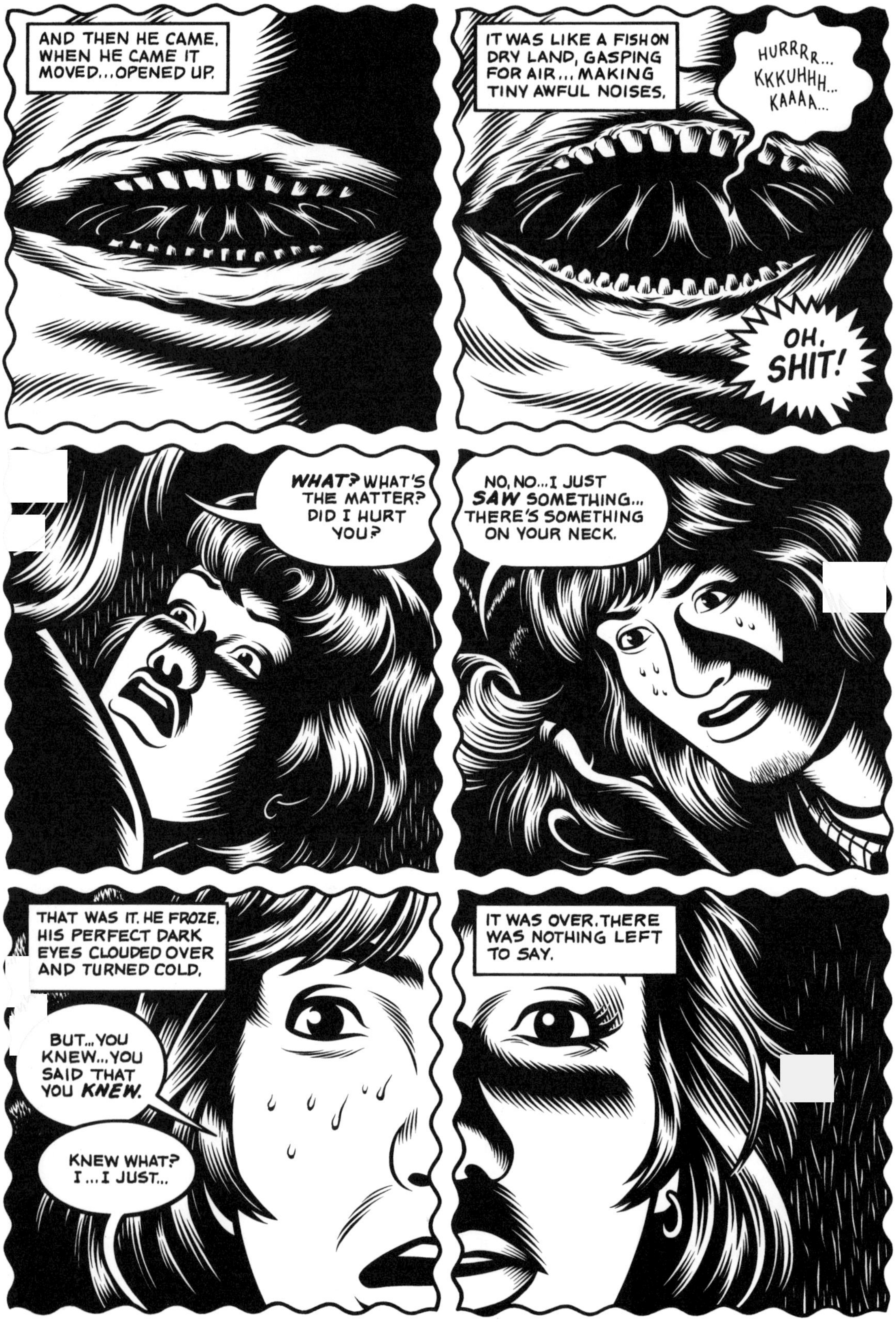
AND THEN HE CAME. WHEN HE CAME IT MOVED... OPENED UP.
IT WAS LIKE A FISH ON DRY LAND, GASPING FOR AIR... MAKING TINY AWFUL NOISES.
HURRRR... KKKUHHH... KAAAA...
OH, SHIT!
WHAT? WHAT'S THE MATTER? DID I HURT YOU?
NO, NO... I JUST SAW SOMETHING... THERE'S SOMETHING ON YOUR NECK.
THAT WAS IT. HE FROZE. HIS PERFECT DARK EYES CLOUDED OVER AND TURNED COLD.
BUT... YOU KNEW... YOU SAID THAT YOU KNEW.
KNEW WHAT? I... I JUST...
IT WAS OVER. THERE WAS NOTHING LEFT TO SAY.

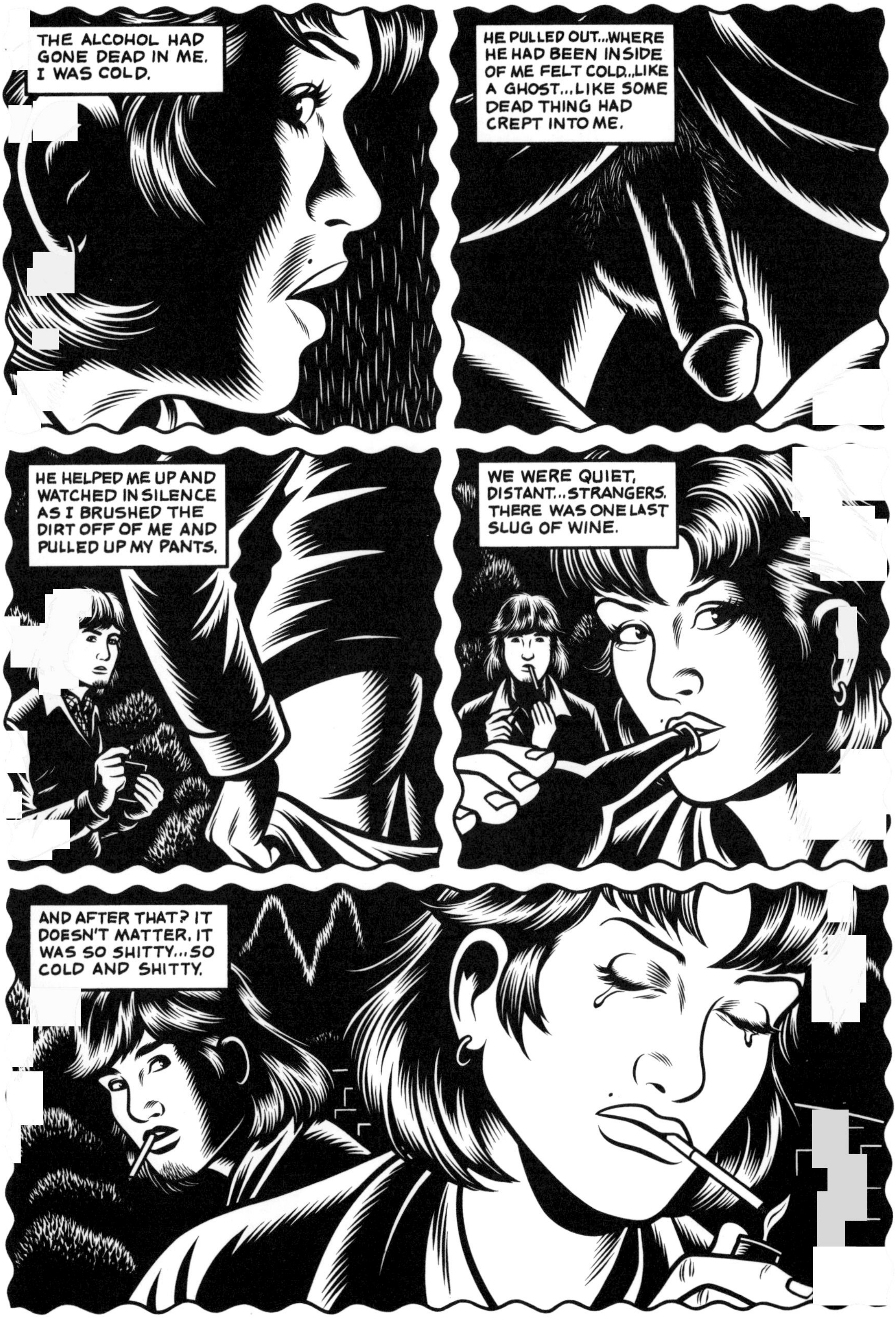
THE ALCOHOL HAD GONE DEAD IN ME. I WAS COLD.
HE PULLED OUT...WHERE HE HAD BEEN INSIDE OF ME FELT COLD...LIKE A GHOST...LIKE SOME DEAD THING HAD CREPT INTO ME.
HE HELPED ME UP AND WATCHED IN SILENCE AS I BRUSHED THE DIRT OFF OF ME AND PULLED UP MY PANTS.
WE WERE QUIET, DISTANT...STRANGERS. THERE WAS ONE LAST SLUG OF WINE.
AND AFTER THAT? IT DOESN'T MATTER. IT WAS SO SHITTY...SO COLD AND SHITTY.

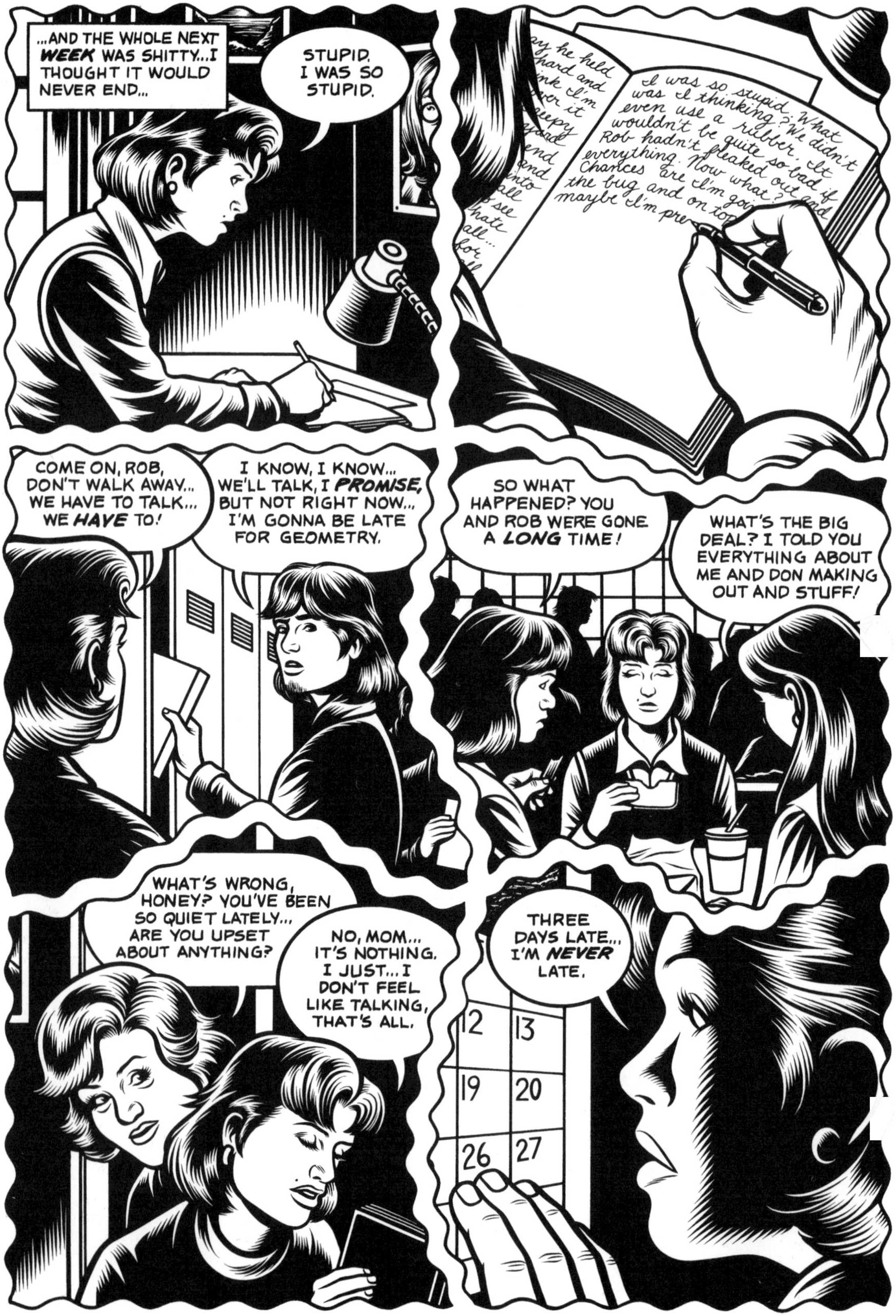
...AND THE WHOLE NEXT **WEEK** WAS SHITTY...I THOUGHT IT WOULD NEVER END...
STUPID. I WAS SO STUPID.
COME ON, ROB, DON'T WALK AWAY... WE HAVE TO TALK... WE **HAVE** TO!
I KNOW, I KNOW... WE'LL TALK, I **PROMISE,** BUT NOT RIGHT NOW... I'M GONNA BE LATE FOR GEOMETRY.
SO WHAT HAPPENED? YOU AND ROB WERE GONE A **LONG** TIME!
WHAT'S THE BIG DEAL? I TOLD YOU EVERYTHING ABOUT ME AND DON MAKING OUT AND STUFF!
WHAT'S WRONG, HONEY? YOU'VE BEEN SO QUIET LATELY... ARE YOU UPSET ABOUT ANYTHING?
NO, MOM... IT'S NOTHING. I JUST... I DON'T FEEL LIKE TALKING, THAT'S ALL.
THREE DAYS LATE... I'M **NEVER** LATE.
12 13
19 20
26 27

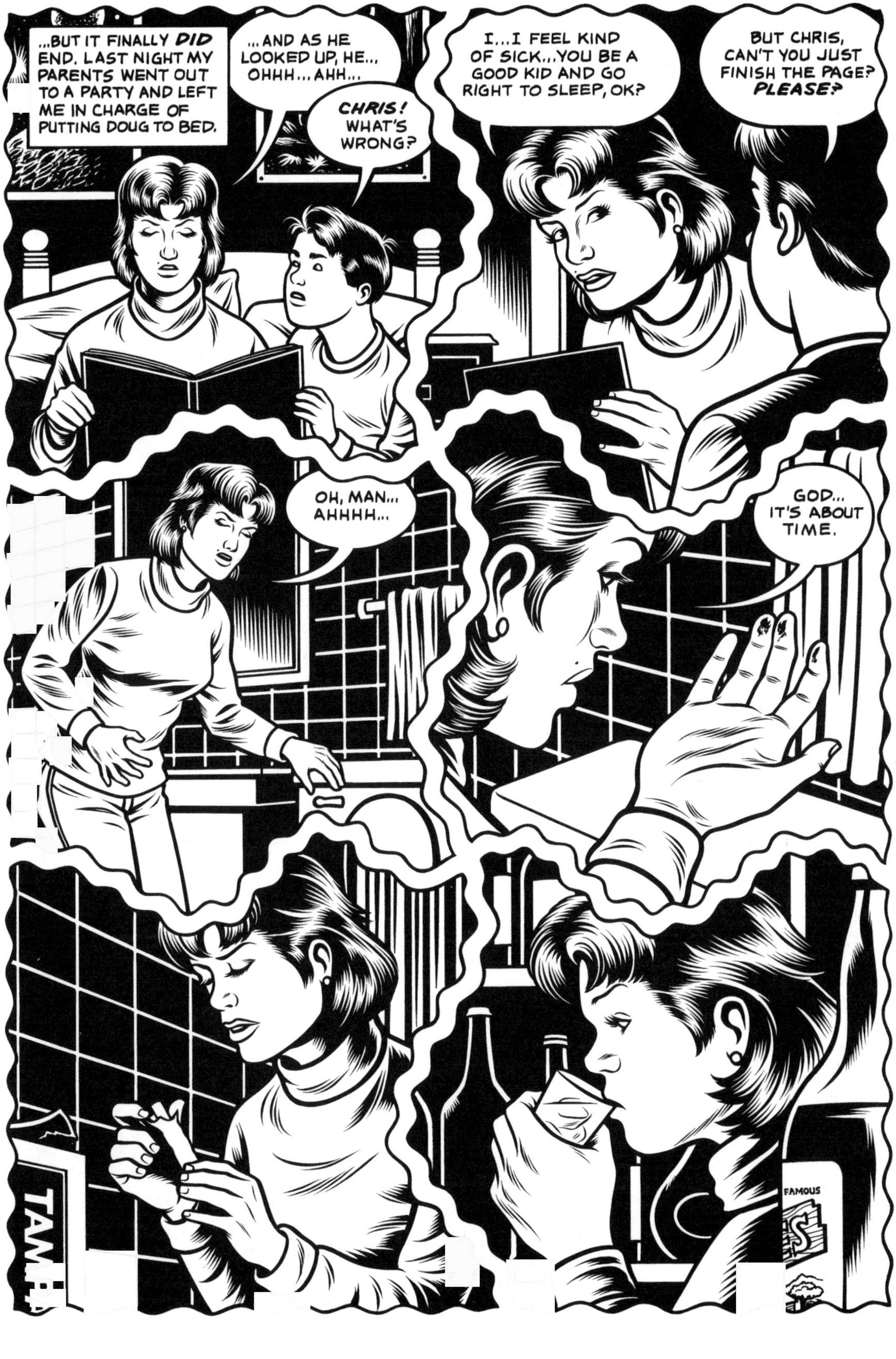
...BUT IT FINALLY *DID* END. LAST NIGHT MY PARENTS WENT OUT TO A PARTY AND LEFT ME IN CHARGE OF PUTTING DOUG TO BED.
...AND AS HE LOOKED UP, HE... OHHH... AHH...
CHRIS! WHAT'S WRONG?
I...I FEEL KIND OF SICK...YOU BE A GOOD KID AND GO RIGHT TO SLEEP, OK?
BUT CHRIS, CAN'T YOU JUST FINISH THE PAGE? *PLEASE?*
OH, MAN... AHHHH...
GOD... IT'S ABOUT TIME.
FAMOUS

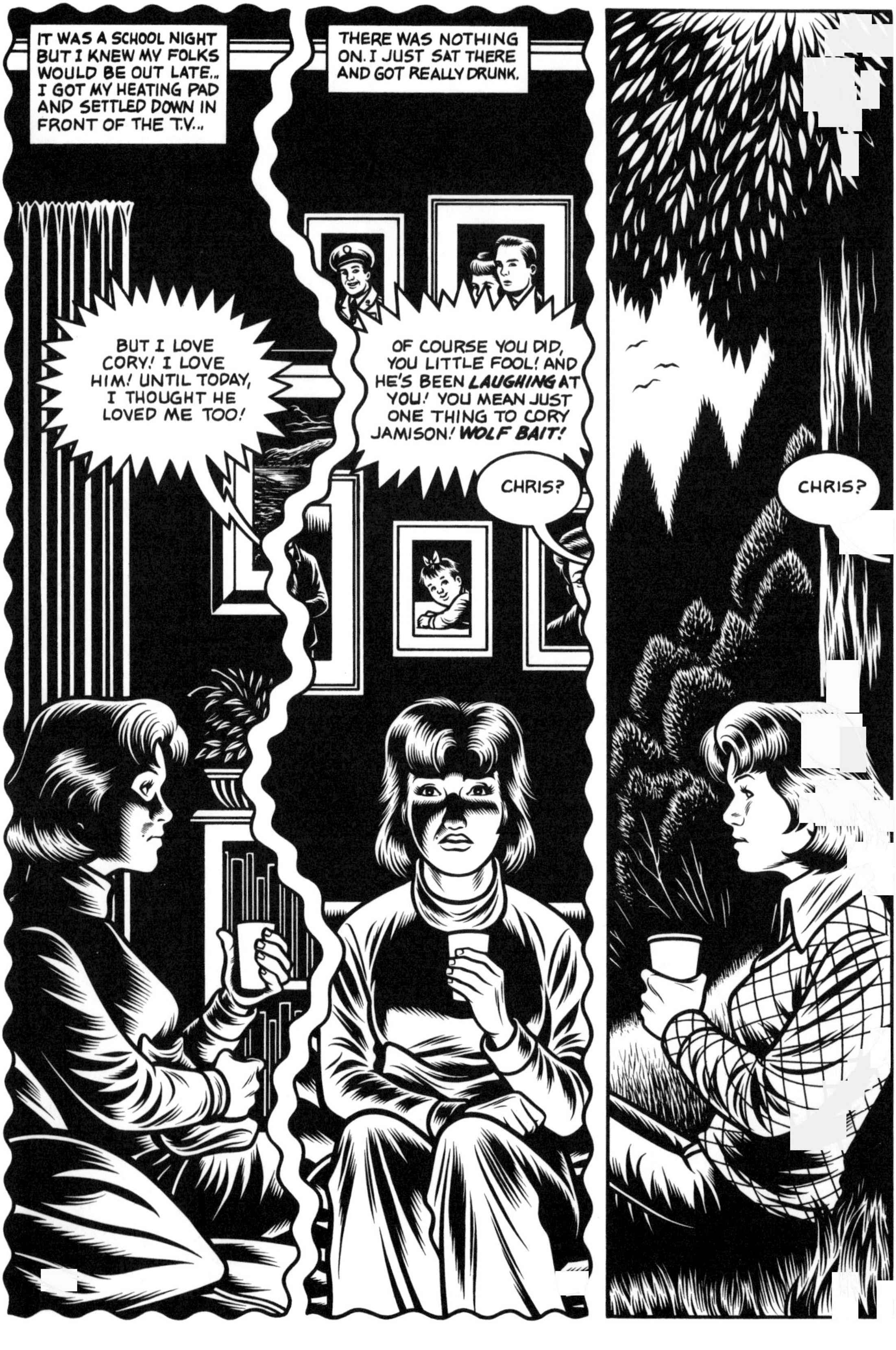

IT WAS A SCHOOL NIGHT BUT I KNEW MY FOLKS WOULD BE OUT LATE... I GOT MY HEATING PAD AND SETTLED DOWN IN FRONT OF THE T.V...
BUT I LOVE CORY! I LOVE HIM! UNTIL TODAY, I THOUGHT HE LOVED ME TOO!
THERE WAS NOTHING ON. I JUST SAT THERE AND GOT REALLY DRUNK.
OF COURSE YOU DID, YOU LITTLE FOOL! AND HE'S BEEN LAUGHING AT YOU! YOU MEAN JUST ONE THING TO CORY JAMISON! WOLF BAIT!
CHRIS?
CHRIS?

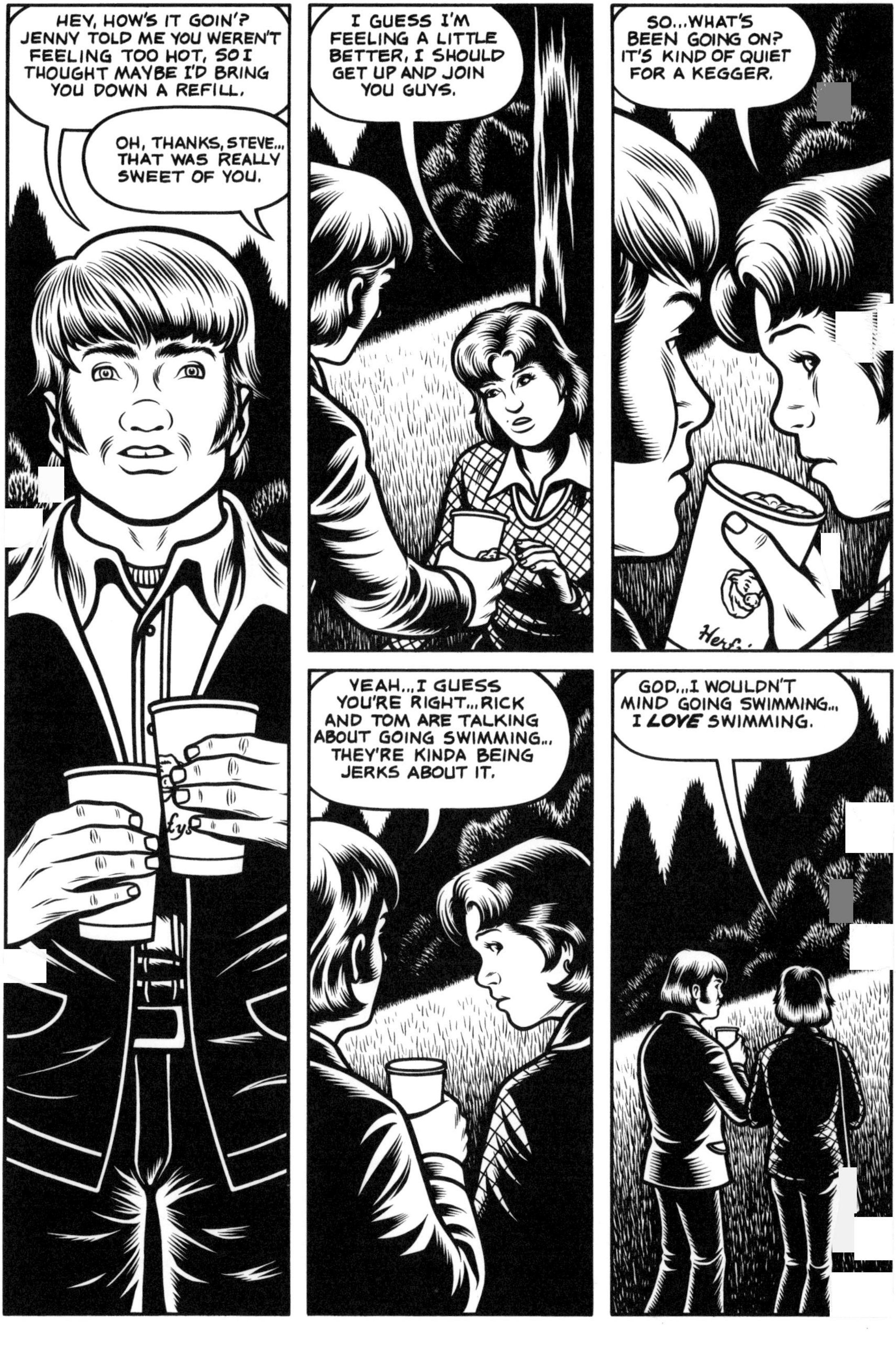
HEY, HOW'S IT GOIN'? JENNY TOLD ME YOU WEREN'T FEELING TOO HOT, SO I THOUGHT MAYBE I'D BRING YOU DOWN A REFILL.
OH, THANKS, STEVE... THAT WAS REALLY SWEET OF YOU.
I GUESS I'M FEELING A LITTLE BETTER, I SHOULD GET UP AND JOIN YOU GUYS.
SO...WHAT'S BEEN GOING ON? IT'S KIND OF QUIET FOR A KEGGER.
YEAH...I GUESS YOU'RE RIGHT...RICK AND TOM ARE TALKING ABOUT GOING SWIMMING... THEY'RE KINDA BEING JERKS ABOUT IT.
GOD...I WOULDN'T MIND GOING SWIMMING... I LOVE SWIMMING.

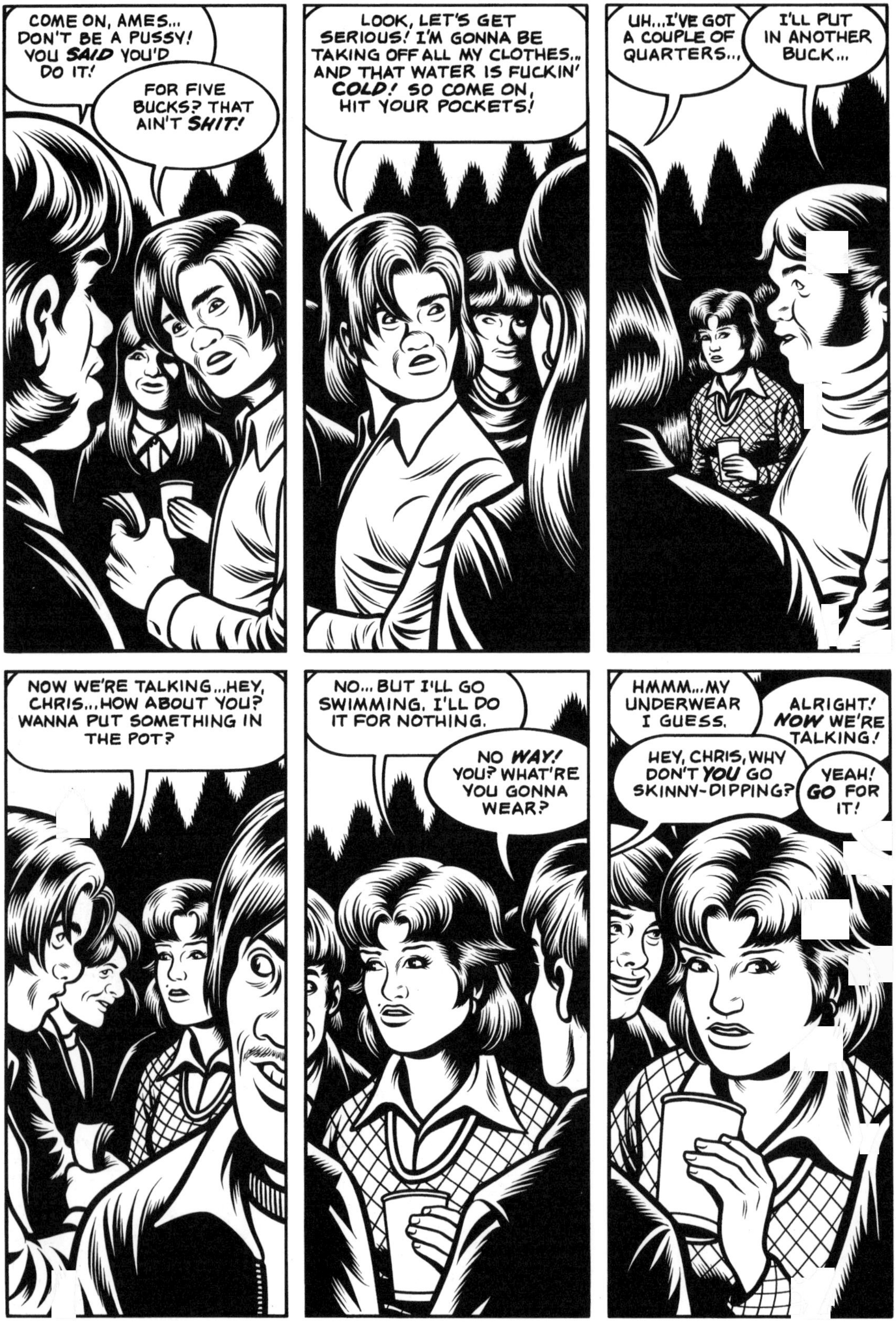
COME ON, AMES... DON'T BE A PUSSY! YOU SAID YOU'D DO IT!
FOR FIVE BUCKS? THAT AIN'T SHIT!
LOOK, LET'S GET SERIOUS! I'M GONNA BE TAKING OFF ALL MY CLOTHES... AND THAT WATER IS FUCKIN' COLD! SO COME ON, HIT YOUR POCKETS!
UH...I'VE GOT A COUPLE OF QUARTERS...
I'LL PUT IN ANOTHER BUCK...
NOW WE'RE TALKING...HEY, CHRIS...HOW ABOUT YOU? WANNA PUT SOMETHING IN THE POT?
NO... BUT I'LL GO SWIMMING. I'LL DO IT FOR NOTHING.
NO WAY! YOU? WHAT'RE YOU GONNA WEAR?
HMMM...MY UNDERWEAR I GUESS.
ALRIGHT! NOW WE'RE TALKING!
HEY, CHRIS, WHY DON'T YOU GO SKINNY-DIPPING?
YEAH! GO FOR IT!

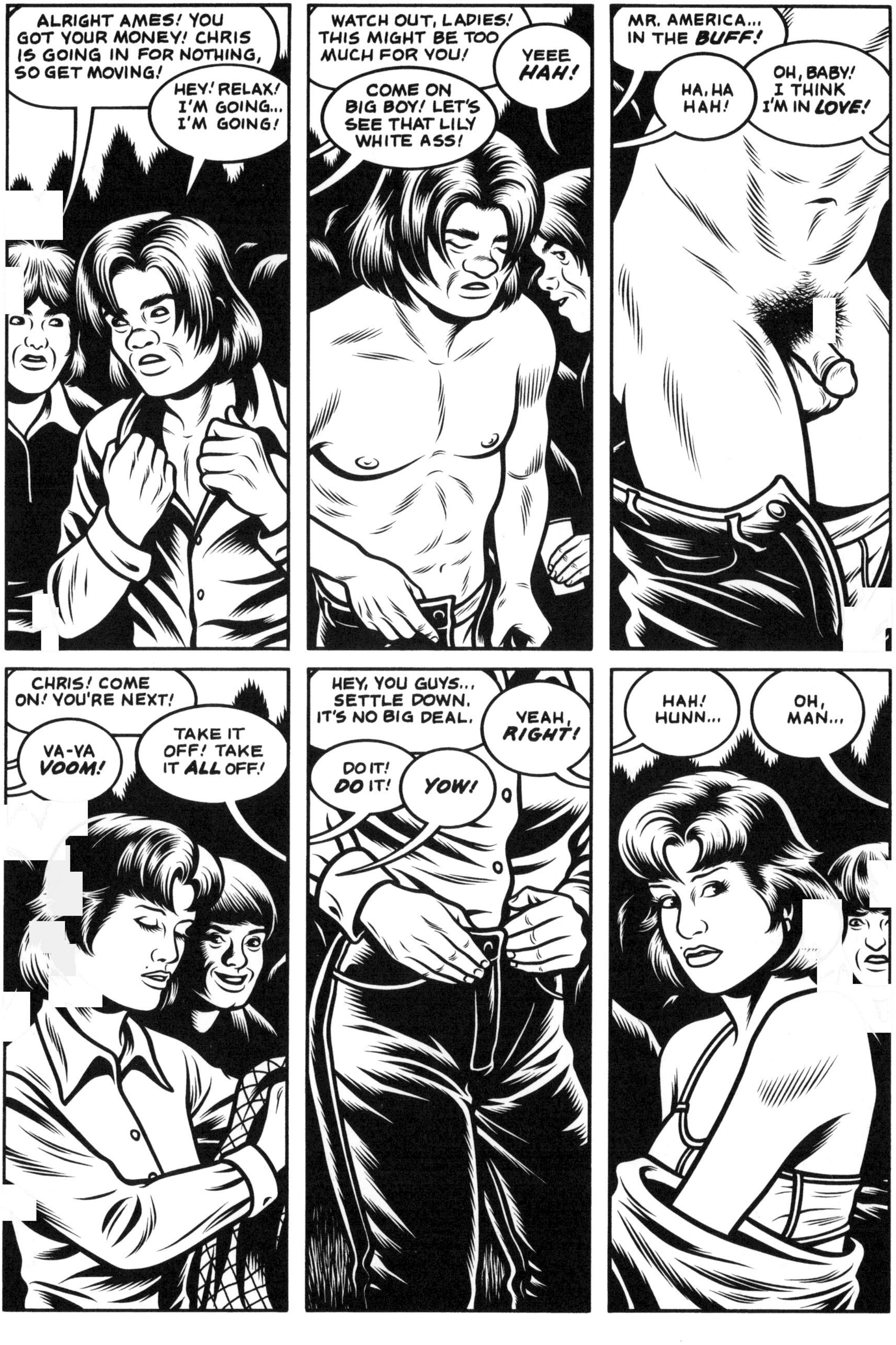
ALRIGHT AMES! YOU GOT YOUR MONEY! CHRIS IS GOING IN FOR NOTHING, SO GET MOVING!
HEY! RELAX! I'M GOING... I'M GOING!
WATCH OUT, LADIES! THIS MIGHT BE TOO MUCH FOR YOU!
YEEE HAH!
COME ON BIG BOY! LET'S SEE THAT LILY WHITE ASS!
MR. AMERICA... IN THE BUFF!
HA, HA HAH!
OH, BABY! I THINK I'M IN LOVE!
CHRIS! COME ON! YOU'RE NEXT!
VA-VA VOOM!
TAKE IT OFF! TAKE IT ALL OFF!
HEY, YOU GUYS... SETTLE DOWN. IT'S NO BIG DEAL.
YEAH, RIGHT!
DO IT! DO IT!
YOW!
HAH! HUNN...
OH, MAN...

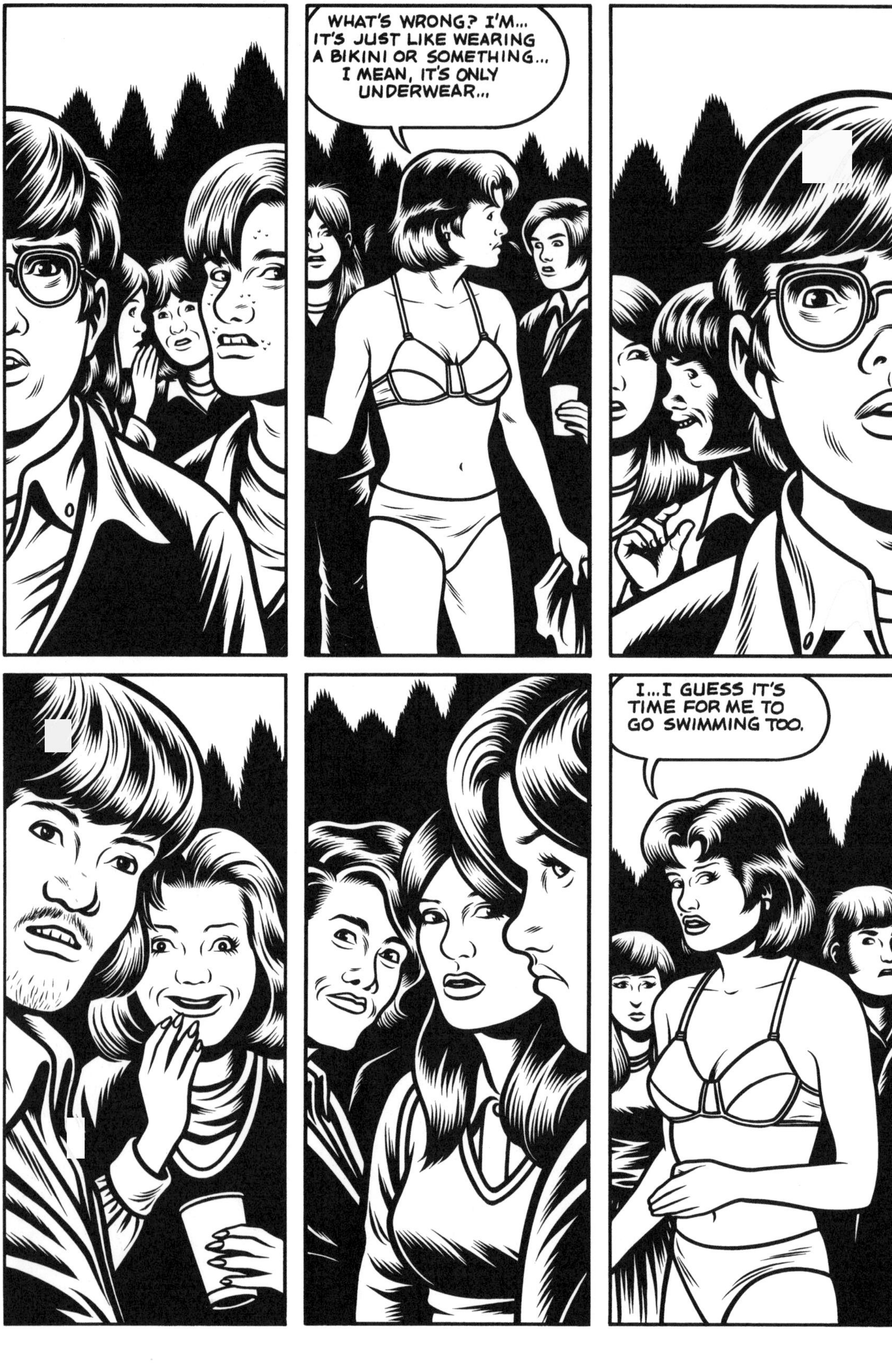
WHAT'S WRONG? I'M... IT'S JUST LIKE WEARING A BIKINI OR SOMETHING... I MEAN, IT'S ONLY UNDERWEAR...
I...I GUESS IT'S TIME FOR ME TO GO SWIMMING TOO.

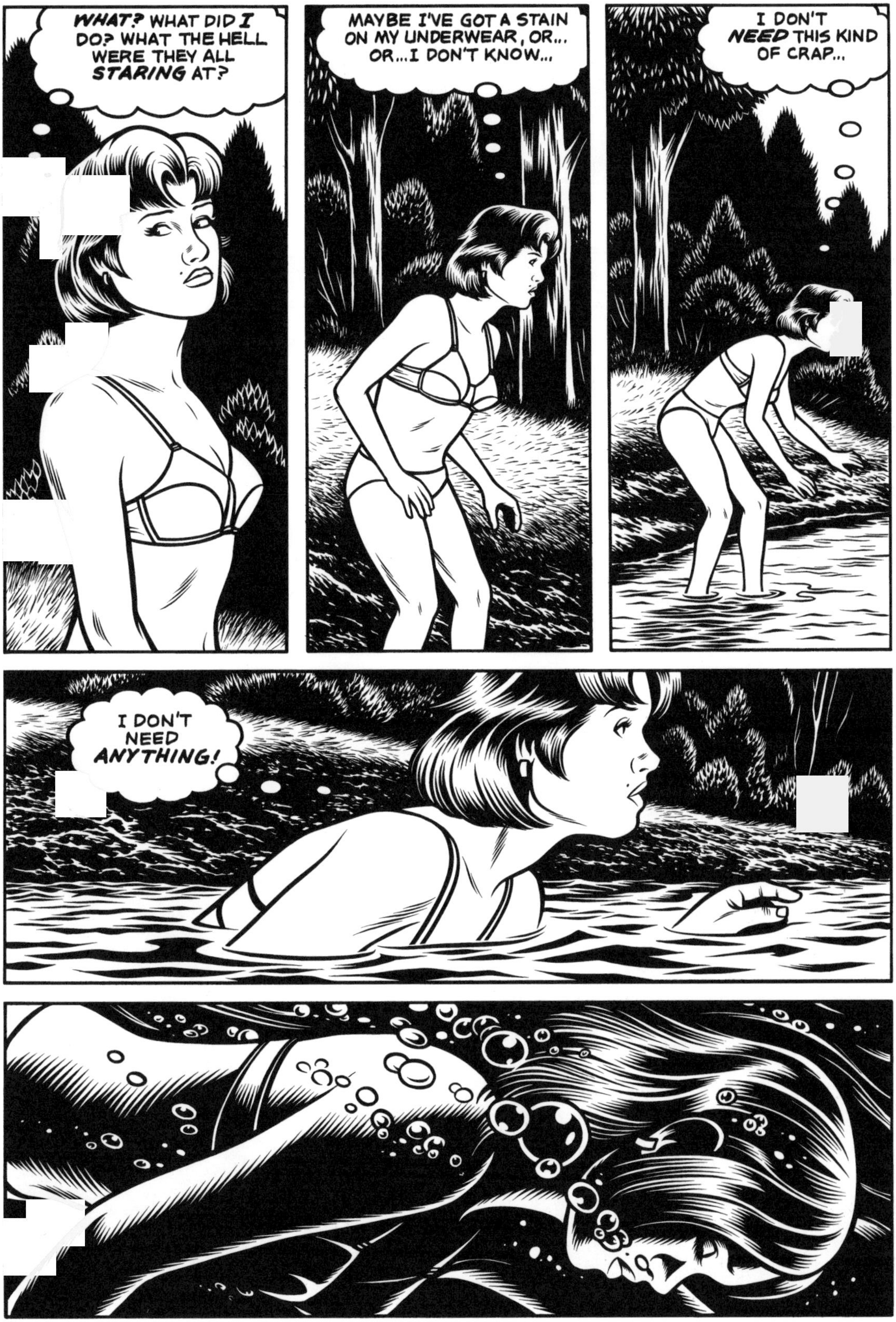
WHAT? WHAT DID I DO? WHAT THE HELL WERE THEY ALL STARING AT?
MAYBE I'VE GOT A STAIN ON MY UNDERWEAR, OR... OR... I DON'T KNOW...
I DON'T NEED THIS KIND OF CRAP...
I DON'T NEED ANYTHING!

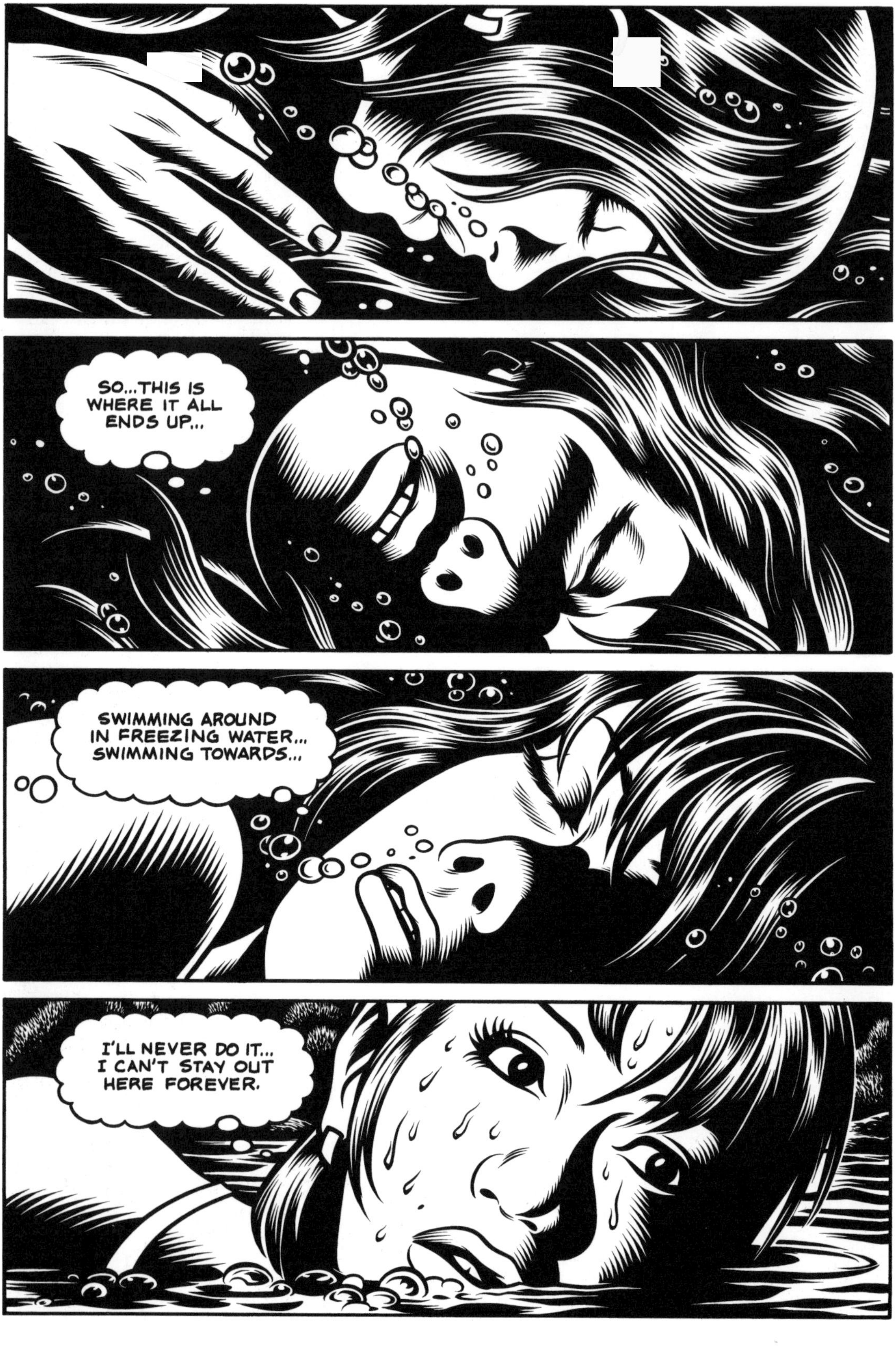
SO...THIS IS WHERE IT ALL ENDS UP...
SWIMMING AROUND IN FREEZING WATER... SWIMMING TOWARDS...
I'LL NEVER DO IT... I CAN'T STAY OUT HERE FOREVER.

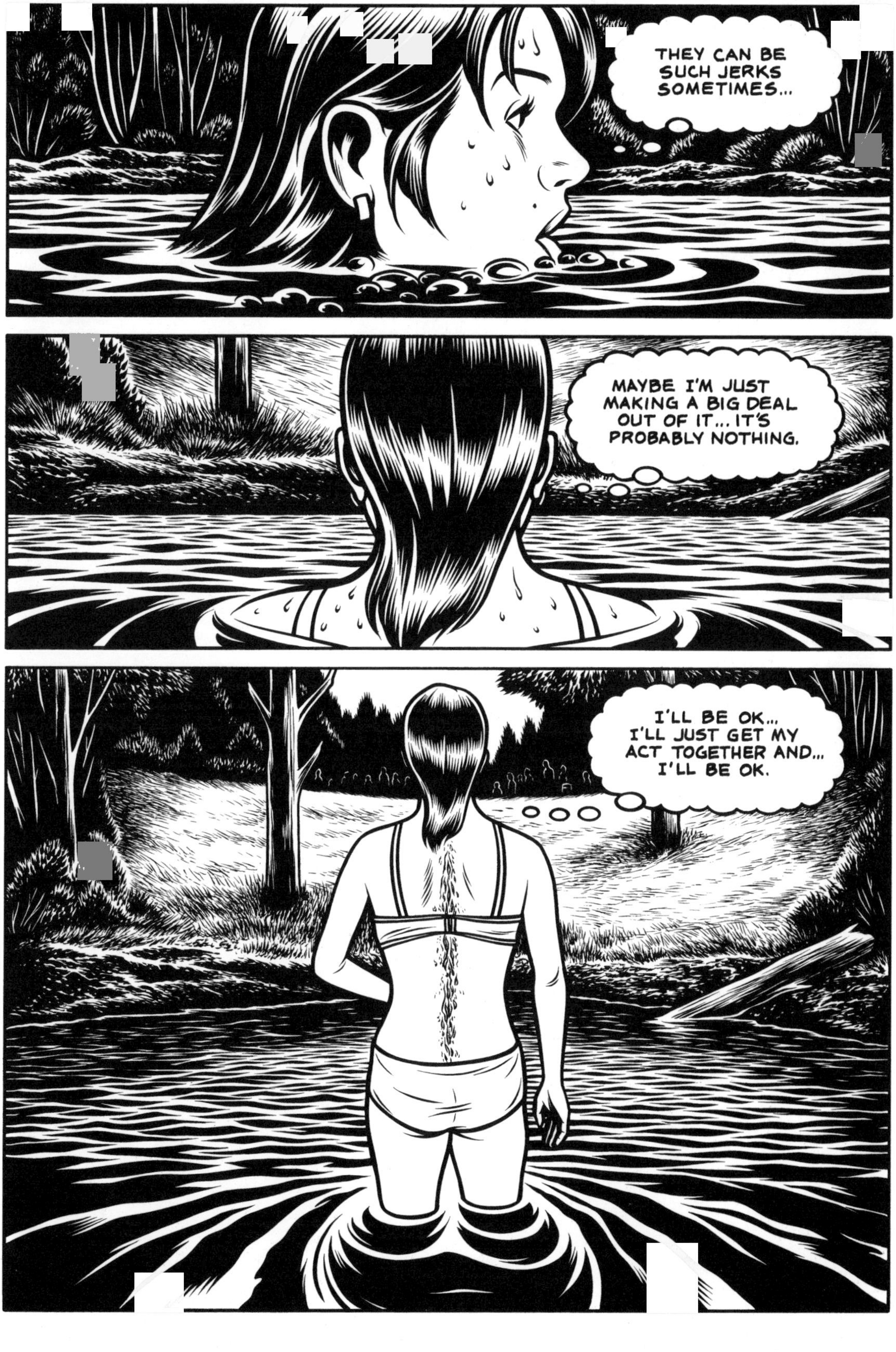
THEY CAN BE SUCH JERKS SOMETIMES...
MAYBE I'M JUST MAKING A BIG DEAL OUT OF IT... IT'S PROBABLY NOTHING.
I'LL BE OK... I'LL JUST GET MY ACT TOGETHER AND... I'LL BE OK.

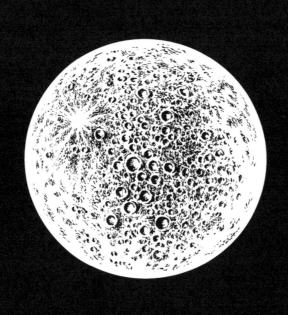

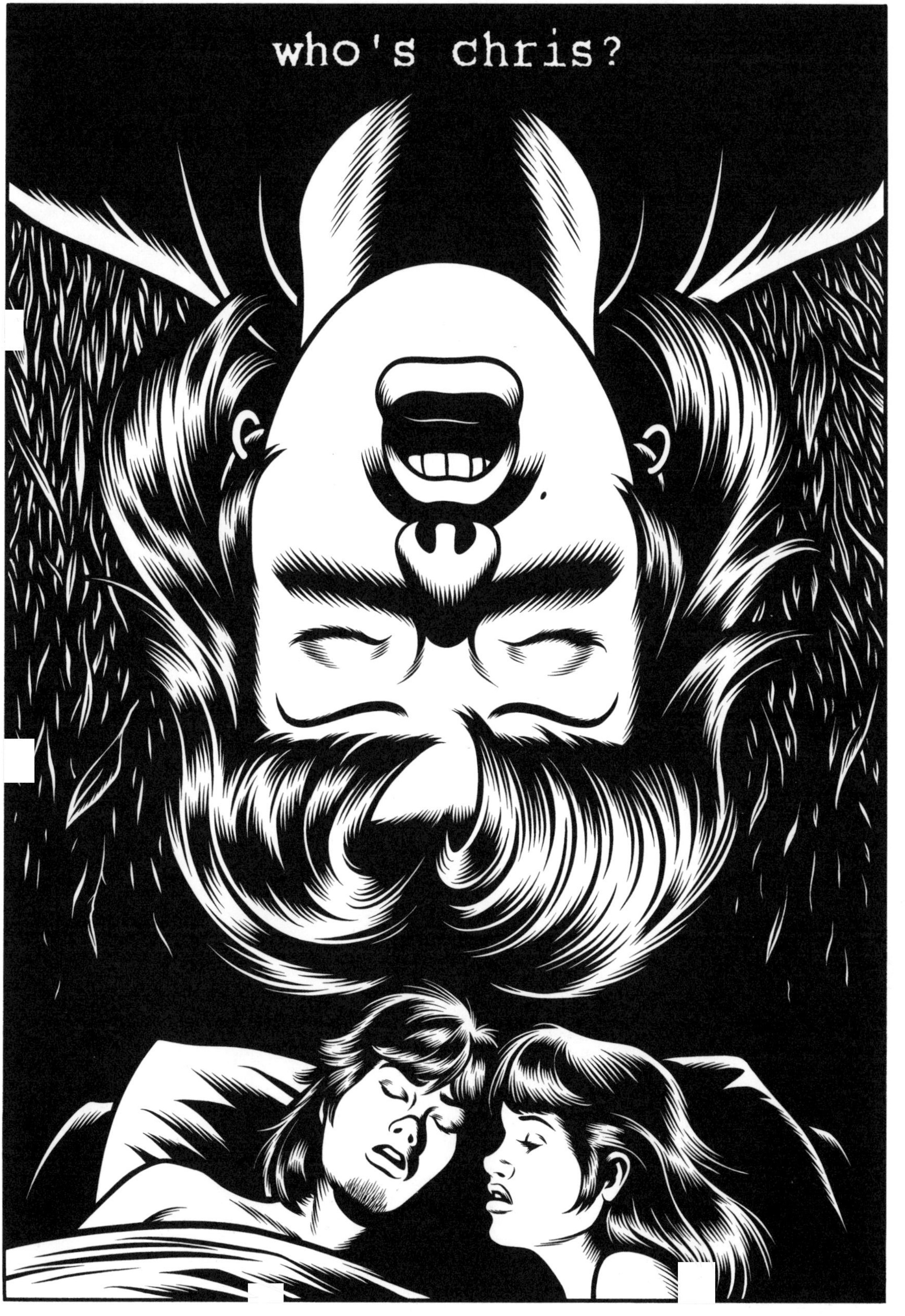
who's chris?

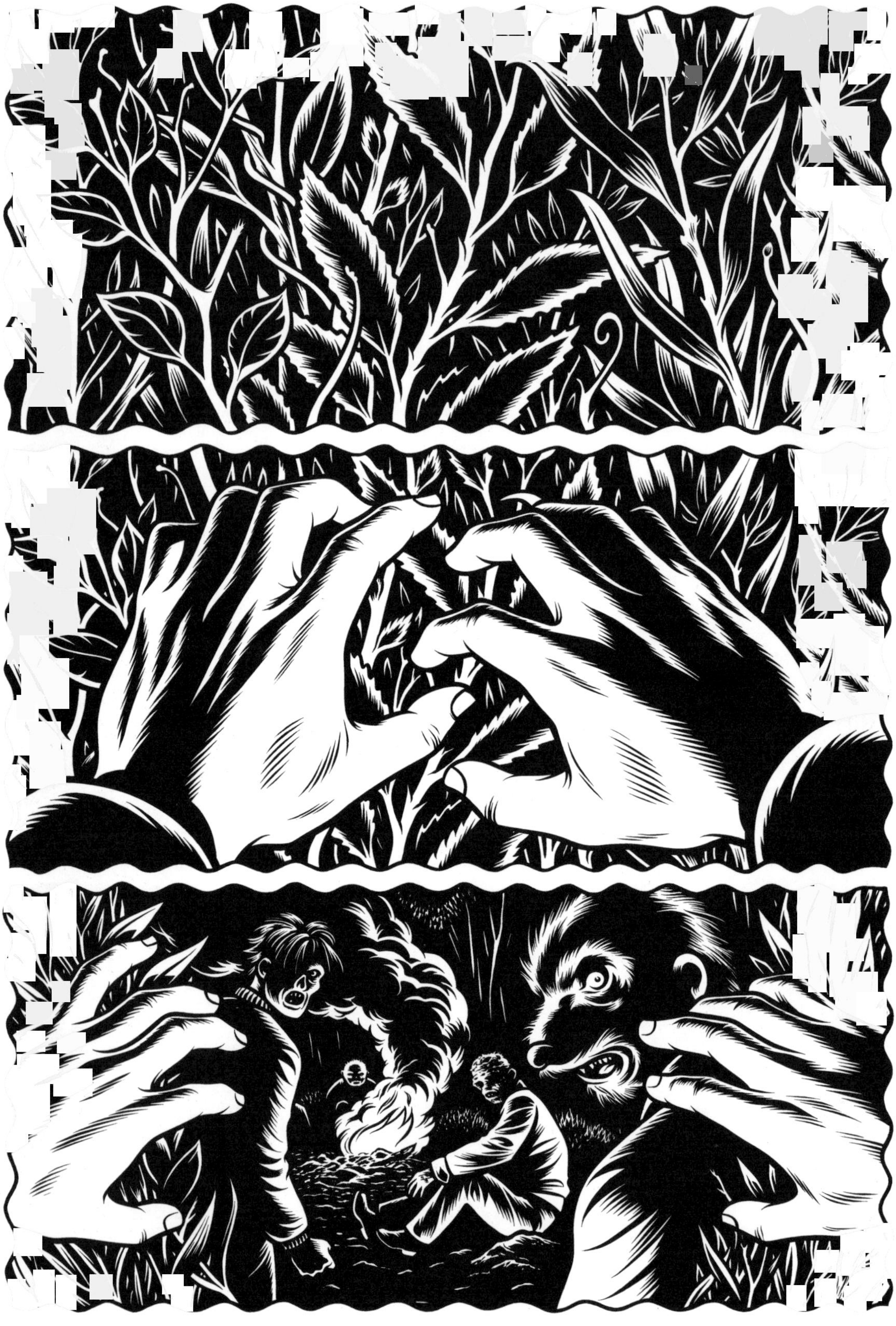

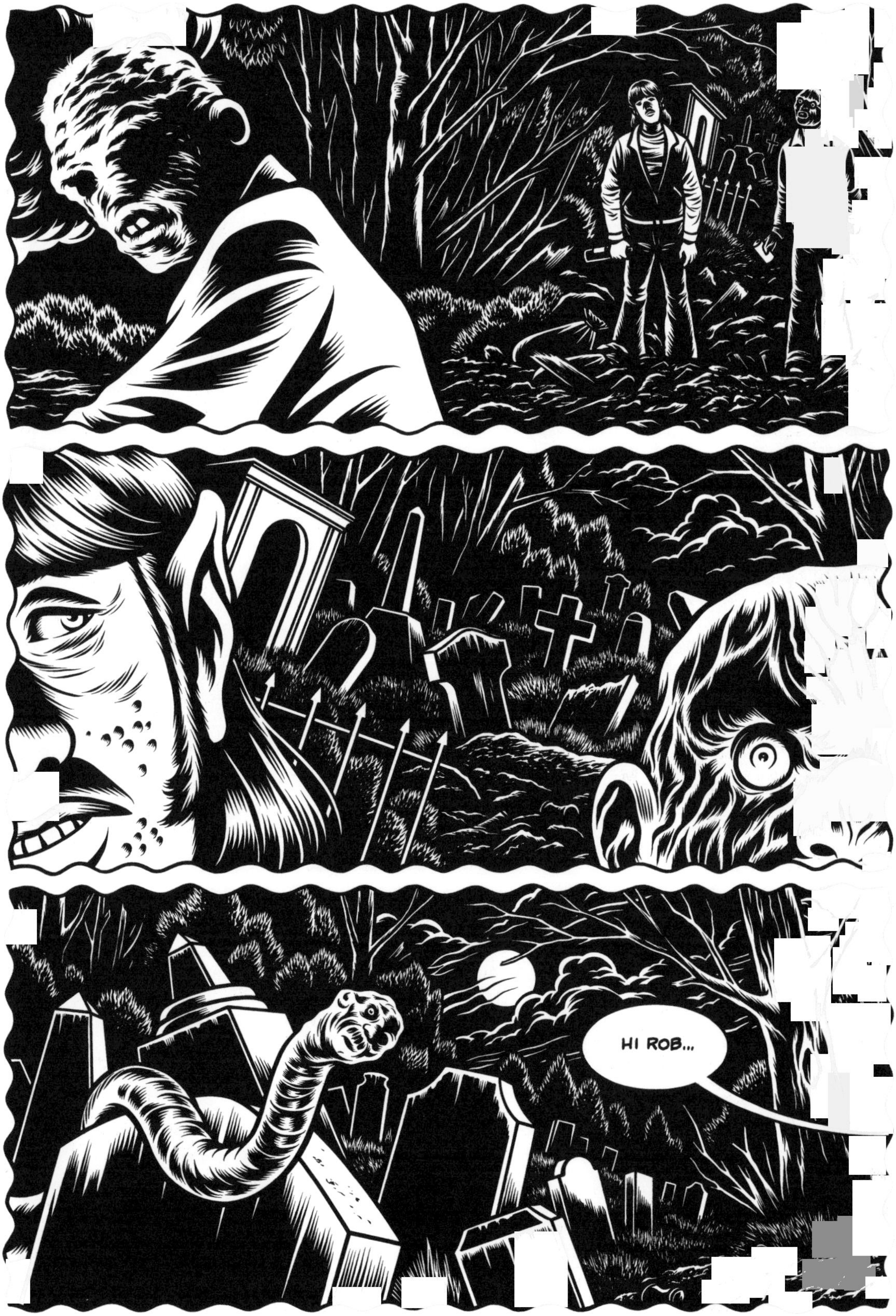
HI ROB...

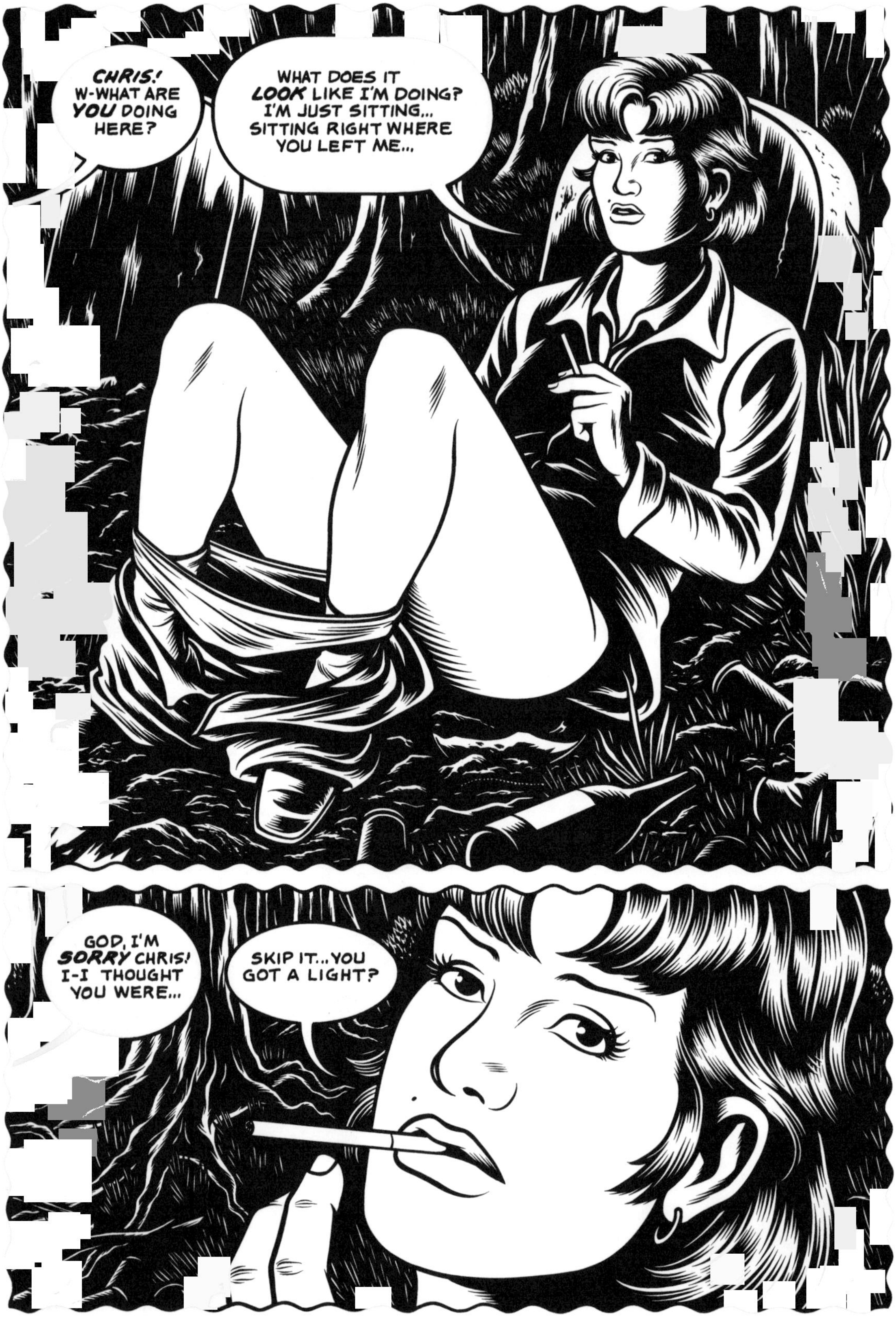
CHRIS! W-WHAT ARE YOU DOING HERE?
WHAT DOES IT LOOK LIKE I'M DOING? I'M JUST SITTING... SITTING RIGHT WHERE YOU LEFT ME...
GOD, I'M SORRY CHRIS! I-I THOUGHT YOU WERE...
SKIP IT... YOU GOT A LIGHT?

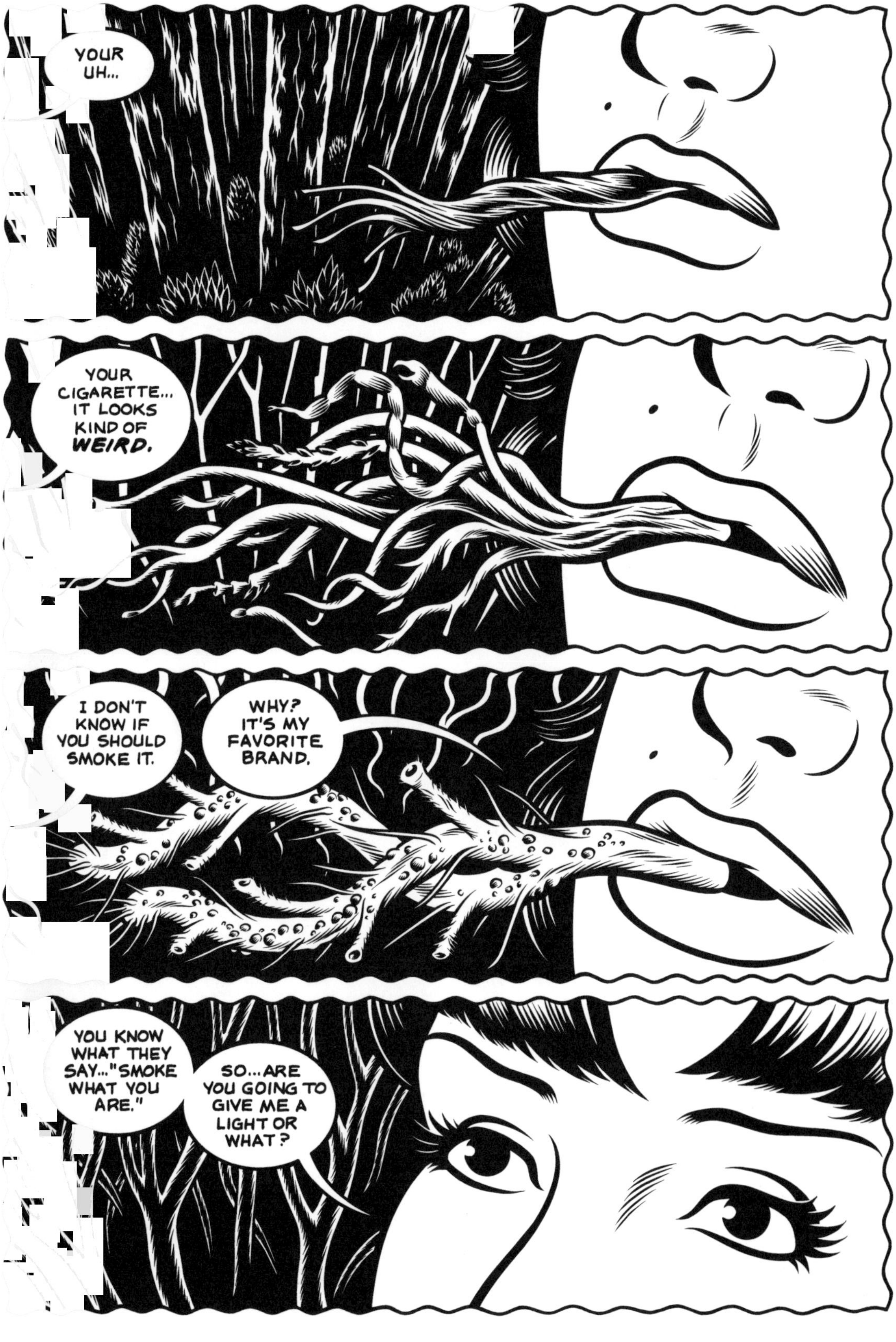
YOUR UH...
YOUR CIGARETTE... IT LOOKS KIND OF WEIRD.
I DON'T KNOW IF YOU SHOULD SMOKE IT.
WHY? IT'S MY FAVORITE BRAND.
YOU KNOW WHAT THEY SAY..."SMOKE WHAT YOU ARE."
SO...ARE YOU GOING TO GIVE ME A LIGHT OR WHAT?

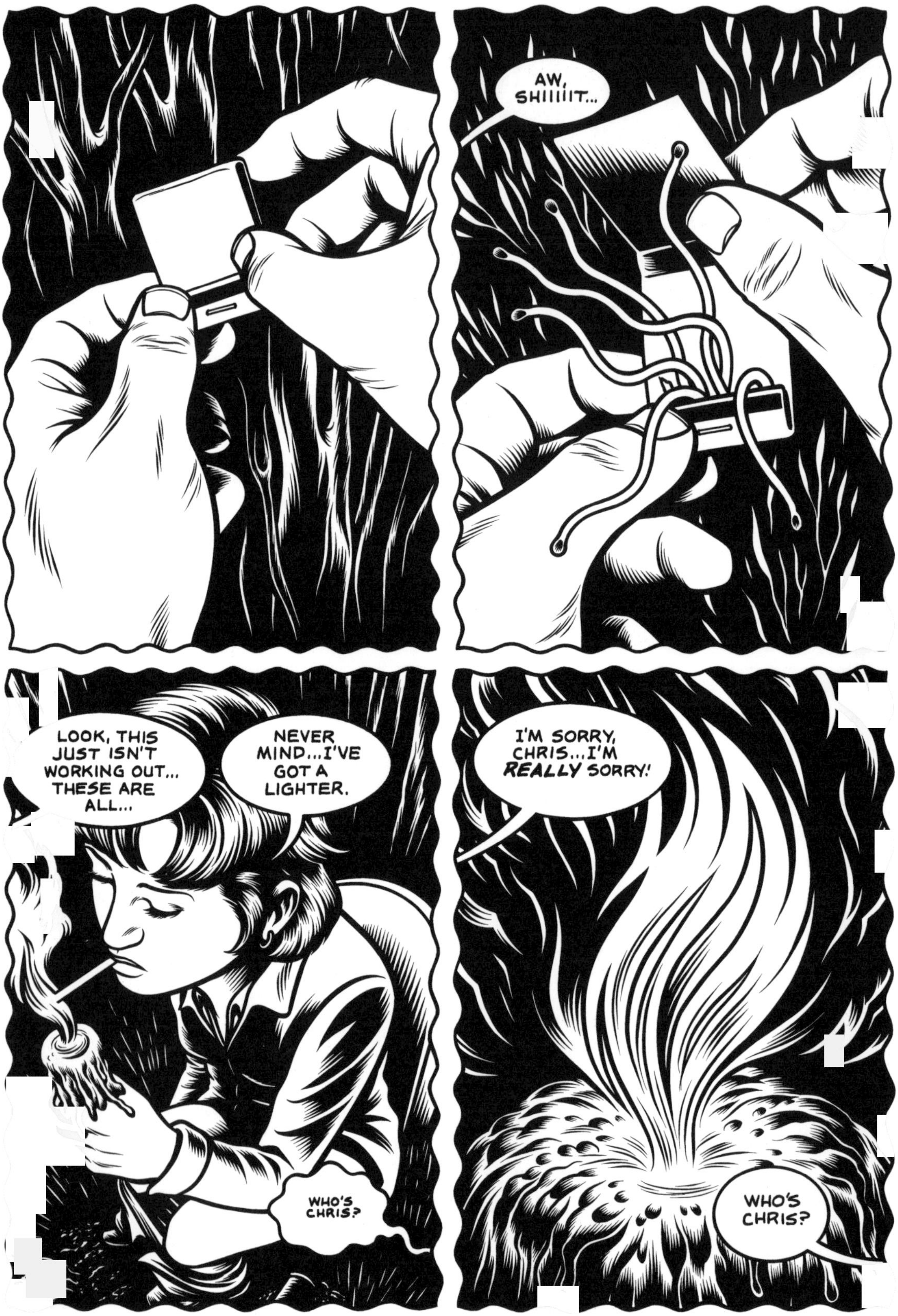
AW, SHIIIIIT...
LOOK, THIS JUST ISN'T WORKING OUT... THESE ARE ALL...
NEVER MIND...I'VE GOT A LIGHTER.
WHO'S CHRIS?
I'M SORRY, CHRIS...I'M *REALLY* SORRY!
WHO'S CHRIS?

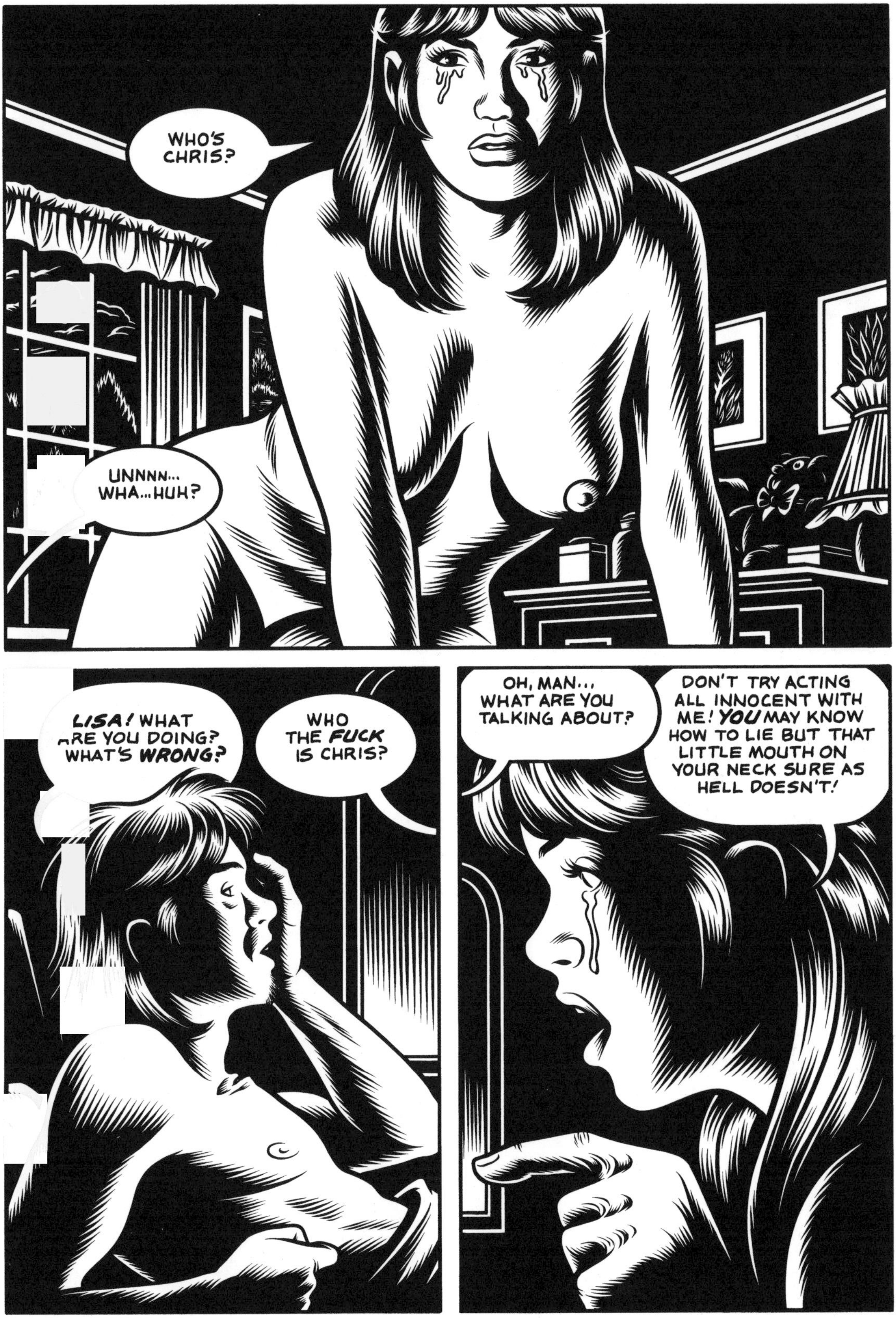
WHO'S CHRIS?
UNNNN... WHA...HUH?
LISA! WHAT ARE YOU DOING? WHAT'S WRONG?
WHO THE FUCK IS CHRIS?
OH, MAN... WHAT ARE YOU TALKING ABOUT?
DON'T TRY ACTING ALL INNOCENT WITH ME! YOU MAY KNOW HOW TO LIE BUT THAT LITTLE MOUTH ON YOUR NECK SURE AS HELL DOESN'T!

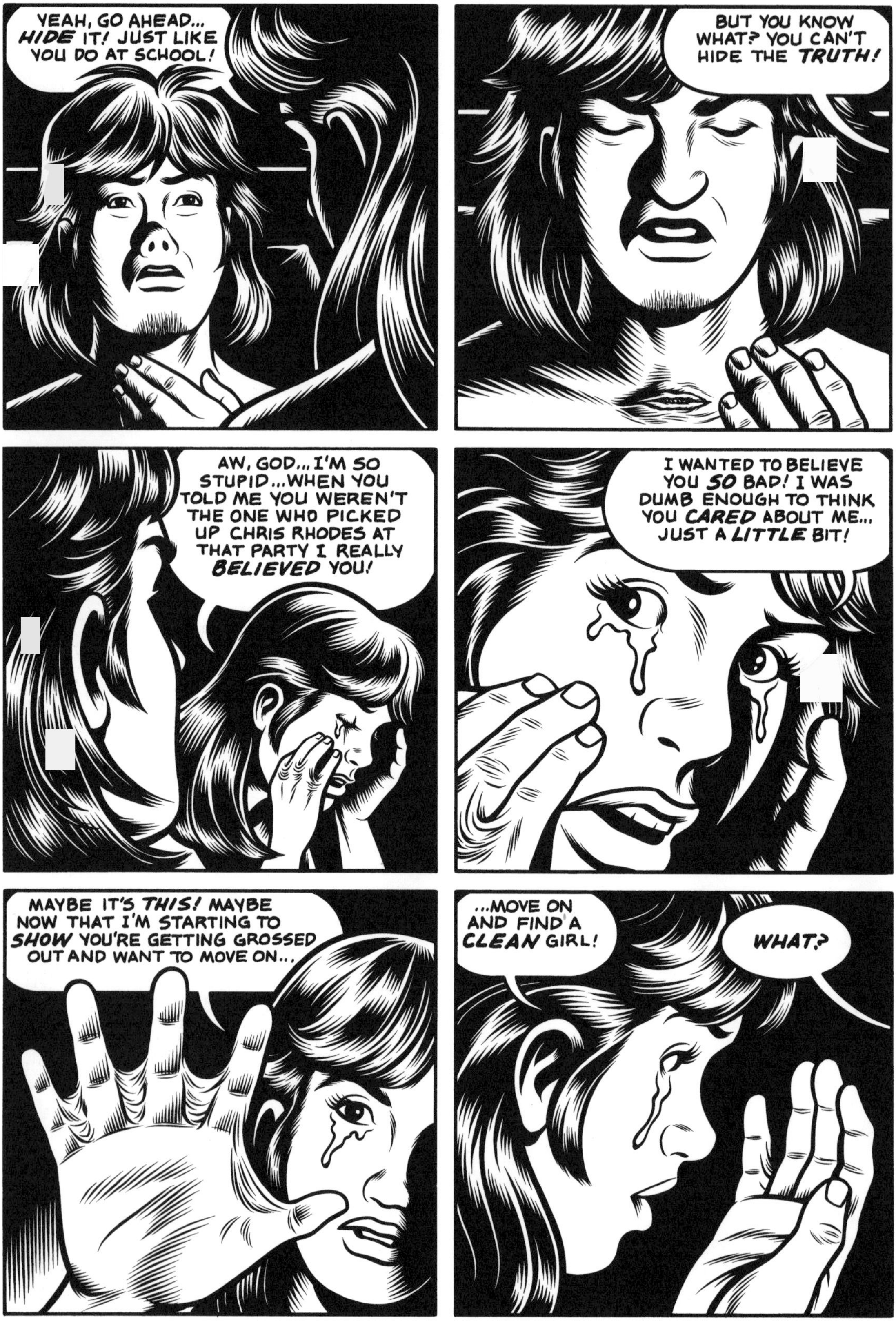
YEAH, GO AHEAD... HIDE IT! JUST LIKE YOU DO AT SCHOOL!
BUT YOU KNOW WHAT? YOU CAN'T HIDE THE TRUTH!
AW, GOD... I'M SO STUPID... WHEN YOU TOLD ME YOU WEREN'T THE ONE WHO PICKED UP CHRIS RHODES AT THAT PARTY I REALLY BELIEVED YOU!
I WANTED TO BELIEVE YOU SO BAD! I WAS DUMB ENOUGH TO THINK YOU CARED ABOUT ME... JUST A LITTLE BIT!
MAYBE IT'S THIS! MAYBE NOW THAT I'M STARTING TO SHOW YOU'RE GETTING GROSSED OUT AND WANT TO MOVE ON...
...MOVE ON AND FIND A CLEAN GIRL!
WHAT?

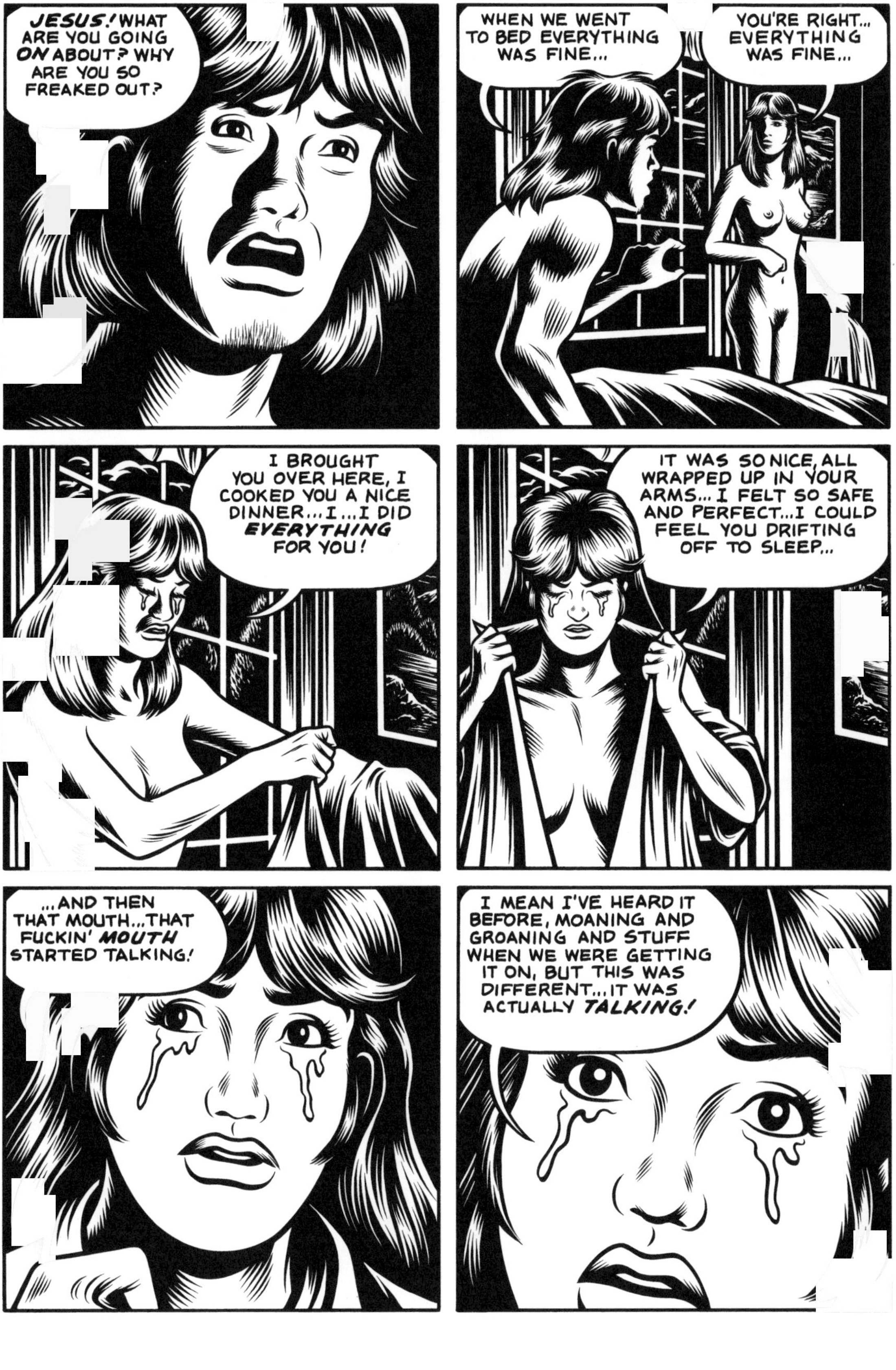
JESUS! WHAT ARE YOU GOING ON ABOUT? WHY ARE YOU SO FREAKED OUT?
WHEN WE WENT TO BED EVERYTHING WAS FINE...
YOU'RE RIGHT... EVERYTHING WAS FINE...
I BROUGHT YOU OVER HERE, I COOKED YOU A NICE DINNER... I... I DID EVERYTHING FOR YOU!
IT WAS SO NICE, ALL WRAPPED UP IN YOUR ARMS... I FELT SO SAFE AND PERFECT... I COULD FEEL YOU DRIFTING OFF TO SLEEP...
...AND THEN THAT MOUTH... THAT FUCKIN' MOUTH STARTED TALKING!
I MEAN I'VE HEARD IT BEFORE, MOANING AND GROANING AND STUFF WHEN WE WERE GETTING IT ON, BUT THIS WAS DIFFERENT... IT WAS ACTUALLY TALKING!

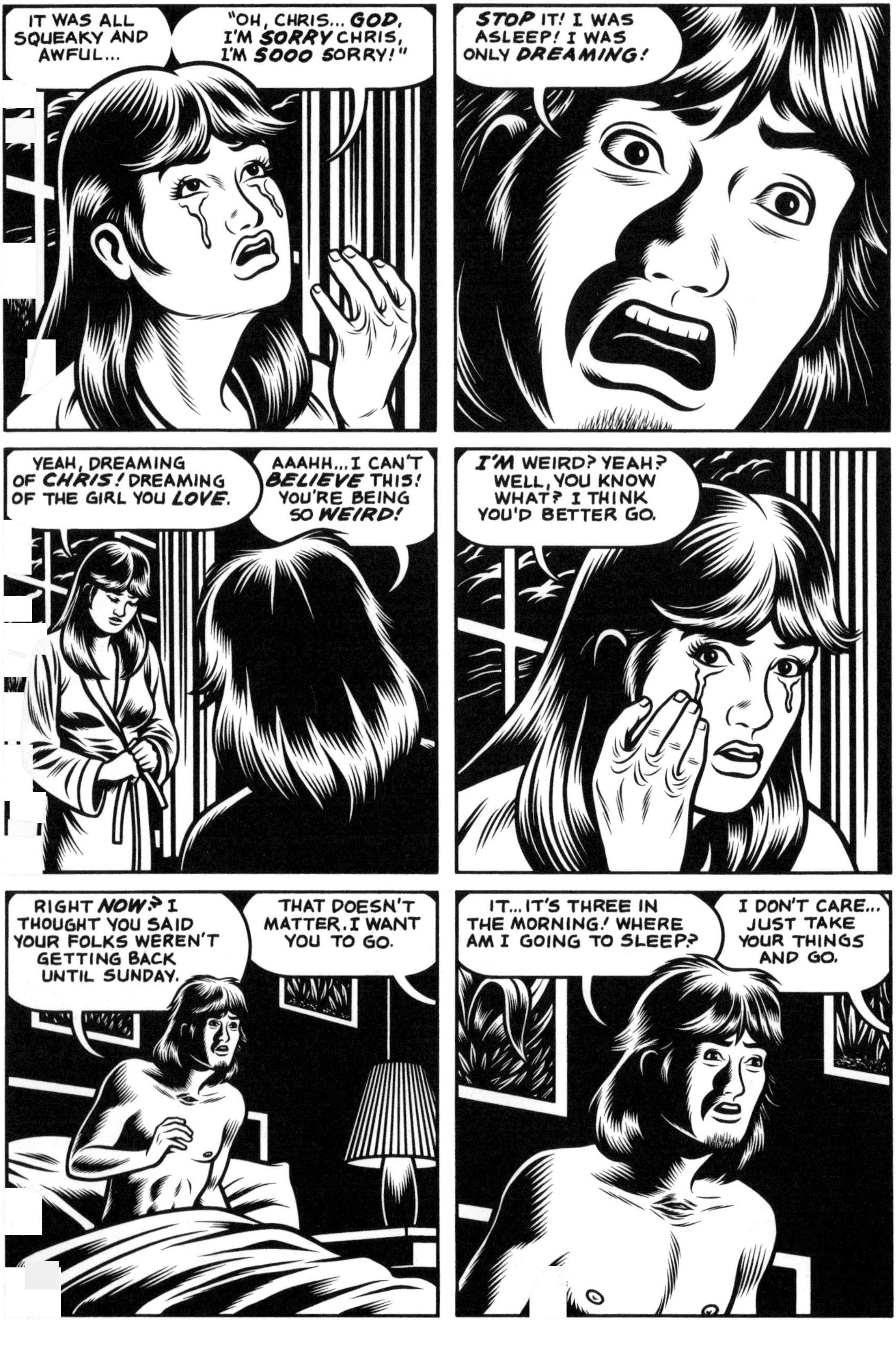
IT WAS ALL SQUEAKY AND AWFUL...
"OH, CHRIS... GOD, I'M SORRY CHRIS, I'M SOOO SORRY!"
STOP IT! I WAS ASLEEP! I WAS ONLY DREAMING!
YEAH, DREAMING OF CHRIS! DREAMING OF THE GIRL YOU LOVE.
AAAHH... I CAN'T BELIEVE THIS! YOU'RE BEING SO WEIRD!
I'M WEIRD? YEAH? WELL, YOU KNOW WHAT? I THINK YOU'D BETTER GO.
RIGHT NOW?! I THOUGHT YOU SAID YOUR FOLKS WEREN'T GETTING BACK UNTIL SUNDAY.
THAT DOESN'T MATTER. I WANT YOU TO GO.
IT... IT'S THREE IN THE MORNING! WHERE AM I GOING TO SLEEP?
I DON'T CARE... JUST TAKE YOUR THINGS AND GO.

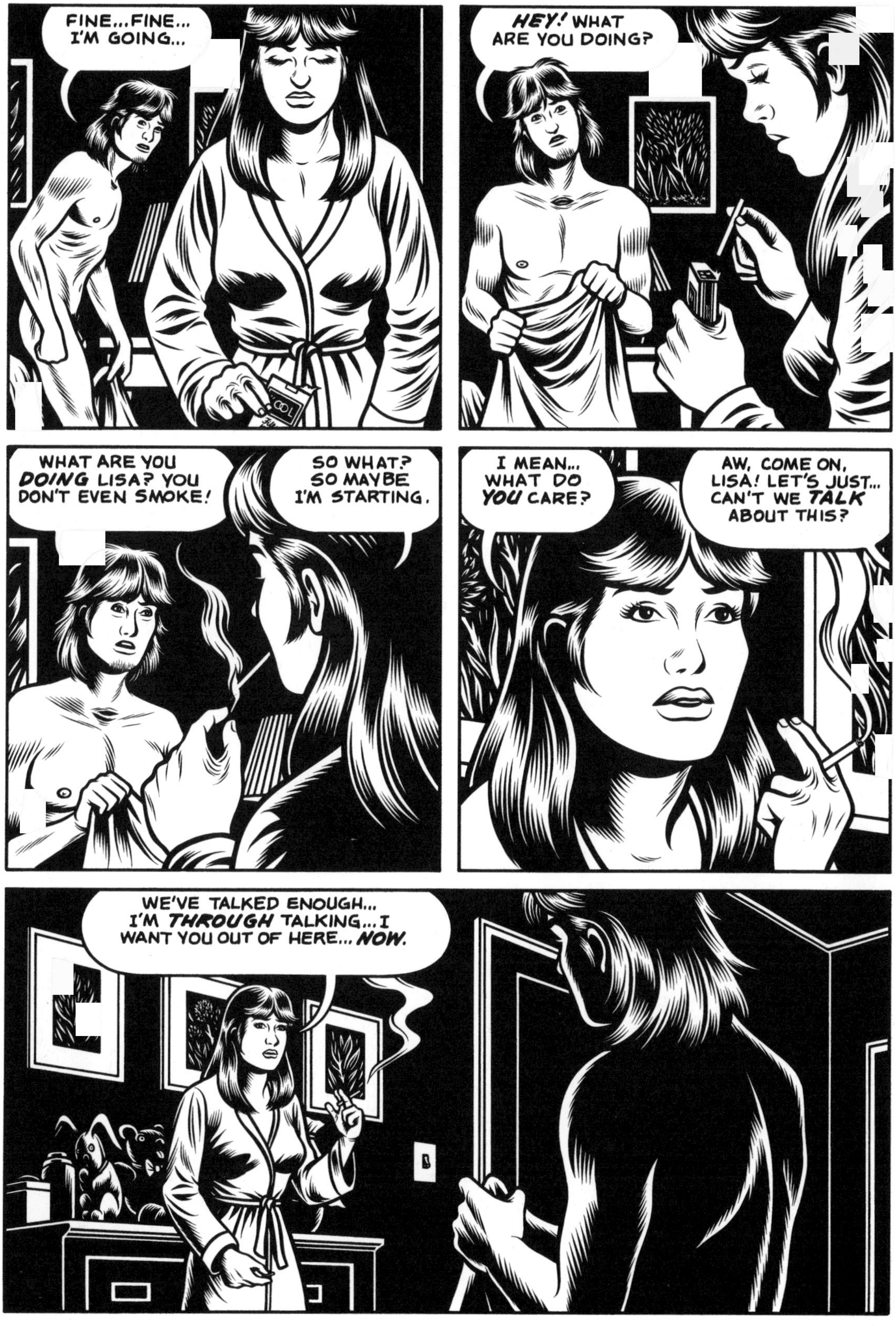
FINE... FINE... I'M GOING...
HEY! WHAT ARE YOU DOING?
WHAT ARE YOU DOING LISA? YOU DON'T EVEN SMOKE!
SO WHAT? SO MAYBE I'M STARTING.
I MEAN... WHAT DO YOU CARE?
AW, COME ON, LISA! LET'S JUST... CAN'T WE TALK ABOUT THIS?
WE'VE TALKED ENOUGH... I'M THROUGH TALKING... I WANT YOU OUT OF HERE... NOW.

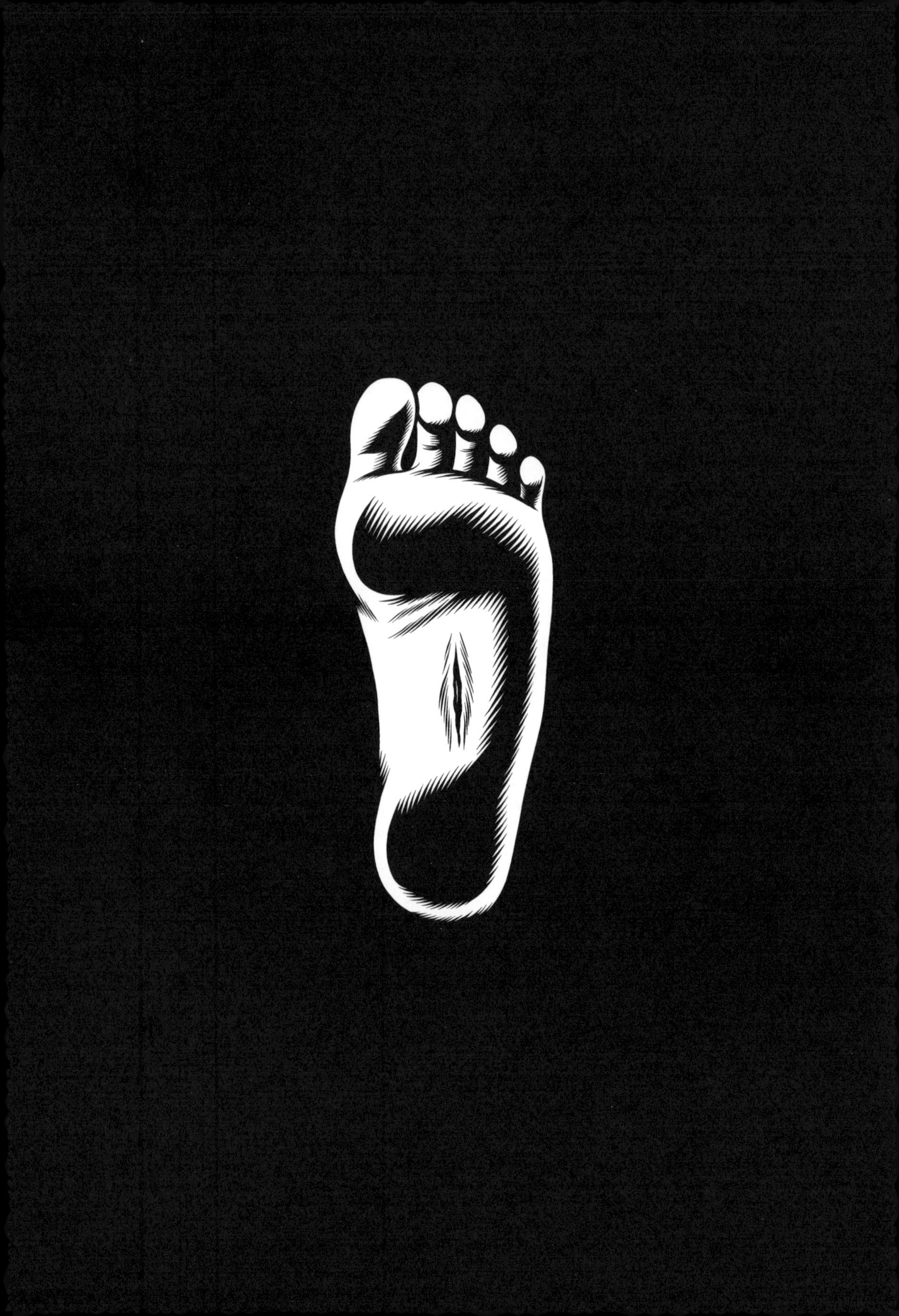

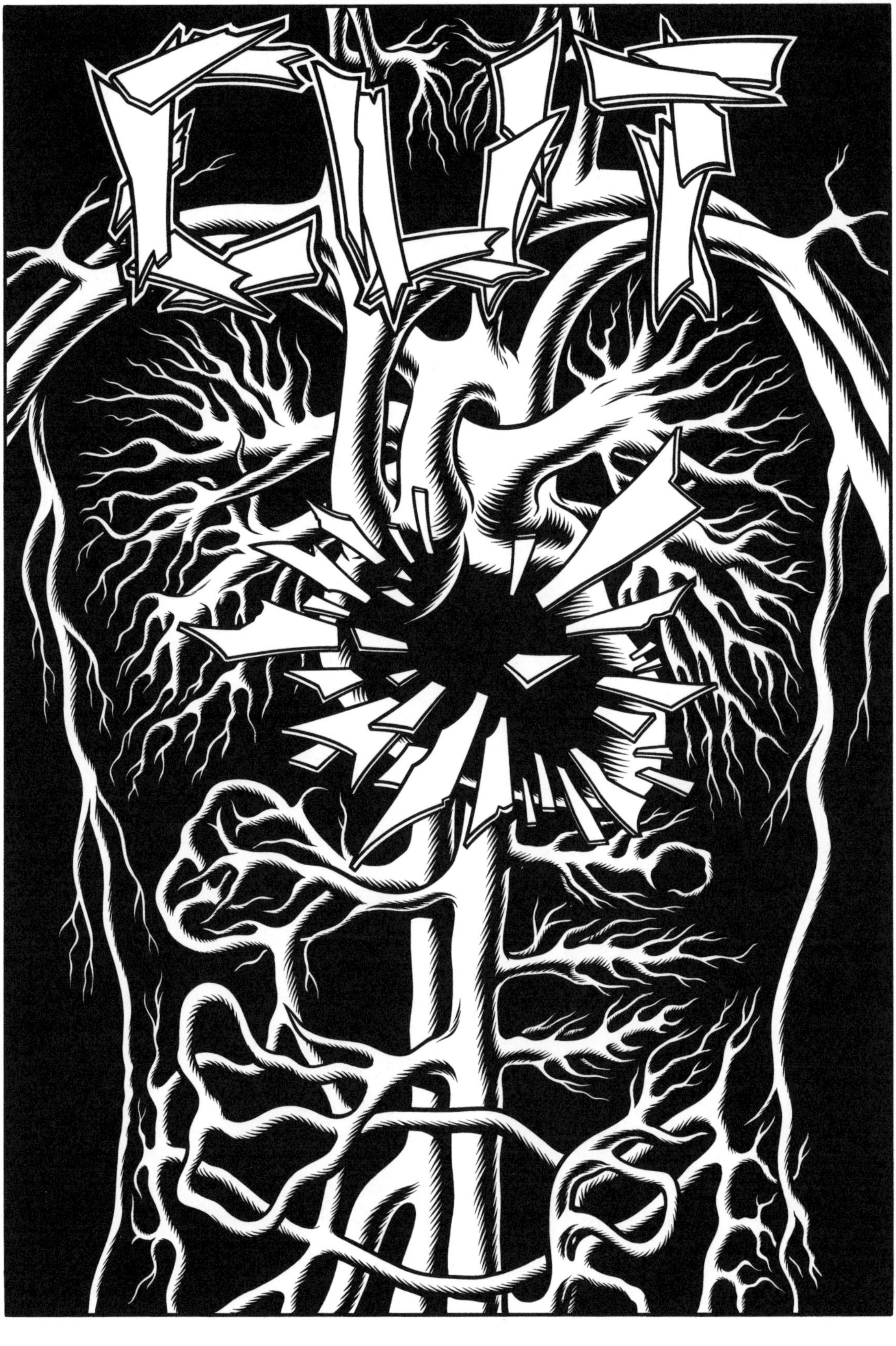
CUT

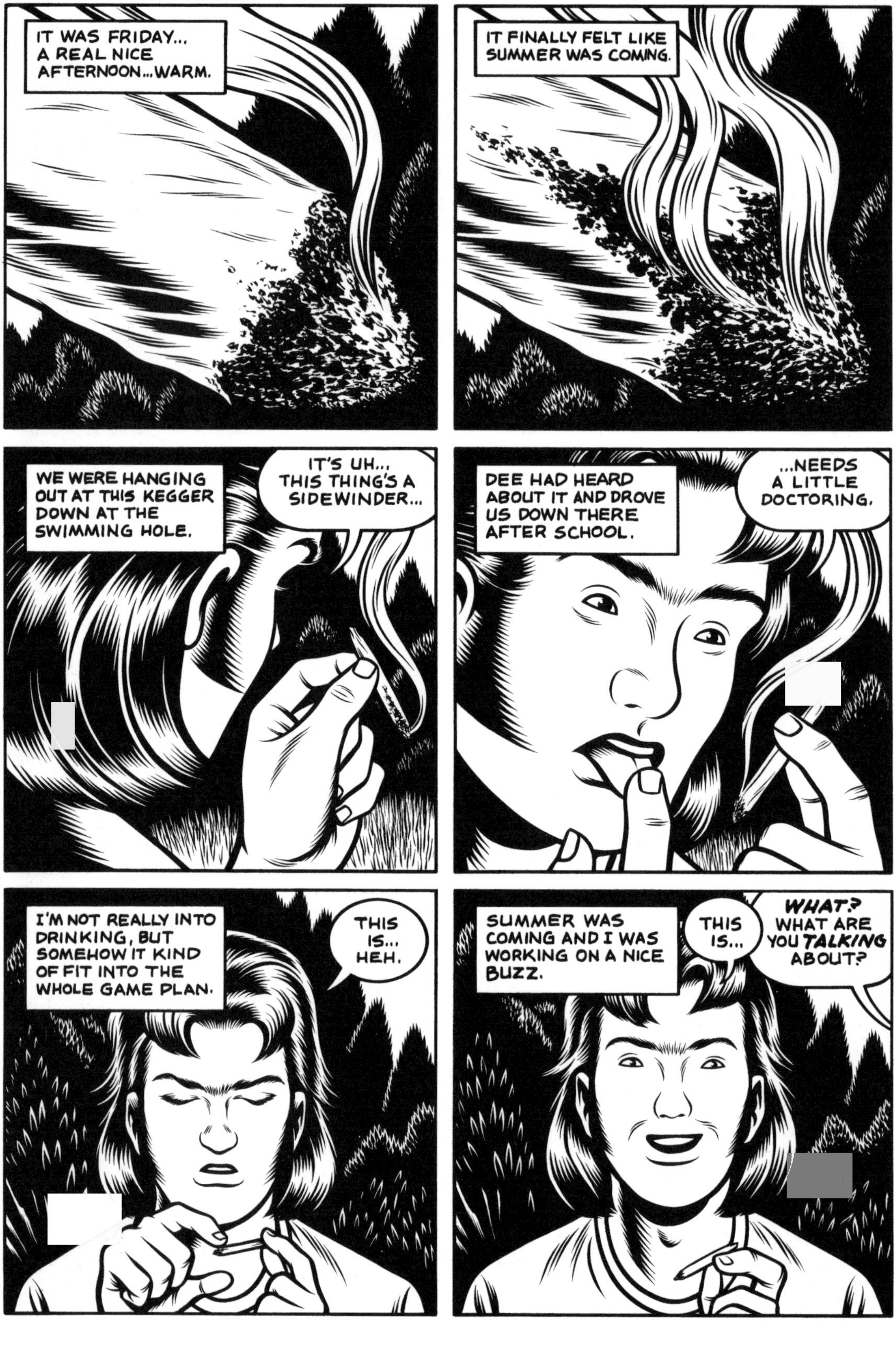
IT WAS FRIDAY... A REAL NICE AFTERNOON...WARM.
IT FINALLY FELT LIKE SUMMER WAS COMING.
WE WERE HANGING OUT AT THIS KEGGER DOWN AT THE SWIMMING HOLE.
IT'S UH... THIS THING'S A SIDEWINDER...
DEE HAD HEARD ABOUT IT AND DROVE US DOWN THERE AFTER SCHOOL.
...NEEDS A LITTLE DOCTORING.
I'M NOT REALLY INTO DRINKING, BUT SOMEHOW IT KIND OF FIT INTO THE WHOLE GAME PLAN.
THIS IS... HEH.
SUMMER WAS COMING AND I WAS WORKING ON A NICE BUZZ.
THIS IS...
WHAT? WHAT ARE YOU TALKING ABOUT?

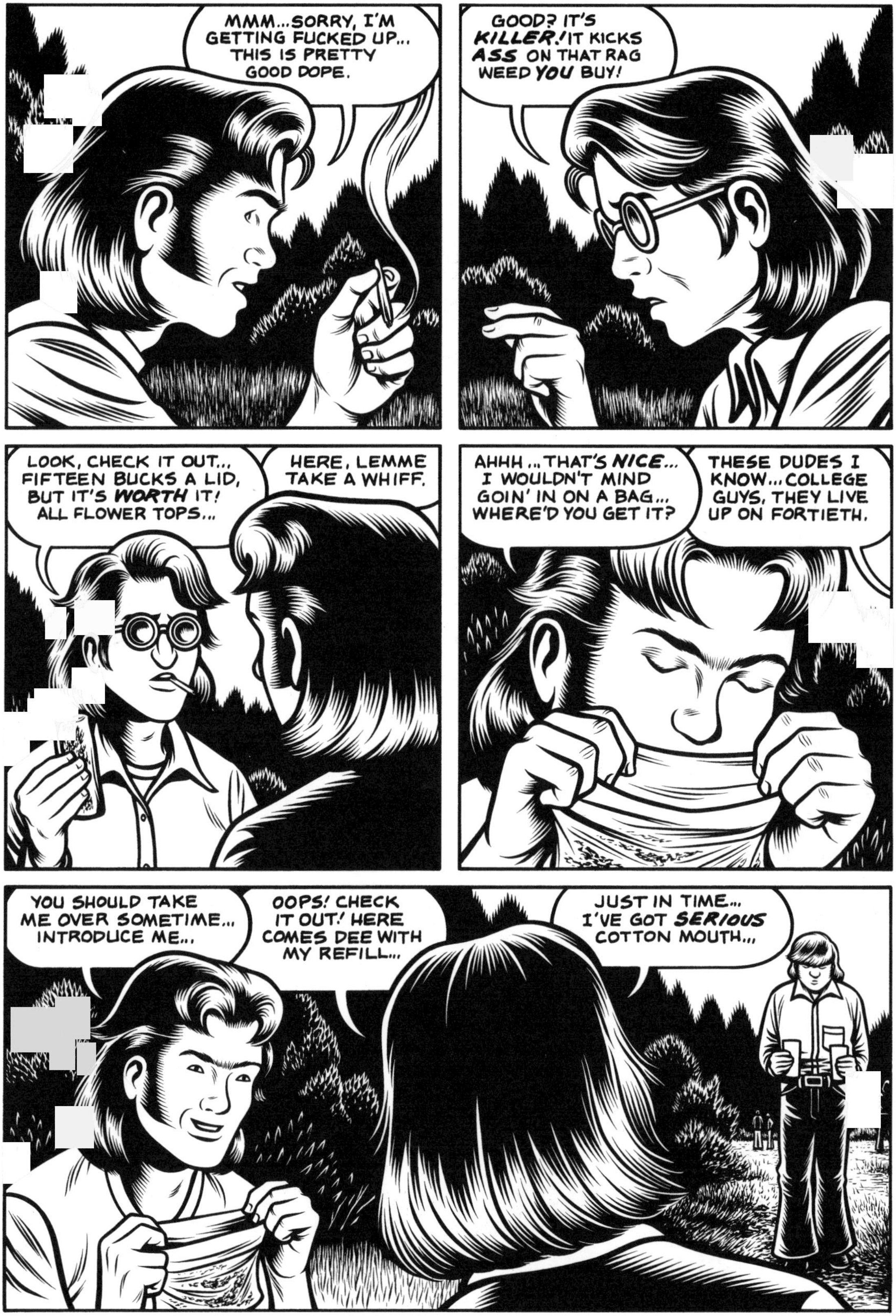
MMM... SORRY, I'M GETTING FUCKED UP... THIS IS PRETTY GOOD DOPE.
GOOD? IT'S KILLER! IT KICKS ASS ON THAT RAG WEED YOU BUY!
LOOK, CHECK IT OUT... FIFTEEN BUCKS A LID, BUT IT'S WORTH IT! ALL FLOWER TOPS...
HERE, LEMME TAKE A WHIFF.
AHHH... THAT'S NICE... I WOULDN'T MIND GOIN' IN ON A BAG... WHERE'D YOU GET IT?
THESE DUDES I KNOW... COLLEGE GUYS, THEY LIVE UP ON FORTIETH.
YOU SHOULD TAKE ME OVER SOMETIME... INTRODUCE ME...
OOPS! CHECK IT OUT! HERE COMES DEE WITH MY REFILL...
JUST IN TIME... I'VE GOT SERIOUS COTTON MOUTH...

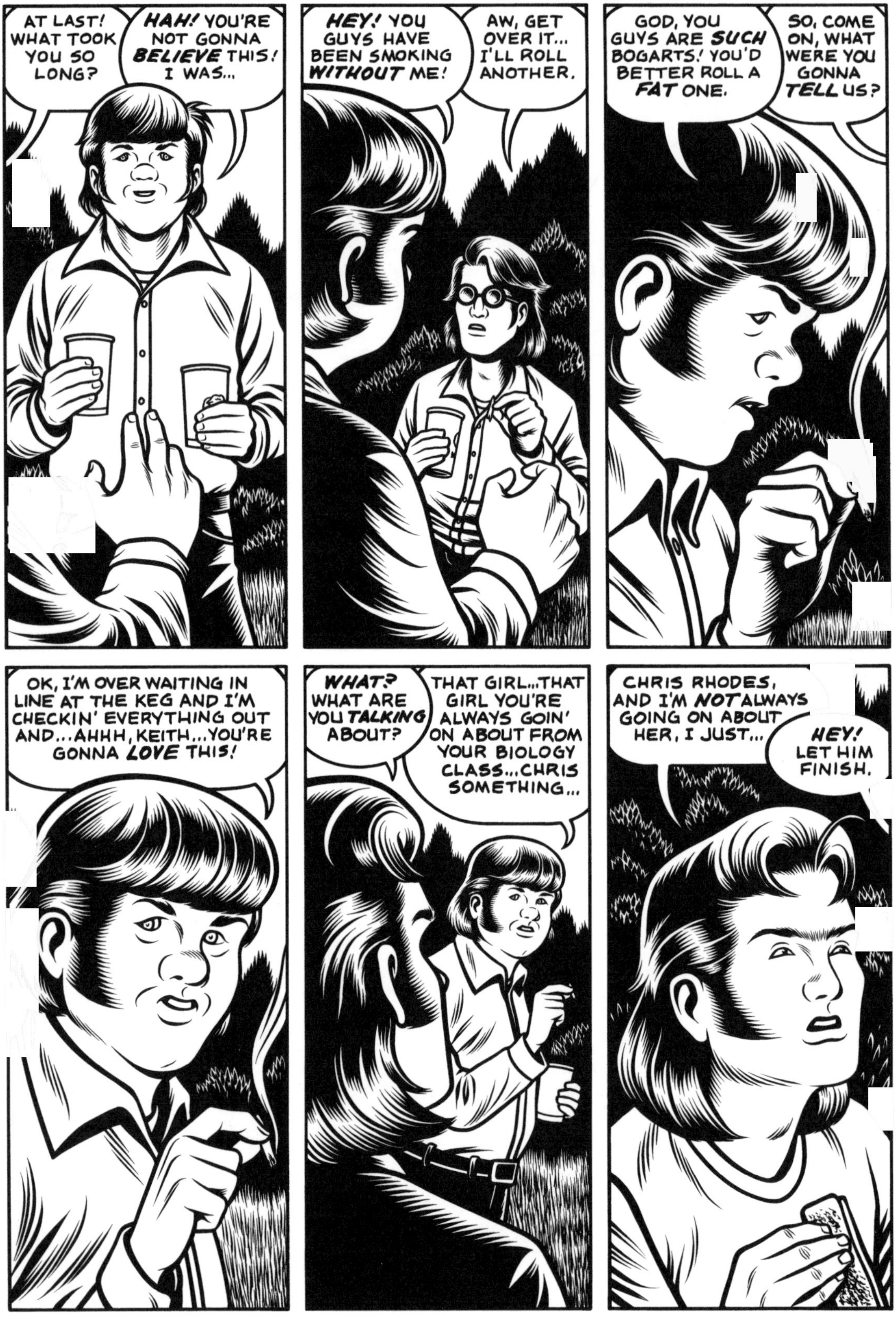
AT LAST! WHAT TOOK YOU SO LONG?
HAH! YOU'RE NOT GONNA BELIEVE THIS! I WAS...
HEY! YOU GUYS HAVE BEEN SMOKING WITHOUT ME!
AW, GET OVER IT... I'LL ROLL ANOTHER.
GOD, YOU GUYS ARE SUCH BOGARTS! YOU'D BETTER ROLL A FAT ONE.
SO, COME ON, WHAT WERE YOU GONNA TELL US?
OK, I'M OVER WAITING IN LINE AT THE KEG AND I'M CHECKIN' EVERYTHING OUT AND... AHHH, KEITH... YOU'RE GONNA LOVE THIS!
WHAT? WHAT ARE YOU TALKING ABOUT?
THAT GIRL... THAT GIRL YOU'RE ALWAYS GOIN' ON ABOUT FROM YOUR BIOLOGY CLASS... CHRIS SOMETHING...
CHRIS RHODES, AND I'M NOT ALWAYS GOING ON ABOUT HER, I JUST...
HEY! LET HIM FINISH.

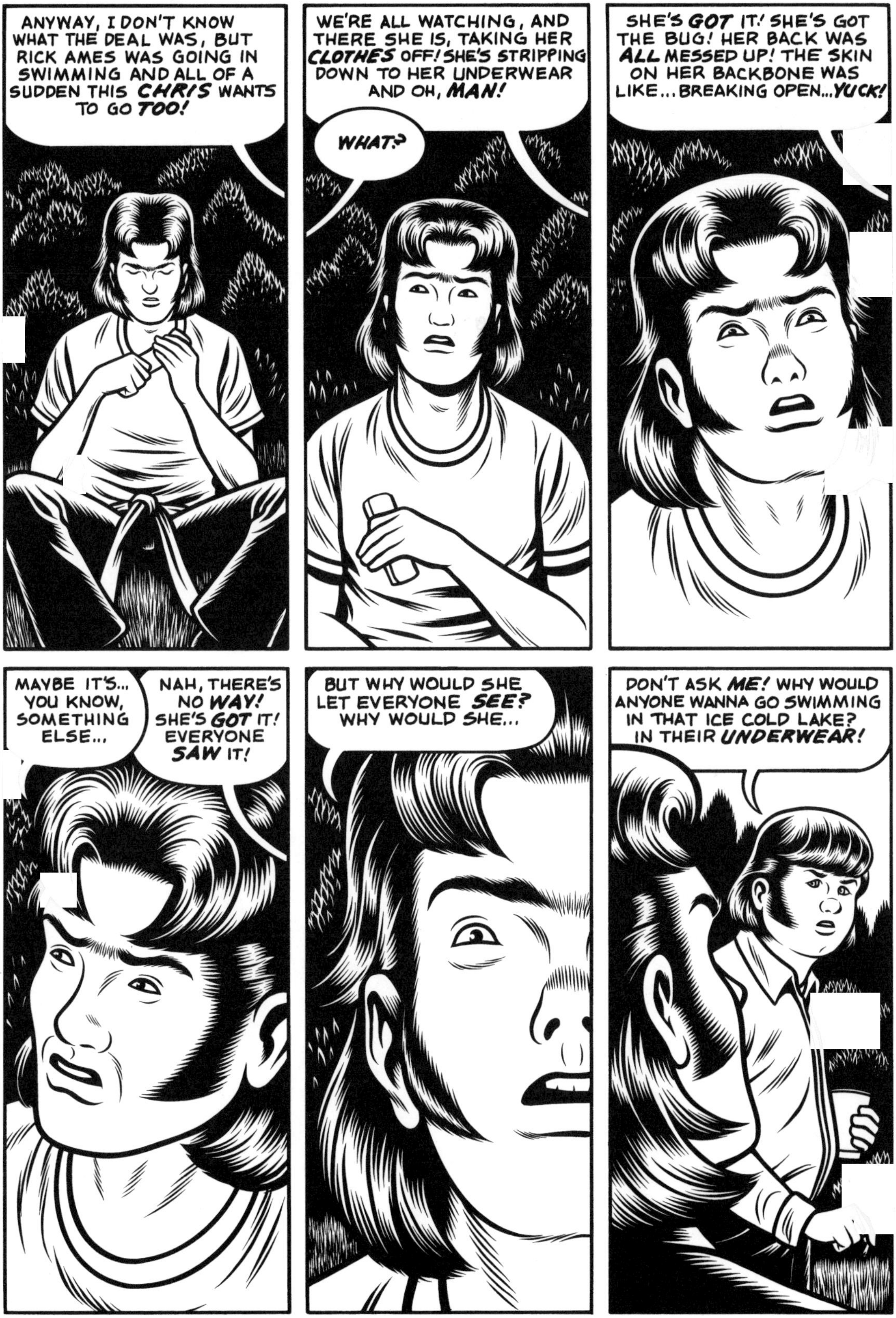
ANYWAY, I DON'T KNOW WHAT THE DEAL WAS, BUT RICK AMES WAS GOING IN SWIMMING AND ALL OF A SUDDEN THIS CHRIS WANTS TO GO TOO!
WE'RE ALL WATCHING, AND THERE SHE IS, TAKING HER CLOTHES OFF! SHE'S STRIPPING DOWN TO HER UNDERWEAR AND OH, MAN!
WHAT?
SHE'S GOT IT! SHE'S GOT THE BUG! HER BACK WAS ALL MESSED UP! THE SKIN ON HER BACKBONE WAS LIKE... BREAKING OPEN... YUCK!
MAYBE IT'S... YOU KNOW, SOMETHING ELSE...
NAH, THERE'S NO WAY! SHE'S GOT IT! EVERYONE SAW IT!
BUT WHY WOULD SHE LET EVERYONE SEE? WHY WOULD SHE...
DON'T ASK ME! WHY WOULD ANYONE WANNA GO SWIMMING IN THAT ICE COLD LAKE? IN THEIR UNDERWEAR!

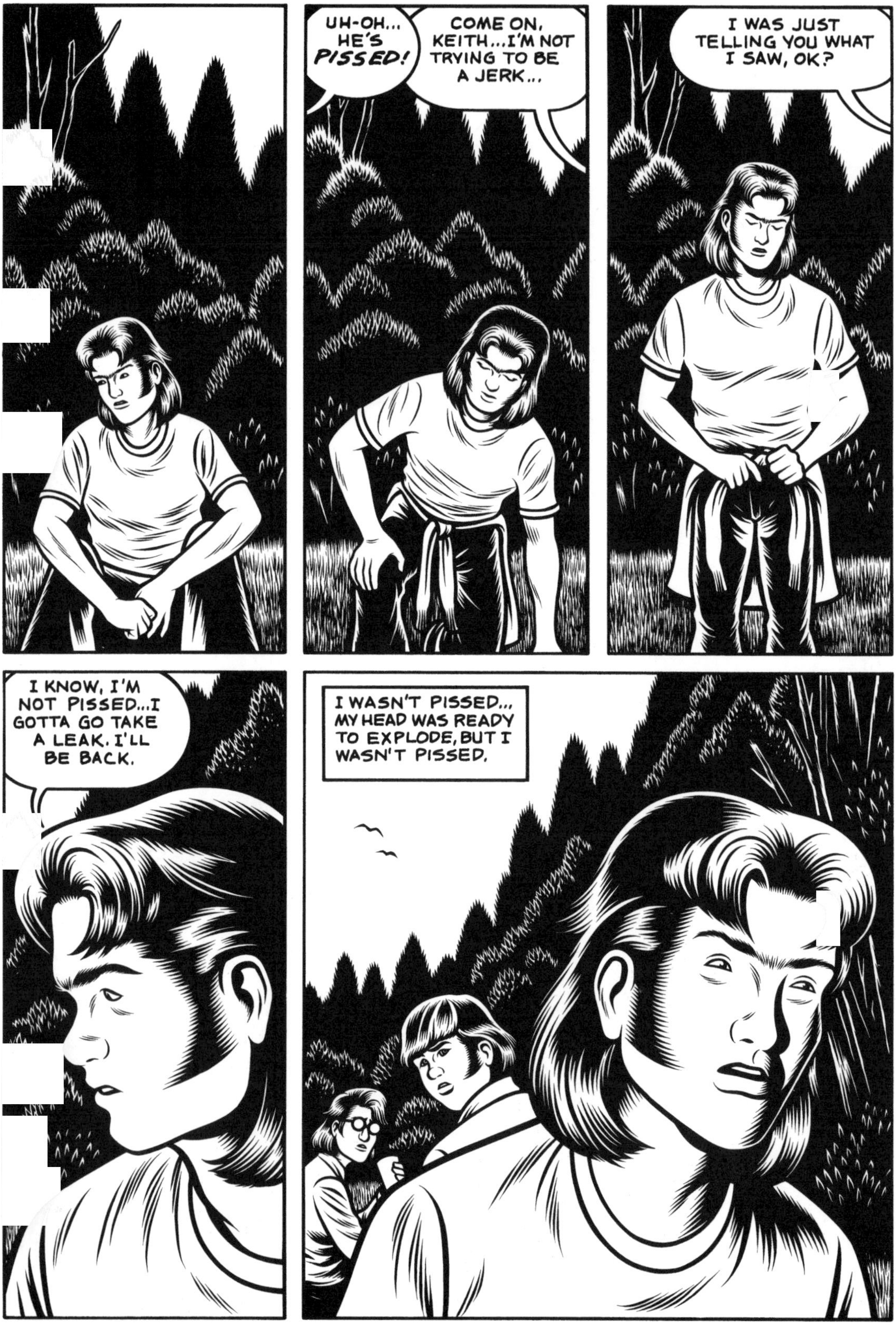
UH-OH... HE'S *PISSED!*
COME ON, KEITH... I'M NOT TRYING TO BE A JERK...
I WAS JUST TELLING YOU WHAT I SAW, OK?
I KNOW, I'M NOT PISSED... I GOTTA GO TAKE A LEAK. I'LL BE BACK.
I WASN'T PISSED... MY HEAD WAS READY TO EXPLODE, BUT I WASN'T PISSED.

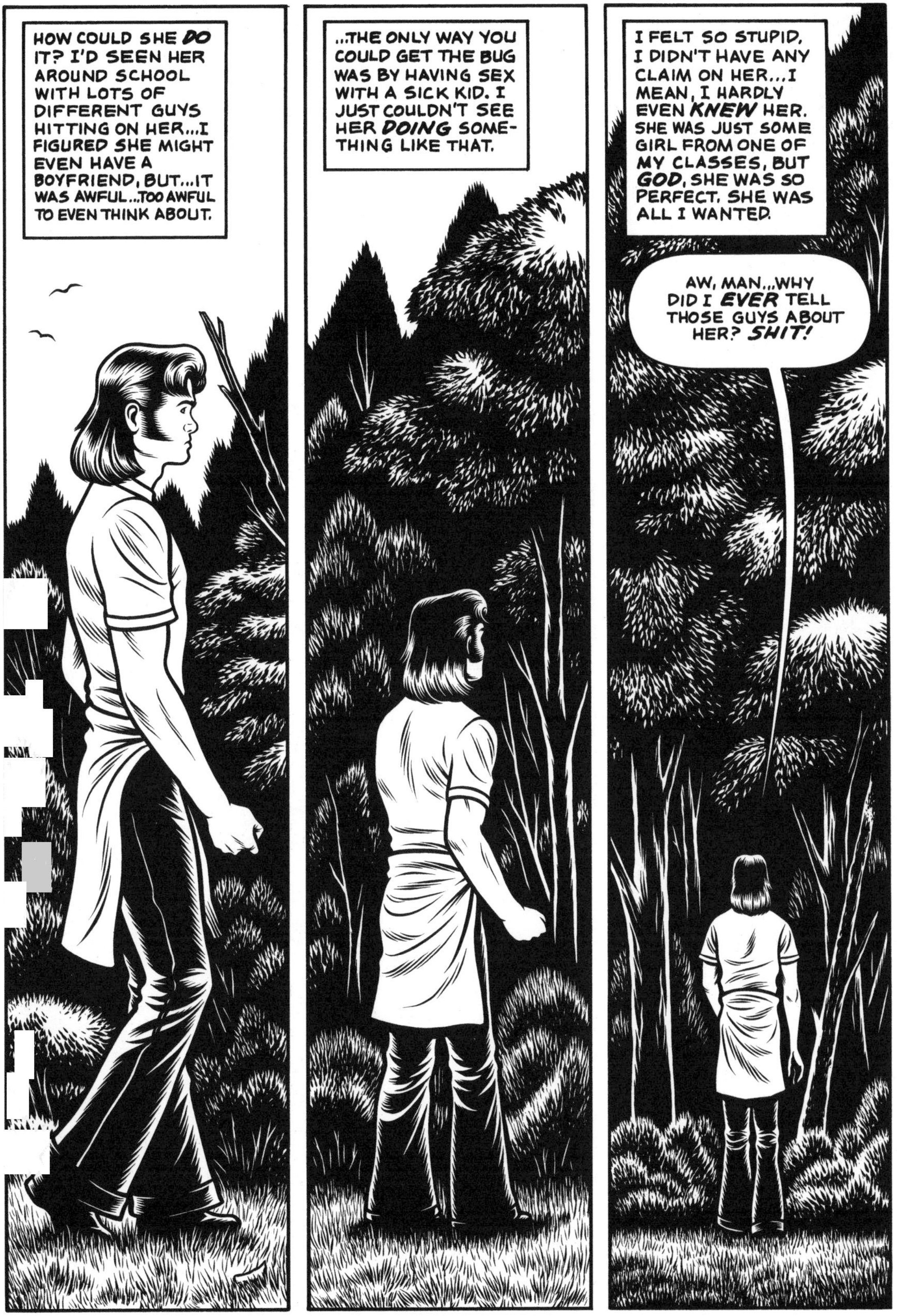
HOW COULD SHE DO IT? I'D SEEN HER AROUND SCHOOL WITH LOTS OF DIFFERENT GUYS HITTING ON HER...I FIGURED SHE MIGHT EVEN HAVE A BOYFRIEND, BUT...IT WAS AWFUL...TOO AWFUL TO EVEN THINK ABOUT.
...THE ONLY WAY YOU COULD GET THE BUG WAS BY HAVING SEX WITH A SICK KID. I JUST COULDN'T SEE HER DOING SOMETHING LIKE THAT.
I FELT SO STUPID, I DIDN'T HAVE ANY CLAIM ON HER...I MEAN, I HARDLY EVEN KNEW HER. SHE WAS JUST SOME GIRL FROM ONE OF MY CLASSES, BUT GOD, SHE WAS SO PERFECT. SHE WAS ALL I WANTED.
AW, MAN...WHY DID I EVER TELL THOSE GUYS ABOUT HER? SHIT!

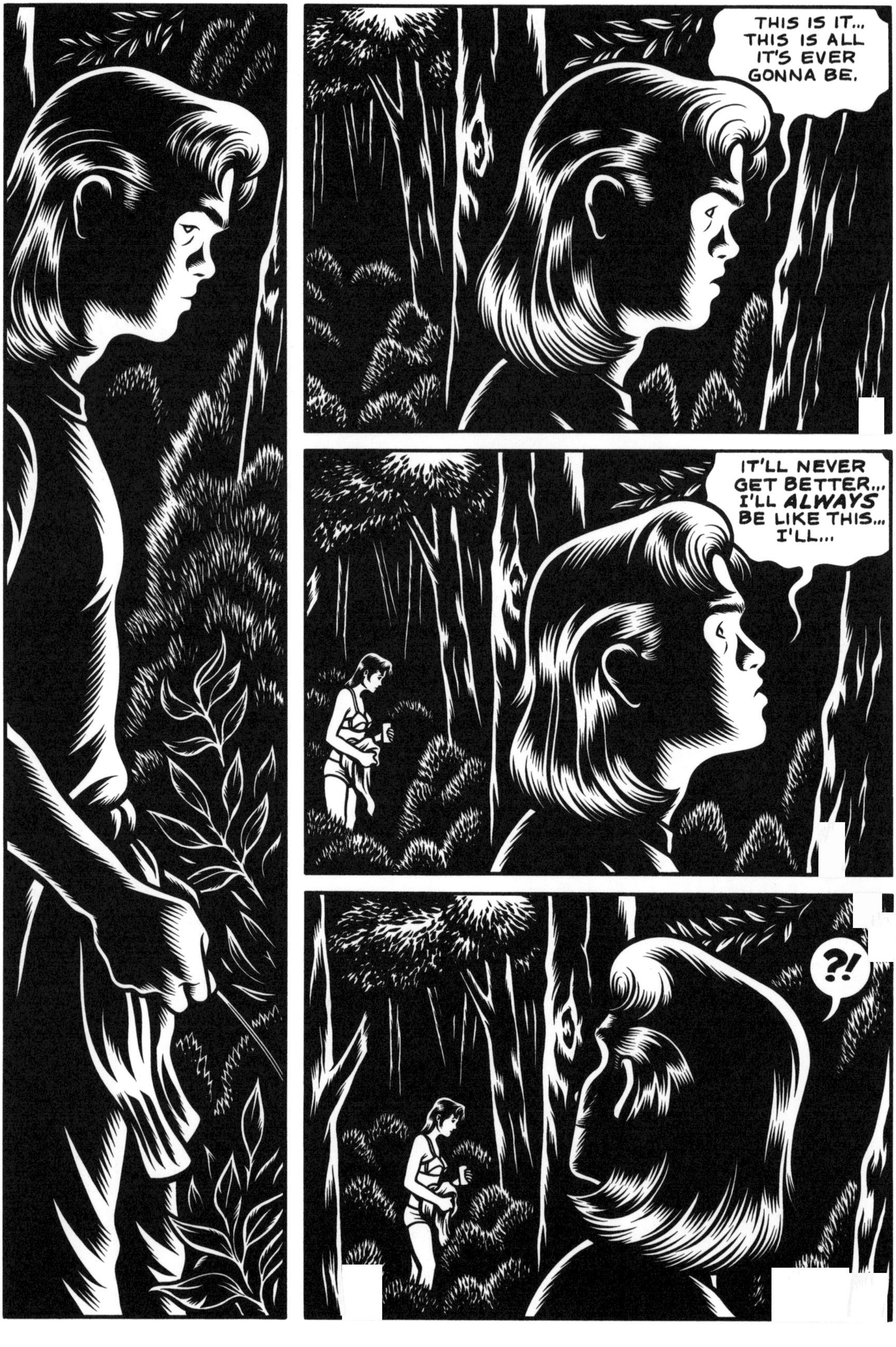
THIS IS IT... THIS IS ALL IT'S EVER GONNA BE.
IT'LL NEVER GET BETTER... I'LL *ALWAYS* BE LIKE THIS... I'LL...
?!

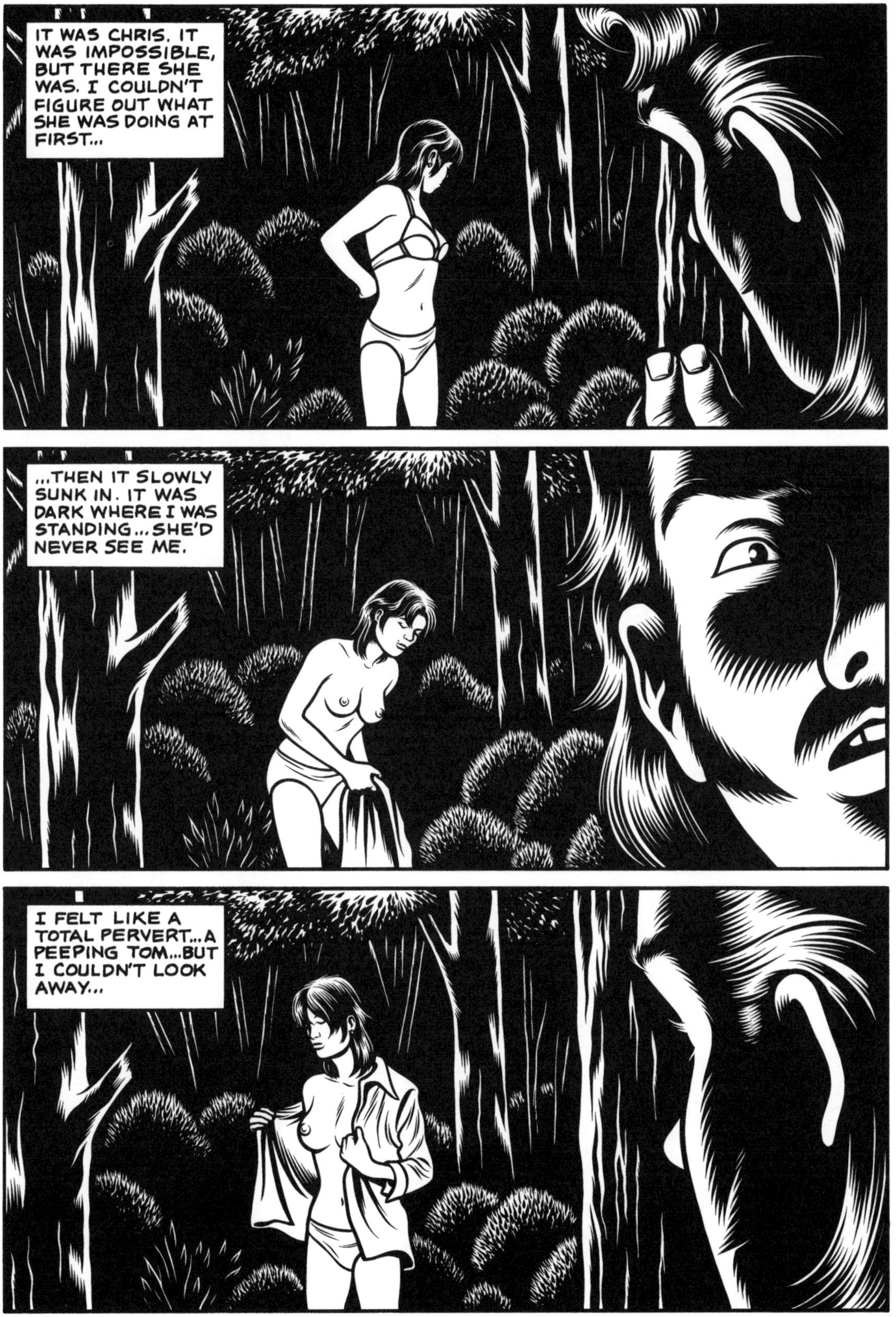
IT WAS CHRIS. IT WAS IMPOSSIBLE, BUT THERE SHE WAS. I COULDN'T FIGURE OUT WHAT SHE WAS DOING AT FIRST...
...THEN IT SLOWLY SUNK IN. IT WAS DARK WHERE I WAS STANDING...SHE'D NEVER SEE ME.
I FELT LIKE A TOTAL PERVERT...A PEEPING TOM...BUT I COULDN'T LOOK AWAY...

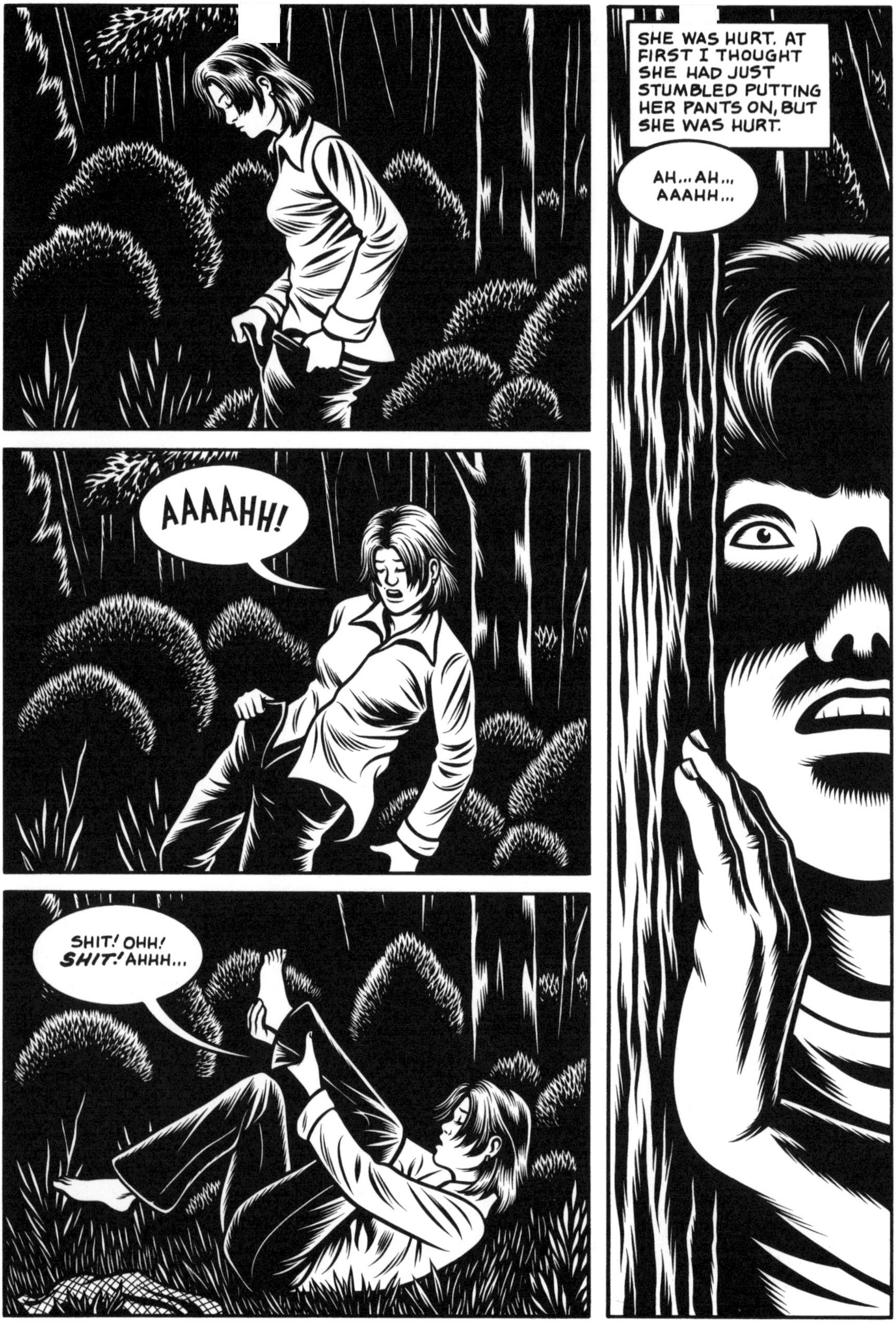
AAAAHH!
SHIT! OHH! SHIT! AHHH...
SHE WAS HURT. AT FIRST I THOUGHT SHE HAD JUST STUMBLED PUTTING HER PANTS ON, BUT SHE WAS HURT.
AH... AH... AAAHH...

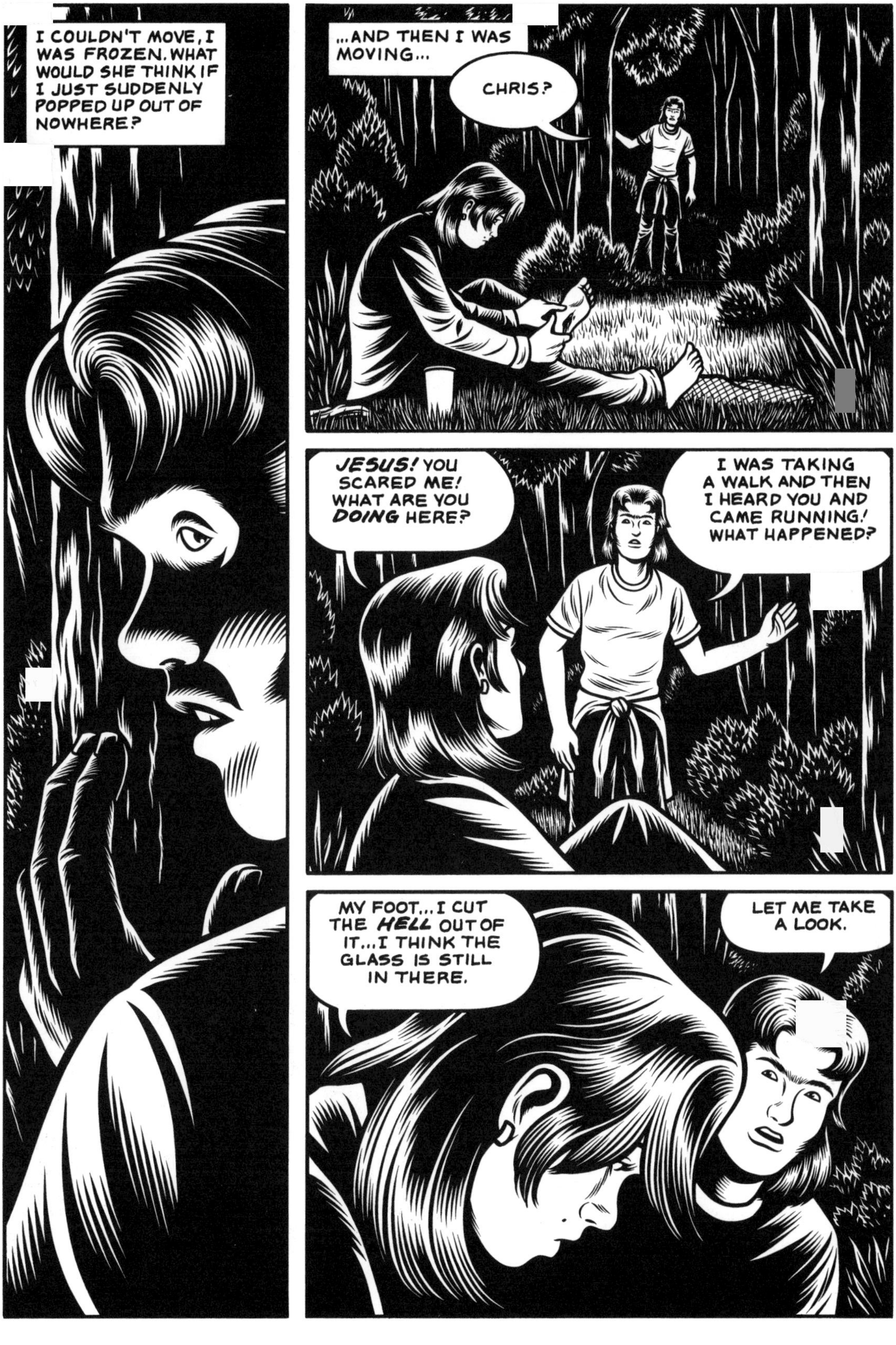
I COULDN'T MOVE, I WAS FROZEN. WHAT WOULD SHE THINK IF I JUST SUDDENLY POPPED UP OUT OF NOWHERE?
...AND THEN I WAS MOVING...
CHRIS?
JESUS! YOU SCARED ME! WHAT ARE YOU DOING HERE?
I WAS TAKING A WALK AND THEN I HEARD YOU AND CAME RUNNING! WHAT HAPPENED?
MY FOOT... I CUT THE HELL OUT OF IT... I THINK THE GLASS IS STILL IN THERE.
LET ME TAKE A LOOK.

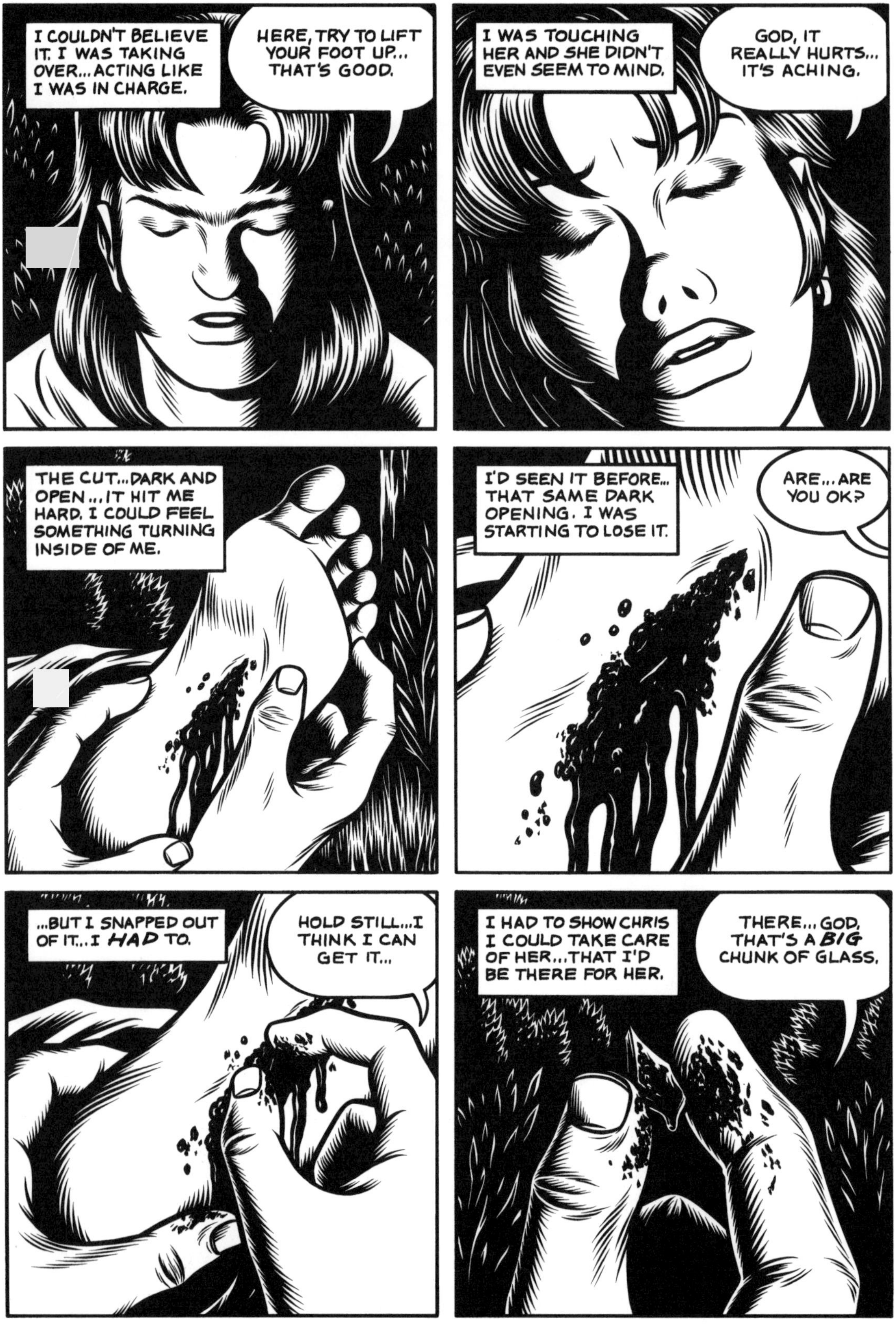
I COULDN'T BELIEVE IT. I WAS TAKING OVER... ACTING LIKE I WAS IN CHARGE.
HERE, TRY TO LIFT YOUR FOOT UP... THAT'S GOOD.
I WAS TOUCHING HER AND SHE DIDN'T EVEN SEEM TO MIND.
GOD, IT REALLY HURTS... IT'S ACHING.
THE CUT... DARK AND OPEN... IT HIT ME HARD. I COULD FEEL SOMETHING TURNING INSIDE OF ME.
I'D SEEN IT BEFORE... THAT SAME DARK OPENING. I WAS STARTING TO LOSE IT.
ARE... ARE YOU OK?
...BUT I SNAPPED OUT OF IT... I *HAD* TO.
HOLD STILL... I THINK I CAN GET IT...
I HAD TO SHOW CHRIS I COULD TAKE CARE OF HER... THAT I'D BE THERE FOR HER.
THERE... GOD, THAT'S A *BIG* CHUNK OF GLASS.

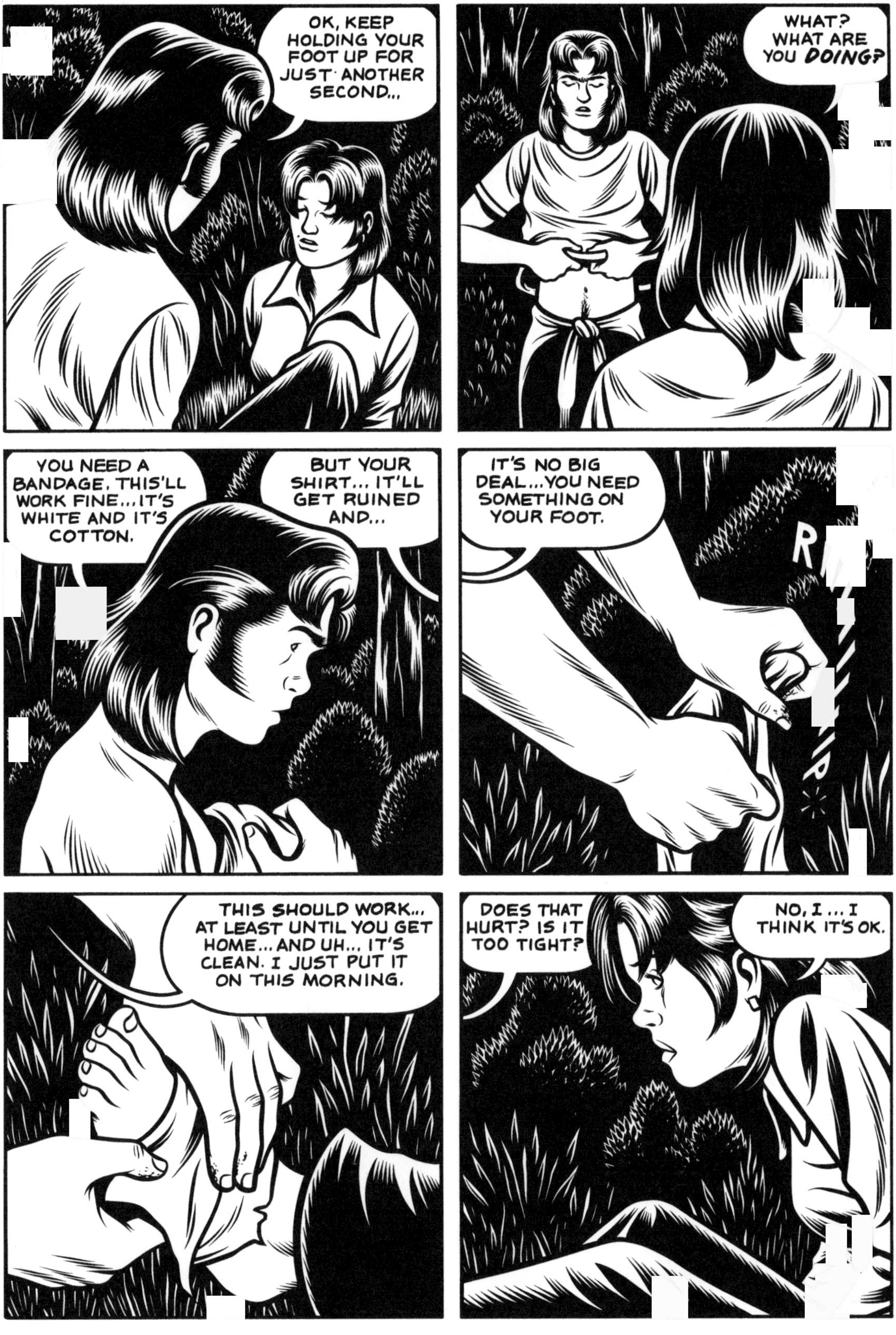
OK, KEEP HOLDING YOUR FOOT UP FOR JUST ANOTHER SECOND...
WHAT? WHAT ARE YOU *DOING*?
YOU NEED A BANDAGE. THIS'LL WORK FINE... IT'S WHITE AND IT'S COTTON.
BUT YOUR SHIRT... IT'LL GET RUINED AND...
IT'S NO BIG DEAL... YOU NEED SOMETHING ON YOUR FOOT.
THIS SHOULD WORK... AT LEAST UNTIL YOU GET HOME... AND UH... IT'S CLEAN. I JUST PUT IT ON THIS MORNING.
DOES THAT HURT? IS IT TOO TIGHT?
NO, I ... I THINK IT'S OK.

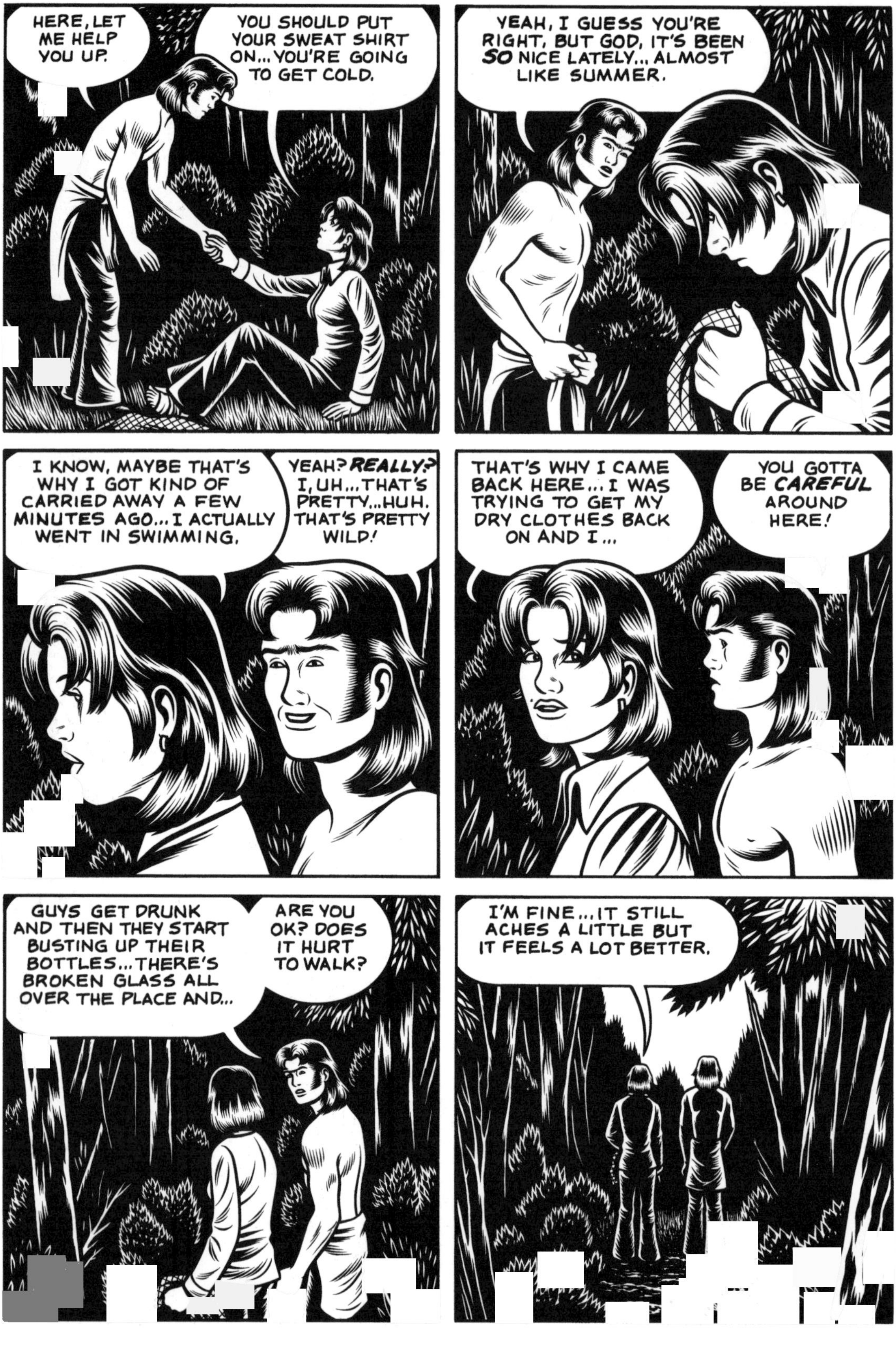
HERE, LET ME HELP YOU UP.
YOU SHOULD PUT YOUR SWEAT SHIRT ON... YOU'RE GOING TO GET COLD.
YEAH, I GUESS YOU'RE RIGHT, BUT GOD, IT'S BEEN SO NICE LATELY... ALMOST LIKE SUMMER.
I KNOW, MAYBE THAT'S WHY I GOT KIND OF CARRIED AWAY A FEW MINUTES AGO... I ACTUALLY WENT IN SWIMMING.
YEAH? REALLY? I, UH... THAT'S PRETTY... HUH. THAT'S PRETTY WILD!
THAT'S WHY I CAME BACK HERE... I WAS TRYING TO GET MY DRY CLOTHES BACK ON AND I...
YOU GOTTA BE CAREFUL AROUND HERE!
GUYS GET DRUNK AND THEN THEY START BUSTING UP THEIR BOTTLES... THERE'S BROKEN GLASS ALL OVER THE PLACE AND...
ARE YOU OK? DOES IT HURT TO WALK?
I'M FINE... IT STILL ACHES A LITTLE BUT IT FEELS A LOT BETTER.

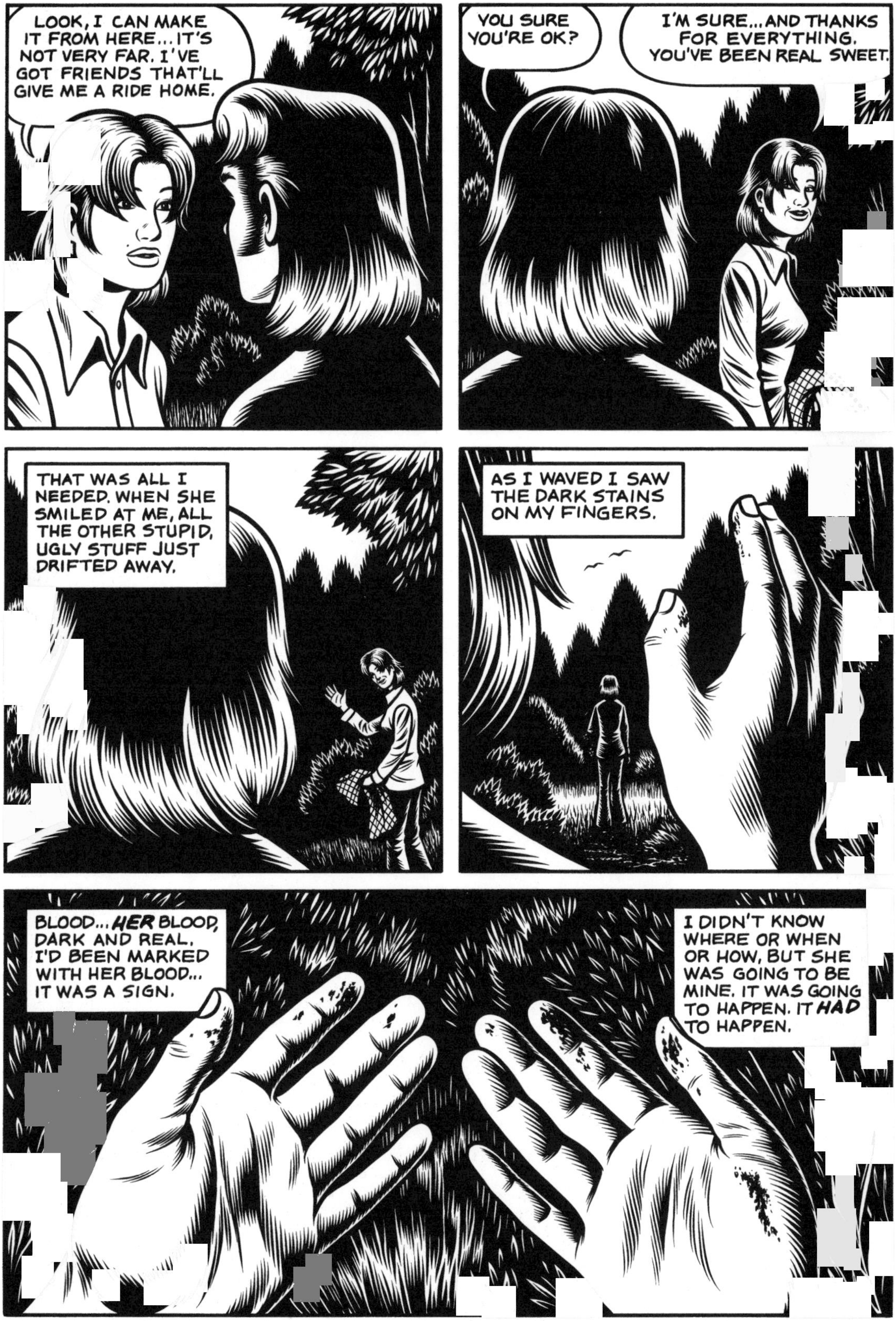
LOOK, I CAN MAKE IT FROM HERE... IT'S NOT VERY FAR. I'VE GOT FRIENDS THAT'LL GIVE ME A RIDE HOME.
YOU SURE YOU'RE OK?
I'M SURE... AND THANKS FOR EVERYTHING. YOU'VE BEEN REAL SWEET.
THAT WAS ALL I NEEDED. WHEN SHE SMILED AT ME, ALL THE OTHER STUPID, UGLY STUFF JUST DRIFTED AWAY.
AS I WAVED I SAW THE DARK STAINS ON MY FINGERS.
BLOOD... **HER** BLOOD, DARK AND REAL. I'D BEEN MARKED WITH HER BLOOD... IT WAS A SIGN.
I DIDN'T KNOW WHERE OR WHEN OR HOW, BUT SHE WAS GOING TO BE MINE. IT WAS GOING TO HAPPEN. IT ***HAD*** TO HAPPEN.

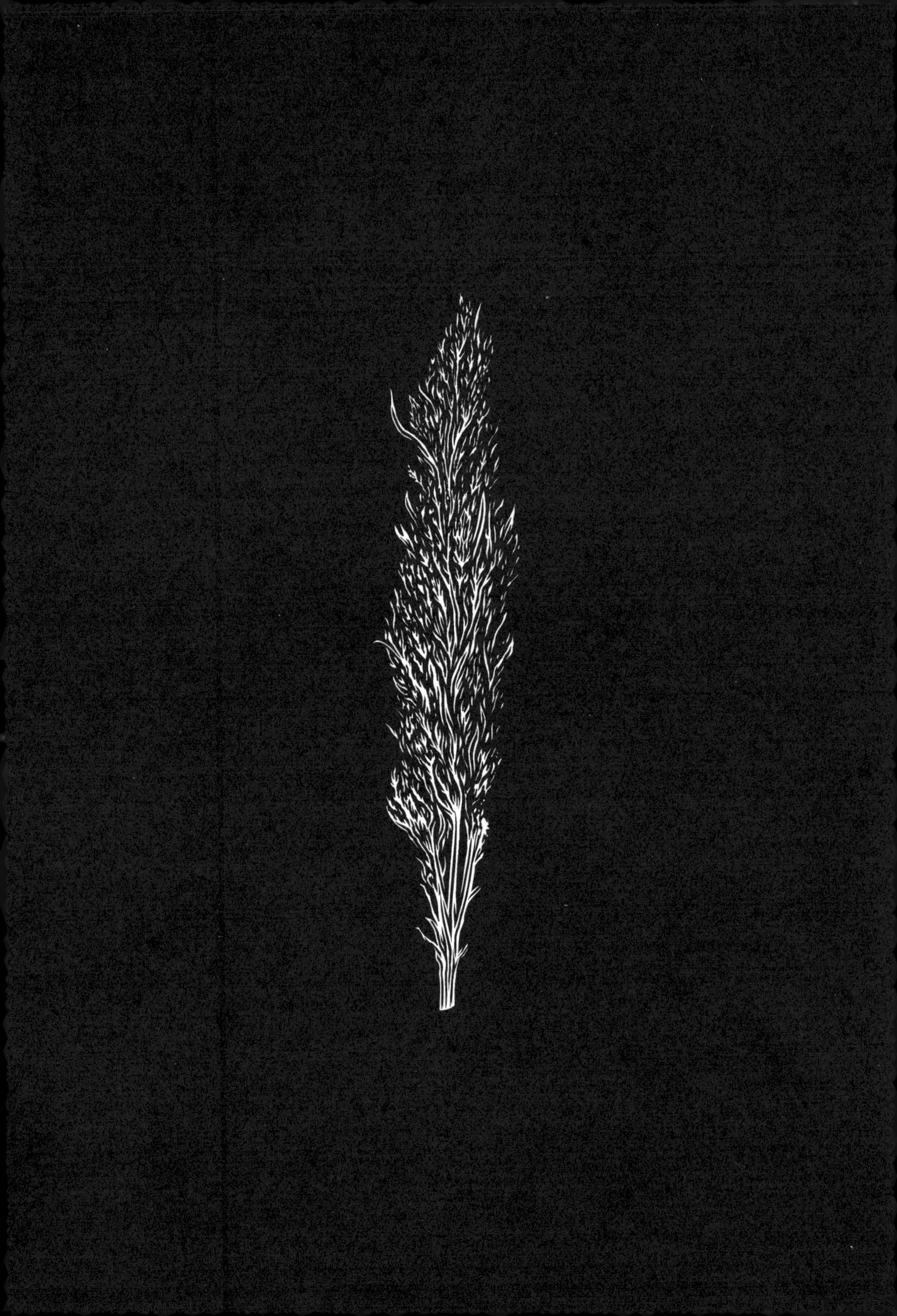

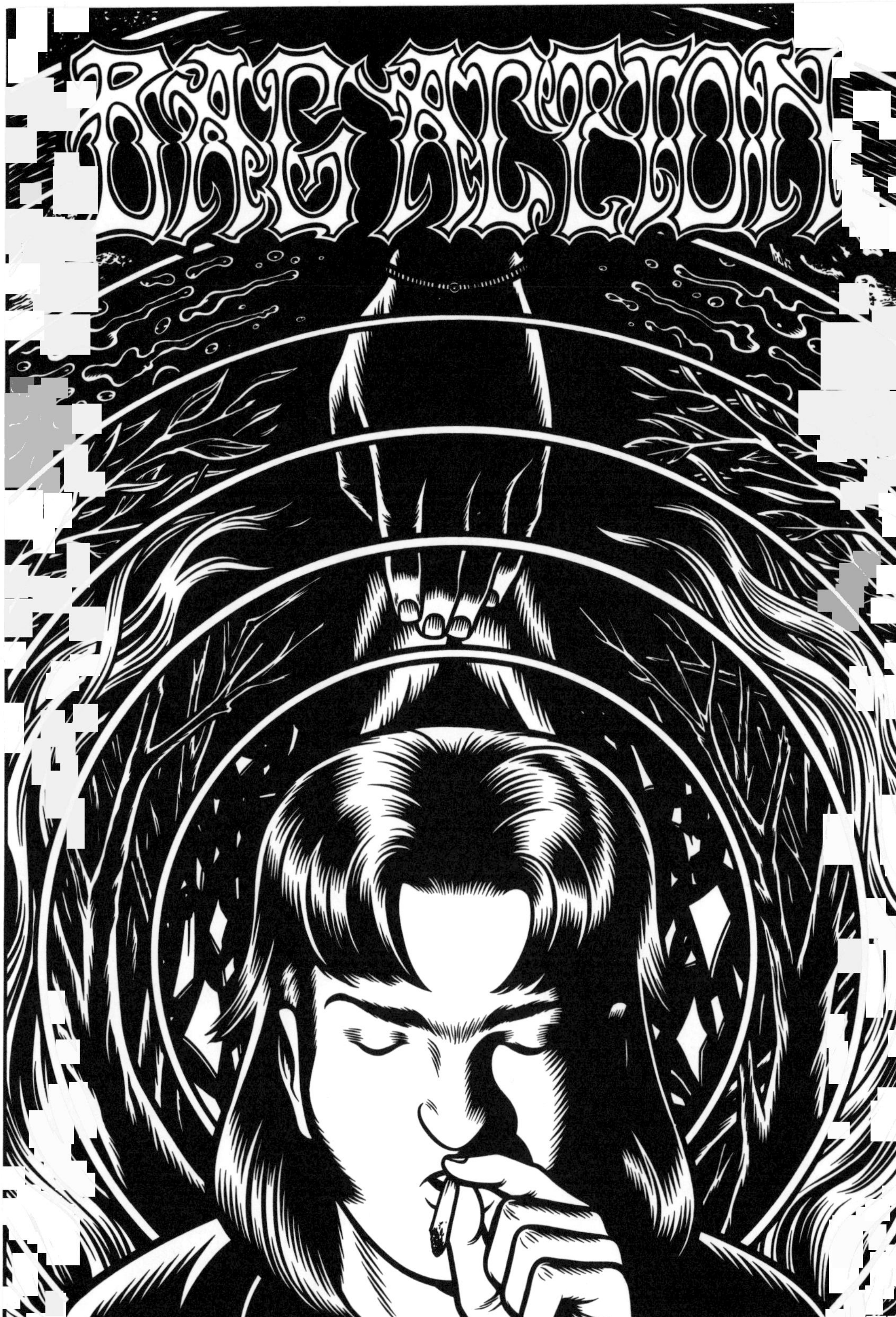

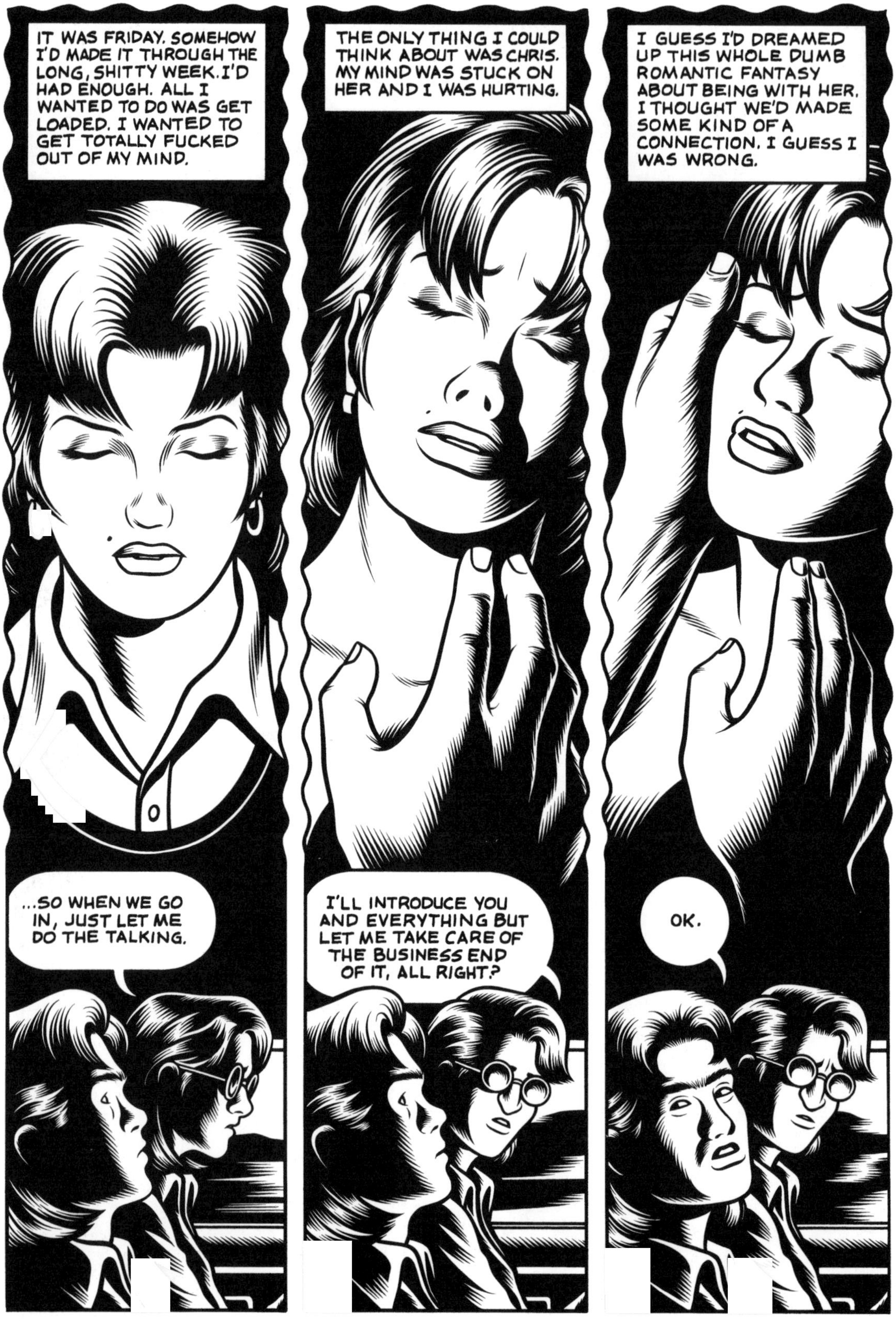
IT WAS FRIDAY. SOMEHOW I'D MADE IT THROUGH THE LONG, SHITTY WEEK. I'D HAD ENOUGH. ALL I WANTED TO DO WAS GET LOADED. I WANTED TO GET TOTALLY FUCKED OUT OF MY MIND.
...SO WHEN WE GO IN, JUST LET ME DO THE TALKING.
THE ONLY THING I COULD THINK ABOUT WAS CHRIS. MY MIND WAS STUCK ON HER AND I WAS HURTING.
I'LL INTRODUCE YOU AND EVERYTHING BUT LET ME TAKE CARE OF THE BUSINESS END OF IT, ALL RIGHT?
I GUESS I'D DREAMED UP THIS WHOLE DUMB ROMANTIC FANTASY ABOUT BEING WITH HER. I THOUGHT WE'D MADE SOME KIND OF A CONNECTION. I GUESS I WAS WRONG.
OK.

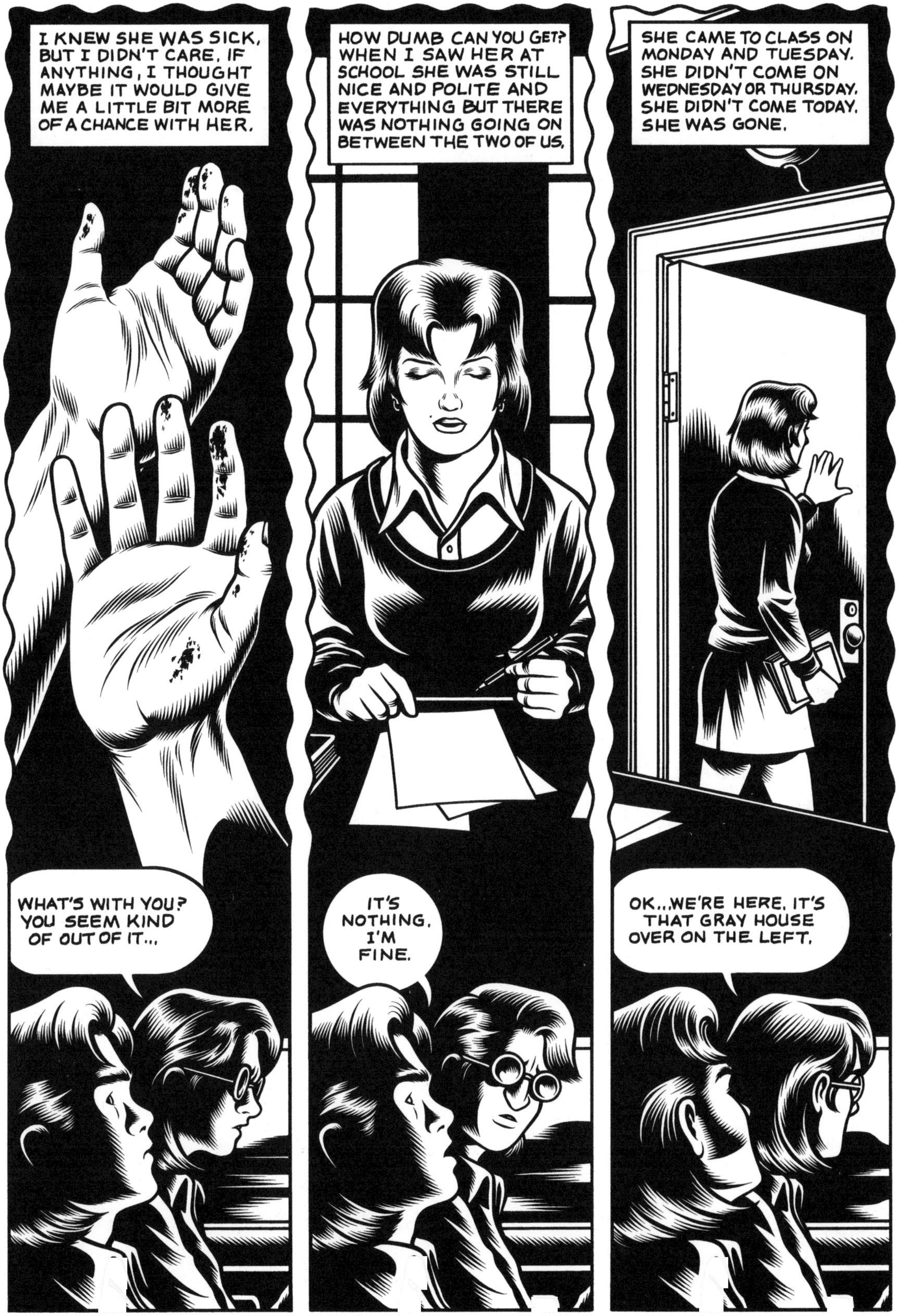
I KNEW SHE WAS SICK, BUT I DIDN'T CARE. IF ANYTHING, I THOUGHT MAYBE IT WOULD GIVE ME A LITTLE BIT MORE OF A CHANCE WITH HER.
HOW DUMB CAN YOU GET? WHEN I SAW HER AT SCHOOL SHE WAS STILL NICE AND POLITE AND EVERYTHING BUT THERE WAS NOTHING GOING ON BETWEEN THE TWO OF US.
SHE CAME TO CLASS ON MONDAY AND TUESDAY. SHE DIDN'T COME ON WEDNESDAY OR THURSDAY. SHE DIDN'T COME TODAY. SHE WAS GONE.
WHAT'S WITH YOU? YOU SEEM KIND OF OUT OF IT...
IT'S NOTHING. I'M FINE.
OK...WE'RE HERE. IT'S THAT GRAY HOUSE OVER ON THE LEFT.

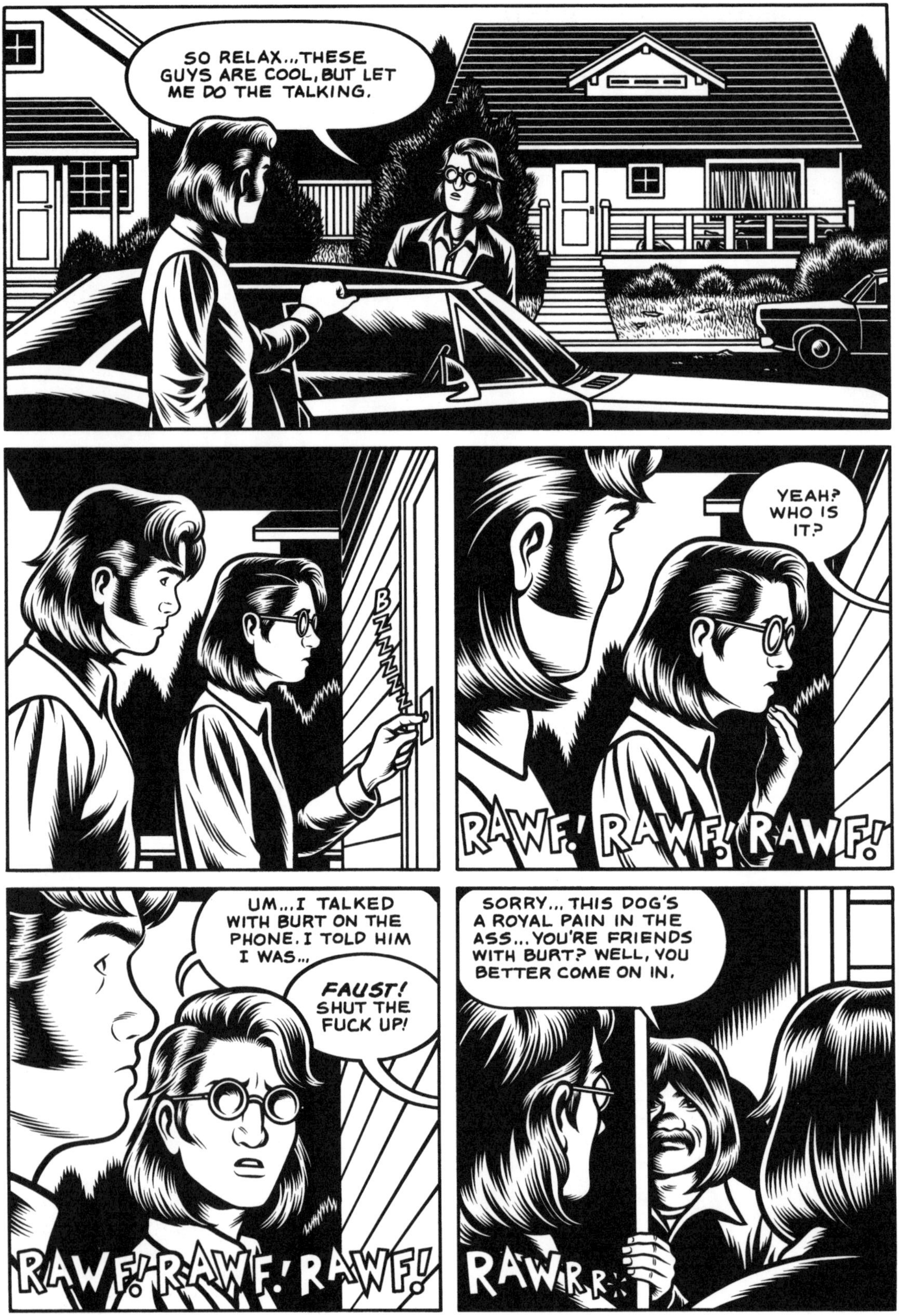
SO RELAX...THESE GUYS ARE COOL, BUT LET ME DO THE TALKING.
BZZZZZZ
YEAH? WHO IS IT?
RAWF! RAWF! RAWF!
UM...I TALKED WITH BURT ON THE PHONE. I TOLD HIM I WAS...
FAUST! SHUT THE FUCK UP!
RAWF! RAWF! RAWF!
SORRY...THIS DOG'S A ROYAL PAIN IN THE ASS...YOU'RE FRIENDS WITH BURT? WELL, YOU BETTER COME ON IN.
RAWRRR

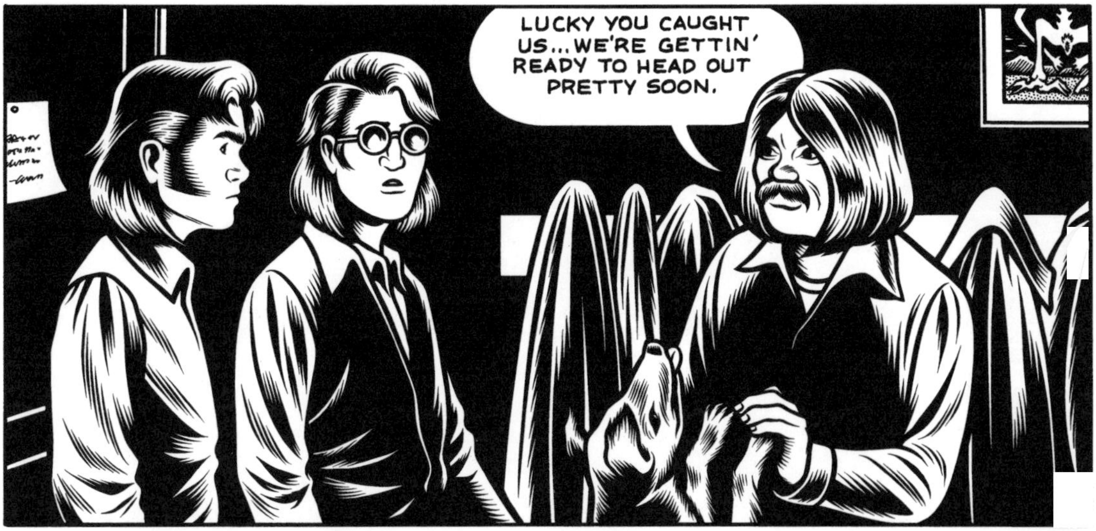
LUCKY YOU CAUGHT US... WE'RE GETTIN' READY TO HEAD OUT PRETTY SOON.

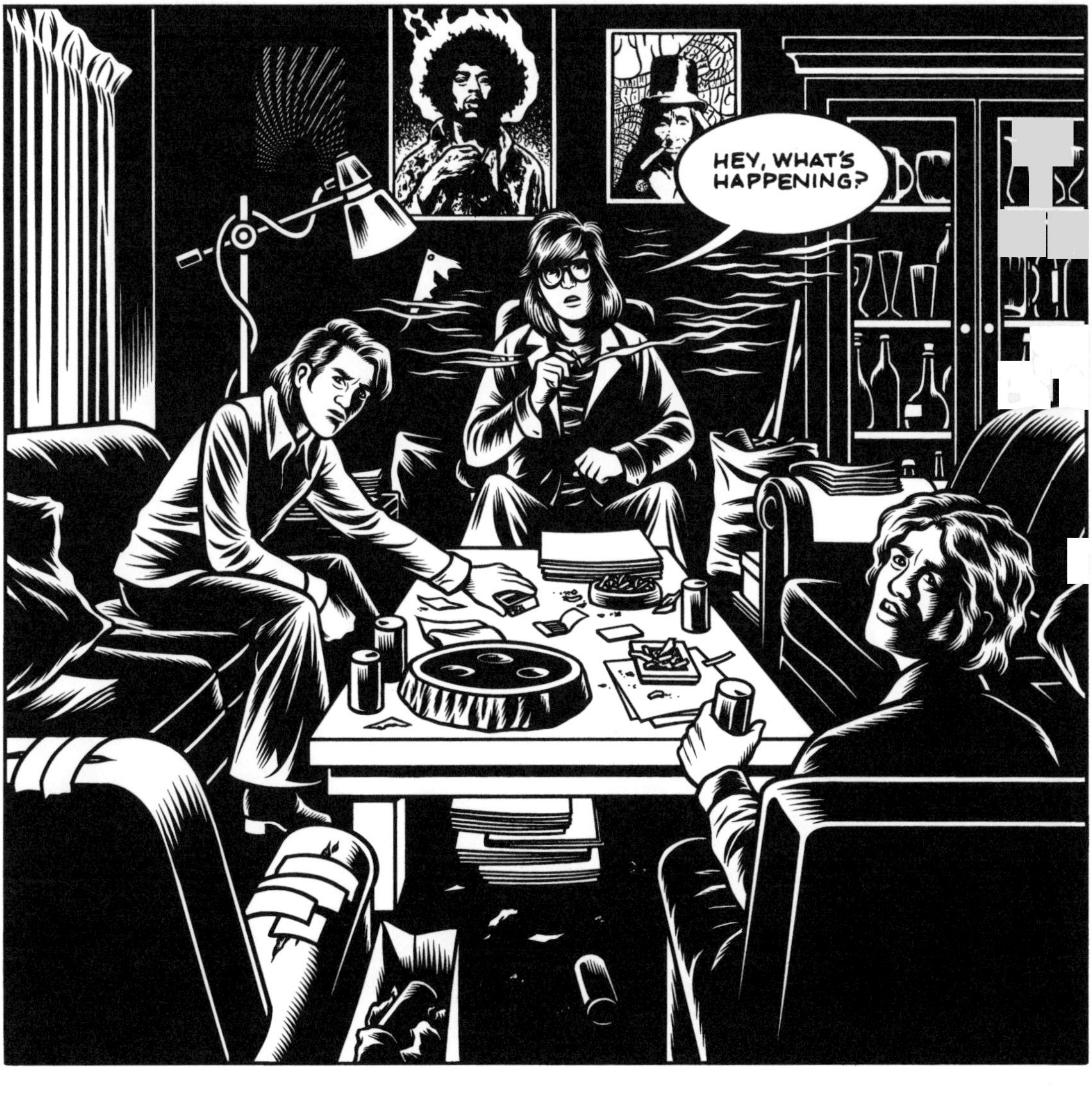
HEY, WHAT'S HAPPENING?

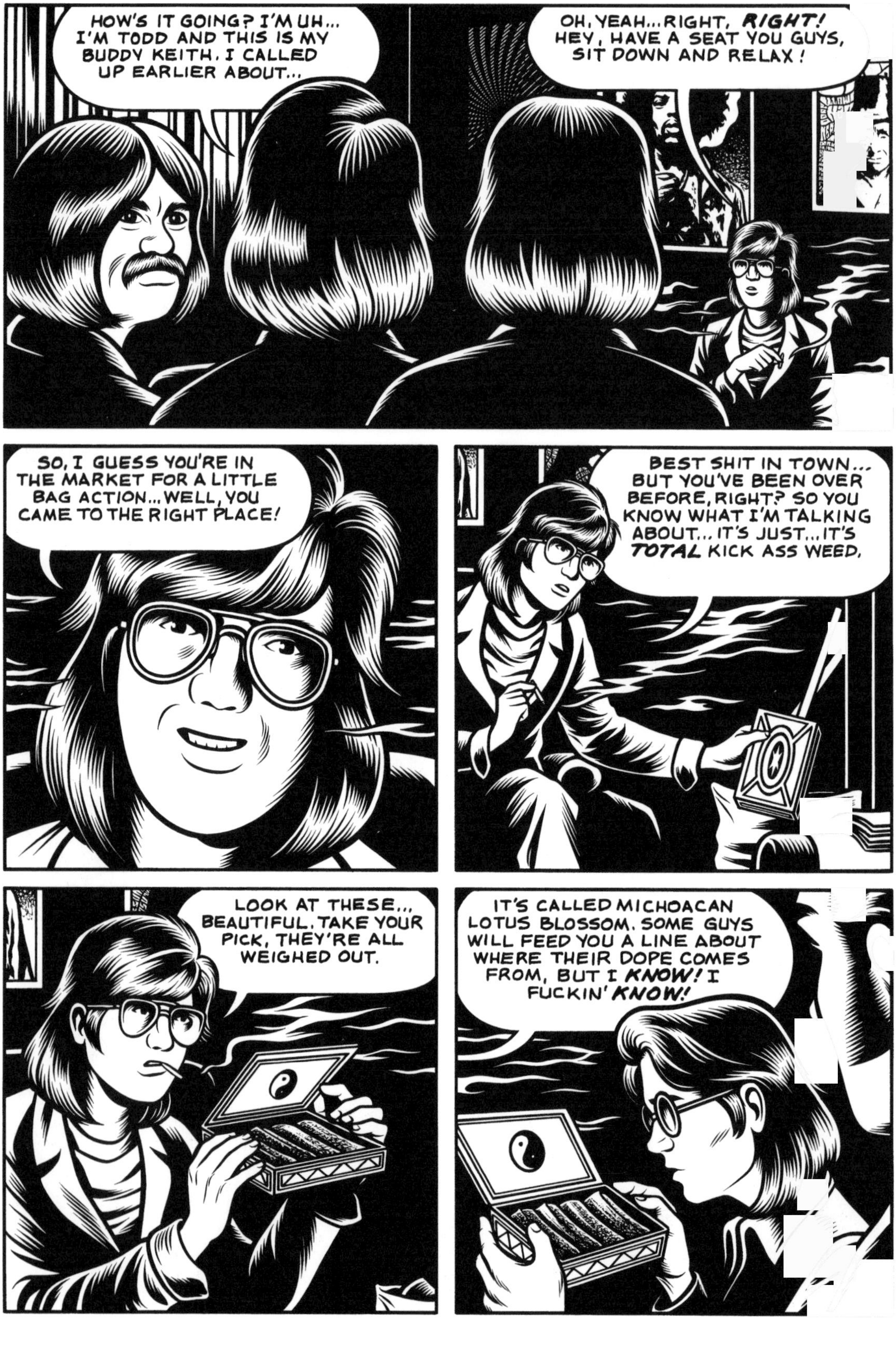
HOW'S IT GOING? I'M UH... I'M TODD AND THIS IS MY BUDDY KEITH. I CALLED UP EARLIER ABOUT...
OH, YEAH... RIGHT, RIGHT! HEY, HAVE A SEAT YOU GUYS, SIT DOWN AND RELAX!
SO, I GUESS YOU'RE IN THE MARKET FOR A LITTLE BAG ACTION... WELL, YOU CAME TO THE RIGHT PLACE!
BEST SHIT IN TOWN... BUT YOU'VE BEEN OVER BEFORE, RIGHT? SO YOU KNOW WHAT I'M TALKING ABOUT... IT'S JUST... IT'S TOTAL KICK ASS WEED.
LOOK AT THESE... BEAUTIFUL. TAKE YOUR PICK, THEY'RE ALL WEIGHED OUT.
IT'S CALLED MICHOACAN LOTUS BLOSSOM. SOME GUYS WILL FEED YOU A LINE ABOUT WHERE THEIR DOPE COMES FROM, BUT I KNOW! I FUCKIN' KNOW!

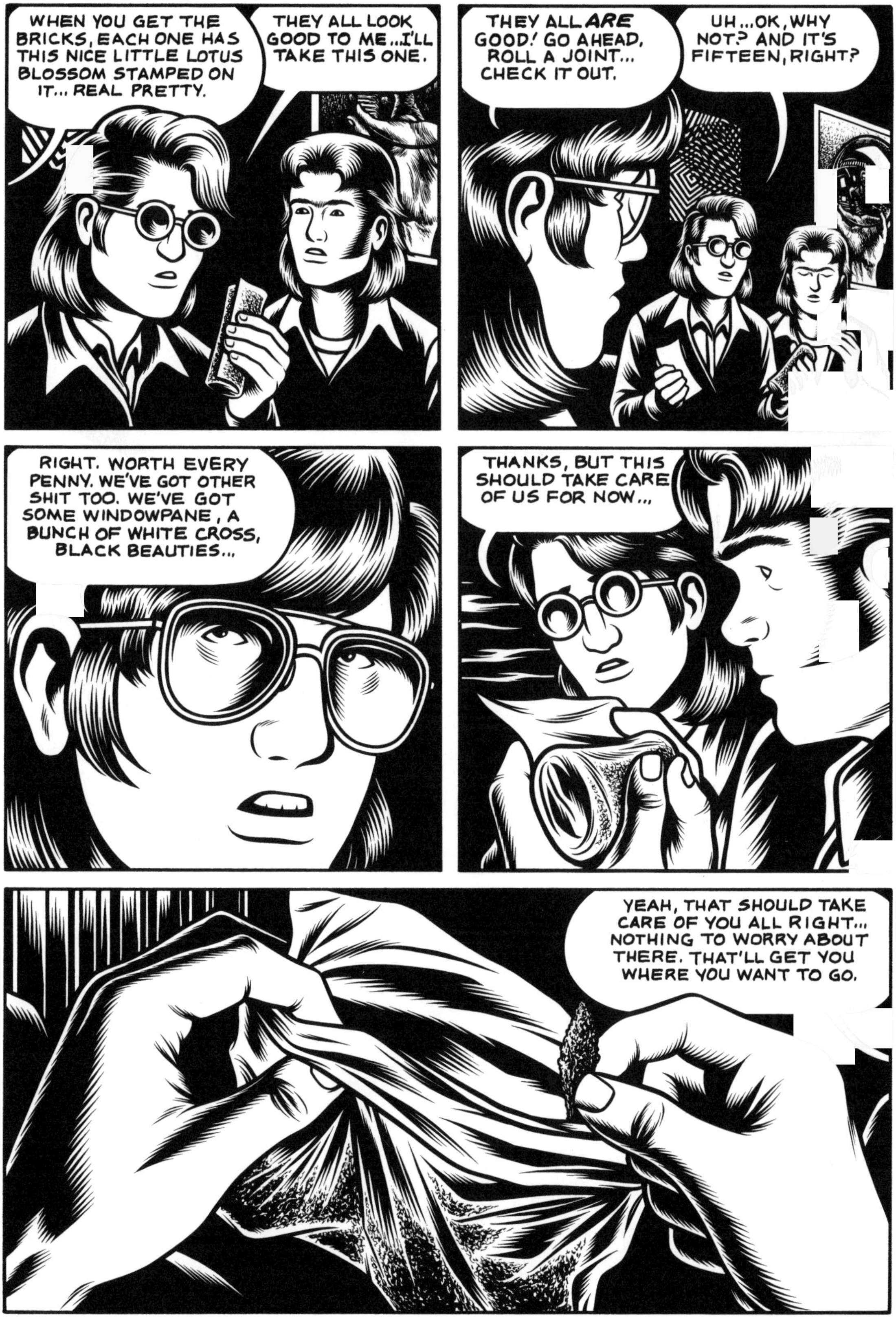
WHEN YOU GET THE BRICKS, EACH ONE HAS THIS NICE LITTLE LOTUS BLOSSOM STAMPED ON IT... REAL PRETTY.
THEY ALL LOOK GOOD TO ME...I'LL TAKE THIS ONE.
THEY ALL ARE GOOD! GO AHEAD, ROLL A JOINT... CHECK IT OUT.
UH...OK, WHY NOT? AND IT'S FIFTEEN, RIGHT?
RIGHT. WORTH EVERY PENNY. WE'VE GOT OTHER SHIT TOO. WE'VE GOT SOME WINDOWPANE, A BUNCH OF WHITE CROSS, BLACK BEAUTIES...
THANKS, BUT THIS SHOULD TAKE CARE OF US FOR NOW...
YEAH, THAT SHOULD TAKE CARE OF YOU ALL RIGHT... NOTHING TO WORRY ABOUT THERE. THAT'LL GET YOU WHERE YOU WANT TO GO.

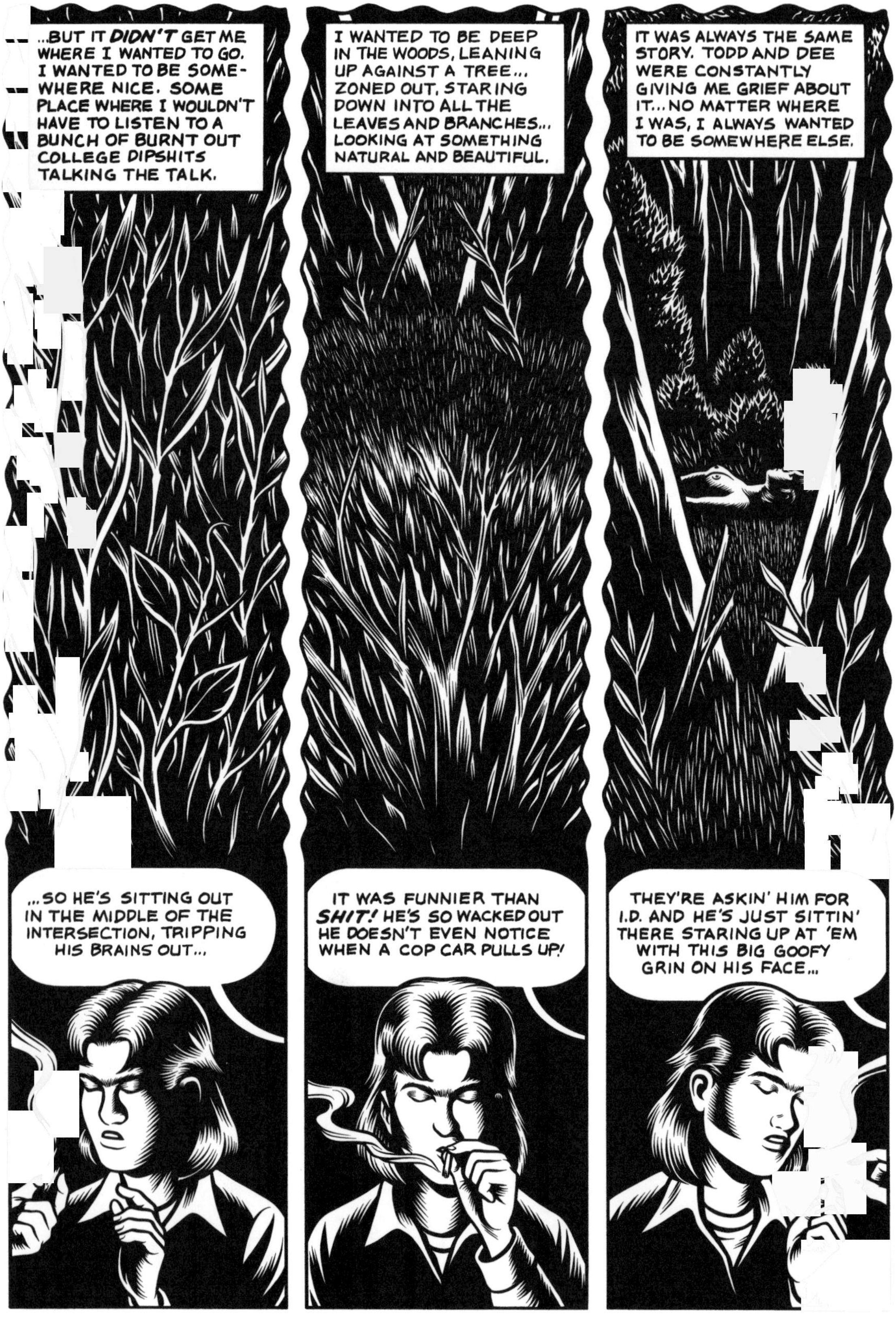
...BUT IT DIDN'T GET ME WHERE I WANTED TO GO. I WANTED TO BE SOME-WHERE NICE. SOME PLACE WHERE I WOULDN'T HAVE TO LISTEN TO A BUNCH OF BURNT OUT COLLEGE DIPSHITS TALKING THE TALK.
I WANTED TO BE DEEP IN THE WOODS, LEANING UP AGAINST A TREE... ZONED OUT, STARING DOWN INTO ALL THE LEAVES AND BRANCHES... LOOKING AT SOMETHING NATURAL AND BEAUTIFUL.
IT WAS ALWAYS THE SAME STORY. TODD AND DEE WERE CONSTANTLY GIVING ME GRIEF ABOUT IT... NO MATTER WHERE I WAS, I ALWAYS WANTED TO BE SOMEWHERE ELSE.
...SO HE'S SITTING OUT IN THE MIDDLE OF THE INTERSECTION, TRIPPING HIS BRAINS OUT...
IT WAS FUNNIER THAN SHIT! HE'S SO WACKED OUT HE DOESN'T EVEN NOTICE WHEN A COP CAR PULLS UP!
THEY'RE ASKIN' HIM FOR I.D. AND HE'S JUST SITTIN' THERE STARING UP AT 'EM WITH THIS BIG GOOFY GRIN ON HIS FACE...

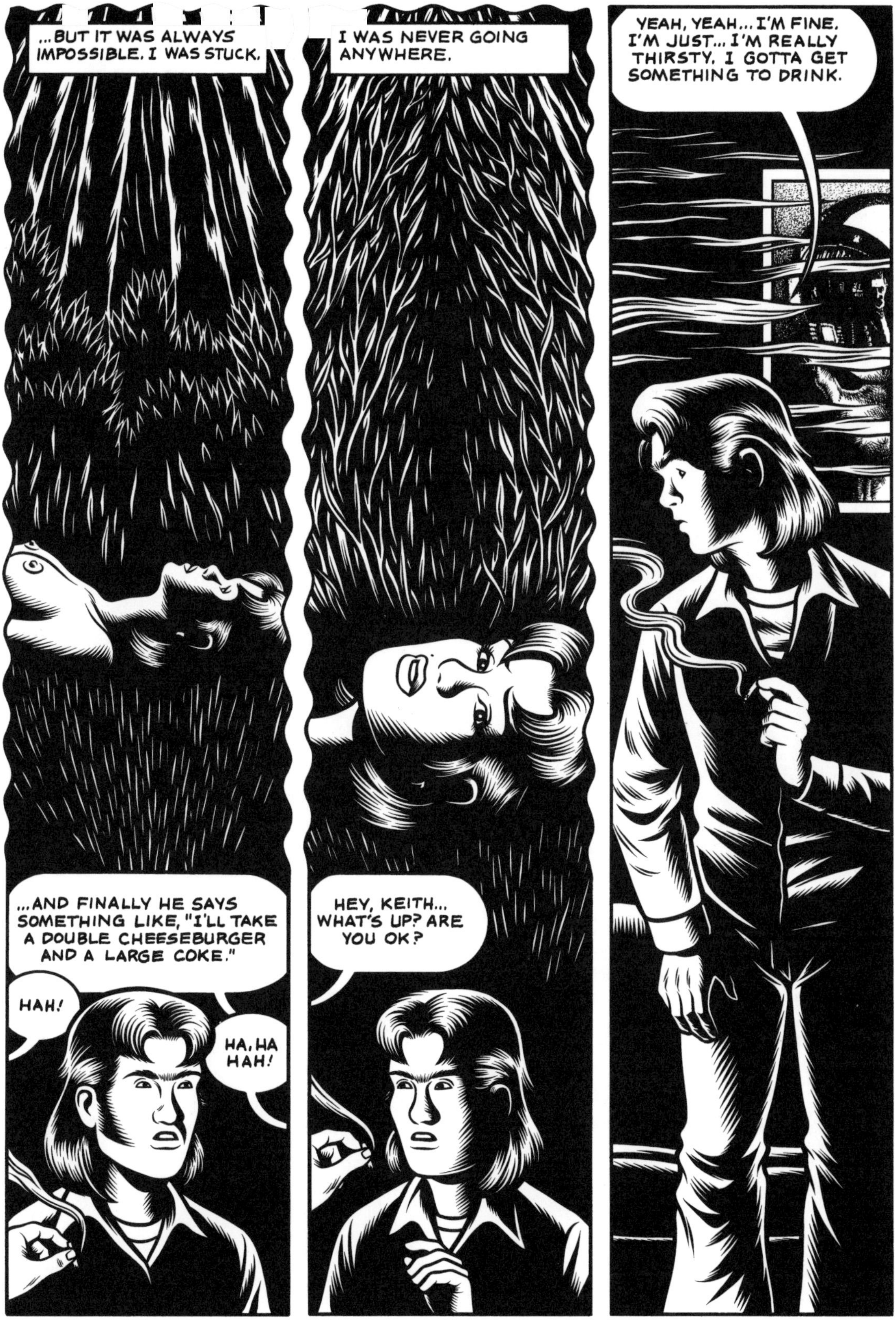
...BUT IT WAS ALWAYS IMPOSSIBLE. I WAS STUCK,
...AND FINALLY HE SAYS SOMETHING LIKE, "I'LL TAKE A DOUBLE CHEESEBURGER AND A LARGE COKE."
HAH!
HA, HA HAH!
I WAS NEVER GOING ANYWHERE.
HEY, KEITH... WHAT'S UP? ARE YOU OK?
YEAH, YEAH... I'M FINE. I'M JUST... I'M REALLY THIRSTY. I GOTTA GET SOMETHING TO DRINK.

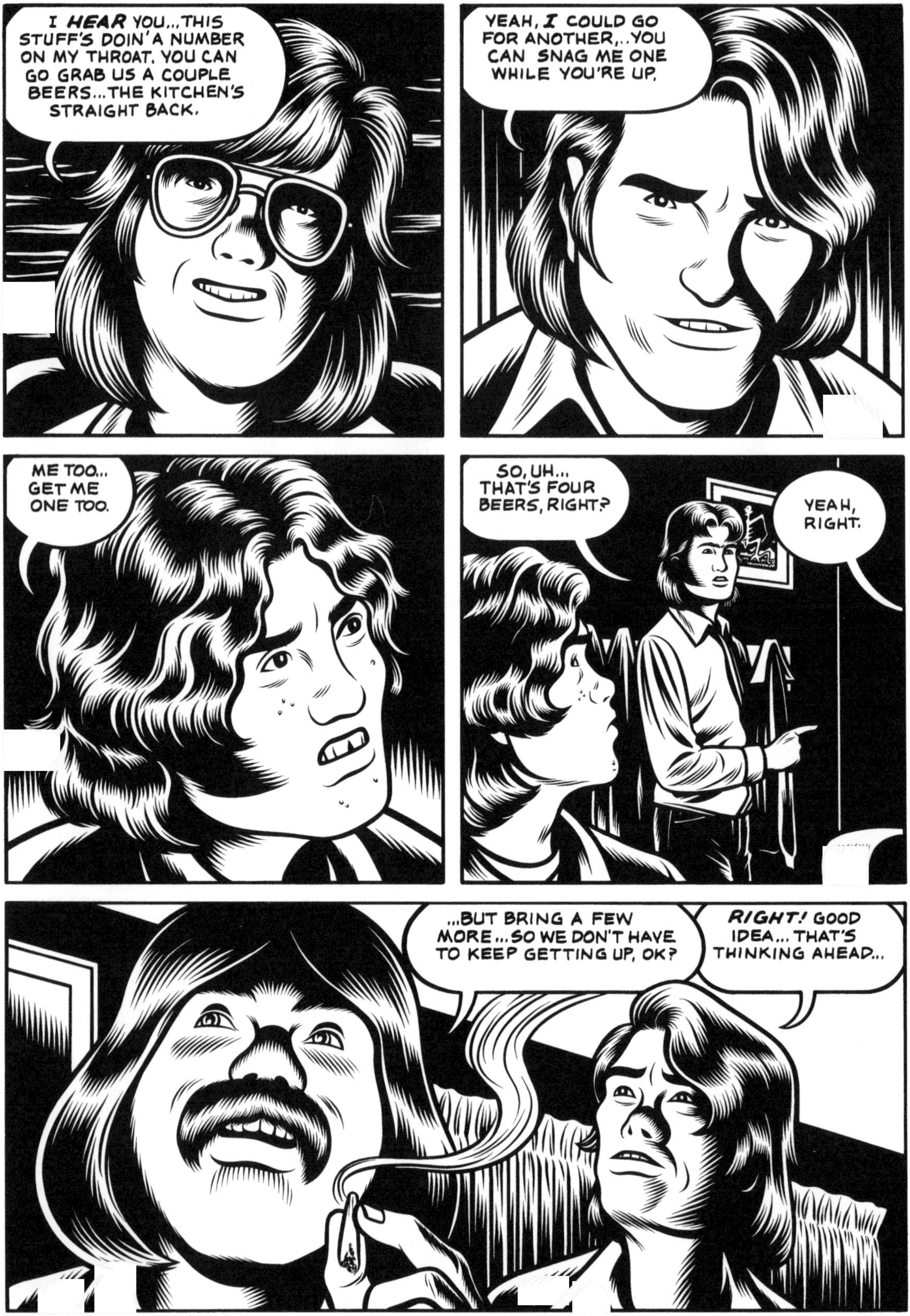
I HEAR YOU... THIS STUFF'S DOIN' A NUMBER ON MY THROAT. YOU CAN GO GRAB US A COUPLE BEERS... THE KITCHEN'S STRAIGHT BACK.
YEAH, I COULD GO FOR ANOTHER... YOU CAN SNAG ME ONE WHILE YOU'RE UP.
ME TOO... GET ME ONE TOO.
SO, UH... THAT'S FOUR BEERS, RIGHT?
YEAH, RIGHT.
...BUT BRING A FEW MORE... SO WE DON'T HAVE TO KEEP GETTING UP, OK?
RIGHT! GOOD IDEA... THAT'S THINKING AHEAD...

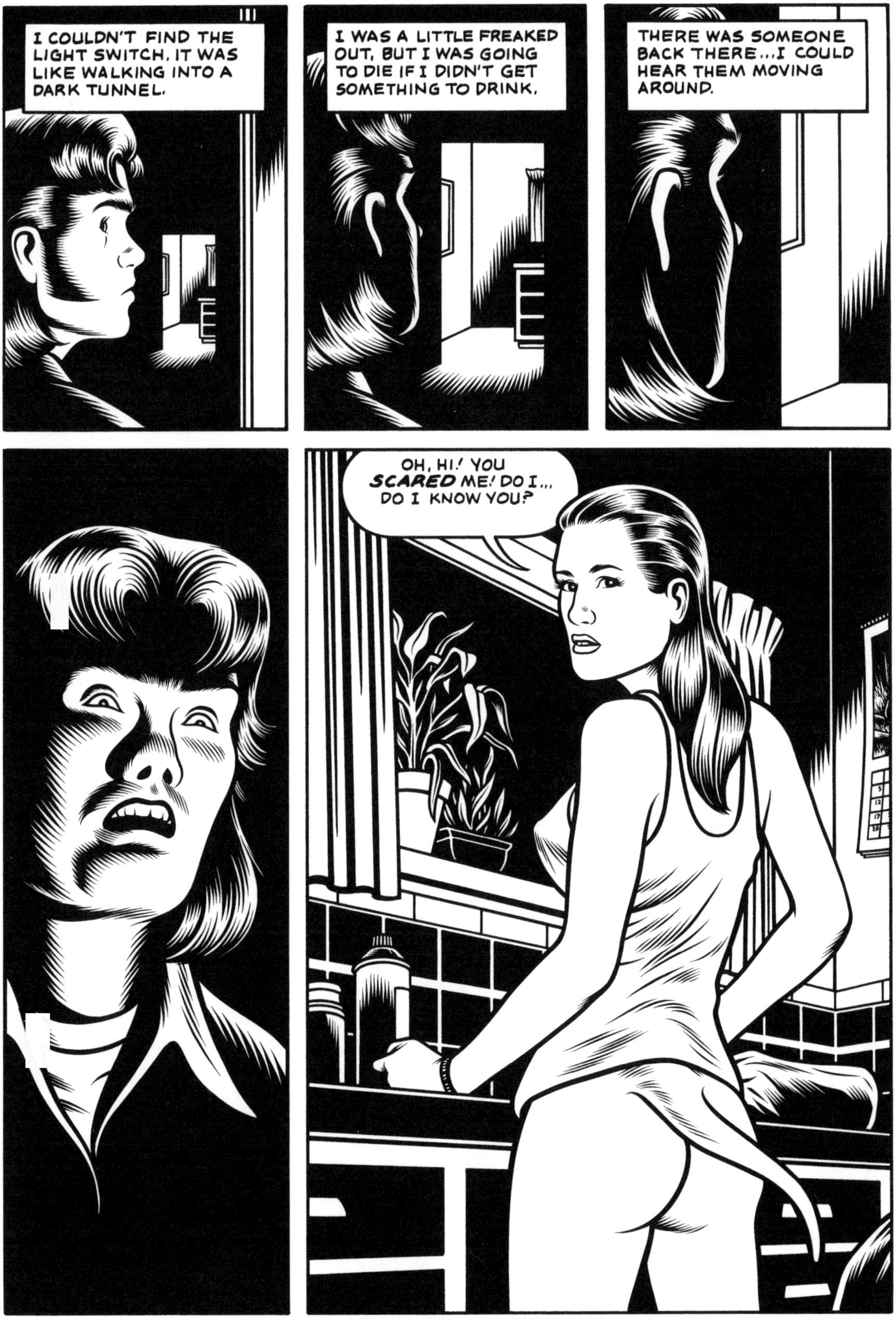
I COULDN'T FIND THE LIGHT SWITCH. IT WAS LIKE WALKING INTO A DARK TUNNEL.
I WAS A LITTLE FREAKED OUT, BUT I WAS GOING TO DIE IF I DIDN'T GET SOMETHING TO DRINK.
THERE WAS SOMEONE BACK THERE...I COULD HEAR THEM MOVING AROUND.
OH, HI! YOU SCARED ME! DO I... DO I KNOW YOU?

SHE TURNED TOWARDS ME AND I JUST STOOD THERE LIKE AN IDIOT...STARING.

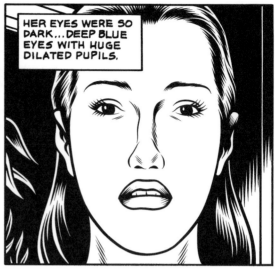

HER EYES WERE SO DARK...DEEP BLUE EYES WITH HUGE DILATED PUPILS.

BLACK HAIR AGAINST WHITE SKIN. THE BRIGHT FLUORESCENT LIGHT IN THE KITCHEN MADE IT LOOK EVEN WHITER.

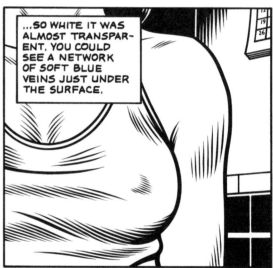

...SO WHITE IT WAS ALMOST TRANSPARENT. YOU COULD SEE A NETWORK OF SOFT BLUE VEINS JUST UNDER THE SURFACE.

SHE HAD TURNED BUT I HAD SEEN IT ALREADY...I'D SEEN WHAT WAS BACK THERE.

OOPS!

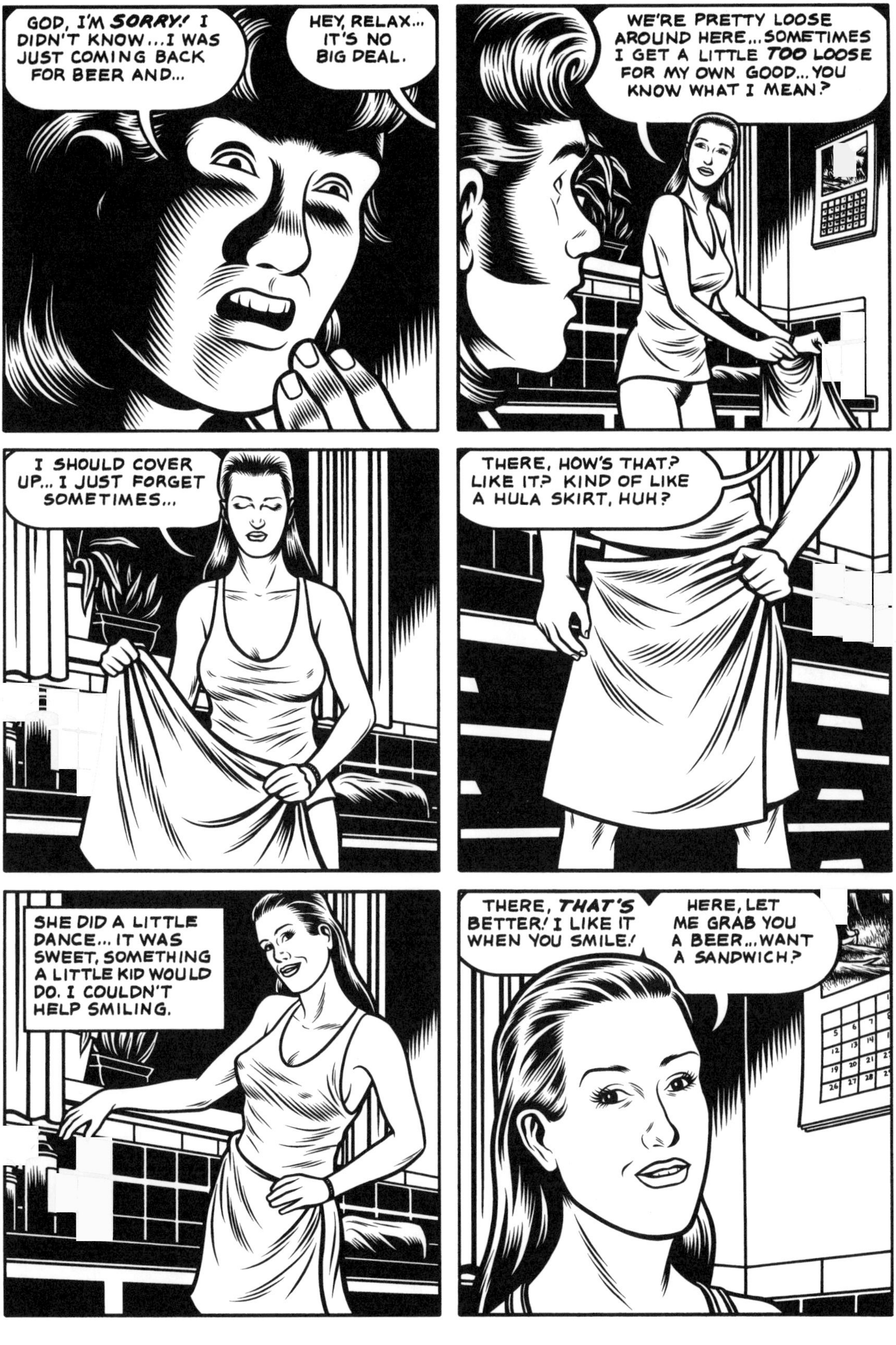

GOD, I'M SORRY! I DIDN'T KNOW... I WAS JUST COMING BACK FOR BEER AND...
HEY, RELAX... IT'S NO BIG DEAL.
WE'RE PRETTY LOOSE AROUND HERE... SOMETIMES I GET A LITTLE TOO LOOSE FOR MY OWN GOOD... YOU KNOW WHAT I MEAN?
I SHOULD COVER UP... I JUST FORGET SOMETIMES...
THERE, HOW'S THAT? LIKE IT? KIND OF LIKE A HULA SKIRT, HUH?
SHE DID A LITTLE DANCE... IT WAS SWEET, SOMETHING A LITTLE KID WOULD DO. I COULDN'T HELP SMILING.
THERE, THAT'S BETTER! I LIKE IT WHEN YOU SMILE!
HERE, LET ME GRAB YOU A BEER... WANT A SANDWICH?

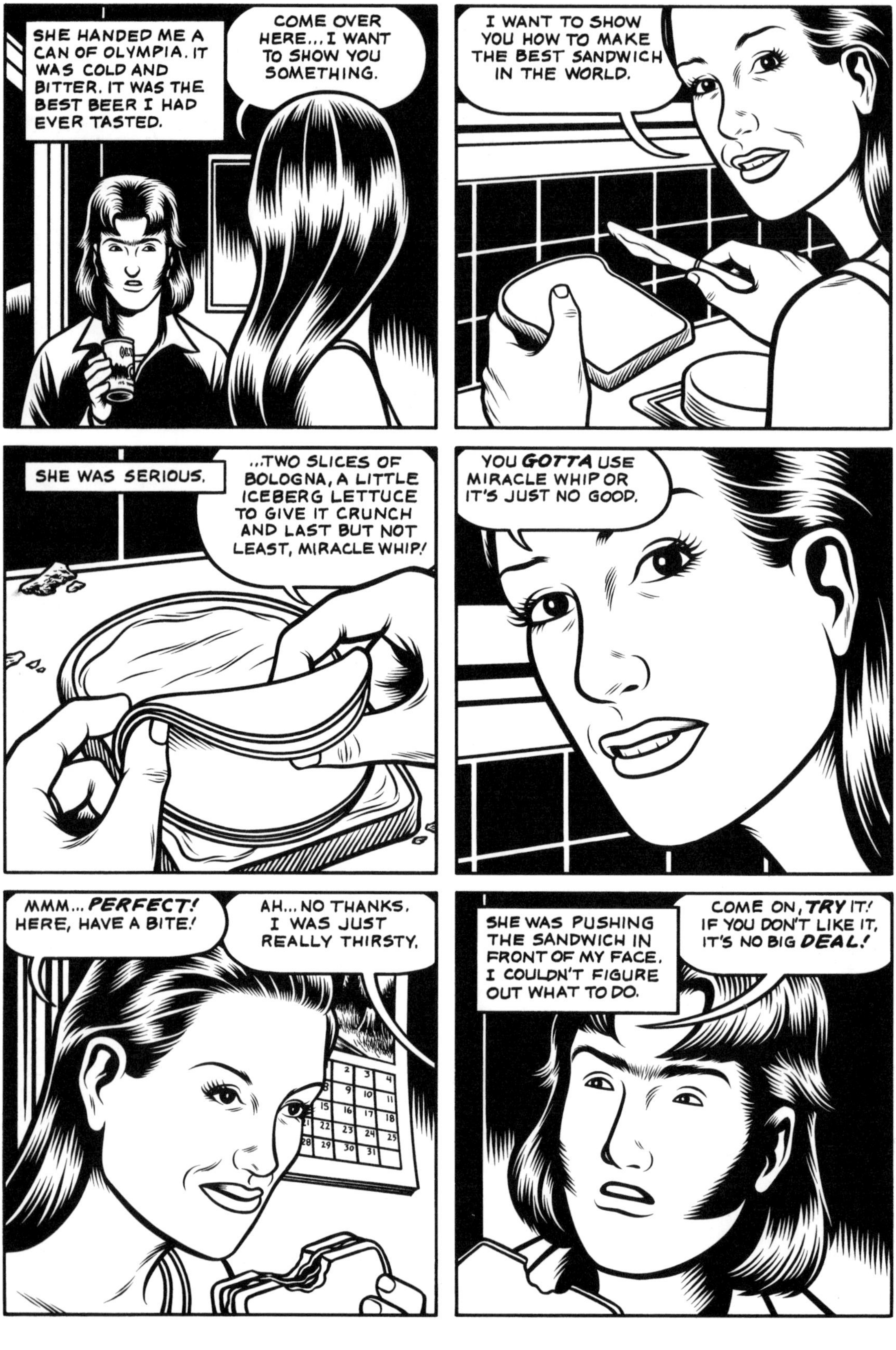
SHE HANDED ME A CAN OF OLYMPIA. IT WAS COLD AND BITTER. IT WAS THE BEST BEER I HAD EVER TASTED.
COME OVER HERE... I WANT TO SHOW YOU SOMETHING.
I WANT TO SHOW YOU HOW TO MAKE THE BEST SANDWICH IN THE WORLD.
SHE WAS SERIOUS.
...TWO SLICES OF BOLOGNA, A LITTLE ICEBERG LETTUCE TO GIVE IT CRUNCH AND LAST BUT NOT LEAST, MIRACLE WHIP!
YOU GOTTA USE MIRACLE WHIP OR IT'S JUST NO GOOD.
MMM... PERFECT! HERE, HAVE A BITE!
AH... NO THANKS. I WAS JUST REALLY THIRSTY.
SHE WAS PUSHING THE SANDWICH IN FRONT OF MY FACE. I COULDN'T FIGURE OUT WHAT TO DO.
COME ON, TRY IT! IF YOU DON'T LIKE IT, IT'S NO BIG DEAL!

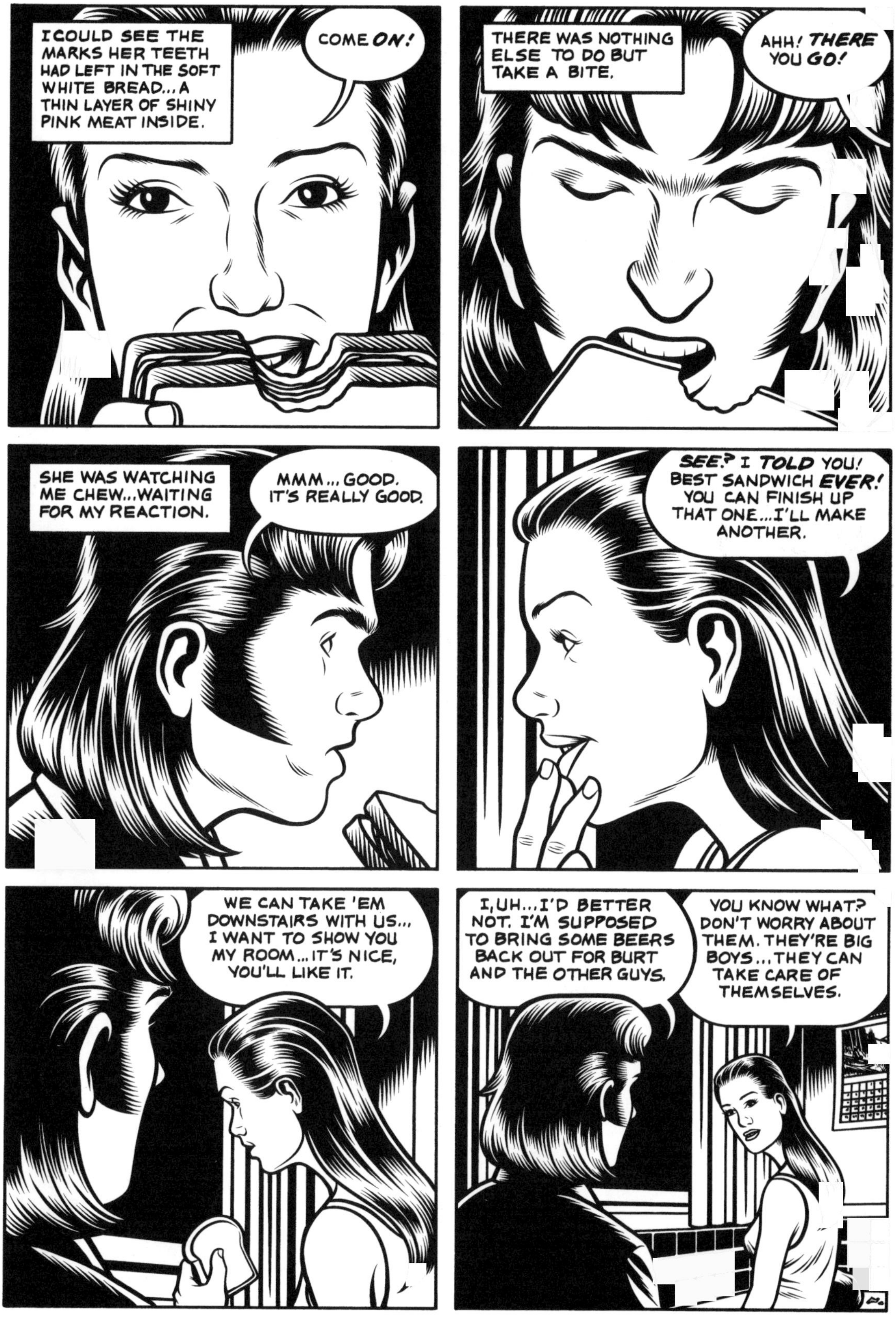
I COULD SEE THE MARKS HER TEETH HAD LEFT IN THE SOFT WHITE BREAD... A THIN LAYER OF SHINY PINK MEAT INSIDE.
COME ON!
THERE WAS NOTHING ELSE TO DO BUT TAKE A BITE.
AHH! THERE YOU GO!
SHE WAS WATCHING ME CHEW... WAITING FOR MY REACTION.
MMM... GOOD. IT'S REALLY GOOD.
SEE? I TOLD YOU! BEST SANDWICH EVER! YOU CAN FINISH UP THAT ONE... I'LL MAKE ANOTHER.
WE CAN TAKE 'EM DOWNSTAIRS WITH US... I WANT TO SHOW YOU MY ROOM... IT'S NICE, YOU'LL LIKE IT.
I, UH... I'D BETTER NOT. I'M SUPPOSED TO BRING SOME BEERS BACK OUT FOR BURT AND THE OTHER GUYS.
YOU KNOW WHAT? DON'T WORRY ABOUT THEM. THEY'RE BIG BOYS... THEY CAN TAKE CARE OF THEMSELVES.

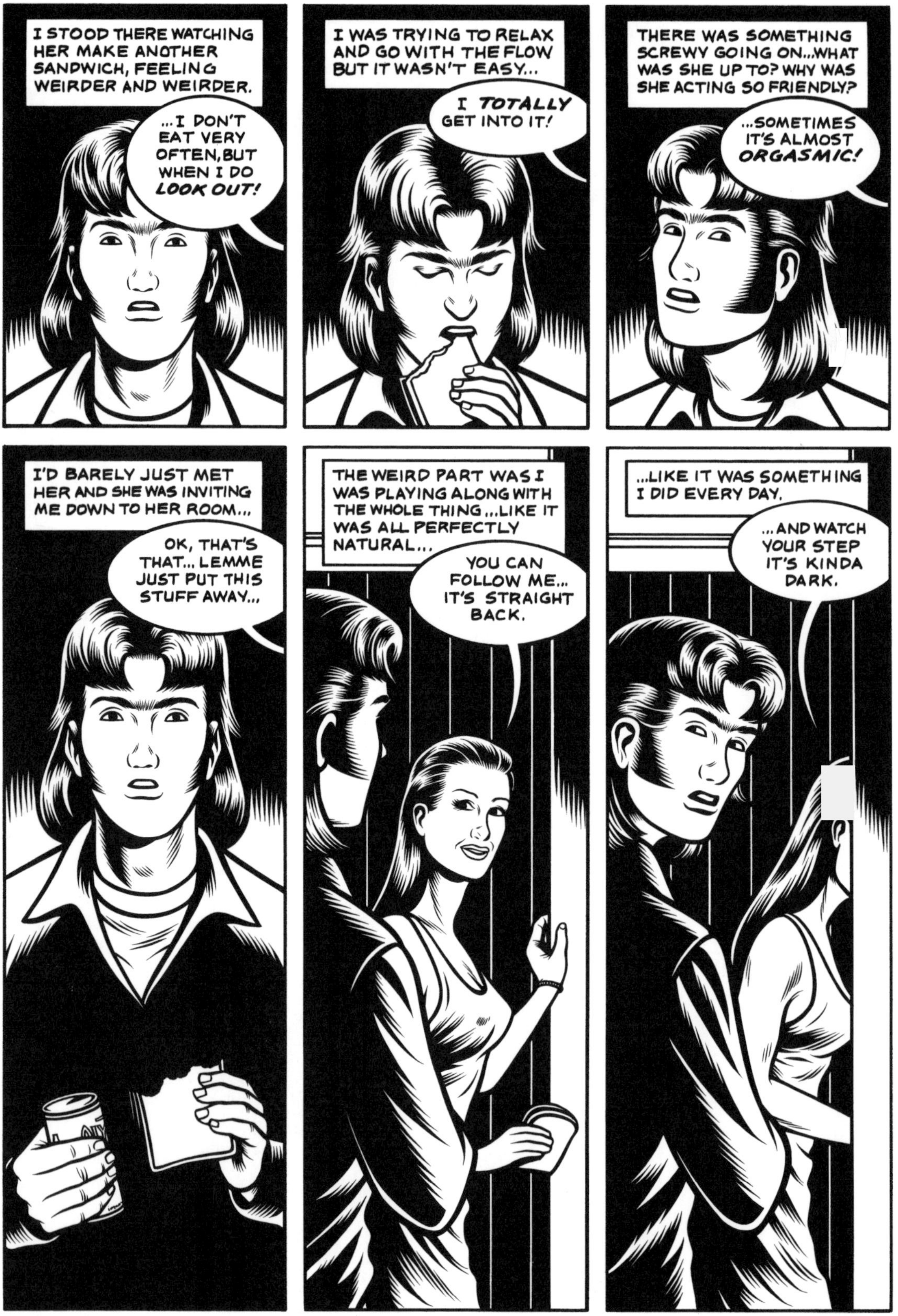
I STOOD THERE WATCHING HER MAKE ANOTHER SANDWICH, FEELING WEIRDER AND WEIRDER.
...I DON'T EAT VERY OFTEN, BUT WHEN I DO LOOK OUT!
I WAS TRYING TO RELAX AND GO WITH THE FLOW BUT IT WASN'T EASY...
I TOTALLY GET INTO IT!
THERE WAS SOMETHING SCREWY GOING ON...WHAT WAS SHE UP TO? WHY WAS SHE ACTING SO FRIENDLY?
...SOMETIMES IT'S ALMOST ORGASMIC!
I'D BARELY JUST MET HER AND SHE WAS INVITING ME DOWN TO HER ROOM...
OK, THAT'S THAT... LEMME JUST PUT THIS STUFF AWAY...
THE WEIRD PART WAS I WAS PLAYING ALONG WITH THE WHOLE THING...LIKE IT WAS ALL PERFECTLY NATURAL...
YOU CAN FOLLOW ME... IT'S STRAIGHT BACK.
...LIKE IT WAS SOMETHING I DID EVERY DAY.
...AND WATCH YOUR STEP IT'S KINDA DARK.

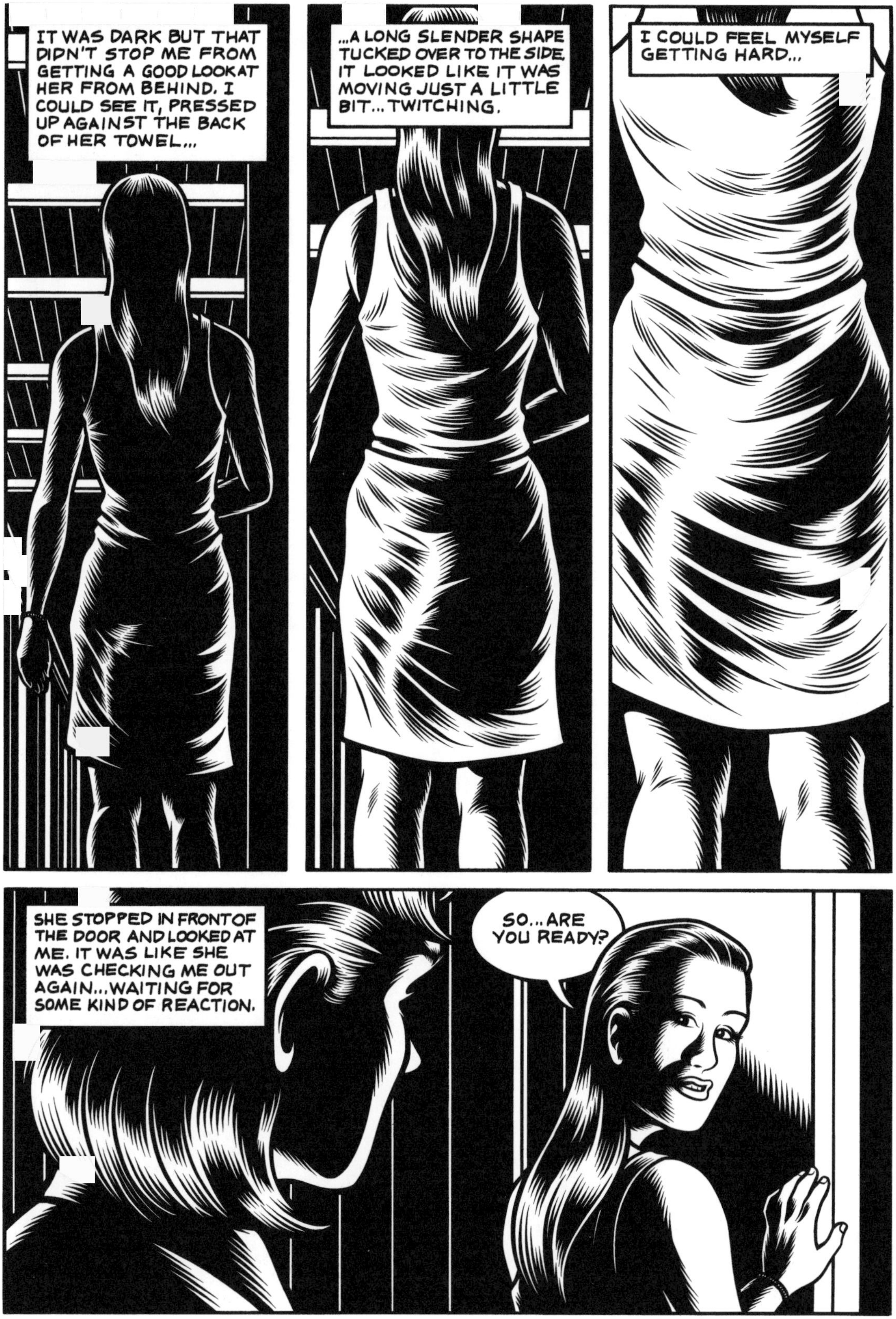
IT WAS DARK BUT THAT DIDN'T STOP ME FROM GETTING A GOOD LOOK AT HER FROM BEHIND. I COULD SEE IT, PRESSED UP AGAINST THE BACK OF HER TOWEL...
...A LONG SLENDER SHAPE TUCKED OVER TO THE SIDE. IT LOOKED LIKE IT WAS MOVING JUST A LITTLE BIT... TWITCHING.
I COULD FEEL MYSELF GETTING HARD...
SHE STOPPED IN FRONT OF THE DOOR AND LOOKED AT ME. IT WAS LIKE SHE WAS CHECKING ME OUT AGAIN... WAITING FOR SOME KIND OF REACTION.
SO... ARE YOU READY?

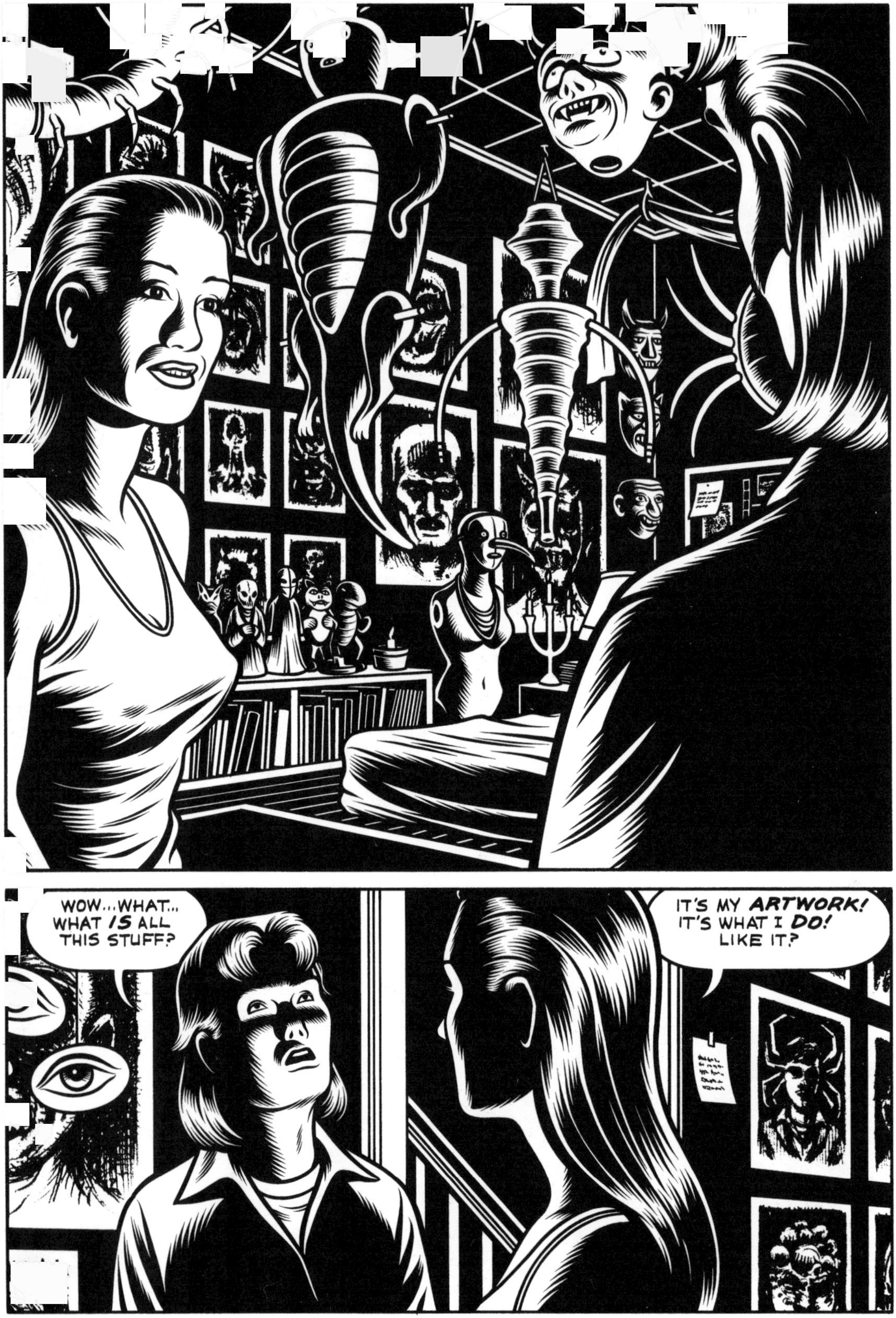
WOW...WHAT...
WHAT *IS* ALL
THIS STUFF?
IT'S MY **ARTWORK!**
IT'S WHAT I **DO!**
LIKE IT?

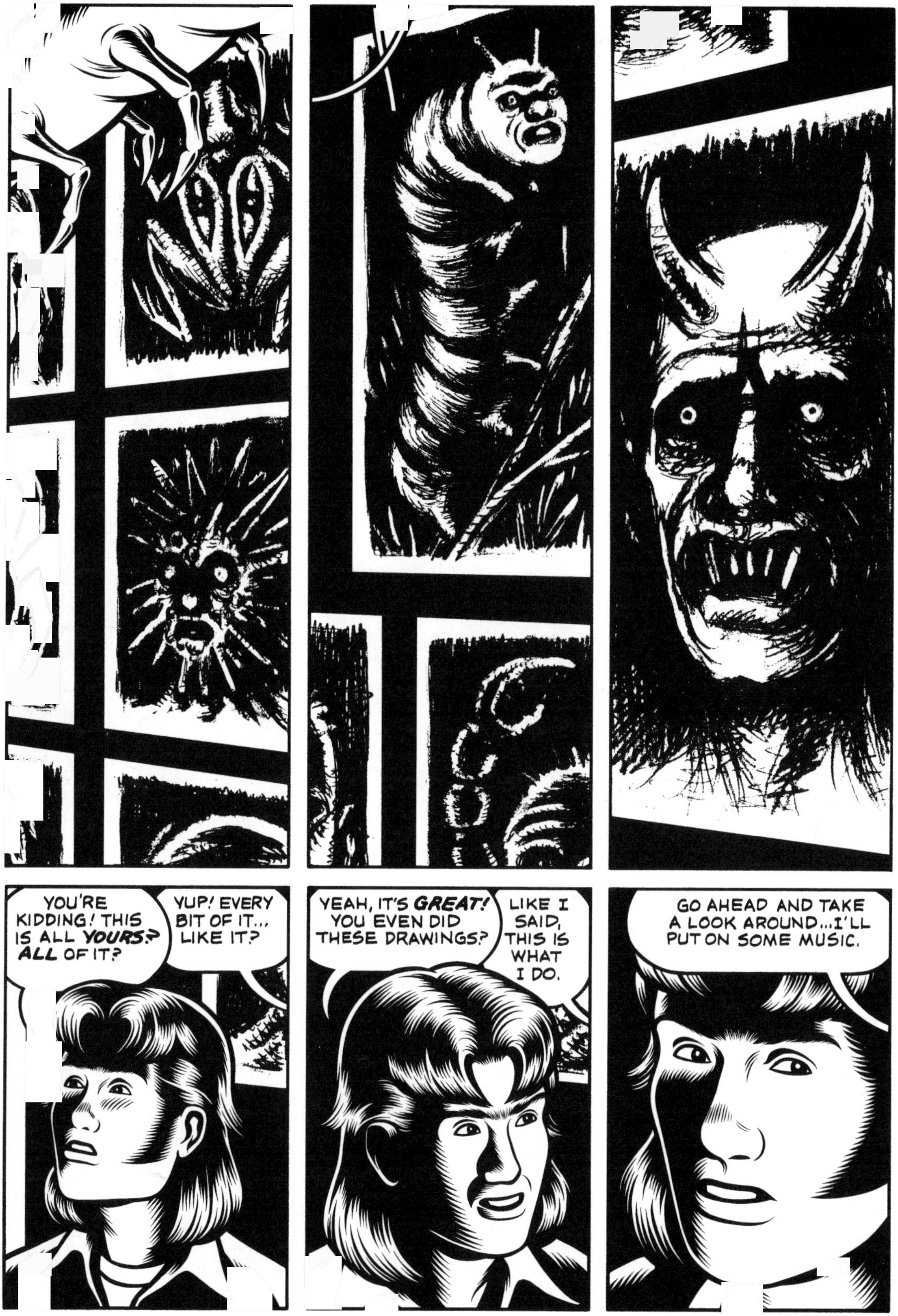
YOU'RE KIDDING! THIS IS ALL *YOURS?* *ALL* OF IT?
YUP! EVERY BIT OF IT... LIKE IT?
YEAH, IT'S *GREAT!* YOU EVEN DID THESE DRAWINGS?
LIKE I SAID, THIS IS WHAT I DO.
GO AHEAD AND TAKE A LOOK AROUND...I'LL PUT ON SOME MUSIC.

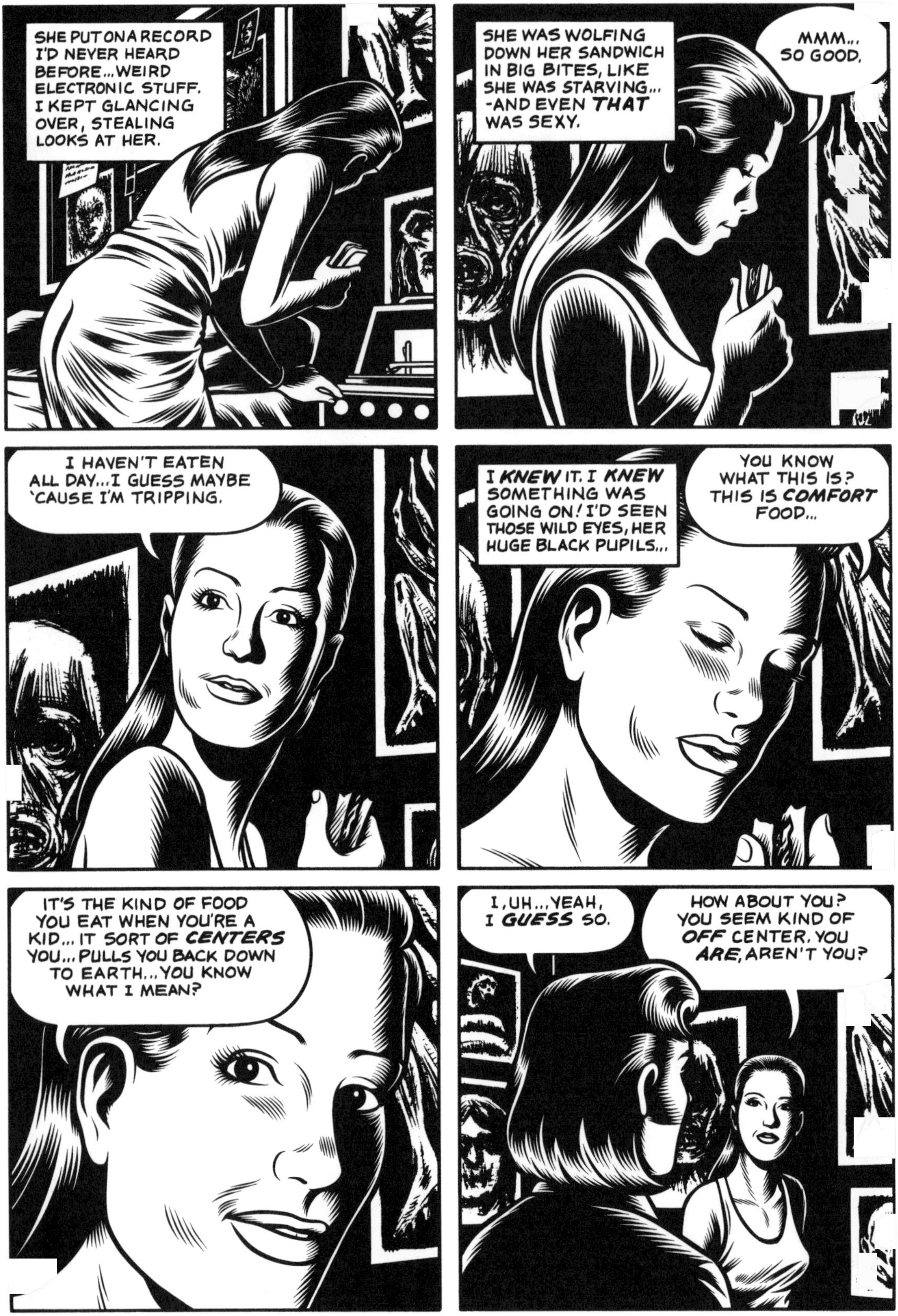
SHE PUT ON A RECORD I'D NEVER HEARD BEFORE... WEIRD ELECTRONIC STUFF. I KEPT GLANCING OVER, STEALING LOOKS AT HER.
SHE WAS WOLFING DOWN HER SANDWICH IN BIG BITES, LIKE SHE WAS STARVING... -AND EVEN THAT WAS SEXY.
MMM... SO GOOD.
I HAVEN'T EATEN ALL DAY... I GUESS MAYBE 'CAUSE I'M TRIPPING.
I KNEW IT. I KNEW SOMETHING WAS GOING ON! I'D SEEN THOSE WILD EYES, HER HUGE BLACK PUPILS...
YOU KNOW WHAT THIS IS? THIS IS COMFORT FOOD...
IT'S THE KIND OF FOOD YOU EAT WHEN YOU'RE A KID... IT SORT OF CENTERS YOU... PULLS YOU BACK DOWN TO EARTH... YOU KNOW WHAT I MEAN?
I, UH... YEAH, I GUESS SO.
HOW ABOUT YOU? YOU SEEM KIND OF OFF CENTER. YOU ARE, AREN'T YOU?

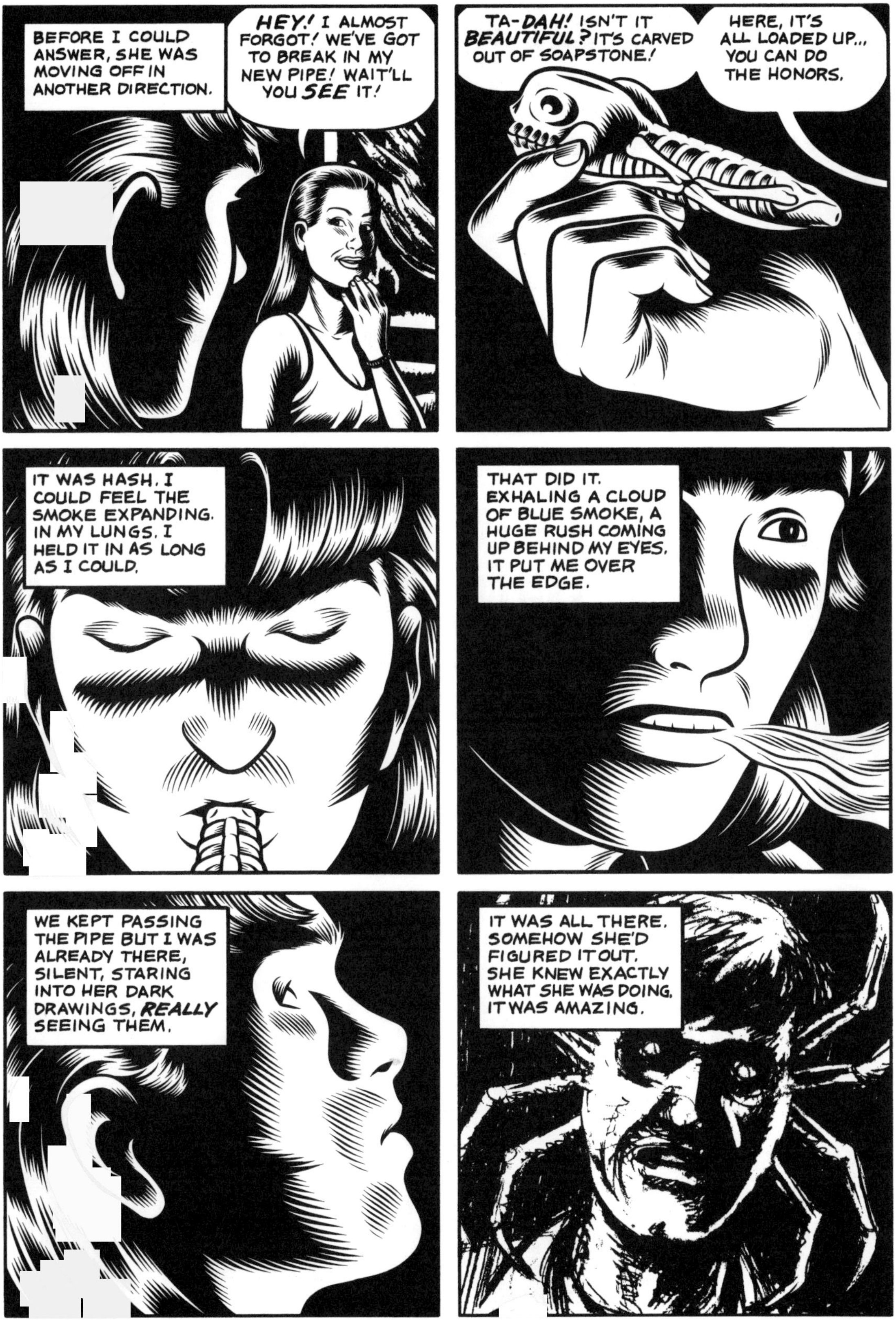
BEFORE I COULD ANSWER, SHE WAS MOVING OFF IN ANOTHER DIRECTION.
HEY! I ALMOST FORGOT! WE'VE GOT TO BREAK IN MY NEW PIPE! WAIT'LL YOU SEE IT!
TA-DAH! ISN'T IT BEAUTIFUL? IT'S CARVED OUT OF SOAPSTONE!
HERE, IT'S ALL LOADED UP... YOU CAN DO THE HONORS.
IT WAS HASH. I COULD FEEL THE SMOKE EXPANDING IN MY LUNGS. I HELD IT IN AS LONG AS I COULD.
THAT DID IT. EXHALING A CLOUD OF BLUE SMOKE, A HUGE RUSH COMING UP BEHIND MY EYES, IT PUT ME OVER THE EDGE.
WE KEPT PASSING THE PIPE BUT I WAS ALREADY THERE, SILENT, STARING INTO HER DARK DRAWINGS, REALLY SEEING THEM.
IT WAS ALL THERE. SOMEHOW SHE'D FIGURED IT OUT. SHE KNEW EXACTLY WHAT SHE WAS DOING. IT WAS AMAZING.

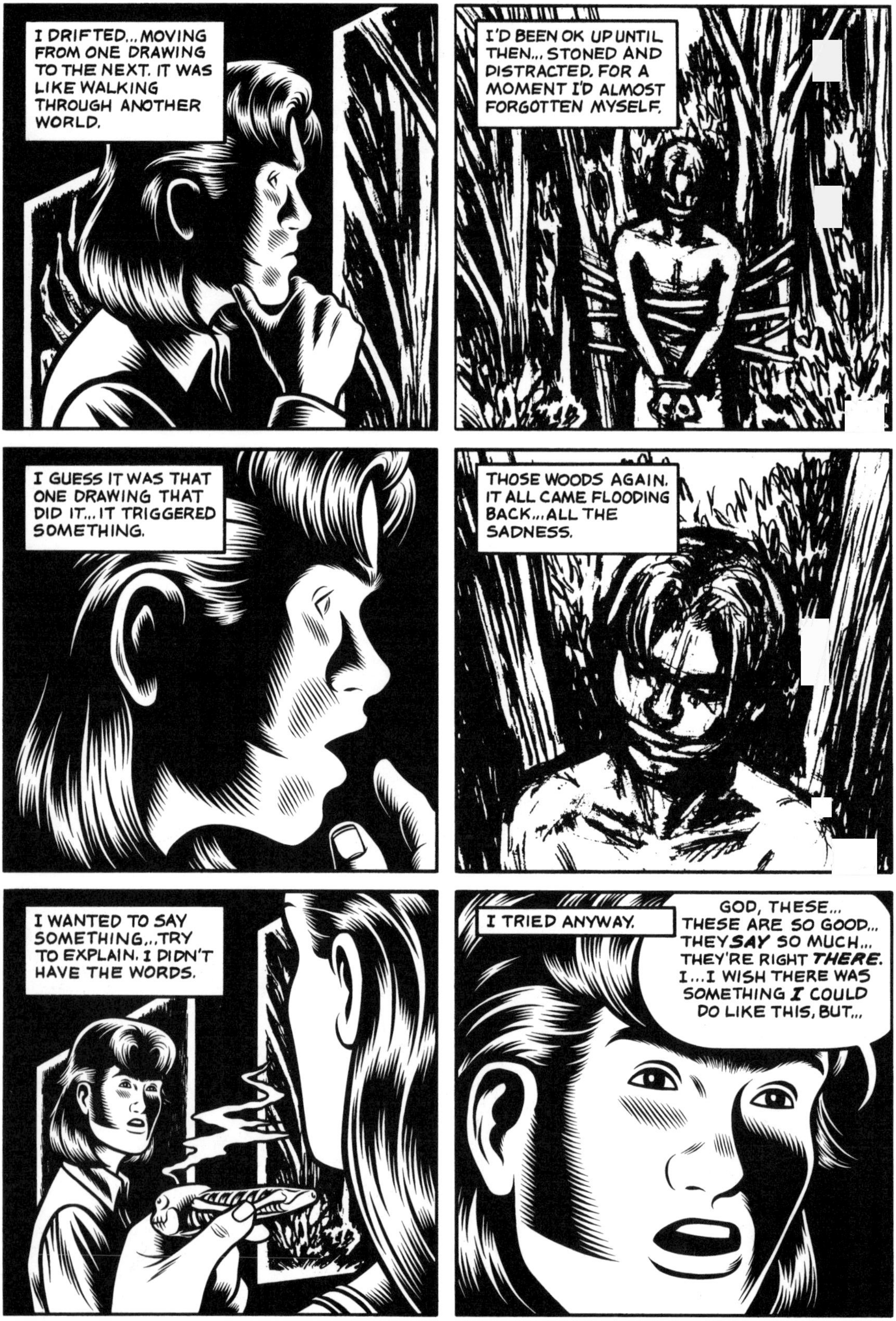

I DRIFTED... MOVING FROM ONE DRAWING TO THE NEXT. IT WAS LIKE WALKING THROUGH ANOTHER WORLD.
I'D BEEN OK UP UNTIL THEN... STONED AND DISTRACTED. FOR A MOMENT I'D ALMOST FORGOTTEN MYSELF.
I GUESS IT WAS THAT ONE DRAWING THAT DID IT... IT TRIGGERED SOMETHING.
THOSE WOODS AGAIN. IT ALL CAME FLOODING BACK... ALL THE SADNESS.
I WANTED TO SAY SOMETHING... TRY TO EXPLAIN. I DIDN'T HAVE THE WORDS.
I TRIED ANYWAY.
GOD, THESE... THESE ARE SO GOOD... THEY *SAY* SO MUCH... THEY'RE RIGHT *THERE*. I... I WISH THERE WAS SOMETHING *I* COULD DO LIKE THIS, BUT...

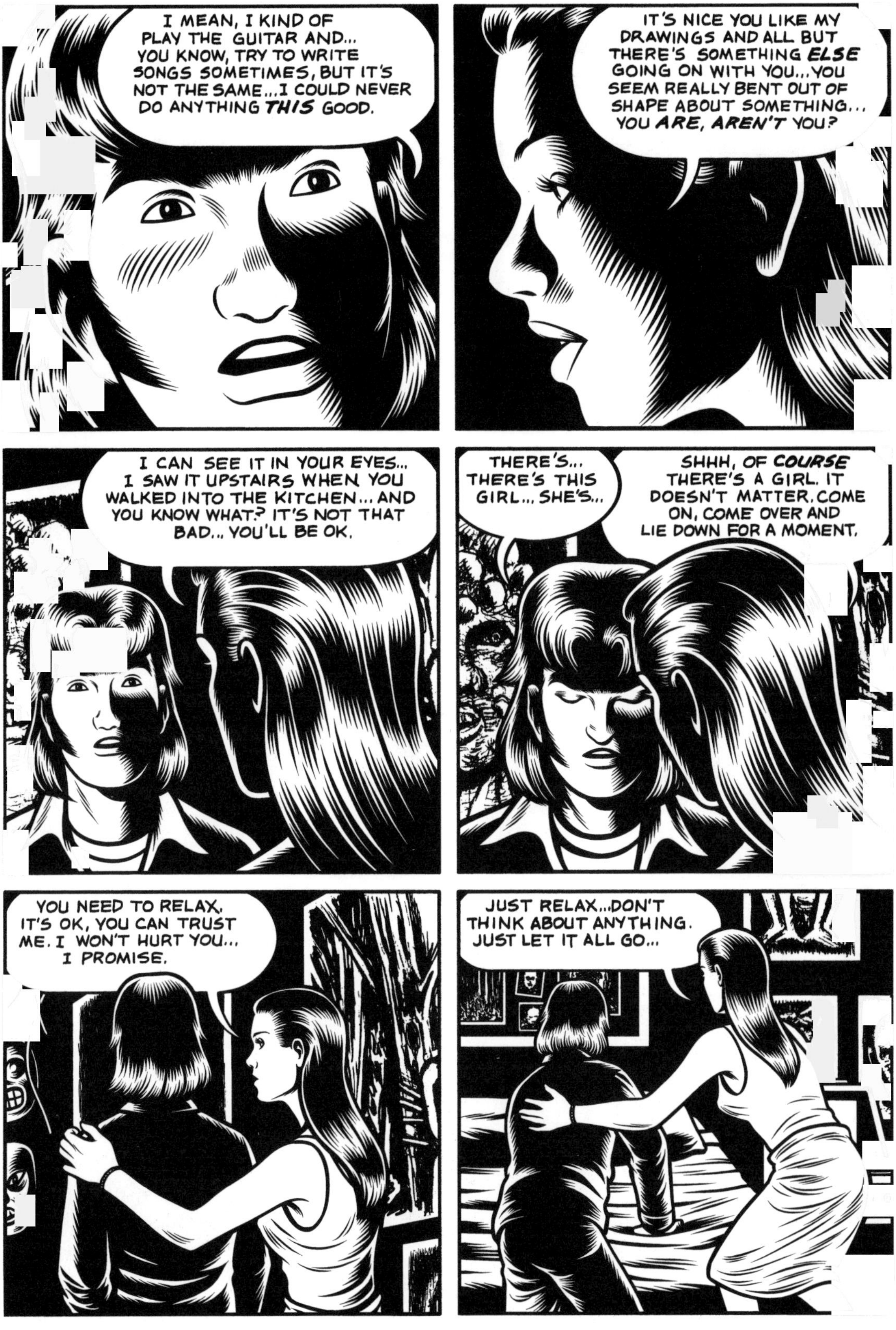
I MEAN, I KIND OF PLAY THE GUITAR AND... YOU KNOW, TRY TO WRITE SONGS SOMETIMES, BUT IT'S NOT THE SAME... I COULD NEVER DO ANYTHING THIS GOOD.
IT'S NICE YOU LIKE MY DRAWINGS AND ALL BUT THERE'S SOMETHING ELSE GOING ON WITH YOU... YOU SEEM REALLY BENT OUT OF SHAPE ABOUT SOMETHING... YOU ARE, AREN'T YOU?
I CAN SEE IT IN YOUR EYES... I SAW IT UPSTAIRS WHEN YOU WALKED INTO THE KITCHEN... AND YOU KNOW WHAT? IT'S NOT THAT BAD... YOU'LL BE OK.
THERE'S... THERE'S THIS GIRL... SHE'S...
SHHH, OF COURSE THERE'S A GIRL. IT DOESN'T MATTER. COME ON, COME OVER AND LIE DOWN FOR A MOMENT.
YOU NEED TO RELAX. IT'S OK, YOU CAN TRUST ME. I WON'T HURT YOU... I PROMISE.
JUST RELAX...DON'T THINK ABOUT ANYTHING. JUST LET IT ALL GO...

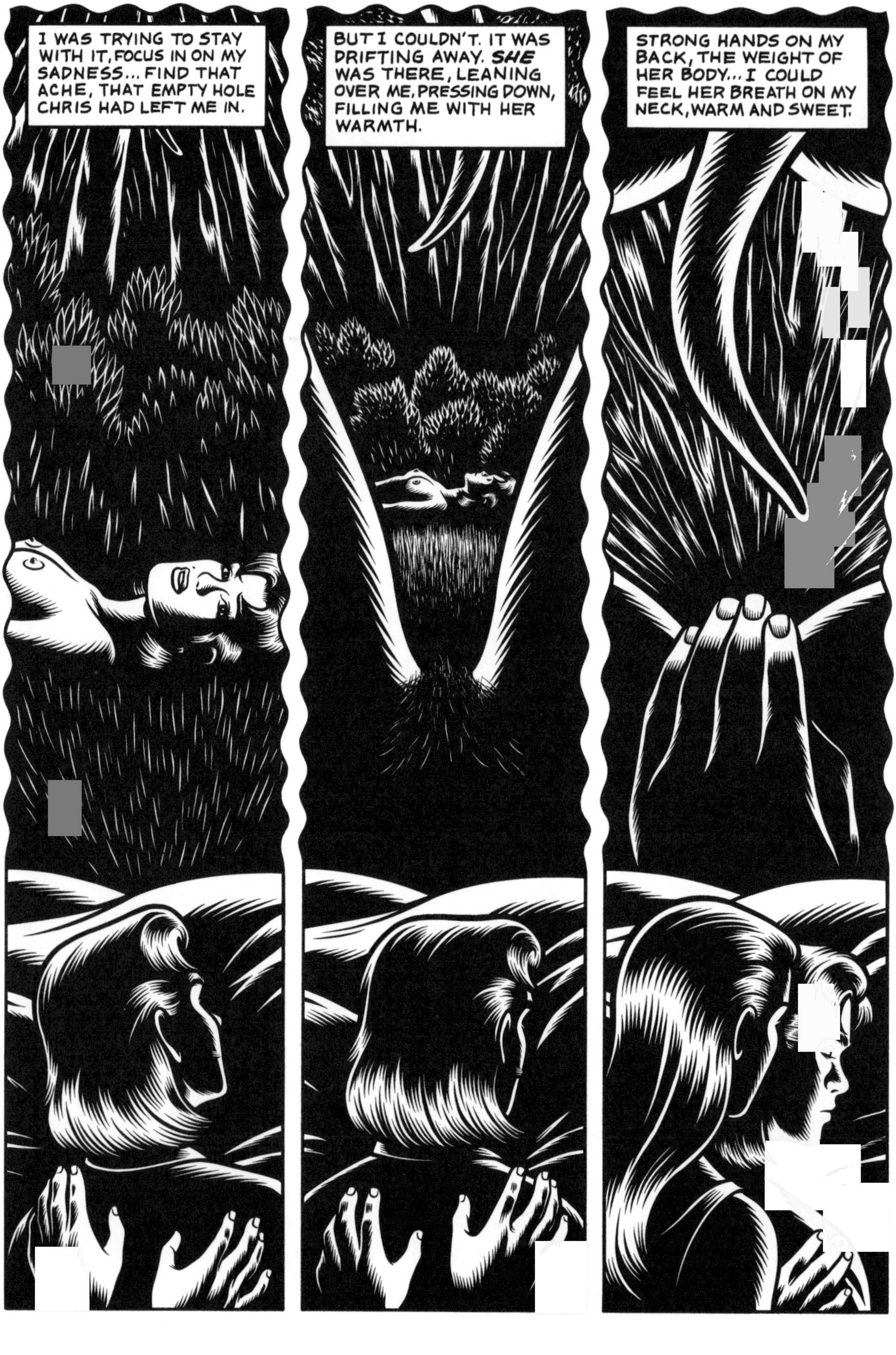
I WAS TRYING TO STAY WITH IT, FOCUS IN ON MY SADNESS... FIND THAT ACHE, THAT EMPTY HOLE CHRIS HAD LEFT ME IN.
BUT I COULDN'T. IT WAS DRIFTING AWAY. *SHE* WAS THERE, LEANING OVER ME, PRESSING DOWN, FILLING ME WITH HER WARMTH.
STRONG HANDS ON MY BACK, THE WEIGHT OF HER BODY... I COULD FEEL HER BREATH ON MY NECK, WARM AND SWEET.

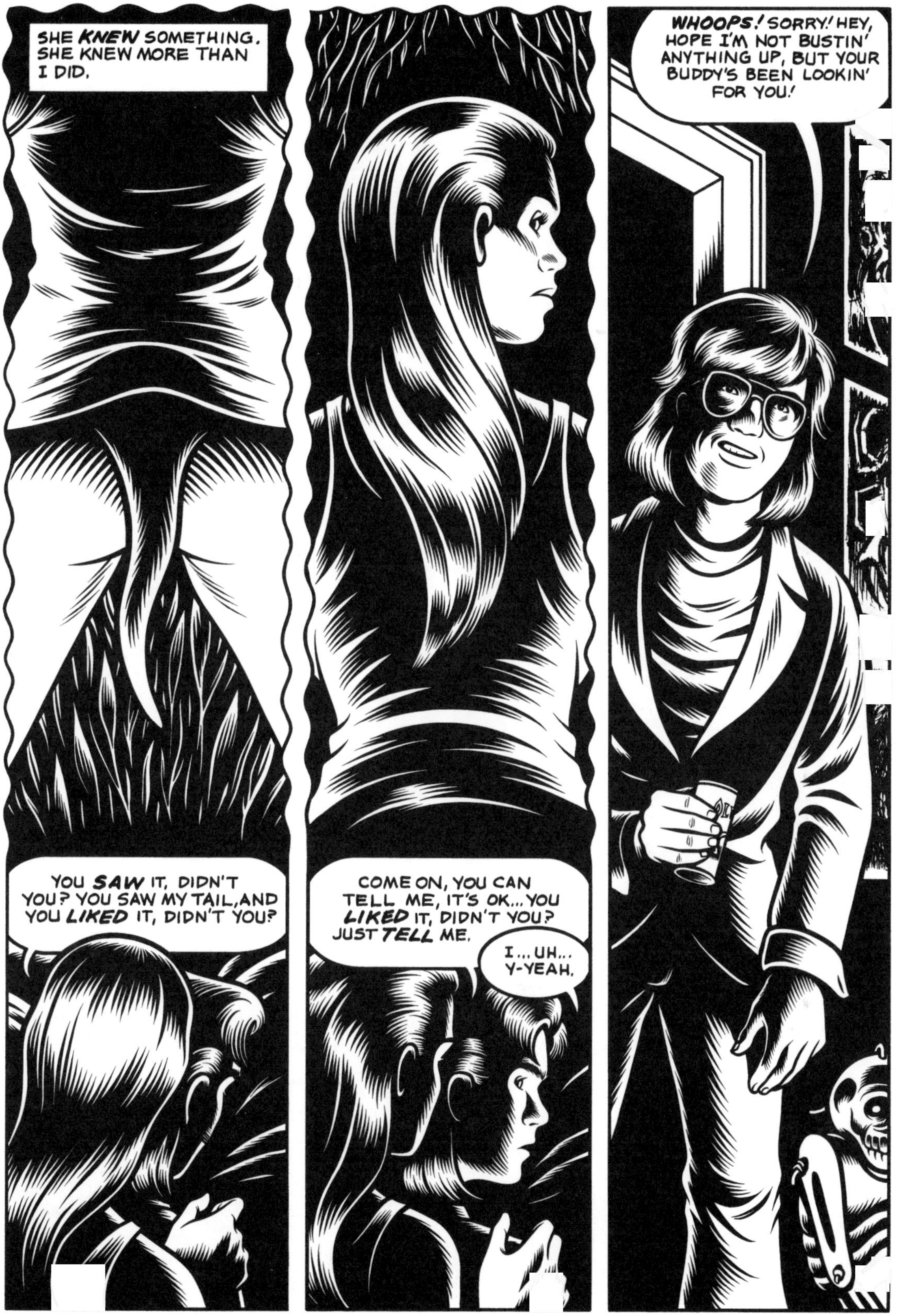
SHE KNEW SOMETHING. SHE KNEW MORE THAN I DID.
YOU SAW IT, DIDN'T YOU? YOU SAW MY TAIL, AND YOU LIKED IT, DIDN'T YOU?
COME ON, YOU CAN TELL ME, IT'S OK... YOU LIKED IT, DIDN'T YOU? JUST TELL ME.
I... UH... Y-YEAH.
WHOOPS! SORRY! HEY, HOPE I'M NOT BUSTIN' ANYTHING UP, BUT YOUR BUDDY'S BEEN LOOKIN' FOR YOU!

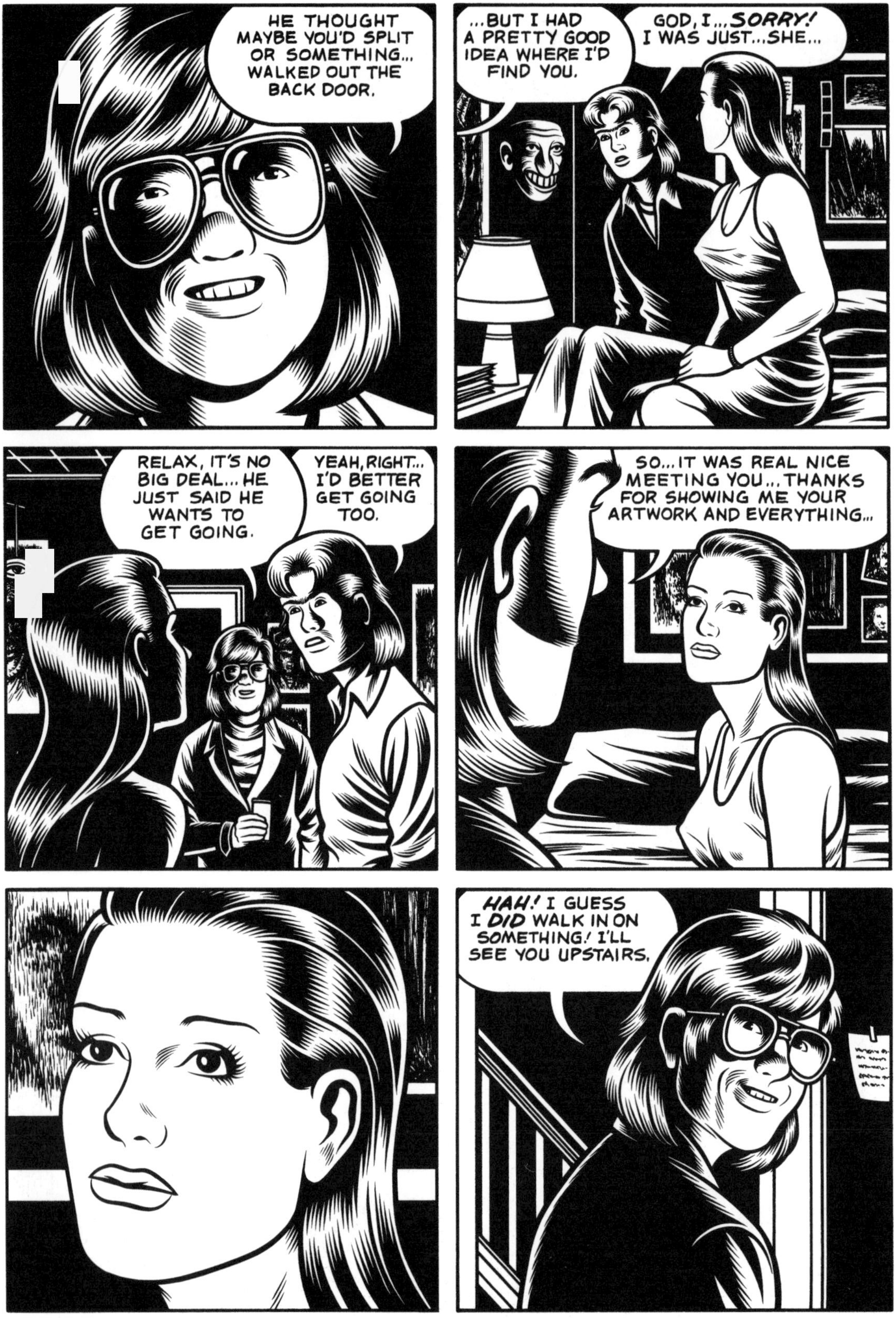
HE THOUGHT MAYBE YOU'D SPLIT OR SOMETHING... WALKED OUT THE BACK DOOR.
...BUT I HAD A PRETTY GOOD IDEA WHERE I'D FIND YOU.
GOD, I... SORRY! I WAS JUST...SHE...
RELAX, IT'S NO BIG DEAL... HE JUST SAID HE WANTS TO GET GOING.
YEAH, RIGHT... I'D BETTER GET GOING TOO.
SO... IT WAS REAL NICE MEETING YOU... THANKS FOR SHOWING ME YOUR ARTWORK AND EVERYTHING...
HAH! I GUESS I DID WALK IN ON SOMETHING! I'LL SEE YOU UPSTAIRS.

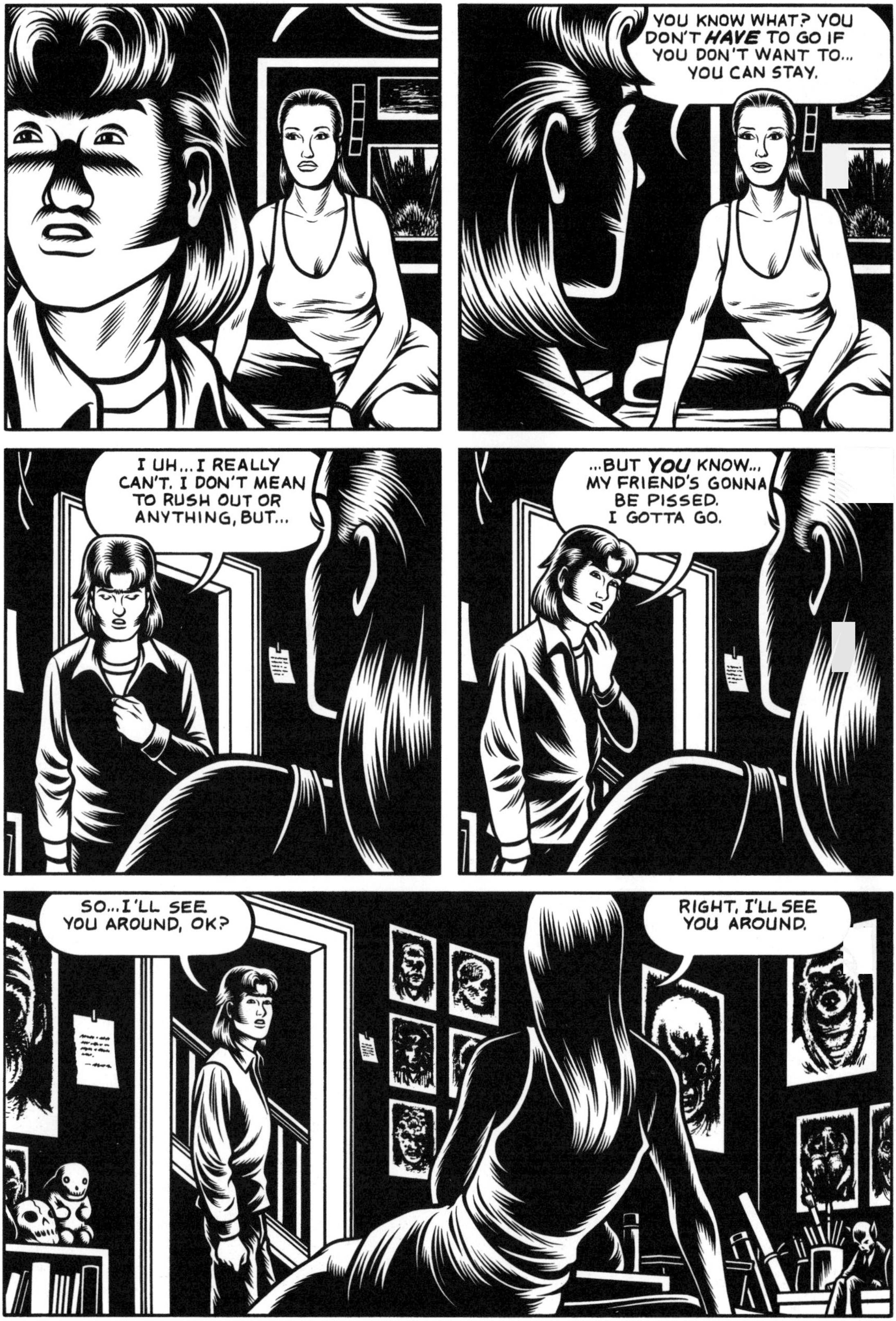

YOU KNOW WHAT? YOU DON'T *HAVE* TO GO IF YOU DON'T WANT TO... YOU CAN STAY.
I UH... I REALLY CAN'T. I DON'T MEAN TO RUSH OUT OR ANYTHING, BUT...
...BUT *YOU* KNOW... MY FRIEND'S GONNA BE PISSED. I GOTTA GO.
SO... I'LL SEE YOU AROUND, OK?
RIGHT, I'LL SEE YOU AROUND.

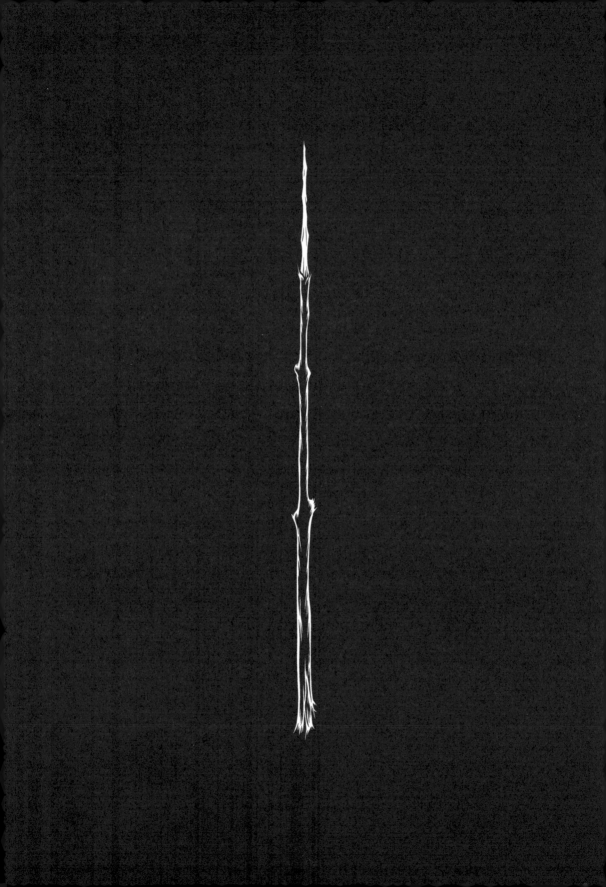

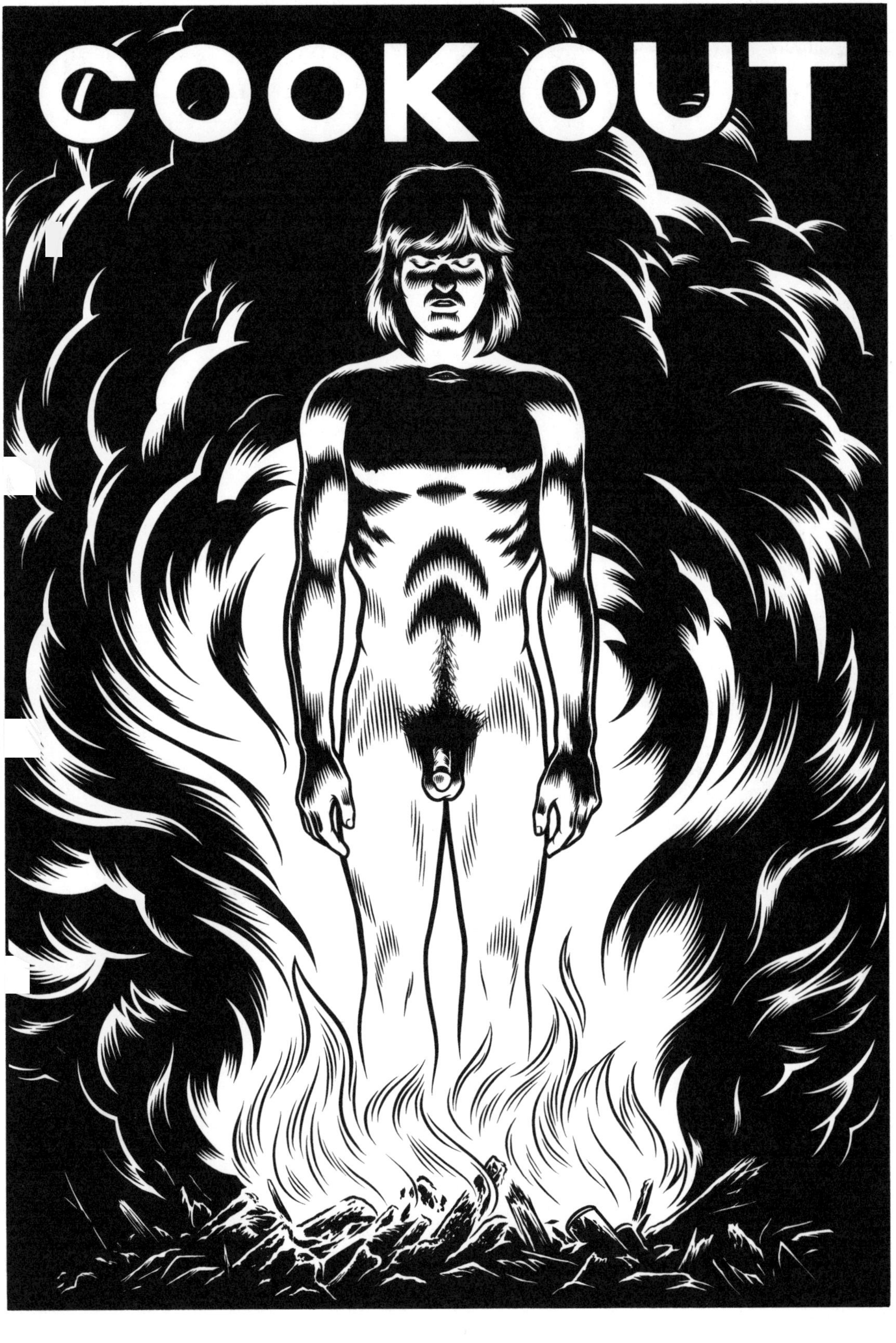
COOK OUT

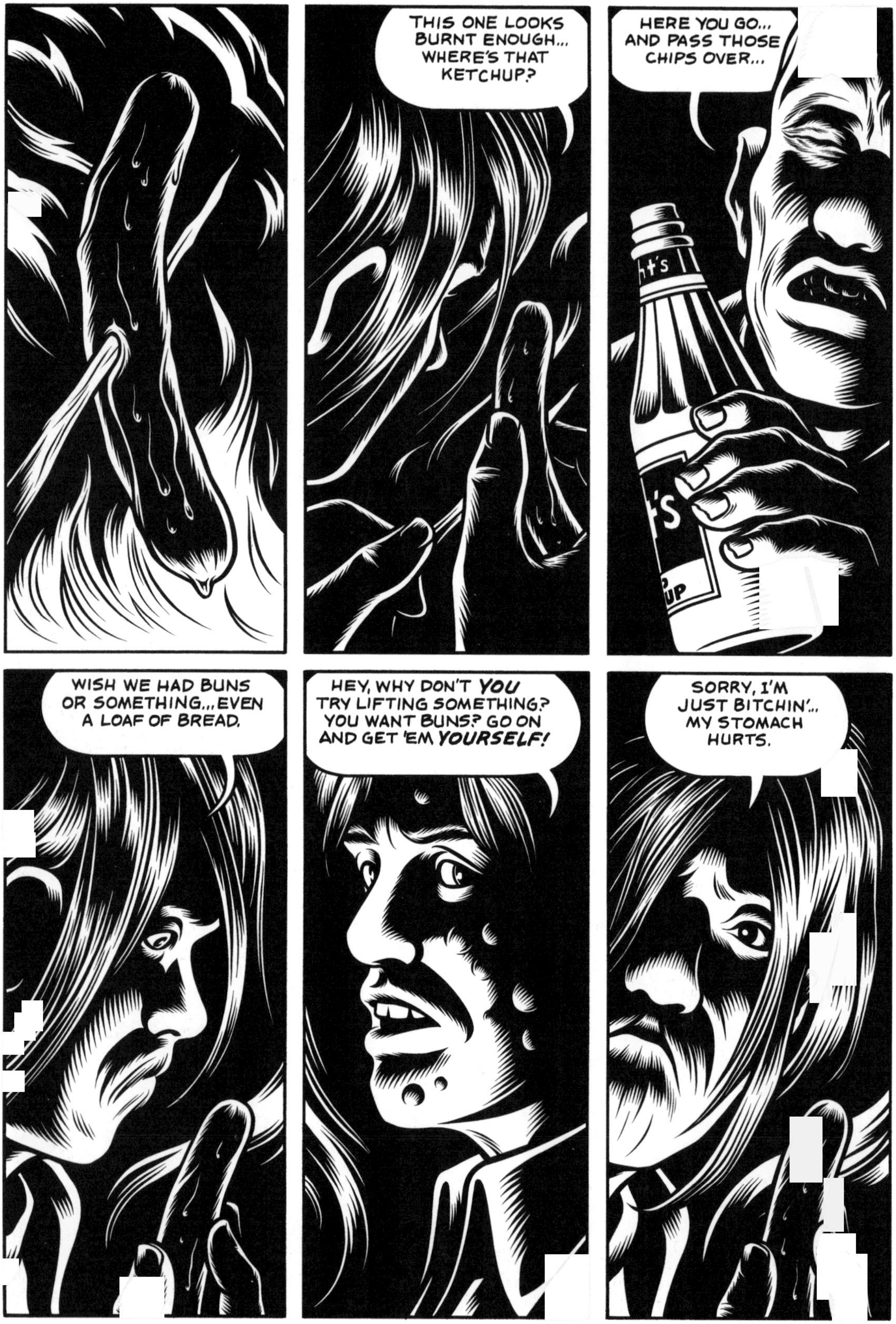
THIS ONE LOOKS BURNT ENOUGH... WHERE'S THAT KETCHUP?
HERE YOU GO... AND PASS THOSE CHIPS OVER...
WISH WE HAD BUNS OR SOMETHING... EVEN A LOAF OF BREAD.
HEY, WHY DON'T *YOU* TRY LIFTING SOMETHING? YOU WANT BUNS? GO ON AND GET 'EM *YOURSELF!*
SORRY, I'M JUST BITCHIN'... MY STOMACH HURTS.

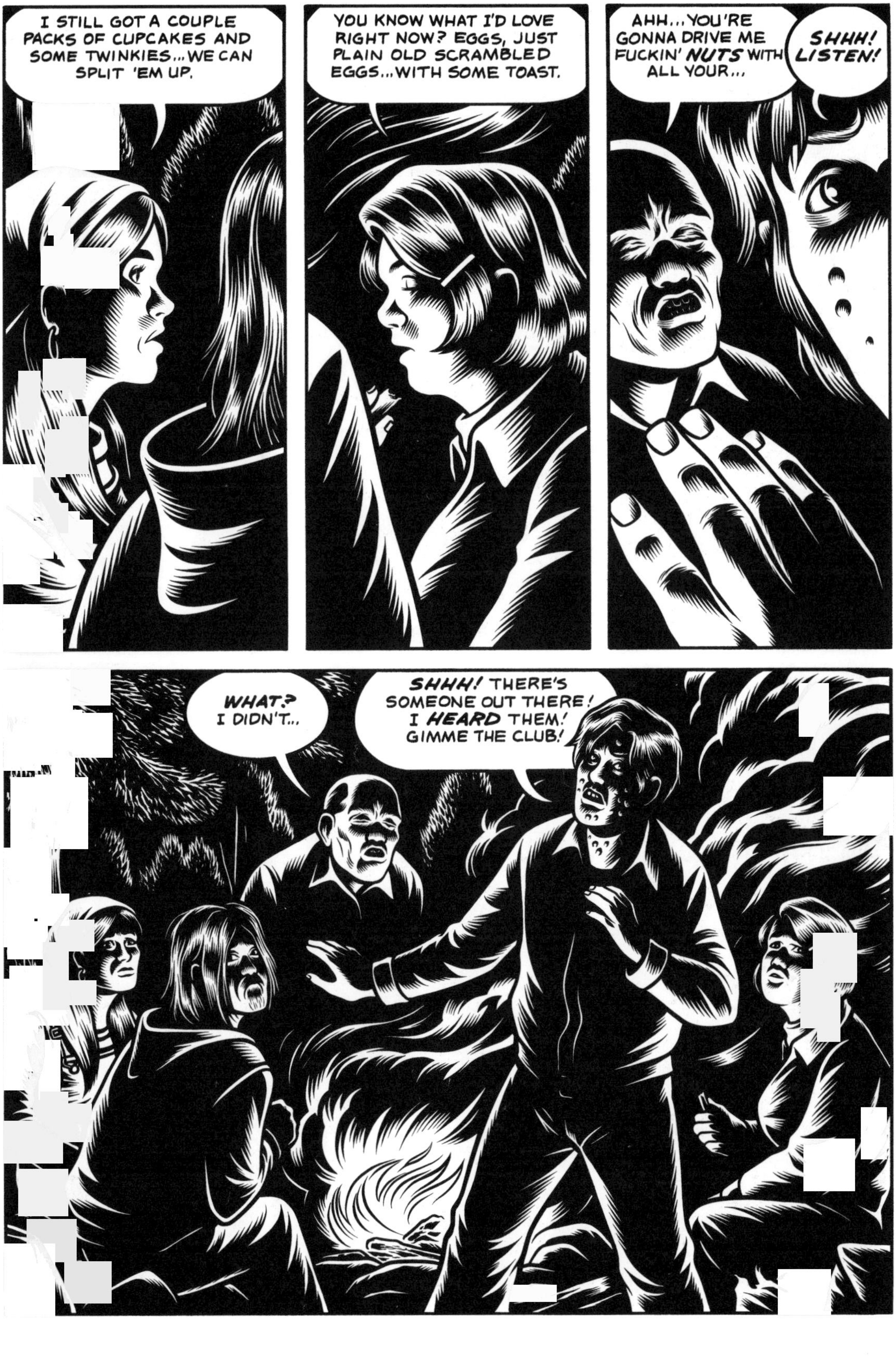
I STILL GOT A COUPLE PACKS OF CUPCAKES AND SOME TWINKIES... WE CAN SPLIT 'EM UP.
YOU KNOW WHAT I'D LOVE RIGHT NOW? EGGS, JUST PLAIN OLD SCRAMBLED EGGS... WITH SOME TOAST.
AHH... YOU'RE GONNA DRIVE ME FUCKIN' NUTS WITH ALL YOUR...
SHHH! LISTEN!
WHAT? I DIDN'T...
SHHH! THERE'S SOMEONE OUT THERE! I HEARD THEM! GIMME THE CLUB!

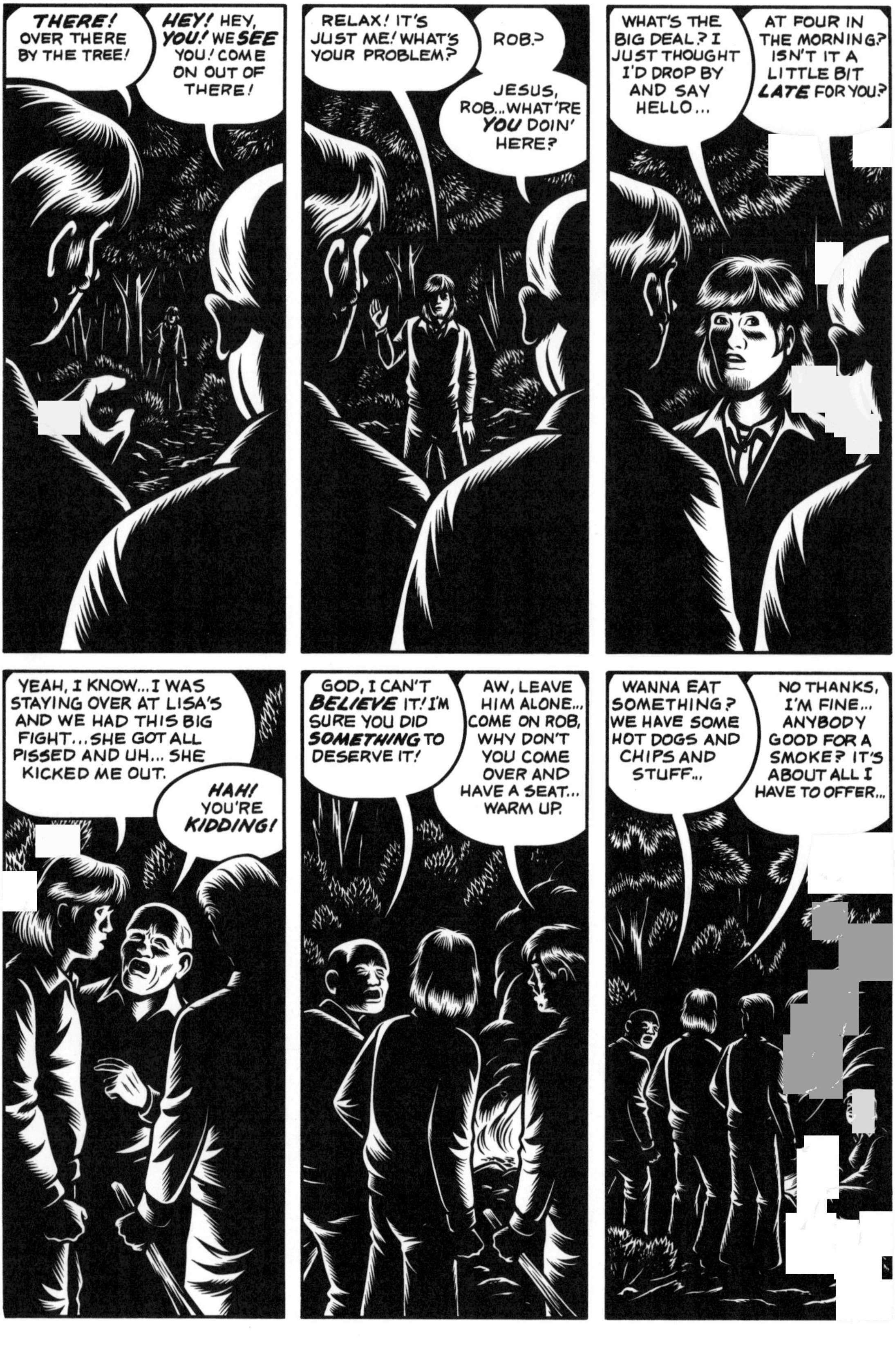
THERE! OVER THERE BY THE TREE!
HEY! HEY, YOU! WE SEE YOU! COME ON OUT OF THERE!
RELAX! IT'S JUST ME! WHAT'S YOUR PROBLEM?
ROB?
JESUS, ROB... WHAT'RE YOU DOIN' HERE?
WHAT'S THE BIG DEAL? I JUST THOUGHT I'D DROP BY AND SAY HELLO...
AT FOUR IN THE MORNING? ISN'T IT A LITTLE BIT LATE FOR YOU?
YEAH, I KNOW... I WAS STAYING OVER AT LISA'S AND WE HAD THIS BIG FIGHT... SHE GOT ALL PISSED AND UH... SHE KICKED ME OUT.
HAH! YOU'RE KIDDING!
GOD, I CAN'T BELIEVE IT! I'M SURE YOU DID SOMETHING TO DESERVE IT!
AW, LEAVE HIM ALONE... COME ON ROB, WHY DON'T YOU COME OVER AND HAVE A SEAT... WARM UP.
WANNA EAT SOMETHING? WE HAVE SOME HOT DOGS AND CHIPS AND STUFF...
NO THANKS, I'M FINE... ANYBODY GOOD FOR A SMOKE? IT'S ABOUT ALL I HAVE TO OFFER...

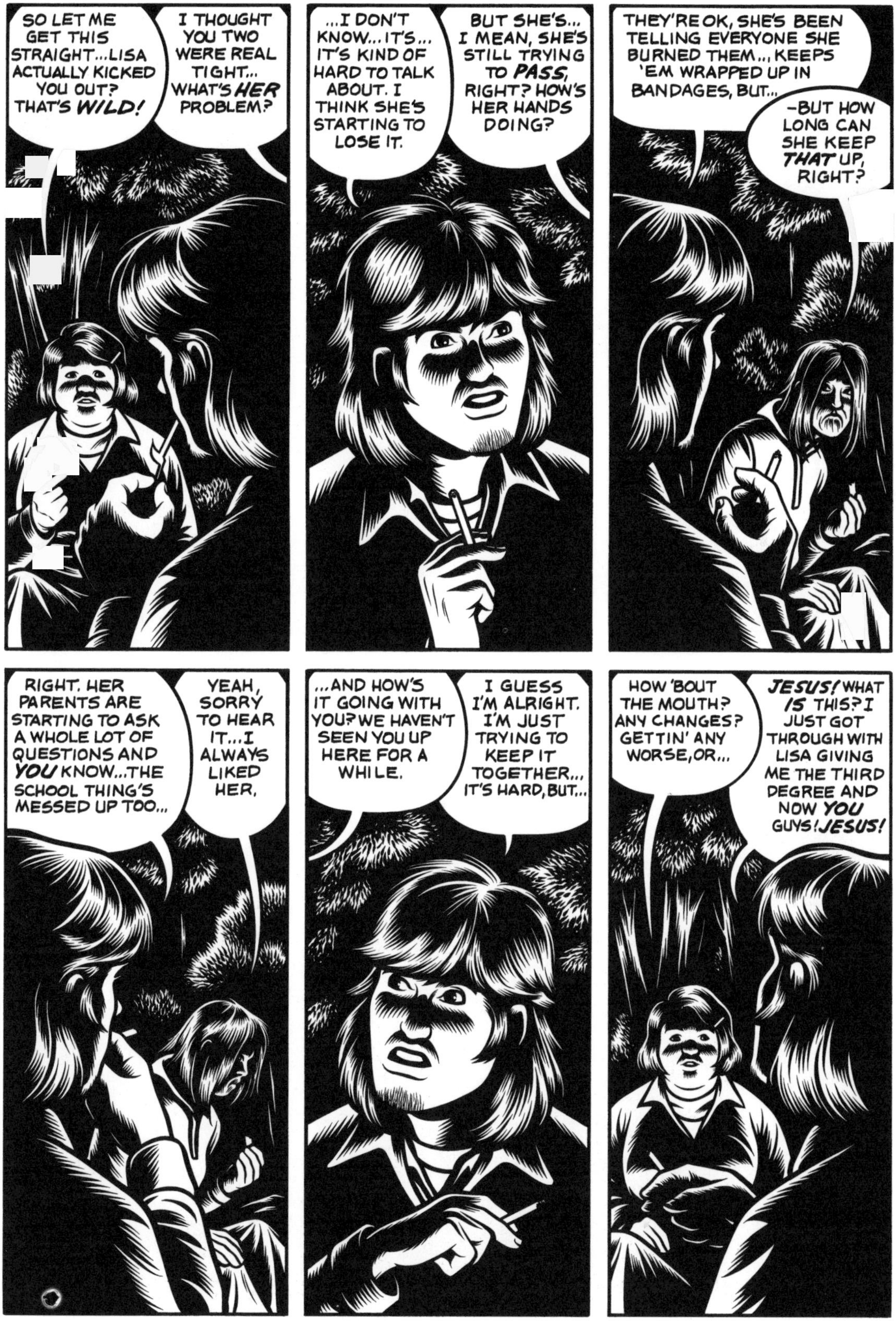
SO LET ME GET THIS STRAIGHT...LISA ACTUALLY KICKED YOU OUT? THAT'S **WILD!**
I THOUGHT YOU TWO WERE REAL TIGHT... WHAT'S **HER** PROBLEM?
...I DON'T KNOW... IT'S... IT'S KIND OF HARD TO TALK ABOUT. I THINK SHE'S STARTING TO LOSE IT.
BUT SHE'S... I MEAN, SHE'S STILL TRYING TO **PASS**, RIGHT? HOW'S HER HANDS DOING?
THEY'RE OK, SHE'S BEEN TELLING EVERYONE SHE BURNED THEM..., KEEPS 'EM WRAPPED UP IN BANDAGES, BUT...
–BUT HOW LONG CAN SHE KEEP **THAT** UP, RIGHT?
RIGHT. HER PARENTS ARE STARTING TO ASK A WHOLE LOT OF QUESTIONS AND **YOU** KNOW...THE SCHOOL THING'S MESSED UP TOO...
YEAH, SORRY TO HEAR IT...I ALWAYS LIKED HER.
...AND HOW'S IT GOING WITH YOU? WE HAVEN'T SEEN YOU UP HERE FOR A WHILE.
I GUESS I'M ALRIGHT. I'M JUST TRYING TO KEEP IT TOGETHER... IT'S HARD, BUT...
HOW 'BOUT THE MOUTH? ANY CHANGES? GETTIN' ANY WORSE, OR...
JESUS! WHAT **IS** THIS? I JUST GOT THROUGH WITH LISA GIVING ME THE THIRD DEGREE AND NOW **YOU** GUYS! **JESUS!**

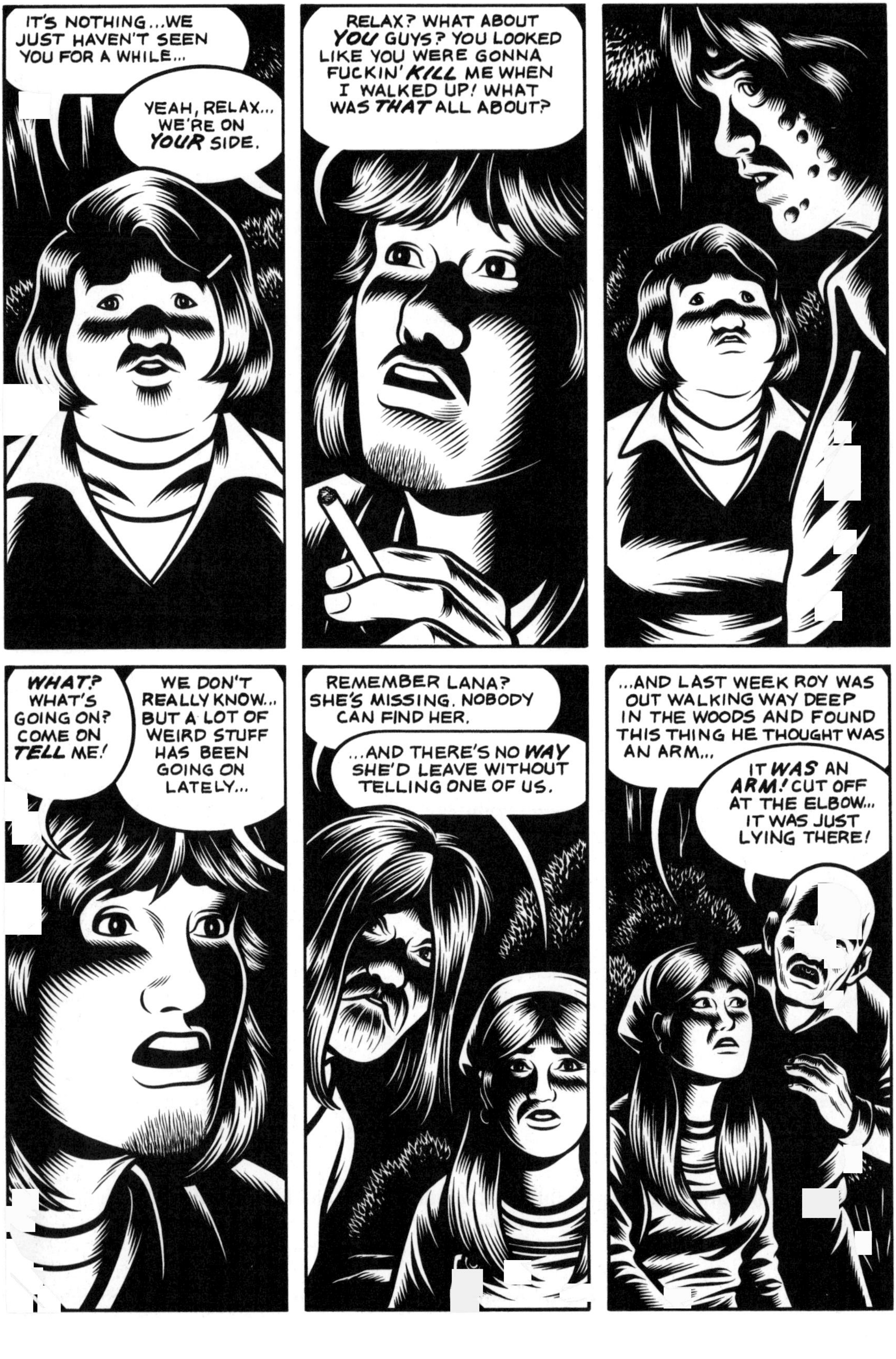
IT'S NOTHING...WE JUST HAVEN'T SEEN YOU FOR A WHILE...
YEAH, RELAX... WE'RE ON YOUR SIDE.
RELAX? WHAT ABOUT YOU GUYS? YOU LOOKED LIKE YOU WERE GONNA FUCKIN' KILL ME WHEN I WALKED UP! WHAT WAS THAT ALL ABOUT?
WHAT? WHAT'S GOING ON? COME ON TELL ME!
WE DON'T REALLY KNOW... BUT A LOT OF WEIRD STUFF HAS BEEN GOING ON LATELY...
REMEMBER LANA? SHE'S MISSING. NOBODY CAN FIND HER.
...AND THERE'S NO WAY SHE'D LEAVE WITHOUT TELLING ONE OF US.
...AND LAST WEEK ROY WAS OUT WALKING WAY DEEP IN THE WOODS AND FOUND THIS THING HE THOUGHT WAS AN ARM...
IT WAS AN ARM! CUT OFF AT THE ELBOW... IT WAS JUST LYING THERE!

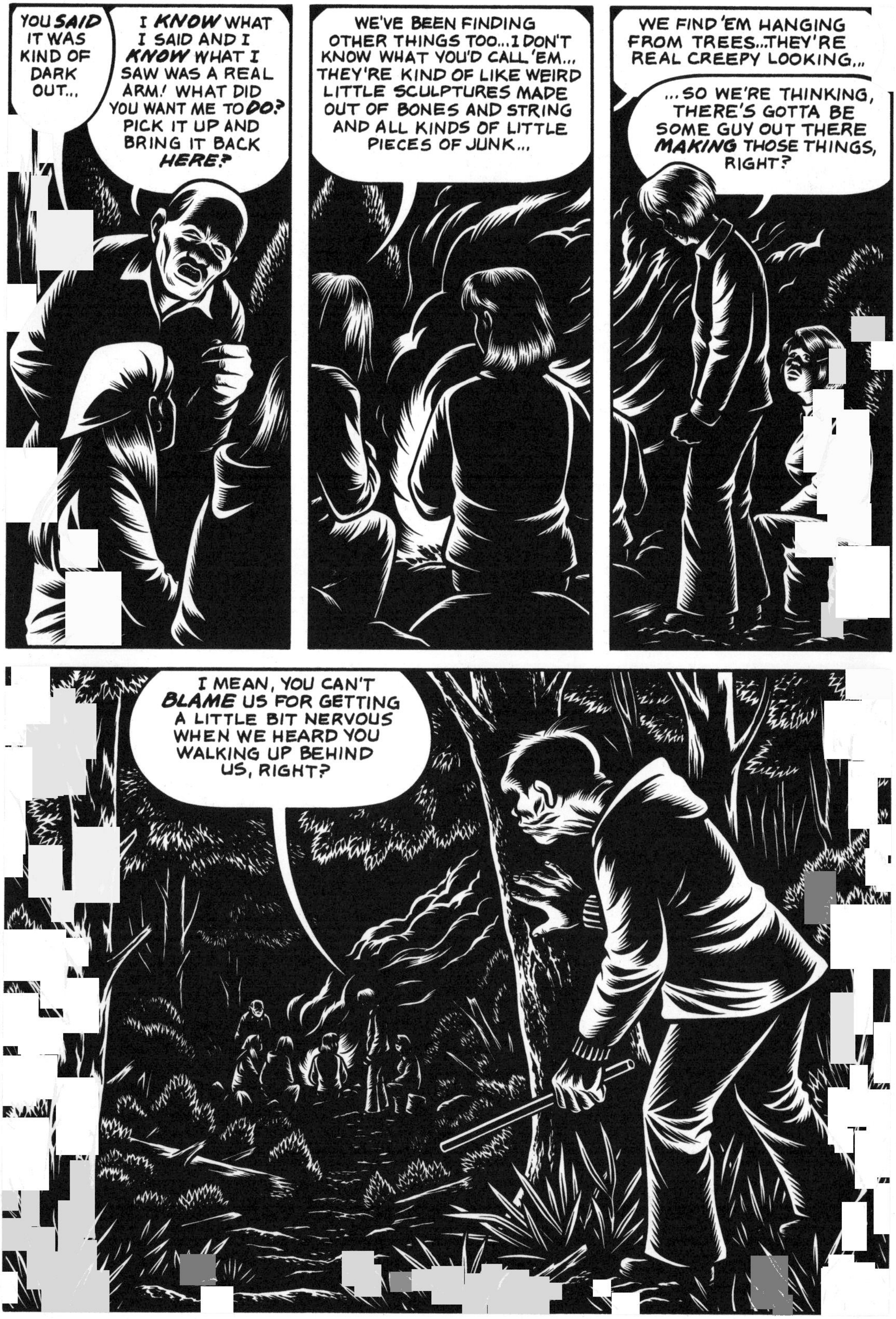
YOU SAID IT WAS KIND OF DARK OUT...
I KNOW WHAT I SAID AND I KNOW WHAT I SAW WAS A REAL ARM! WHAT DID YOU WANT ME TO DO? PICK IT UP AND BRING IT BACK HERE?
WE'VE BEEN FINDING OTHER THINGS TOO... I DON'T KNOW WHAT YOU'D CALL 'EM... THEY'RE KIND OF LIKE WEIRD LITTLE SCULPTURES MADE OUT OF BONES AND STRING AND ALL KINDS OF LITTLE PIECES OF JUNK...
WE FIND 'EM HANGING FROM TREES... THEY'RE REAL CREEPY LOOKING...
...SO WE'RE THINKING, THERE'S GOTTA BE SOME GUY OUT THERE MAKING THOSE THINGS, RIGHT?
I MEAN, YOU CAN'T BLAME US FOR GETTING A LITTLE BIT NERVOUS WHEN WE HEARD YOU WALKING UP BEHIND US, RIGHT?

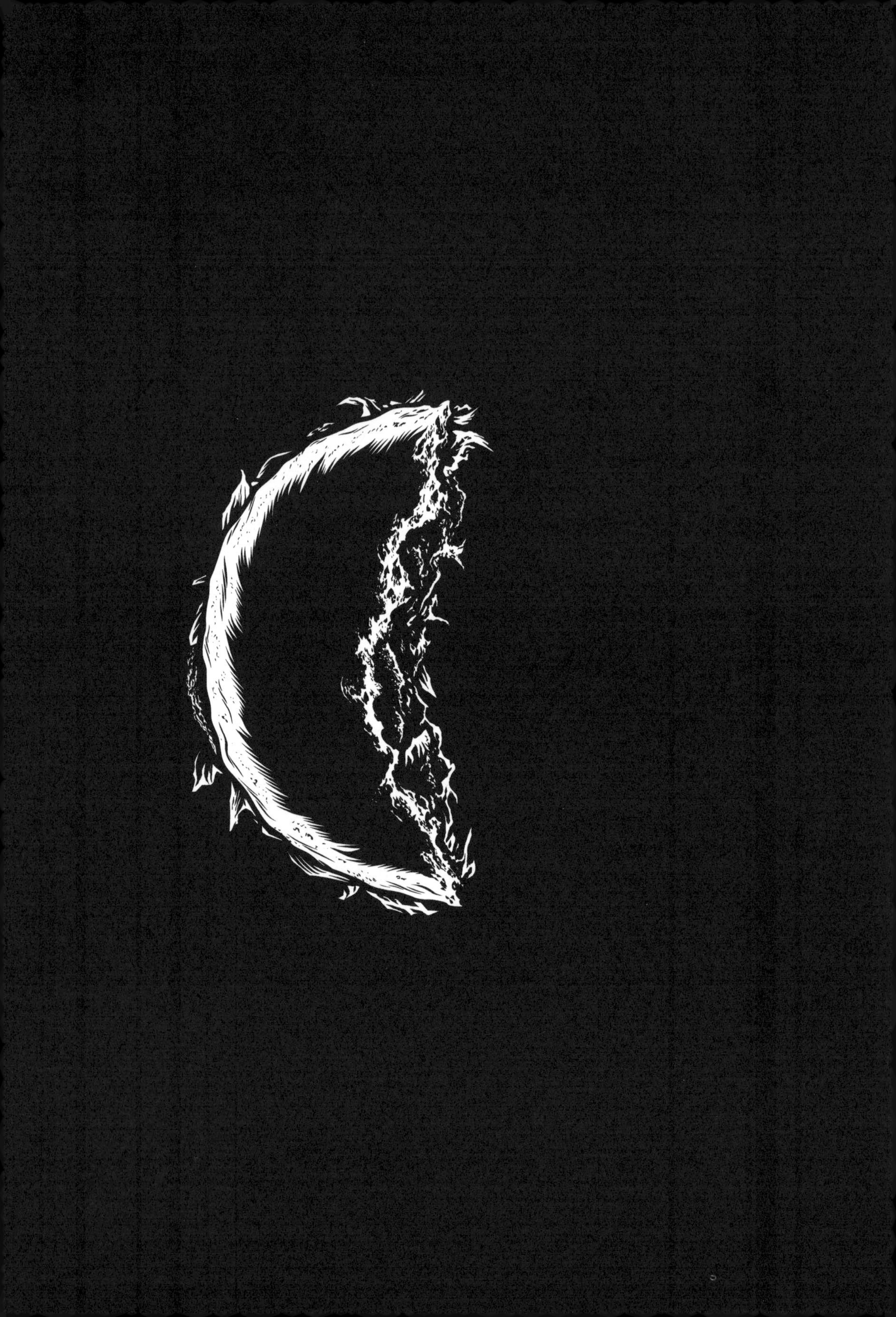

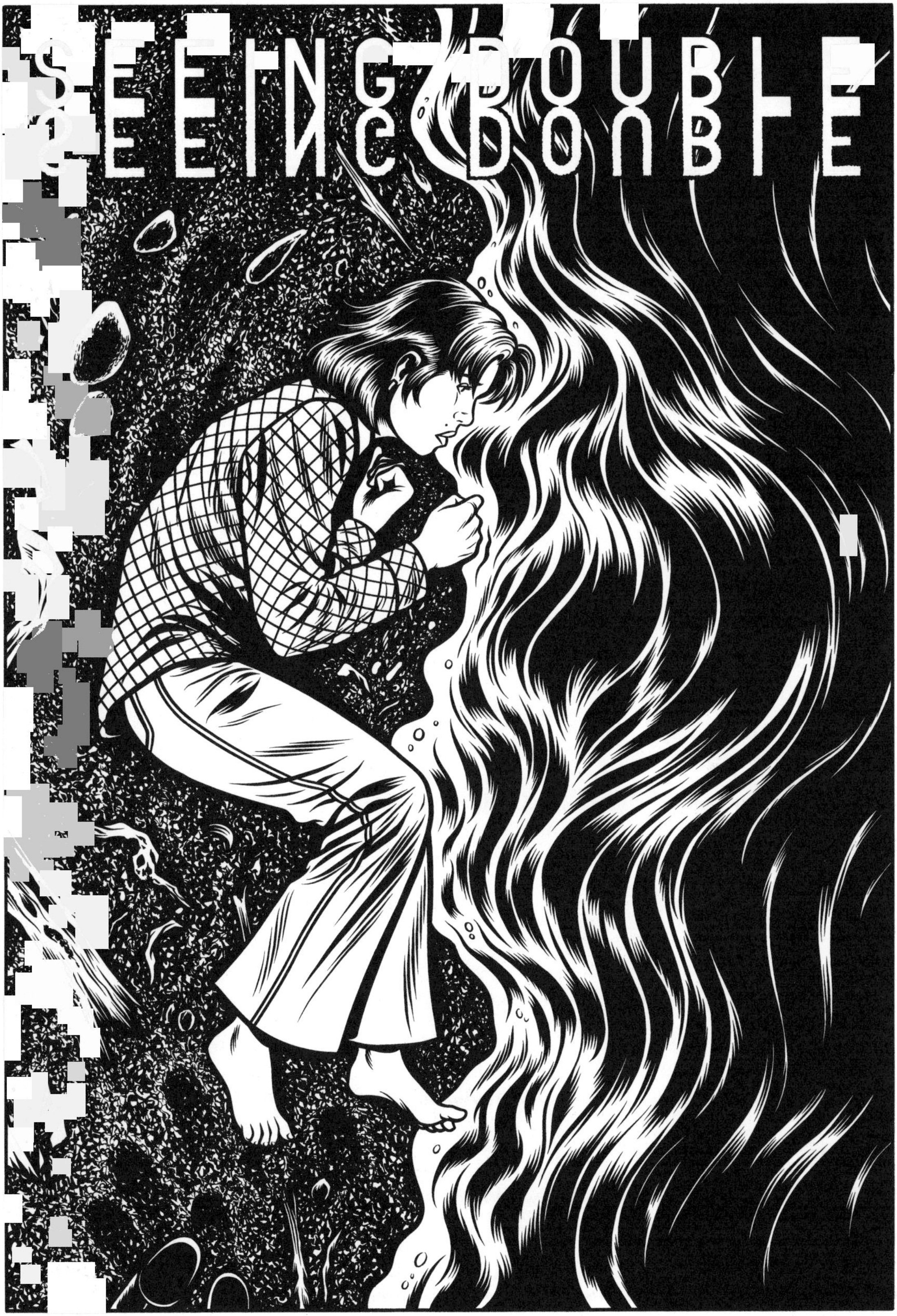
SEEING DOUBLE

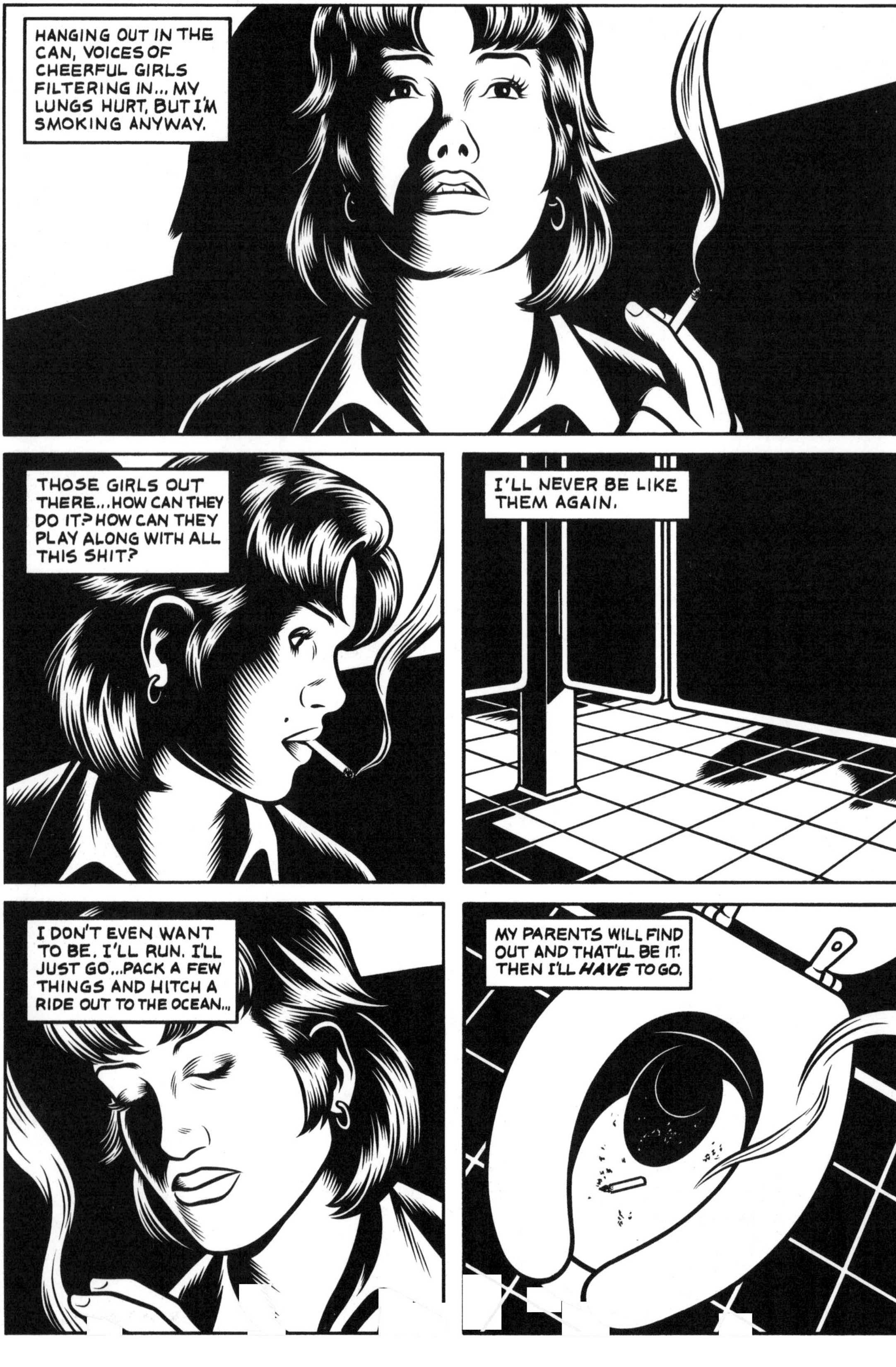
HANGING OUT IN THE CAN, VOICES OF CHEERFUL GIRLS FILTERING IN... MY LUNGS HURT, BUT I'M SMOKING ANYWAY.
THOSE GIRLS OUT THERE... HOW CAN THEY DO IT? HOW CAN THEY PLAY ALONG WITH ALL THIS SHIT?
I'LL NEVER BE LIKE THEM AGAIN.
I DON'T EVEN WANT TO BE. I'LL RUN. I'LL JUST GO... PACK A FEW THINGS AND HITCH A RIDE OUT TO THE OCEAN...
MY PARENTS WILL FIND OUT AND THAT'LL BE IT. THEN I'LL ***HAVE*** TO GO.

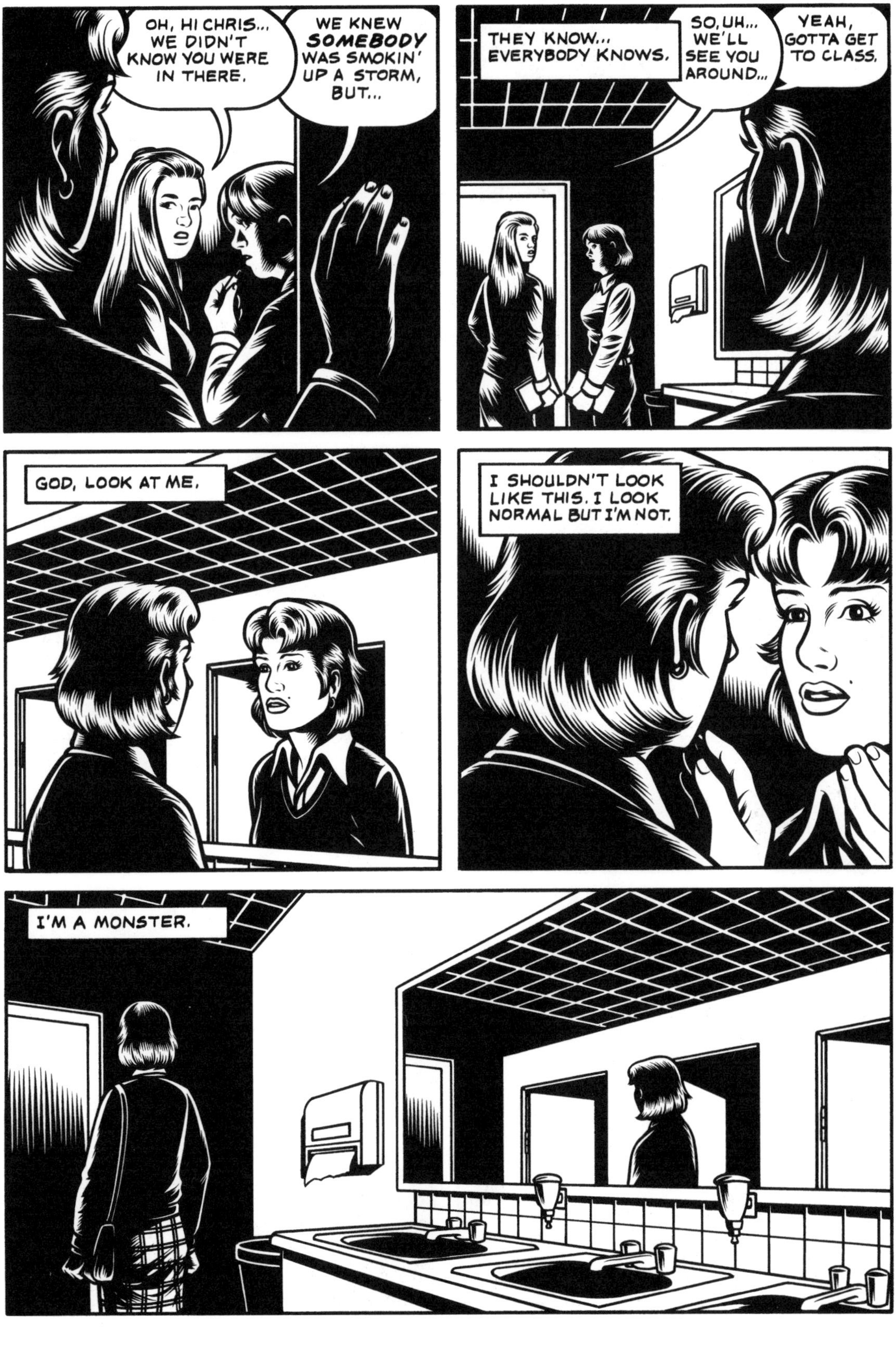
OH, HI CHRIS... WE DIDN'T KNOW YOU WERE IN THERE.
WE KNEW SOMEBODY WAS SMOKIN' UP A STORM, BUT...
THEY KNOW... EVERYBODY KNOWS.
SO, UH... WE'LL SEE YOU AROUND...
YEAH, GOTTA GET TO CLASS.
GOD, LOOK AT ME.
I SHOULDN'T LOOK LIKE THIS. I LOOK NORMAL BUT I'M NOT.
I'M A MONSTER.

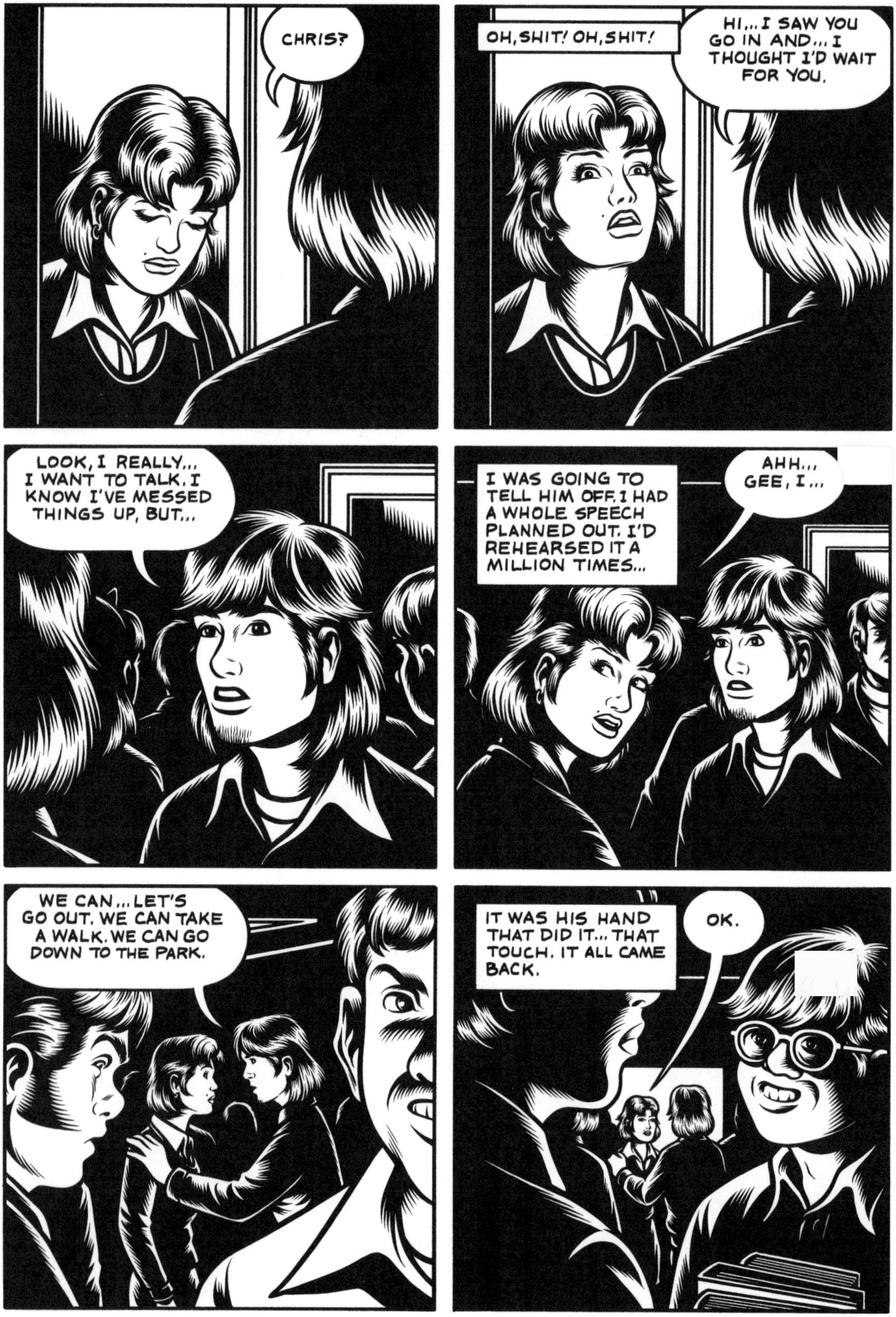
CHRIS?
OH, SHIT! OH, SHIT!
HI... I SAW YOU GO IN AND... I THOUGHT I'D WAIT FOR YOU.
LOOK, I REALLY... I WANT TO TALK. I KNOW I'VE MESSED THINGS UP, BUT...
I WAS GOING TO TELL HIM OFF. I HAD A WHOLE SPEECH PLANNED OUT. I'D REHEARSED IT A MILLION TIMES...
AHH... GEE, I...
WE CAN... LET'S GO OUT. WE CAN TAKE A WALK. WE CAN GO DOWN TO THE PARK.
IT WAS HIS HAND THAT DID IT... THAT TOUCH. IT ALL CAME BACK.
OK.

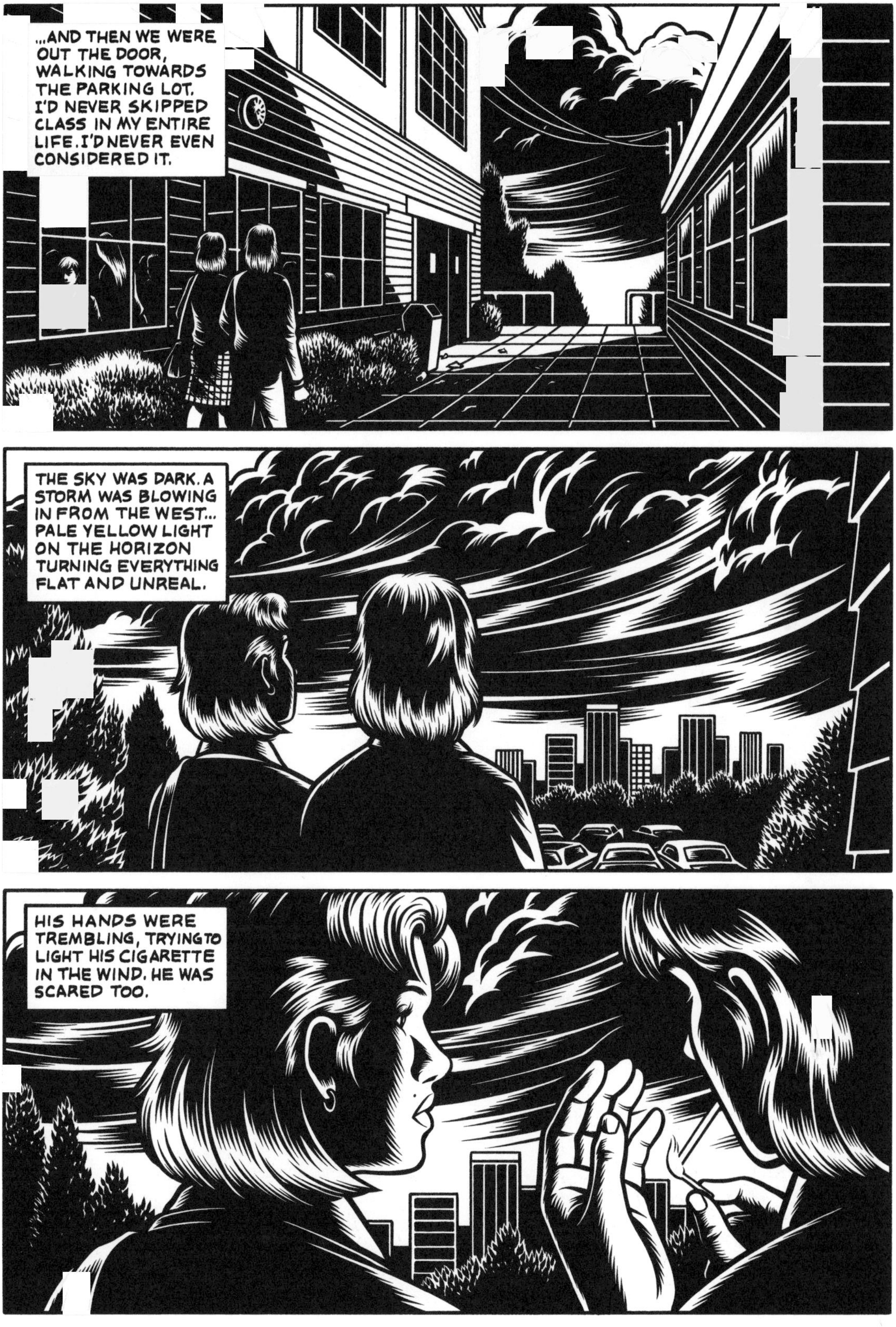
...AND THEN WE WERE OUT THE DOOR, WALKING TOWARDS THE PARKING LOT. I'D NEVER SKIPPED CLASS IN MY ENTIRE LIFE. I'D NEVER EVEN CONSIDERED IT.
THE SKY WAS DARK. A STORM WAS BLOWING IN FROM THE WEST... PALE YELLOW LIGHT ON THE HORIZON TURNING EVERYTHING FLAT AND UNREAL.
HIS HANDS WERE TREMBLING, TRYING TO LIGHT HIS CIGARETTE IN THE WIND. HE WAS SCARED TOO.

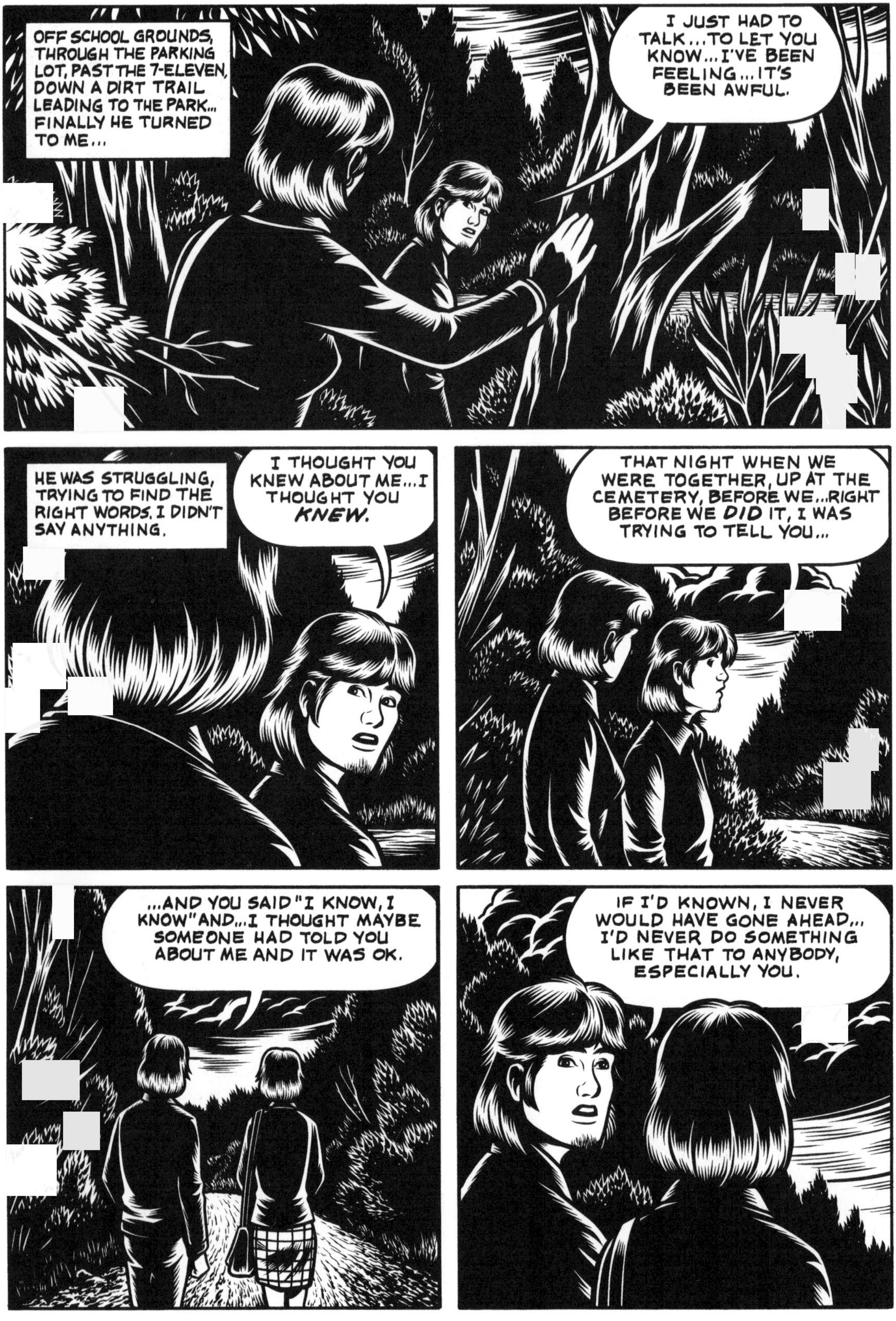
OFF SCHOOL GROUNDS, THROUGH THE PARKING LOT, PAST THE 7-ELEVEN, DOWN A DIRT TRAIL LEADING TO THE PARK... FINALLY HE TURNED TO ME...
I JUST HAD TO TALK... TO LET YOU KNOW... I'VE BEEN FEELING... IT'S BEEN AWFUL.
HE WAS STRUGGLING, TRYING TO FIND THE RIGHT WORDS. I DIDN'T SAY ANYTHING.
I THOUGHT YOU KNEW ABOUT ME... I THOUGHT YOU *KNEW.*
THAT NIGHT WHEN WE WERE TOGETHER, UP AT THE CEMETERY, BEFORE WE... RIGHT BEFORE WE *DID* IT, I WAS TRYING TO TELL YOU...
...AND YOU SAID "I KNOW, I KNOW" AND... I THOUGHT MAYBE SOMEONE HAD TOLD YOU ABOUT ME AND IT WAS OK.
IF I'D KNOWN, I NEVER WOULD HAVE GONE AHEAD... I'D NEVER DO SOMETHING LIKE THAT TO ANYBODY, ESPECIALLY YOU.

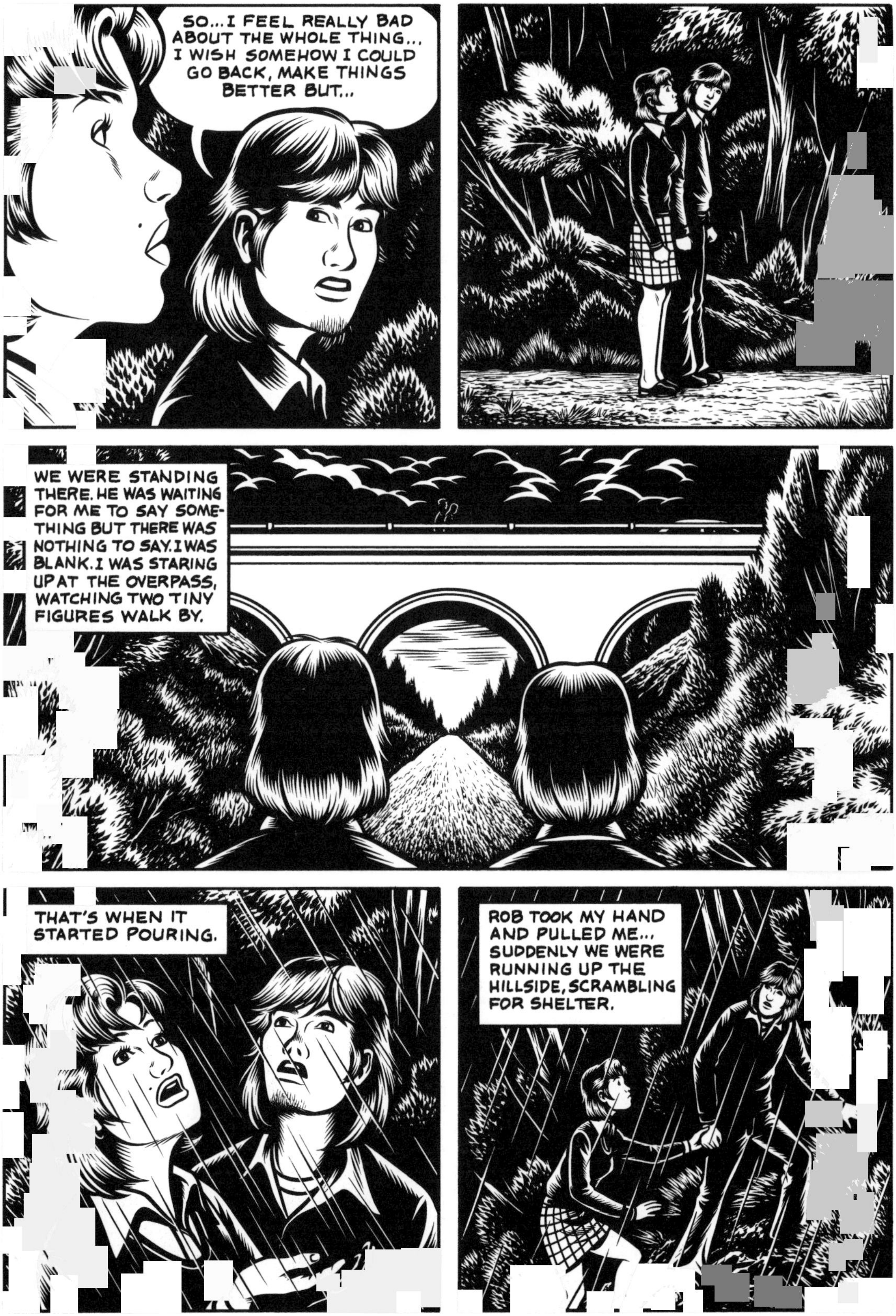
SO... I FEEL REALLY BAD ABOUT THE WHOLE THING... I WISH SOMEHOW I COULD GO BACK, MAKE THINGS BETTER BUT...
WE WERE STANDING THERE. HE WAS WAITING FOR ME TO SAY SOMETHING BUT THERE WAS NOTHING TO SAY. I WAS BLANK. I WAS STARING UP AT THE OVERPASS, WATCHING TWO TINY FIGURES WALK BY.
THAT'S WHEN IT STARTED POURING.
ROB TOOK MY HAND AND PULLED ME... SUDDENLY WE WERE RUNNING UP THE HILLSIDE, SCRAMBLING FOR SHELTER.

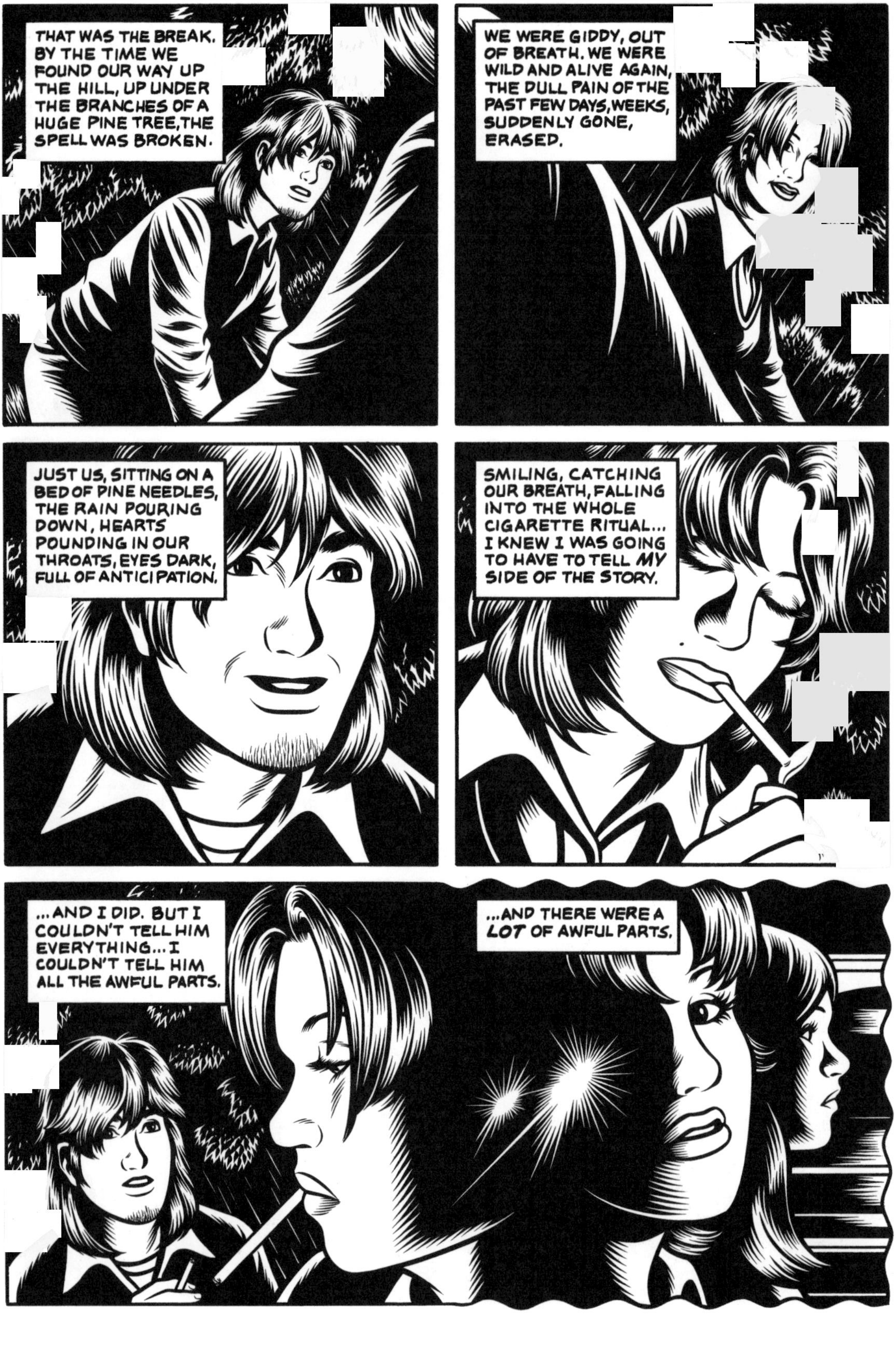
THAT WAS THE BREAK. BY THE TIME WE FOUND OUR WAY UP THE HILL, UP UNDER THE BRANCHES OF A HUGE PINE TREE, THE SPELL WAS BROKEN.
WE WERE GIDDY, OUT OF BREATH. WE WERE WILD AND ALIVE AGAIN, THE DULL PAIN OF THE PAST FEW DAYS, WEEKS, SUDDENLY GONE, ERASED.
JUST US, SITTING ON A BED OF PINE NEEDLES, THE RAIN POURING DOWN, HEARTS POUNDING IN OUR THROATS, EYES DARK, FULL OF ANTICIPATION.
SMILING, CATCHING OUR BREATH, FALLING INTO THE WHOLE CIGARETTE RITUAL... I KNEW I WAS GOING TO HAVE TO TELL *MY* SIDE OF THE STORY.
...AND I DID. BUT I COULDN'T TELL HIM EVERYTHING... I COULDN'T TELL HIM ALL THE AWFUL PARTS.
...AND THERE WERE A *LOT* OF AWFUL PARTS.

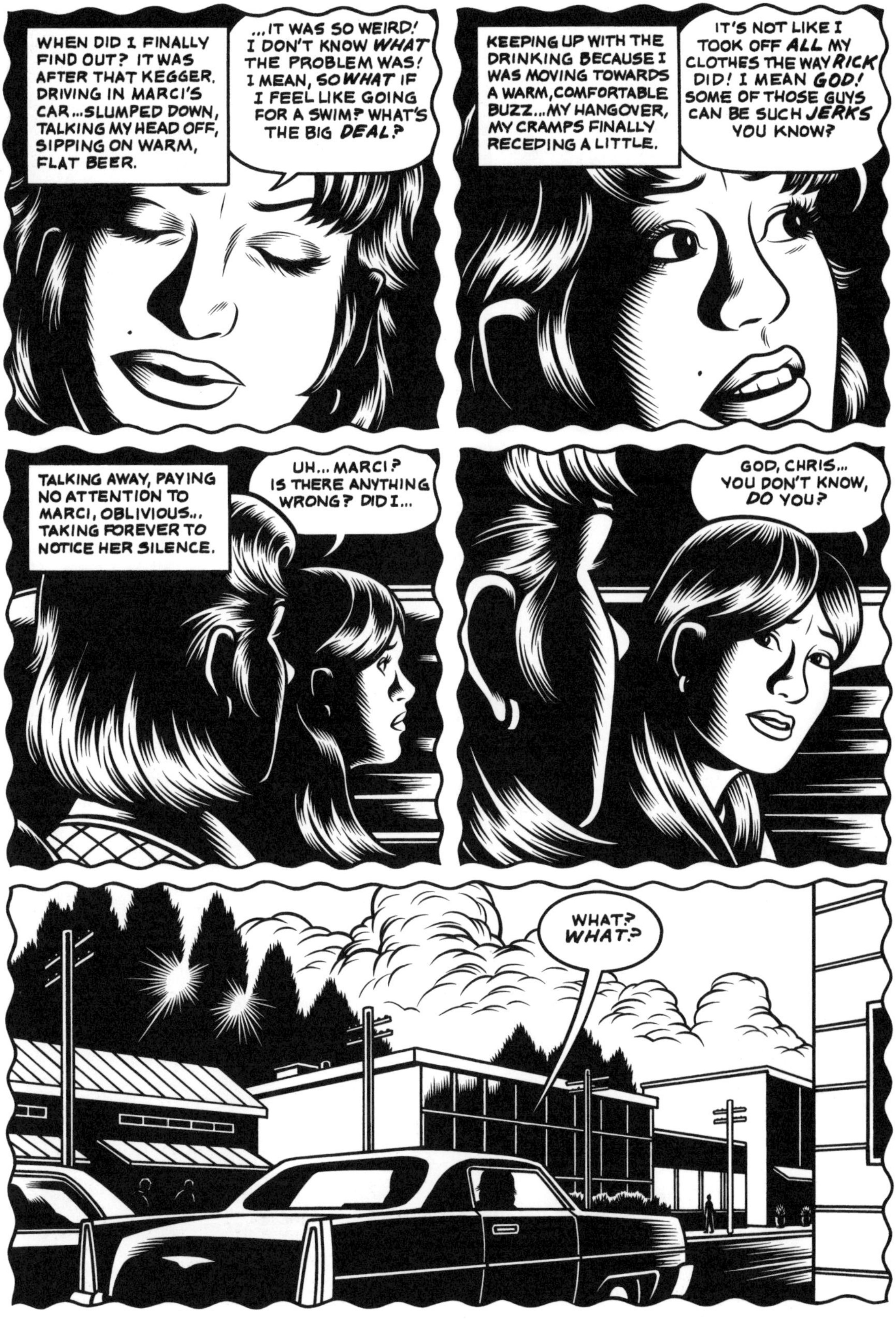
WHEN DID I FINALLY FIND OUT? IT WAS AFTER THAT KEGGER. DRIVING IN MARCI'S CAR...SLUMPED DOWN, TALKING MY HEAD OFF, SIPPING ON WARM, FLAT BEER.
...IT WAS SO WEIRD! I DON'T KNOW *WHAT* THE PROBLEM WAS! I MEAN, SO *WHAT* IF I FEEL LIKE GOING FOR A SWIM? WHAT'S THE BIG *DEAL*?
KEEPING UP WITH THE DRINKING BECAUSE I WAS MOVING TOWARDS A WARM, COMFORTABLE BUZZ...MY HANGOVER, MY CRAMPS FINALLY RECEDING A LITTLE.
IT'S NOT LIKE I TOOK OFF *ALL* MY CLOTHES THE WAY *RICK* DID! I MEAN *GOD!* SOME OF THOSE GUYS CAN BE SUCH *JERKS* YOU KNOW?
TALKING AWAY, PAYING NO ATTENTION TO MARCI, OBLIVIOUS... TAKING FOREVER TO NOTICE HER SILENCE.
UH... MARCI? IS THERE ANYTHING WRONG? DID I...
GOD, CHRIS... YOU DON'T KNOW, *DO* YOU?
WHAT? *WHAT?*

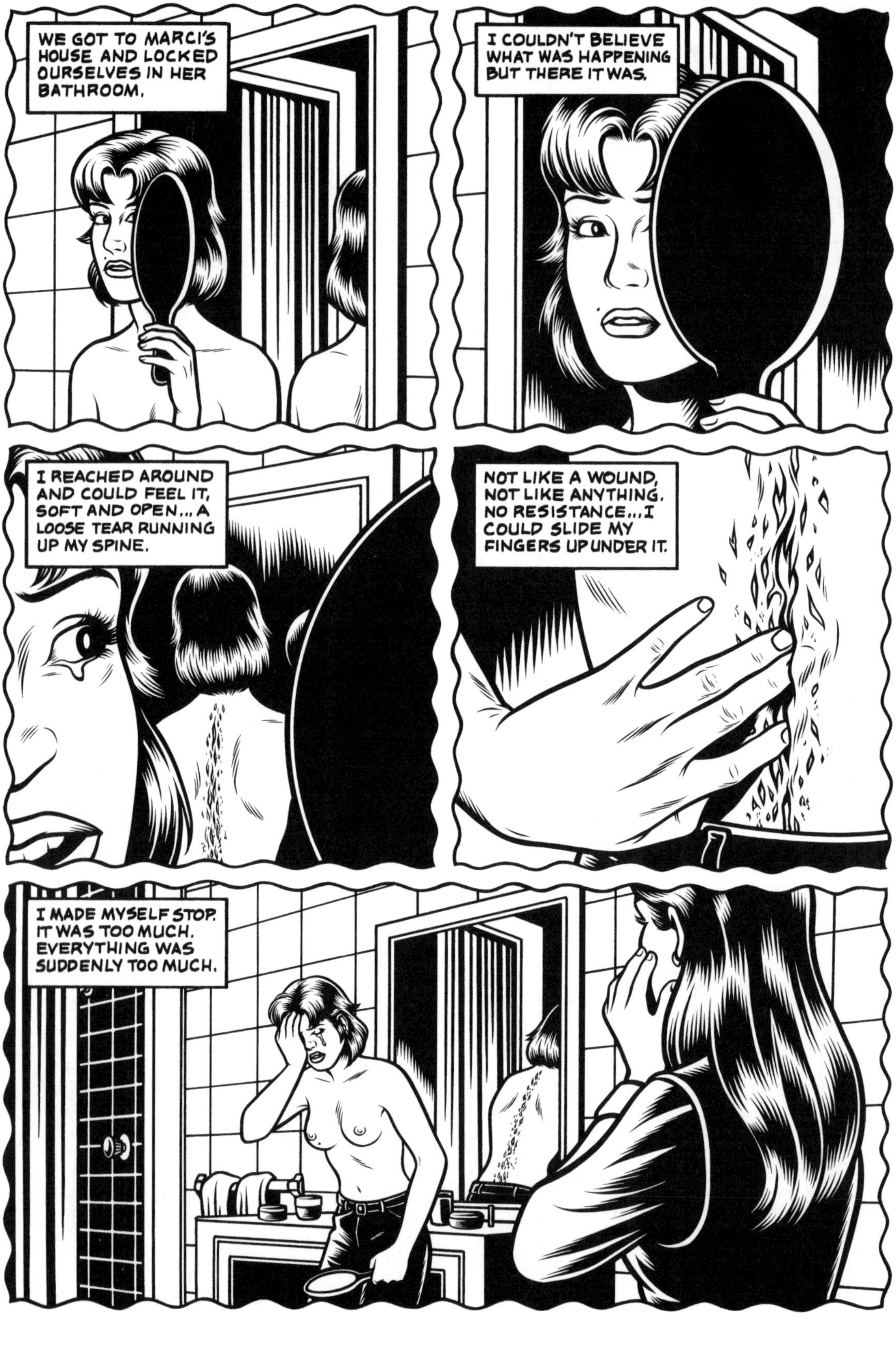
WE GOT TO MARCI'S HOUSE AND LOCKED OURSELVES IN HER BATHROOM.
I COULDN'T BELIEVE WHAT WAS HAPPENING BUT THERE IT WAS.
I REACHED AROUND AND COULD FEEL IT, SOFT AND OPEN... A LOOSE TEAR RUNNING UP MY SPINE.
NOT LIKE A WOUND, NOT LIKE ANYTHING. NO RESISTANCE... I COULD SLIDE MY FINGERS UP UNDER IT.
I MADE MYSELF STOP. IT WAS TOO MUCH. EVERYTHING WAS SUDDENLY TOO MUCH.

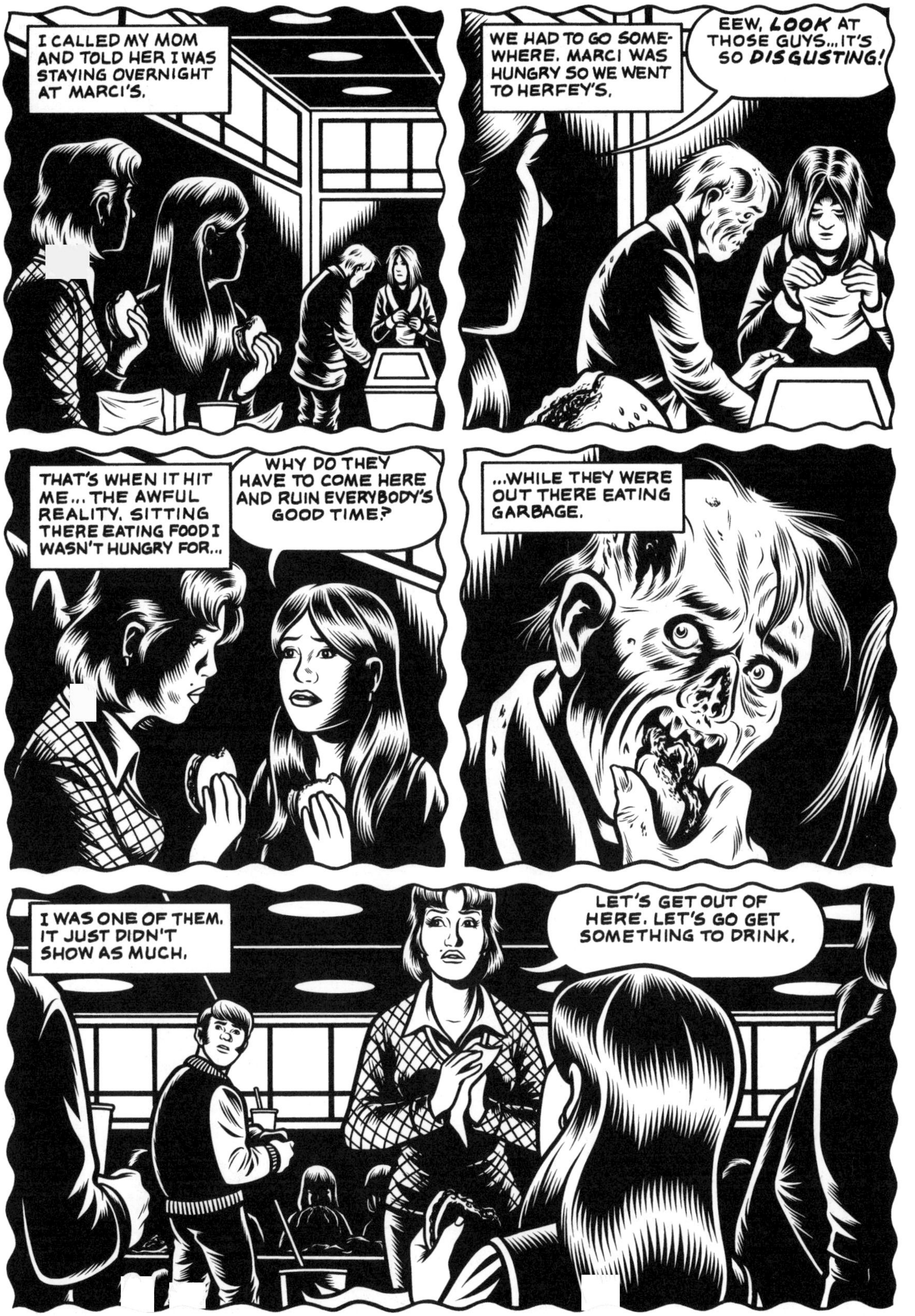
I CALLED MY MOM AND TOLD HER I WAS STAYING OVERNIGHT AT MARCI'S.
WE HAD TO GO SOMEWHERE. MARCI WAS HUNGRY SO WE WENT TO HERFEY'S.
EEW, **LOOK** AT THOSE GUYS...IT'S SO **DISGUSTING**!
THAT'S WHEN IT HIT ME... THE AWFUL REALITY. SITTING THERE EATING FOOD I WASN'T HUNGRY FOR...
WHY DO THEY HAVE TO COME HERE AND RUIN EVERYBODY'S GOOD TIME?
...WHILE THEY WERE OUT THERE EATING GARBAGE.
I WAS ONE OF THEM. IT JUST DIDN'T SHOW AS MUCH.
LET'S GET OUT OF HERE. LET'S GO GET SOMETHING TO DRINK.

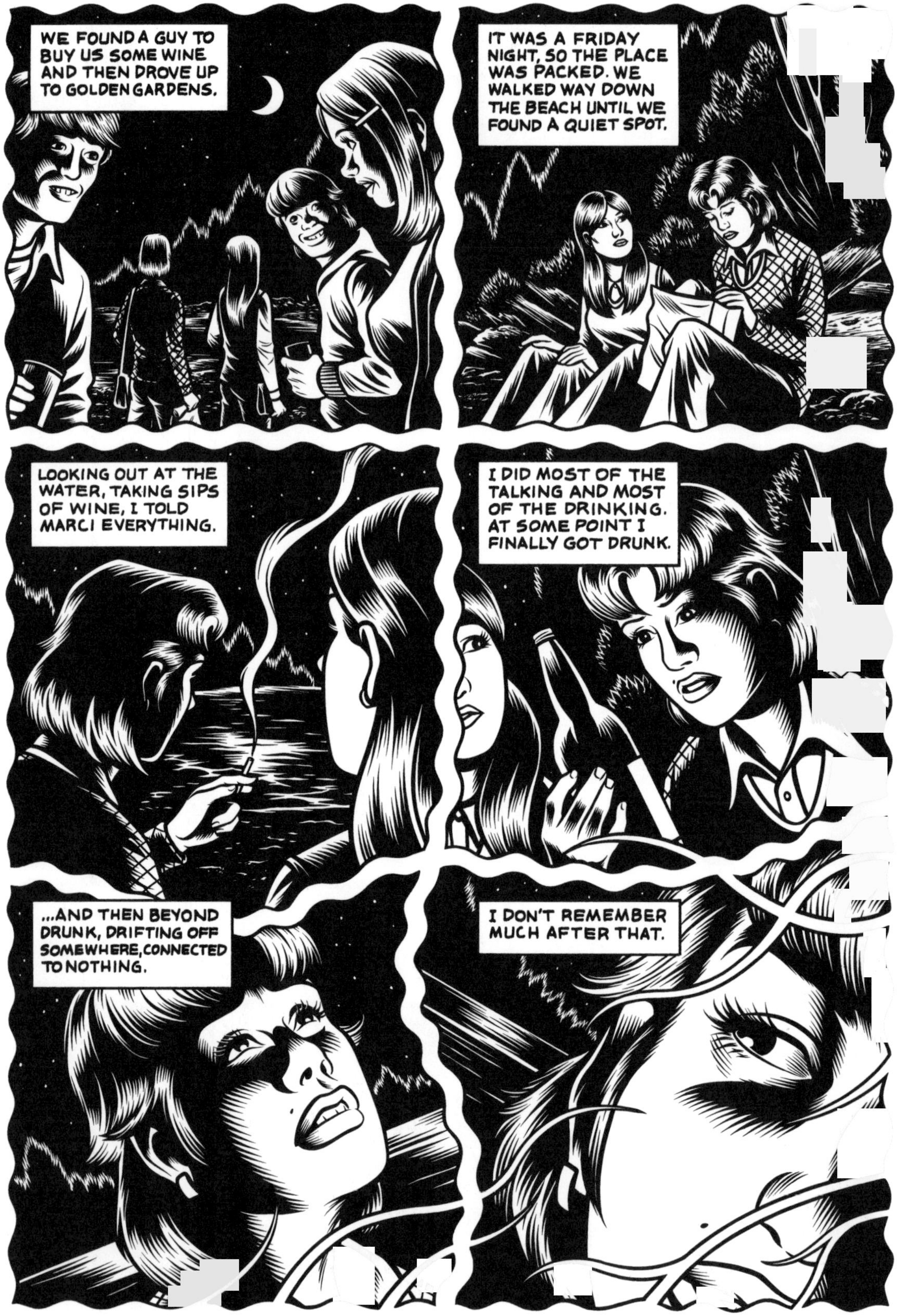
WE FOUND A GUY TO BUY US SOME WINE AND THEN DROVE UP TO GOLDEN GARDENS.
IT WAS A FRIDAY NIGHT, SO THE PLACE WAS PACKED. WE WALKED WAY DOWN THE BEACH UNTIL WE FOUND A QUIET SPOT.
LOOKING OUT AT THE WATER, TAKING SIPS OF WINE, I TOLD MARCI EVERYTHING.
I DID MOST OF THE TALKING AND MOST OF THE DRINKING. AT SOME POINT I FINALLY GOT DRUNK.
...AND THEN BEYOND DRUNK, DRIFTING OFF SOMEWHERE, CONNECTED TO NOTHING.
I DON'T REMEMBER MUCH AFTER THAT.

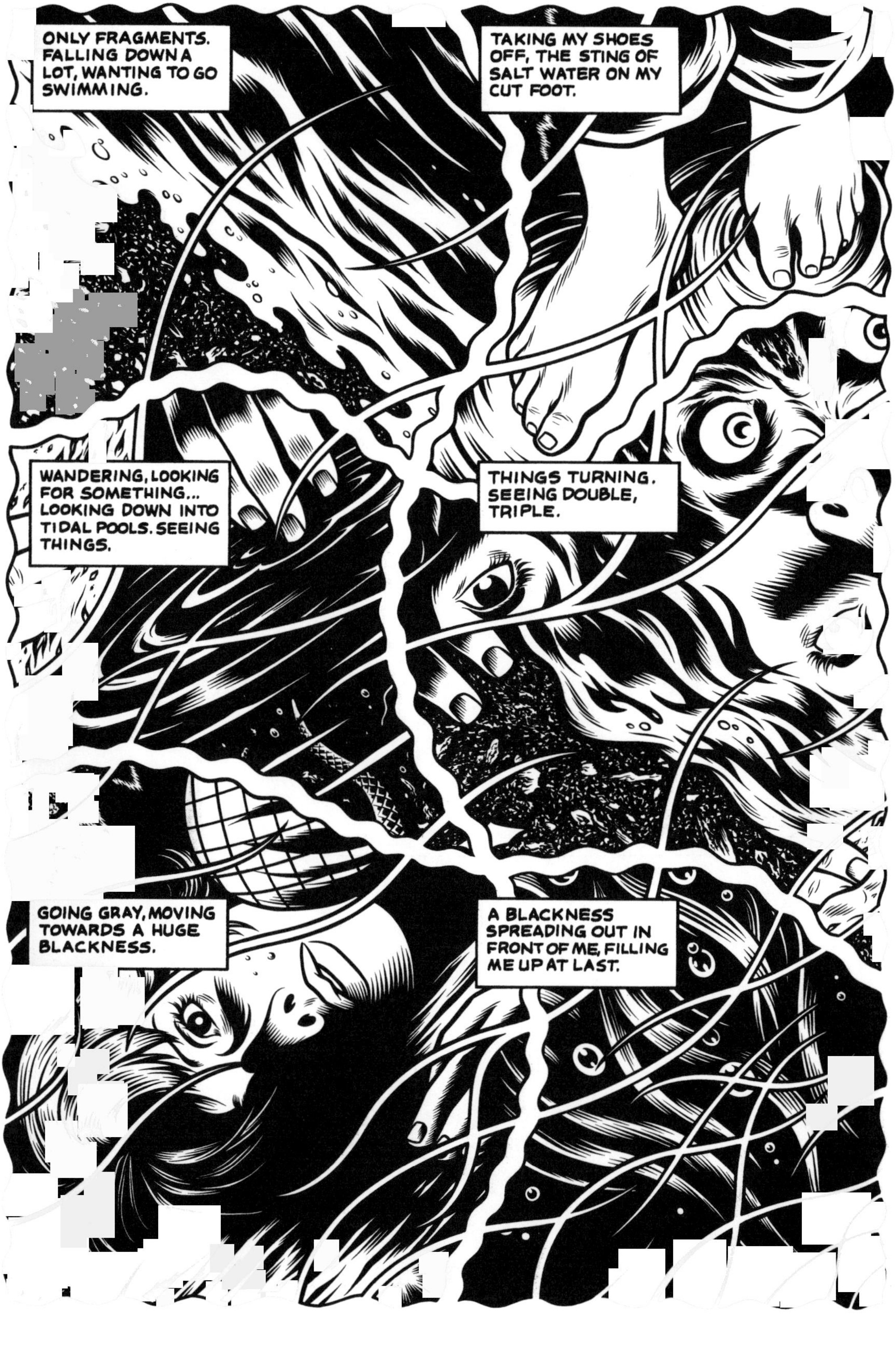
ONLY FRAGMENTS. FALLING DOWN A LOT, WANTING TO GO SWIMMING.
TAKING MY SHOES OFF, THE STING OF SALT WATER ON MY CUT FOOT.
WANDERING, LOOKING FOR SOMETHING... LOOKING DOWN INTO TIDAL POOLS. SEEING THINGS.
THINGS TURNING. SEEING DOUBLE, TRIPLE.
GOING GRAY, MOVING TOWARDS A HUGE BLACKNESS.
A BLACKNESS SPREADING OUT IN FRONT OF ME, FILLING ME UP AT LAST.

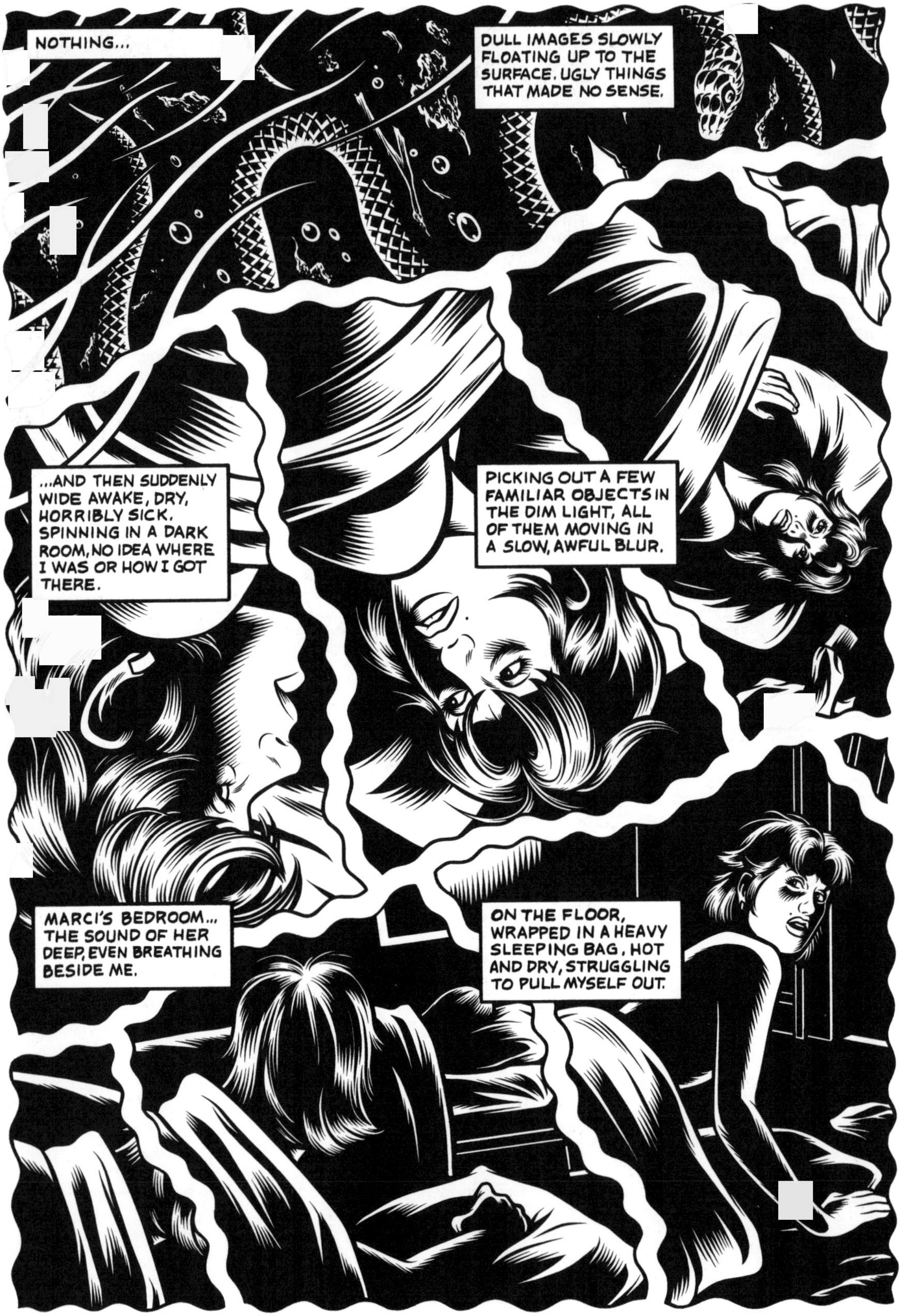
NOTHING...
DULL IMAGES SLOWLY FLOATING UP TO THE SURFACE. UGLY THINGS THAT MADE NO SENSE.
...AND THEN SUDDENLY WIDE AWAKE, DRY, HORRIBLY SICK, SPINNING IN A DARK ROOM, NO IDEA WHERE I WAS OR HOW I GOT THERE.
PICKING OUT A FEW FAMILIAR OBJECTS IN THE DIM LIGHT, ALL OF THEM MOVING IN A SLOW, AWFUL BLUR.
MARCI'S BEDROOM... THE SOUND OF HER DEEP, EVEN BREATHING BESIDE ME.
ON THE FLOOR, WRAPPED IN A HEAVY SLEEPING BAG, HOT AND DRY, STRUGGLING TO PULL MYSELF OUT.

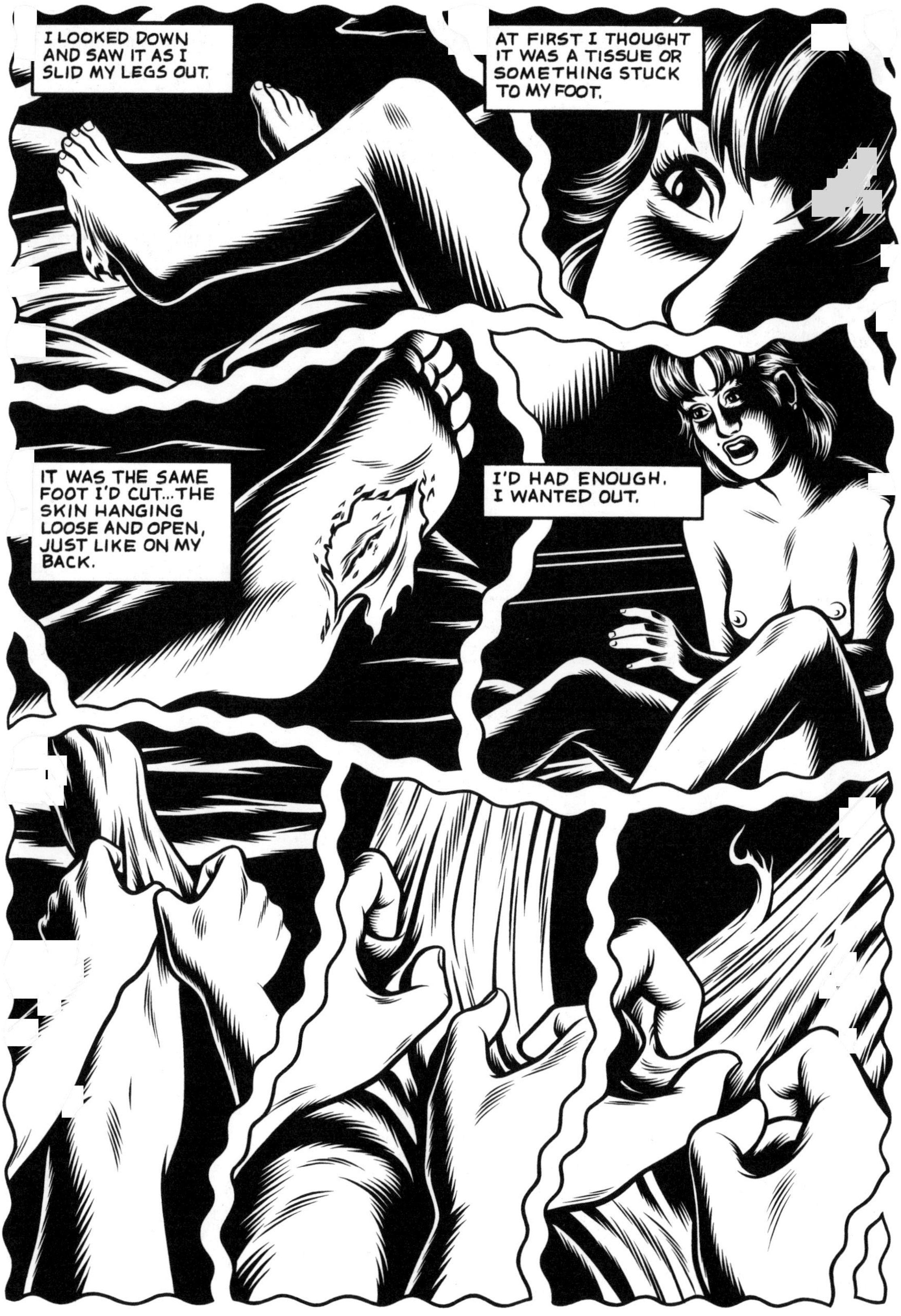
I LOOKED DOWN AND SAW IT AS I SLID MY LEGS OUT.
AT FIRST I THOUGHT IT WAS A TISSUE OR SOMETHING STUCK TO MY FOOT.
IT WAS THE SAME FOOT I'D CUT...THE SKIN HANGING LOOSE AND OPEN, JUST LIKE ON MY BACK.
I'D HAD ENOUGH. I WANTED OUT.

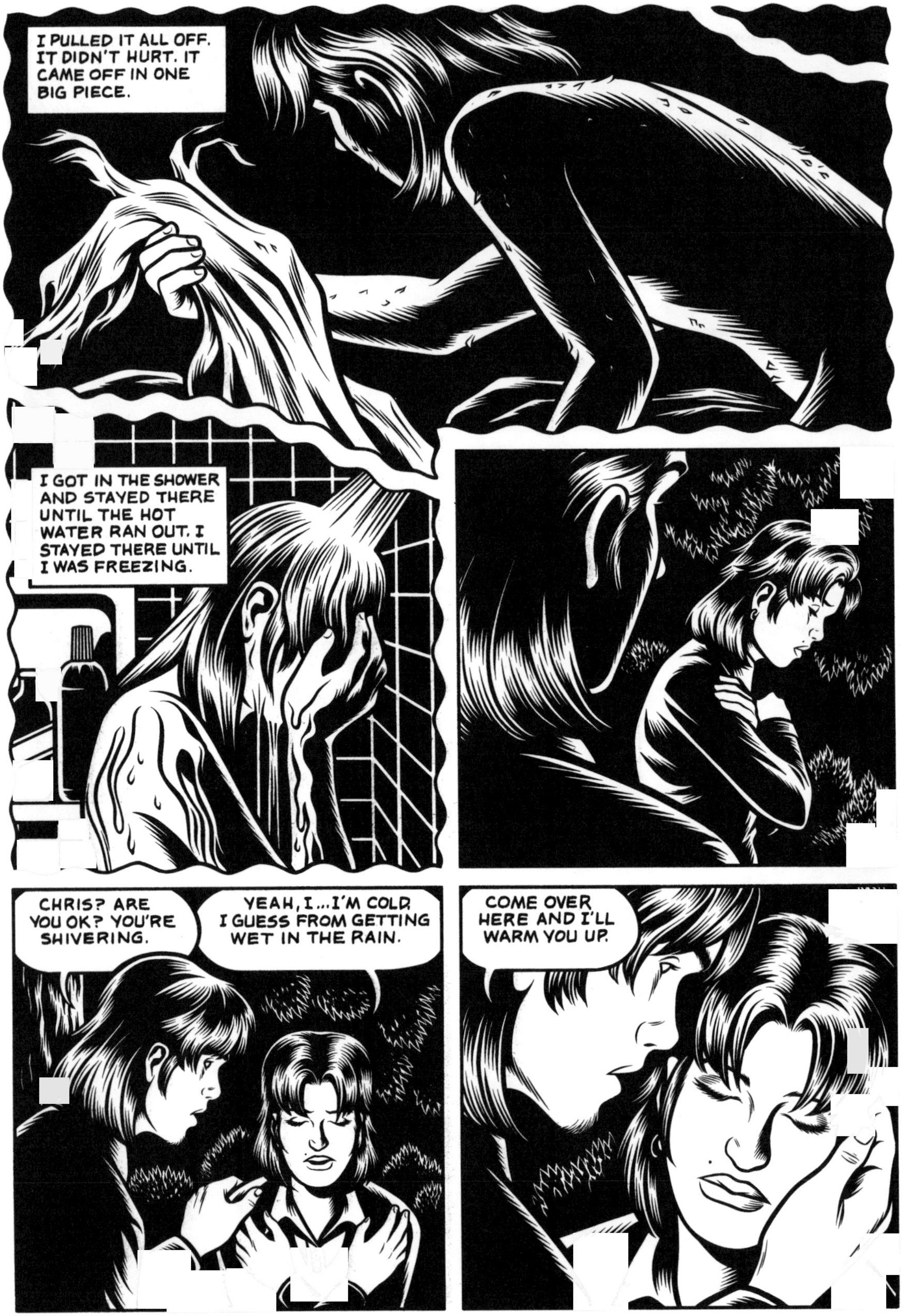
I PULLED IT ALL OFF. IT DIDN'T HURT. IT CAME OFF IN ONE BIG PIECE.
I GOT IN THE SHOWER AND STAYED THERE UNTIL THE HOT WATER RAN OUT. I STAYED THERE UNTIL I WAS FREEZING.
CHRIS? ARE YOU OK? YOU'RE SHIVERING.
YEAH, I...I'M COLD. I GUESS FROM GETTING WET IN THE RAIN.
COME OVER HERE AND I'LL WARM YOU UP.

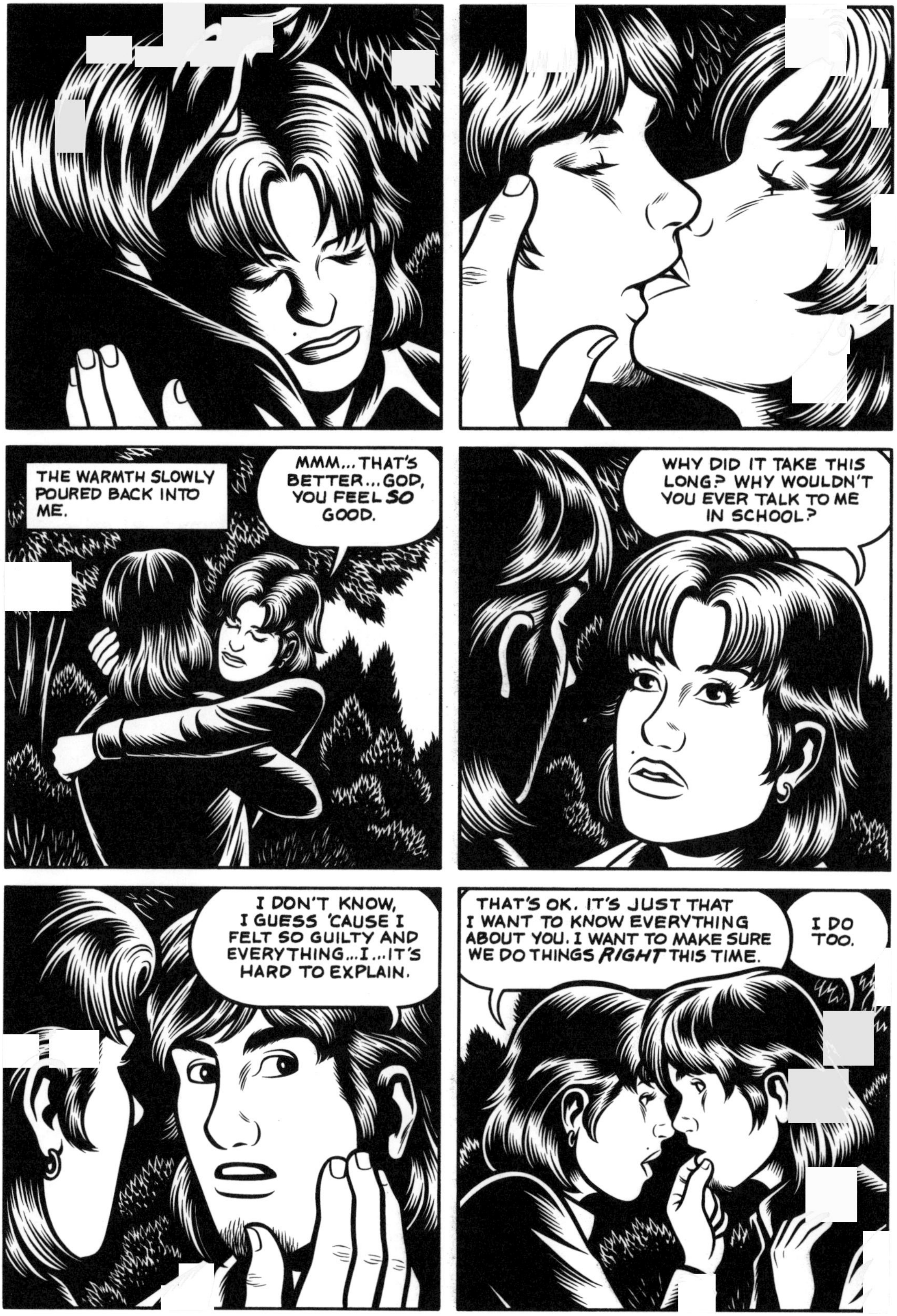

THE WARMTH SLOWLY POURED BACK INTO ME.
MMM... THAT'S BETTER... GOD, YOU FEEL *SO* GOOD.
WHY DID IT TAKE THIS LONG? WHY WOULDN'T YOU EVER TALK TO ME IN SCHOOL?
I DON'T KNOW, I GUESS 'CAUSE I FELT SO GUILTY AND EVERYTHING... I... IT'S HARD TO EXPLAIN.
THAT'S OK. IT'S JUST THAT I WANT TO KNOW EVERYTHING ABOUT YOU. I WANT TO MAKE SURE WE DO THINGS *RIGHT* THIS TIME.
I DO TOO.

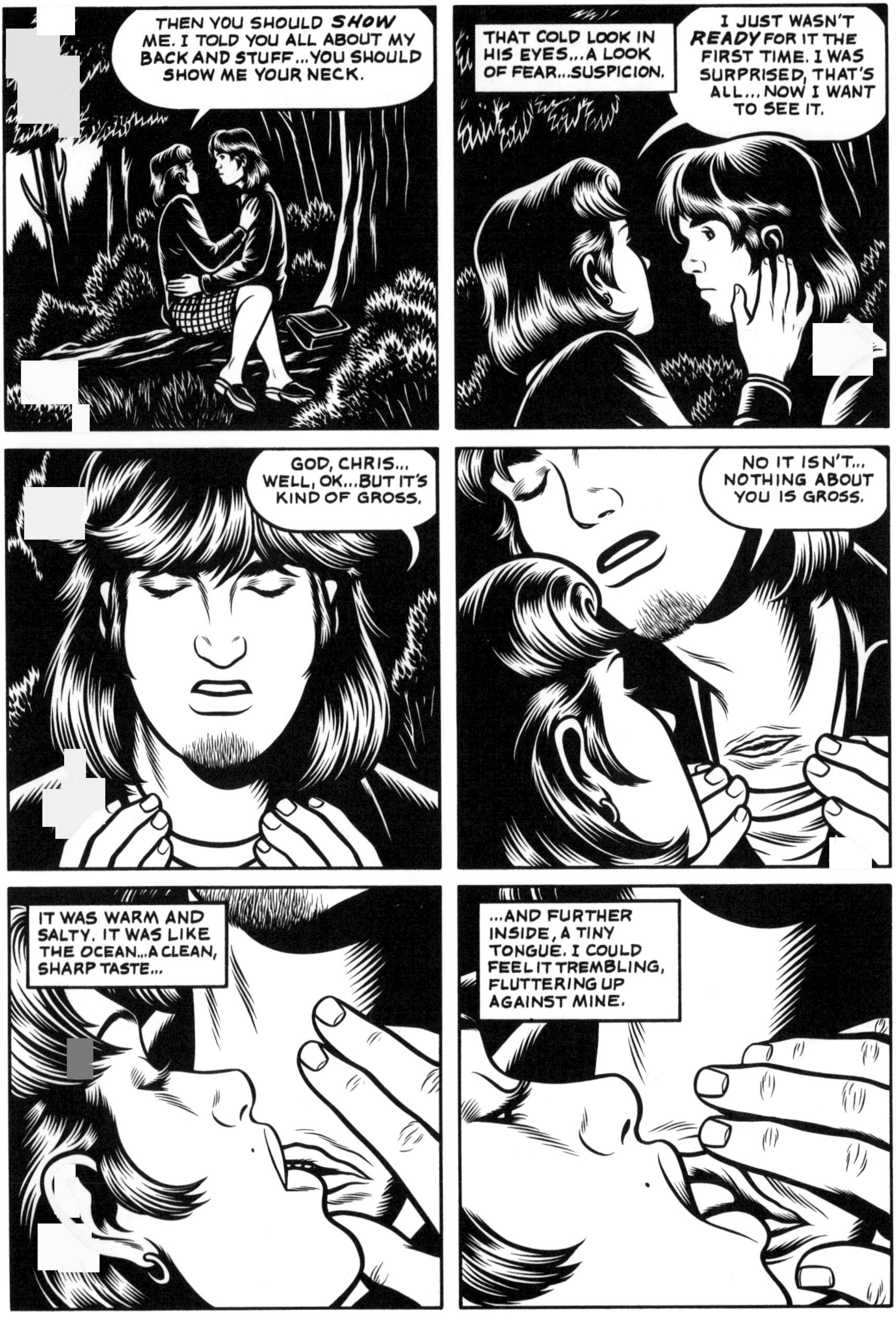
THEN YOU SHOULD SHOW ME. I TOLD YOU ALL ABOUT MY BACK AND STUFF... YOU SHOULD SHOW ME YOUR NECK.
THAT COLD LOOK IN HIS EYES... A LOOK OF FEAR... SUSPICION.
I JUST WASN'T READY FOR IT THE FIRST TIME. I WAS SURPRISED, THAT'S ALL... NOW I WANT TO SEE IT.
GOD, CHRIS... WELL, OK... BUT IT'S KIND OF GROSS.
NO IT ISN'T... NOTHING ABOUT YOU IS GROSS.
IT WAS WARM AND SALTY. IT WAS LIKE THE OCEAN... A CLEAN, SHARP TASTE...
...AND FURTHER INSIDE, A TINY TONGUE. I COULD FEEL IT TREMBLING, FLUTTERING UP AGAINST MINE.

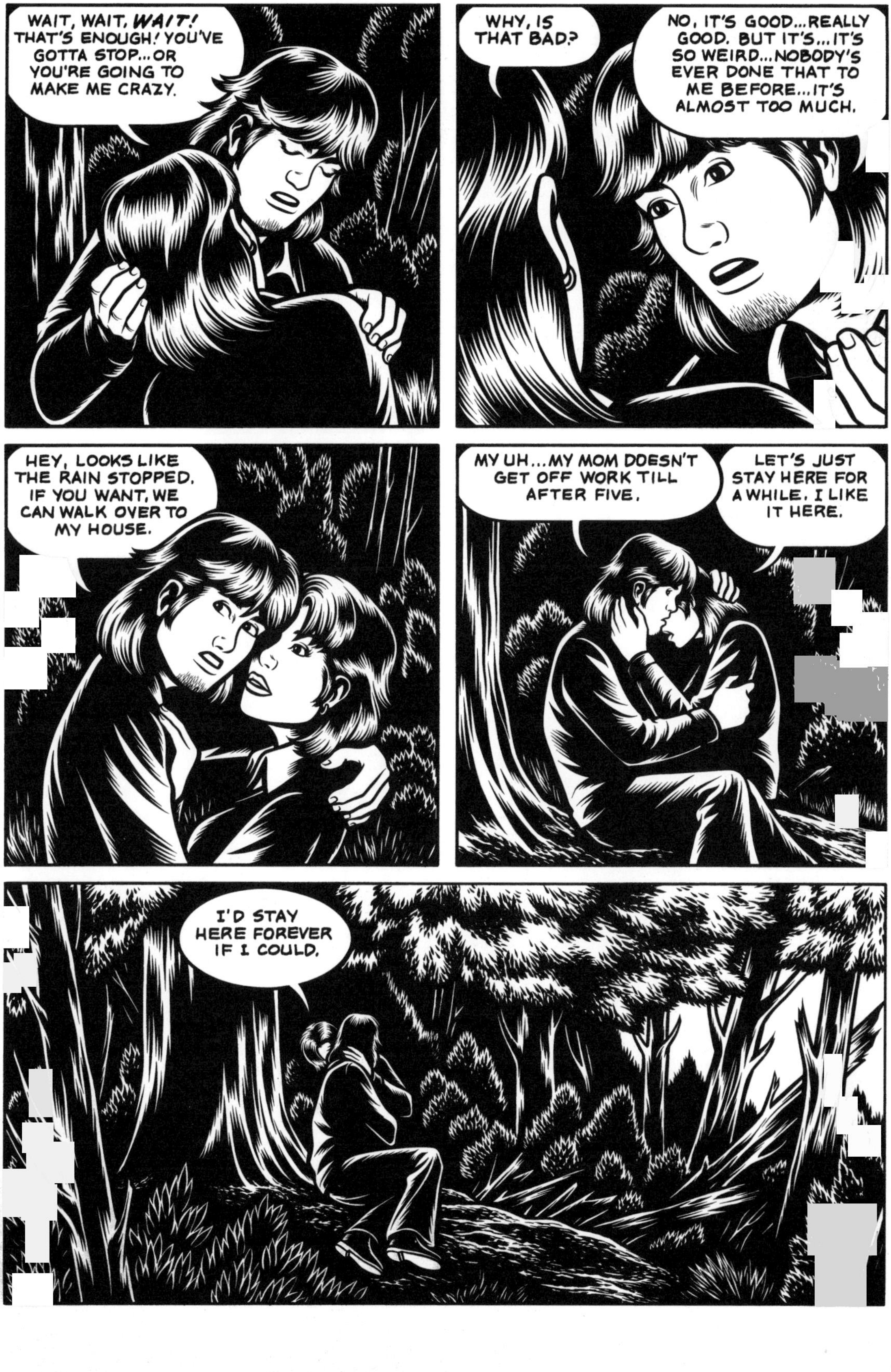
WAIT, WAIT, WAIT! THAT'S ENOUGH! YOU'VE GOTTA STOP...OR YOU'RE GOING TO MAKE ME CRAZY.
WHY, IS THAT BAD?
NO, IT'S GOOD...REALLY GOOD. BUT IT'S...IT'S SO WEIRD...NOBODY'S EVER DONE THAT TO ME BEFORE...IT'S ALMOST TOO MUCH.
HEY, LOOKS LIKE THE RAIN STOPPED. IF YOU WANT, WE CAN WALK OVER TO MY HOUSE.
MY UH...MY MOM DOESN'T GET OFF WORK TILL AFTER FIVE.
LET'S JUST STAY HERE FOR A WHILE. I LIKE IT HERE.
I'D STAY HERE FOREVER IF I COULD.

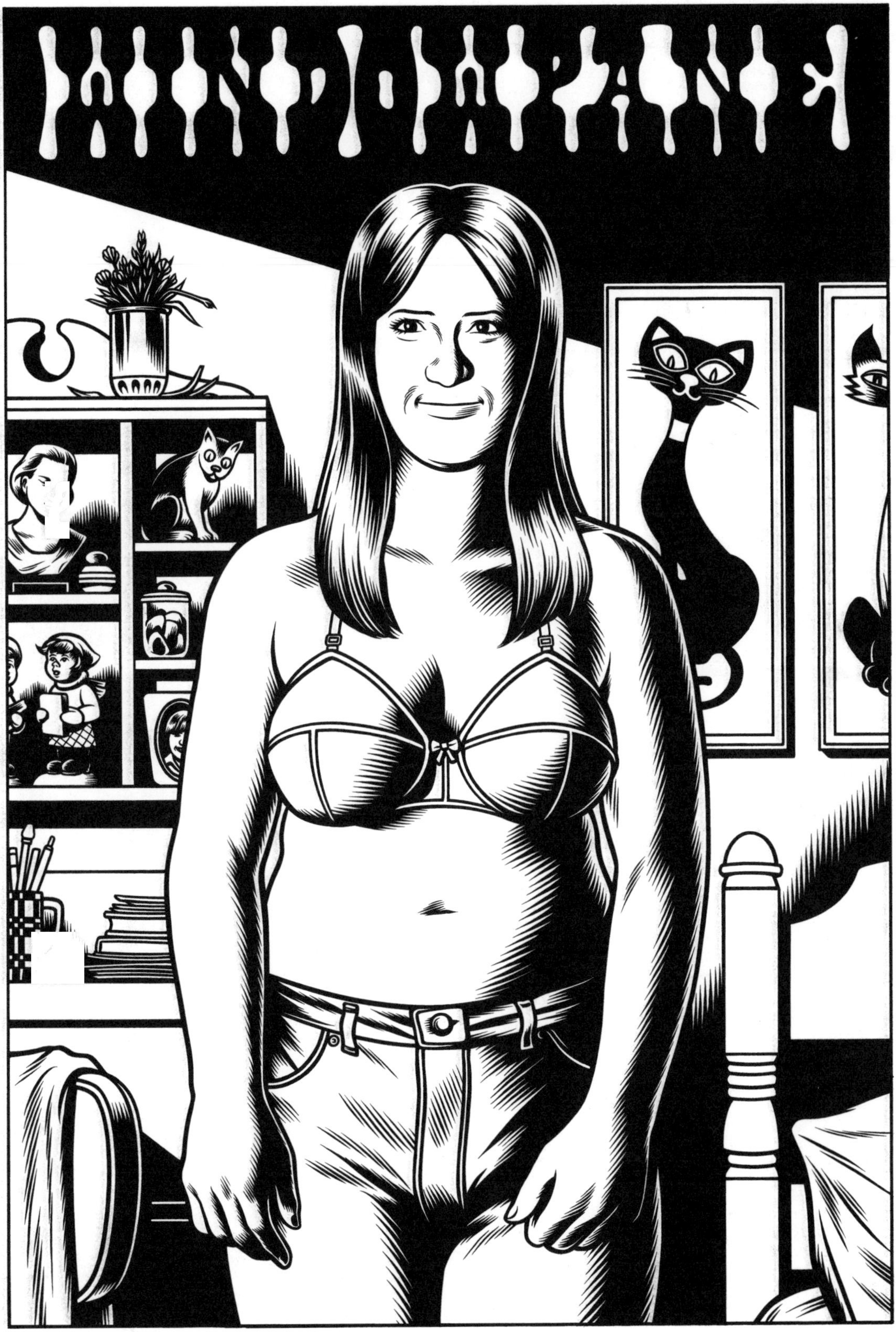

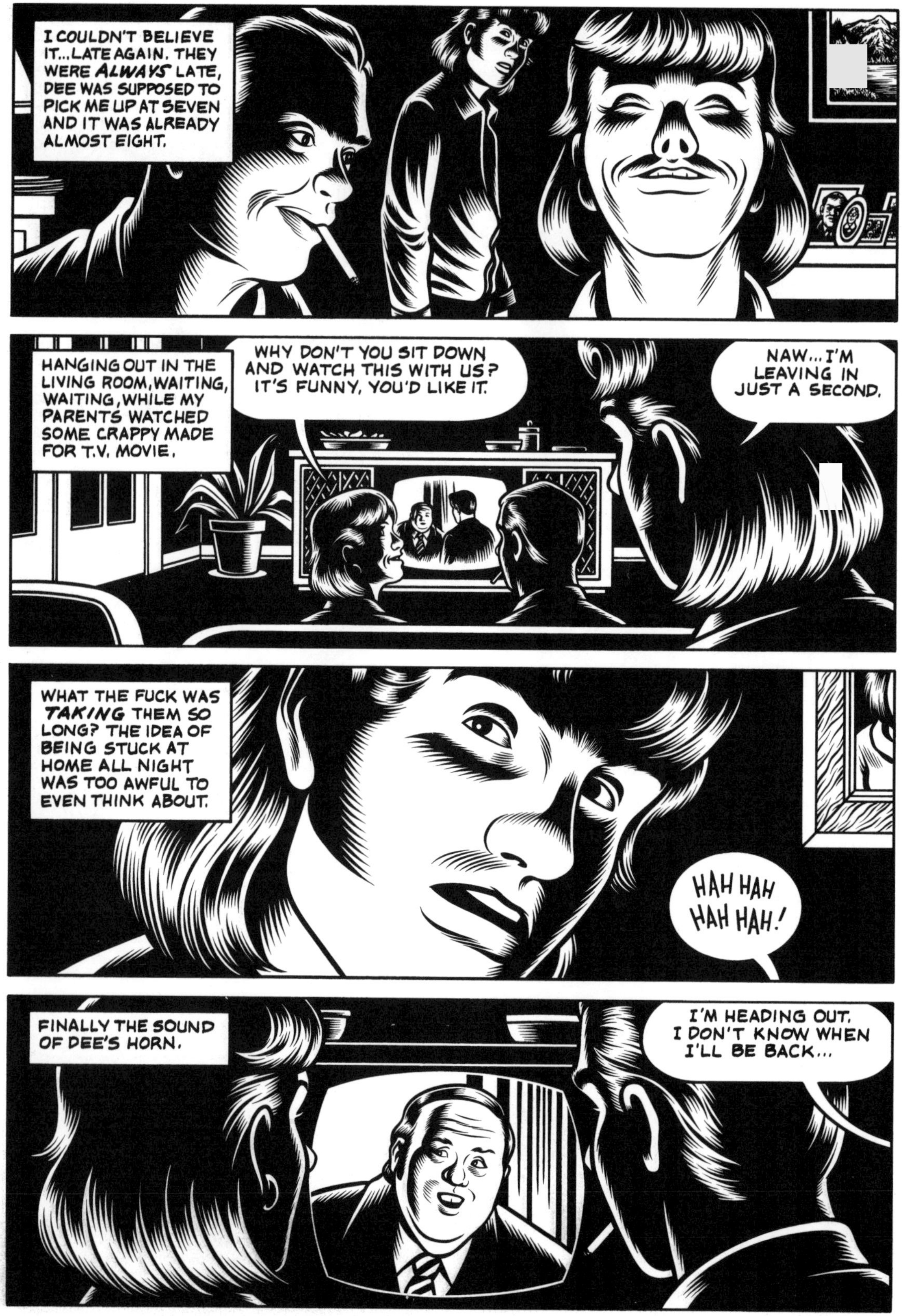
I COULDN'T BELIEVE IT... LATE AGAIN. THEY WERE *ALWAYS* LATE, DEE WAS SUPPOSED TO PICK ME UP AT SEVEN AND IT WAS ALREADY ALMOST EIGHT.
HANGING OUT IN THE LIVING ROOM, WAITING, WAITING, WHILE MY PARENTS WATCHED SOME CRAPPY MADE FOR T.V. MOVIE.
WHY DON'T YOU SIT DOWN AND WATCH THIS WITH US? IT'S FUNNY, YOU'D LIKE IT.
NAW... I'M LEAVING IN JUST A SECOND.
WHAT THE FUCK WAS *TAKING* THEM SO LONG? THE IDEA OF BEING STUCK AT HOME ALL NIGHT WAS TOO AWFUL TO EVEN THINK ABOUT.
HAH HAH HAH HAH!
FINALLY THE SOUND OF DEE'S HORN.
I'M HEADING OUT. I DON'T KNOW WHEN I'LL BE BACK...

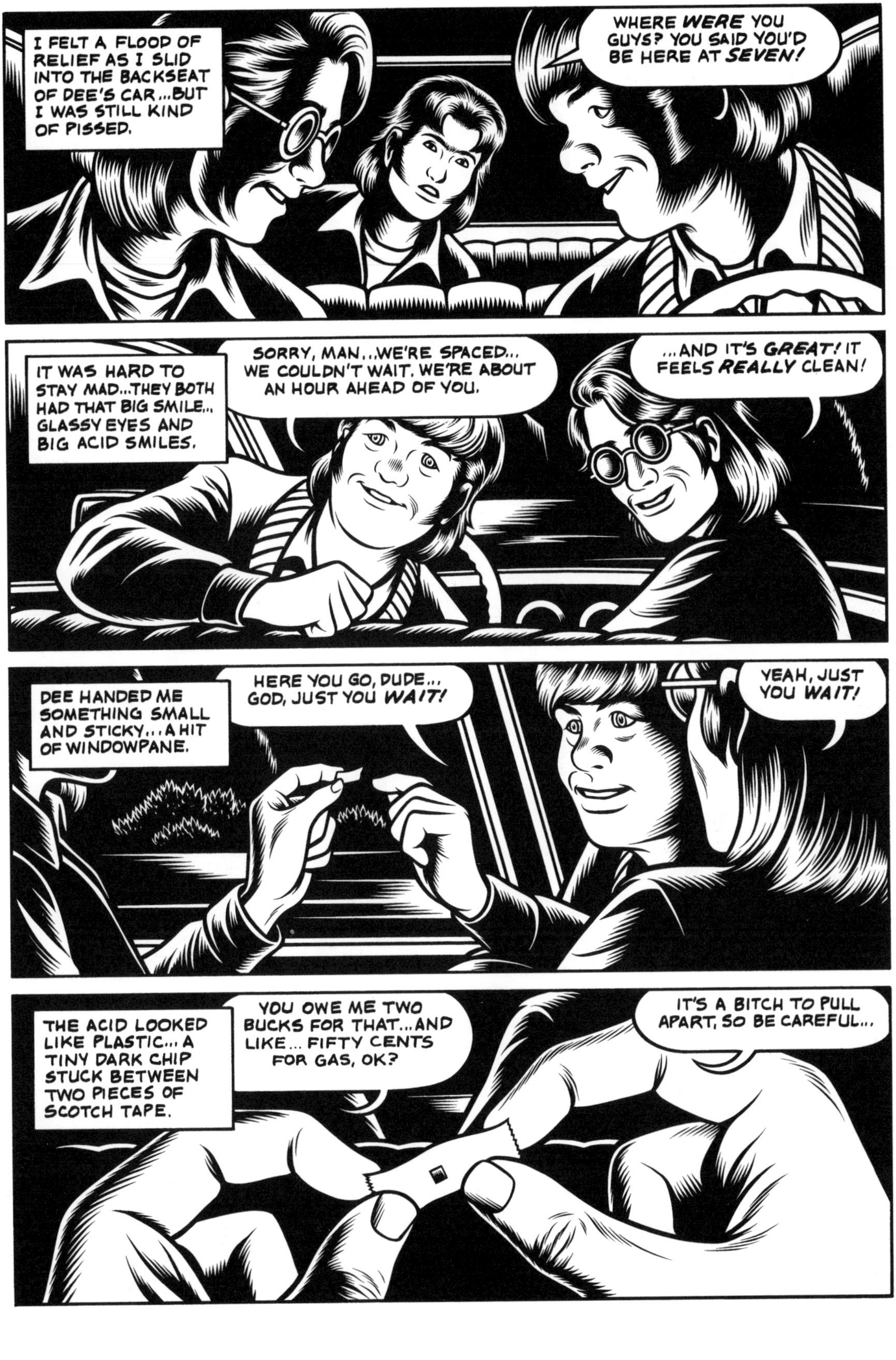
I FELT A FLOOD OF RELIEF AS I SLID INTO THE BACKSEAT OF DEE'S CAR...BUT I WAS STILL KIND OF PISSED.
WHERE *WERE* YOU GUYS? YOU SAID YOU'D BE HERE AT *SEVEN!*
IT WAS HARD TO STAY MAD...THEY BOTH HAD THAT BIG SMILE... GLASSY EYES AND BIG ACID SMILES.
SORRY, MAN...WE'RE SPACED... WE COULDN'T WAIT. WE'RE ABOUT AN HOUR AHEAD OF YOU.
...AND IT'S *GREAT!* IT FEELS *REALLY* CLEAN!
DEE HANDED ME SOMETHING SMALL AND STICKY... A HIT OF WINDOWPANE.
HERE YOU GO, DUDE... GOD, JUST YOU *WAIT!*
YEAH, JUST YOU *WAIT!*
THE ACID LOOKED LIKE PLASTIC... A TINY DARK CHIP STUCK BETWEEN TWO PIECES OF SCOTCH TAPE.
YOU OWE ME TWO BUCKS FOR THAT...AND LIKE... FIFTY CENTS FOR GAS, OK?
IT'S A BITCH TO PULL APART, SO BE CAREFUL...

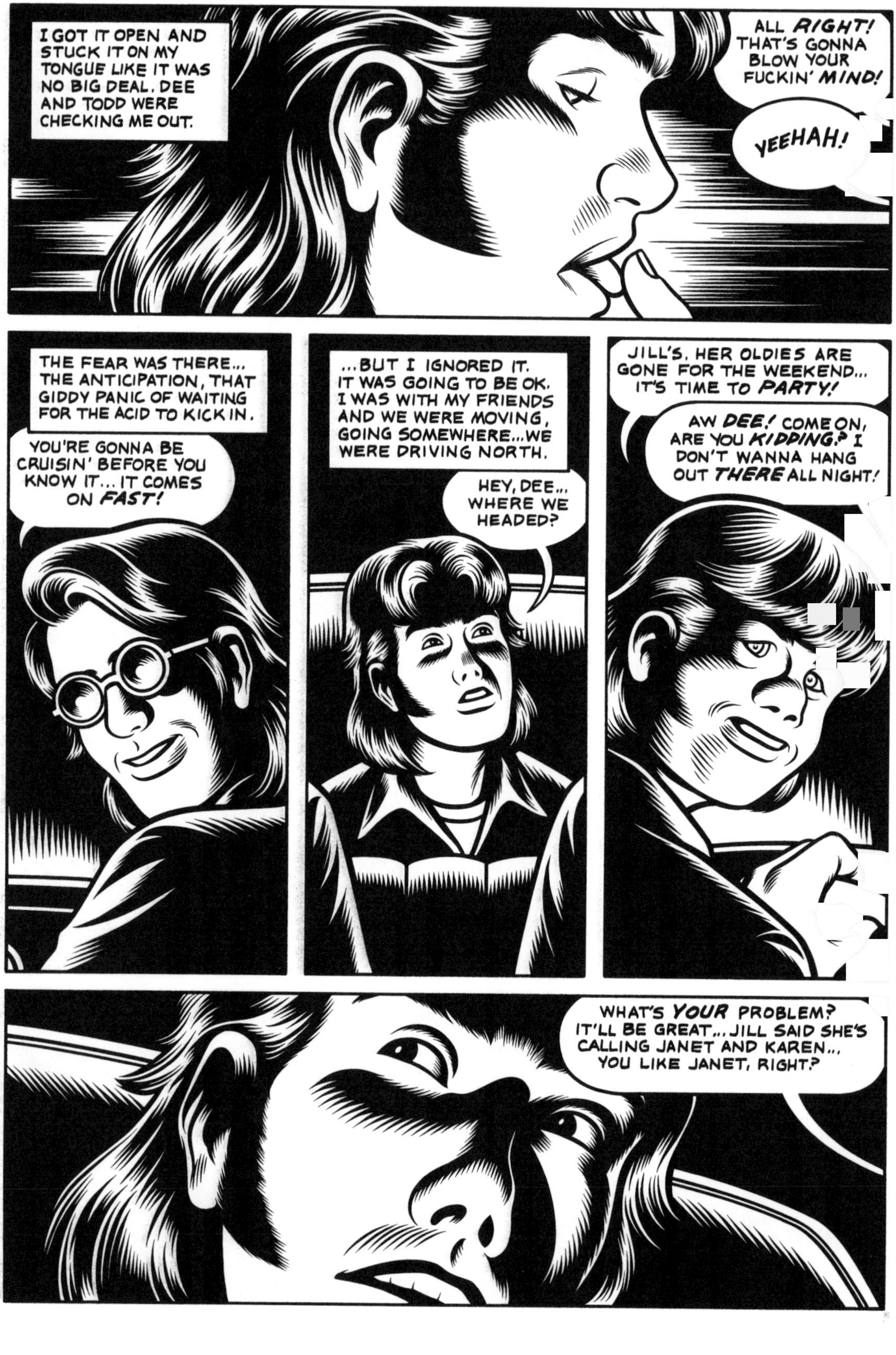
I GOT IT OPEN AND STUCK IT ON MY TONGUE LIKE IT WAS NO BIG DEAL. DEE AND TODD WERE CHECKING ME OUT.
ALL RIGHT! THAT'S GONNA BLOW YOUR FUCKIN' MIND!
YEEHAH!
THE FEAR WAS THERE... THE ANTICIPATION, THAT GIDDY PANIC OF WAITING FOR THE ACID TO KICK IN.
YOU'RE GONNA BE CRUISIN' BEFORE YOU KNOW IT... IT COMES ON FAST!
...BUT I IGNORED IT. IT WAS GOING TO BE OK. I WAS WITH MY FRIENDS AND WE WERE MOVING, GOING SOMEWHERE... WE WERE DRIVING NORTH.
HEY, DEE... WHERE WE HEADED?
JILL'S. HER OLDIES ARE GONE FOR THE WEEKEND... IT'S TIME TO PARTY!
AW DEE! COME ON, ARE YOU KIDDING? I DON'T WANNA HANG OUT THERE ALL NIGHT!
WHAT'S YOUR PROBLEM? IT'LL BE GREAT... JILL SAID SHE'S CALLING JANET AND KAREN... YOU LIKE JANET, RIGHT?

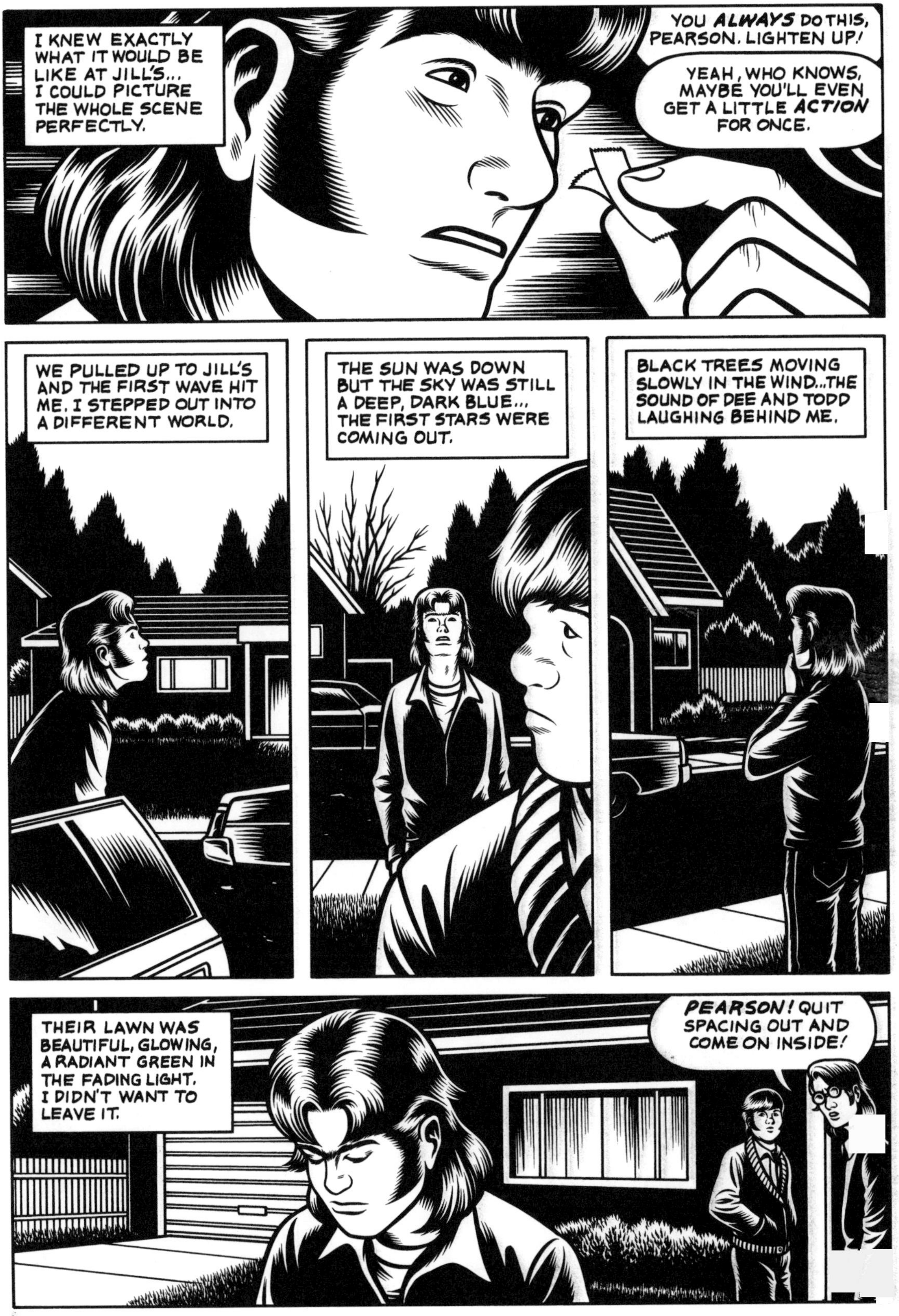

I KNEW EXACTLY WHAT IT WOULD BE LIKE AT JILL'S... I COULD PICTURE THE WHOLE SCENE PERFECTLY.
YOU ALWAYS DO THIS, PEARSON. LIGHTEN UP!
YEAH, WHO KNOWS, MAYBE YOU'LL EVEN GET A LITTLE ACTION FOR ONCE.
WE PULLED UP TO JILL'S AND THE FIRST WAVE HIT ME. I STEPPED OUT INTO A DIFFERENT WORLD.
THE SUN WAS DOWN BUT THE SKY WAS STILL A DEEP, DARK BLUE... THE FIRST STARS WERE COMING OUT.
BLACK TREES MOVING SLOWLY IN THE WIND...THE SOUND OF DEE AND TODD LAUGHING BEHIND ME.
THEIR LAWN WAS BEAUTIFUL, GLOWING, A RADIANT GREEN IN THE FADING LIGHT. I DIDN'T WANT TO LEAVE IT.
PEARSON! QUIT SPACING OUT AND COME ON INSIDE!

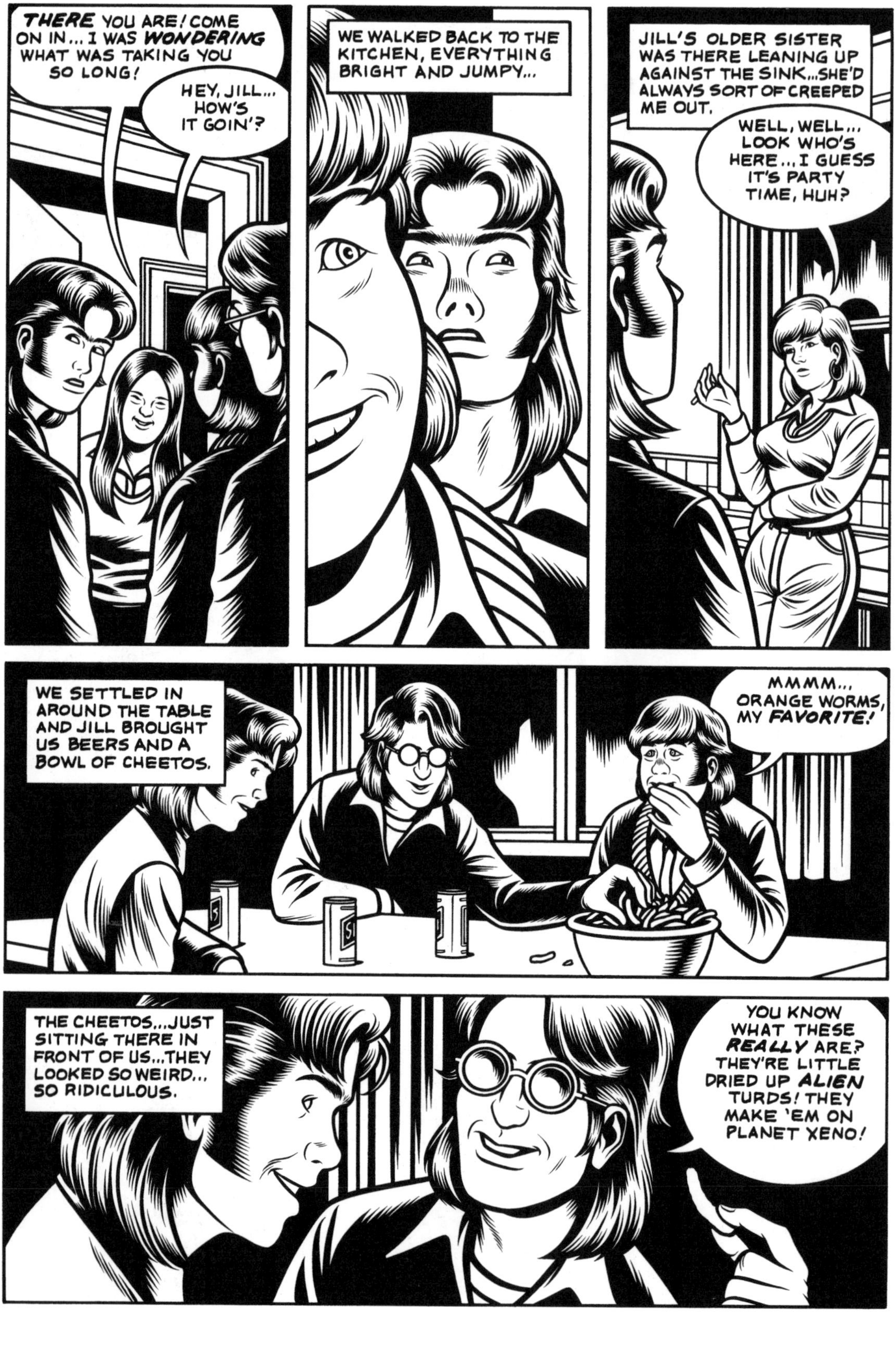
THERE YOU ARE! COME ON IN... I WAS WONDERING WHAT WAS TAKING YOU SO LONG!
HEY, JILL... HOW'S IT GOIN'?
WE WALKED BACK TO THE KITCHEN, EVERYTHING BRIGHT AND JUMPY...
JILL'S OLDER SISTER WAS THERE LEANING UP AGAINST THE SINK...SHE'D ALWAYS SORT OF CREEPED ME OUT.
WELL, WELL... LOOK WHO'S HERE... I GUESS IT'S PARTY TIME, HUH?
WE SETTLED IN AROUND THE TABLE AND JILL BROUGHT US BEERS AND A BOWL OF CHEETOS.
MMMM... ORANGE WORMS, MY FAVORITE!
THE CHEETOS...JUST SITTING THERE IN FRONT OF US...THEY LOOKED SO WEIRD... SO RIDICULOUS.
YOU KNOW WHAT THESE REALLY ARE? THEY'RE LITTLE DRIED UP ALIEN TURDS! THEY MAKE 'EM ON PLANET XENO!

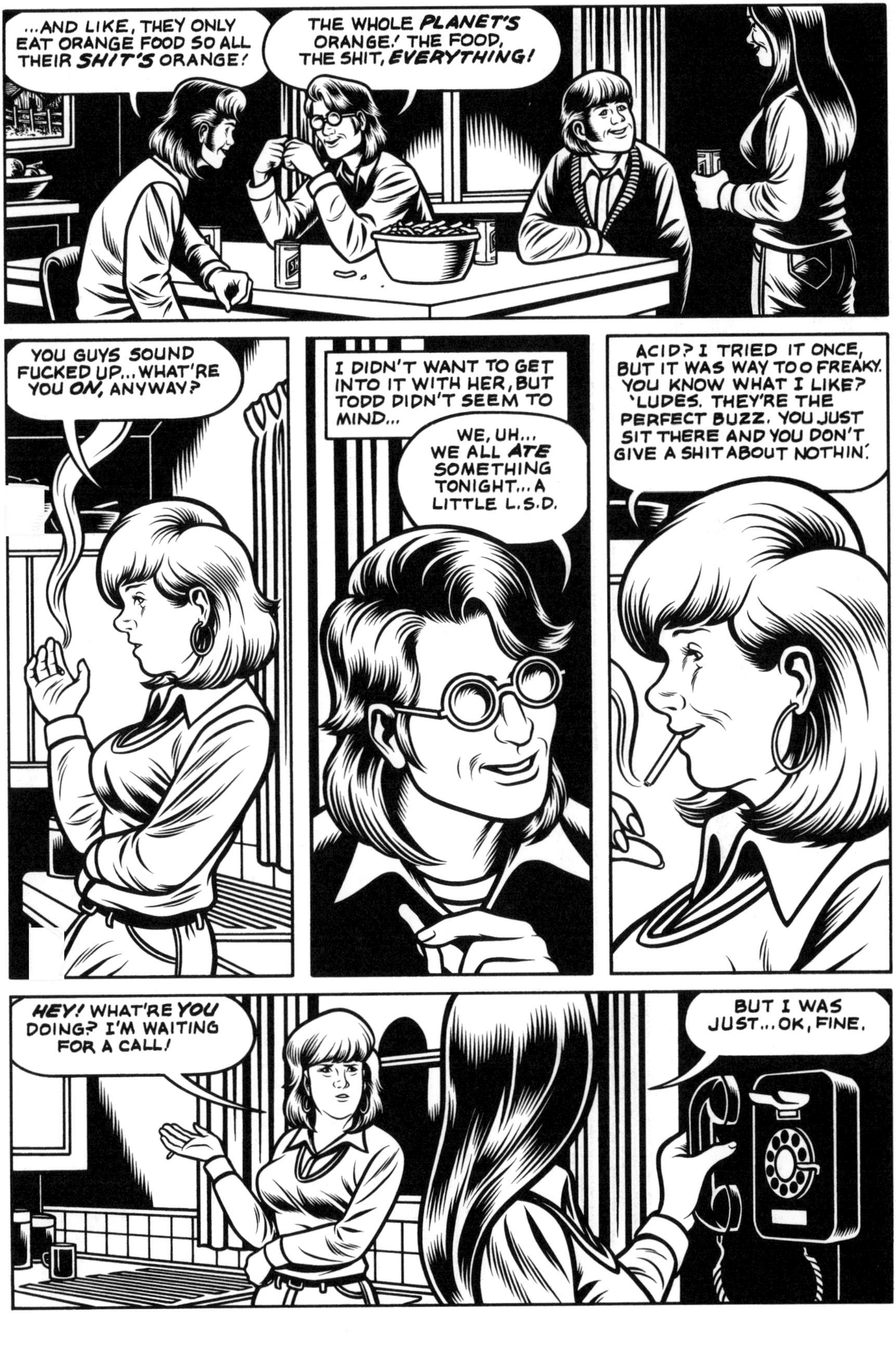
...AND LIKE, THEY ONLY EAT ORANGE FOOD SO ALL THEIR SHIT'S ORANGE!
THE WHOLE PLANET'S ORANGE! THE FOOD, THE SHIT, EVERYTHING!
YOU GUYS SOUND FUCKED UP... WHAT'RE YOU ON, ANYWAY?
I DIDN'T WANT TO GET INTO IT WITH HER, BUT TODD DIDN'T SEEM TO MIND...
WE, UH... WE ALL ATE SOMETHING TONIGHT... A LITTLE L.S.D.
ACID? I TRIED IT ONCE, BUT IT WAS WAY TOO FREAKY. YOU KNOW WHAT I LIKE? 'LUDES. THEY'RE THE PERFECT BUZZ. YOU JUST SIT THERE AND YOU DON'T GIVE A SHIT ABOUT NOTHIN'.
HEY! WHAT'RE YOU DOING? I'M WAITING FOR A CALL!
BUT I WAS JUST... OK, FINE.

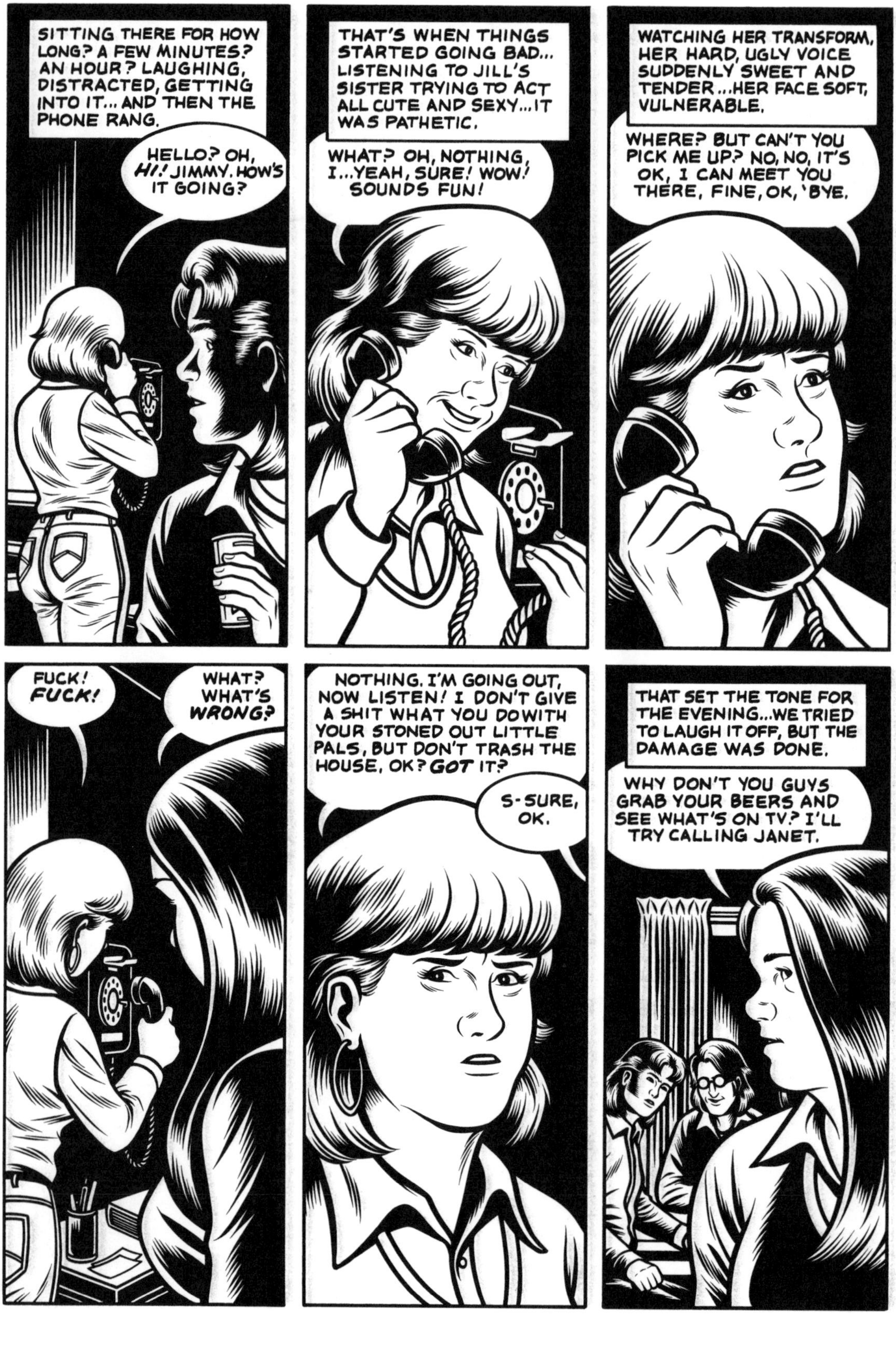
SITTING THERE FOR HOW LONG? A FEW MINUTES? AN HOUR? LAUGHING, DISTRACTED, GETTING INTO IT... AND THEN THE PHONE RANG.
HELLO? OH, HI! JIMMY. HOW'S IT GOING?
THAT'S WHEN THINGS STARTED GOING BAD... LISTENING TO JILL'S SISTER TRYING TO ACT ALL CUTE AND SEXY... IT WAS PATHETIC.
WHAT? OH, NOTHING, I...YEAH, SURE! WOW! SOUNDS FUN!
WATCHING HER TRANSFORM, HER HARD, UGLY VOICE SUDDENLY SWEET AND TENDER...HER FACE SOFT, VULNERABLE.
WHERE? BUT CAN'T YOU PICK ME UP? NO, NO, IT'S OK, I CAN MEET YOU THERE, FINE, OK, 'BYE.
FUCK! FUCK!
WHAT? WHAT'S WRONG?
NOTHING. I'M GOING OUT, NOW LISTEN! I DON'T GIVE A SHIT WHAT YOU DO WITH YOUR STONED OUT LITTLE PALS, BUT DON'T TRASH THE HOUSE, OK? GOT IT?
S-SURE, OK.
THAT SET THE TONE FOR THE EVENING...WE TRIED TO LAUGH IT OFF, BUT THE DAMAGE WAS DONE.
WHY DON'T YOU GUYS GRAB YOUR BEERS AND SEE WHAT'S ON TV? I'LL TRY CALLING JANET.

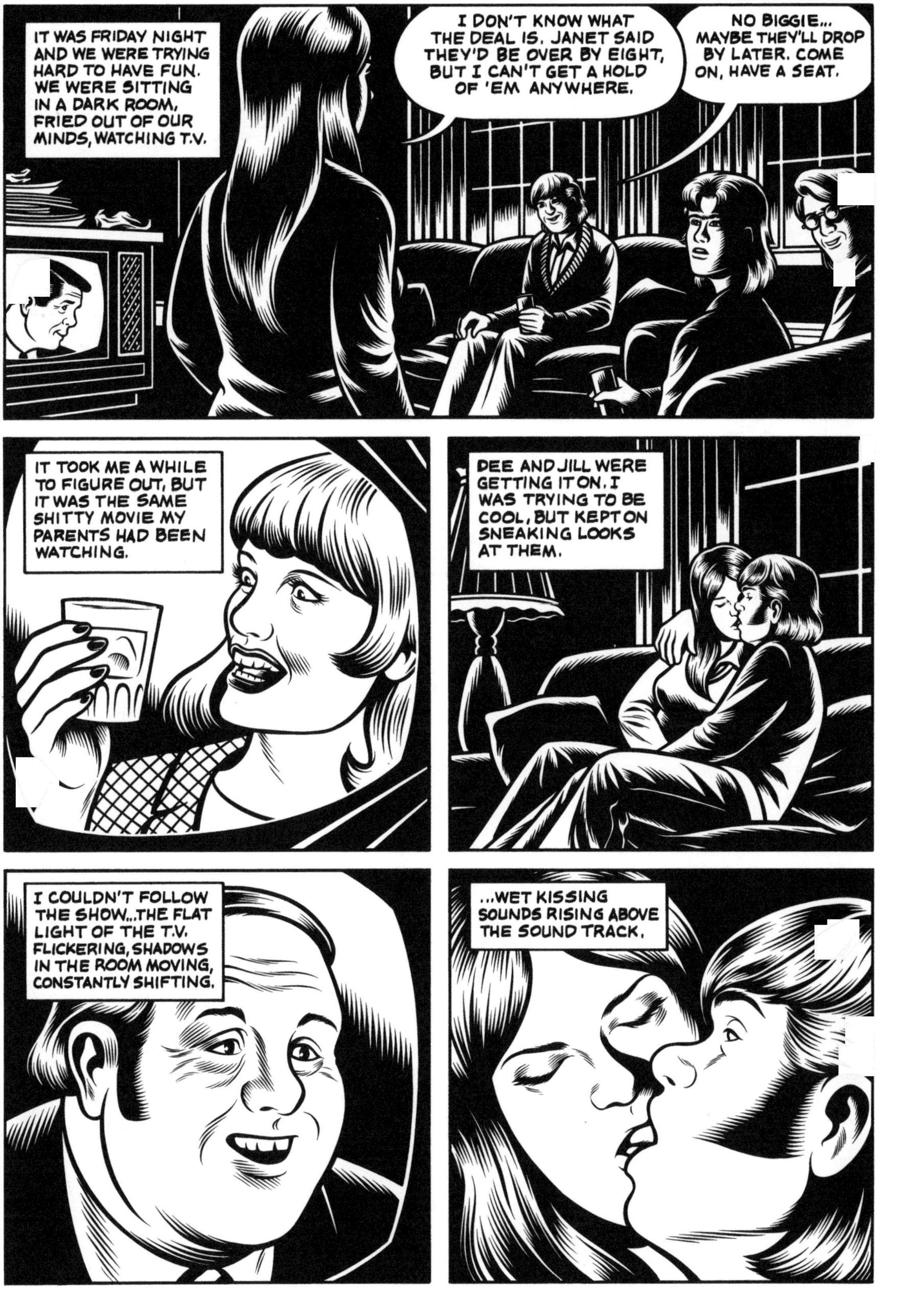
IT WAS FRIDAY NIGHT AND WE WERE TRYING HARD TO HAVE FUN. WE WERE SITTING IN A DARK ROOM, FRIED OUT OF OUR MINDS, WATCHING T.V.
I DON'T KNOW WHAT THE DEAL IS. JANET SAID THEY'D BE OVER BY EIGHT, BUT I CAN'T GET A HOLD OF 'EM ANYWHERE.
NO BIGGIE... MAYBE THEY'LL DROP BY LATER. COME ON, HAVE A SEAT.
IT TOOK ME A WHILE TO FIGURE OUT, BUT IT WAS THE SAME SHITTY MOVIE MY PARENTS HAD BEEN WATCHING.
DEE AND JILL WERE GETTING IT ON. I WAS TRYING TO BE COOL, BUT KEPT ON SNEAKING LOOKS AT THEM.
I COULDN'T FOLLOW THE SHOW...THE FLAT LIGHT OF THE T.V. FLICKERING, SHADOWS IN THE ROOM MOVING, CONSTANTLY SHIFTING.
...WET KISSING SOUNDS RISING ABOVE THE SOUND TRACK.

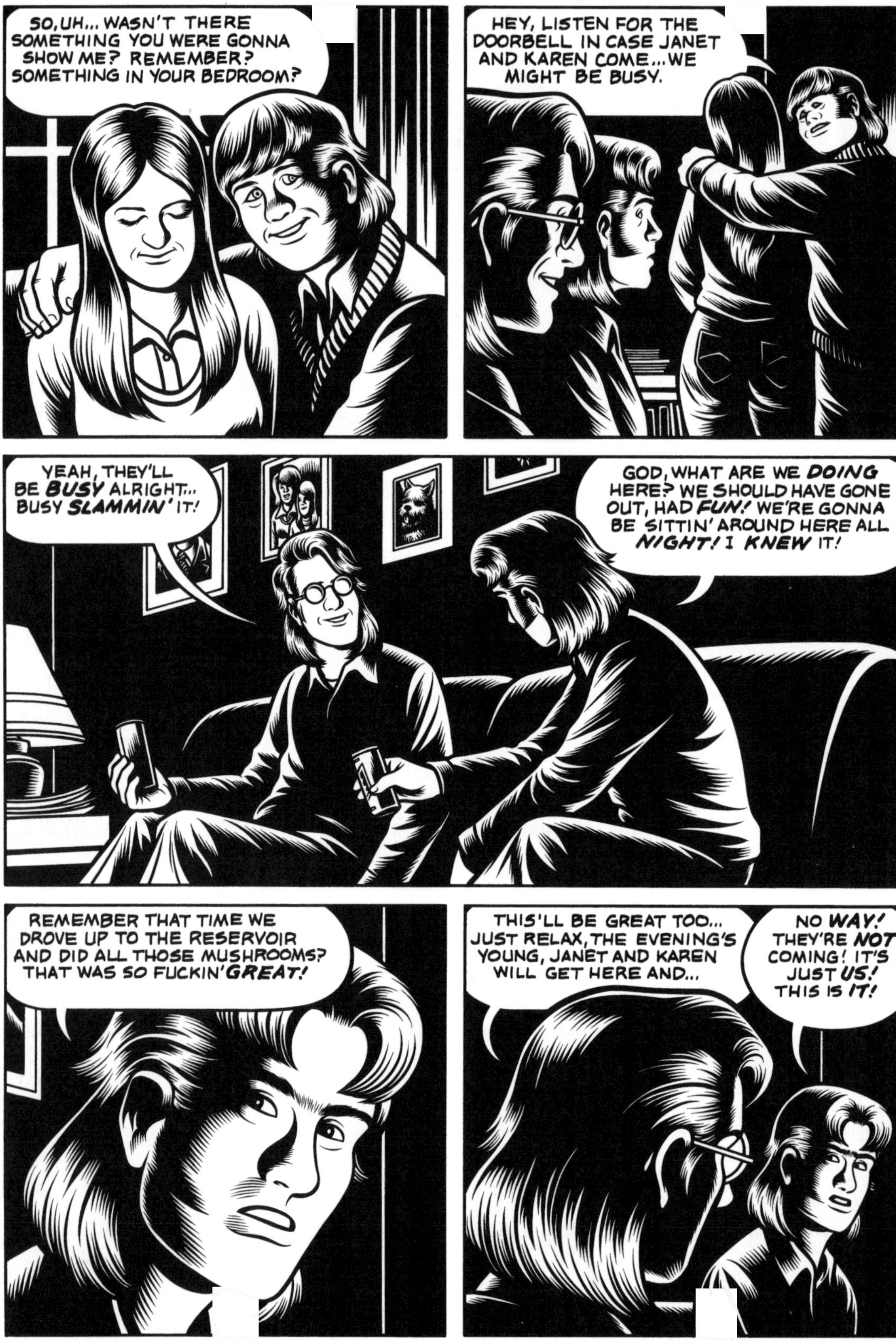
SO, UH... WASN'T THERE SOMETHING YOU WERE GONNA SHOW ME? REMEMBER? SOMETHING IN YOUR BEDROOM?
HEY, LISTEN FOR THE DOORBELL IN CASE JANET AND KAREN COME... WE MIGHT BE BUSY.
YEAH, THEY'LL BE *BUSY* ALRIGHT... BUSY *SLAMMIN'* IT!
GOD, WHAT ARE WE *DOING* HERE? WE SHOULD HAVE GONE OUT, HAD *FUN!* WE'RE GONNA BE SITTIN' AROUND HERE ALL *NIGHT!* I *KNEW* IT!
REMEMBER THAT TIME WE DROVE UP TO THE RESERVOIR AND DID ALL THOSE MUSHROOMS? THAT WAS SO FUCKIN' *GREAT!*
THIS'LL BE GREAT TOO... JUST RELAX, THE EVENING'S YOUNG, JANET AND KAREN WILL GET HERE AND...
NO *WAY!* THEY'RE *NOT* COMING! IT'S JUST *US!* THIS IS *IT!*

KEITH, LISTEN TO ME... YOU ALWAYS DO THIS! YOU ALWAYS WANT TO BE SOMEWHERE ELSE! WHAT ARE WE GONNA DO, JUST SPLIT? LEAVE DEE HERE?
I THOUGHT YOU WANTED TO HANG OUT. YOU'VE BEEN MOPING AROUND BY YOURSELF FOR A WEEK... TWO WEEKS! YOU'VE BEEN ACTING LIKE A TOTAL MARTYR!
...AND WHY? 'CAUSE THAT GIRL, SOME GIRL YOU HARDLY EVEN KNOW DIDN'T FALL MADLY IN LOVE WITH YOU!
YOU DON'T UNDERSTAND.
NO, YOU DON'T UNDERSTAND! SHE'S GONE! YOU NEVER HAD ANYTHING GOIN' WITH HER IN THE FIRST PLACE, AND EVEN IF YOU DID, SHE'S GOT THE BUG!
LOOK, JUST GET OVER IT, ALRIGHT? THINK ABOUT JANET AND KAREN. MAYBE THEY'RE A BIT LATE BUT SO WHAT? THEY'LL BE HERE.
HEY, WHERE YOU GOIN'?
I GOTTA TAKE A PISS... I'LL BE RIGHT BACK.

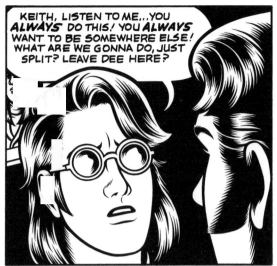

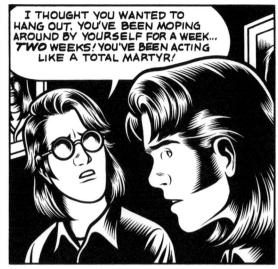

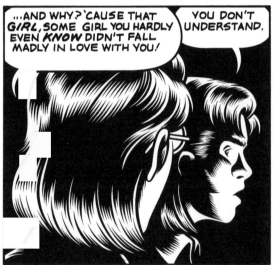

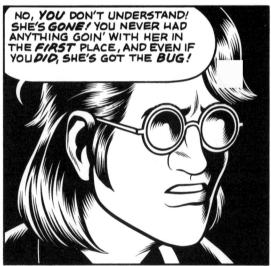

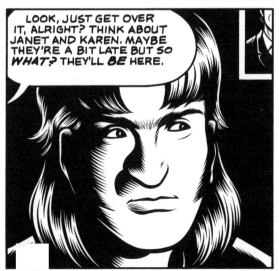

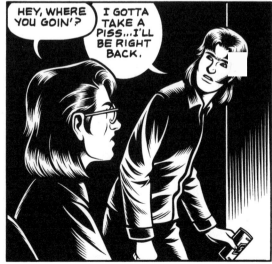

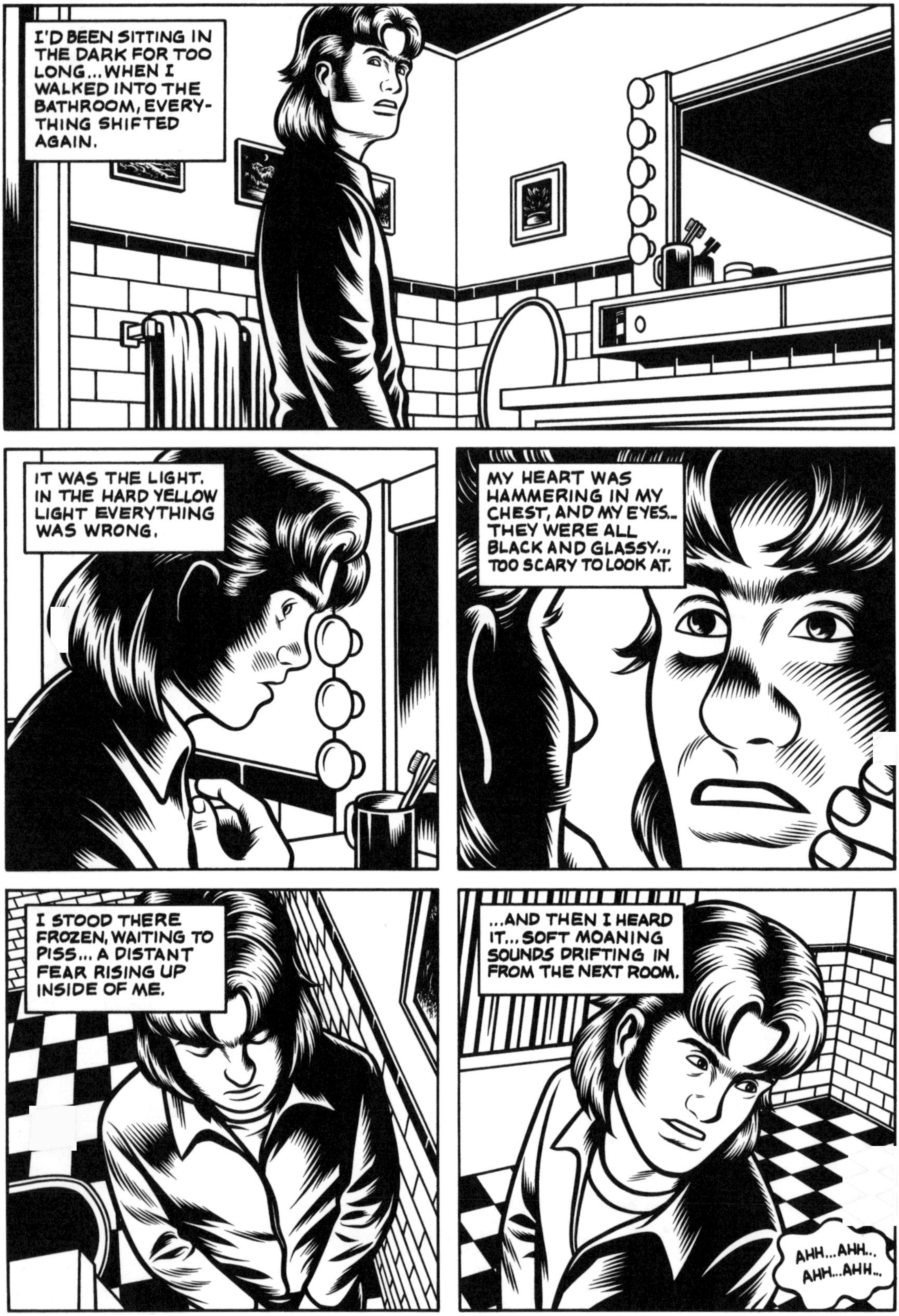
I'D BEEN SITTING IN THE DARK FOR TOO LONG... WHEN I WALKED INTO THE BATHROOM, EVERYTHING SHIFTED AGAIN.
IT WAS THE LIGHT. IN THE HARD YELLOW LIGHT EVERYTHING WAS WRONG.
MY HEART WAS HAMMERING IN MY CHEST, AND MY EYES.. THEY WERE ALL BLACK AND GLASSY... TOO SCARY TO LOOK AT.
I STOOD THERE FROZEN, WAITING TO PISS... A DISTANT FEAR RISING UP INSIDE OF ME.
...AND THEN I HEARD IT... SOFT MOANING SOUNDS DRIFTING IN FROM THE NEXT ROOM.
AHH...AHH... AHH...AHH...

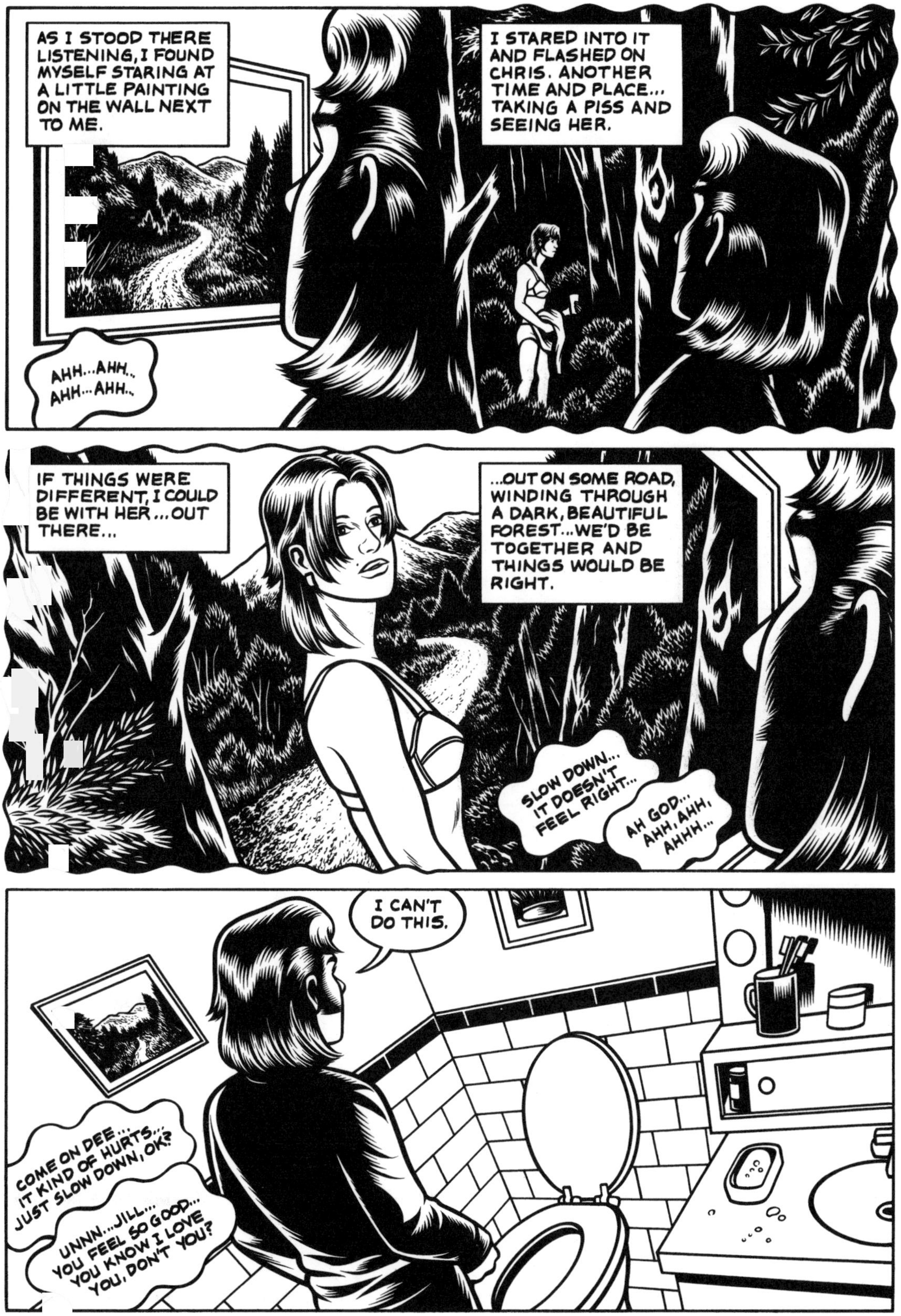

AS I STOOD THERE LISTENING, I FOUND MYSELF STARING AT A LITTLE PAINTING ON THE WALL NEXT TO ME.
AHH...AHH.. AHH...AHH..
I STARED INTO IT AND FLASHED ON CHRIS. ANOTHER TIME AND PLACE... TAKING A PISS AND SEEING HER.
IF THINGS WERE DIFFERENT, I COULD BE WITH HER...OUT THERE...
...OUT ON SOME ROAD, WINDING THROUGH A DARK, BEAUTIFUL FOREST...WE'D BE TOGETHER AND THINGS WOULD BE RIGHT.
SLOW DOWN... IT DOESN'T FEEL RIGHT...
AH GOD... AHH, AHH, AHHH...
I CAN'T DO THIS.
COME ON DEE... IT KIND OF HURTS... JUST SLOW DOWN, OK?
UNNN...JILL... YOU FEEL SO GOOD... YOU KNOW I LOVE YOU, DON'T YOU?

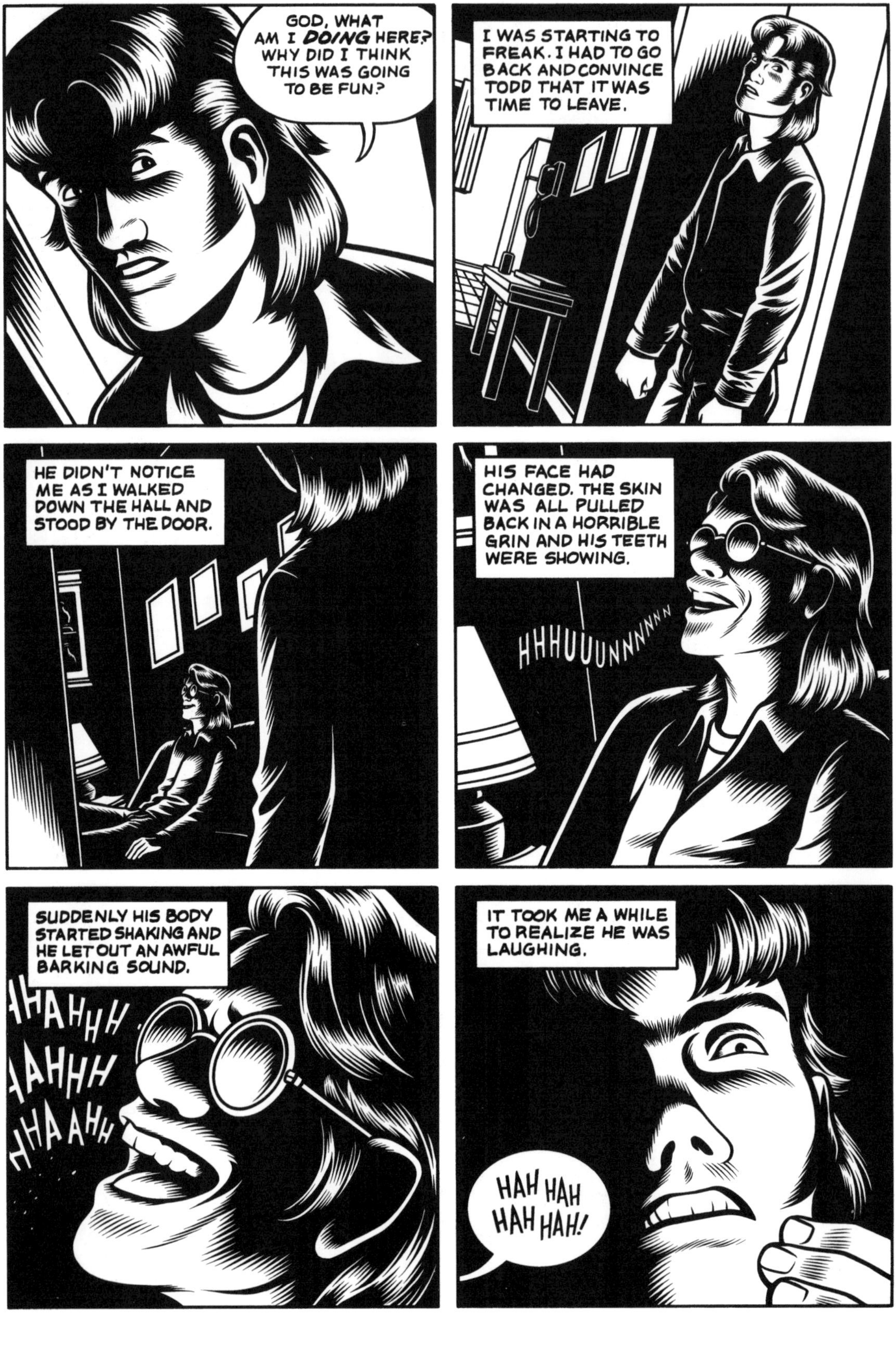
GOD, WHAT AM I DOING HERE? WHY DID I THINK THIS WAS GOING TO BE FUN?
I WAS STARTING TO FREAK. I HAD TO GO BACK AND CONVINCE TODD THAT IT WAS TIME TO LEAVE.
HE DIDN'T NOTICE ME AS I WALKED DOWN THE HALL AND STOOD BY THE DOOR.
HIS FACE HAD CHANGED. THE SKIN WAS ALL PULLED BACK IN A HORRIBLE GRIN AND HIS TEETH WERE SHOWING.
HHHUUUNNNNNN
SUDDENLY HIS BODY STARTED SHAKING AND HE LET OUT AN AWFUL BARKING SOUND.
HAHHH AHHHH HHA AHH
IT TOOK ME A WHILE TO REALIZE HE WAS LAUGHING.
HAH HAH HAH HAH!

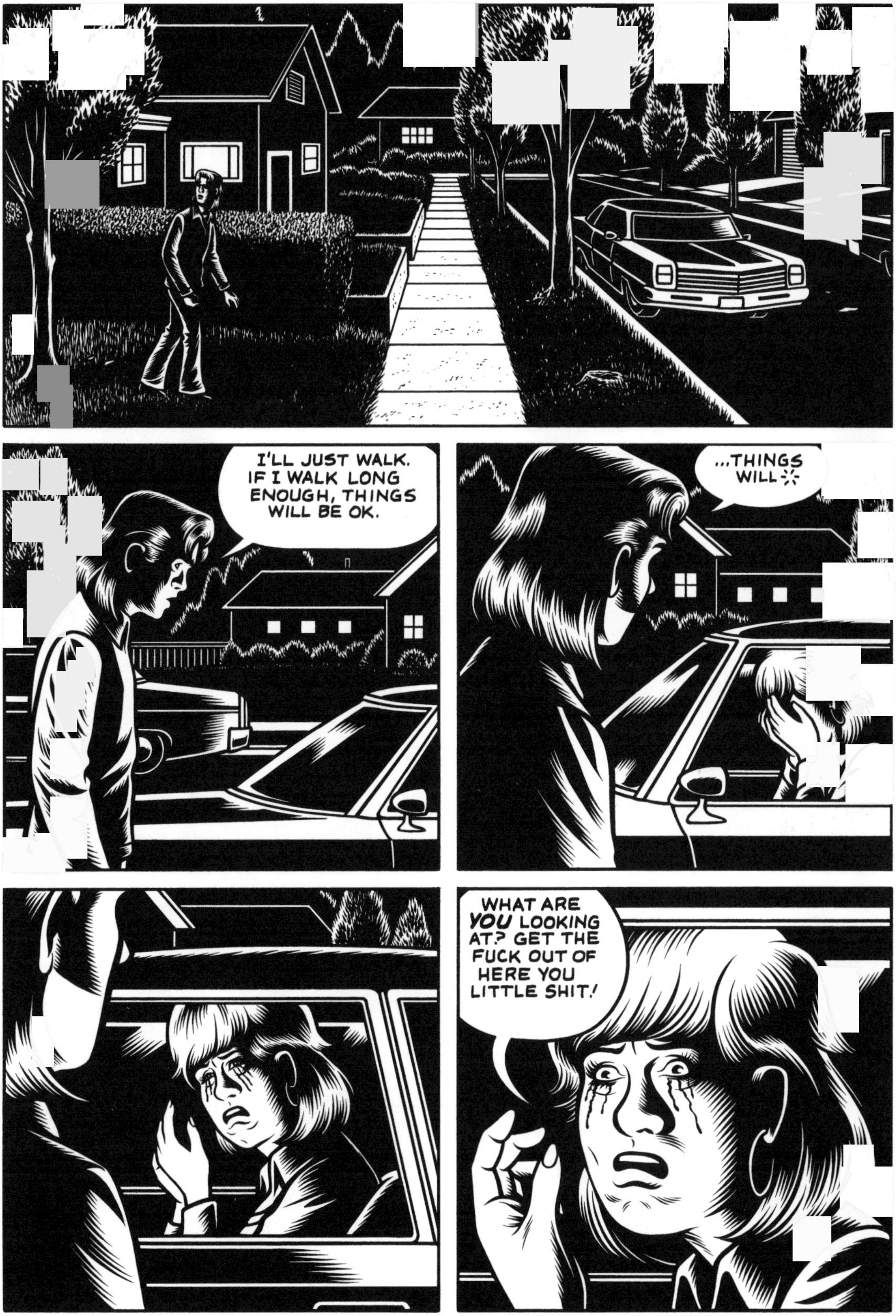
I'LL JUST WALK. IF I WALK LONG ENOUGH, THINGS WILL BE OK.
...THINGS WILL
WHAT ARE YOU LOOKING AT? GET THE FUCK OUT OF HERE YOU LITTLE SHIT!

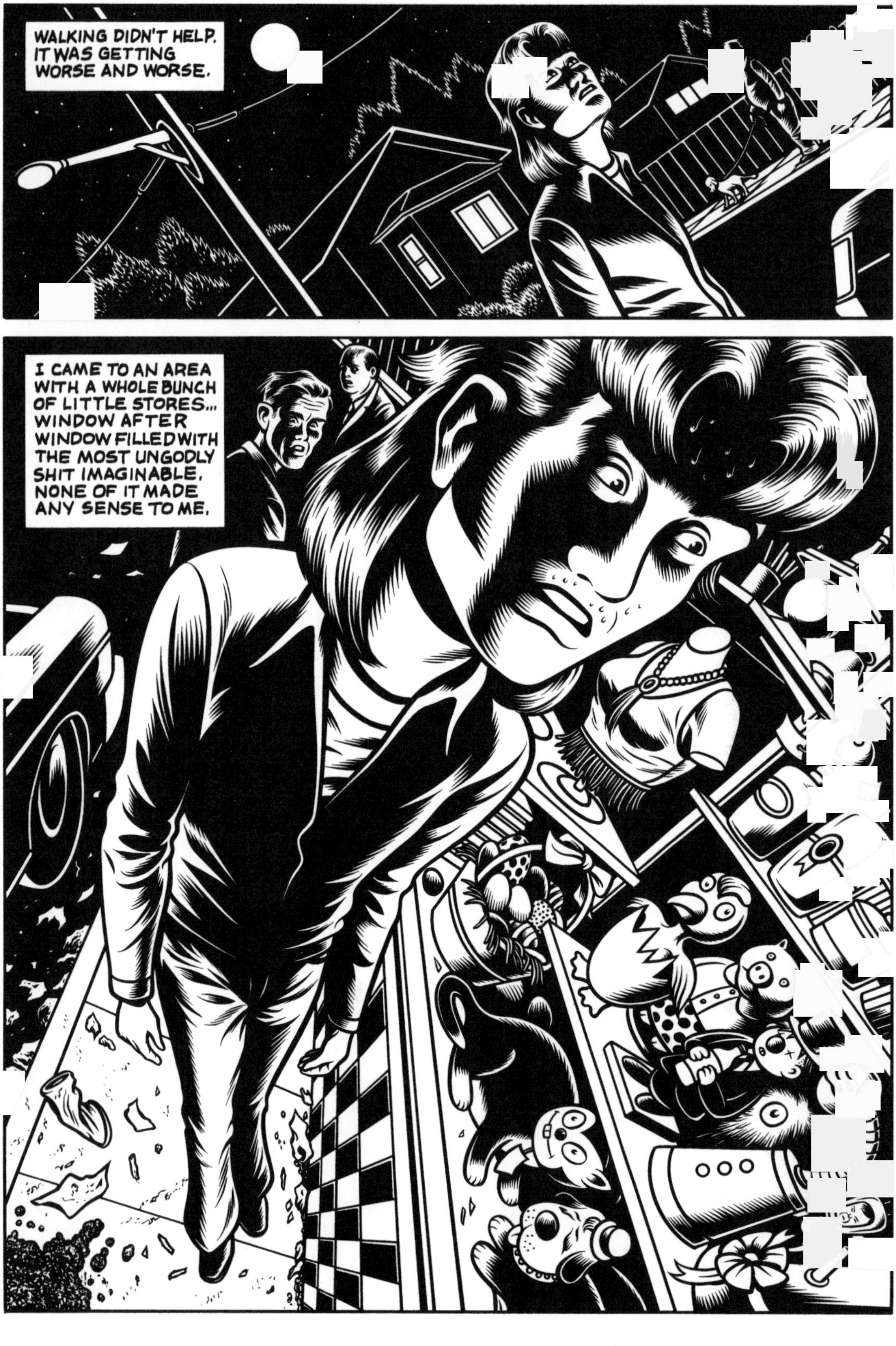
WALKING DIDN'T HELP. IT WAS GETTING WORSE AND WORSE.
I CAME TO AN AREA WITH A WHOLE BUNCH OF LITTLE STORES... WINDOW AFTER WINDOW FILLED WITH THE MOST UNGODLY SHIT IMAGINABLE. NONE OF IT MADE ANY SENSE TO ME.

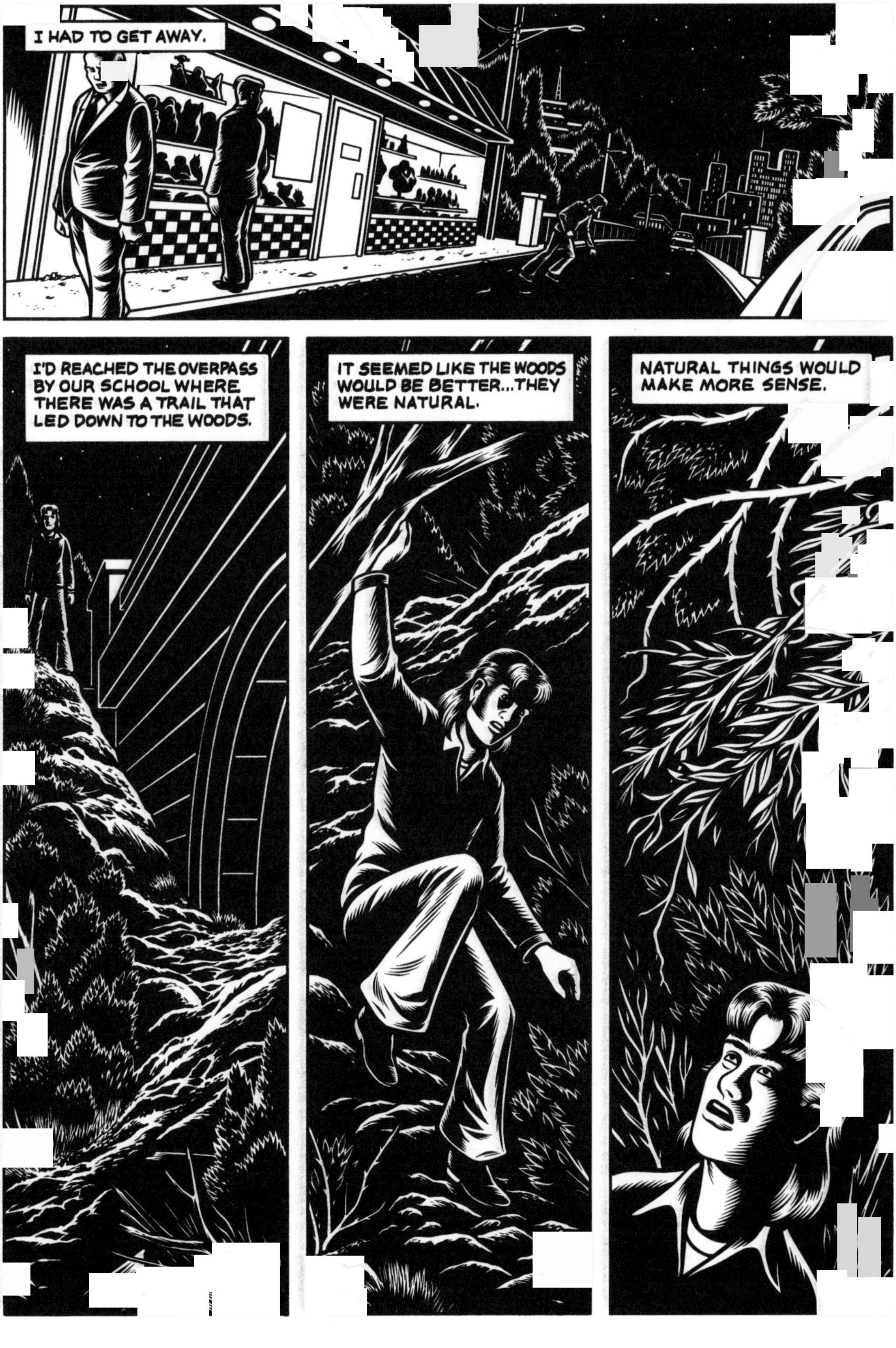
I HAD TO GET AWAY.
I'D REACHED THE OVERPASS BY OUR SCHOOL WHERE THERE WAS A TRAIL THAT LED DOWN TO THE WOODS.
IT SEEMED LIKE THE WOODS WOULD BE BETTER... THEY WERE NATURAL.
NATURAL THINGS WOULD MAKE MORE SENSE.

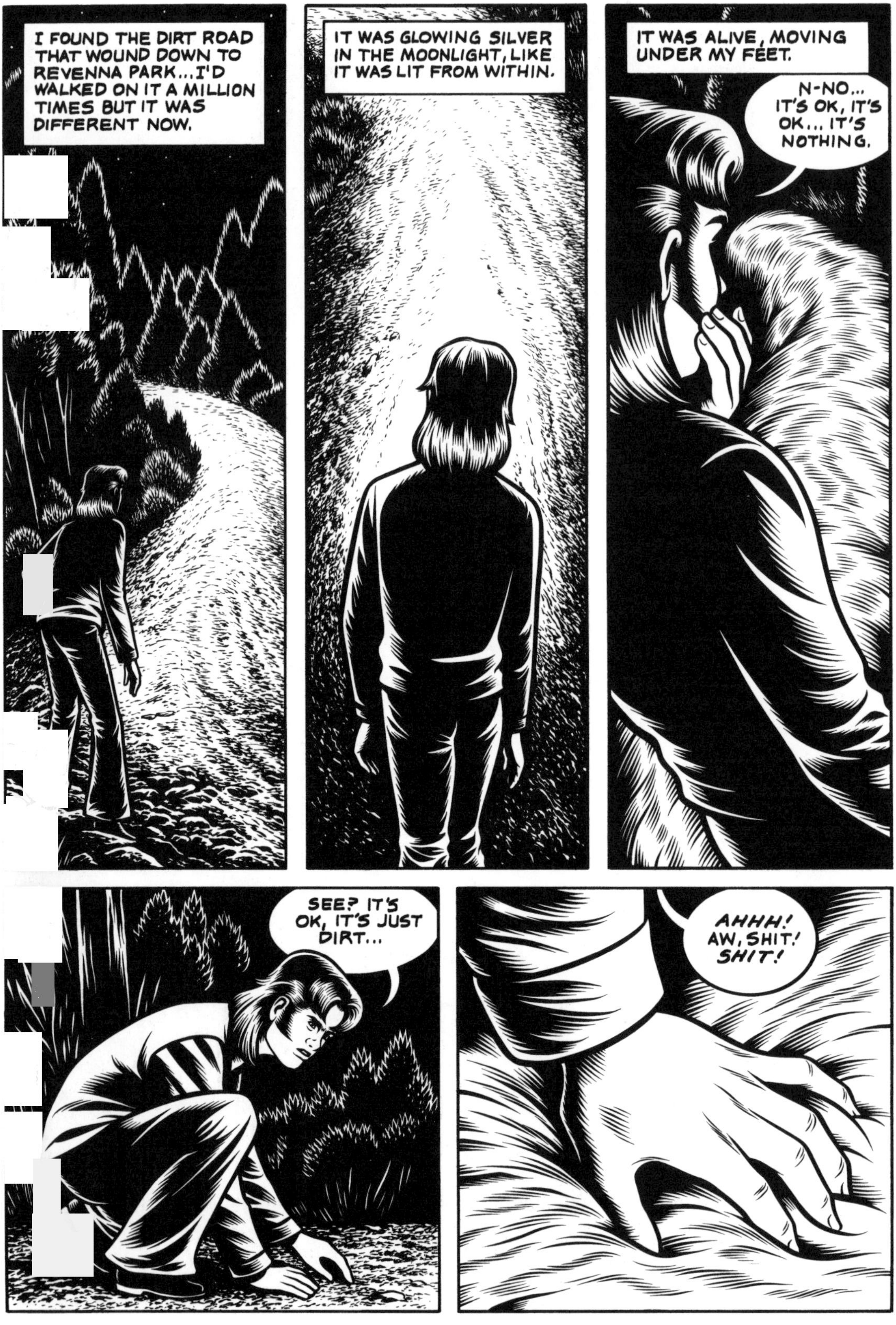
I FOUND THE DIRT ROAD THAT WOUND DOWN TO REVENNA PARK... I'D WALKED ON IT A MILLION TIMES BUT IT WAS DIFFERENT NOW.
IT WAS GLOWING SILVER IN THE MOONLIGHT, LIKE IT WAS LIT FROM WITHIN.
IT WAS ALIVE, MOVING UNDER MY FEET.
N-NO... IT'S OK, IT'S OK... IT'S NOTHING.
SEE? IT'S OK, IT'S JUST DIRT...
AHHH! AW, SHIT! SHIT!

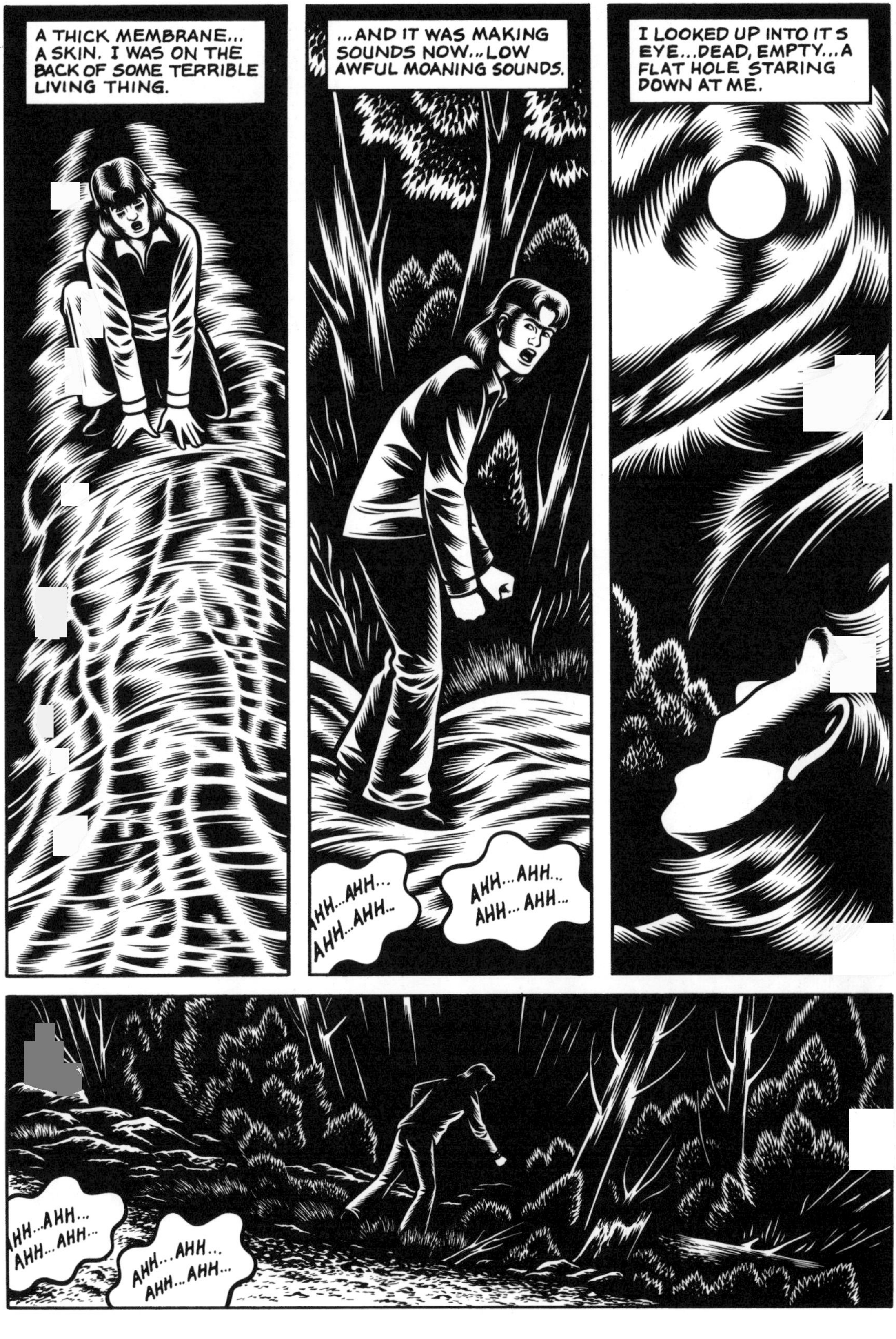
A THICK MEMBRANE... A SKIN. I WAS ON THE BACK OF SOME TERRIBLE LIVING THING.
...AND IT WAS MAKING SOUNDS NOW... LOW AWFUL MOANING SOUNDS.
AHH...AHH... AHH...AHH...
AHH...AHH... AHH...AHH...
I LOOKED UP INTO ITS EYE...DEAD, EMPTY...A FLAT HOLE STARING DOWN AT ME.
AHH...AHH... AHH...AHH...
AHH...AHH... AHH...AHH...

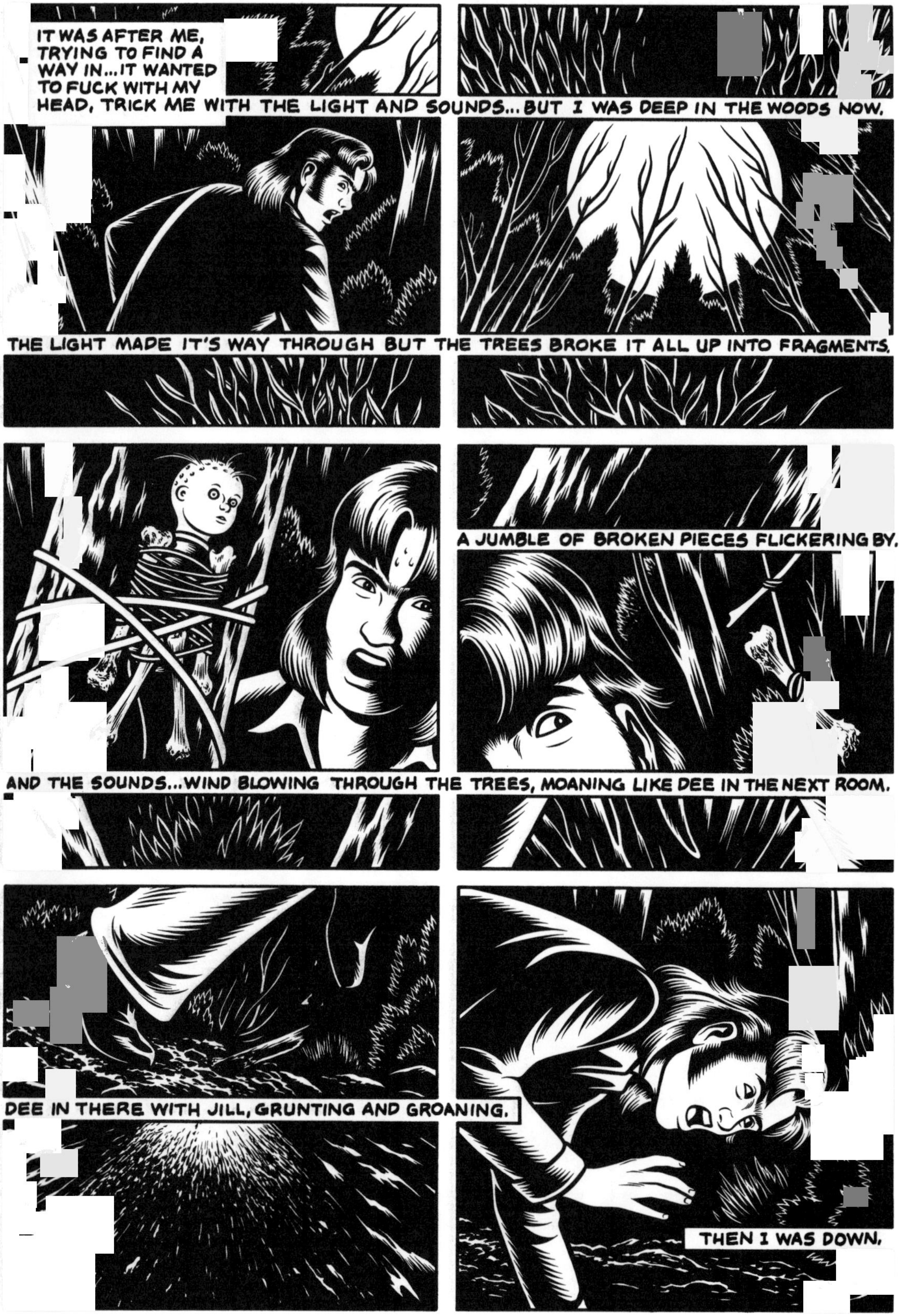
IT WAS AFTER ME, TRYING TO FIND A WAY IN... IT WANTED TO FUCK WITH MY HEAD, TRICK ME WITH THE LIGHT AND SOUNDS... BUT I WAS DEEP IN THE WOODS NOW.
THE LIGHT MADE IT'S WAY THROUGH BUT THE TREES BROKE IT ALL UP INTO FRAGMENTS.
A JUMBLE OF BROKEN PIECES FLICKERING BY.
AND THE SOUNDS... WIND BLOWING THROUGH THE TREES, MOANING LIKE DEE IN THE NEXT ROOM.
DEE IN THERE WITH JILL, GRUNTING AND GROANING.
THEN I WAS DOWN.

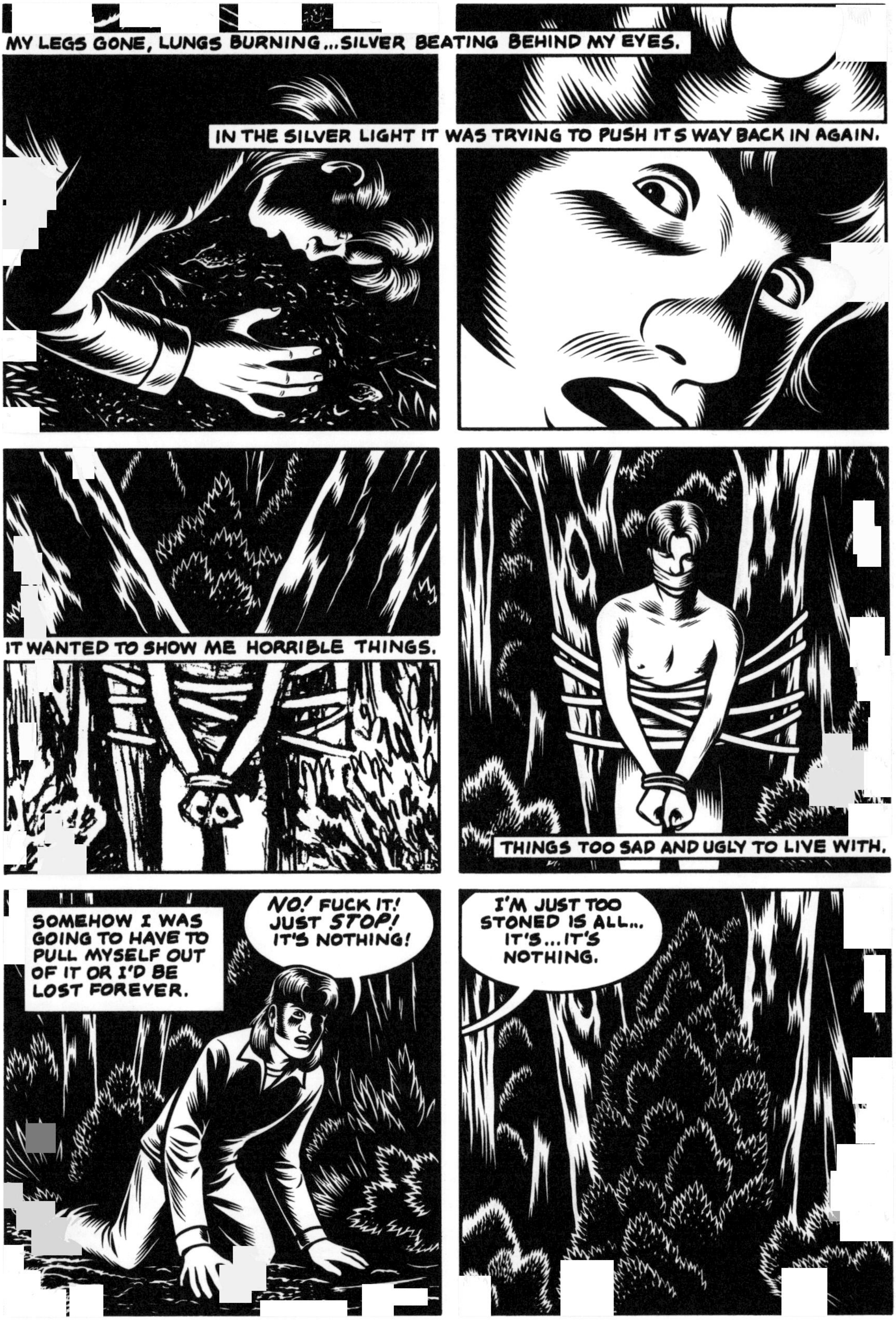
MY LEGS GONE, LUNGS BURNING... SILVER BEATING BEHIND MY EYES.
IN THE SILVER LIGHT IT WAS TRYING TO PUSH ITS WAY BACK IN AGAIN.
IT WANTED TO SHOW ME HORRIBLE THINGS.
THINGS TOO SAD AND UGLY TO LIVE WITH.
SOMEHOW I WAS GOING TO HAVE TO PULL MYSELF OUT OF IT OR I'D BE LOST FOREVER.
NO! FUCK IT! JUST STOP! IT'S NOTHING!
I'M JUST TOO STONED IS ALL... IT'S... IT'S NOTHING.

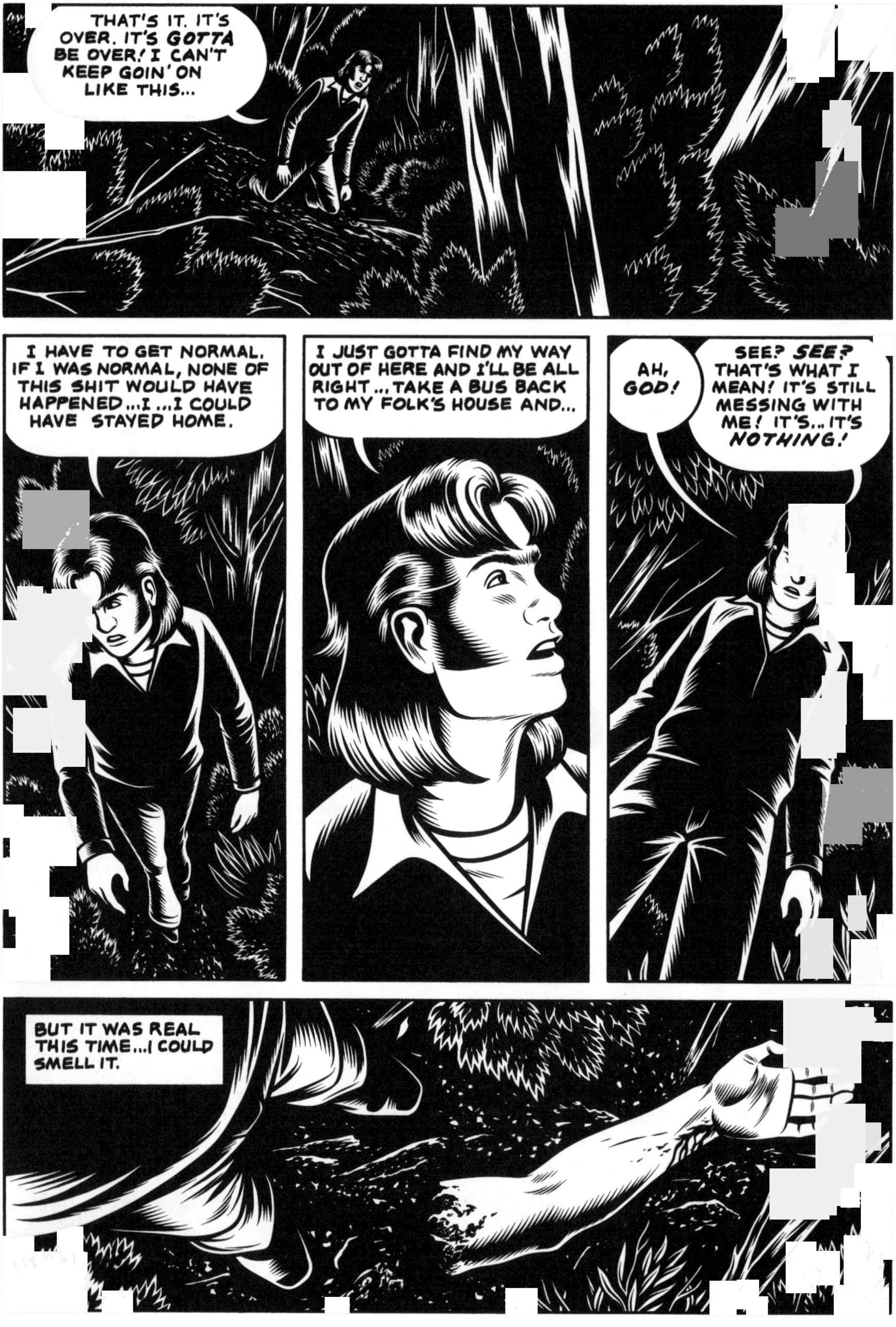
THAT'S IT. IT'S OVER. IT'S GOTTA BE OVER! I CAN'T KEEP GOIN' ON LIKE THIS...
I HAVE TO GET NORMAL. IF I WAS NORMAL, NONE OF THIS SHIT WOULD HAVE HAPPENED...I...I COULD HAVE STAYED HOME.
I JUST GOTTA FIND MY WAY OUT OF HERE AND I'LL BE ALL RIGHT...TAKE A BUS BACK TO MY FOLK'S HOUSE AND...
AH, GOD!
SEE? SEE? THAT'S WHAT I MEAN! IT'S STILL MESSING WITH ME! IT'S...IT'S NOTHING!
BUT IT WAS REAL THIS TIME...I COULD SMELL IT.

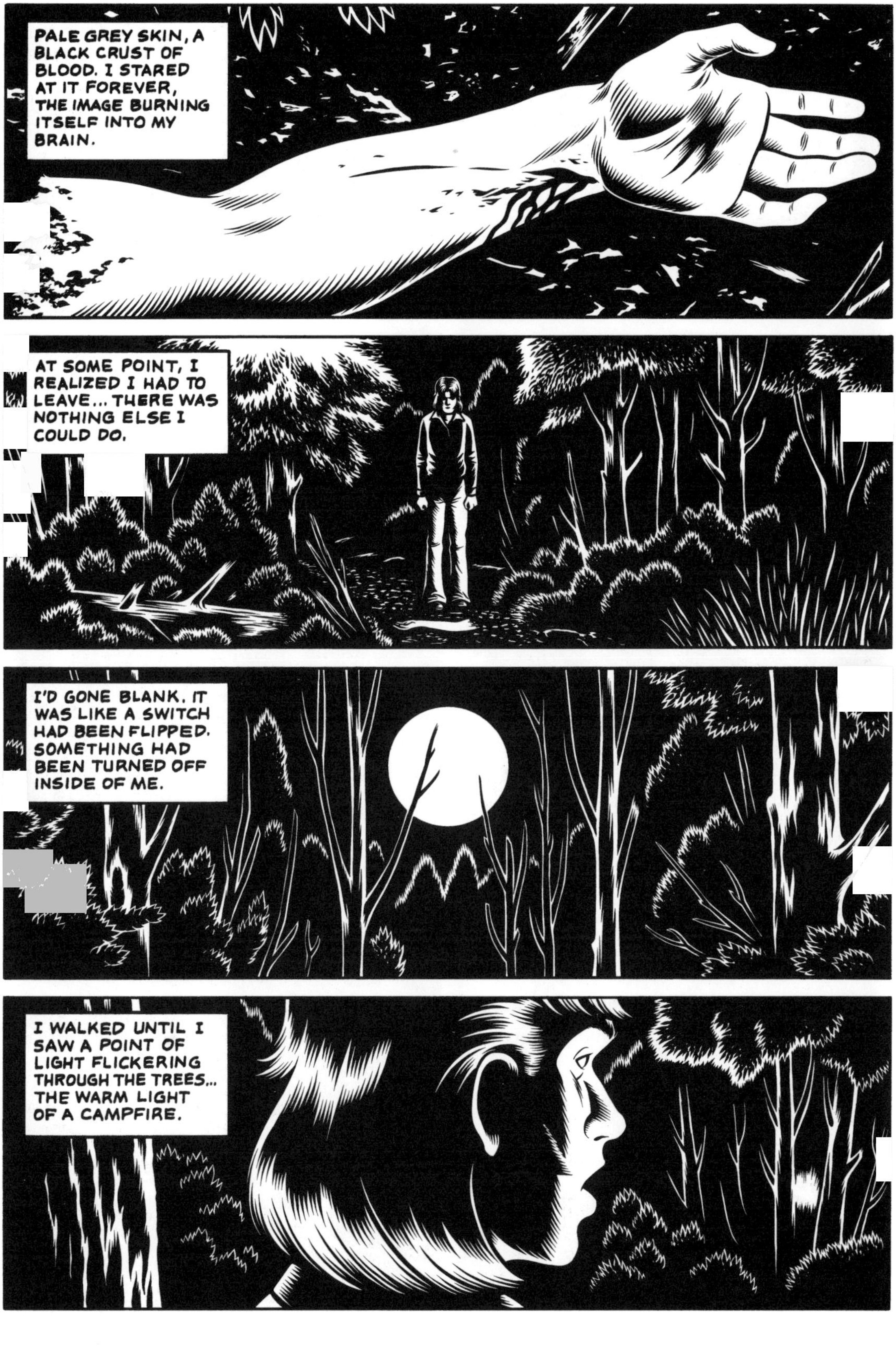
PALE GREY SKIN, A BLACK CRUST OF BLOOD. I STARED AT IT FOREVER, THE IMAGE BURNING ITSELF INTO MY BRAIN.
AT SOME POINT, I REALIZED I HAD TO LEAVE... THERE WAS NOTHING ELSE I COULD DO.
I'D GONE BLANK. IT WAS LIKE A SWITCH HAD BEEN FLIPPED. SOMETHING HAD BEEN TURNED OFF INSIDE OF ME.
I WALKED UNTIL I SAW A POINT OF LIGHT FLICKERING THROUGH THE TREES... THE WARM LIGHT OF A CAMPFIRE.

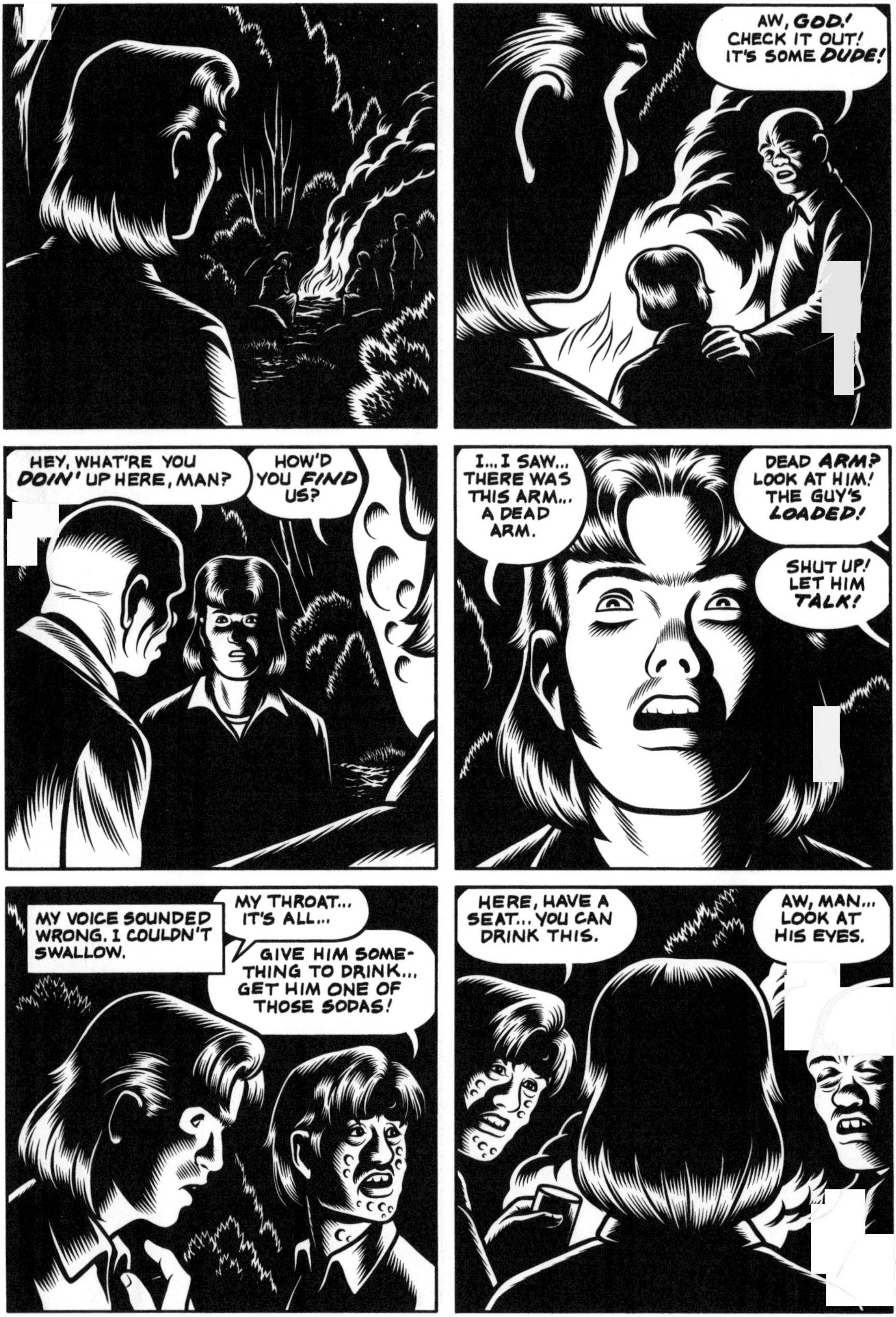

AW, GOD! CHECK IT OUT! IT'S SOME DUDE!
HEY, WHAT'RE YOU DOIN' UP HERE, MAN?
HOW'D YOU FIND US?
I... I SAW... THERE WAS THIS ARM... A DEAD ARM.
DEAD ARM? LOOK AT HIM! THE GUY'S LOADED!
SHUT UP! LET HIM TALK!
MY VOICE SOUNDED WRONG. I COULDN'T SWALLOW.
MY THROAT... IT'S ALL...
GIVE HIM SOMETHING TO DRINK... GET HIM ONE OF THOSE SODAS!
HERE, HAVE A SEAT... YOU CAN DRINK THIS.
AW, MAN... LOOK AT HIS EYES.

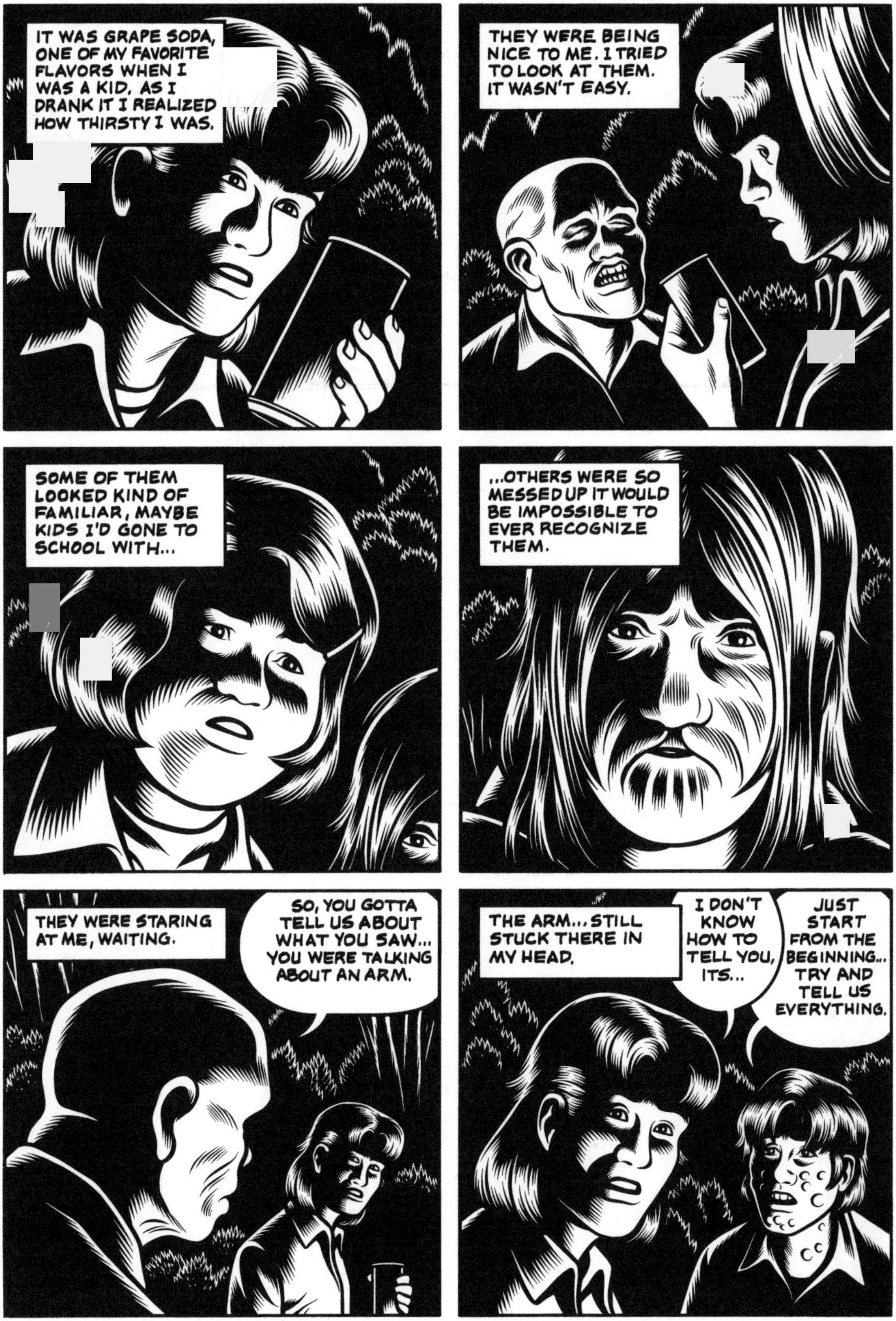
IT WAS GRAPE SODA, ONE OF MY FAVORITE FLAVORS WHEN I WAS A KID. AS I DRANK IT I REALIZED HOW THIRSTY I WAS.
THEY WERE BEING NICE TO ME. I TRIED TO LOOK AT THEM. IT WASN'T EASY.
SOME OF THEM LOOKED KIND OF FAMILIAR, MAYBE KIDS I'D GONE TO SCHOOL WITH...
...OTHERS WERE SO MESSED UP IT WOULD BE IMPOSSIBLE TO EVER RECOGNIZE THEM.
THEY WERE STARING AT ME, WAITING.
SO, YOU GOTTA TELL US ABOUT WHAT YOU SAW... YOU WERE TALKING ABOUT AN ARM.
THE ARM... STILL STUCK THERE IN MY HEAD.
I DON'T KNOW HOW TO TELL YOU, ITS...
JUST START FROM THE BEGINNING... TRY AND TELL US EVERYTHING.

AS I STARTED TO TALK, I FELT SOMETHING SWELLING IN MY CHEST, STRAINING TO GET OUT.

MY FRIENDS AND I... WE UH, WE DID SOME DRUGS TONIGHT AND... THINGS STARTED GOING BAD.

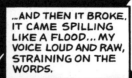

...AND THEN IT BROKE, IT CAME SPILLING LIKE A FLOOD... MY VOICE LOUD AND RAW, STRAINING ON THE WORDS.

OK, OK, I *KNOW*... THINGS HAVE BEEN WRONG FOR A LONG TIME, BUT THIS WAS *DIFFERENT*, RIGHT? THIS WAS...TOO MUCH!

I DON'T KNOW WHY, BUT I FELT LIKE I HAD TO TELL THEM EVERYTHING.

...AND WHEN I WALKED OUT, HER SISTER WAS SITTING THERE IN THE CAR CRYING...H-HER MAKE UP ALL RUNNING DOWN HER FACE...

EVERYTHING. EVERY LAST DETAIL.

...BUT I WASN'T SEEING THINGS THIS TIME...IT WAS REAL. YOU COULD SMELL IT... THIS AWFUL SMELL OF ROTTEN MEAT.

WHEN I WAS DONE I WAS EMPTY. IT WAS SILENT EXCEPT FOR THE CRACKLING OF THE FIRE.

IT WAS FINALLY ALL OUT OF ME...I WAS AS PURE AND EMPTY AS THE FLAMES MOVING IN FRONT OF ME.

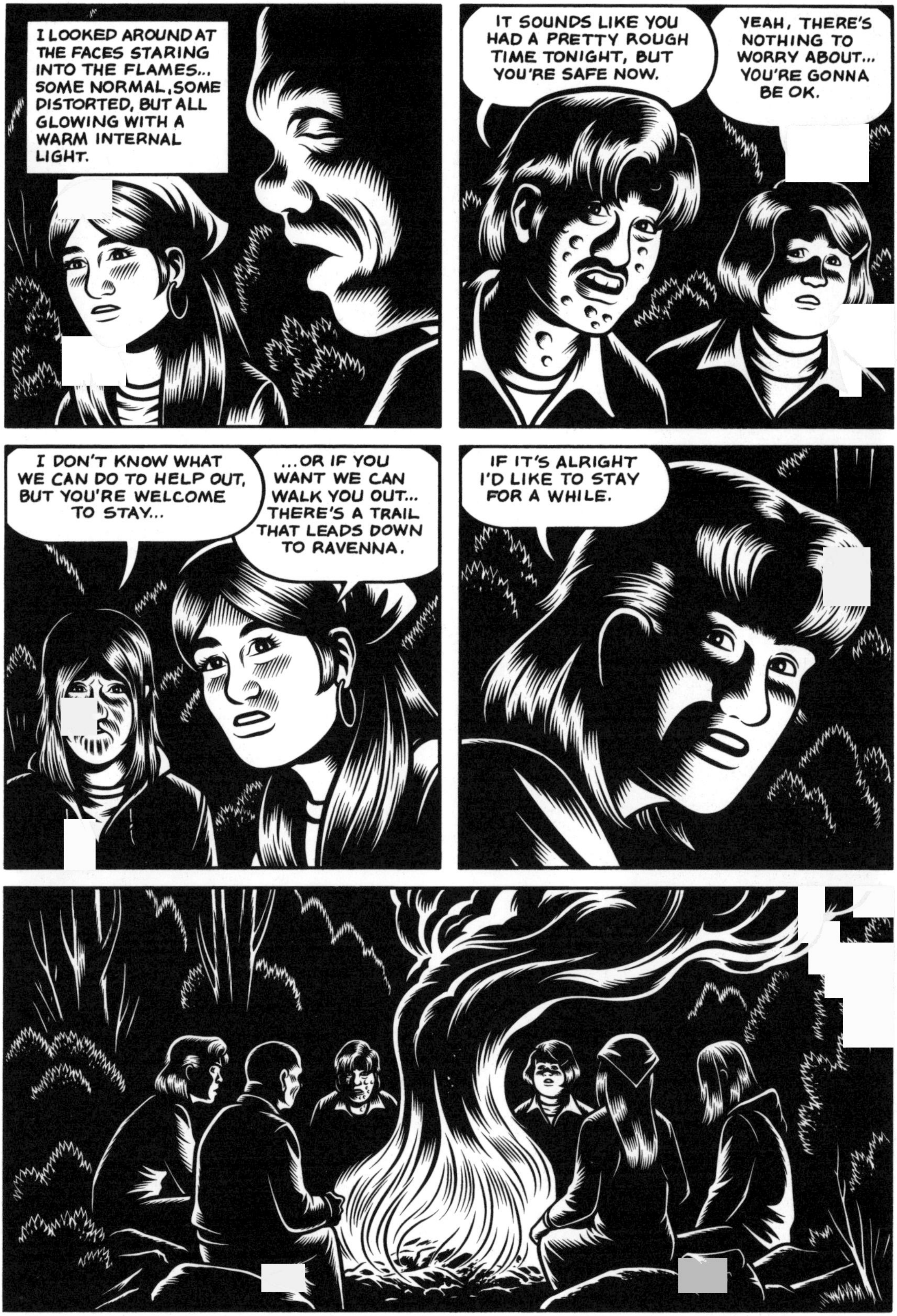
I LOOKED AROUND AT THE FACES STARING INTO THE FLAMES... SOME NORMAL, SOME DISTORTED, BUT ALL GLOWING WITH A WARM INTERNAL LIGHT.
IT SOUNDS LIKE YOU HAD A PRETTY ROUGH TIME TONIGHT, BUT YOU'RE SAFE NOW.
YEAH, THERE'S NOTHING TO WORRY ABOUT... YOU'RE GONNA BE OK.
I DON'T KNOW WHAT WE CAN DO TO HELP OUT, BUT YOU'RE WELCOME TO STAY...
...OR IF YOU WANT WE CAN WALK YOU OUT... THERE'S A TRAIL THAT LEADS DOWN TO RAVENNA.
IF IT'S ALRIGHT I'D LIKE TO STAY FOR A WHILE.

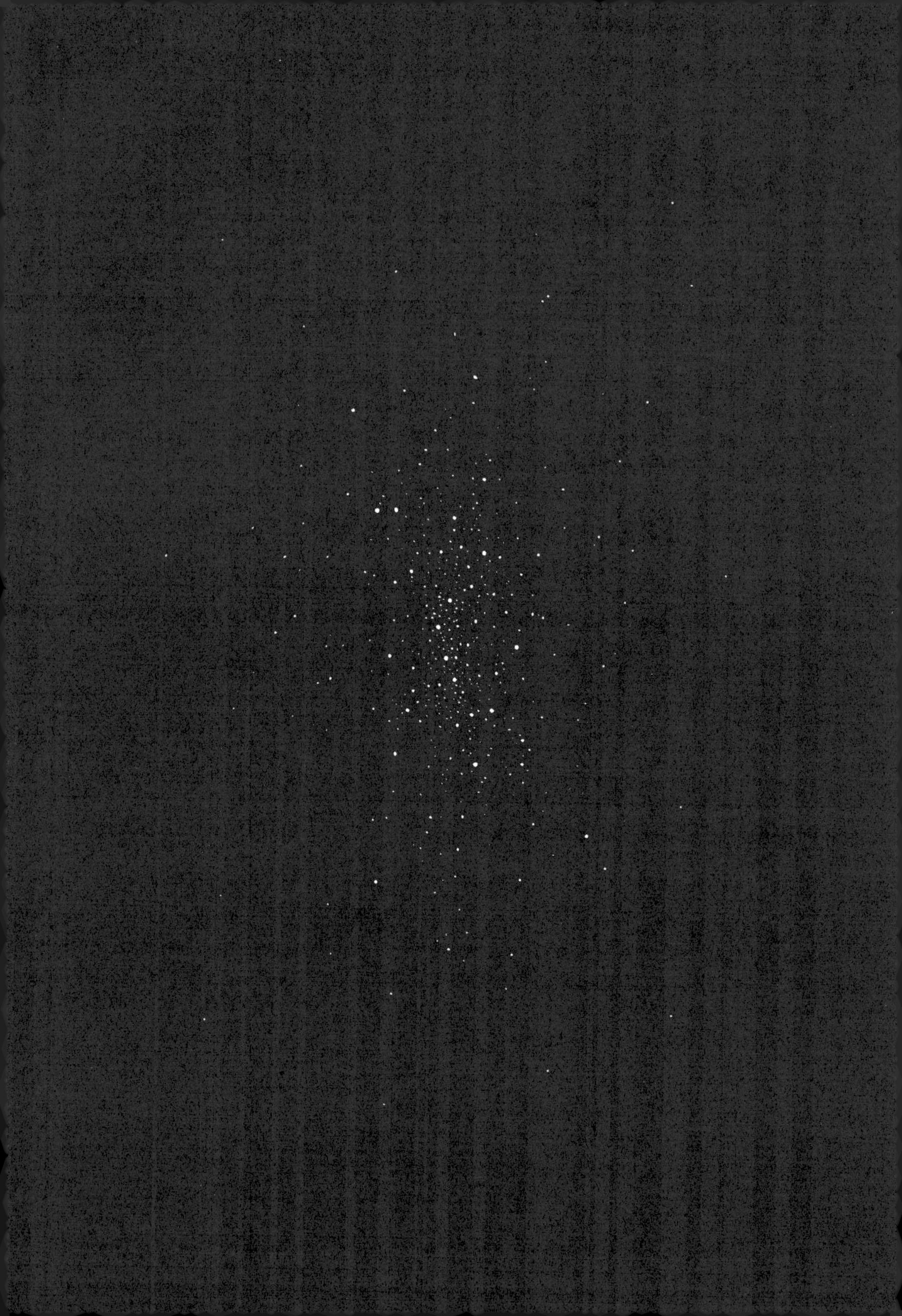

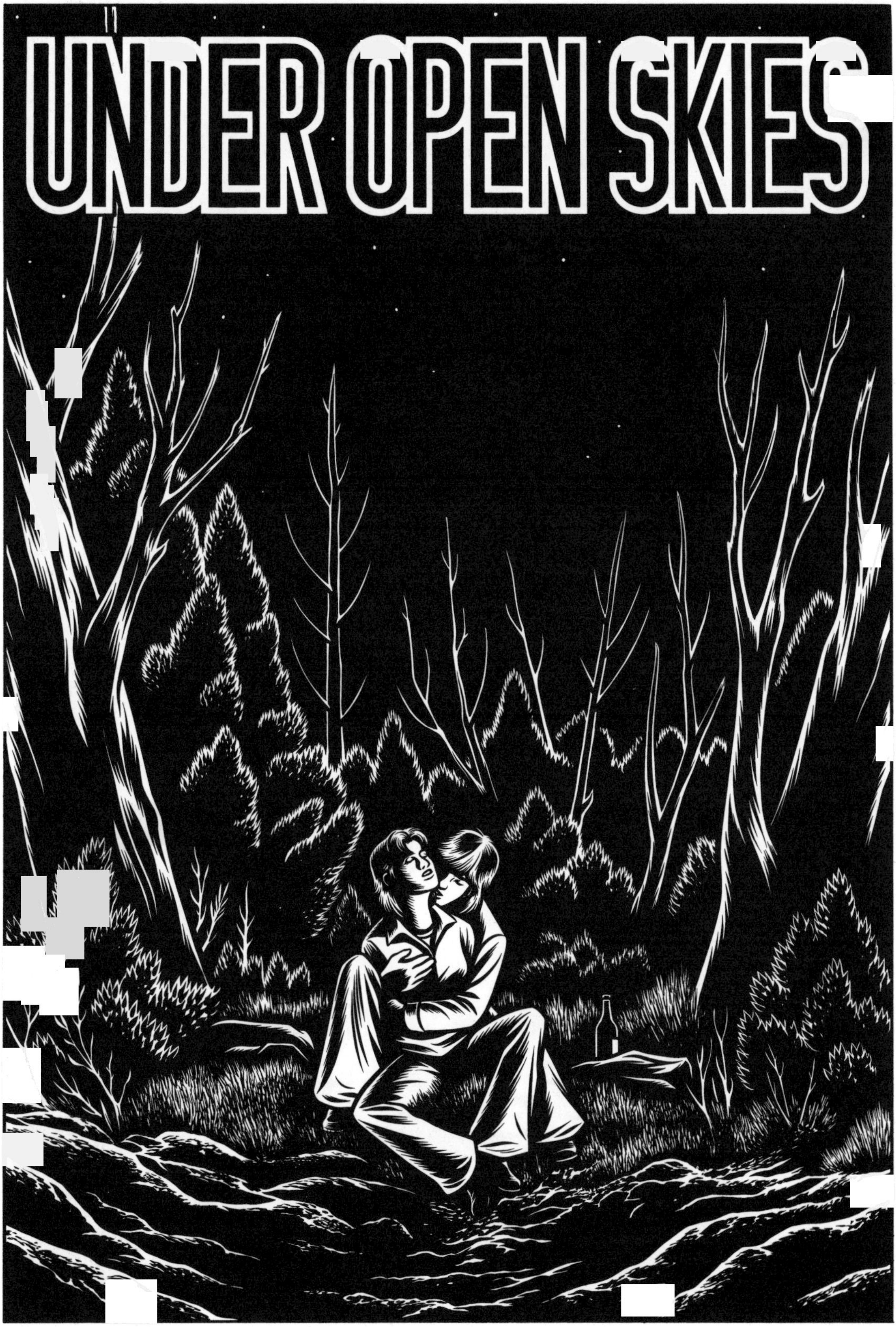
UNDER OPEN SKIES

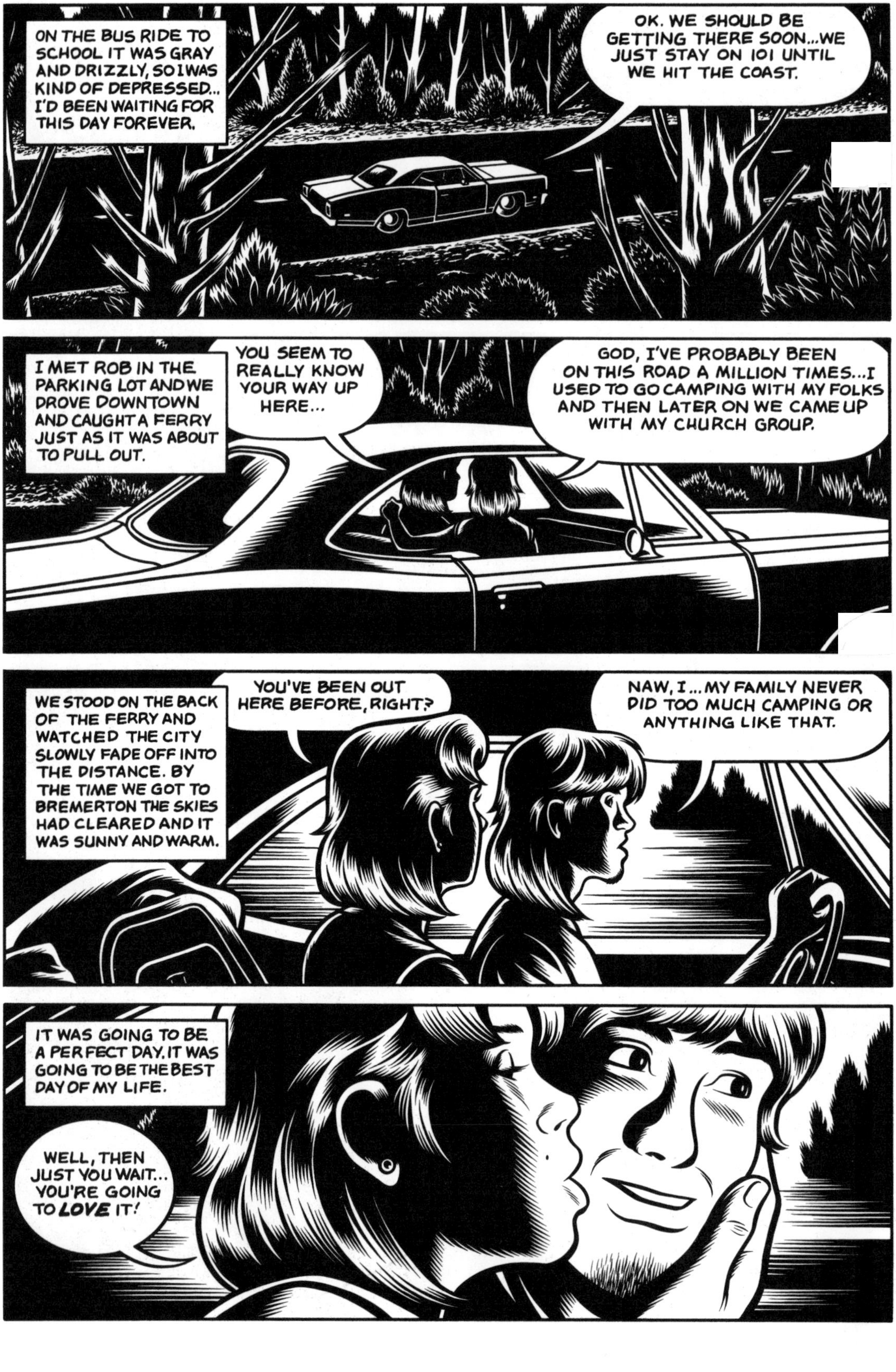
ON THE BUS RIDE TO SCHOOL IT WAS GRAY AND DRIZZLY, SO I WAS KIND OF DEPRESSED... I'D BEEN WAITING FOR THIS DAY FOREVER.
OK. WE SHOULD BE GETTING THERE SOON...WE JUST STAY ON 101 UNTIL WE HIT THE COAST.
I MET ROB IN THE PARKING LOT AND WE DROVE DOWNTOWN AND CAUGHT A FERRY JUST AS IT WAS ABOUT TO PULL OUT.
YOU SEEM TO REALLY KNOW YOUR WAY UP HERE...
GOD, I'VE PROBABLY BEEN ON THIS ROAD A MILLION TIMES...I USED TO GO CAMPING WITH MY FOLKS AND THEN LATER ON WE CAME UP WITH MY CHURCH GROUP.
WE STOOD ON THE BACK OF THE FERRY AND WATCHED THE CITY SLOWLY FADE OFF INTO THE DISTANCE. BY THE TIME WE GOT TO BREMERTON THE SKIES HAD CLEARED AND IT WAS SUNNY AND WARM.
YOU'VE BEEN OUT HERE BEFORE, RIGHT?
NAW, I... MY FAMILY NEVER DID TOO MUCH CAMPING OR ANYTHING LIKE THAT.
IT WAS GOING TO BE A PERFECT DAY. IT WAS GOING TO BE THE BEST DAY OF MY LIFE.
WELL, THEN JUST YOU WAIT... YOU'RE GOING TO *LOVE* IT!

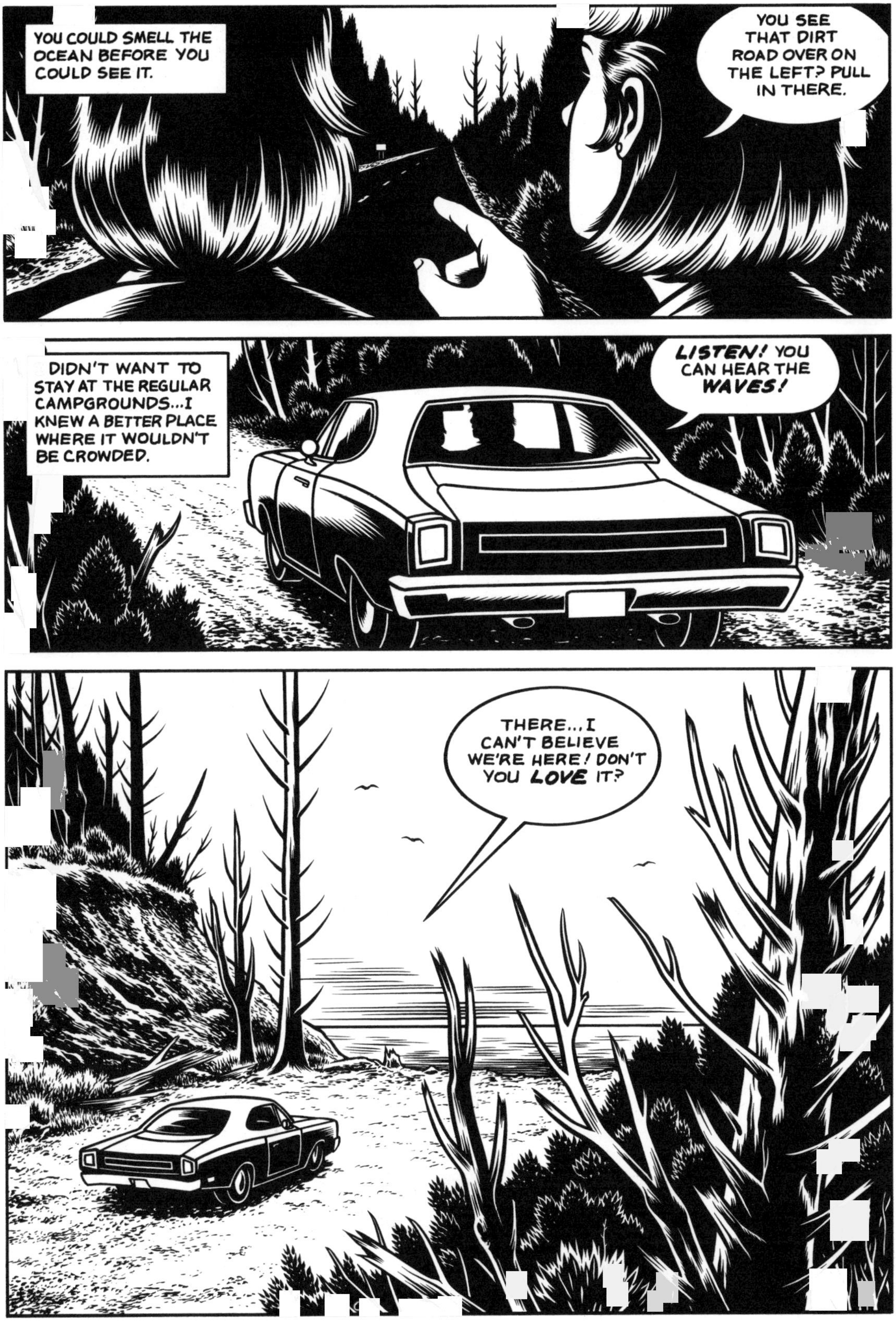
YOU COULD SMELL THE OCEAN BEFORE YOU COULD SEE IT.
YOU SEE THAT DIRT ROAD OVER ON THE LEFT? PULL IN THERE.
DIDN'T WANT TO STAY AT THE REGULAR CAMPGROUNDS...I KNEW A BETTER PLACE WHERE IT WOULDN'T BE CROWDED.
LISTEN! YOU CAN HEAR THE WAVES!
THERE...I CAN'T BELIEVE WE'RE HERE! DON'T YOU LOVE IT?

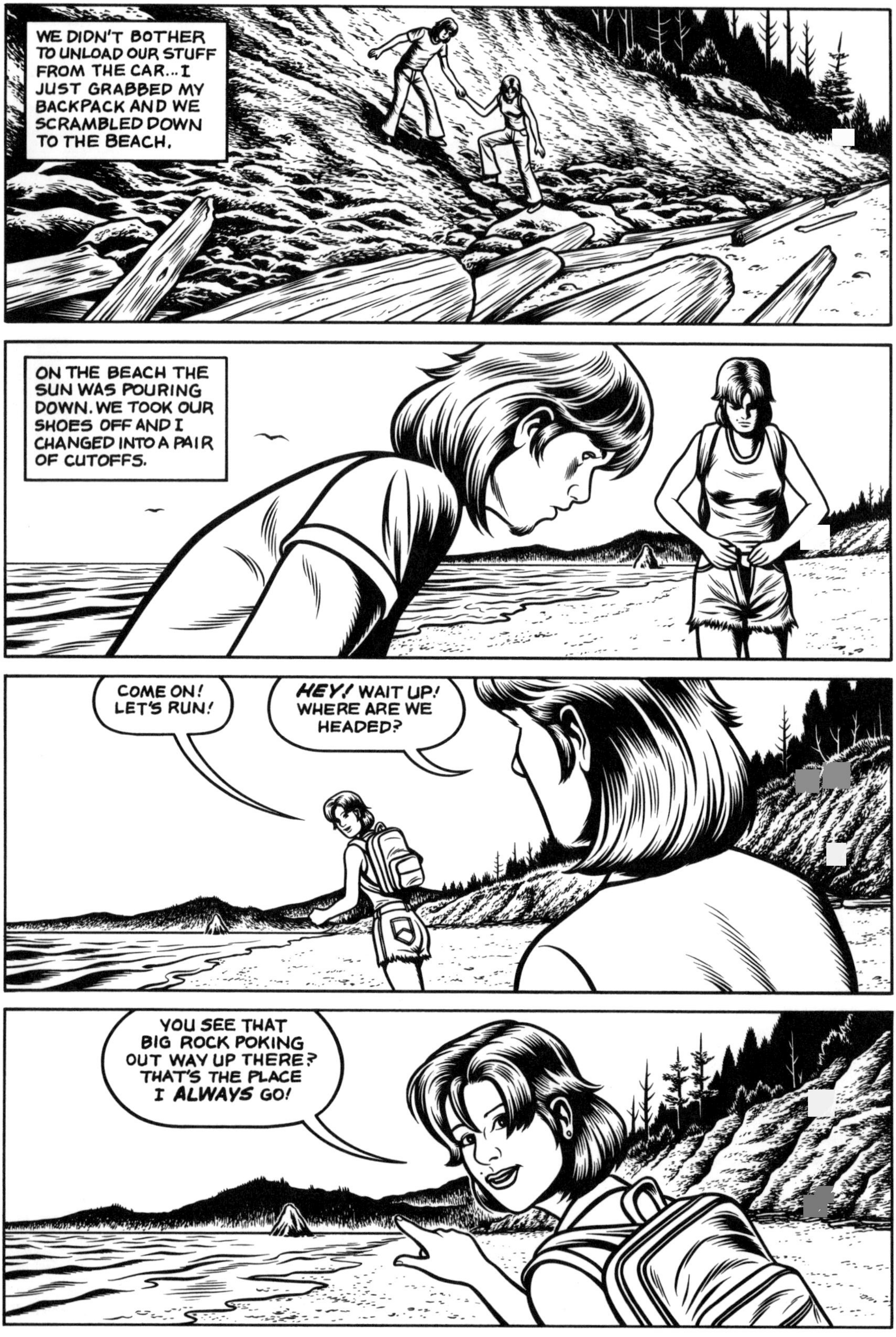
WE DIDN'T BOTHER TO UNLOAD OUR STUFF FROM THE CAR... I JUST GRABBED MY BACKPACK AND WE SCRAMBLED DOWN TO THE BEACH.
ON THE BEACH THE SUN WAS POURING DOWN. WE TOOK OUR SHOES OFF AND I CHANGED INTO A PAIR OF CUTOFFS.
COME ON! LET'S RUN!
HEY! WAIT UP! WHERE ARE WE HEADED?
YOU SEE THAT BIG ROCK POKING OUT WAY UP THERE? THAT'S THE PLACE I ALWAYS GO!

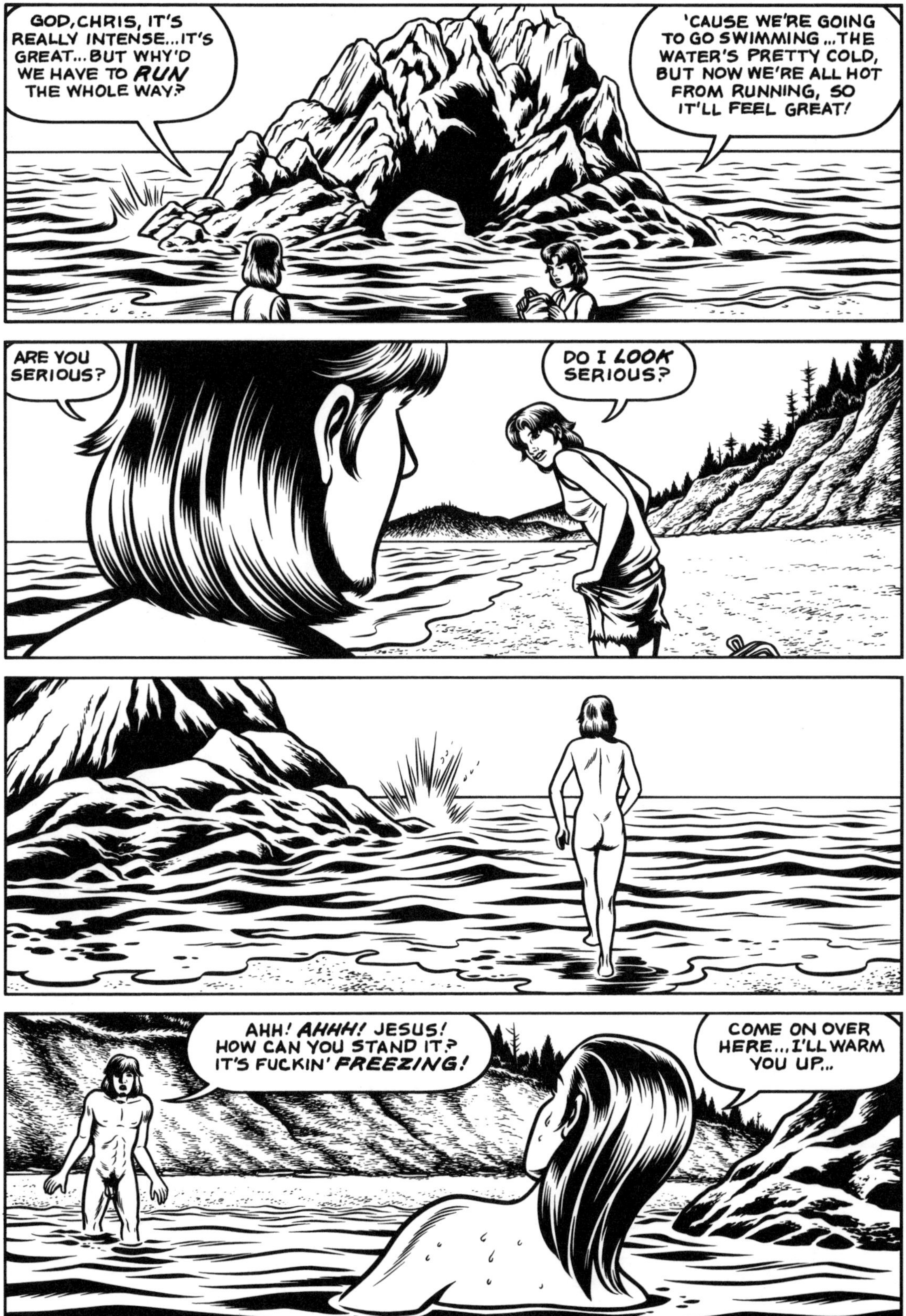
GOD, CHRIS, IT'S REALLY INTENSE...IT'S GREAT...BUT WHY'D WE HAVE TO RUN THE WHOLE WAY?
'CAUSE WE'RE GOING TO GO SWIMMING...THE WATER'S PRETTY COLD, BUT NOW WE'RE ALL HOT FROM RUNNING, SO IT'LL FEEL GREAT!
ARE YOU SERIOUS?
DO I LOOK SERIOUS?
AHH! AHHH! JESUS! HOW CAN YOU STAND IT? IT'S FUCKIN' FREEZING!
COME ON OVER HERE...I'LL WARM YOU UP...

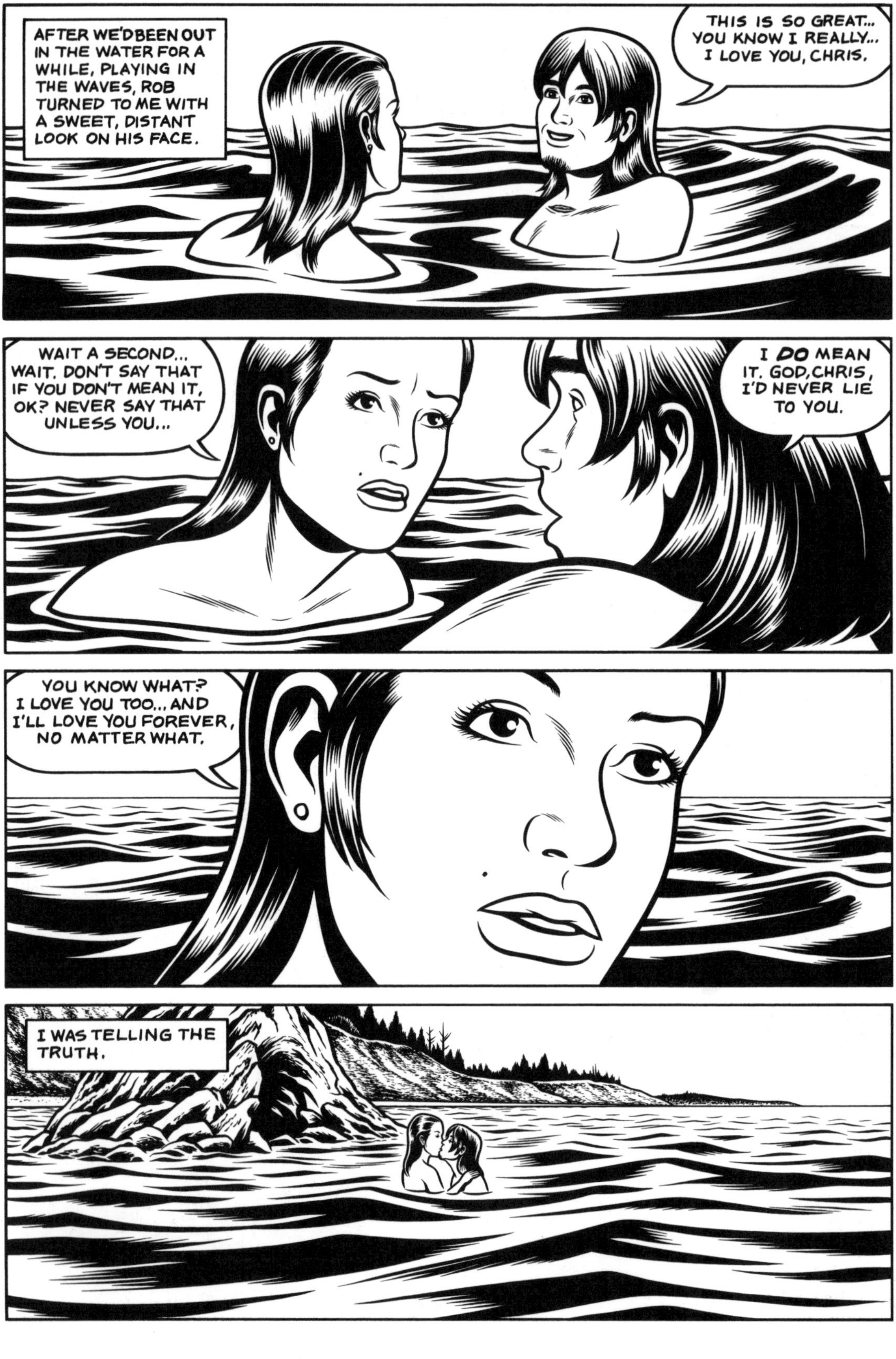
AFTER WE'D BEEN OUT IN THE WATER FOR A WHILE, PLAYING IN THE WAVES, ROB TURNED TO ME WITH A SWEET, DISTANT LOOK ON HIS FACE.
THIS IS SO GREAT... YOU KNOW I REALLY... I LOVE YOU, CHRIS.
WAIT A SECOND... WAIT. DON'T SAY THAT IF YOU DON'T MEAN IT, OK? NEVER SAY THAT UNLESS YOU...
I DO MEAN IT. GOD, CHRIS, I'D NEVER LIE TO YOU.
YOU KNOW WHAT? I LOVE YOU TOO... AND I'LL LOVE YOU FOREVER, NO MATTER WHAT.
I WAS TELLING THE TRUTH.

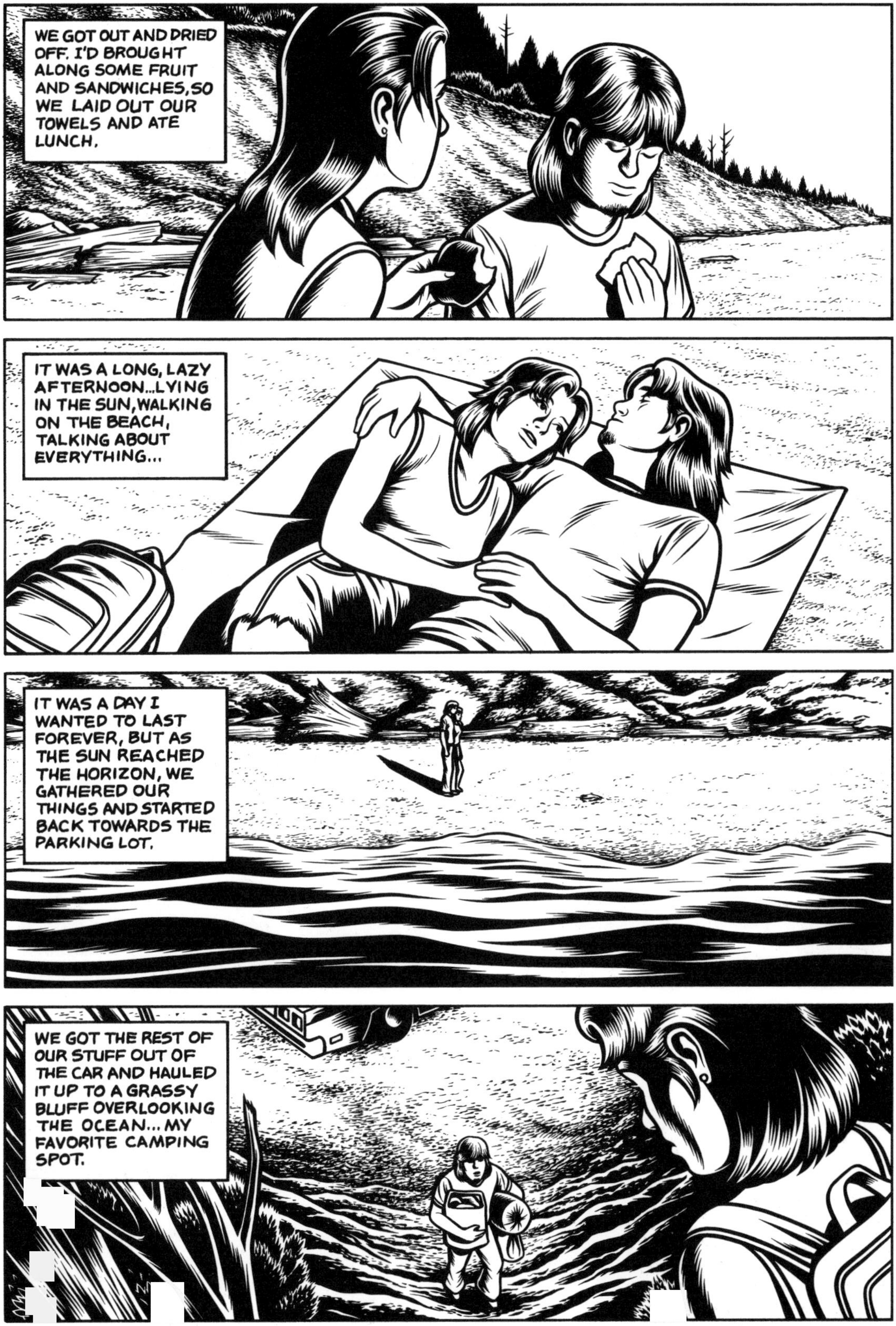
WE GOT OUT AND DRIED OFF. I'D BROUGHT ALONG SOME FRUIT AND SANDWICHES, SO WE LAID OUT OUR TOWELS AND ATE LUNCH.
IT WAS A LONG, LAZY AFTERNOON...LYING IN THE SUN, WALKING ON THE BEACH, TALKING ABOUT EVERYTHING...
IT WAS A DAY I WANTED TO LAST FOREVER, BUT AS THE SUN REACHED THE HORIZON, WE GATHERED OUR THINGS AND STARTED BACK TOWARDS THE PARKING LOT.
WE GOT THE REST OF OUR STUFF OUT OF THE CAR AND HAULED IT UP TO A GRASSY BLUFF OVERLOOKING THE OCEAN... MY FAVORITE CAMPING SPOT.

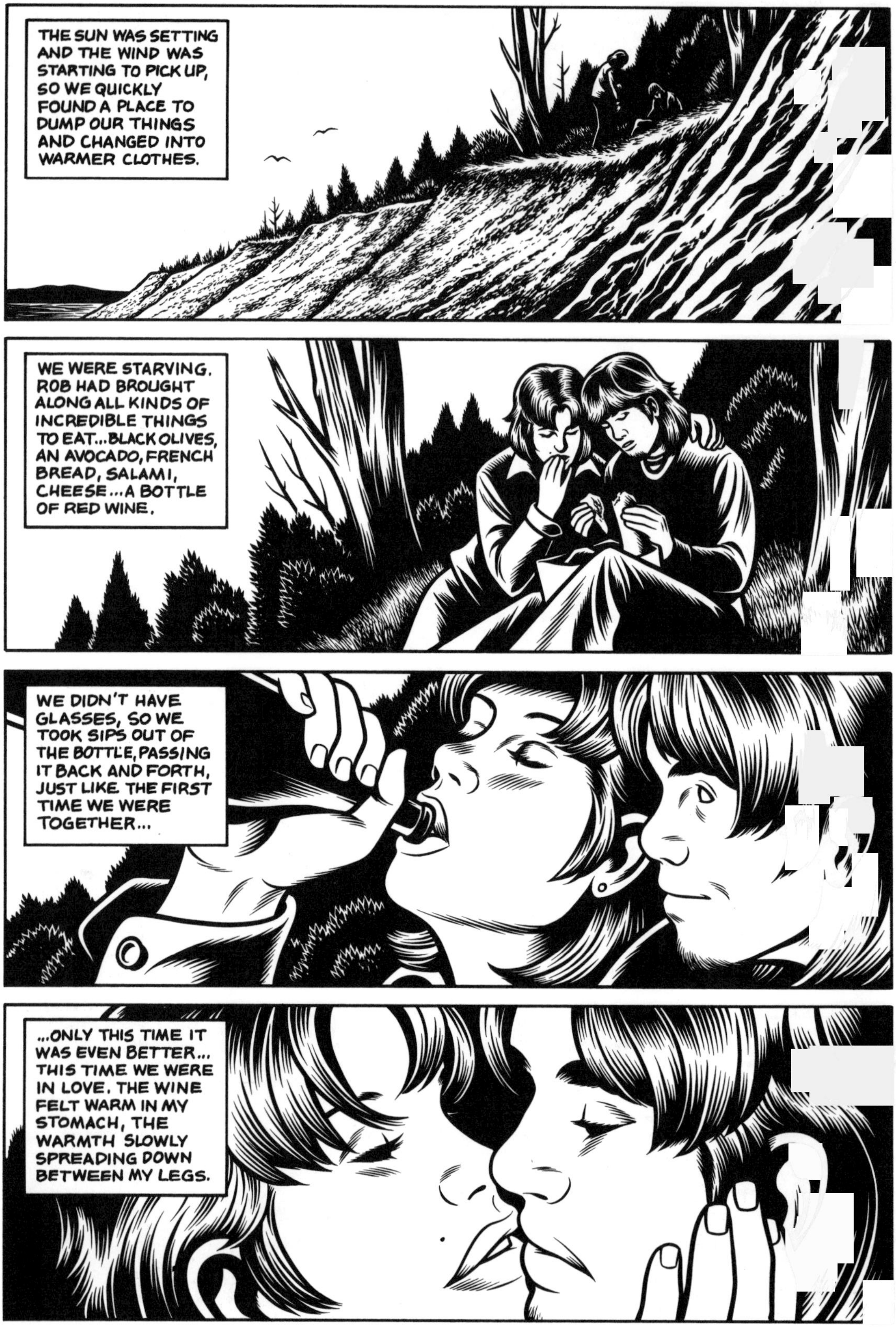
THE SUN WAS SETTING AND THE WIND WAS STARTING TO PICK UP, SO WE QUICKLY FOUND A PLACE TO DUMP OUR THINGS AND CHANGED INTO WARMER CLOTHES.
WE WERE STARVING. ROB HAD BROUGHT ALONG ALL KINDS OF INCREDIBLE THINGS TO EAT... BLACK OLIVES, AN AVOCADO, FRENCH BREAD, SALAMI, CHEESE... A BOTTLE OF RED WINE.
WE DIDN'T HAVE GLASSES, SO WE TOOK SIPS OUT OF THE BOTTLE, PASSING IT BACK AND FORTH, JUST LIKE THE FIRST TIME WE WERE TOGETHER...
...ONLY THIS TIME IT WAS EVEN BETTER... THIS TIME WE WERE IN LOVE. THE WINE FELT WARM IN MY STOMACH, THE WARMTH SLOWLY SPREADING DOWN BETWEEN MY LEGS.

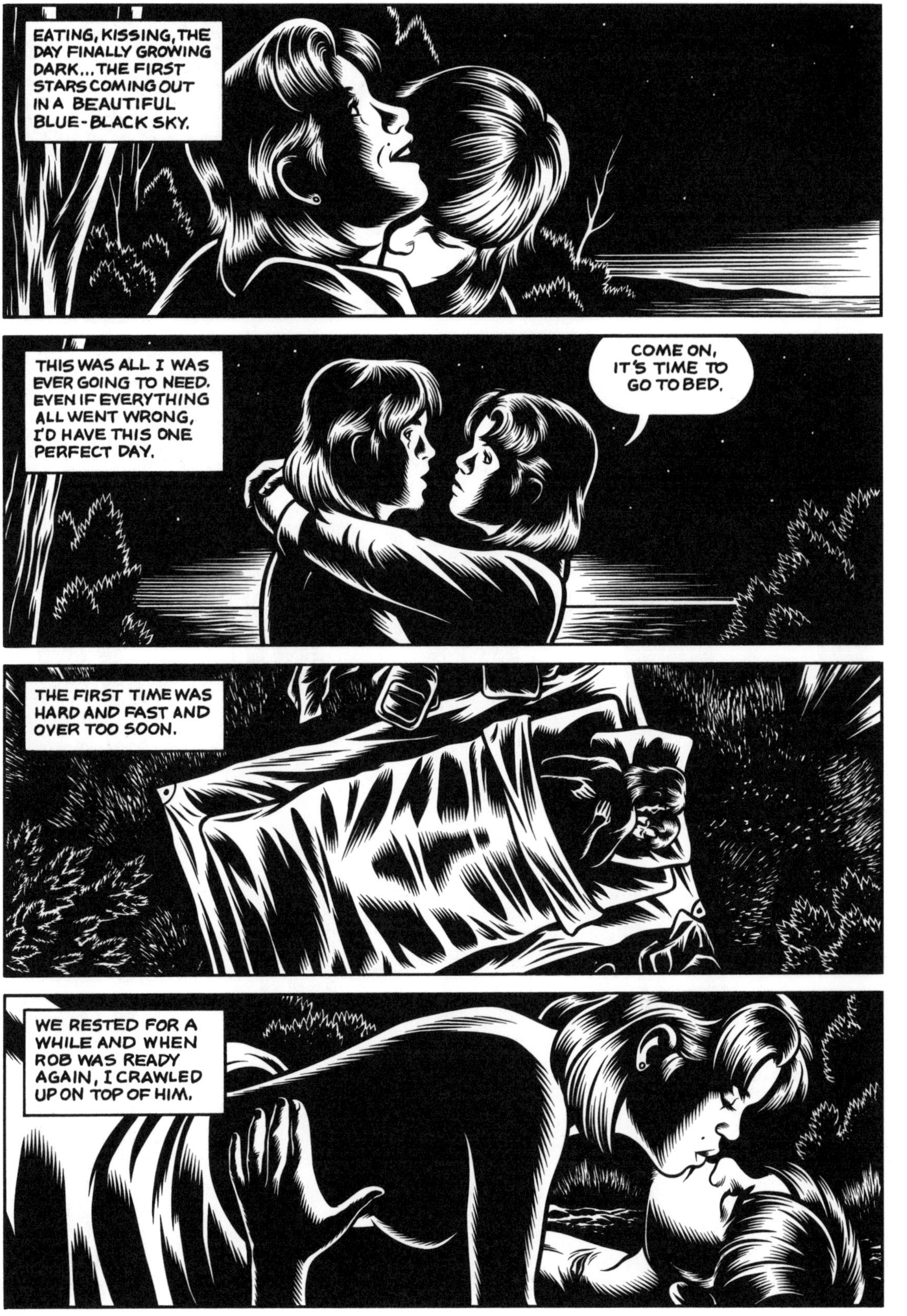
EATING, KISSING, THE DAY FINALLY GROWING DARK... THE FIRST STARS COMING OUT IN A BEAUTIFUL BLUE-BLACK SKY.
THIS WAS ALL I WAS EVER GOING TO NEED. EVEN IF EVERYTHING ALL WENT WRONG, I'D HAVE THIS ONE PERFECT DAY.
COME ON, IT'S TIME TO GO TO BED.
THE FIRST TIME WAS HARD AND FAST AND OVER TOO SOON.
WE RESTED FOR A WHILE AND WHEN ROB WAS READY AGAIN, I CRAWLED UP ON TOP OF HIM.

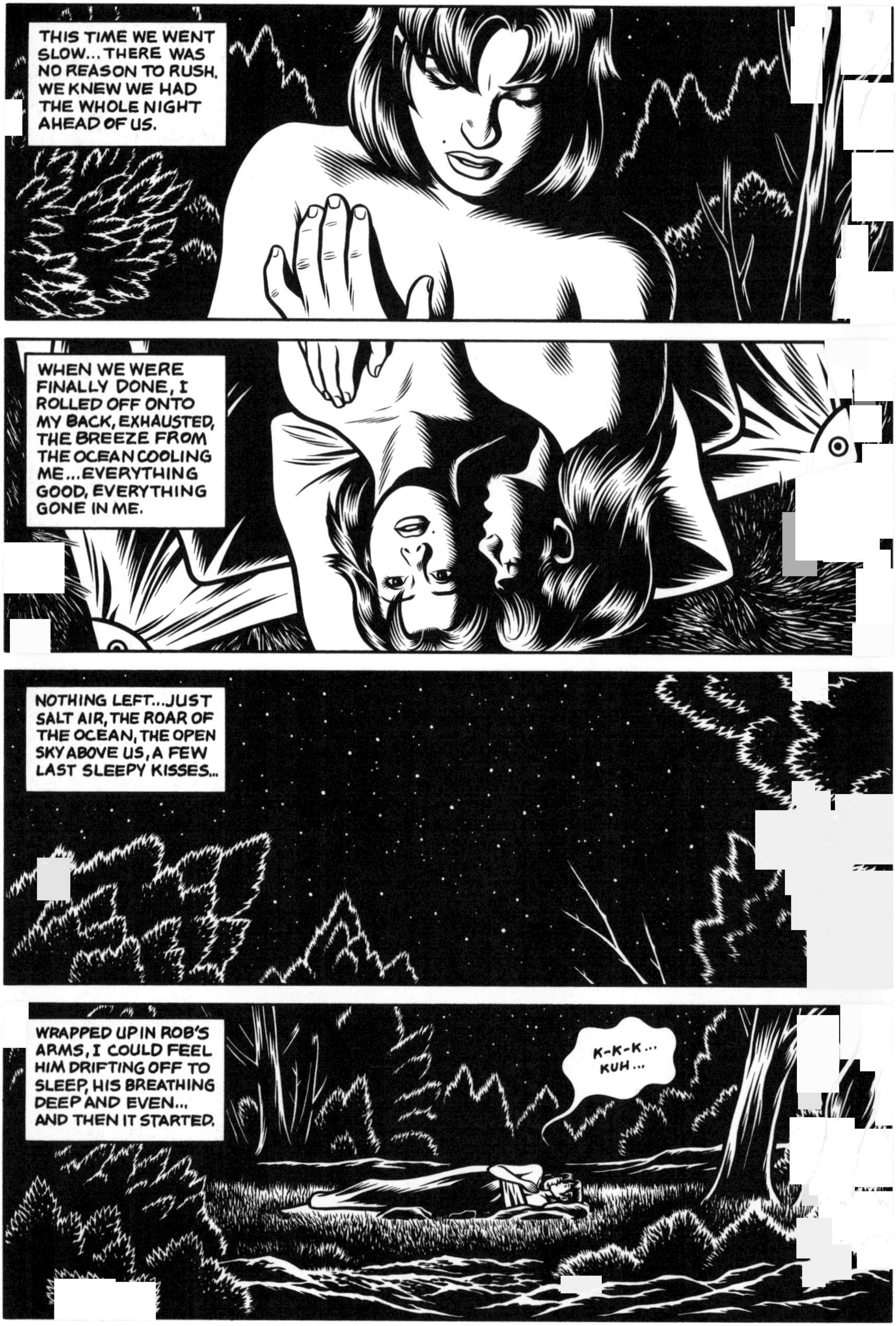
THIS TIME WE WENT SLOW... THERE WAS NO REASON TO RUSH. WE KNEW WE HAD THE WHOLE NIGHT AHEAD OF US.
WHEN WE WERE FINALLY DONE, I ROLLED OFF ONTO MY BACK, EXHAUSTED, THE BREEZE FROM THE OCEAN COOLING ME... EVERYTHING GOOD, EVERYTHING GONE IN ME.
NOTHING LEFT... JUST SALT AIR, THE ROAR OF THE OCEAN, THE OPEN SKY ABOVE US, A FEW LAST SLEEPY KISSES...
WRAPPED UP IN ROB'S ARMS, I COULD FEEL HIM DRIFTING OFF TO SLEEP, HIS BREATHING DEEP AND EVEN... AND THEN IT STARTED.
K-K-K... KUH...

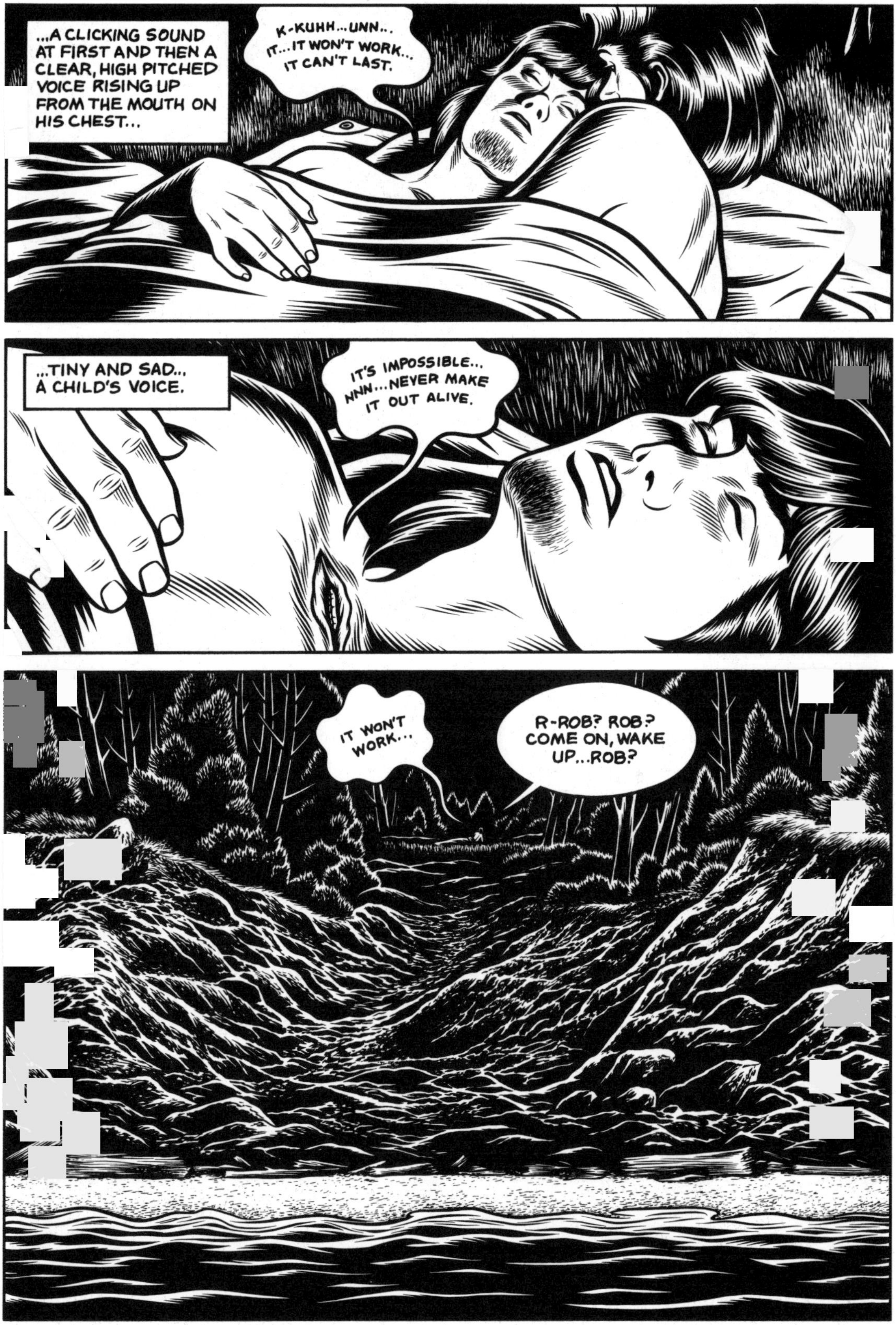
...A CLICKING SOUND AT FIRST AND THEN A CLEAR, HIGH PITCHED VOICE RISING UP FROM THE MOUTH ON HIS CHEST...
K-KUHH...UNN... IT...IT WON'T WORK... IT CAN'T LAST.
...TINY AND SAD... A CHILD'S VOICE.
IT'S IMPOSSIBLE... NNN...NEVER MAKE IT OUT ALIVE.
IT WON'T WORK...
R-ROB? ROB? COME ON, WAKE UP...ROB?

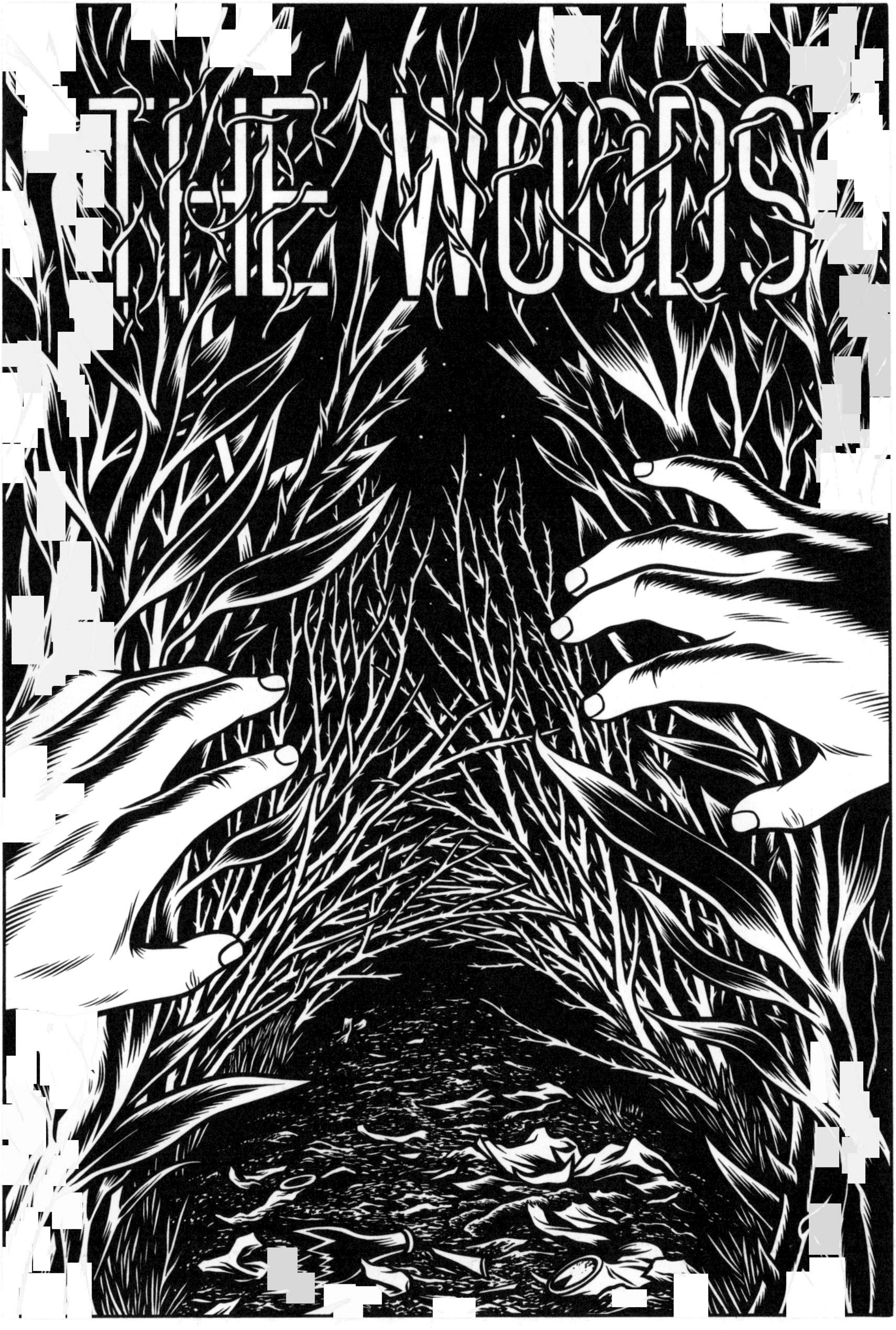
THE WOODS

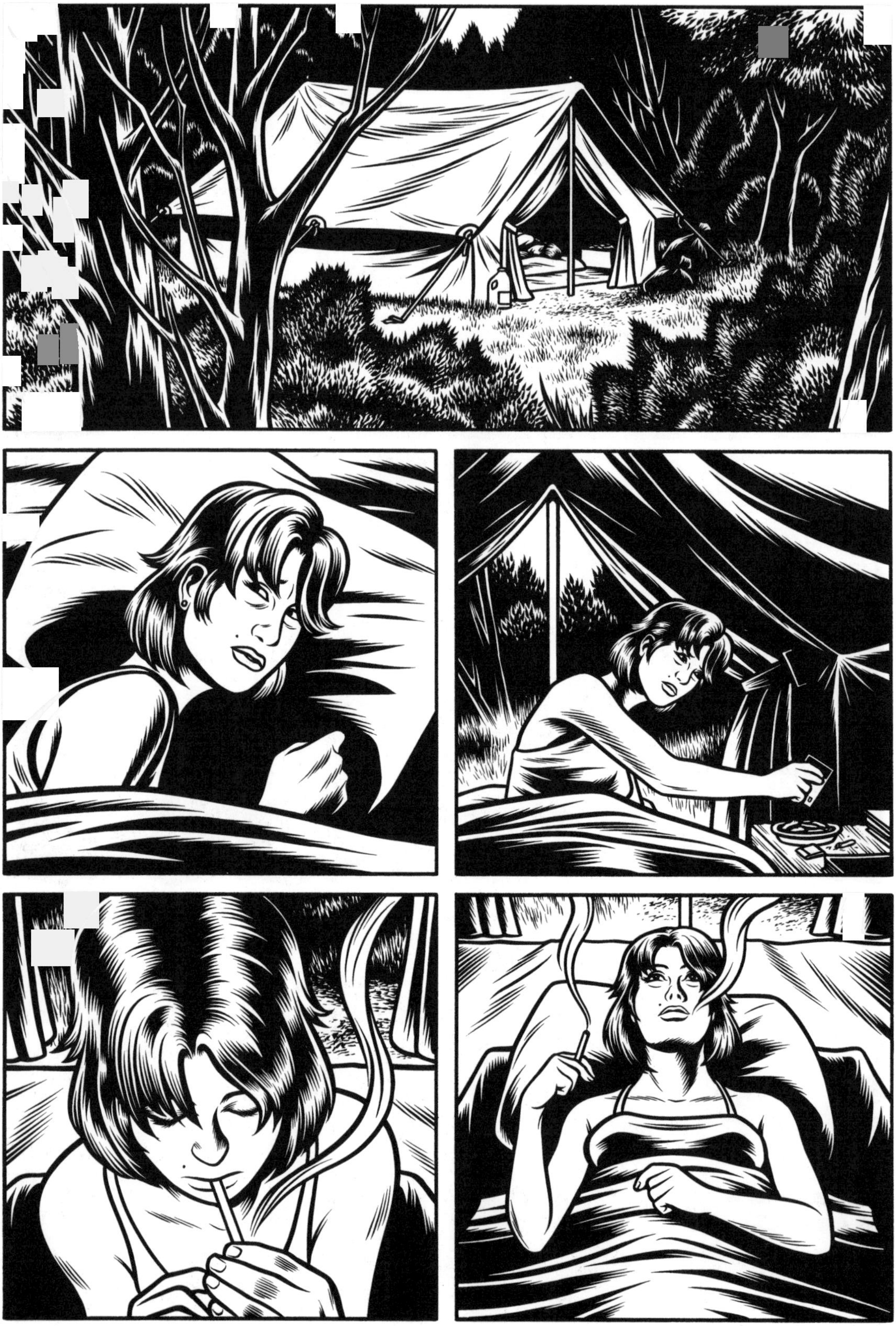

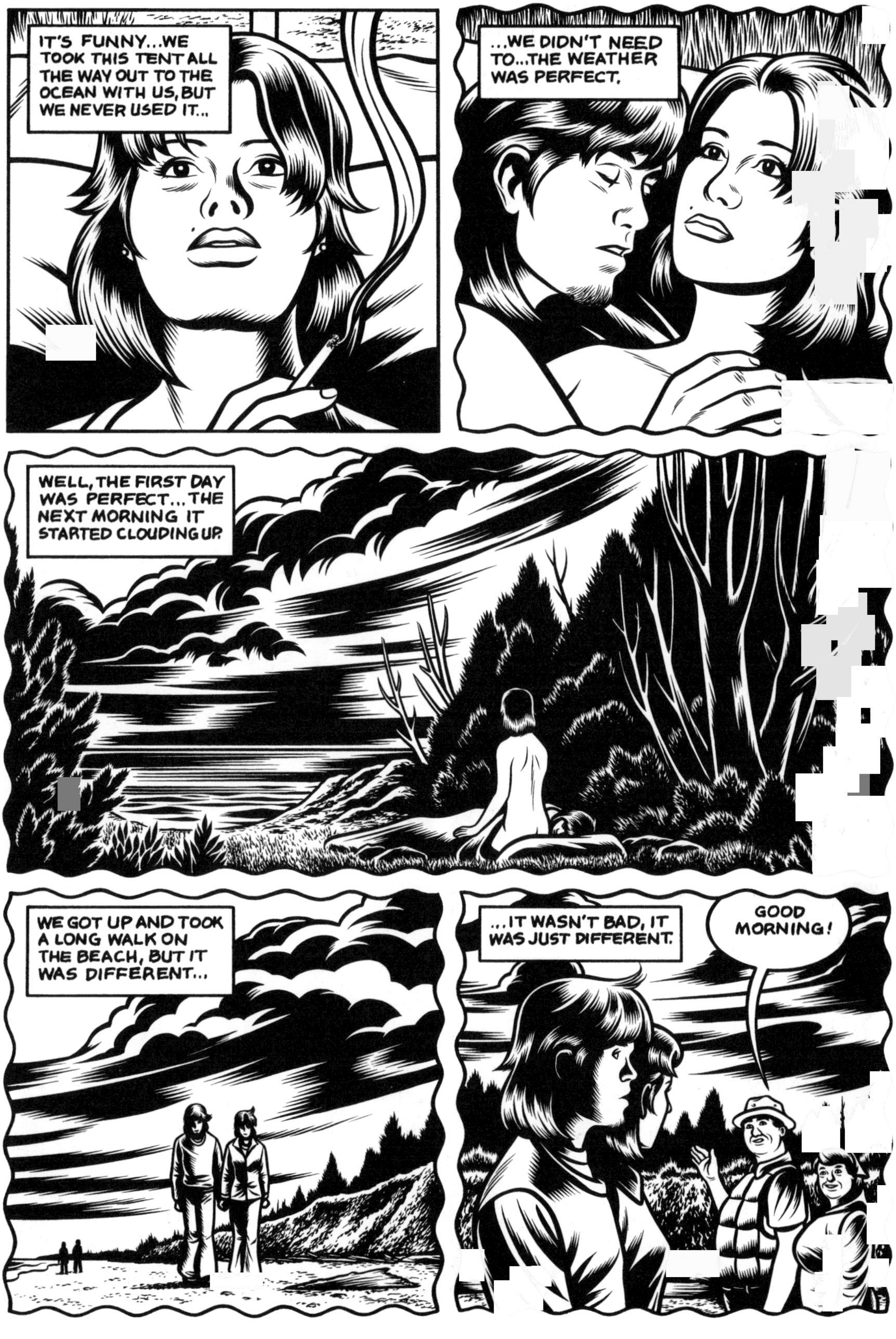
IT'S FUNNY...WE TOOK THIS TENT ALL THE WAY OUT TO THE OCEAN WITH US, BUT WE NEVER USED IT...
...WE DIDN'T NEED TO...THE WEATHER WAS PERFECT.
WELL, THE FIRST DAY WAS PERFECT... THE NEXT MORNING IT STARTED CLOUDING UP.
WE GOT UP AND TOOK A LONG WALK ON THE BEACH, BUT IT WAS DIFFERENT...
...IT WASN'T BAD, IT WAS JUST DIFFERENT.
GOOD MORNING!

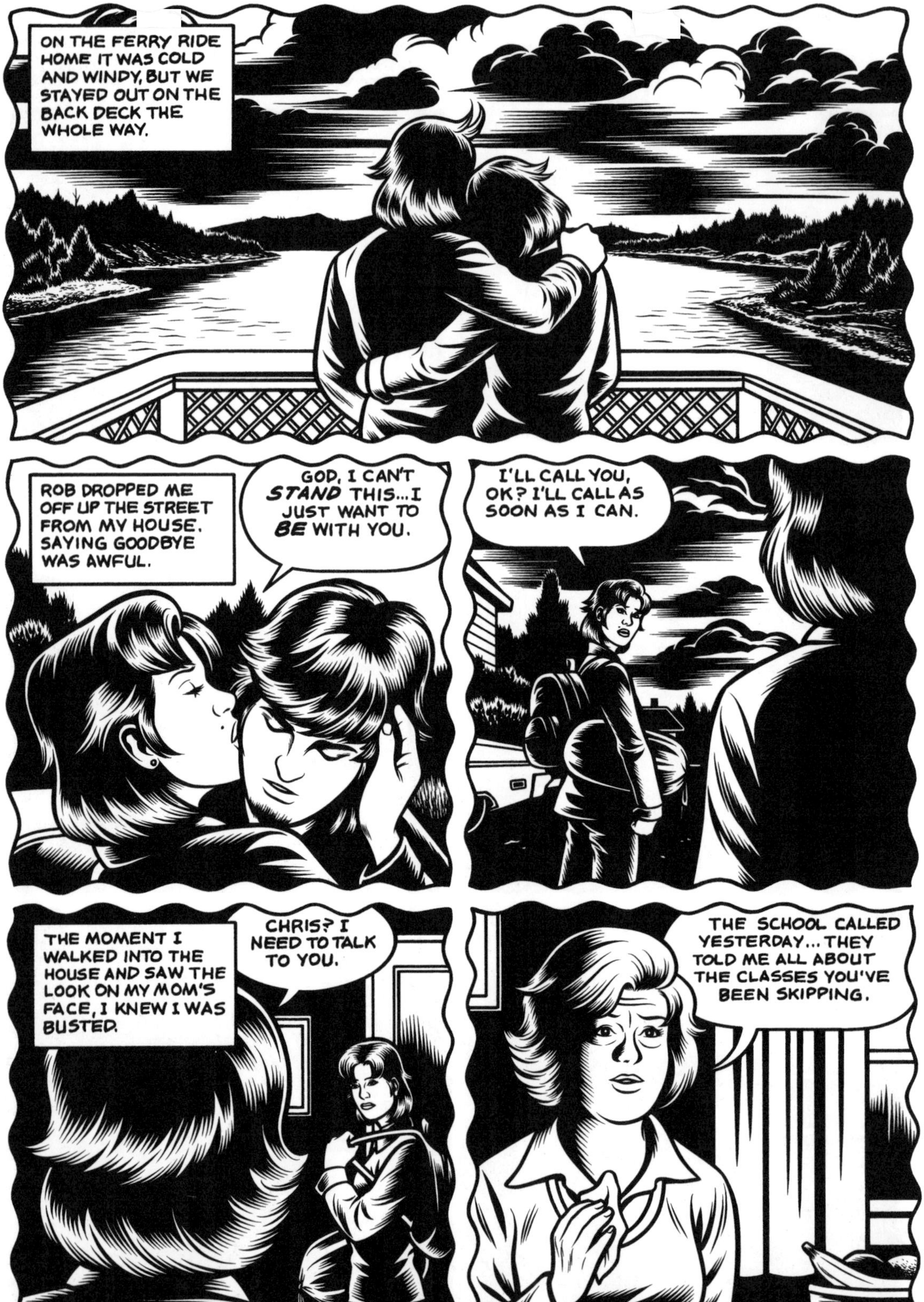
ON THE FERRY RIDE HOME IT WAS COLD AND WINDY, BUT WE STAYED OUT ON THE BACK DECK THE WHOLE WAY.
ROB DROPPED ME OFF UP THE STREET FROM MY HOUSE. SAYING GOODBYE WAS AWFUL.
GOD, I CAN'T *STAND* THIS... I JUST WANT TO *BE* WITH YOU.
I'LL CALL YOU, OK? I'LL CALL AS SOON AS I CAN.
THE MOMENT I WALKED INTO THE HOUSE AND SAW THE LOOK ON MY MOM'S FACE, I KNEW I WAS BUSTED.
CHRIS? I NEED TO TALK TO YOU.
THE SCHOOL CALLED YESTERDAY... THEY TOLD ME ALL ABOUT THE CLASSES YOU'VE BEEN SKIPPING.

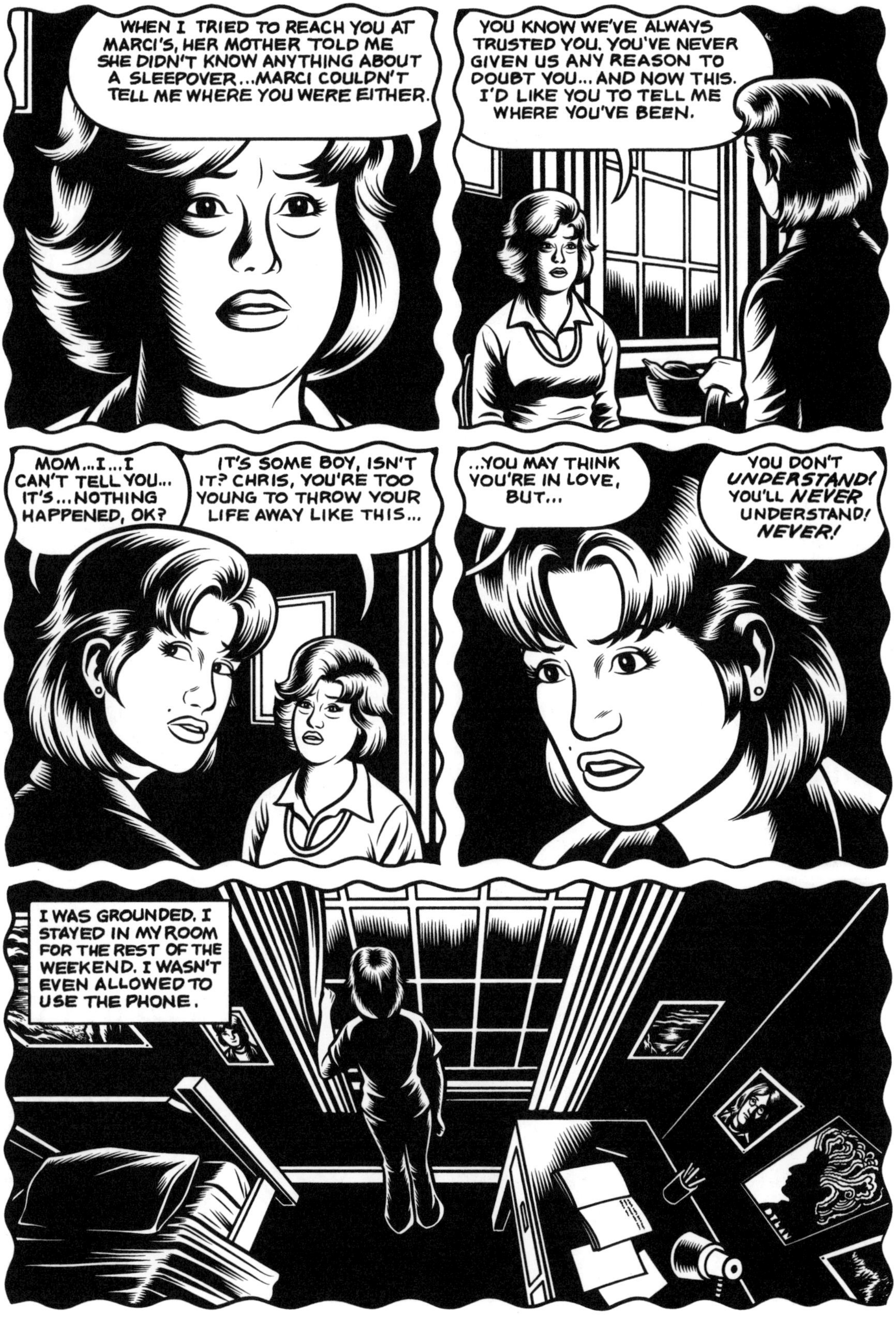
WHEN I TRIED TO REACH YOU AT MARCI'S, HER MOTHER TOLD ME SHE DIDN'T KNOW ANYTHING ABOUT A SLEEPOVER...MARCI COULDN'T TELL ME WHERE YOU WERE EITHER.
YOU KNOW WE'VE ALWAYS TRUSTED YOU. YOU'VE NEVER GIVEN US ANY REASON TO DOUBT YOU... AND NOW THIS. I'D LIKE YOU TO TELL ME WHERE YOU'VE BEEN.
MOM...I...I CAN'T TELL YOU... IT'S...NOTHING HAPPENED, OK?
IT'S SOME BOY, ISN'T IT? CHRIS, YOU'RE TOO YOUNG TO THROW YOUR LIFE AWAY LIKE THIS...
...YOU MAY THINK YOU'RE IN LOVE, BUT...
YOU DON'T *UNDERSTAND!* YOU'LL *NEVER* UNDERSTAND! *NEVER!*
I WAS GROUNDED. I STAYED IN MY ROOM FOR THE REST OF THE WEEKEND. I WASN'T EVEN ALLOWED TO USE THE PHONE.

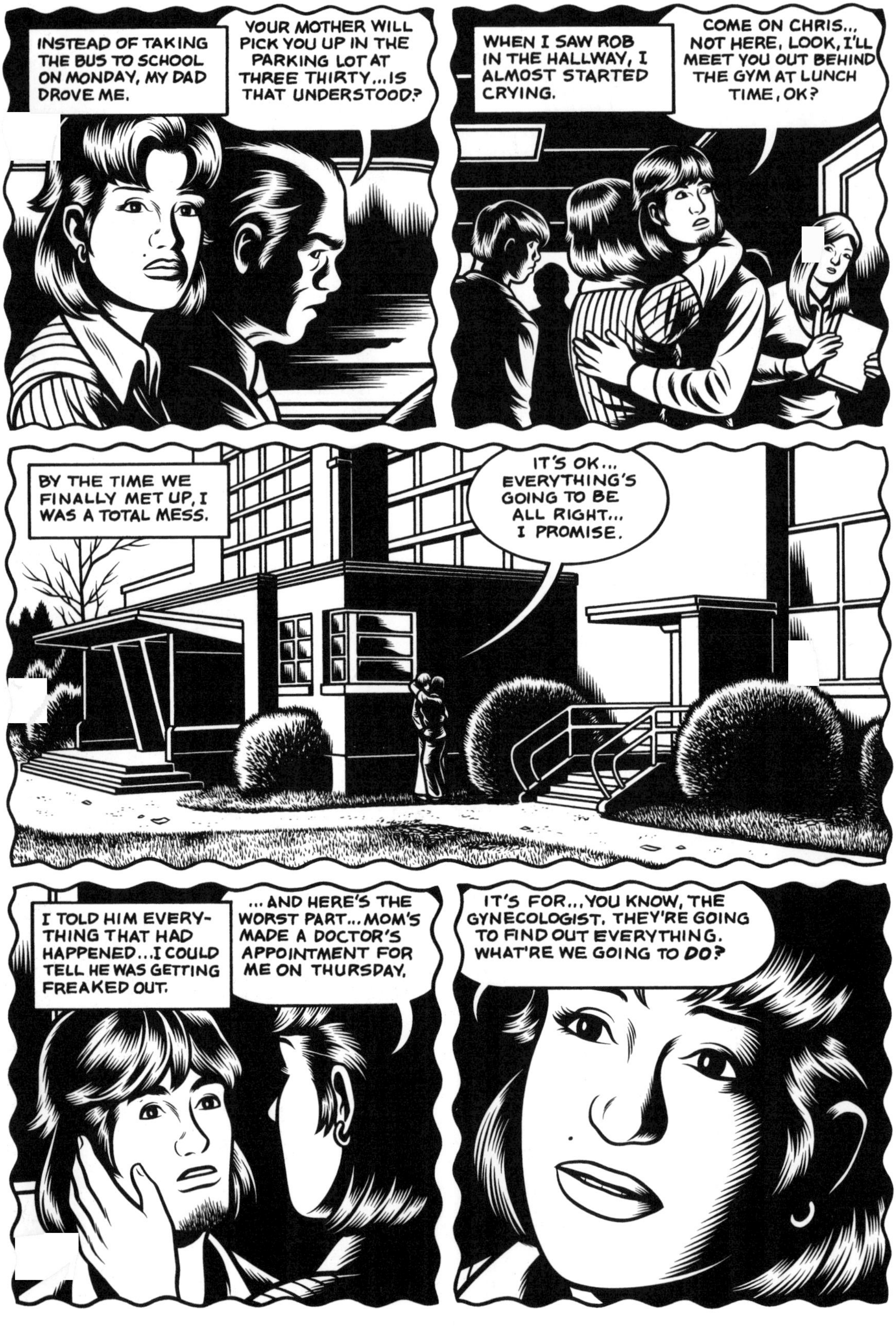
INSTEAD OF TAKING THE BUS TO SCHOOL ON MONDAY, MY DAD DROVE ME.
YOUR MOTHER WILL PICK YOU UP IN THE PARKING LOT AT THREE THIRTY... IS THAT UNDERSTOOD?
WHEN I SAW ROB IN THE HALLWAY, I ALMOST STARTED CRYING.
COME ON CHRIS... NOT HERE, LOOK, I'LL MEET YOU OUT BEHIND THE GYM AT LUNCH TIME, OK?
BY THE TIME WE FINALLY MET UP, I WAS A TOTAL MESS.
IT'S OK... EVERYTHING'S GOING TO BE ALL RIGHT... I PROMISE.
I TOLD HIM EVERYTHING THAT HAD HAPPENED... I COULD TELL HE WAS GETTING FREAKED OUT.
... AND HERE'S THE WORST PART... MOM'S MADE A DOCTOR'S APPOINTMENT FOR ME ON THURSDAY.
IT'S FOR... YOU KNOW, THE GYNECOLOGIST. THEY'RE GOING TO FIND OUT EVERYTHING. WHAT'RE WE GOING TO *DO*?

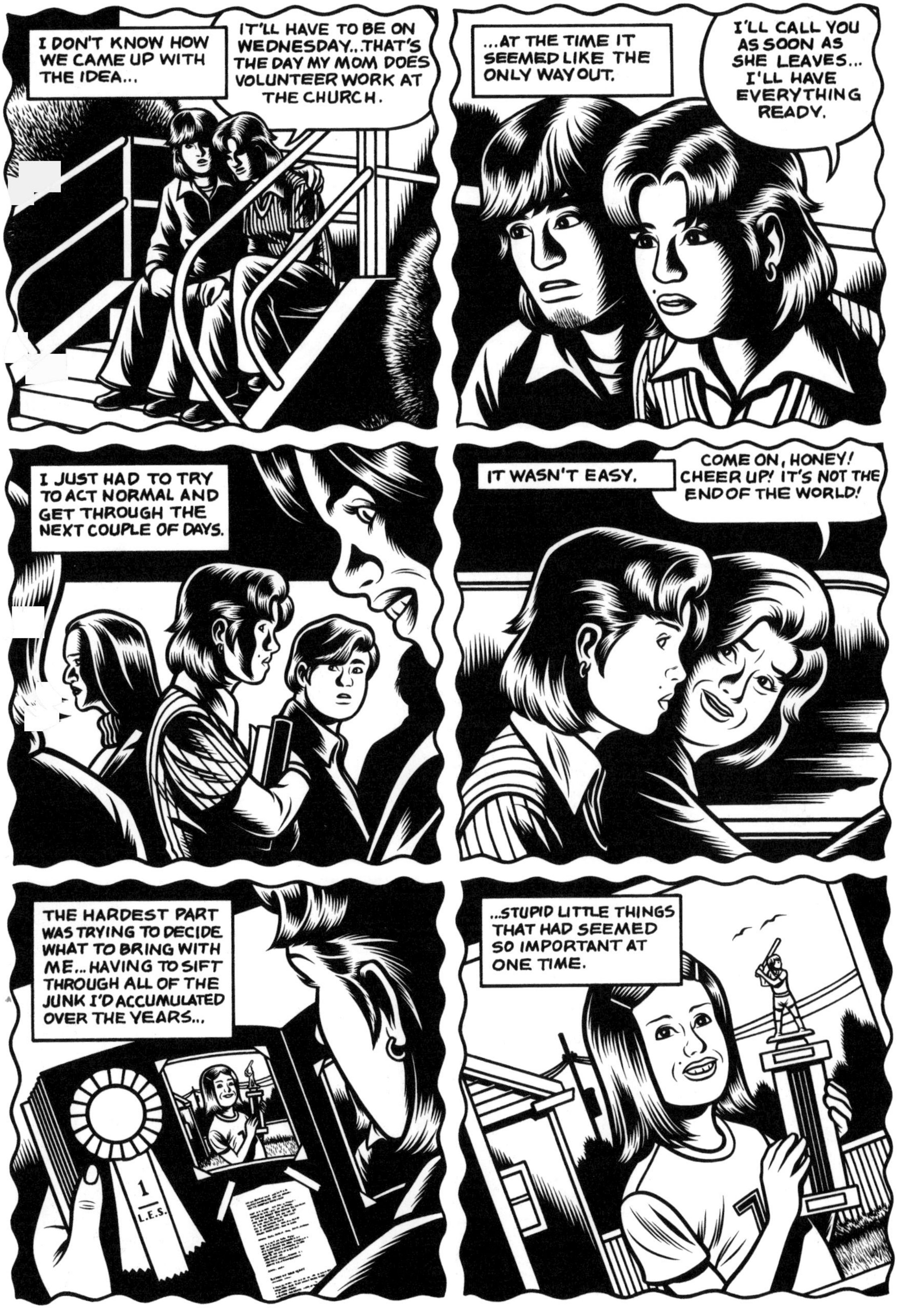
I DON'T KNOW HOW WE CAME UP WITH THE IDEA...
IT'LL HAVE TO BE ON WEDNESDAY...THAT'S THE DAY MY MOM DOES VOLUNTEER WORK AT THE CHURCH.
...AT THE TIME IT SEEMED LIKE THE ONLY WAY OUT.
I'LL CALL YOU AS SOON AS SHE LEAVES... I'LL HAVE EVERYTHING READY.
I JUST HAD TO TRY TO ACT NORMAL AND GET THROUGH THE NEXT COUPLE OF DAYS.
IT WASN'T EASY.
COME ON, HONEY! CHEER UP! IT'S NOT THE END OF THE WORLD!
THE HARDEST PART WAS TRYING TO DECIDE WHAT TO BRING WITH ME... HAVING TO SIFT THROUGH ALL OF THE JUNK I'D ACCUMULATED OVER THE YEARS...
1
L.E.S.
...STUPID LITTLE THINGS THAT HAD SEEMED SO IMPORTANT AT ONE TIME.

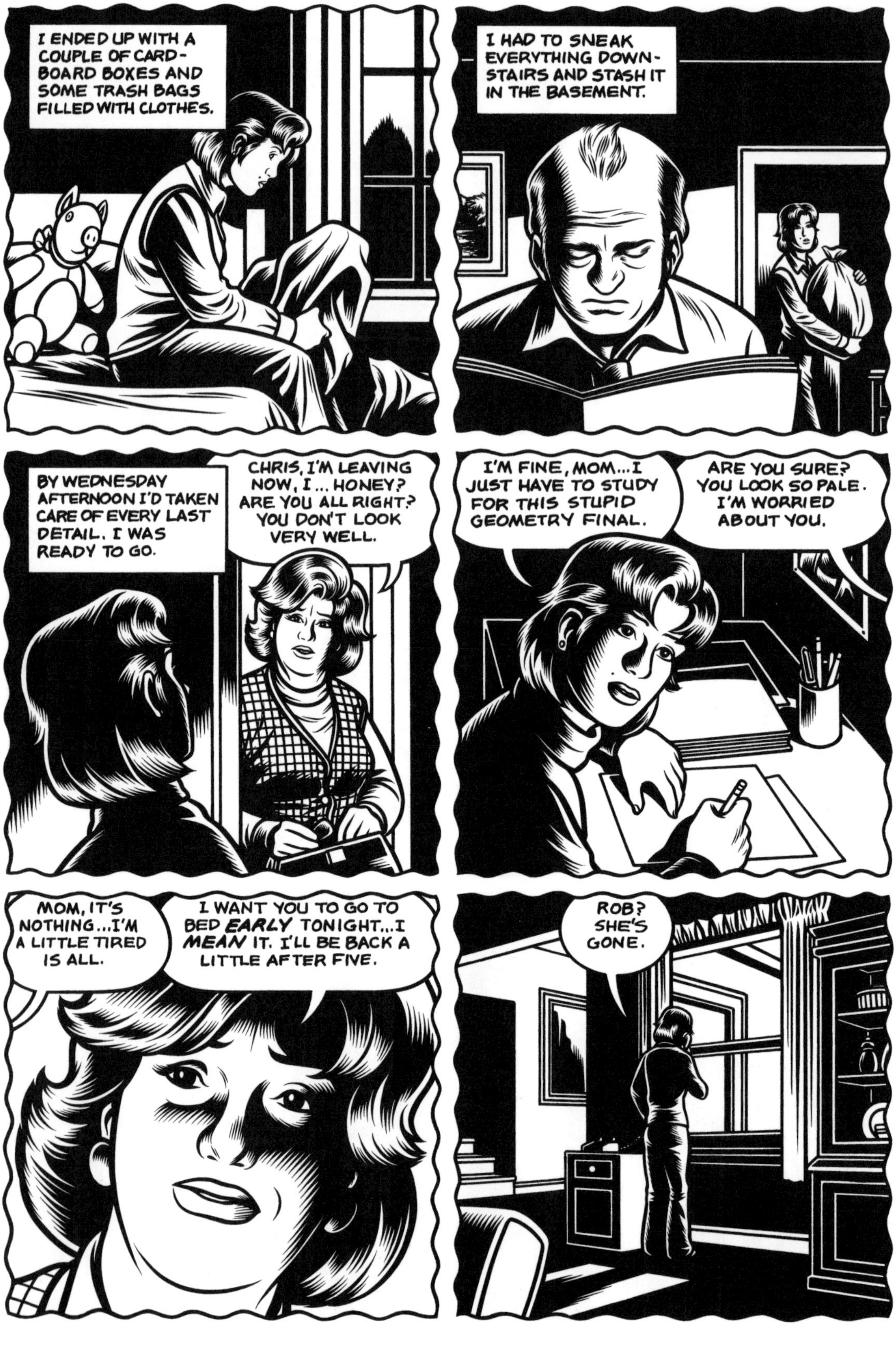
I ENDED UP WITH A COUPLE OF CARD-BOARD BOXES AND SOME TRASH BAGS FILLED WITH CLOTHES.
I HAD TO SNEAK EVERYTHING DOWN-STAIRS AND STASH IT IN THE BASEMENT.
BY WEDNESDAY AFTERNOON I'D TAKEN CARE OF EVERY LAST DETAIL. I WAS READY TO GO.
CHRIS, I'M LEAVING NOW, I ... HONEY? ARE YOU ALL RIGHT? YOU DON'T LOOK VERY WELL.
I'M FINE, MOM... I JUST HAVE TO STUDY FOR THIS STUPID GEOMETRY FINAL.
ARE YOU SURE? YOU LOOK SO PALE. I'M WORRIED ABOUT YOU.
MOM, IT'S NOTHING... I'M A LITTLE TIRED IS ALL.
I WANT YOU TO GO TO BED EARLY TONIGHT... I MEAN IT. I'LL BE BACK A LITTLE AFTER FIVE.
ROB? SHE'S GONE.

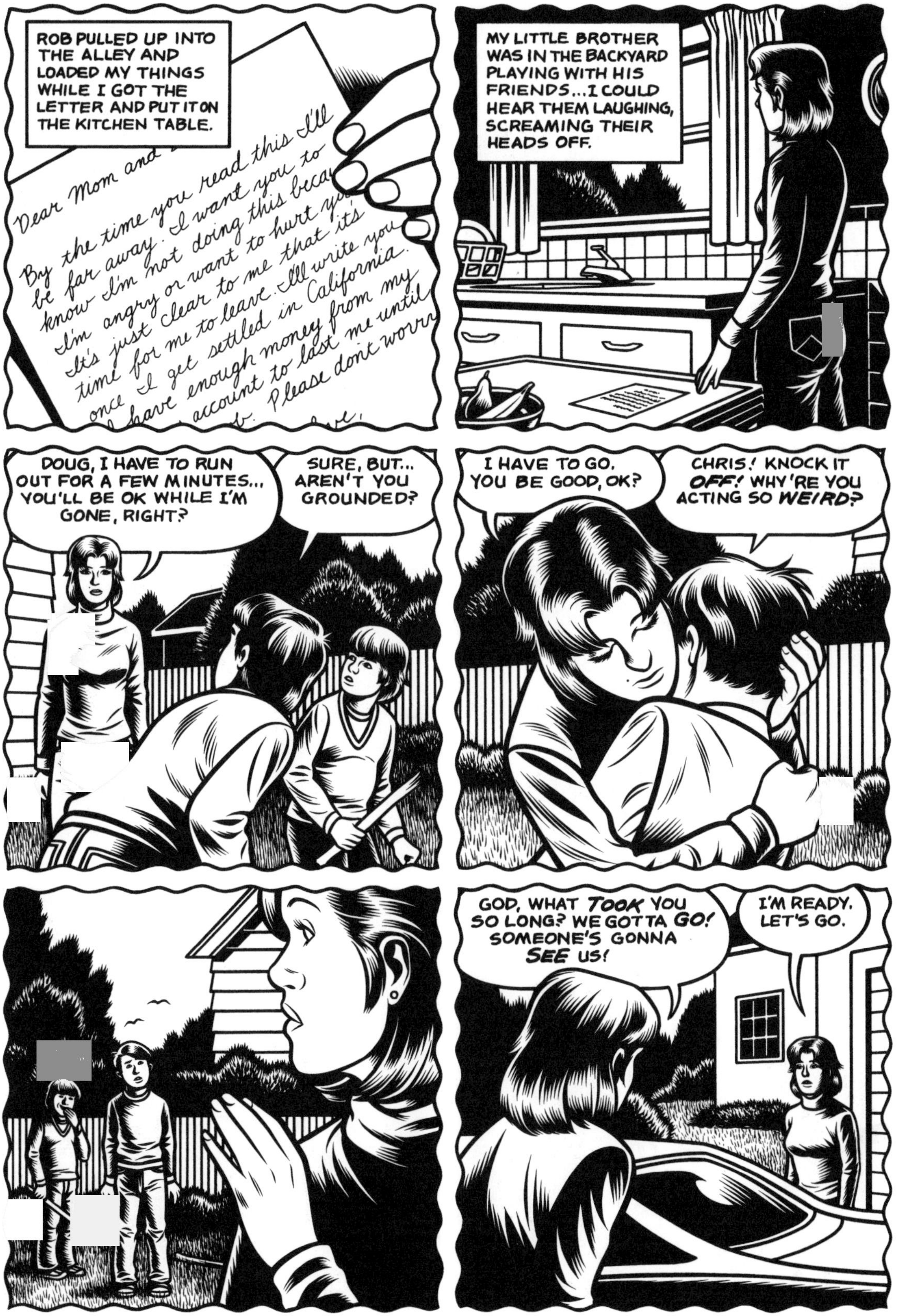
ROB PULLED UP INTO THE ALLEY AND LOADED MY THINGS WHILE I GOT THE LETTER AND PUT IT ON THE KITCHEN TABLE.
Dear Mom and
By the time you read this I'll
be far away. I want you to
know I'm not doing this
I'm angry or want to hurt
It's just clear to me that it's
time for me to leave. I'll write you
once I get settled in California
I have enough money from my
account to last me until
Please don't
MY LITTLE BROTHER WAS IN THE BACKYARD PLAYING WITH HIS FRIENDS... I COULD HEAR THEM LAUGHING, SCREAMING THEIR HEADS OFF.
DOUG, I HAVE TO RUN OUT FOR A FEW MINUTES... YOU'LL BE OK WHILE I'M GONE, RIGHT?
SURE, BUT... AREN'T YOU GROUNDED?
I HAVE TO GO. YOU BE GOOD, OK?
CHRIS! KNOCK IT OFF! WHY'RE YOU ACTING SO WEIRD?
GOD, WHAT TOOK YOU SO LONG? WE GOTTA GO! SOMEONE'S GONNA SEE US!
I'M READY. LET'S GO.

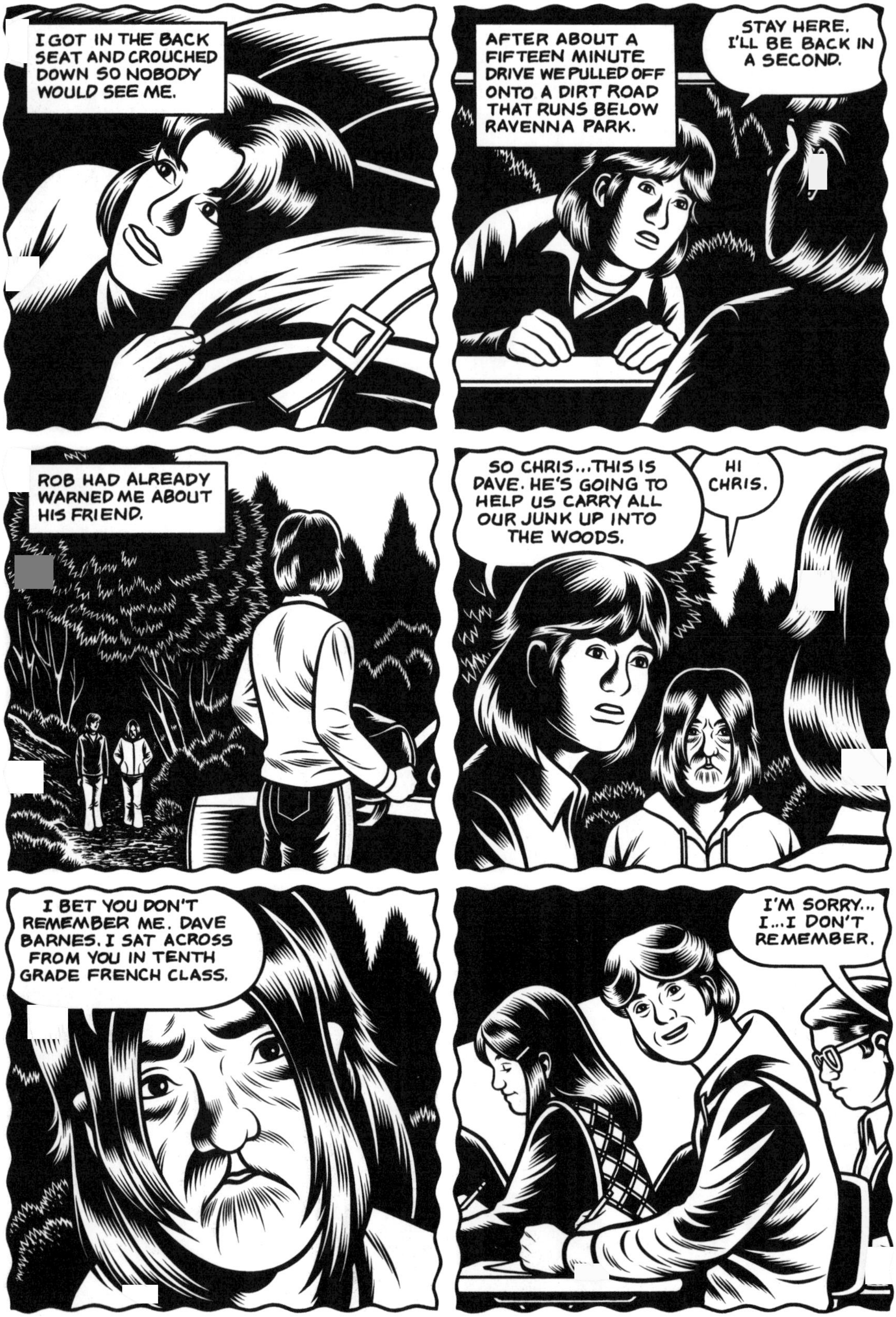
I GOT IN THE BACK SEAT AND CROUCHED DOWN SO NOBODY WOULD SEE ME.
AFTER ABOUT A FIFTEEN MINUTE DRIVE WE PULLED OFF ONTO A DIRT ROAD THAT RUNS BELOW RAVENNA PARK.
STAY HERE. I'LL BE BACK IN A SECOND.
ROB HAD ALREADY WARNED ME ABOUT HIS FRIEND.
SO CHRIS... THIS IS DAVE. HE'S GOING TO HELP US CARRY ALL OUR JUNK UP INTO THE WOODS.
HI CHRIS.
I BET YOU DON'T REMEMBER ME. DAVE BARNES. I SAT ACROSS FROM YOU IN TENTH GRADE FRENCH CLASS.
I'M SORRY... I... I DON'T REMEMBER.

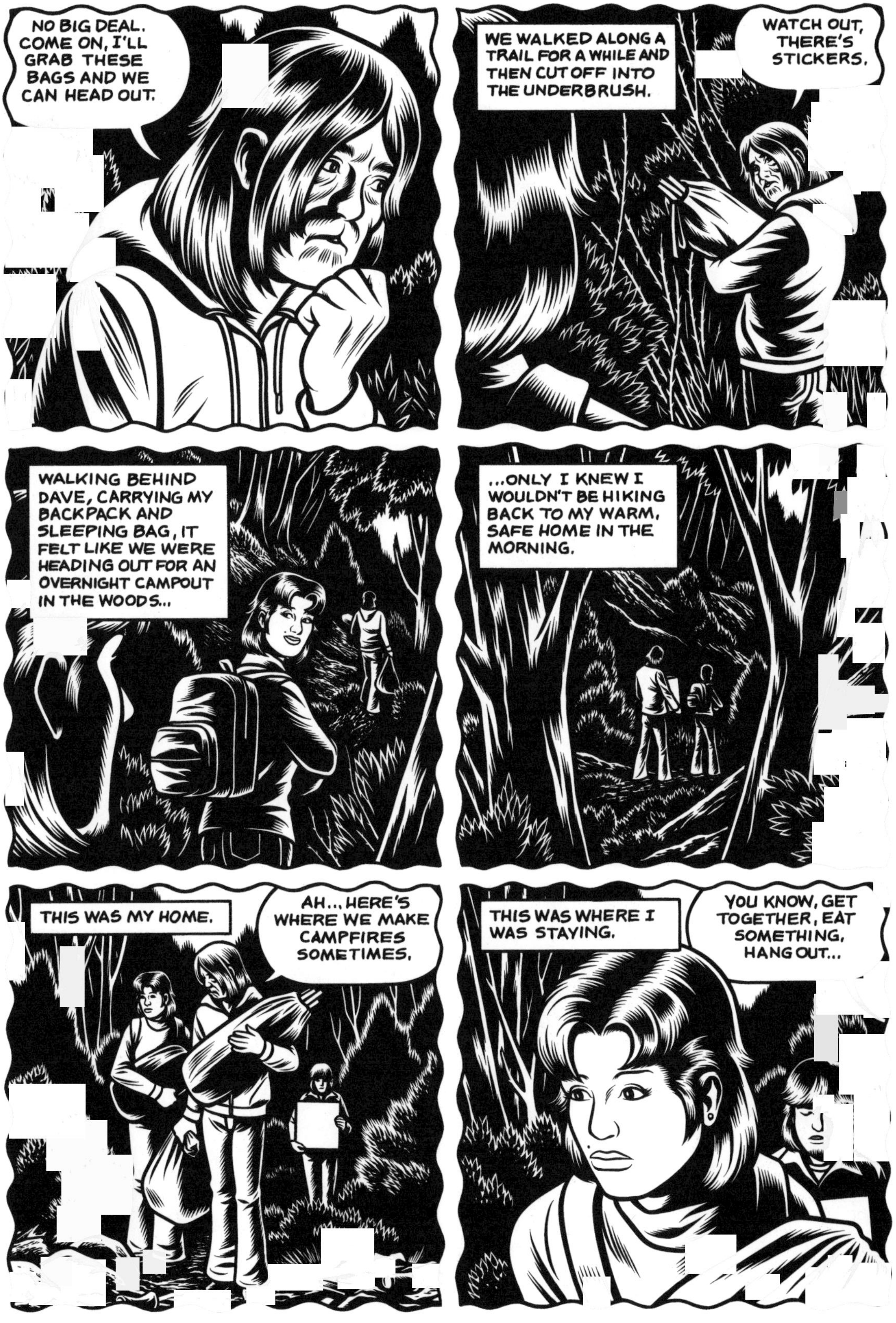
NO BIG DEAL. COME ON, I'LL GRAB THESE BAGS AND WE CAN HEAD OUT.
WE WALKED ALONG A TRAIL FOR A WHILE AND THEN CUT OFF INTO THE UNDERBRUSH.
WATCH OUT, THERE'S STICKERS.
WALKING BEHIND DAVE, CARRYING MY BACKPACK AND SLEEPING BAG, IT FELT LIKE WE WERE HEADING OUT FOR AN OVERNIGHT CAMPOUT IN THE WOODS...
...ONLY I KNEW I WOULDN'T BE HIKING BACK TO MY WARM, SAFE HOME IN THE MORNING.
THIS WAS MY HOME.
AH... HERE'S WHERE WE MAKE CAMPFIRES SOMETIMES.
THIS WAS WHERE I WAS STAYING.
YOU KNOW, GET TOGETHER, EAT SOMETHING, HANG OUT...

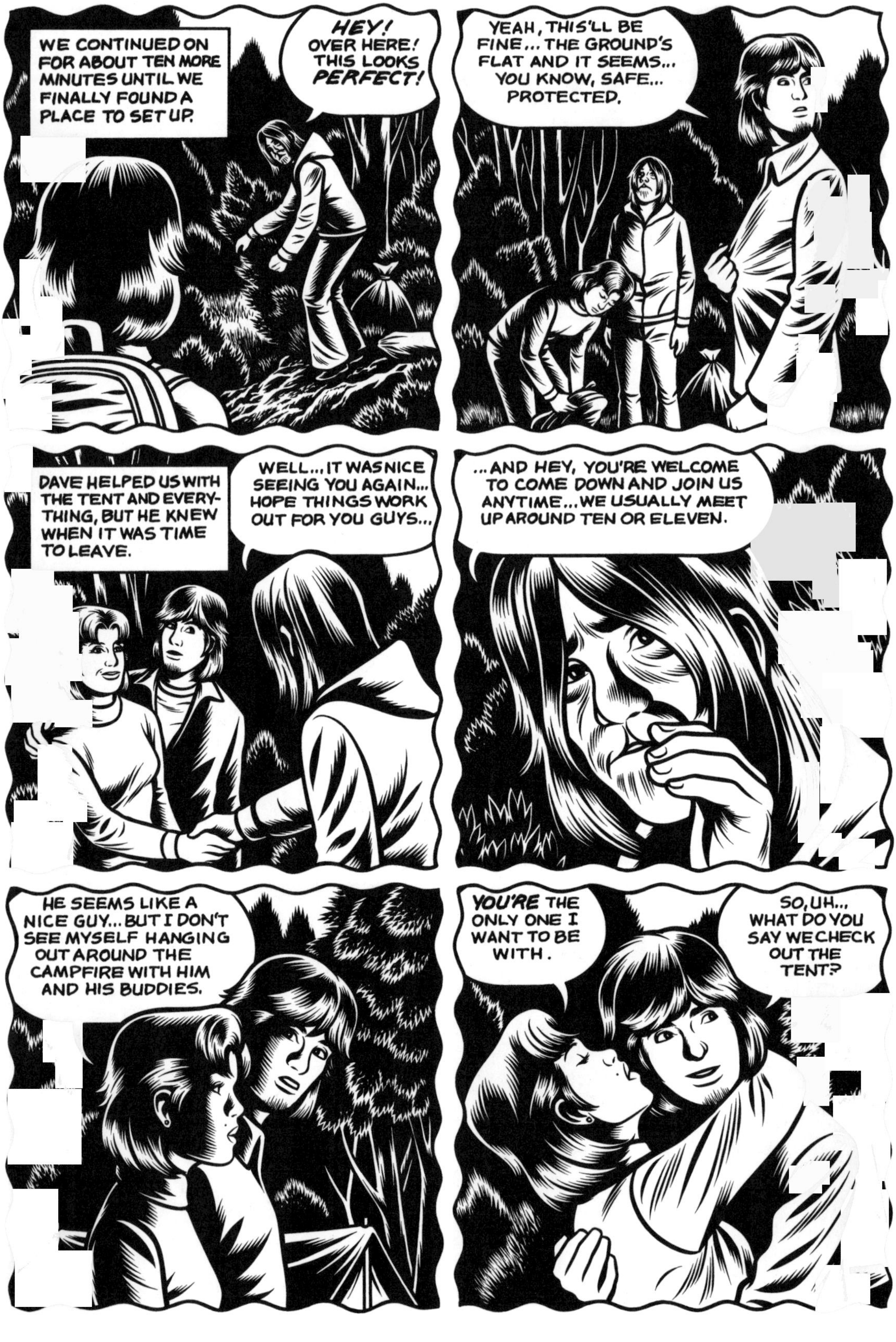
WE CONTINUED ON FOR ABOUT TEN MORE MINUTES UNTIL WE FINALLY FOUND A PLACE TO SET UP.
HEY! OVER HERE! THIS LOOKS PERFECT!
YEAH, THIS'LL BE FINE... THE GROUND'S FLAT AND IT SEEMS... YOU KNOW, SAFE... PROTECTED.
DAVE HELPED US WITH THE TENT AND EVERYTHING, BUT HE KNEW WHEN IT WAS TIME TO LEAVE.
WELL... IT WAS NICE SEEING YOU AGAIN... HOPE THINGS WORK OUT FOR YOU GUYS...
...AND HEY, YOU'RE WELCOME TO COME DOWN AND JOIN US ANYTIME... WE USUALLY MEET UP AROUND TEN OR ELEVEN.
HE SEEMS LIKE A NICE GUY... BUT I DON'T SEE MYSELF HANGING OUT AROUND THE CAMPFIRE WITH HIM AND HIS BUDDIES.
YOU'RE THE ONLY ONE I WANT TO BE WITH.
SO, UH... WHAT DO YOU SAY WE CHECK OUT THE TENT?

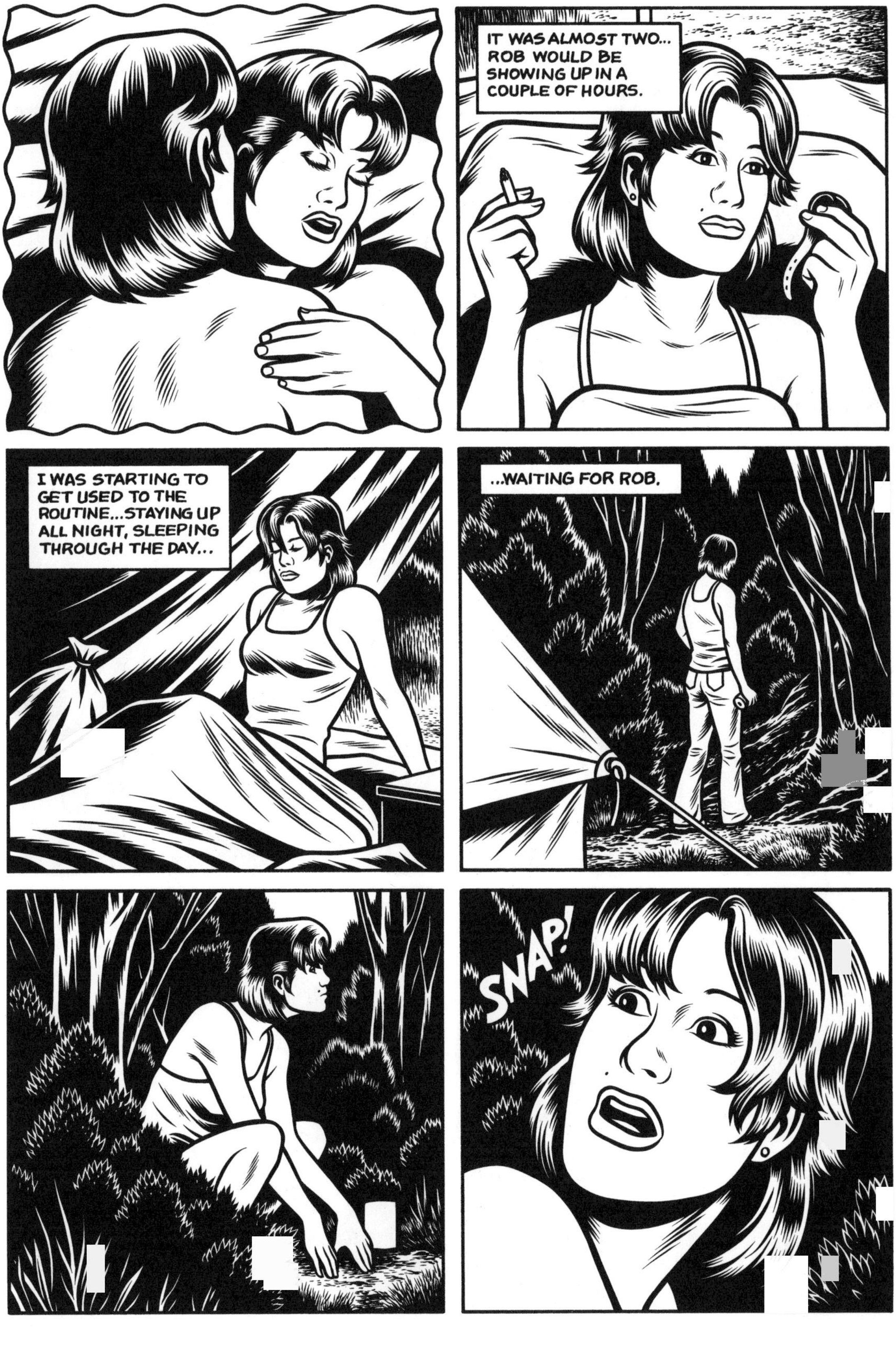
IT WAS ALMOST TWO... ROB WOULD BE SHOWING UP IN A COUPLE OF HOURS.
I WAS STARTING TO GET USED TO THE ROUTINE...STAYING UP ALL NIGHT, SLEEPING THROUGH THE DAY...
...WAITING FOR ROB.
SNAP!

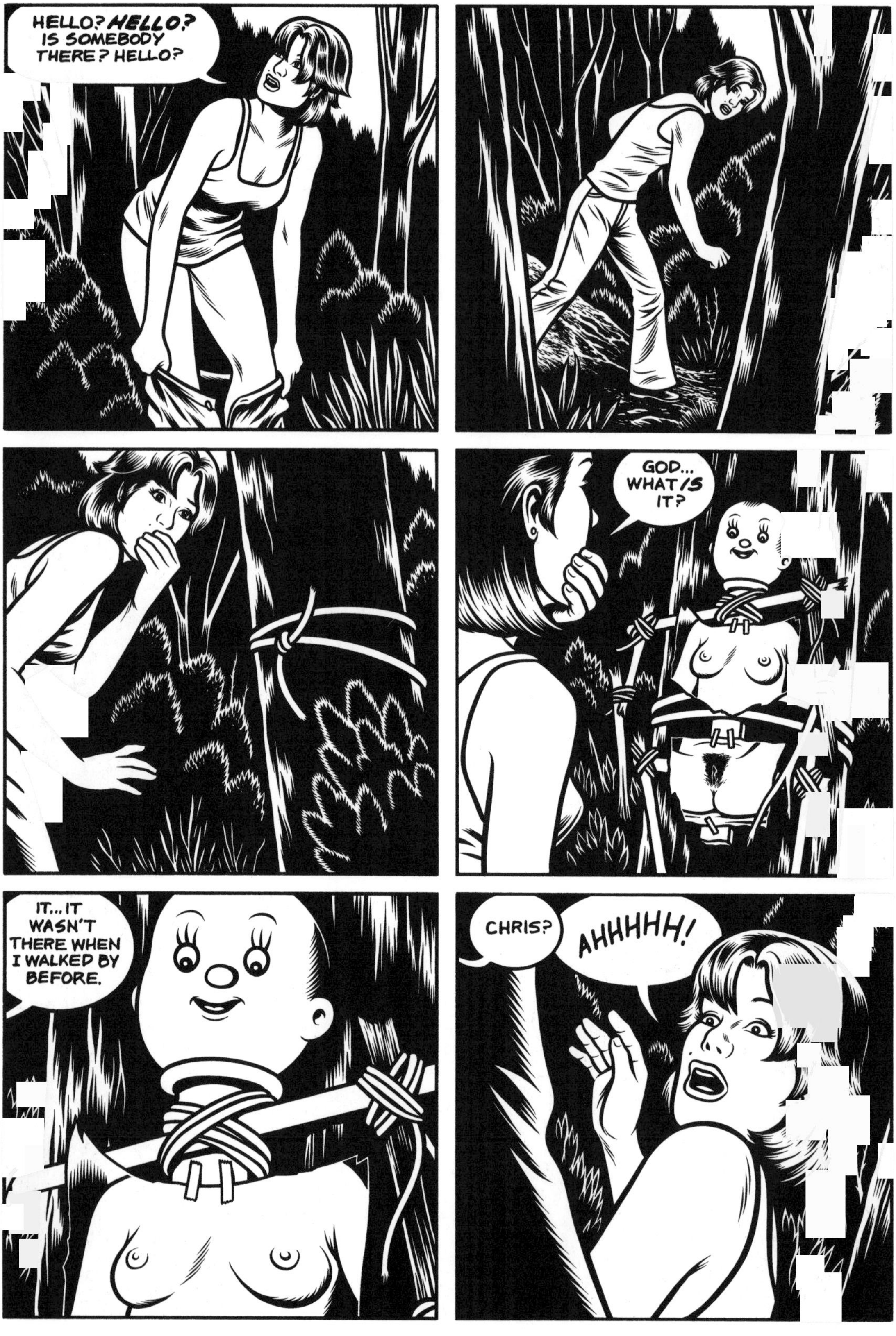
HELLO? HELLO? IS SOMEBODY THERE? HELLO?
GOD... WHAT IS IT?
IT... IT WASN'T THERE WHEN I WALKED BY BEFORE.
CHRIS?
AHHHHH!

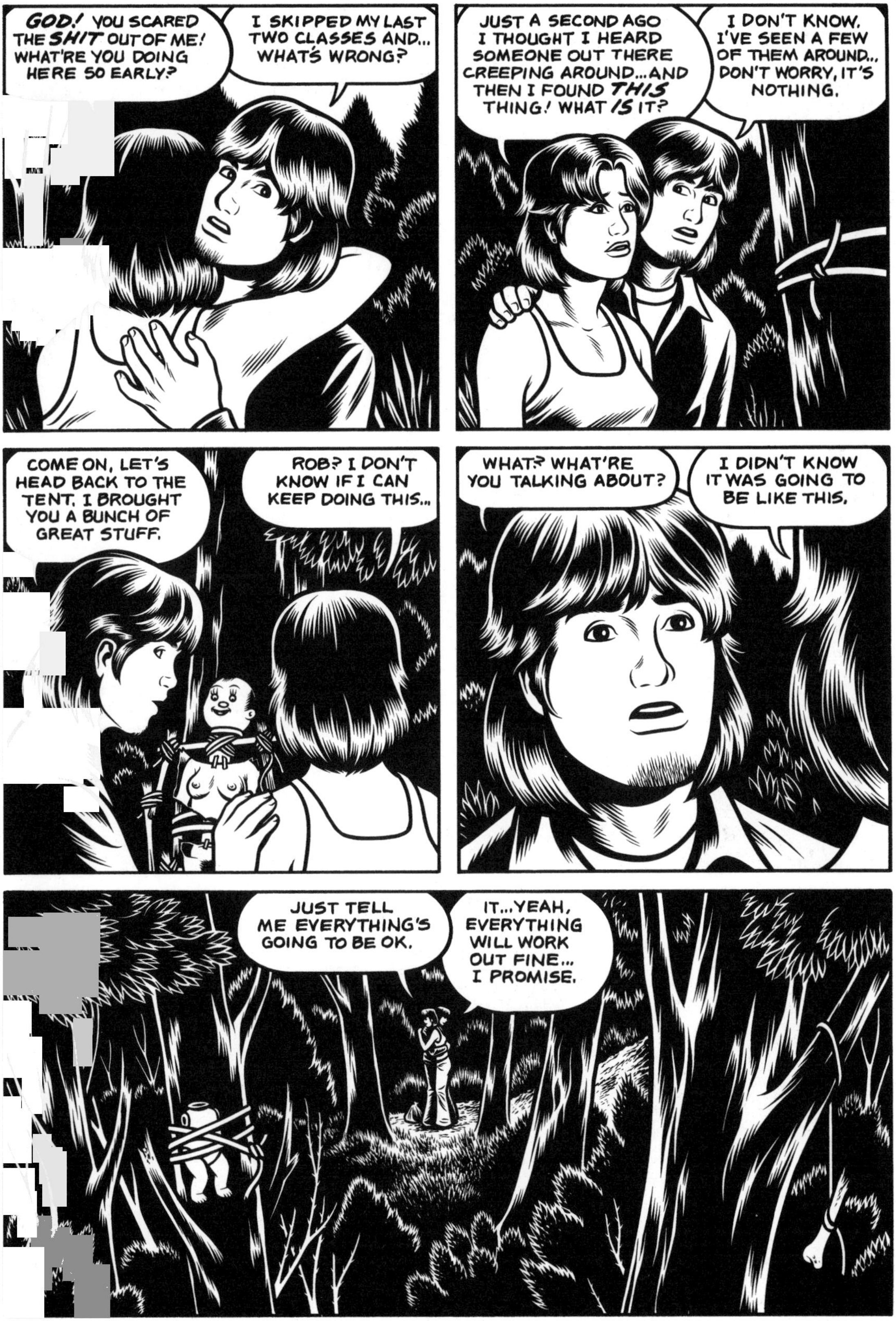

GOD! YOU SCARED THE SHIT OUT OF ME! WHAT'RE YOU DOING HERE SO EARLY?
I SKIPPED MY LAST TWO CLASSES AND... WHAT'S WRONG?
JUST A SECOND AGO I THOUGHT I HEARD SOMEONE OUT THERE CREEPING AROUND...AND THEN I FOUND THIS THING! WHAT IS IT?
I DON'T KNOW. I'VE SEEN A FEW OF THEM AROUND... DON'T WORRY, IT'S NOTHING.
COME ON, LET'S HEAD BACK TO THE TENT. I BROUGHT YOU A BUNCH OF GREAT STUFF.
ROB? I DON'T KNOW IF I CAN KEEP DOING THIS...
WHAT? WHAT'RE YOU TALKING ABOUT?
I DIDN'T KNOW IT WAS GOING TO BE LIKE THIS.
JUST TELL ME EVERYTHING'S GOING TO BE OK.
IT...YEAH, EVERYTHING WILL WORK OUT FINE... I PROMISE.

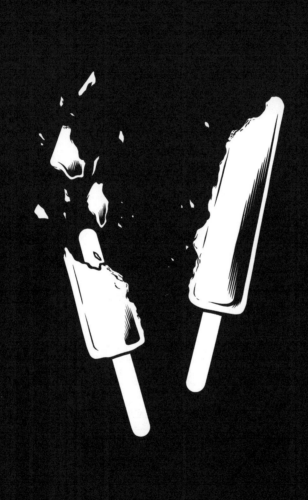

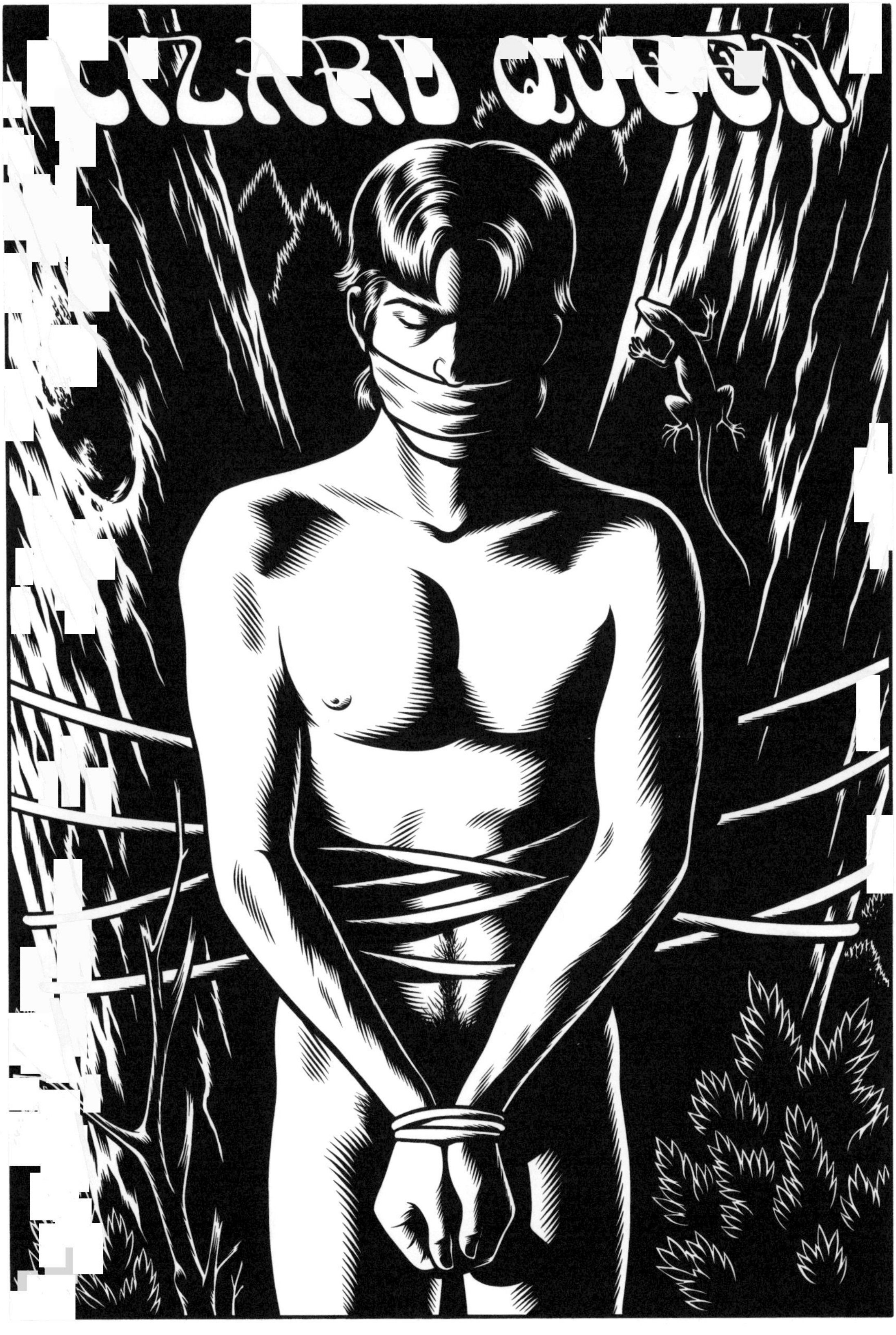
LIZARD QUEEN

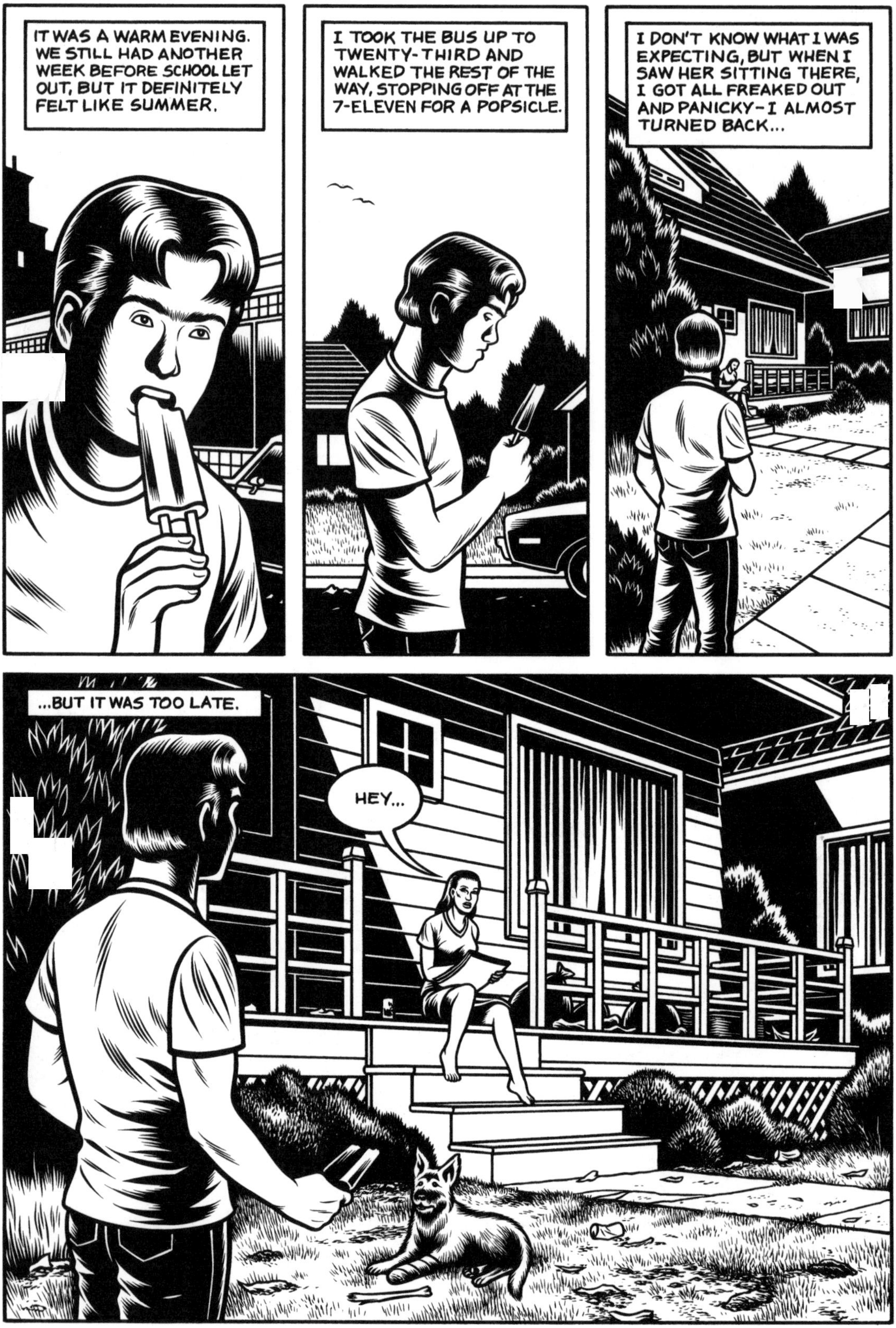
IT WAS A WARM EVENING. WE STILL HAD ANOTHER WEEK BEFORE SCHOOL LET OUT, BUT IT DEFINITELY FELT LIKE SUMMER.
I TOOK THE BUS UP TO TWENTY-THIRD AND WALKED THE REST OF THE WAY, STOPPING OFF AT THE 7-ELEVEN FOR A POPSICLE.
I DON'T KNOW WHAT I WAS EXPECTING, BUT WHEN I SAW HER SITTING THERE, I GOT ALL FREAKED OUT AND PANICKY–I ALMOST TURNED BACK...
...BUT IT WAS TOO LATE.
HEY...

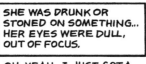

SHE LOOKED DIFFERENT. SOMETHING HAD HAPPENED TO HER.

HEY, LOOK AT YOU...NICE HAIRCUT.

SHE WAS DRUNK OR STONED ON SOMETHING... HER EYES WERE DULL, OUT OF FOCUS.

OH, YEAH...I JUST GOT A PART TIME JOB AT ALBERTSON'S AND THEY'VE GOT THIS DRESS CODE...EVEN MADE ME SHAVE MY SIDEBURNS.

LOOKS GOOD. I'M GETTING REAL TIRED OF THAT SCRAGGLY, LONG HAIRED HIPPIE LOOK.

SO...YOU FINALLY CAME BACK TO SEE ME, HUH?

YEAH, RIGHT...I... BUT I WAS ALSO...

RELAX, I'M JUST GIVIN' YOU SHIT, OK? I KNOW... YOU'RE HERE FOR DRUGS.

THE ONLY PROBLEM IS, KURT AND HIS BUDDIES ARE OUT FOR THE EVENING AND I'M THE ONLY ONE HOLDING DOWN THE FORT...IT'S JUST ME AND FAUST.

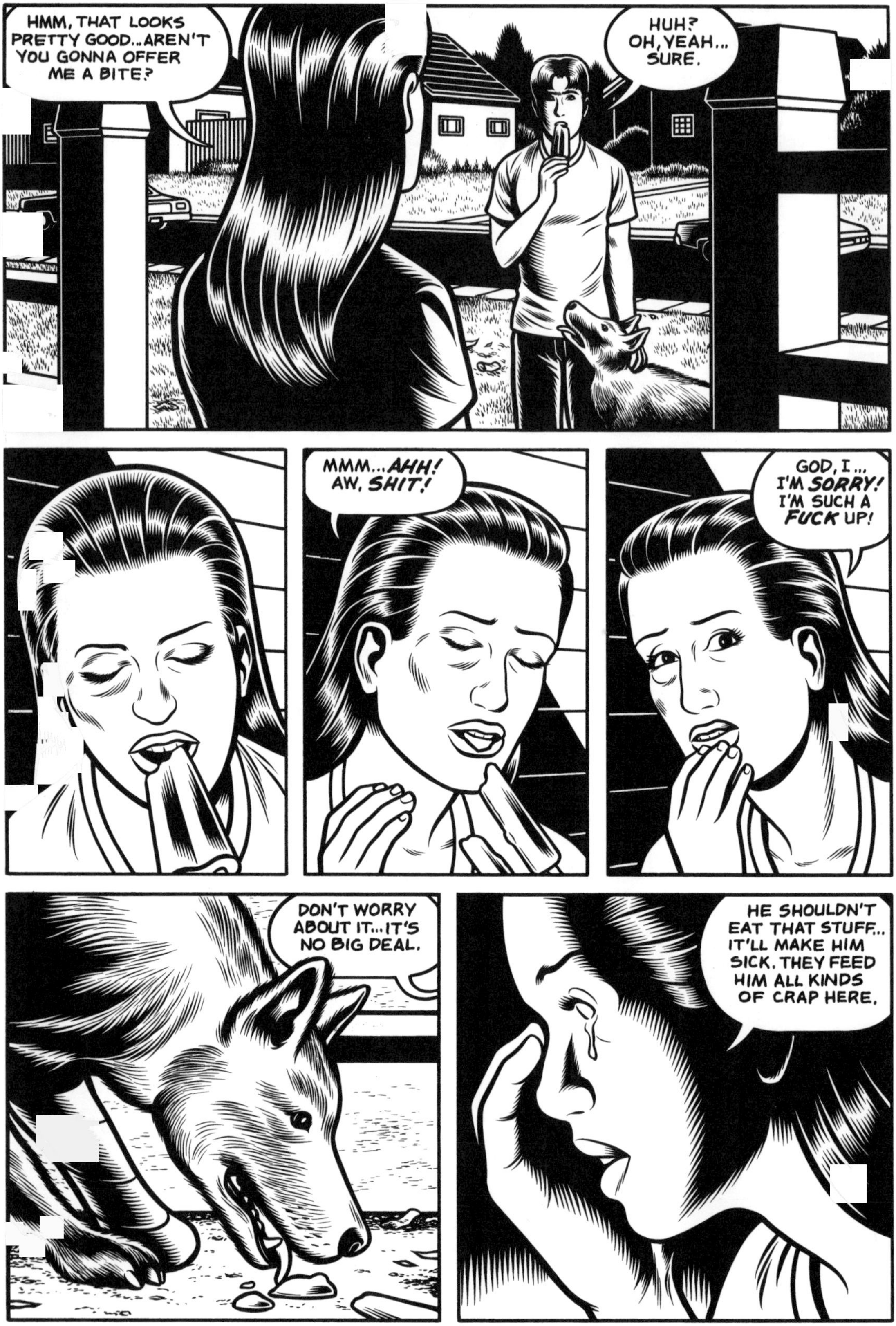
HMM, THAT LOOKS PRETTY GOOD...AREN'T YOU GONNA OFFER ME A BITE?
HUH? OH, YEAH... SURE.
MMM... AHH! AW, SHIT!
GOD, I... I'M SORRY! I'M SUCH A FUCK UP!
DON'T WORRY ABOUT IT... IT'S NO BIG DEAL.
HE SHOULDN'T EAT THAT STUFF... IT'LL MAKE HIM SICK. THEY FEED HIM ALL KINDS OF CRAP HERE.

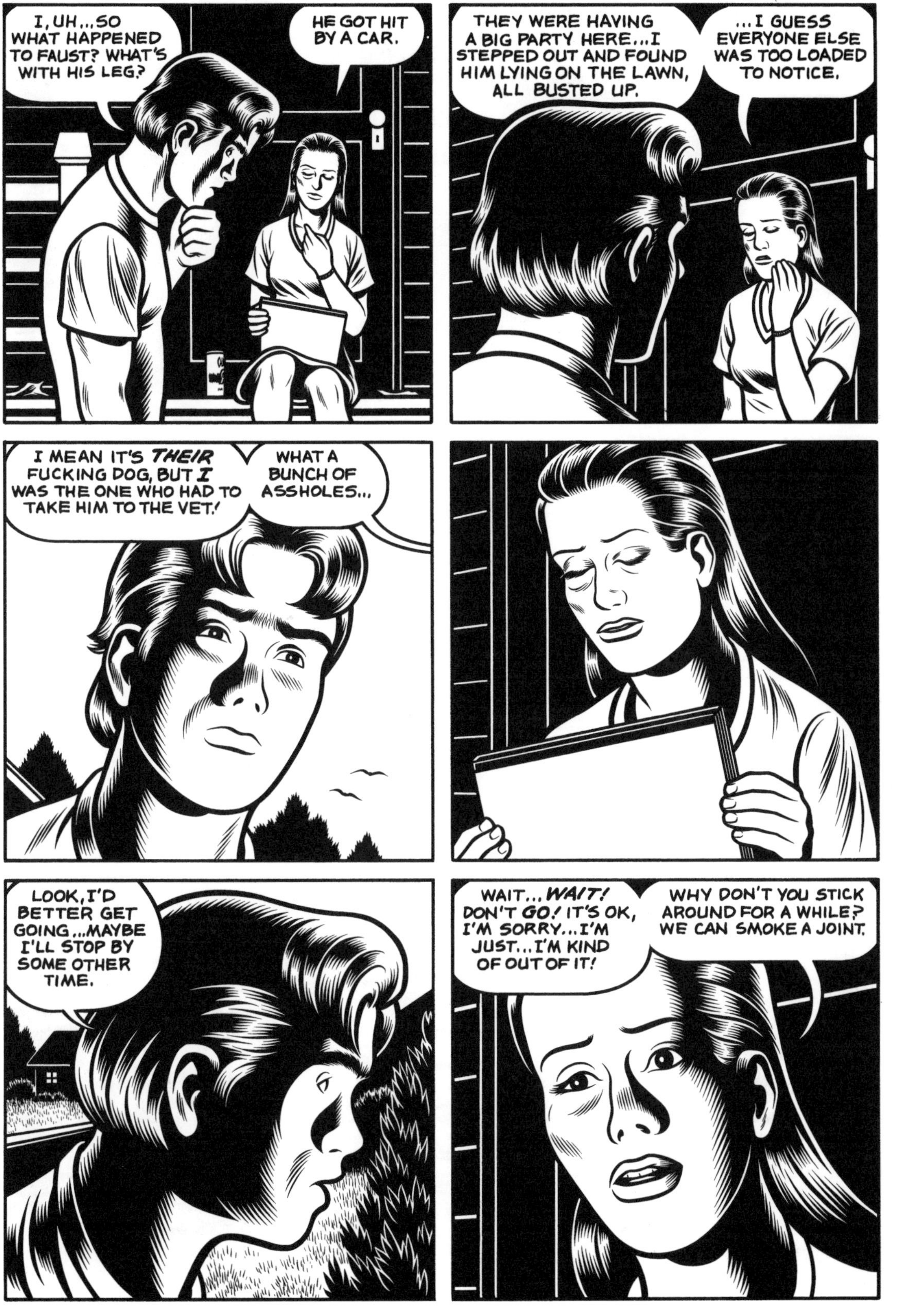
I, UH...SO WHAT HAPPENED TO FAUST? WHAT'S WITH HIS LEG?
HE GOT HIT BY A CAR.
THEY WERE HAVING A BIG PARTY HERE...I STEPPED OUT AND FOUND HIM LYING ON THE LAWN, ALL BUSTED UP.
...I GUESS EVERYONE ELSE WAS TOO LOADED TO NOTICE.
I MEAN IT'S *THEIR* FUCKING DOG, BUT *I* WAS THE ONE WHO HAD TO TAKE HIM TO THE VET!
WHAT A BUNCH OF ASSHOLES...
LOOK, I'D BETTER GET GOING...MAYBE I'LL STOP BY SOME OTHER TIME.
WAIT... *WAIT!* DON'T *GO!* IT'S OK, I'M SORRY...I'M JUST...I'M KIND OF OUT OF IT!
WHY DON'T YOU STICK AROUND FOR A WHILE? WE CAN SMOKE A JOINT.

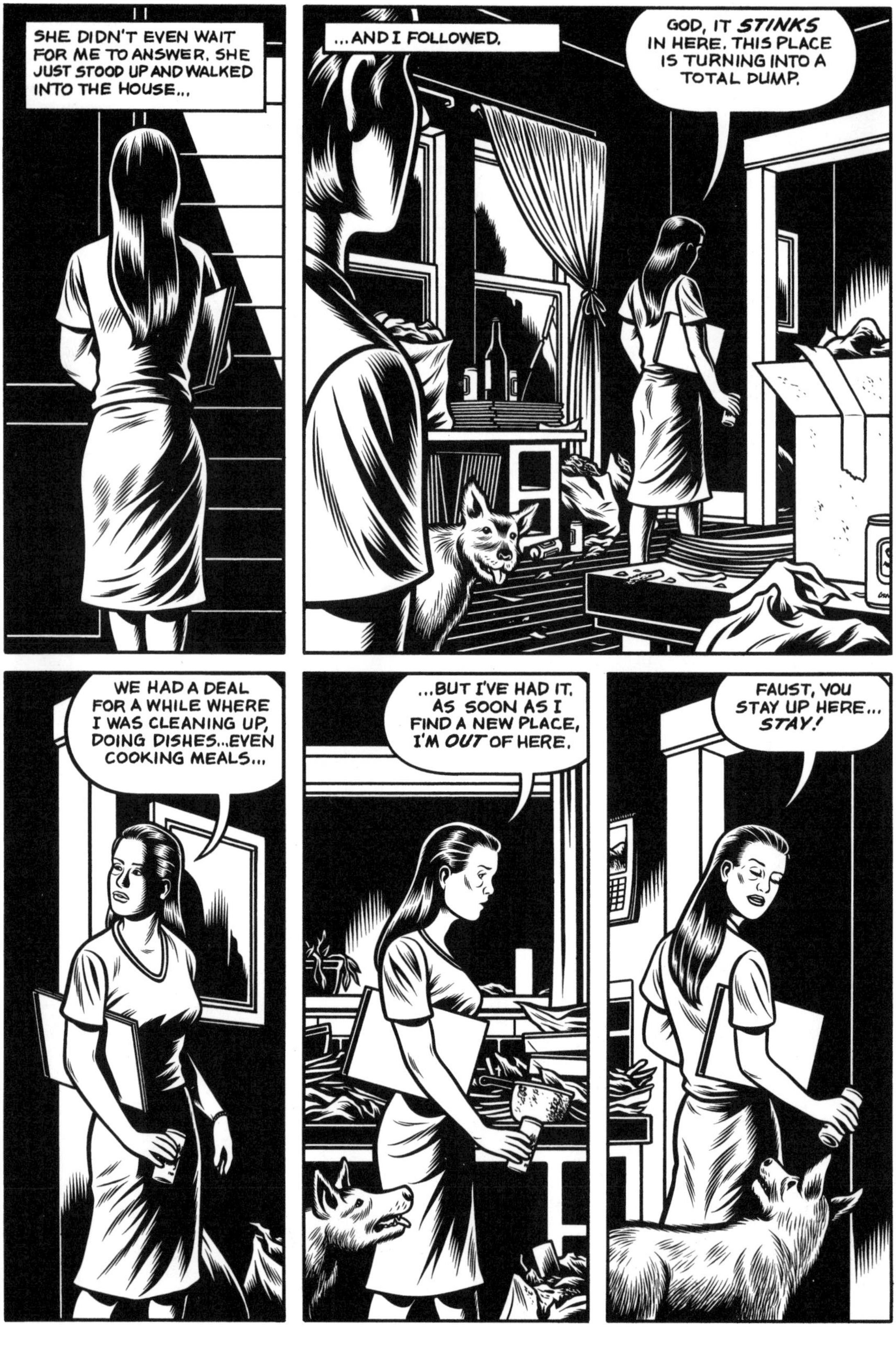
SHE DIDN'T EVEN WAIT FOR ME TO ANSWER. SHE JUST STOOD UP AND WALKED INTO THE HOUSE...
...AND I FOLLOWED.
GOD, IT STINKS IN HERE. THIS PLACE IS TURNING INTO A TOTAL DUMP.
WE HAD A DEAL FOR A WHILE WHERE I WAS CLEANING UP, DOING DISHES...EVEN COOKING MEALS...
...BUT I'VE HAD IT. AS SOON AS I FIND A NEW PLACE, I'M OUT OF HERE.
FAUST, YOU STAY UP HERE... STAY!

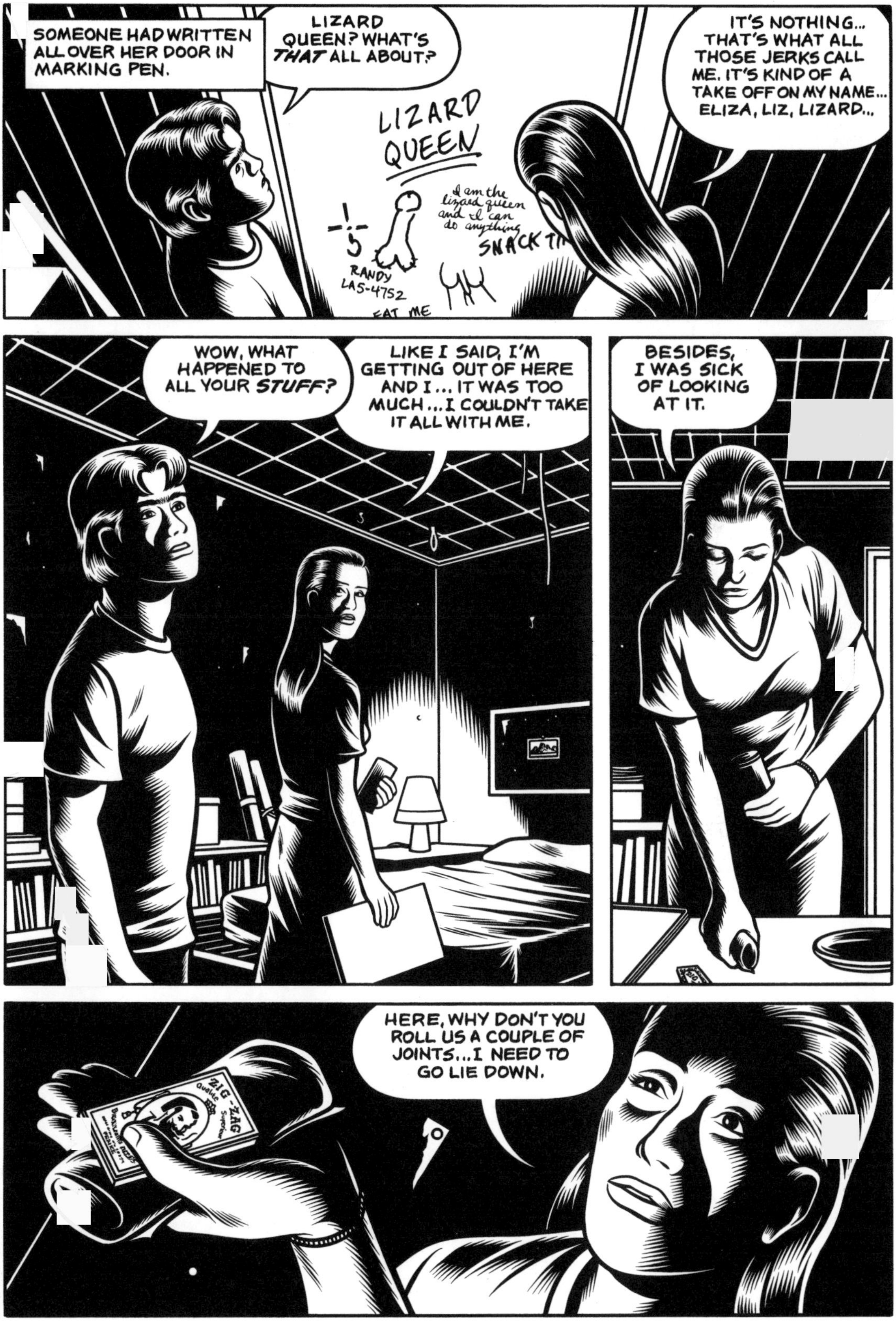
SOMEONE HAD WRITTEN ALL OVER HER DOOR IN MARKING PEN.
LIZARD QUEEN? WHAT'S *THAT* ALL ABOUT?
LIZARD QUEEN
I am the lizard queen and I can do anything
RANDY LA5-4752
EAT ME
IT'S NOTHING... THAT'S WHAT ALL THOSE JERKS CALL ME. IT'S KIND OF A TAKE OFF ON MY NAME... ELIZA, LIZ, LIZARD...
WOW, WHAT HAPPENED TO ALL YOUR *STUFF*?
LIKE I SAID, I'M GETTING OUT OF HERE AND I... IT WAS TOO MUCH... I COULDN'T TAKE IT ALL WITH ME.
BESIDES, I WAS SICK OF LOOKING AT IT.
ZIG-ZAG
HERE, WHY DON'T YOU ROLL US A COUPLE OF JOINTS... I NEED TO GO LIE DOWN.

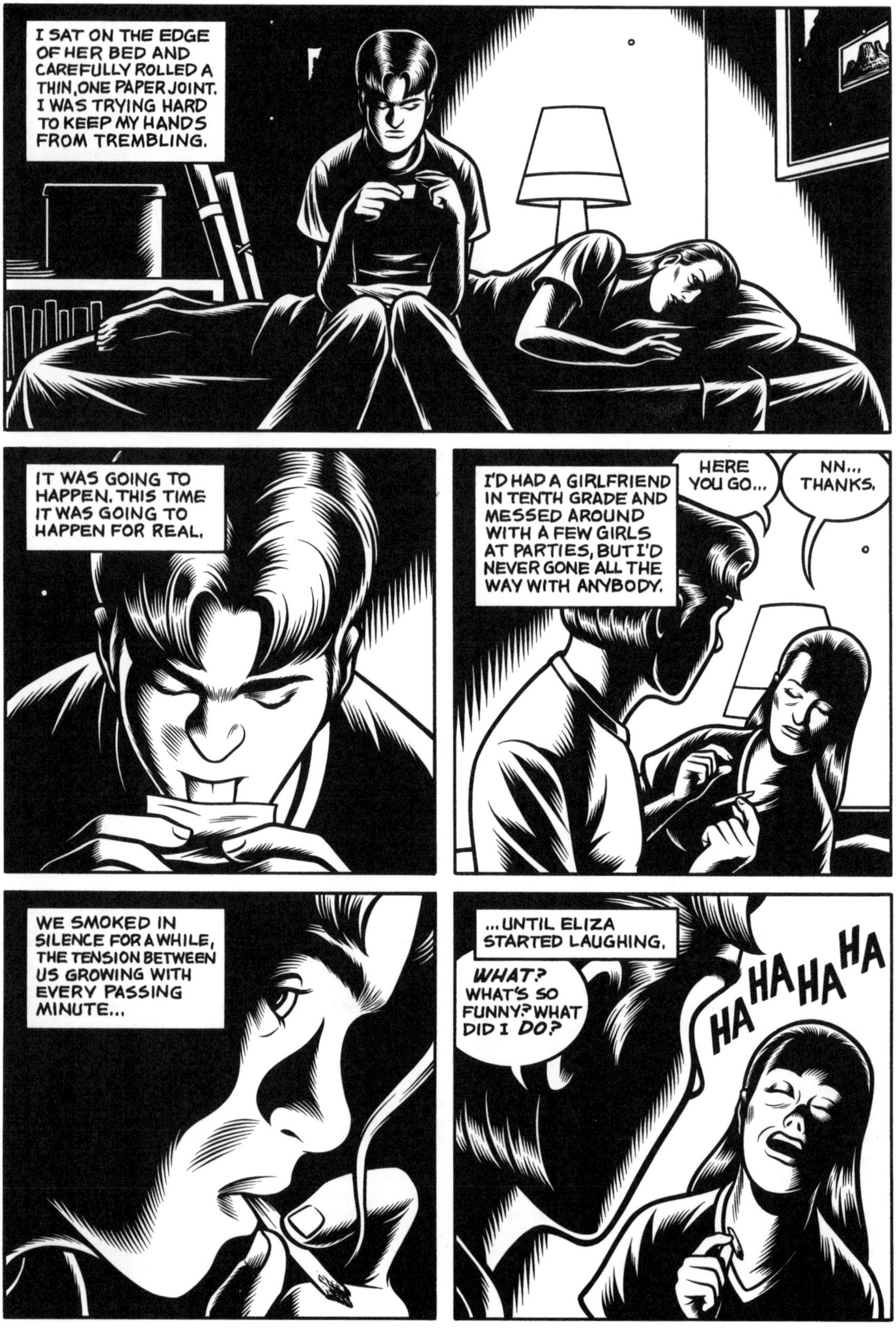
I SAT ON THE EDGE OF HER BED AND CAREFULLY ROLLED A THIN, ONE PAPER JOINT. I WAS TRYING HARD TO KEEP MY HANDS FROM TREMBLING.
IT WAS GOING TO HAPPEN. THIS TIME IT WAS GOING TO HAPPEN FOR REAL.
I'D HAD A GIRLFRIEND IN TENTH GRADE AND MESSED AROUND WITH A FEW GIRLS AT PARTIES, BUT I'D NEVER GONE ALL THE WAY WITH ANYBODY.
HERE YOU GO...
NN... THANKS.
WE SMOKED IN SILENCE FOR A WHILE, THE TENSION BETWEEN US GROWING WITH EVERY PASSING MINUTE...
...UNTIL ELIZA STARTED LAUGHING.
WHAT? WHAT'S SO FUNNY? WHAT DID I DO?
HA HA HA HA HA

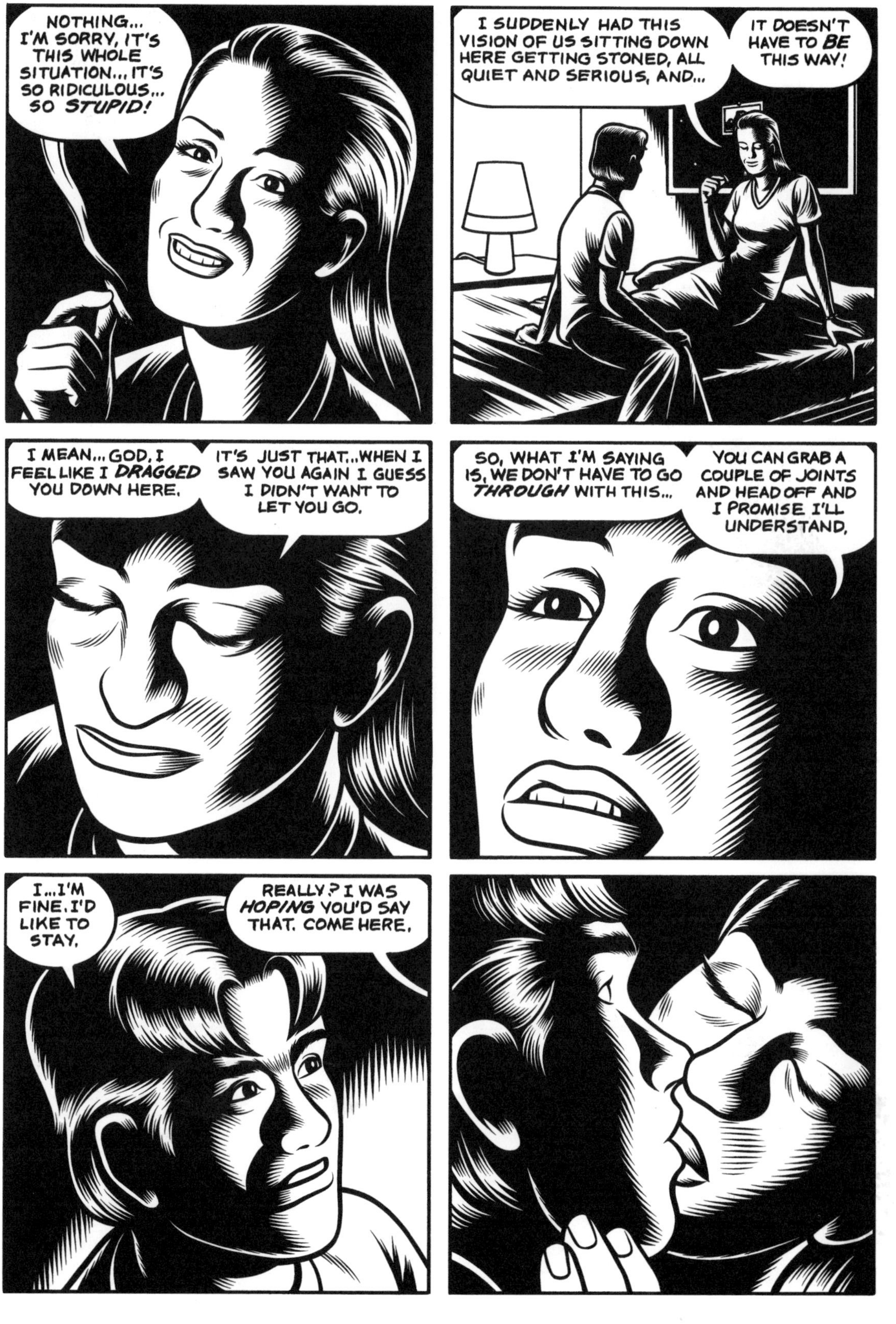
NOTHING... I'M SORRY, IT'S THIS WHOLE SITUATION... IT'S SO RIDICULOUS... SO *STUPID!*
I SUDDENLY HAD THIS VISION OF US SITTING DOWN HERE GETTING STONED, ALL QUIET AND SERIOUS, AND...
IT DOESN'T HAVE TO *BE* THIS WAY!
I MEAN... GOD, I FEEL LIKE I *DRAGGED* YOU DOWN HERE.
IT'S JUST THAT... WHEN I SAW YOU AGAIN I GUESS I DIDN'T WANT TO LET YOU GO.
SO, WHAT I'M SAYING IS, WE DON'T HAVE TO GO *THROUGH* WITH THIS...
YOU CAN GRAB A COUPLE OF JOINTS AND HEAD OFF AND I PROMISE I'LL UNDERSTAND.
I... I'M FINE. I'D LIKE TO STAY.
REALLY? I WAS *HOPING* YOU'D SAY THAT. COME HERE.

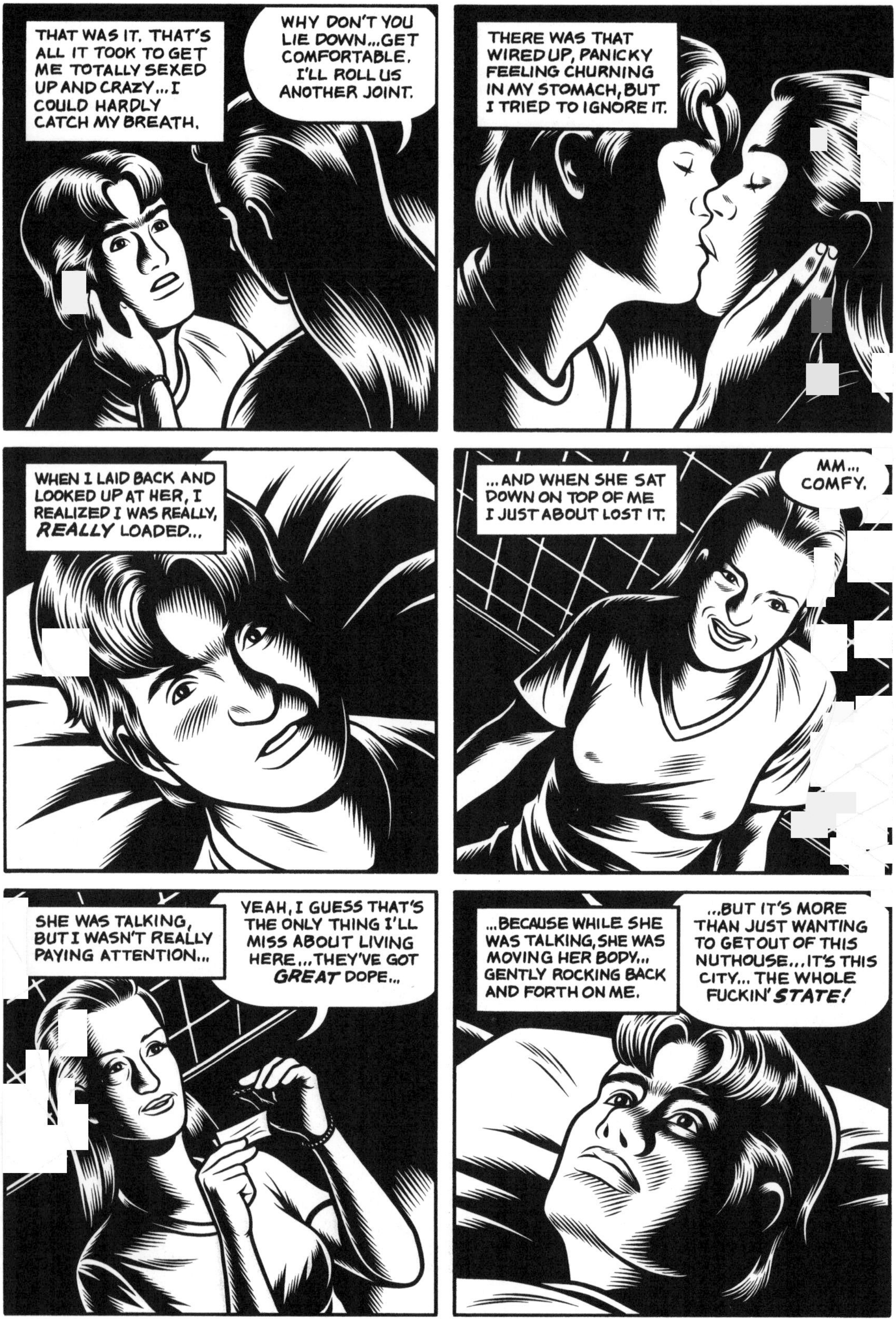
THAT WAS IT. THAT'S ALL IT TOOK TO GET ME TOTALLY SEXED UP AND CRAZY... I COULD HARDLY CATCH MY BREATH.
WHY DON'T YOU LIE DOWN... GET COMFORTABLE. I'LL ROLL US ANOTHER JOINT.
THERE WAS THAT WIRED UP, PANICKY FEELING CHURNING IN MY STOMACH, BUT I TRIED TO IGNORE IT.
WHEN I LAID BACK AND LOOKED UP AT HER, I REALIZED I WAS REALLY, REALLY LOADED...
...AND WHEN SHE SAT DOWN ON TOP OF ME I JUST ABOUT LOST IT.
MM... COMFY.
SHE WAS TALKING, BUT I WASN'T REALLY PAYING ATTENTION...
YEAH, I GUESS THAT'S THE ONLY THING I'LL MISS ABOUT LIVING HERE... THEY'VE GOT GREAT DOPE...
...BECAUSE WHILE SHE WAS TALKING, SHE WAS MOVING HER BODY... GENTLY ROCKING BACK AND FORTH ON ME.
...BUT IT'S MORE THAN JUST WANTING TO GET OUT OF THIS NUTHOUSE... IT'S THIS CITY... THE WHOLE FUCKIN' STATE!

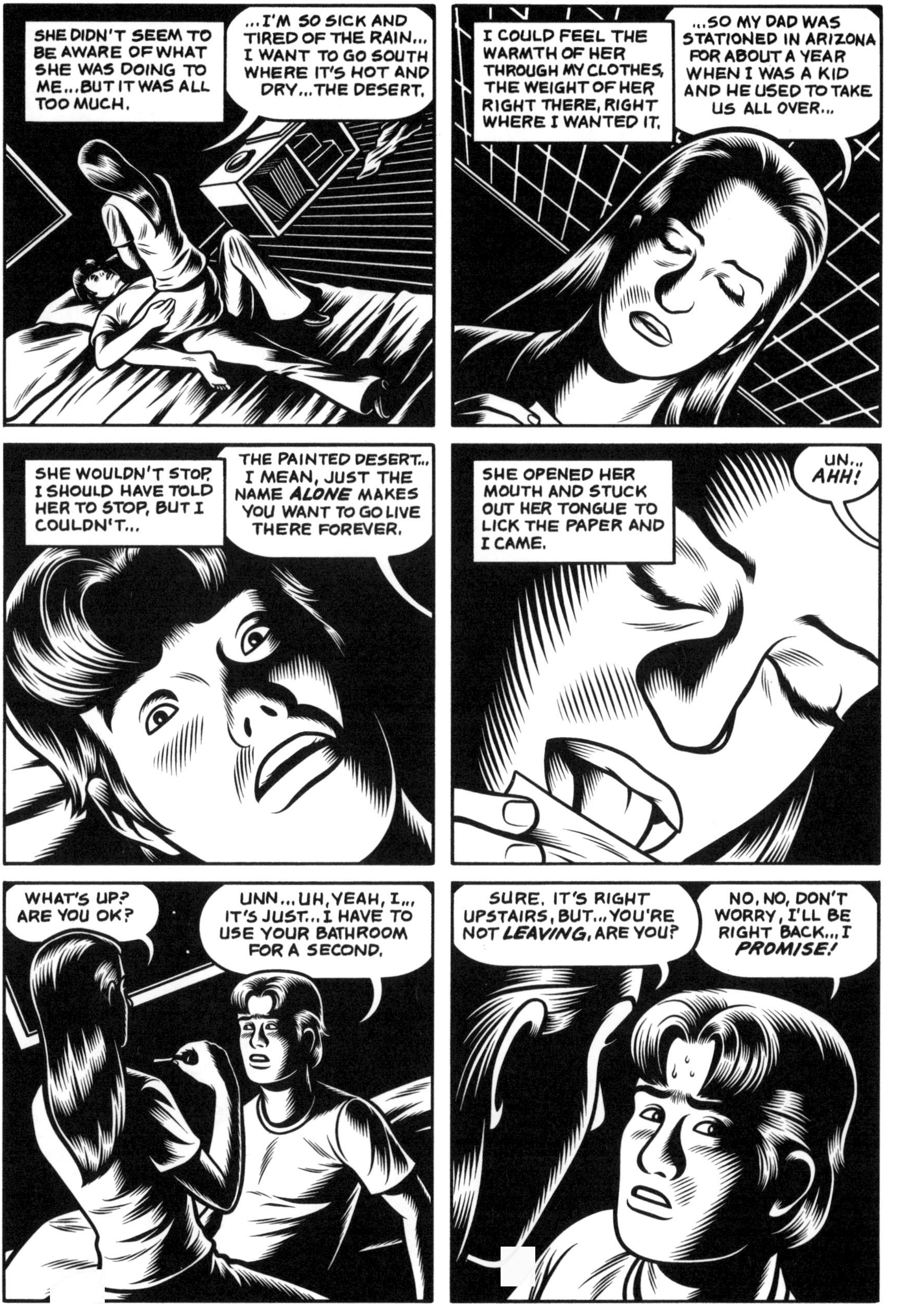
SHE DIDN'T SEEM TO BE AWARE OF WHAT SHE WAS DOING TO ME... BUT IT WAS ALL TOO MUCH.
...I'M SO SICK AND TIRED OF THE RAIN... I WANT TO GO SOUTH WHERE IT'S HOT AND DRY... THE DESERT.
I COULD FEEL THE WARMTH OF HER THROUGH MY CLOTHES, THE WEIGHT OF HER RIGHT THERE, RIGHT WHERE I WANTED IT.
...SO MY DAD WAS STATIONED IN ARIZONA FOR ABOUT A YEAR WHEN I WAS A KID AND HE USED TO TAKE US ALL OVER...
SHE WOULDN'T STOP. I SHOULD HAVE TOLD HER TO STOP, BUT I COULDN'T...
THE PAINTED DESERT... I MEAN, JUST THE NAME ALONE MAKES YOU WANT TO GO LIVE THERE FOREVER.
SHE OPENED HER MOUTH AND STUCK OUT HER TONGUE TO LICK THE PAPER AND I CAME.
UN... AHH!
WHAT'S UP? ARE YOU OK?
UNN... UH, YEAH, I... IT'S JUST... I HAVE TO USE YOUR BATHROOM FOR A SECOND.
SURE. IT'S RIGHT UPSTAIRS, BUT... YOU'RE NOT LEAVING, ARE YOU?
NO, NO, DON'T WORRY, I'LL BE RIGHT BACK... I PROMISE!

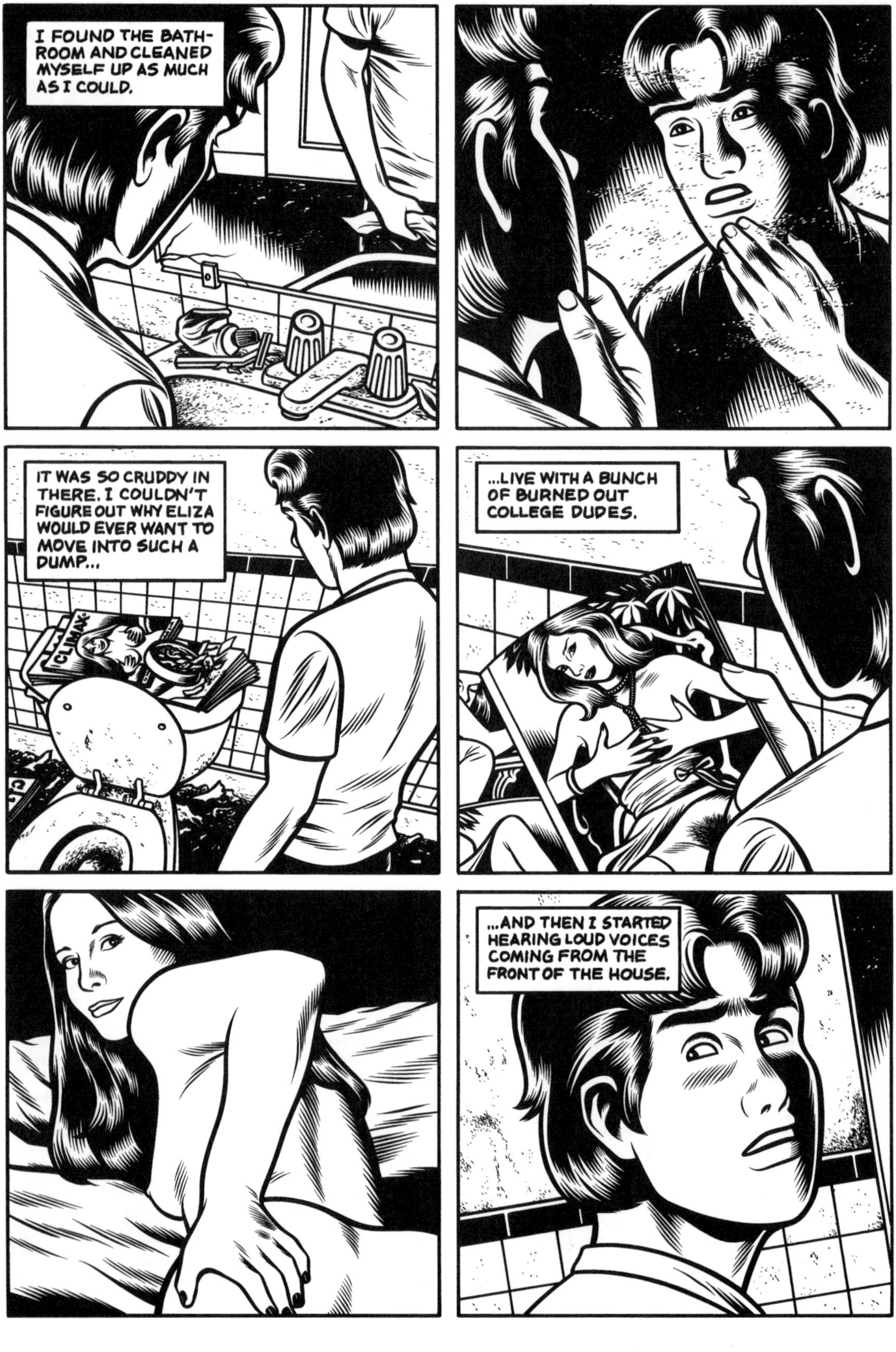
I FOUND THE BATHROOM AND CLEANED MYSELF UP AS MUCH AS I COULD.
IT WAS SO CRUDDY IN THERE. I COULDN'T FIGURE OUT WHY ELIZA WOULD EVER WANT TO MOVE INTO SUCH A DUMP...
CLIMAX
...LIVE WITH A BUNCH OF BURNED OUT COLLEGE DUDES.
...AND THEN I STARTED HEARING LOUD VOICES COMING FROM THE FRONT OF THE HOUSE.

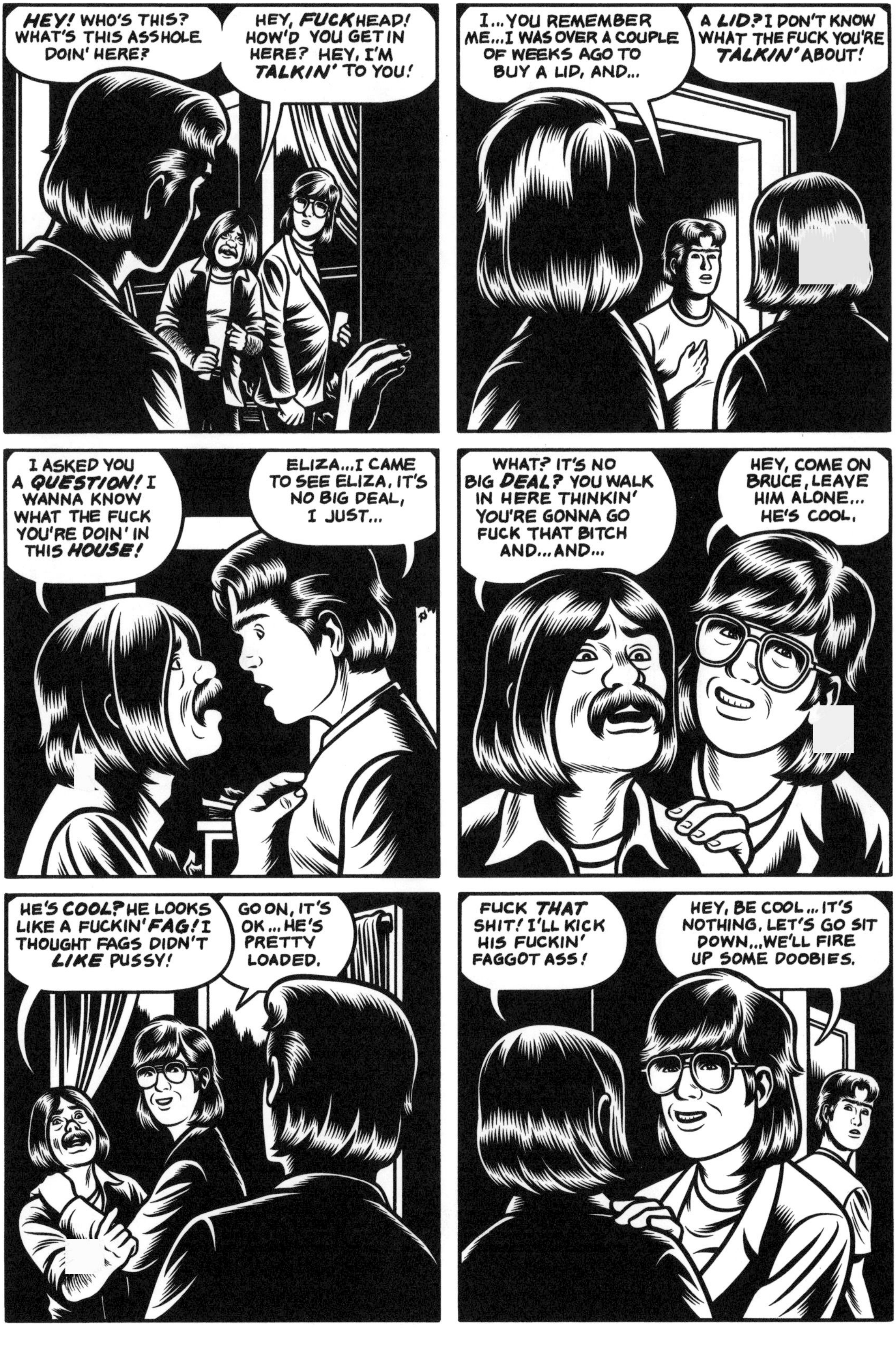
HEY! WHO'S THIS? WHAT'S THIS ASSHOLE DOIN' HERE?
HEY, FUCKHEAD! HOW'D YOU GET IN HERE? HEY, I'M TALKIN' TO YOU!
I... YOU REMEMBER ME... I WAS OVER A COUPLE OF WEEKS AGO TO BUY A LID, AND...
A LID? I DON'T KNOW WHAT THE FUCK YOU'RE TALKIN' ABOUT!
I ASKED YOU A QUESTION! I WANNA KNOW WHAT THE FUCK YOU'RE DOIN' IN THIS HOUSE!
ELIZA... I CAME TO SEE ELIZA, IT'S NO BIG DEAL, I JUST...
WHAT? IT'S NO BIG DEAL? YOU WALK IN HERE THINKIN' YOU'RE GONNA GO FUCK THAT BITCH AND... AND...
HEY, COME ON BRUCE, LEAVE HIM ALONE... HE'S COOL.
HE'S COOL? HE LOOKS LIKE A FUCKIN' FAG! I THOUGHT FAGS DIDN'T LIKE PUSSY!
GO ON, IT'S OK... HE'S PRETTY LOADED.
FUCK THAT SHIT! I'LL KICK HIS FUCKIN' FAGGOT ASS!
HEY, BE COOL... IT'S NOTHING, LET'S GO SIT DOWN... WE'LL FIRE UP SOME DOOBIES.

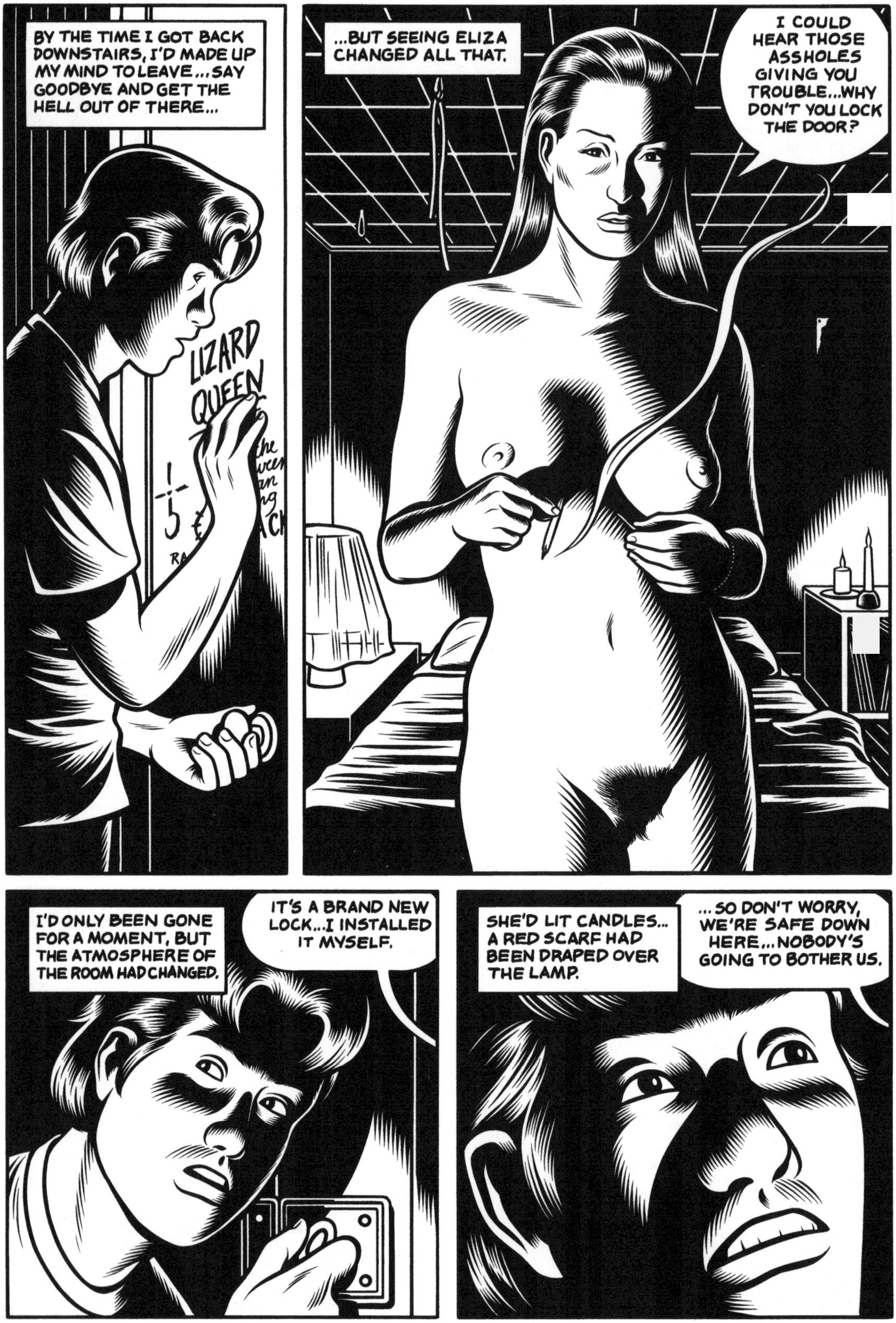
BY THE TIME I GOT BACK DOWNSTAIRS, I'D MADE UP MY MIND TO LEAVE... SAY GOODBYE AND GET THE HELL OUT OF THERE...
LIZARD QUEEN
...BUT SEEING ELIZA CHANGED ALL THAT.
I COULD HEAR THOSE ASSHOLES GIVING YOU TROUBLE...WHY DON'T YOU LOCK THE DOOR?
I'D ONLY BEEN GONE FOR A MOMENT, BUT THE ATMOSPHERE OF THE ROOM HAD CHANGED.
IT'S A BRAND NEW LOCK...I INSTALLED IT MYSELF.
SHE'D LIT CANDLES... A RED SCARF HAD BEEN DRAPED OVER THE LAMP.
...SO DON'T WORRY, WE'RE SAFE DOWN HERE...NOBODY'S GOING TO BOTHER US.

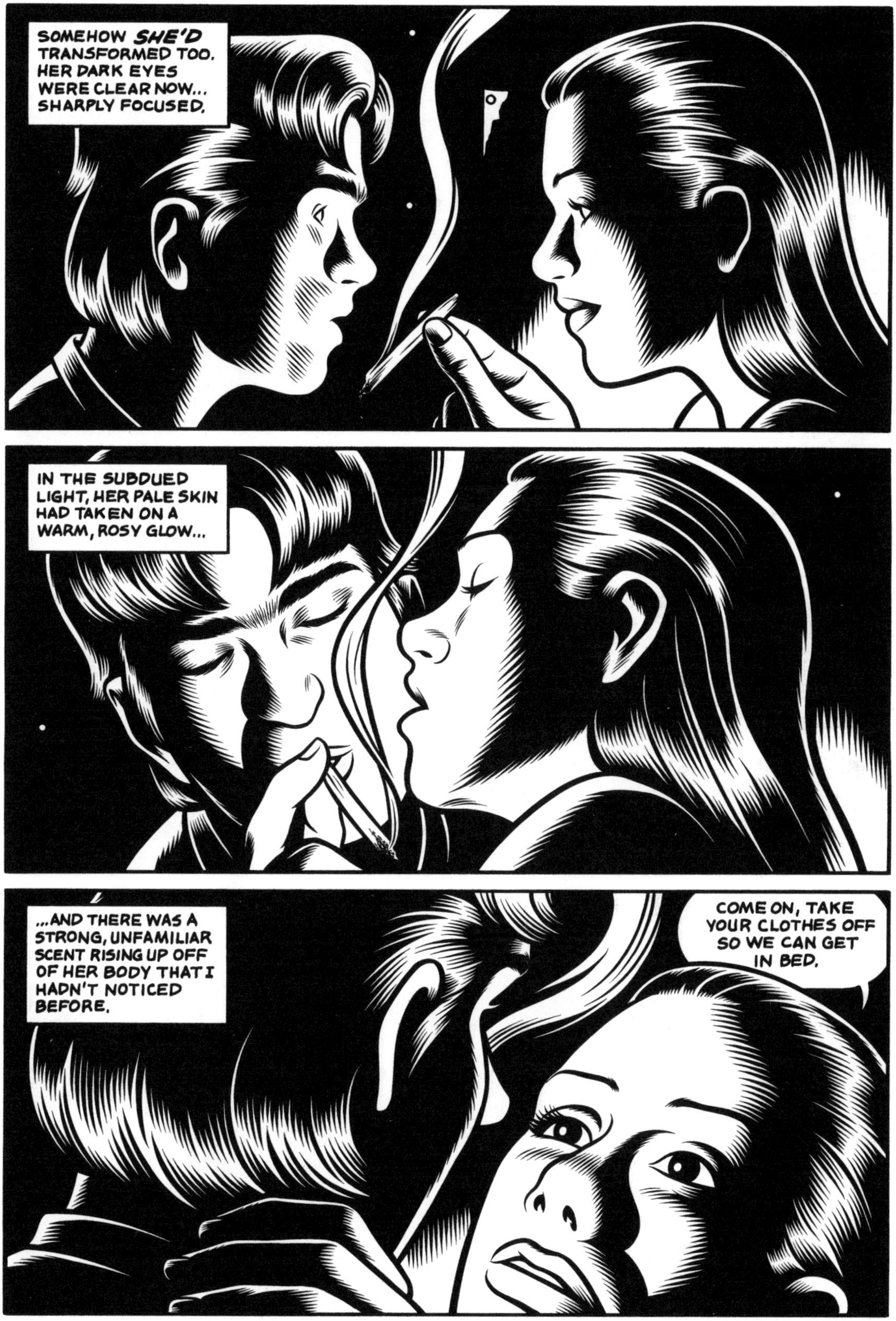
SOMEHOW SHE'D TRANSFORMED TOO. HER DARK EYES WERE CLEAR NOW... SHARPLY FOCUSED.
IN THE SUBDUED LIGHT, HER PALE SKIN HAD TAKEN ON A WARM, ROSY GLOW...
...AND THERE WAS A STRONG, UNFAMILIAR SCENT RISING UP OFF OF HER BODY THAT I HADN'T NOTICED BEFORE.
COME ON, TAKE YOUR CLOTHES OFF SO WE CAN GET IN BED.

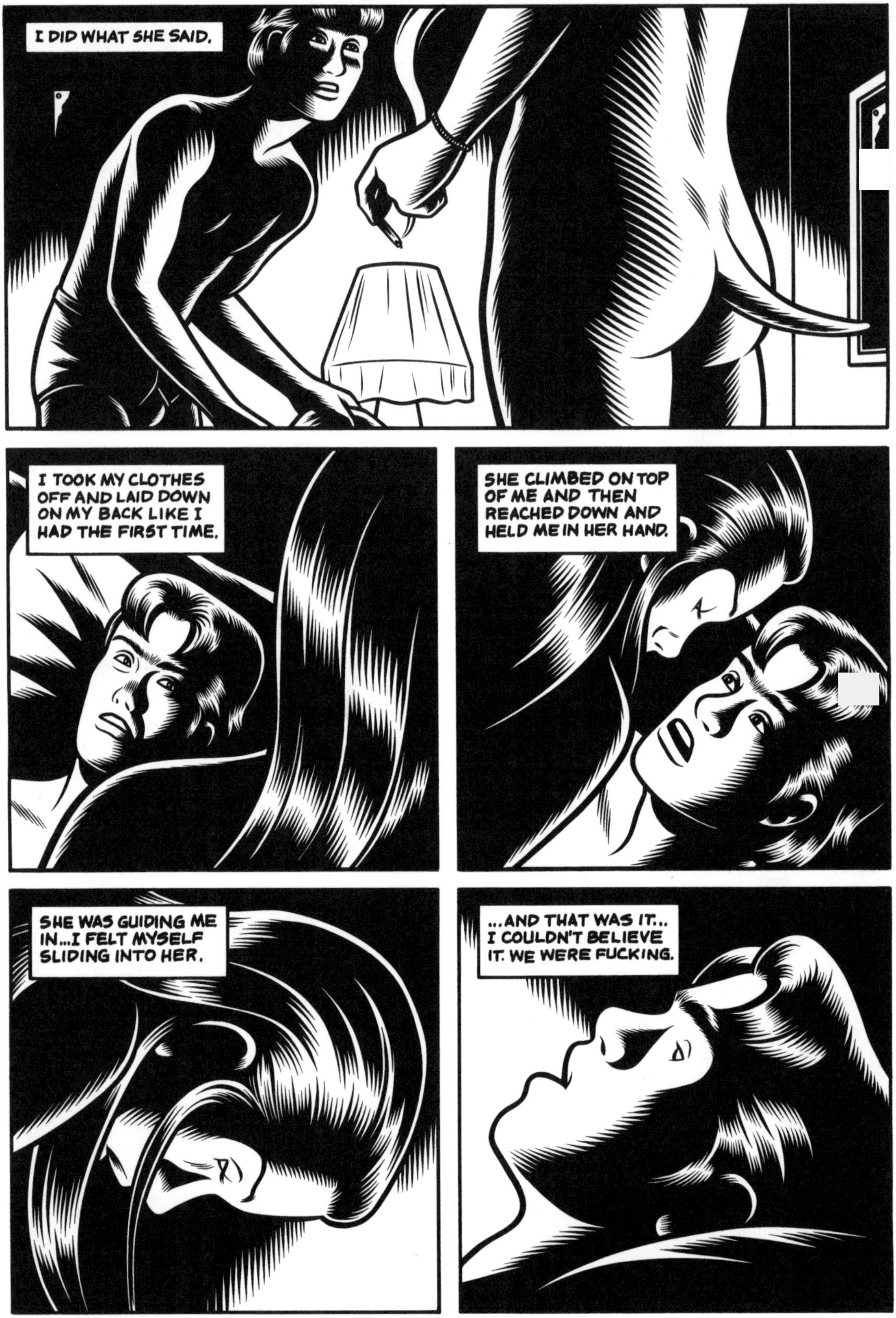
I DID WHAT SHE SAID.
I TOOK MY CLOTHES OFF AND LAID DOWN ON MY BACK LIKE I HAD THE FIRST TIME.
SHE CLIMBED ON TOP OF ME AND THEN REACHED DOWN AND HELD ME IN HER HAND.
SHE WAS GUIDING ME IN...I FELT MYSELF SLIDING INTO HER.
...AND THAT WAS IT... I COULDN'T BELIEVE IT. WE WERE FUCKING.

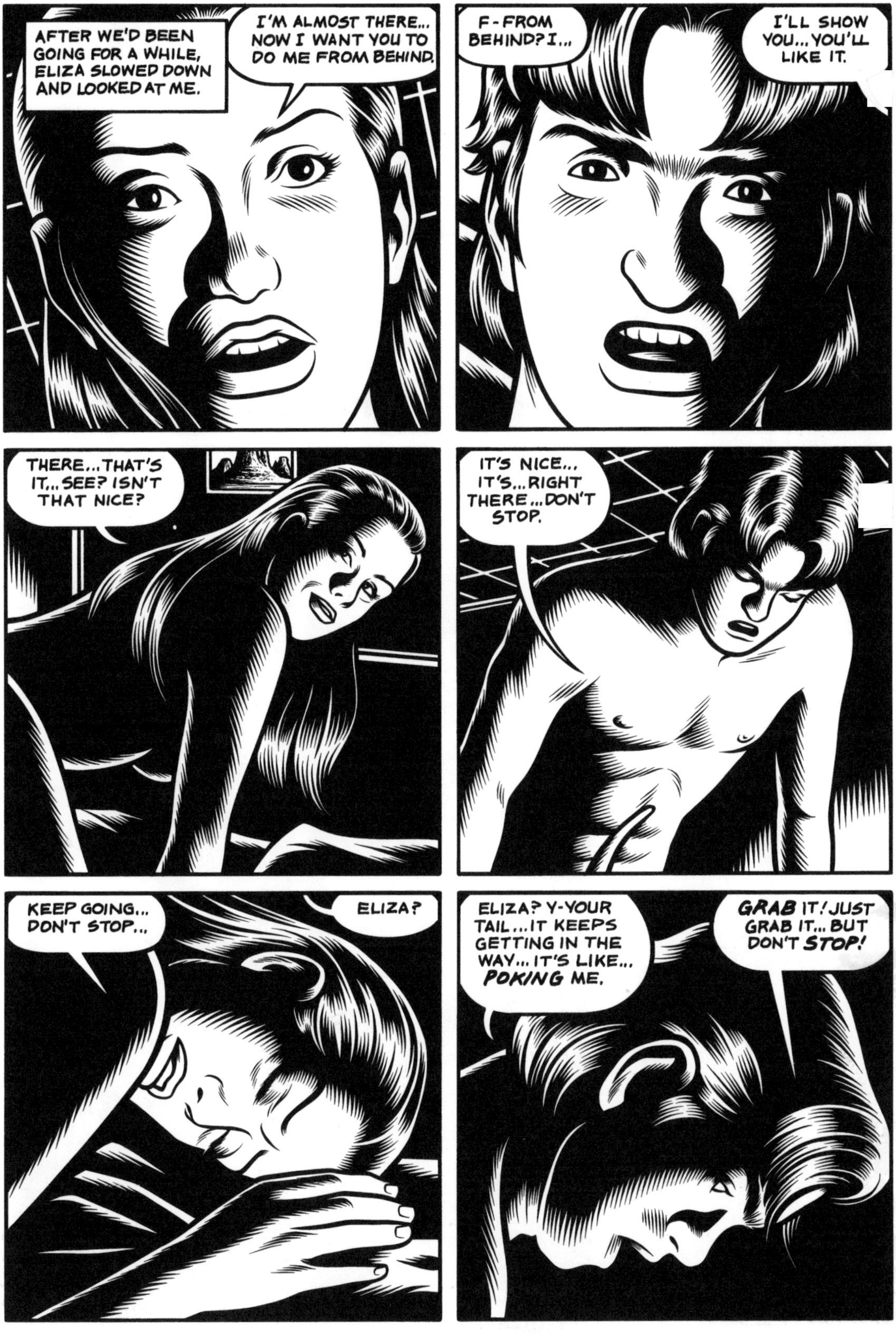
AFTER WE'D BEEN GOING FOR A WHILE, ELIZA SLOWED DOWN AND LOOKED AT ME.
I'M ALMOST THERE... NOW I WANT YOU TO DO ME FROM BEHIND.
F-FROM BEHIND? I...
I'LL SHOW YOU... YOU'LL LIKE IT.
THERE... THAT'S IT... SEE? ISN'T THAT NICE?
IT'S NICE... IT'S... RIGHT THERE... DON'T STOP.
KEEP GOING... DON'T STOP...
ELIZA?
ELIZA? Y-YOUR TAIL... IT KEEPS GETTING IN THE WAY... IT'S LIKE... POKING ME.
GRAB IT! JUST GRAB IT... BUT DON'T STOP!

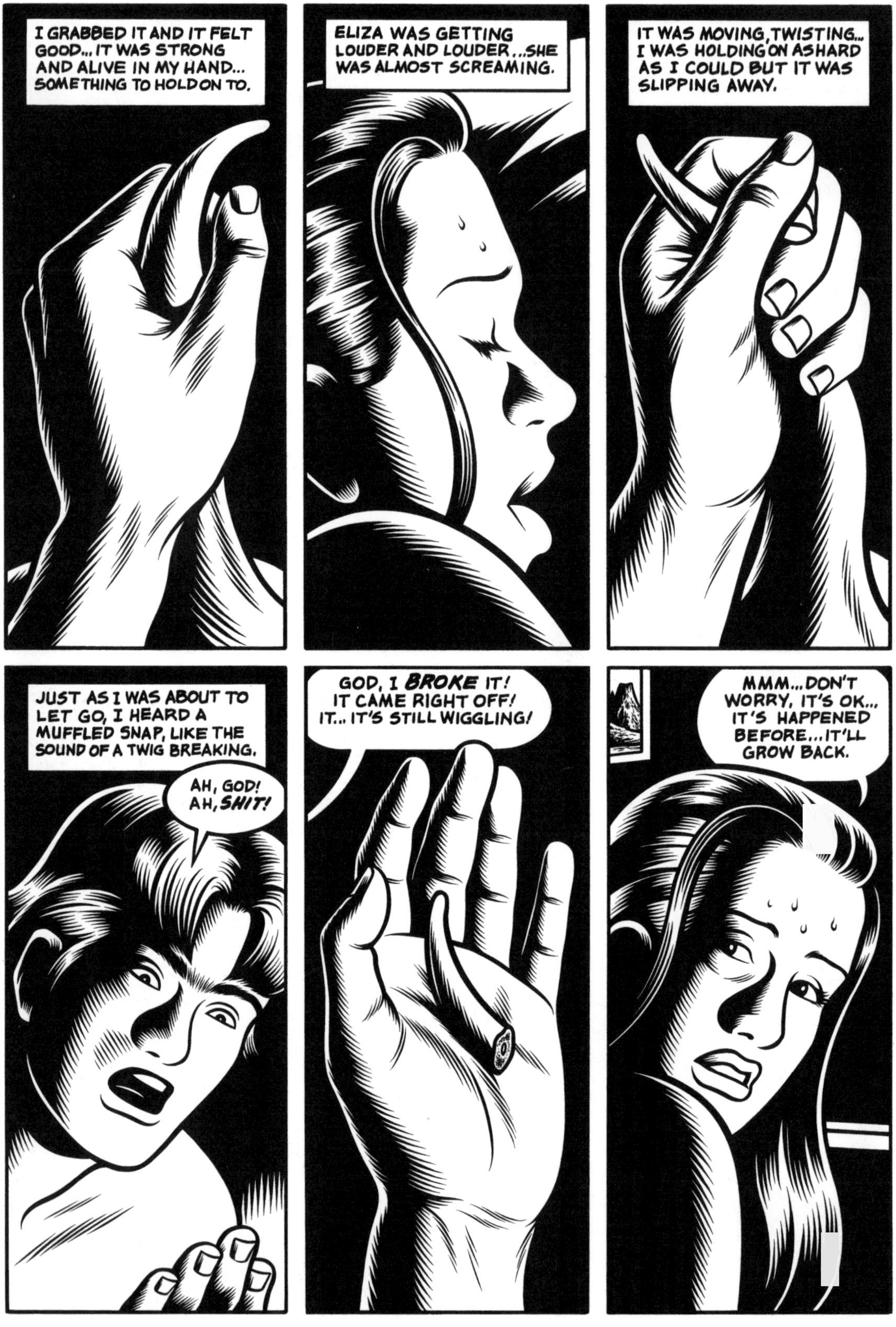
I GRABBED IT AND IT FELT GOOD... IT WAS STRONG AND ALIVE IN MY HAND... SOMETHING TO HOLD ON TO.
ELIZA WAS GETTING LOUDER AND LOUDER... SHE WAS ALMOST SCREAMING.
IT WAS MOVING, TWISTING... I WAS HOLDING ON AS HARD AS I COULD BUT IT WAS SLIPPING AWAY.
JUST AS I WAS ABOUT TO LET GO, I HEARD A MUFFLED SNAP, LIKE THE SOUND OF A TWIG BREAKING.
AH, GOD! AH, *SHIT!*
GOD, I **BROKE** IT! IT CAME RIGHT OFF! IT... IT'S STILL WIGGLING!
MMM... DON'T WORRY, IT'S OK... IT'S HAPPENED BEFORE... IT'LL GROW BACK.

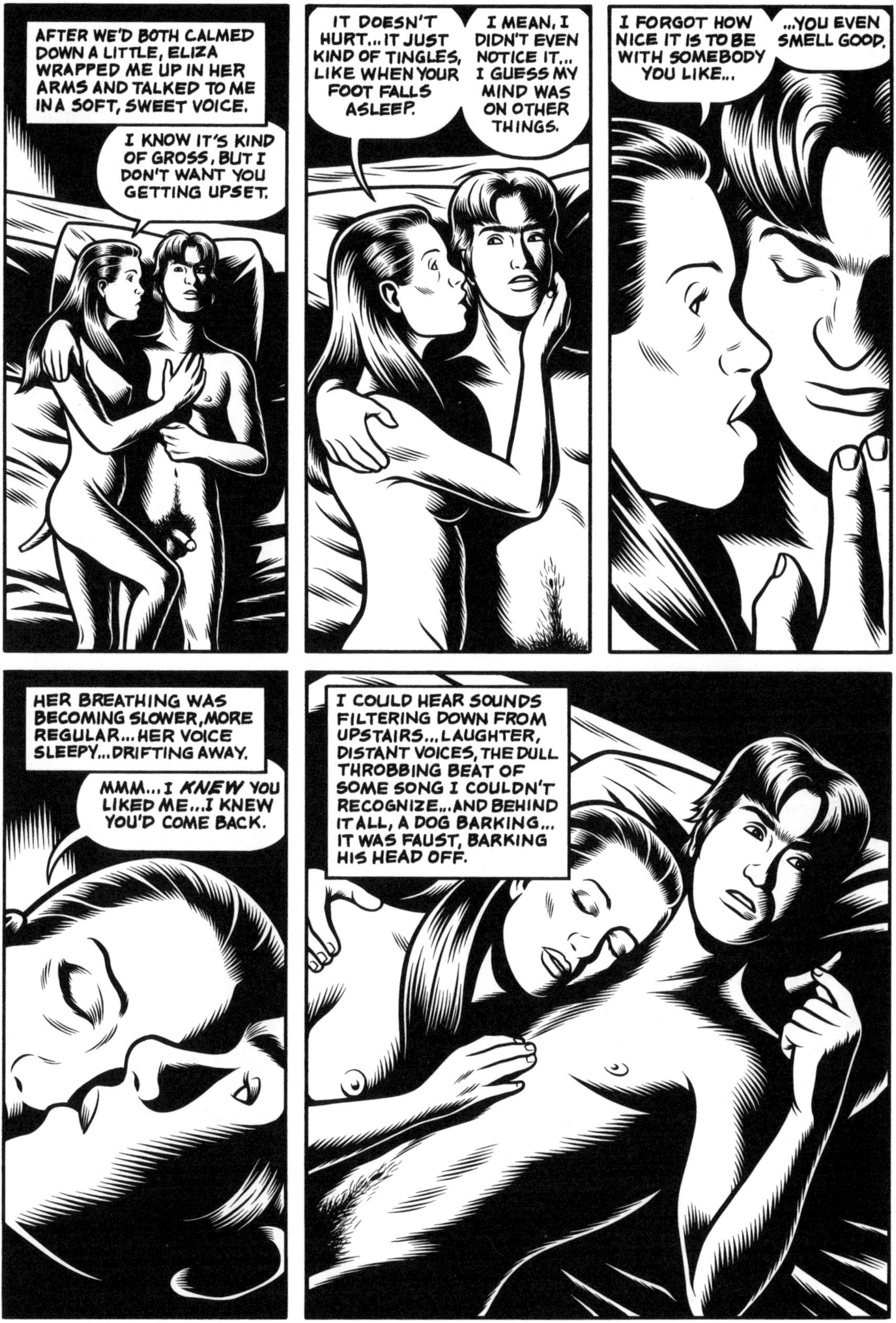
AFTER WE'D BOTH CALMED DOWN A LITTLE, ELIZA WRAPPED ME UP IN HER ARMS AND TALKED TO ME IN A SOFT, SWEET VOICE.
I KNOW IT'S KIND OF GROSS, BUT I DON'T WANT YOU GETTING UPSET.
IT DOESN'T HURT... IT JUST KIND OF TINGLES, LIKE WHEN YOUR FOOT FALLS ASLEEP.
I MEAN, I DIDN'T EVEN NOTICE IT... I GUESS MY MIND WAS ON OTHER THINGS.
I FORGOT HOW NICE IT IS TO BE WITH SOMEBODY YOU LIKE...
...YOU EVEN SMELL GOOD.
HER BREATHING WAS BECOMING SLOWER, MORE REGULAR... HER VOICE SLEEPY... DRIFTING AWAY.
MMM... I *KNEW* YOU LIKED ME... I KNEW YOU'D COME BACK.
I COULD HEAR SOUNDS FILTERING DOWN FROM UPSTAIRS... LAUGHTER, DISTANT VOICES, THE DULL THROBBING BEAT OF SOME SONG I COULDN'T RECOGNIZE... AND BEHIND IT ALL, A DOG BARKING... IT WAS FAUST, BARKING HIS HEAD OFF.

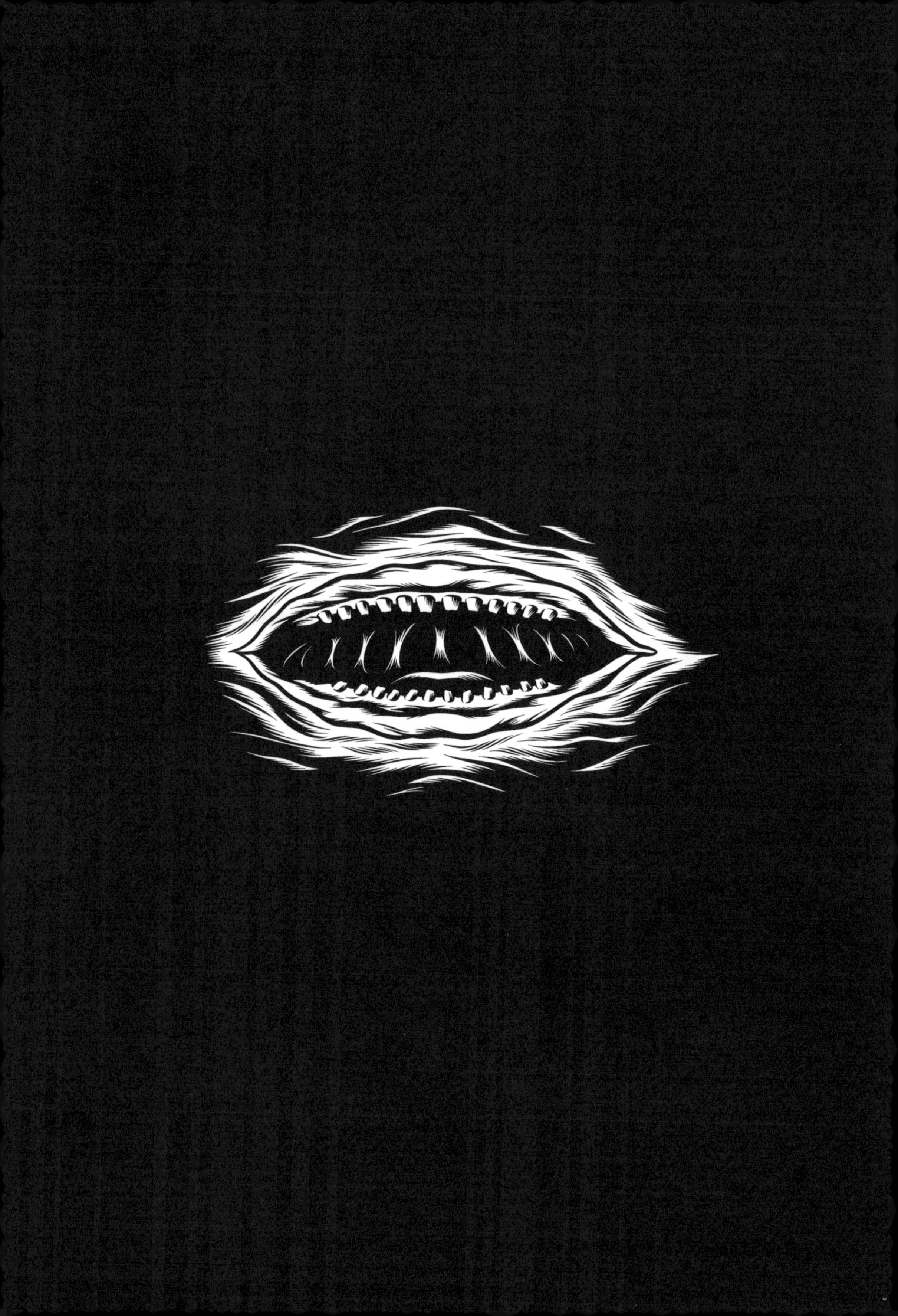

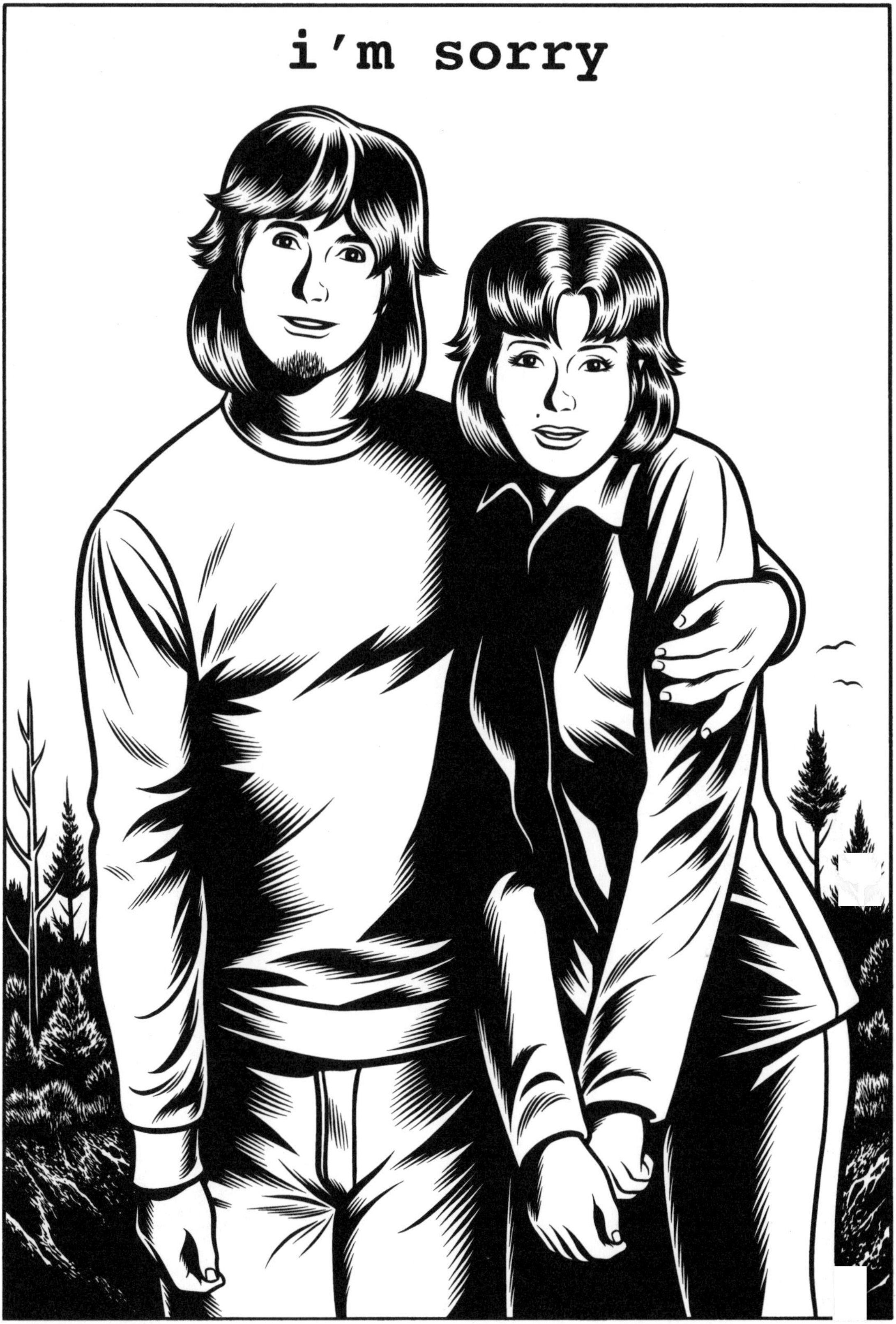
i'm sorry

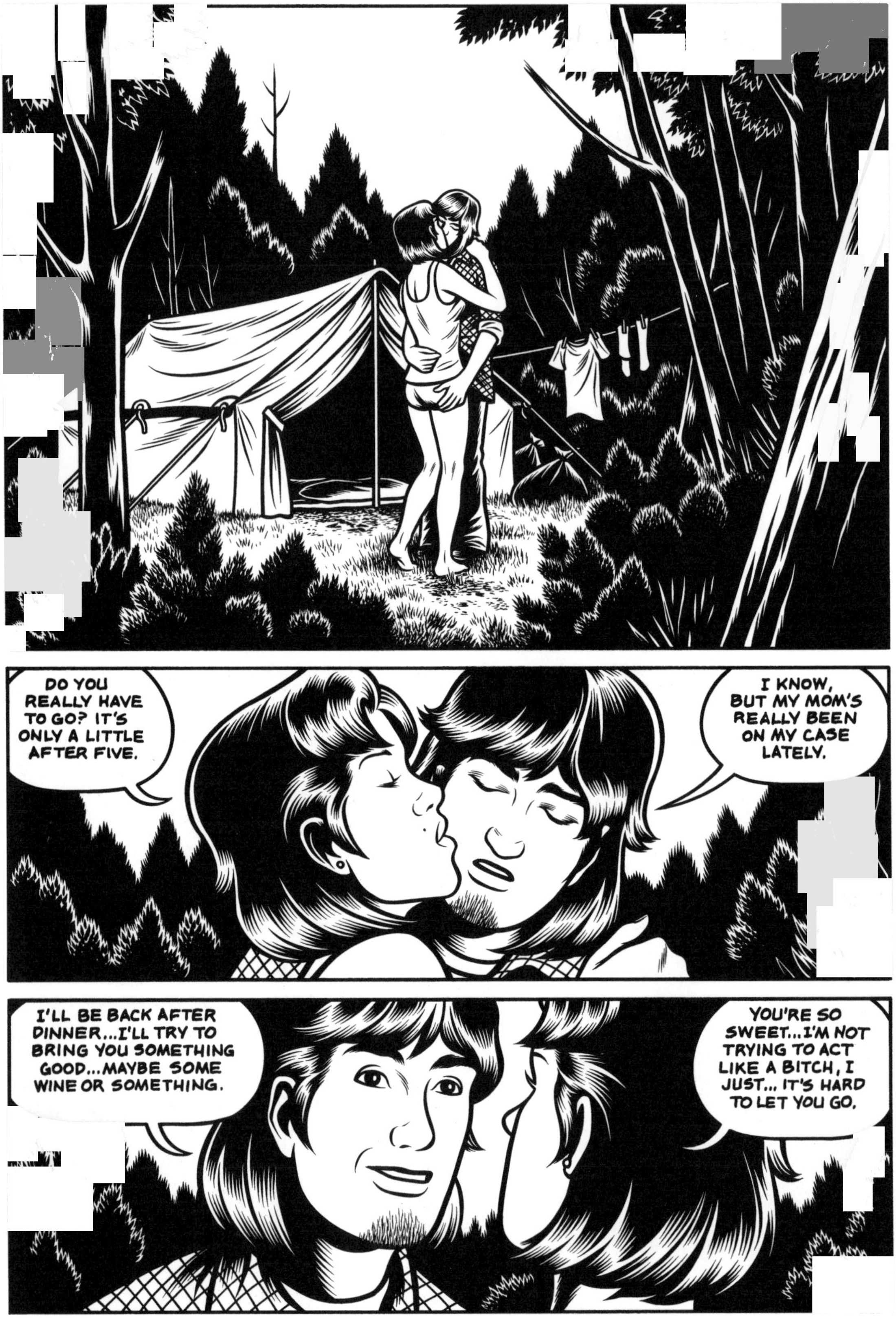
DO YOU REALLY HAVE TO GO? IT'S ONLY A LITTLE AFTER FIVE.
I KNOW, BUT MY MOM'S REALLY BEEN ON MY CASE LATELY.
I'LL BE BACK AFTER DINNER...I'LL TRY TO BRING YOU SOMETHING GOOD...MAYBE SOME WINE OR SOMETHING.
YOU'RE SO SWEET...I'M NOT TRYING TO ACT LIKE A BITCH, I JUST... IT'S HARD TO LET YOU GO.

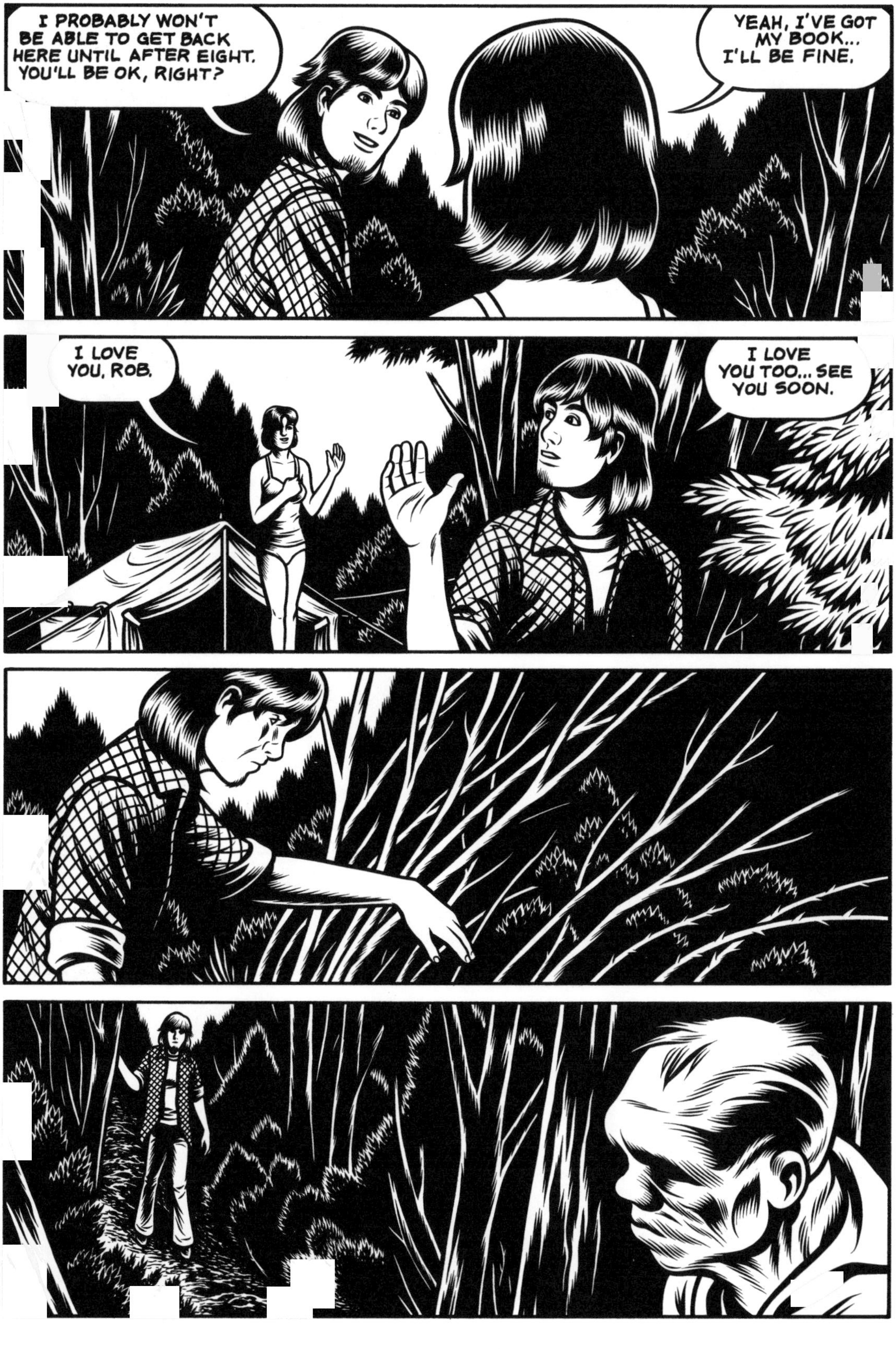
I PROBABLY WON'T BE ABLE TO GET BACK HERE UNTIL AFTER EIGHT. YOU'LL BE OK, RIGHT?
YEAH, I'VE GOT MY BOOK... I'LL BE FINE.
I LOVE YOU, ROB.
I LOVE YOU TOO... SEE YOU SOON.

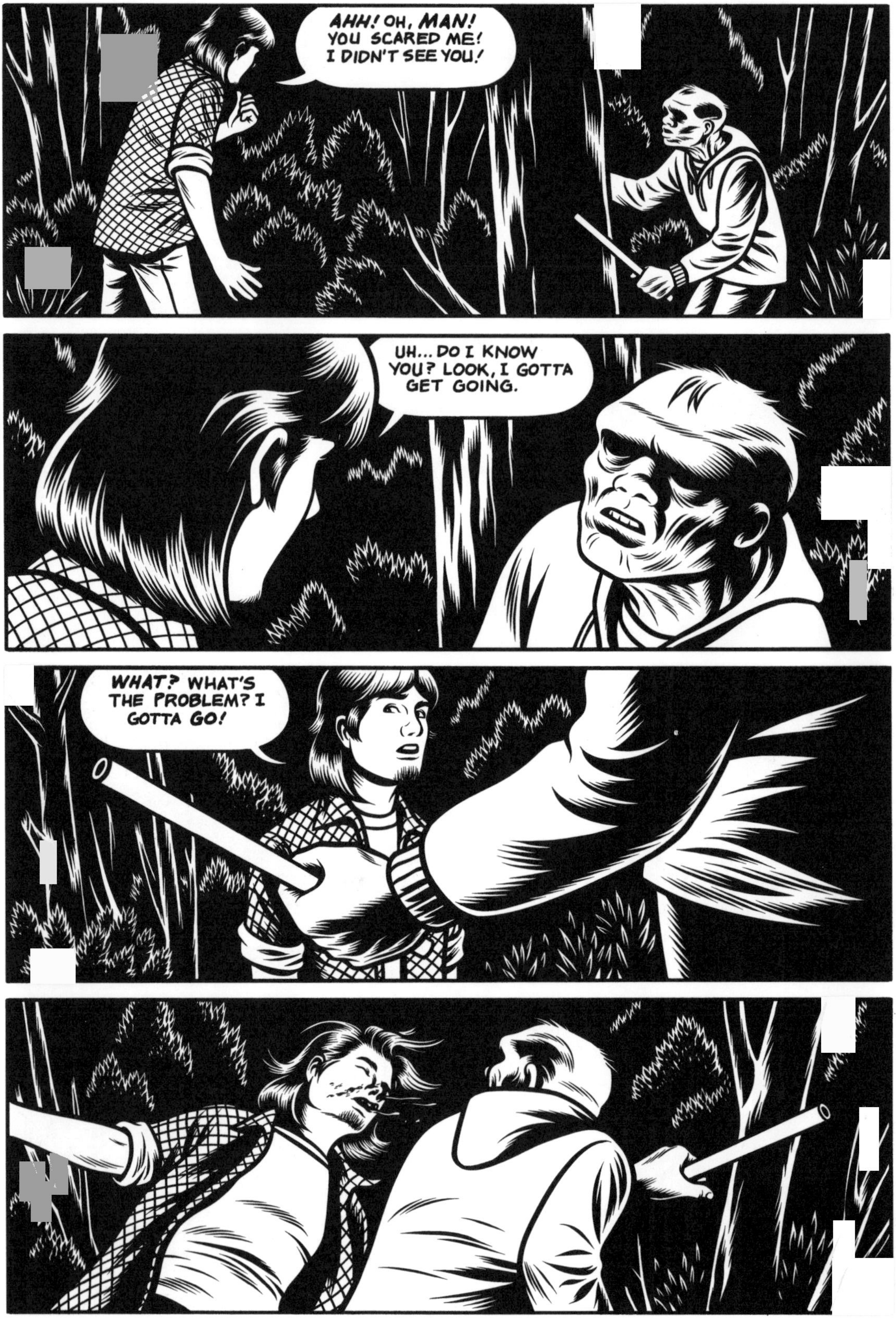
AHH! OH, MAN! YOU SCARED ME! I DIDN'T SEE YOU!
UH... DO I KNOW YOU? LOOK, I GOTTA GET GOING.
WHAT? WHAT'S THE PROBLEM? I GOTTA GO!

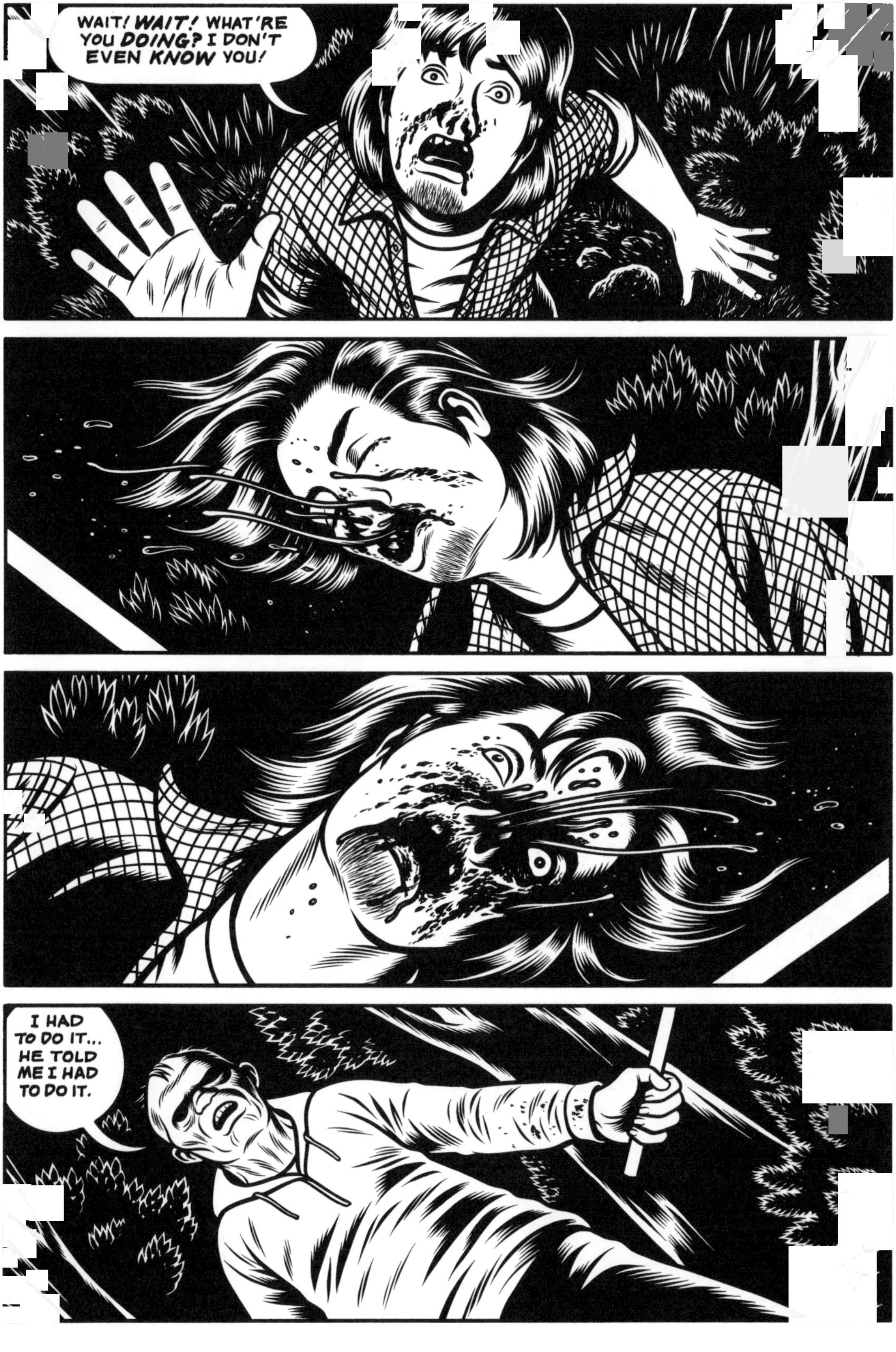
WAIT! WAIT! WHAT'RE YOU DOING? I DON'T EVEN KNOW YOU!
I HAD TO DO IT... HE TOLD ME I HAD TO DO IT.

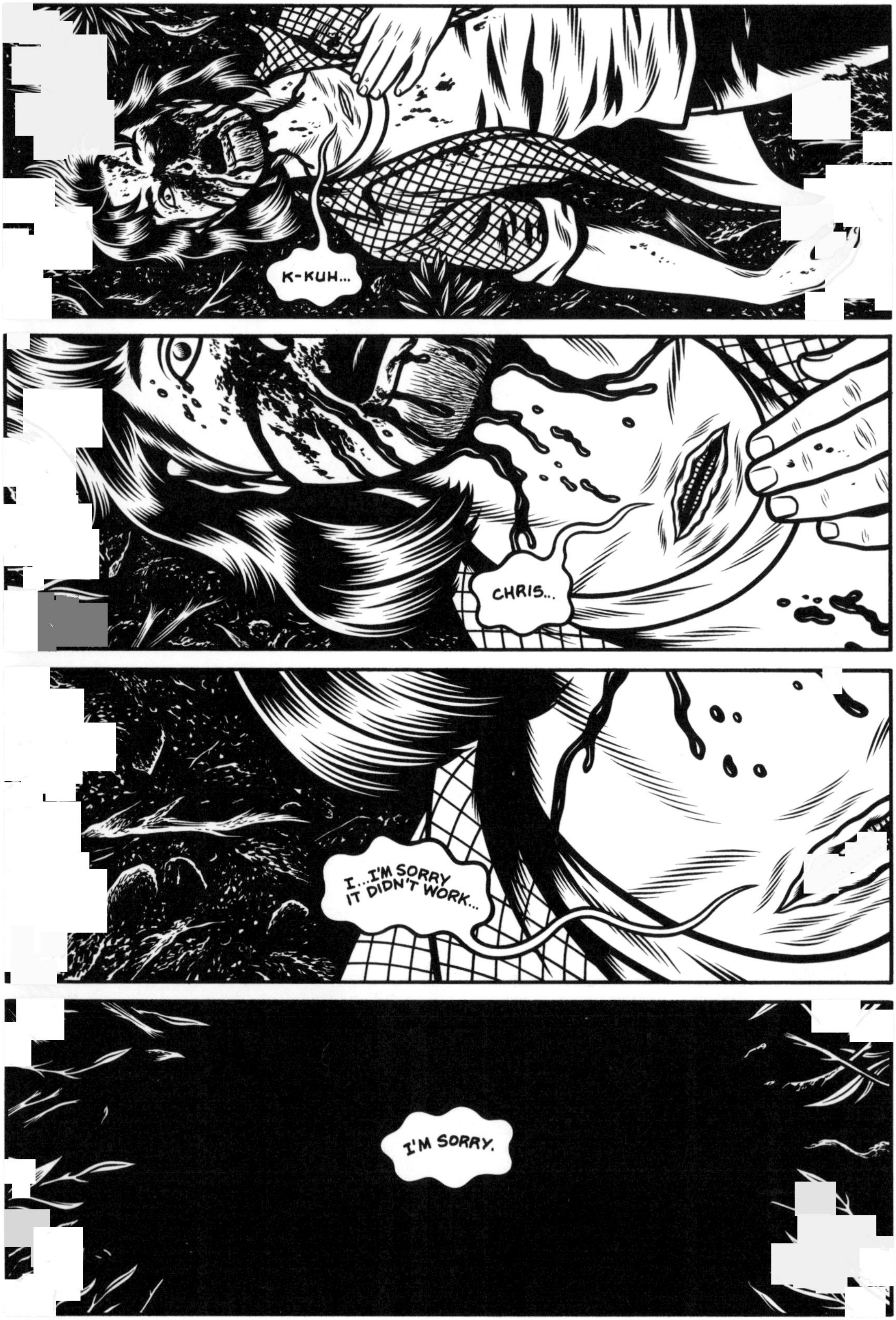
K-KUH...
CHRIS...
I...I'M SORRY
IT DIDN'T WORK...
I'M SORRY.

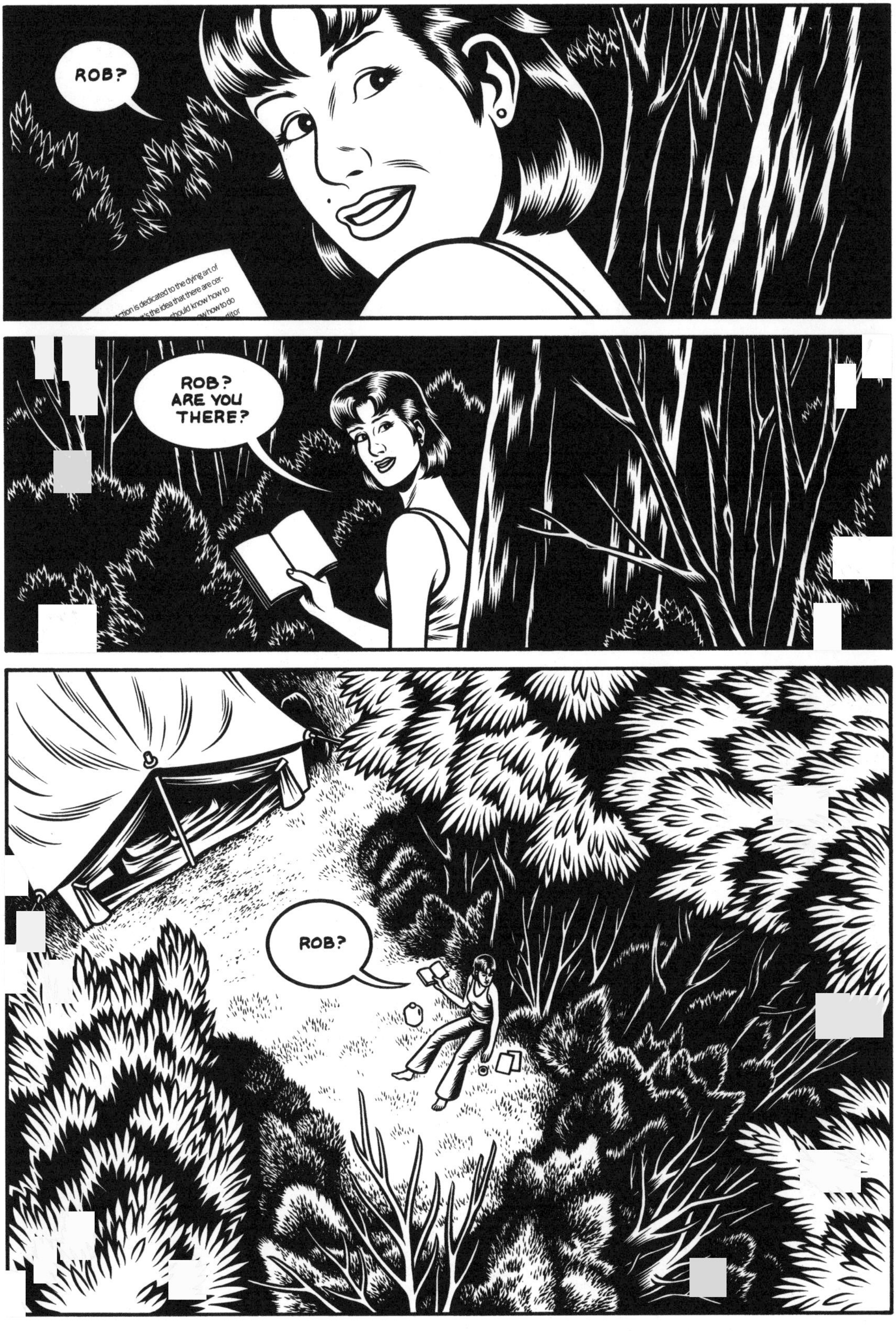
ROB?
ROB? ARE YOU THERE?
ROB?

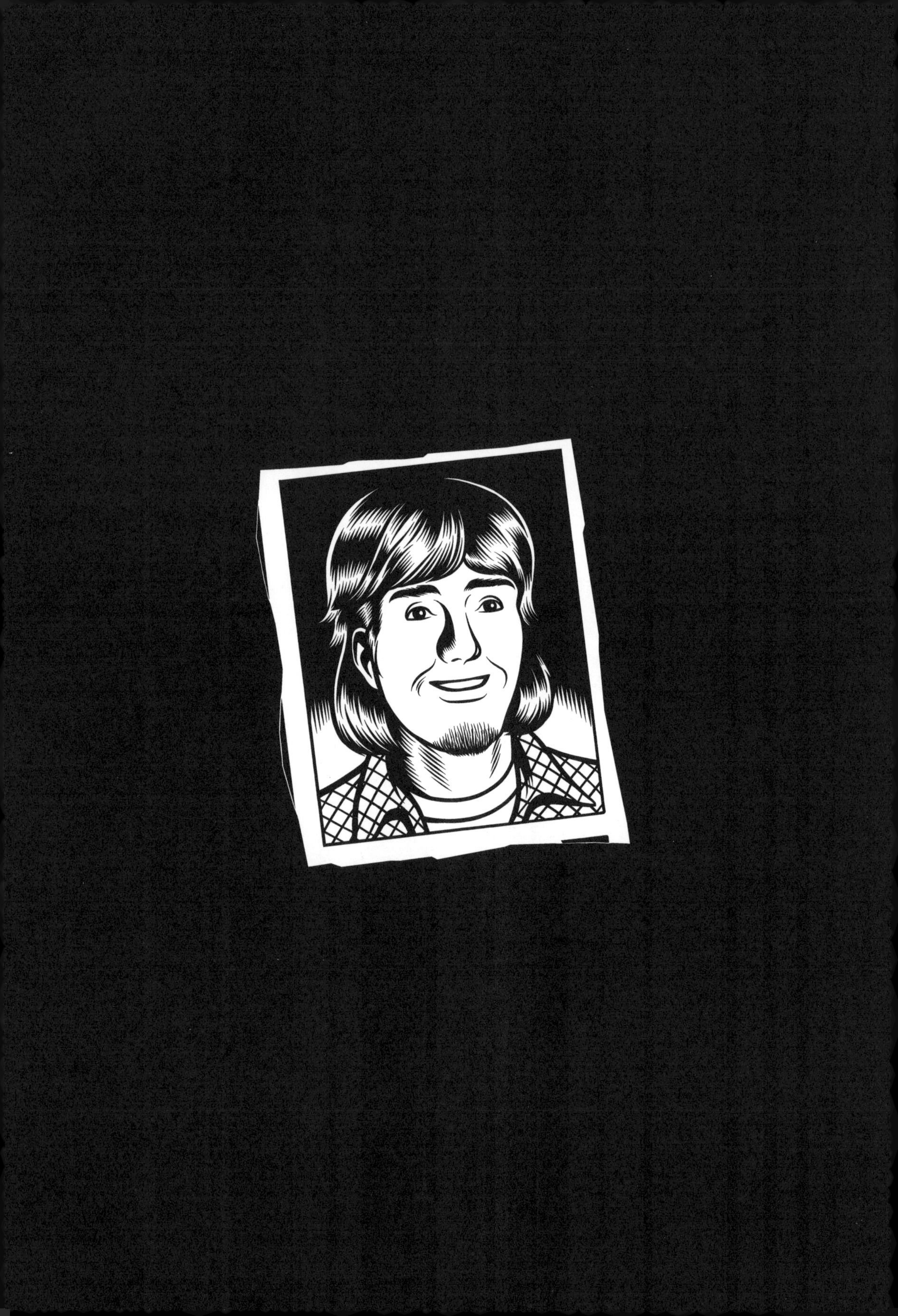

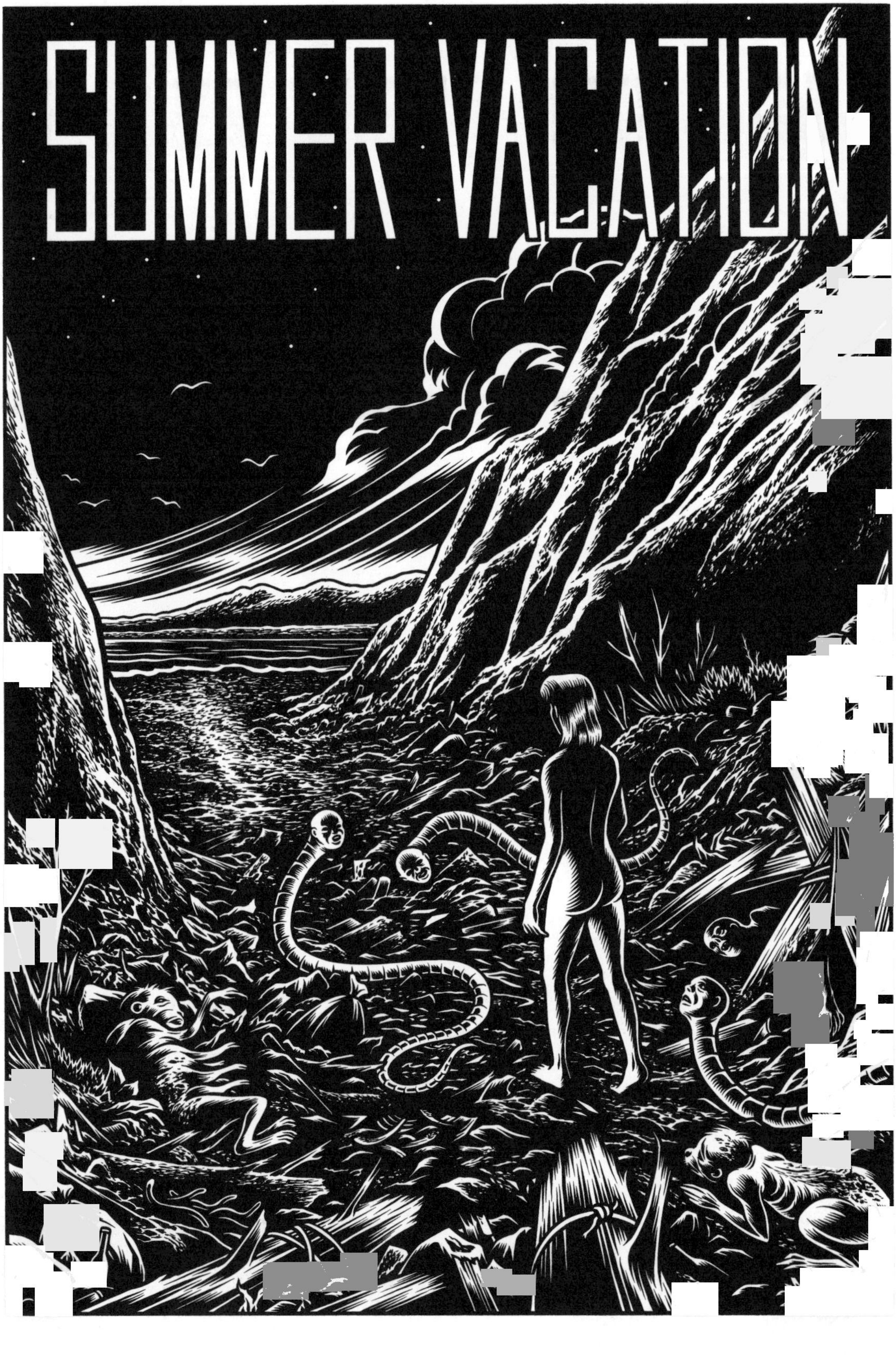
SUMMER VACATION

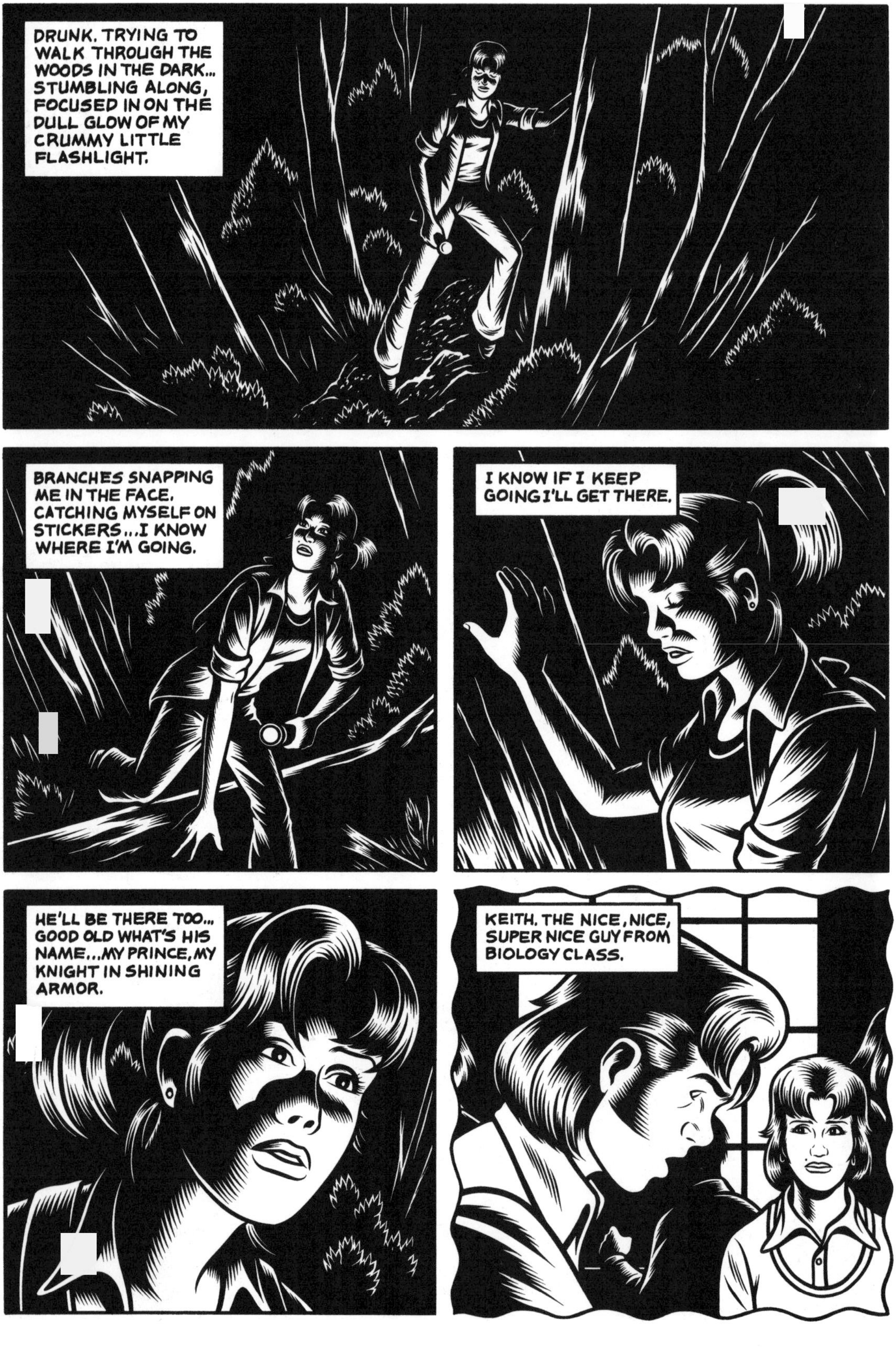
DRUNK. TRYING TO WALK THROUGH THE WOODS IN THE DARK... STUMBLING ALONG, FOCUSED IN ON THE DULL GLOW OF MY CRUMMY LITTLE FLASHLIGHT.
BRANCHES SNAPPING ME IN THE FACE. CATCHING MYSELF ON STICKERS...I KNOW WHERE I'M GOING.
I KNOW IF I KEEP GOING I'LL GET THERE.
HE'LL BE THERE TOO... GOOD OLD WHAT'S HIS NAME...MY PRINCE, MY KNIGHT IN SHINING ARMOR.
KEITH. THE NICE, NICE, SUPER NICE GUY FROM BIOLOGY CLASS.

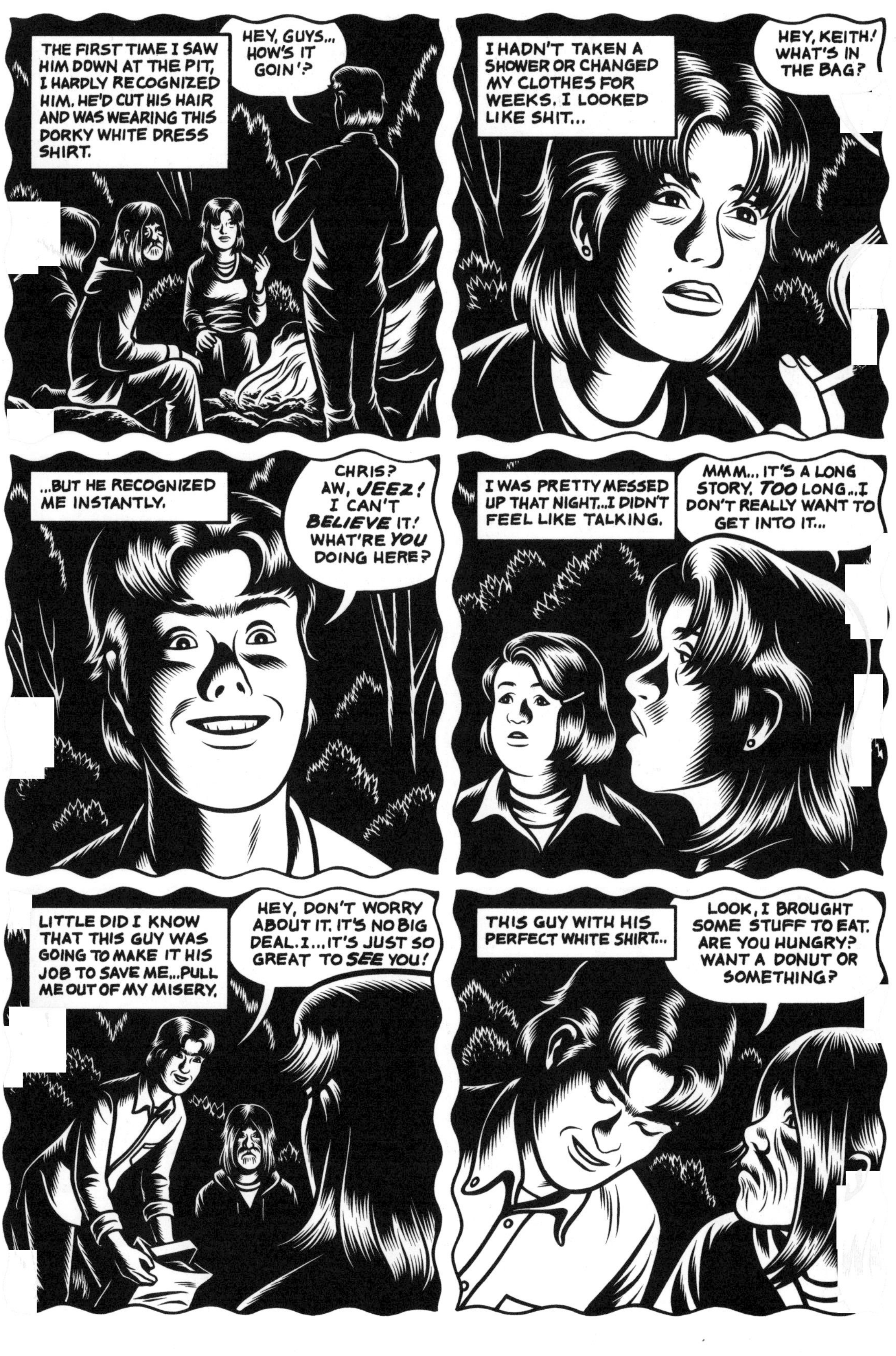

THE FIRST TIME I SAW HIM DOWN AT THE PIT, I HARDLY RECOGNIZED HIM. HE'D CUT HIS HAIR AND WAS WEARING THIS DORKY WHITE DRESS SHIRT.
HEY, GUYS... HOW'S IT GOIN'?
I HADN'T TAKEN A SHOWER OR CHANGED MY CLOTHES FOR WEEKS. I LOOKED LIKE SHIT...
HEY, KEITH! WHAT'S IN THE BAG?
...BUT HE RECOGNIZED ME INSTANTLY.
CHRIS? AW, JEEZ! I CAN'T BELIEVE IT! WHAT'RE YOU DOING HERE?
I WAS PRETTY MESSED UP THAT NIGHT...I DIDN'T FEEL LIKE TALKING.
MMM... IT'S A LONG STORY, TOO LONG...I DON'T REALLY WANT TO GET INTO IT...
LITTLE DID I KNOW THAT THIS GUY WAS GOING TO MAKE IT HIS JOB TO SAVE ME...PULL ME OUT OF MY MISERY.
HEY, DON'T WORRY ABOUT IT. IT'S NO BIG DEAL. I... IT'S JUST SO GREAT TO SEE YOU!
THIS GUY WITH HIS PERFECT WHITE SHIRT...
LOOK, I BROUGHT SOME STUFF TO EAT. ARE YOU HUNGRY? WANT A DONUT OR SOMETHING?

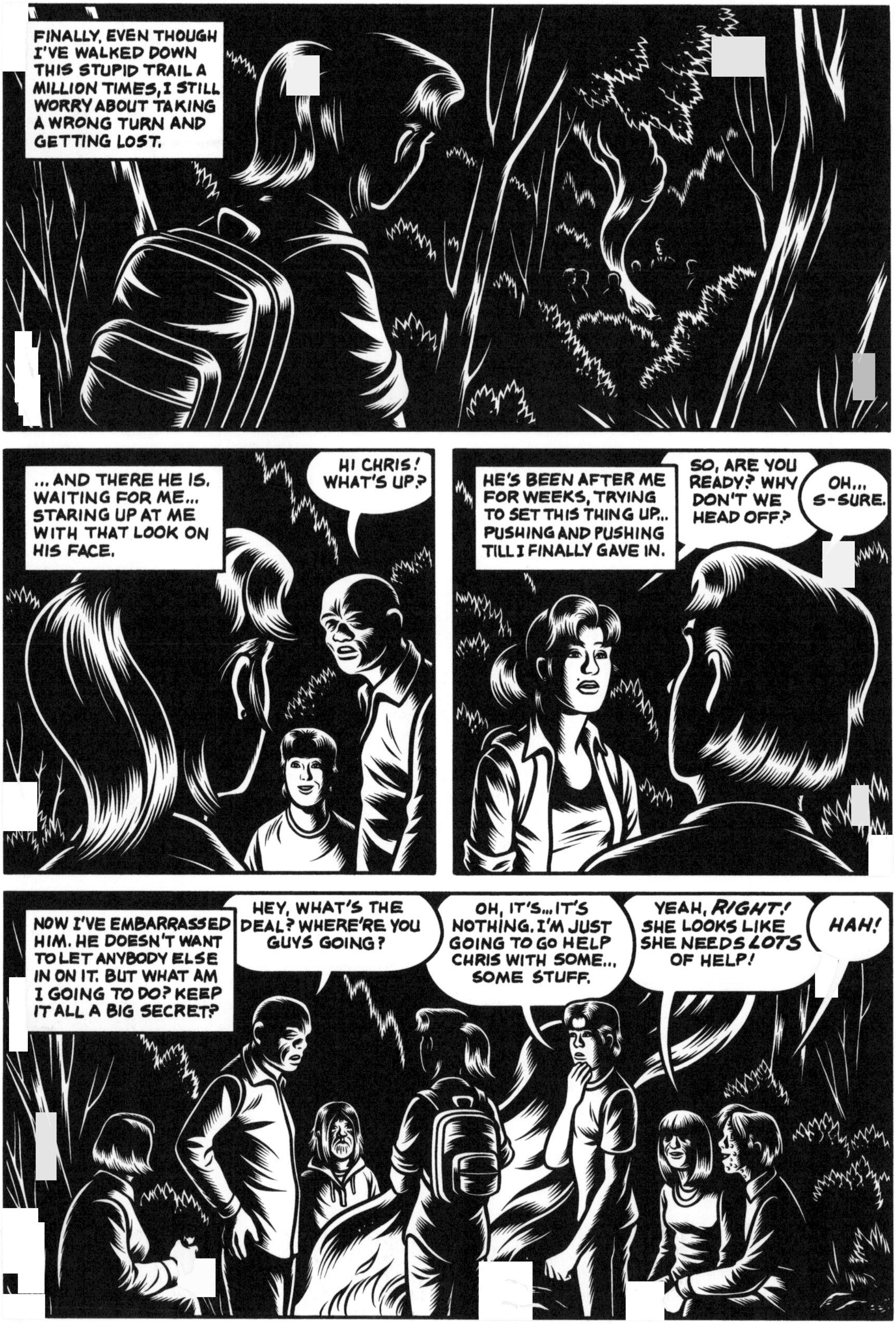
FINALLY, EVEN THOUGH I'VE WALKED DOWN THIS STUPID TRAIL A MILLION TIMES, I STILL WORRY ABOUT TAKING A WRONG TURN AND GETTING LOST.
... AND THERE HE IS. WAITING FOR ME... STARING UP AT ME WITH THAT LOOK ON HIS FACE.
HI CHRIS! WHAT'S UP?
HE'S BEEN AFTER ME FOR WEEKS, TRYING TO SET THIS THING UP... PUSHING AND PUSHING TILL I FINALLY GAVE IN.
SO, ARE YOU READY? WHY DON'T WE HEAD OFF?
OH... S-SURE.
NOW I'VE EMBARRASSED HIM. HE DOESN'T WANT TO LET ANYBODY ELSE IN ON IT. BUT WHAT AM I GOING TO DO? KEEP IT ALL A BIG SECRET?
HEY, WHAT'S THE DEAL? WHERE'RE YOU GUYS GOING?
OH, IT'S... IT'S NOTHING. I'M JUST GOING TO GO HELP CHRIS WITH SOME... SOME STUFF.
YEAH, RIGHT! SHE LOOKS LIKE SHE NEEDS LOTS OF HELP!
HAH!

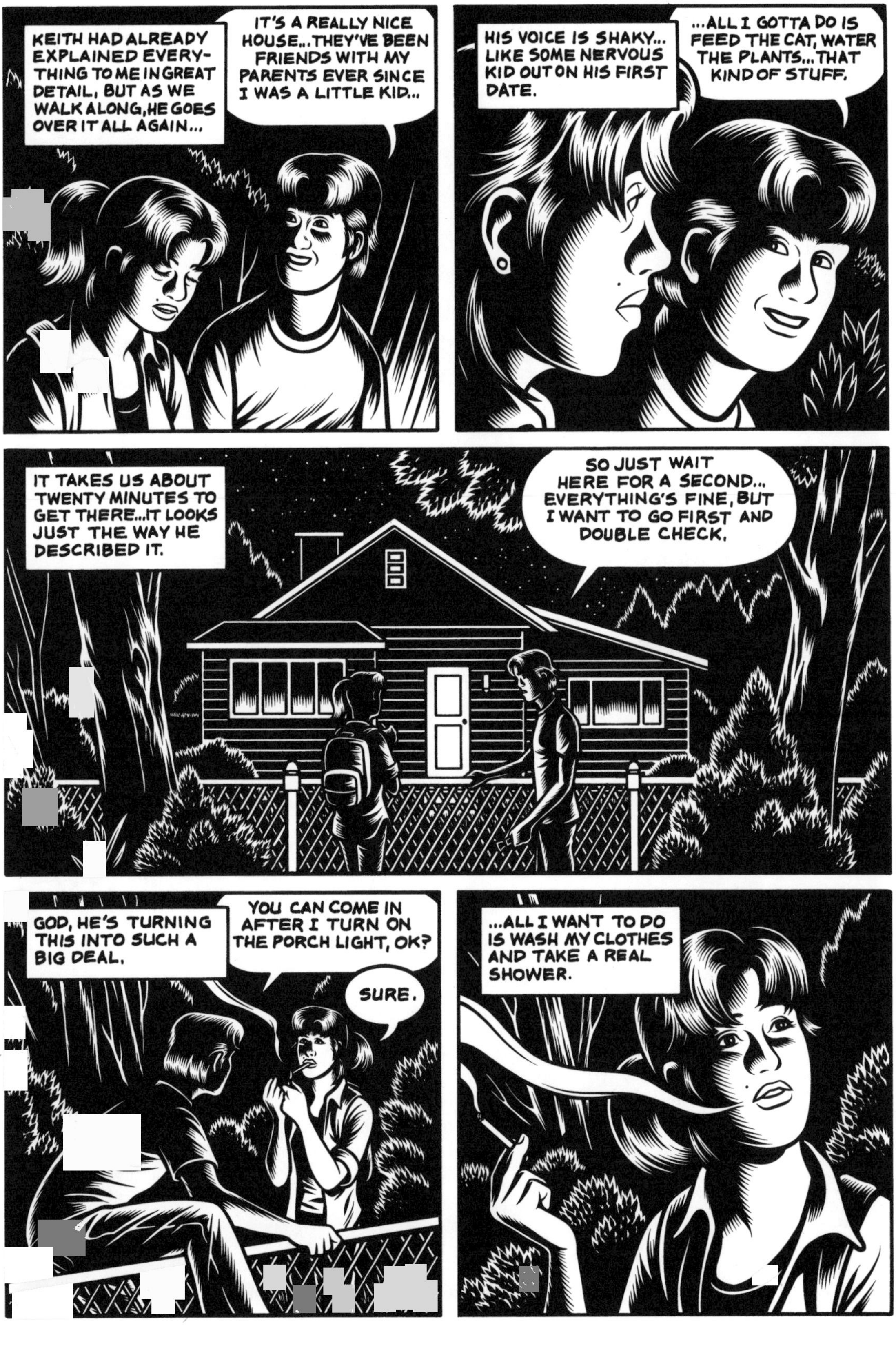

KEITH HAD ALREADY EXPLAINED EVERYTHING TO ME IN GREAT DETAIL, BUT AS WE WALK ALONG, HE GOES OVER IT ALL AGAIN...
IT'S A REALLY NICE HOUSE... THEY'VE BEEN FRIENDS WITH MY PARENTS EVER SINCE I WAS A LITTLE KID...
HIS VOICE IS SHAKY... LIKE SOME NERVOUS KID OUT ON HIS FIRST DATE.
...ALL I GOTTA DO IS FEED THE CAT, WATER THE PLANTS... THAT KIND OF STUFF.
IT TAKES US ABOUT TWENTY MINUTES TO GET THERE... IT LOOKS JUST THE WAY HE DESCRIBED IT.
SO JUST WAIT HERE FOR A SECOND... EVERYTHING'S FINE, BUT I WANT TO GO FIRST AND DOUBLE CHECK.
GOD, HE'S TURNING THIS INTO SUCH A BIG DEAL.
YOU CAN COME IN AFTER I TURN ON THE PORCH LIGHT, OK?
SURE.
...ALL I WANT TO DO IS WASH MY CLOTHES AND TAKE A REAL SHOWER.

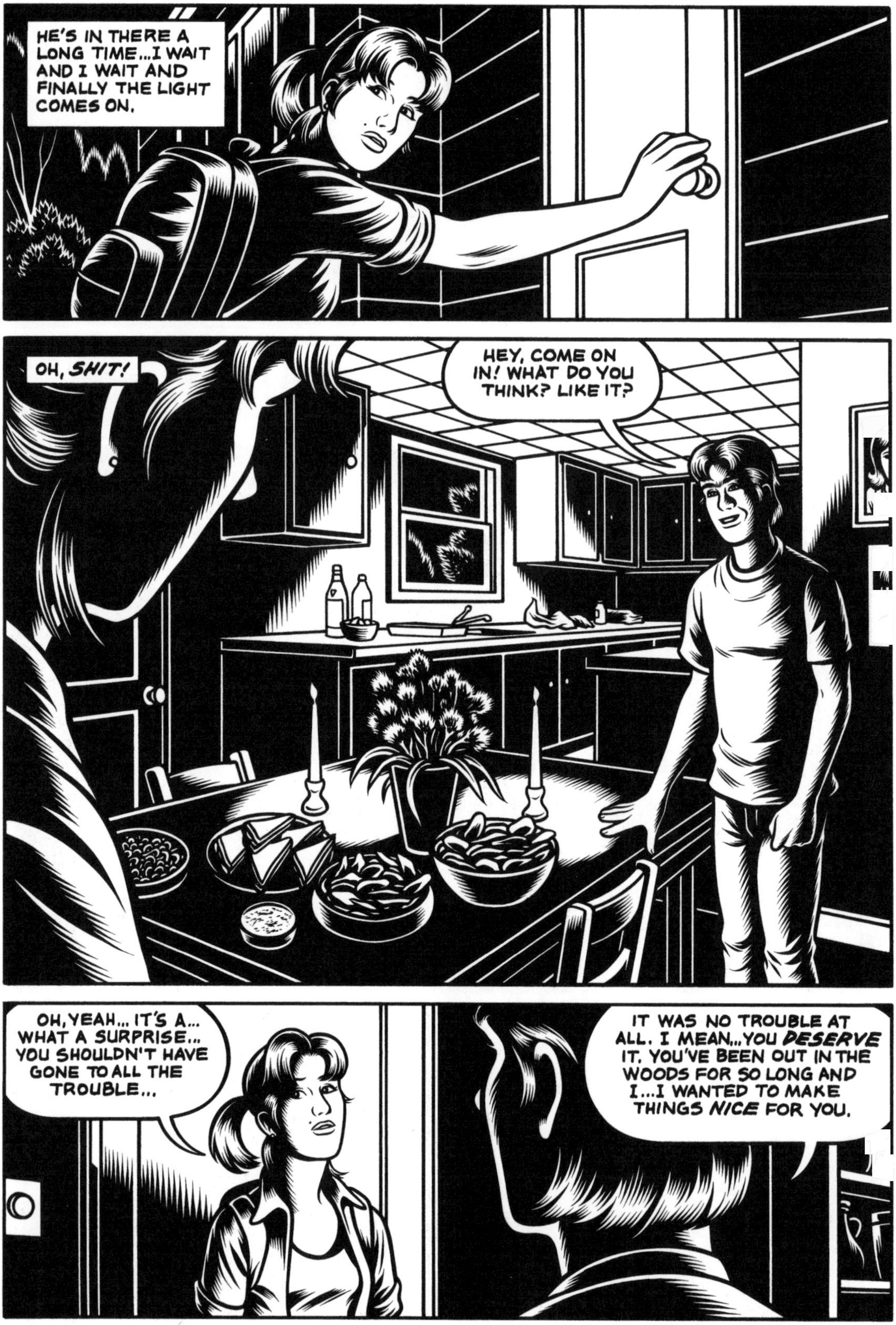
HE'S IN THERE A LONG TIME...I WAIT AND I WAIT AND FINALLY THE LIGHT COMES ON.
OH, *SHIT!*
HEY, COME ON IN! WHAT DO YOU THINK? LIKE IT?
OH, YEAH... IT'S A... WHAT A SURPRISE... YOU SHOULDN'T HAVE GONE TO ALL THE TROUBLE...
IT WAS NO TROUBLE AT ALL. I MEAN,...YOU *DESERVE* IT. YOU'VE BEEN OUT IN THE WOODS FOR SO LONG AND I...I WANTED TO MAKE THINGS *NICE* FOR YOU.

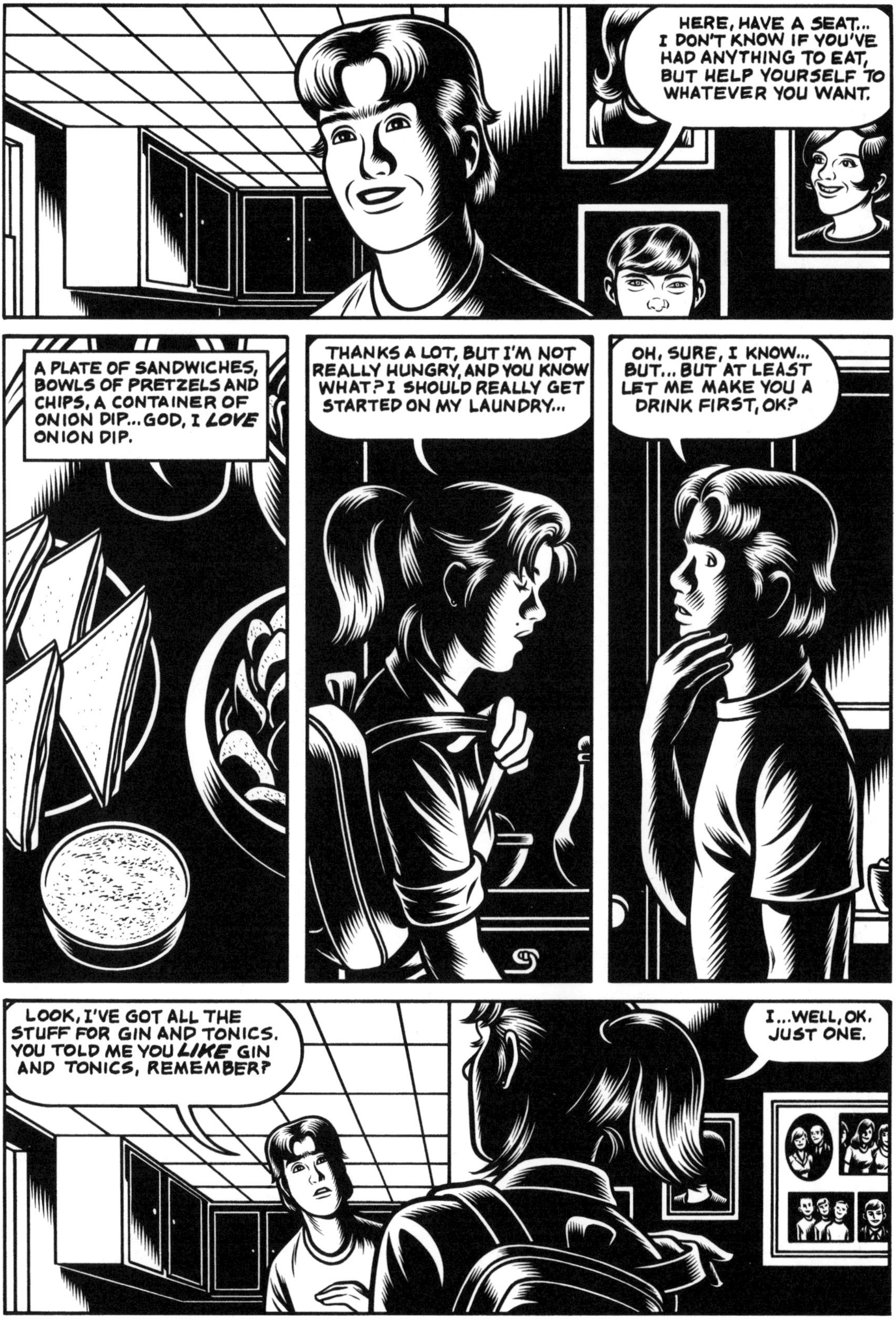
HERE, HAVE A SEAT... I DON'T KNOW IF YOU'VE HAD ANYTHING TO EAT, BUT HELP YOURSELF TO WHATEVER YOU WANT.
A PLATE OF SANDWICHES, BOWLS OF PRETZELS AND CHIPS, A CONTAINER OF ONION DIP... GOD, I *LOVE* ONION DIP.
THANKS A LOT, BUT I'M NOT REALLY HUNGRY, AND YOU KNOW WHAT? I SHOULD REALLY GET STARTED ON MY LAUNDRY...
OH, SURE, I KNOW... BUT... BUT AT LEAST LET ME MAKE YOU A DRINK FIRST, OK?
LOOK, I'VE GOT ALL THE STUFF FOR GIN AND TONICS. YOU TOLD ME YOU *LIKE* GIN AND TONICS, REMEMBER?
I... WELL, OK. JUST ONE.

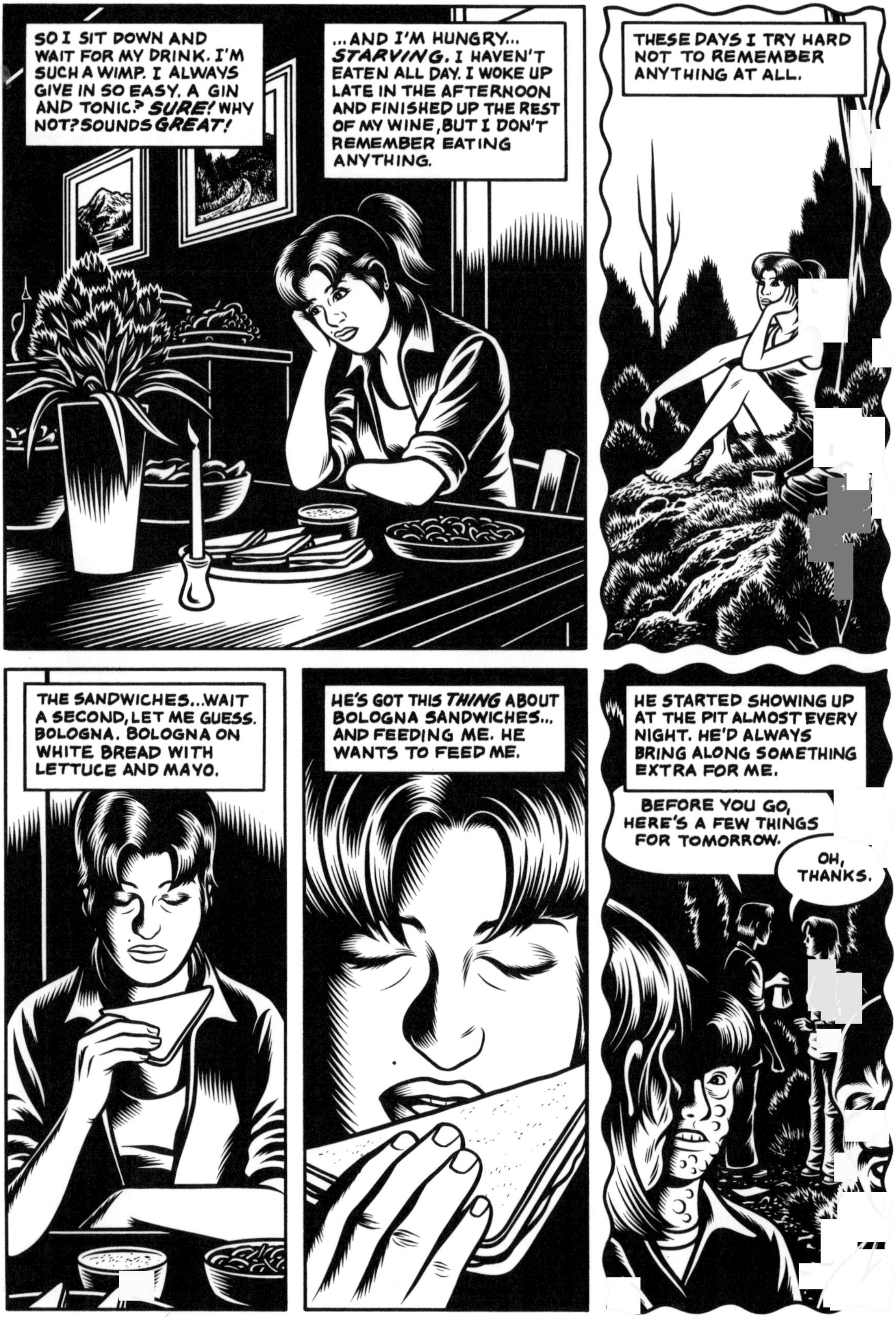
SO I SIT DOWN AND WAIT FOR MY DRINK. I'M SUCH A WIMP. I ALWAYS GIVE IN SO EASY. A GIN AND TONIC? SURE! WHY NOT? SOUNDS GREAT!
...AND I'M HUNGRY... STARVING. I HAVEN'T EATEN ALL DAY. I WOKE UP LATE IN THE AFTERNOON AND FINISHED UP THE REST OF MY WINE, BUT I DON'T REMEMBER EATING ANYTHING.
THESE DAYS I TRY HARD NOT TO REMEMBER ANYTHING AT ALL.
THE SANDWICHES...WAIT A SECOND, LET ME GUESS. BOLOGNA. BOLOGNA ON WHITE BREAD WITH LETTUCE AND MAYO.
HE'S GOT THIS THING ABOUT BOLOGNA SANDWICHES... AND FEEDING ME. HE WANTS TO FEED ME.
HE STARTED SHOWING UP AT THE PIT ALMOST EVERY NIGHT. HE'D ALWAYS BRING ALONG SOMETHING EXTRA FOR ME.
BEFORE YOU GO, HERE'S A FEW THINGS FOR TOMORROW.
OH, THANKS.

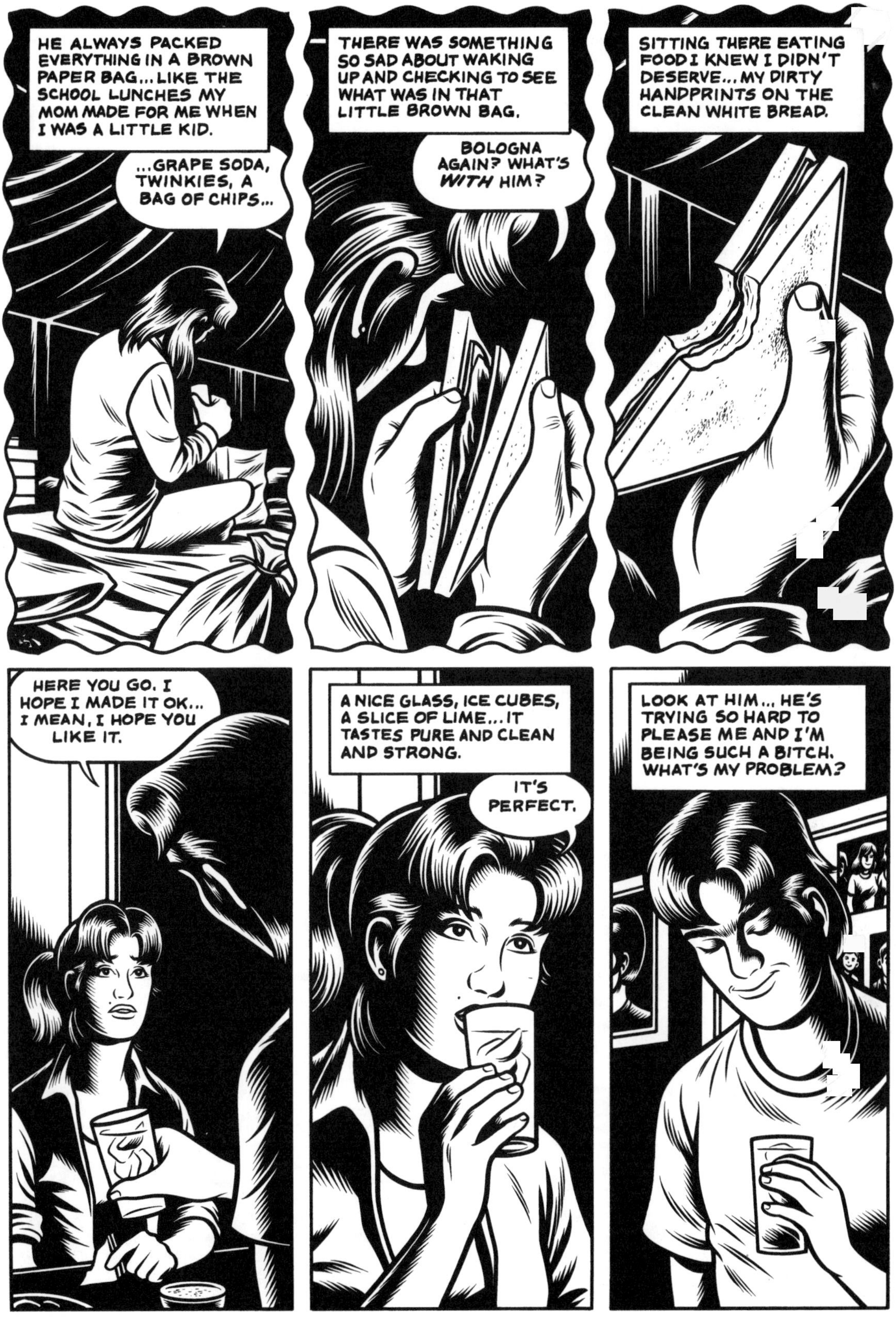
HE ALWAYS PACKED EVERYTHING IN A BROWN PAPER BAG... LIKE THE SCHOOL LUNCHES MY MOM MADE FOR ME WHEN I WAS A LITTLE KID.
...GRAPE SODA, TWINKIES, A BAG OF CHIPS...
THERE WAS SOMETHING SO SAD ABOUT WAKING UP AND CHECKING TO SEE WHAT WAS IN THAT LITTLE BROWN BAG.
BOLOGNA AGAIN? WHAT'S *WITH* HIM?
SITTING THERE EATING FOOD I KNEW I DIDN'T DESERVE... MY DIRTY HANDPRINTS ON THE CLEAN WHITE BREAD.
HERE YOU GO. I HOPE I MADE IT OK... I MEAN, I HOPE YOU LIKE IT.
A NICE GLASS, ICE CUBES, A SLICE OF LIME... IT TASTES PURE AND CLEAN AND STRONG.
IT'S PERFECT.
LOOK AT HIM... HE'S TRYING SO HARD TO PLEASE ME AND I'M BEING SUCH A BITCH. WHAT'S MY PROBLEM?

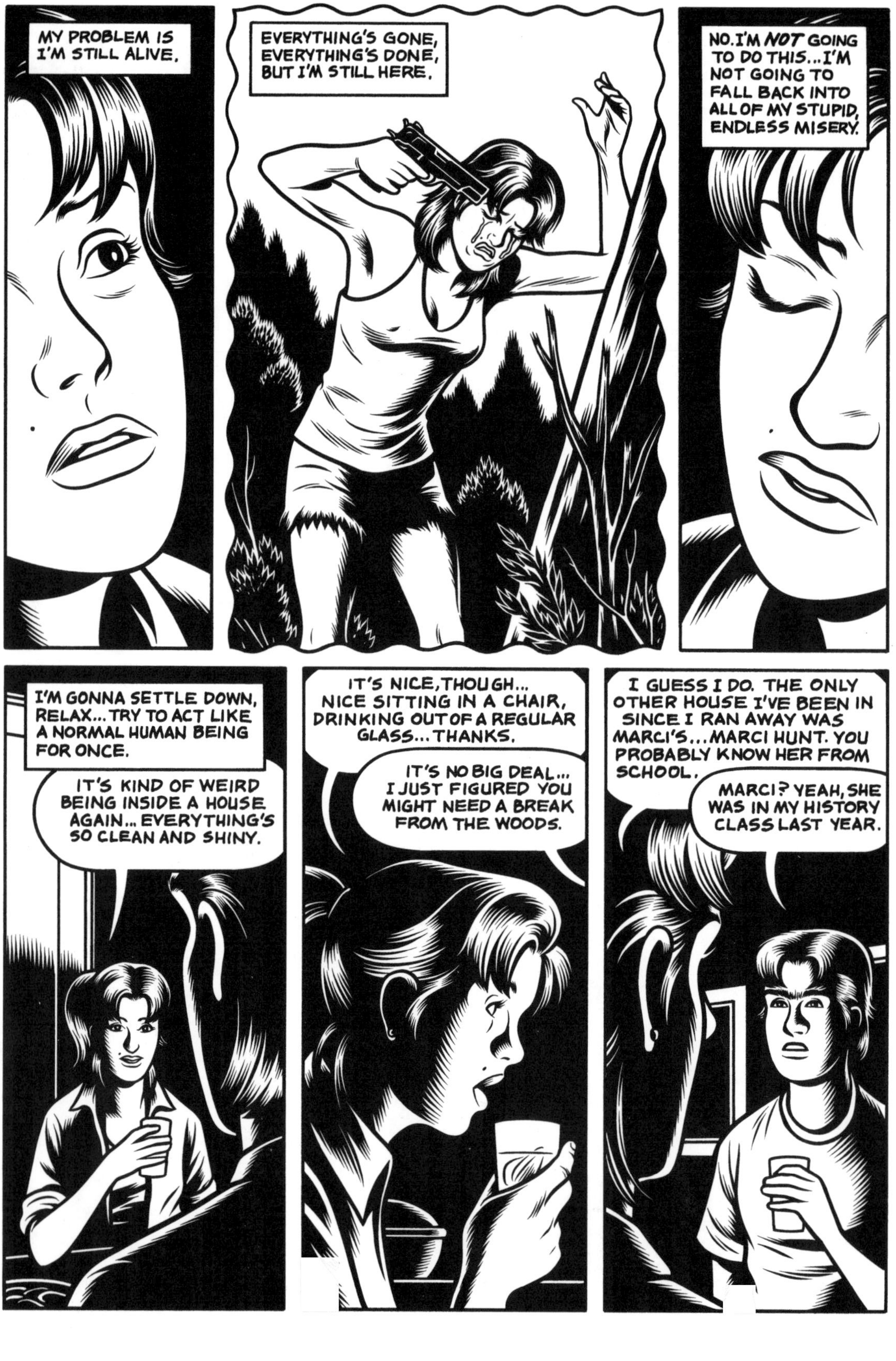
MY PROBLEM IS I'M STILL ALIVE.
EVERYTHING'S GONE, EVERYTHING'S DONE, BUT I'M STILL HERE.
NO. I'M *NOT* GOING TO DO THIS... I'M NOT GOING TO FALL BACK INTO ALL OF MY STUPID, ENDLESS MISERY.
I'M GONNA SETTLE DOWN, RELAX... TRY TO ACT LIKE A NORMAL HUMAN BEING FOR ONCE.
IT'S KIND OF WEIRD BEING INSIDE A HOUSE AGAIN... EVERYTHING'S SO CLEAN AND SHINY.
IT'S NICE, THOUGH... NICE SITTING IN A CHAIR, DRINKING OUT OF A REGULAR GLASS... THANKS.
IT'S NO BIG DEAL... I JUST FIGURED YOU MIGHT NEED A BREAK FROM THE WOODS.
I GUESS I DO. THE ONLY OTHER HOUSE I'VE BEEN IN SINCE I RAN AWAY WAS MARCI'S... MARCI HUNT. YOU PROBABLY KNOW HER FROM SCHOOL.
MARCI? YEAH, SHE WAS IN MY HISTORY CLASS LAST YEAR.

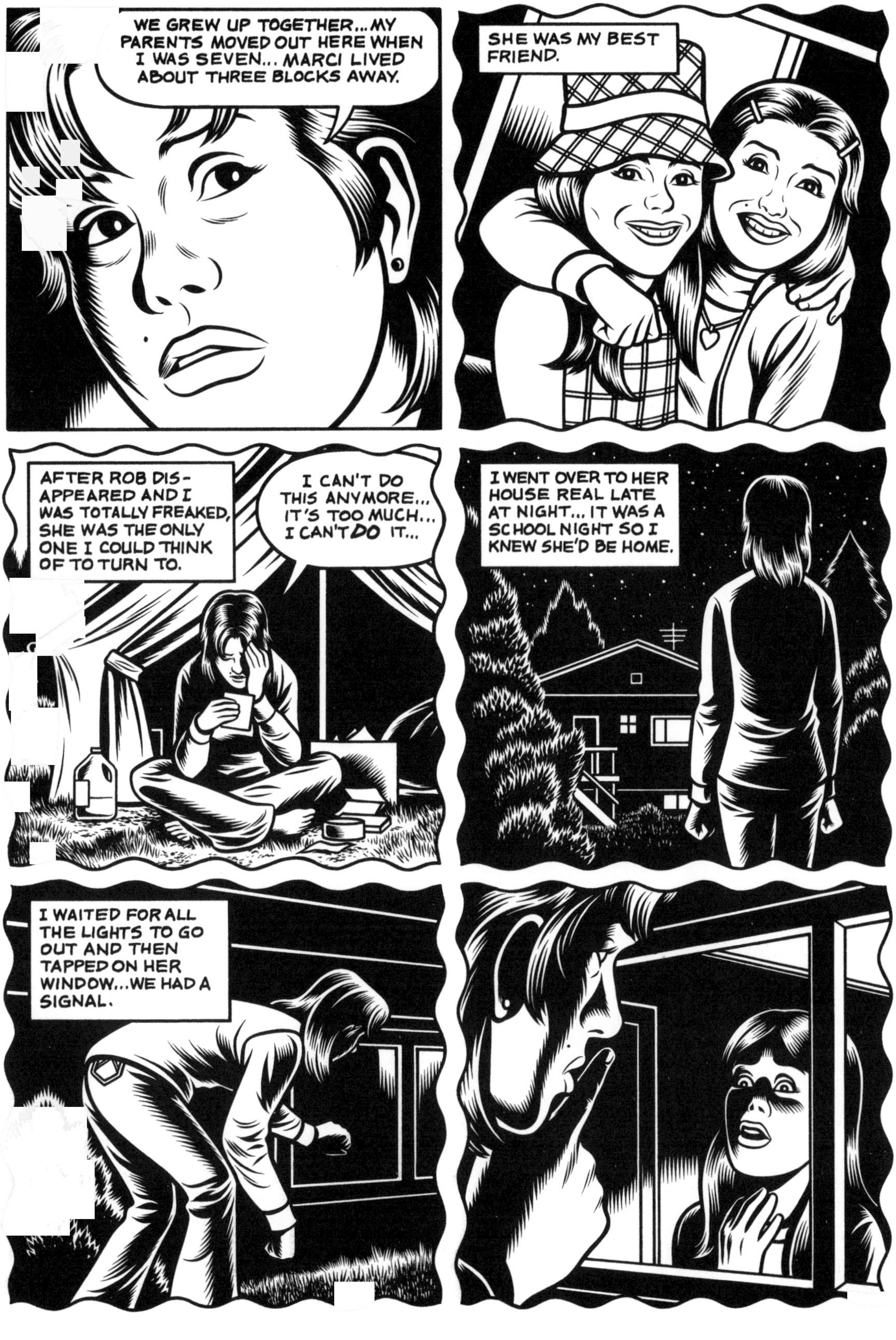

WE GREW UP TOGETHER... MY PARENTS MOVED OUT HERE WHEN I WAS SEVEN... MARCI LIVED ABOUT THREE BLOCKS AWAY.
SHE WAS MY BEST FRIEND.
AFTER ROB DIS-APPEARED AND I WAS TOTALLY FREAKED, SHE WAS THE ONLY ONE I COULD THINK OF TO TURN TO.
I CAN'T DO THIS ANYMORE... IT'S TOO MUCH... I CAN'T DO IT...
I WENT OVER TO HER HOUSE REAL LATE AT NIGHT... IT WAS A SCHOOL NIGHT SO I KNEW SHE'D BE HOME.
I WAITED FOR ALL THE LIGHTS TO GO OUT AND THEN TAPPED ON HER WINDOW... WE HAD A SIGNAL.

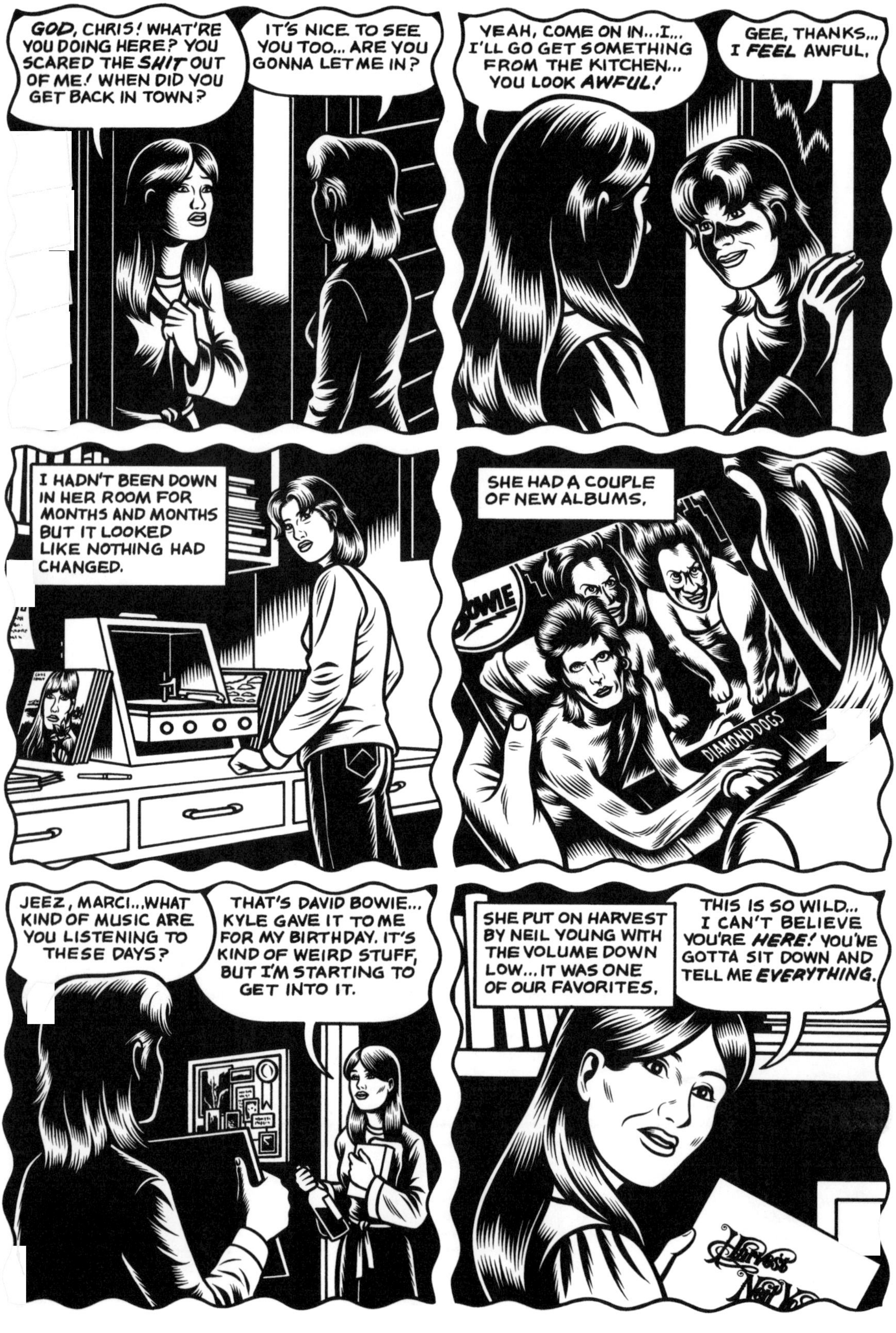
GOD, CHRIS! WHAT'RE YOU DOING HERE? YOU SCARED THE SHIT OUT OF ME! WHEN DID YOU GET BACK IN TOWN?
IT'S NICE TO SEE YOU TOO... ARE YOU GONNA LET ME IN?
YEAH, COME ON IN... I... I'LL GO GET SOMETHING FROM THE KITCHEN... YOU LOOK AWFUL!
GEE, THANKS... I FEEL AWFUL.
I HADN'T BEEN DOWN IN HER ROOM FOR MONTHS AND MONTHS BUT IT LOOKED LIKE NOTHING HAD CHANGED.
SHE HAD A COUPLE OF NEW ALBUMS.
BOWIE
DIAMOND DOGS
JEEZ, MARCI... WHAT KIND OF MUSIC ARE YOU LISTENING TO THESE DAYS?
THAT'S DAVID BOWIE... KYLE GAVE IT TO ME FOR MY BIRTHDAY. IT'S KIND OF WEIRD STUFF, BUT I'M STARTING TO GET INTO IT.
SHE PUT ON HARVEST BY NEIL YOUNG WITH THE VOLUME DOWN LOW... IT WAS ONE OF OUR FAVORITES.
THIS IS SO WILD... I CAN'T BELIEVE YOU'RE HERE! YOU'VE GOTTA SIT DOWN AND TELL ME EVERYTHING.

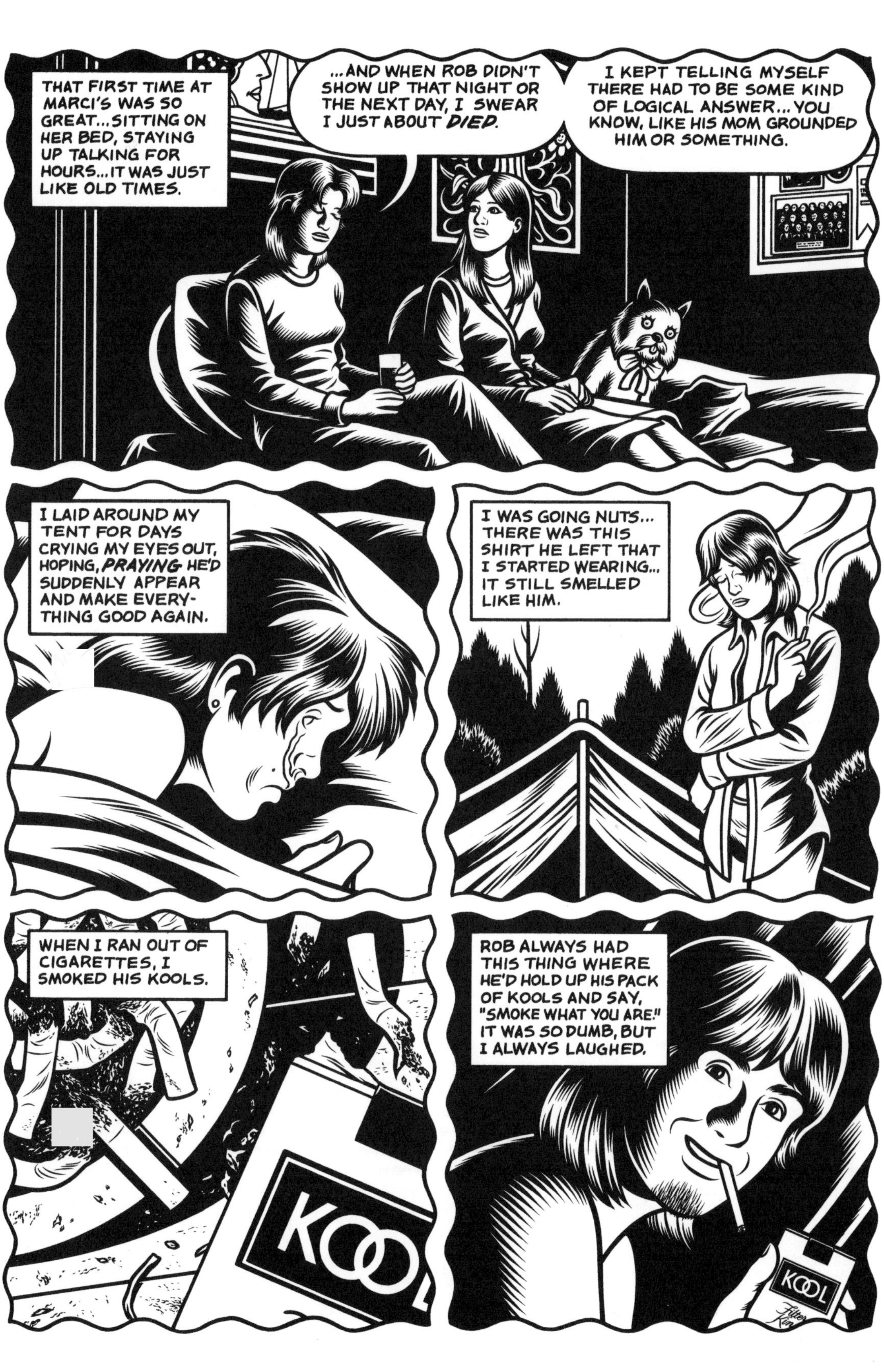
THAT FIRST TIME AT MARCI'S WAS SO GREAT... SITTING ON HER BED, STAYING UP TALKING FOR HOURS... IT WAS JUST LIKE OLD TIMES.
...AND WHEN ROB DIDN'T SHOW UP THAT NIGHT OR THE NEXT DAY, I SWEAR I JUST ABOUT *DIED*.
I KEPT TELLING MYSELF THERE HAD TO BE SOME KIND OF LOGICAL ANSWER... YOU KNOW, LIKE HIS MOM GROUNDED HIM OR SOMETHING.
I LAID AROUND MY TENT FOR DAYS CRYING MY EYES OUT, HOPING, *PRAYING* HE'D SUDDENLY APPEAR AND MAKE EVERY-THING GOOD AGAIN.
I WAS GOING NUTS... THERE WAS THIS SHIRT HE LEFT THAT I STARTED WEARING... IT STILL SMELLED LIKE HIM.
WHEN I RAN OUT OF CIGARETTES, I SMOKED HIS KOOLS.
KOOL
ROB ALWAYS HAD THIS THING WHERE HE'D HOLD UP HIS PACK OF KOOLS AND SAY, "SMOKE WHAT YOU ARE." IT WAS SO DUMB, BUT I ALWAYS LAUGHED.
KOOL

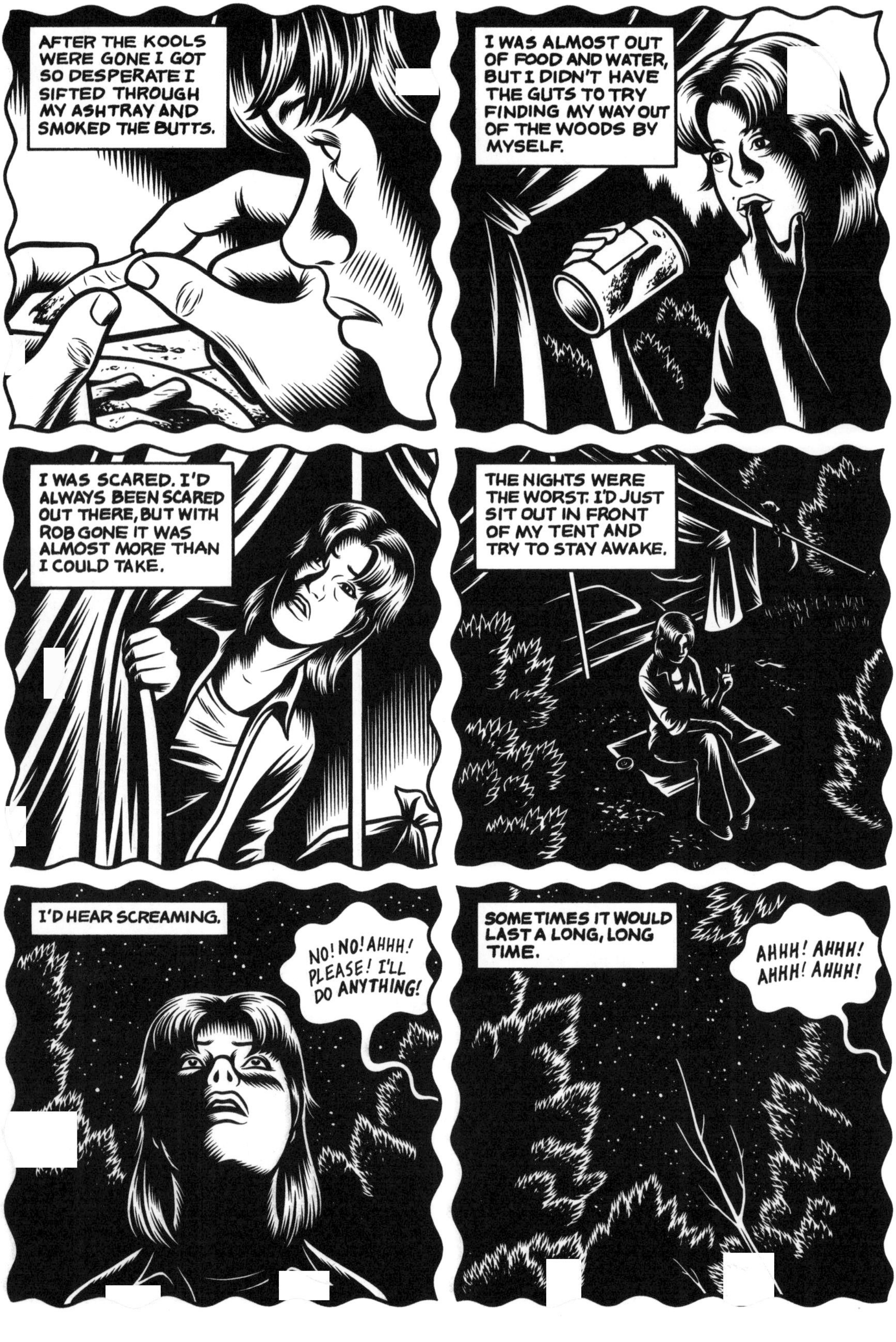
AFTER THE KOOLS WERE GONE I GOT SO DESPERATE I SIFTED THROUGH MY ASHTRAY AND SMOKED THE BUTTS.
I WAS ALMOST OUT OF FOOD AND WATER, BUT I DIDN'T HAVE THE GUTS TO TRY FINDING MY WAY OUT OF THE WOODS BY MYSELF.
I WAS SCARED. I'D ALWAYS BEEN SCARED OUT THERE, BUT WITH ROB GONE IT WAS ALMOST MORE THAN I COULD TAKE.
THE NIGHTS WERE THE WORST. I'D JUST SIT OUT IN FRONT OF MY TENT AND TRY TO STAY AWAKE.
I'D HEAR SCREAMING.
NO! NO! AHHH! PLEASE! I'LL DO ANYTHING!
SOMETIMES IT WOULD LAST A LONG, LONG TIME.
AHHH! AHHH! AHHH! AHHH!

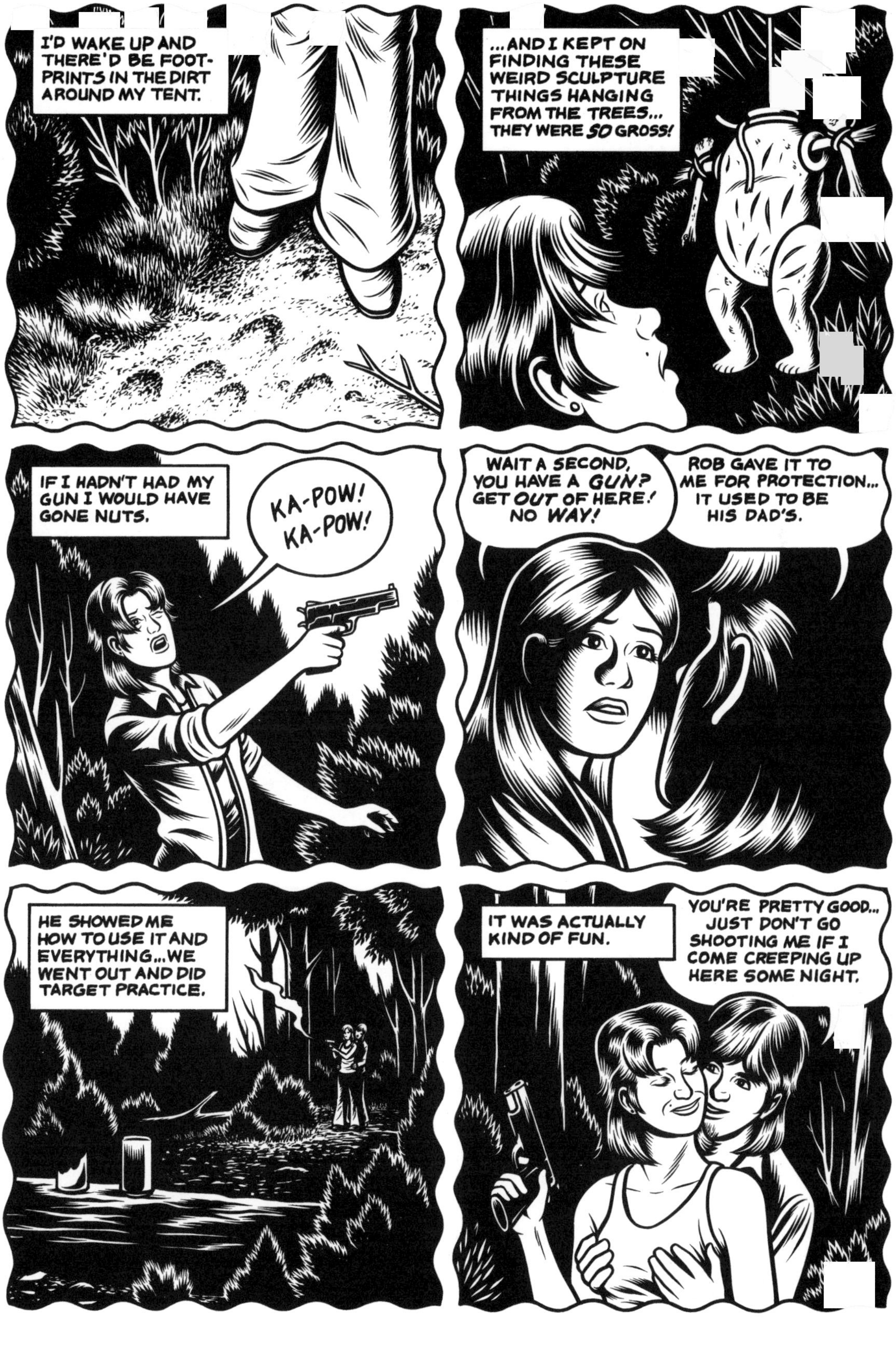
I'D WAKE UP AND THERE'D BE FOOT-PRINTS IN THE DIRT AROUND MY TENT.
...AND I KEPT ON FINDING THESE WEIRD SCULPTURE THINGS HANGING FROM THE TREES... THEY WERE SO GROSS!
IF I HADN'T HAD MY GUN I WOULD HAVE GONE NUTS.
KA-POW! KA-POW!
WAIT A SECOND, YOU HAVE A GUN? GET OUT OF HERE! NO WAY!
ROB GAVE IT TO ME FOR PROTECTION... IT USED TO BE HIS DAD'S.
HE SHOWED ME HOW TO USE IT AND EVERYTHING... WE WENT OUT AND DID TARGET PRACTICE.
IT WAS ACTUALLY KIND OF FUN.
YOU'RE PRETTY GOOD... JUST DON'T GO SHOOTING ME IF I COME CREEPING UP HERE SOME NIGHT.

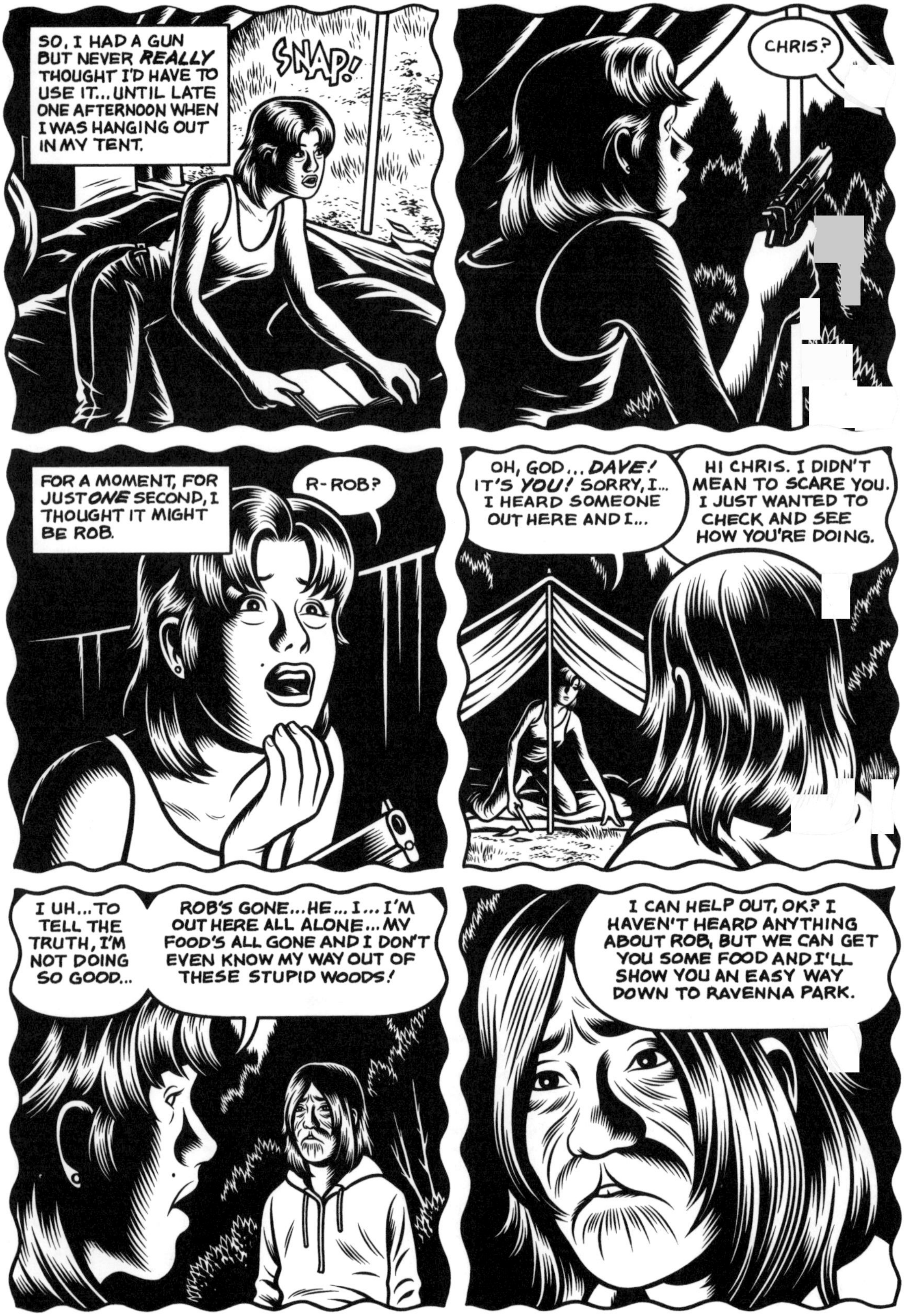
SO, I HAD A GUN BUT NEVER REALLY THOUGHT I'D HAVE TO USE IT... UNTIL LATE ONE AFTERNOON WHEN I WAS HANGING OUT IN MY TENT.
SNAP!
CHRIS?
FOR A MOMENT, FOR JUST ONE SECOND, I THOUGHT IT MIGHT BE ROB.
R-ROB?
OH, GOD... DAVE! IT'S YOU! SORRY, I... I HEARD SOMEONE OUT HERE AND I...
HI CHRIS. I DIDN'T MEAN TO SCARE YOU. I JUST WANTED TO CHECK AND SEE HOW YOU'RE DOING.
I UH... TO TELL THE TRUTH, I'M NOT DOING SO GOOD...
ROB'S GONE... HE... I... I'M OUT HERE ALL ALONE... MY FOOD'S ALL GONE AND I DON'T EVEN KNOW MY WAY OUT OF THESE STUPID WOODS!
I CAN HELP OUT, OK? I HAVEN'T HEARD ANYTHING ABOUT ROB, BUT WE CAN GET YOU SOME FOOD AND I'LL SHOW YOU AN EASY WAY DOWN TO RAVENNA PARK.

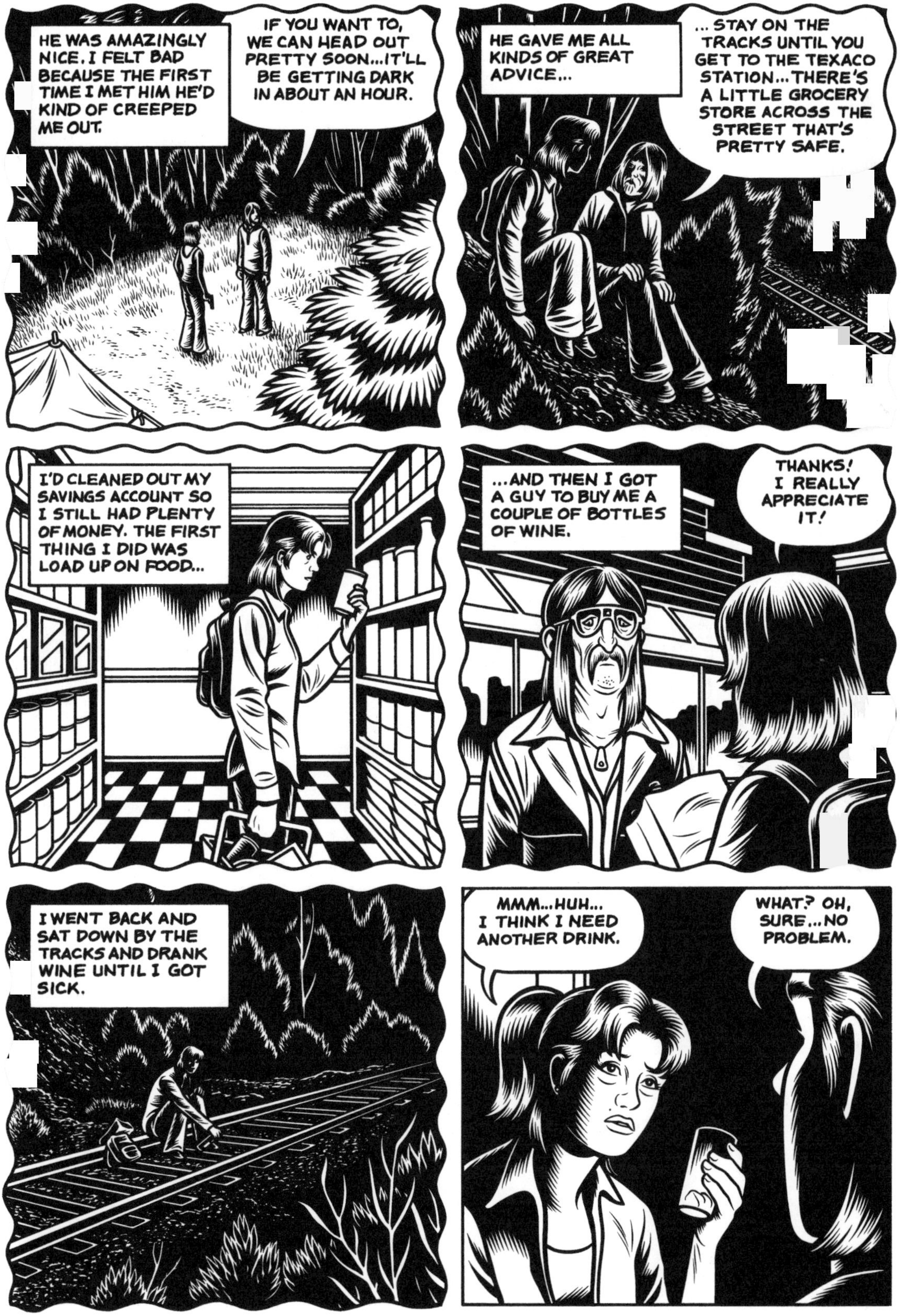
HE WAS AMAZINGLY NICE. I FELT BAD BECAUSE THE FIRST TIME I MET HIM HE'D KIND OF CREEPED ME OUT.
IF YOU WANT TO, WE CAN HEAD OUT PRETTY SOON...IT'LL BE GETTING DARK IN ABOUT AN HOUR.
HE GAVE ME ALL KINDS OF GREAT ADVICE...
...STAY ON THE TRACKS UNTIL YOU GET TO THE TEXACO STATION...THERE'S A LITTLE GROCERY STORE ACROSS THE STREET THAT'S PRETTY SAFE.
I'D CLEANED OUT MY SAVINGS ACCOUNT SO I STILL HAD PLENTY OF MONEY. THE FIRST THING I DID WAS LOAD UP ON FOOD...
...AND THEN I GOT A GUY TO BUY ME A COUPLE OF BOTTLES OF WINE.
THANKS! I REALLY APPRECIATE IT!
I WENT BACK AND SAT DOWN BY THE TRACKS AND DRANK WINE UNTIL I GOT SICK.
MMM...HUH... I THINK I NEED ANOTHER DRINK.
WHAT? OH, SURE...NO PROBLEM.

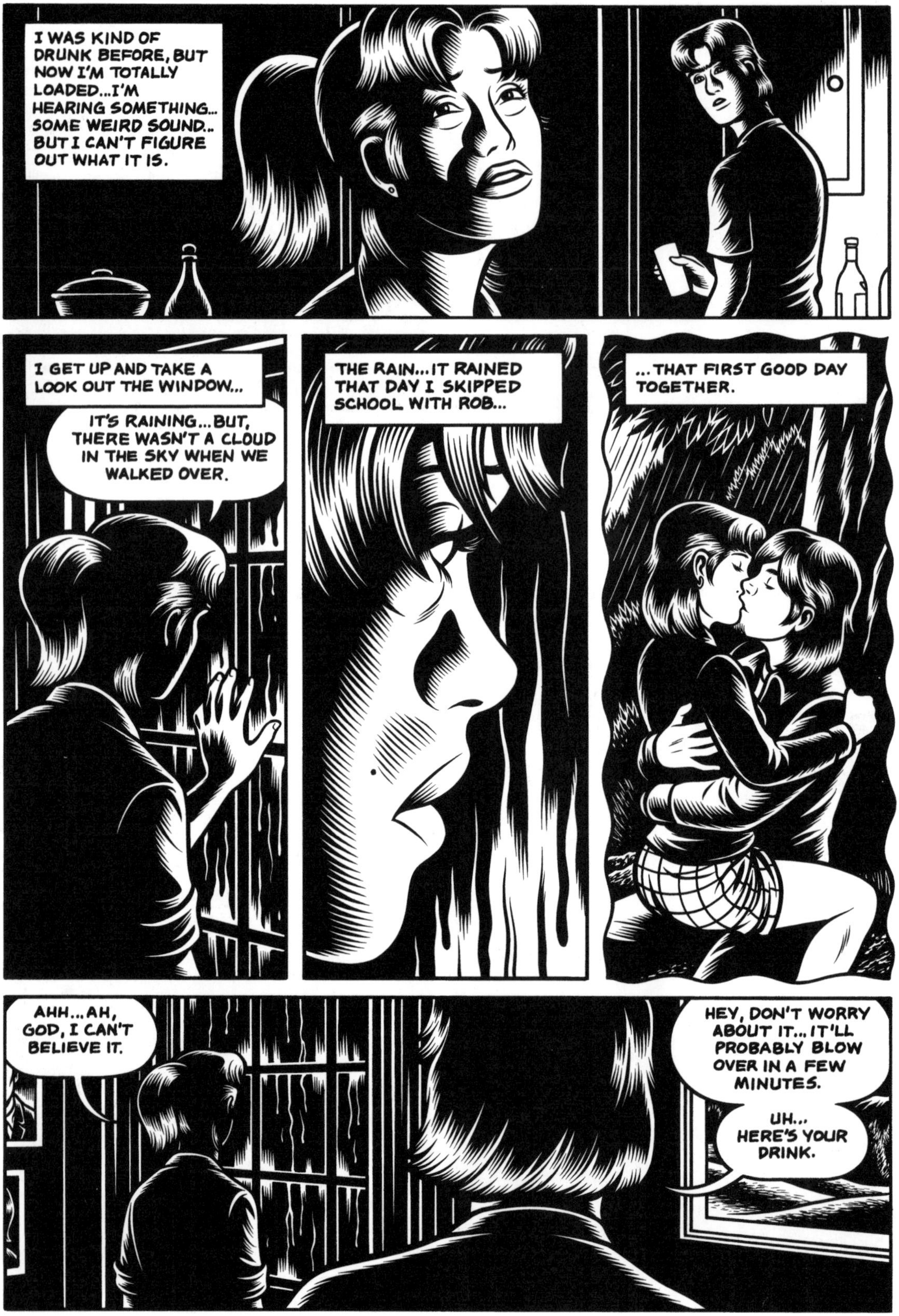
I WAS KIND OF DRUNK BEFORE, BUT NOW I'M TOTALLY LOADED...I'M HEARING SOMETHING... SOME WEIRD SOUND.. BUT I CAN'T FIGURE OUT WHAT IT IS.
I GET UP AND TAKE A LOOK OUT THE WINDOW...
IT'S RAINING...BUT, THERE WASN'T A CLOUD IN THE SKY WHEN WE WALKED OVER.
THE RAIN...IT RAINED THAT DAY I SKIPPED SCHOOL WITH ROB...
...THAT FIRST GOOD DAY TOGETHER.
AHH...AH, GOD, I CAN'T BELIEVE IT.
HEY, DON'T WORRY ABOUT IT...IT'LL PROBABLY BLOW OVER IN A FEW MINUTES.
UH... HERE'S YOUR DRINK.

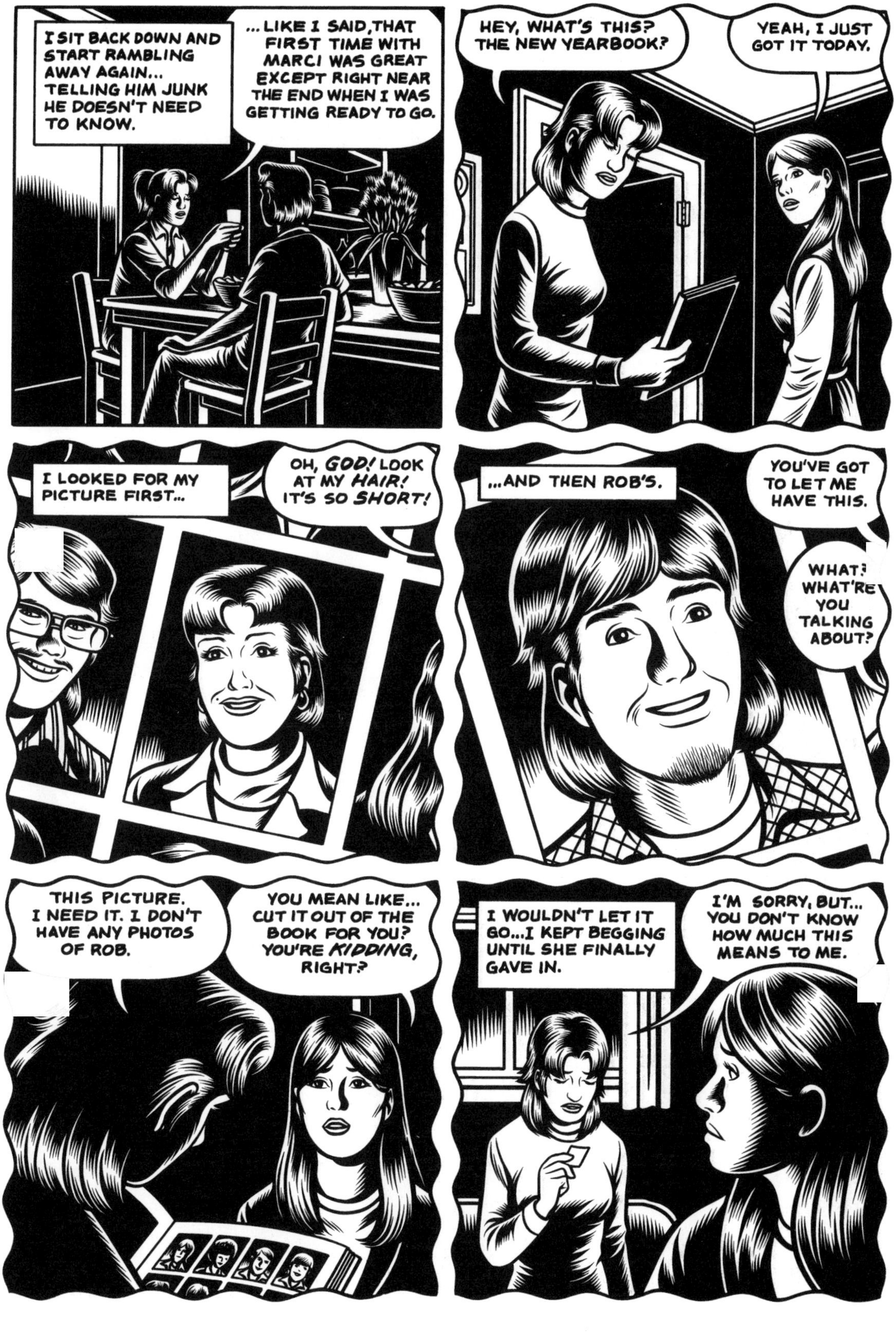
I SIT BACK DOWN AND START RAMBLING AWAY AGAIN... TELLING HIM JUNK HE DOESN'T NEED TO KNOW.
...LIKE I SAID, THAT FIRST TIME WITH MARCI WAS GREAT EXCEPT RIGHT NEAR THE END WHEN I WAS GETTING READY TO GO.
HEY, WHAT'S THIS? THE NEW YEARBOOK?
YEAH, I JUST GOT IT TODAY.
I LOOKED FOR MY PICTURE FIRST...
OH, GOD! LOOK AT MY HAIR! IT'S SO SHORT!
...AND THEN ROB'S.
YOU'VE GOT TO LET ME HAVE THIS.
WHAT? WHAT'RE YOU TALKING ABOUT?
THIS PICTURE. I NEED IT. I DON'T HAVE ANY PHOTOS OF ROB.
YOU MEAN LIKE... CUT IT OUT OF THE BOOK FOR YOU? YOU'RE KIDDING, RIGHT?
I WOULDN'T LET IT GO...I KEPT BEGGING UNTIL SHE FINALLY GAVE IN.
I'M SORRY, BUT... YOU DON'T KNOW HOW MUCH THIS MEANS TO ME.

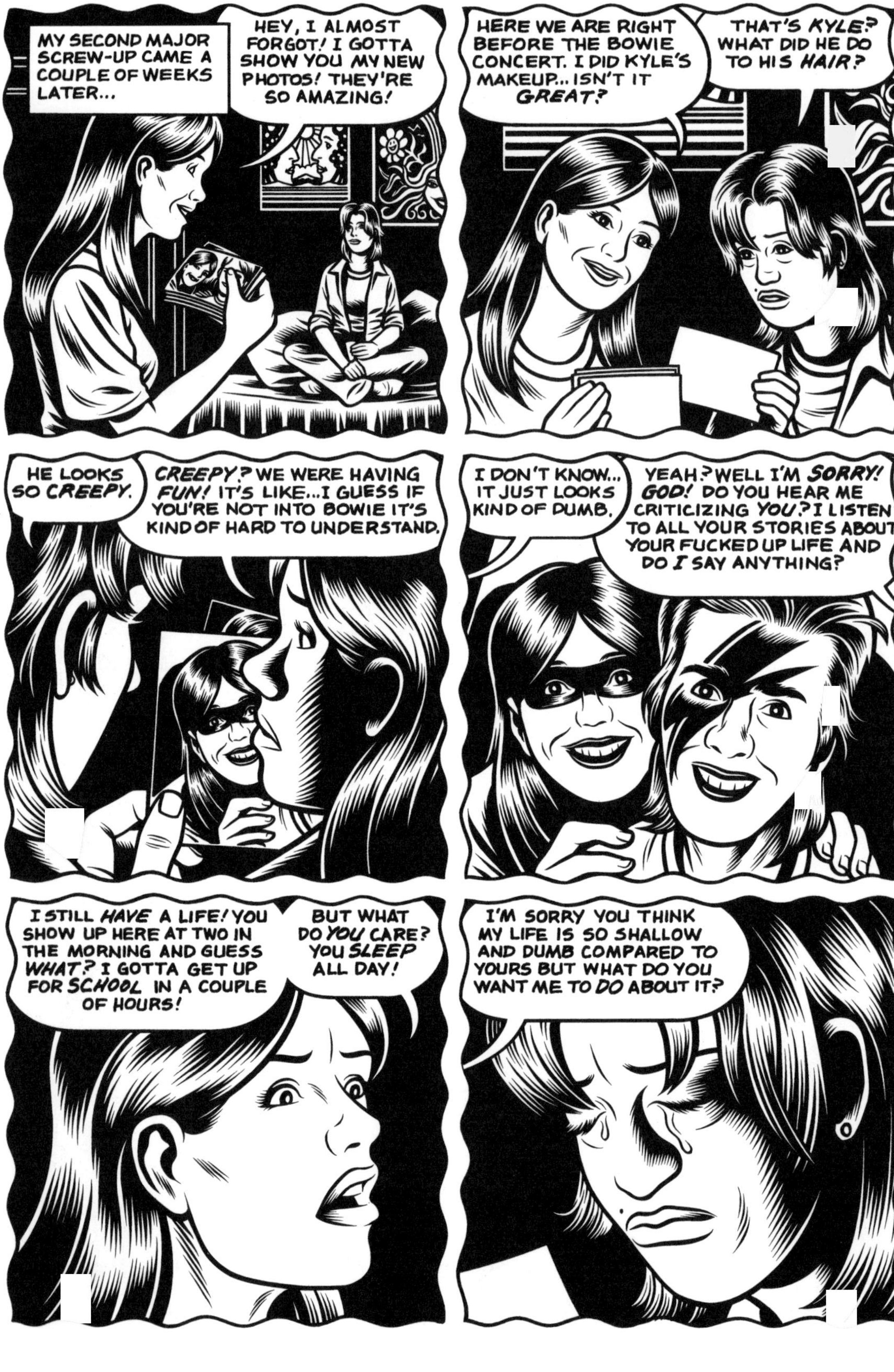

MY SECOND MAJOR SCREW-UP CAME A COUPLE OF WEEKS LATER...
HEY, I ALMOST FORGOT! I GOTTA SHOW YOU MY NEW PHOTOS! THEY'RE SO AMAZING!
HERE WE ARE RIGHT BEFORE THE BOWIE CONCERT. I DID KYLE'S MAKEUP... ISN'T IT GREAT?
THAT'S KYLE? WHAT DID HE DO TO HIS HAIR?
HE LOOKS SO CREEPY.
CREEPY? WE WERE HAVING FUN! IT'S LIKE...I GUESS IF YOU'RE NOT INTO BOWIE IT'S KIND OF HARD TO UNDERSTAND.
I DON'T KNOW... IT JUST LOOKS KIND OF DUMB.
YEAH? WELL I'M SORRY! GOD! DO YOU HEAR ME CRITICIZING YOU? I LISTEN TO ALL YOUR STORIES ABOUT YOUR FUCKED UP LIFE AND DO I SAY ANYTHING?
I STILL HAVE A LIFE! YOU SHOW UP HERE AT TWO IN THE MORNING AND GUESS WHAT? I GOTTA GET UP FOR SCHOOL IN A COUPLE OF HOURS!
BUT WHAT DO YOU CARE? YOU SLEEP ALL DAY!
I'M SORRY YOU THINK MY LIFE IS SO SHALLOW AND DUMB COMPARED TO YOURS BUT WHAT DO YOU WANT ME TO DO ABOUT IT?

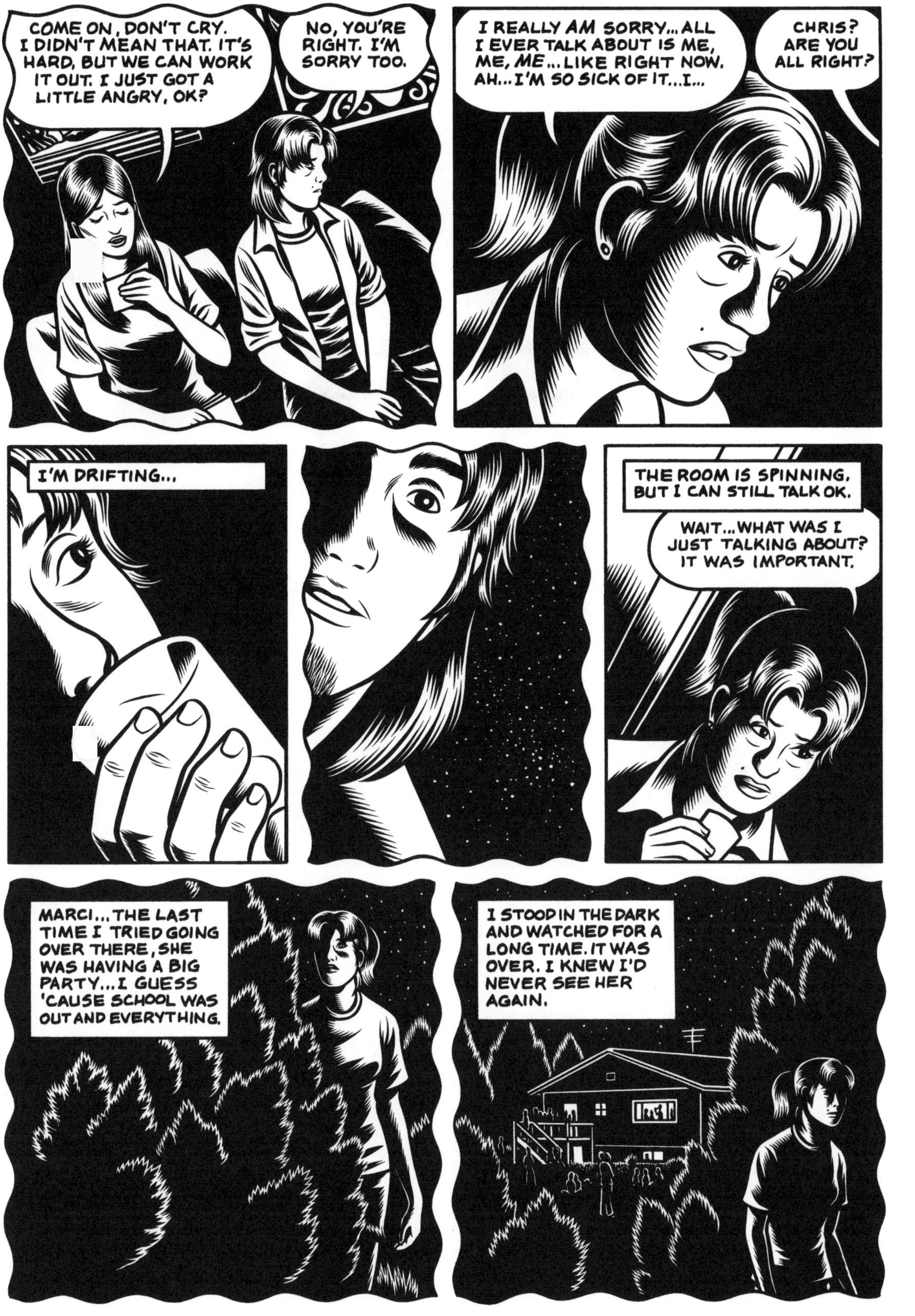
COME ON, DON'T CRY. I DIDN'T MEAN THAT. IT'S HARD, BUT WE CAN WORK IT OUT. I JUST GOT A LITTLE ANGRY, OK?
NO, YOU'RE RIGHT. I'M SORRY TOO.
I REALLY AM SORRY... ALL I EVER TALK ABOUT IS ME, ME, ME... LIKE RIGHT NOW. AH... I'M SO SICK OF IT... I...
CHRIS? ARE YOU ALL RIGHT?
I'M DRIFTING...
THE ROOM IS SPINNING, BUT I CAN STILL TALK OK.
WAIT... WHAT WAS I JUST TALKING ABOUT? IT WAS IMPORTANT.
MARCI... THE LAST TIME I TRIED GOING OVER THERE, SHE WAS HAVING A BIG PARTY... I GUESS 'CAUSE SCHOOL WAS OUT AND EVERYTHING.
I STOOD IN THE DARK AND WATCHED FOR A LONG TIME. IT WAS OVER. I KNEW I'D NEVER SEE HER AGAIN.

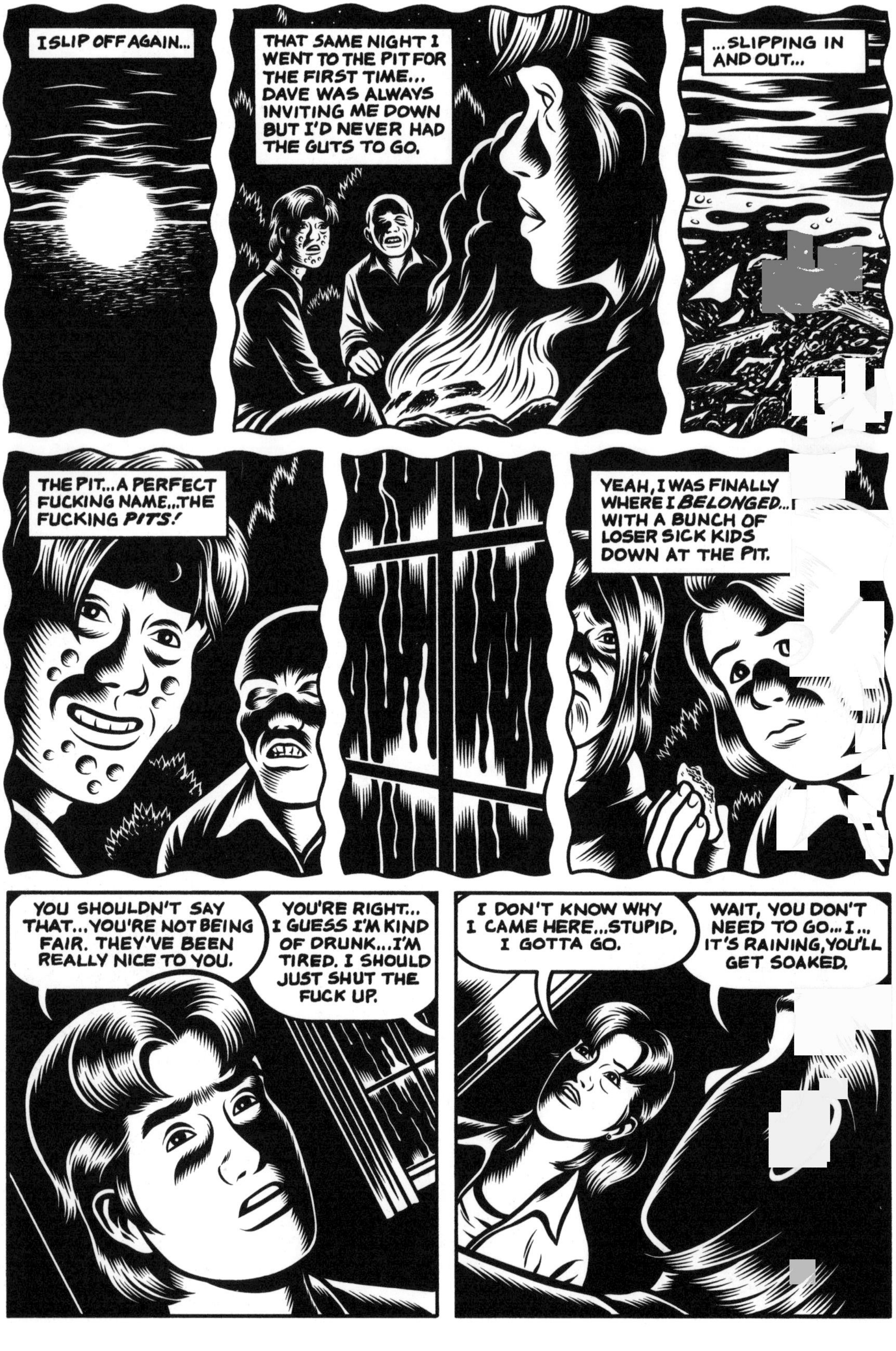
I SLIP OFF AGAIN...
THAT SAME NIGHT I WENT TO THE PIT FOR THE FIRST TIME... DAVE WAS ALWAYS INVITING ME DOWN BUT I'D NEVER HAD THE GUTS TO GO.
...SLIPPING IN AND OUT...
THE PIT...A PERFECT FUCKING NAME...THE FUCKING PITS!
YEAH, I WAS FINALLY WHERE I BELONGED... WITH A BUNCH OF LOSER SICK KIDS DOWN AT THE PIT.
YOU SHOULDN'T SAY THAT... YOU'RE NOT BEING FAIR. THEY'VE BEEN REALLY NICE TO YOU.
YOU'RE RIGHT... I GUESS I'M KIND OF DRUNK... I'M TIRED. I SHOULD JUST SHUT THE FUCK UP.
I DON'T KNOW WHY I CAME HERE... STUPID. I GOTTA GO.
WAIT, YOU DON'T NEED TO GO... I... IT'S RAINING, YOU'LL GET SOAKED.

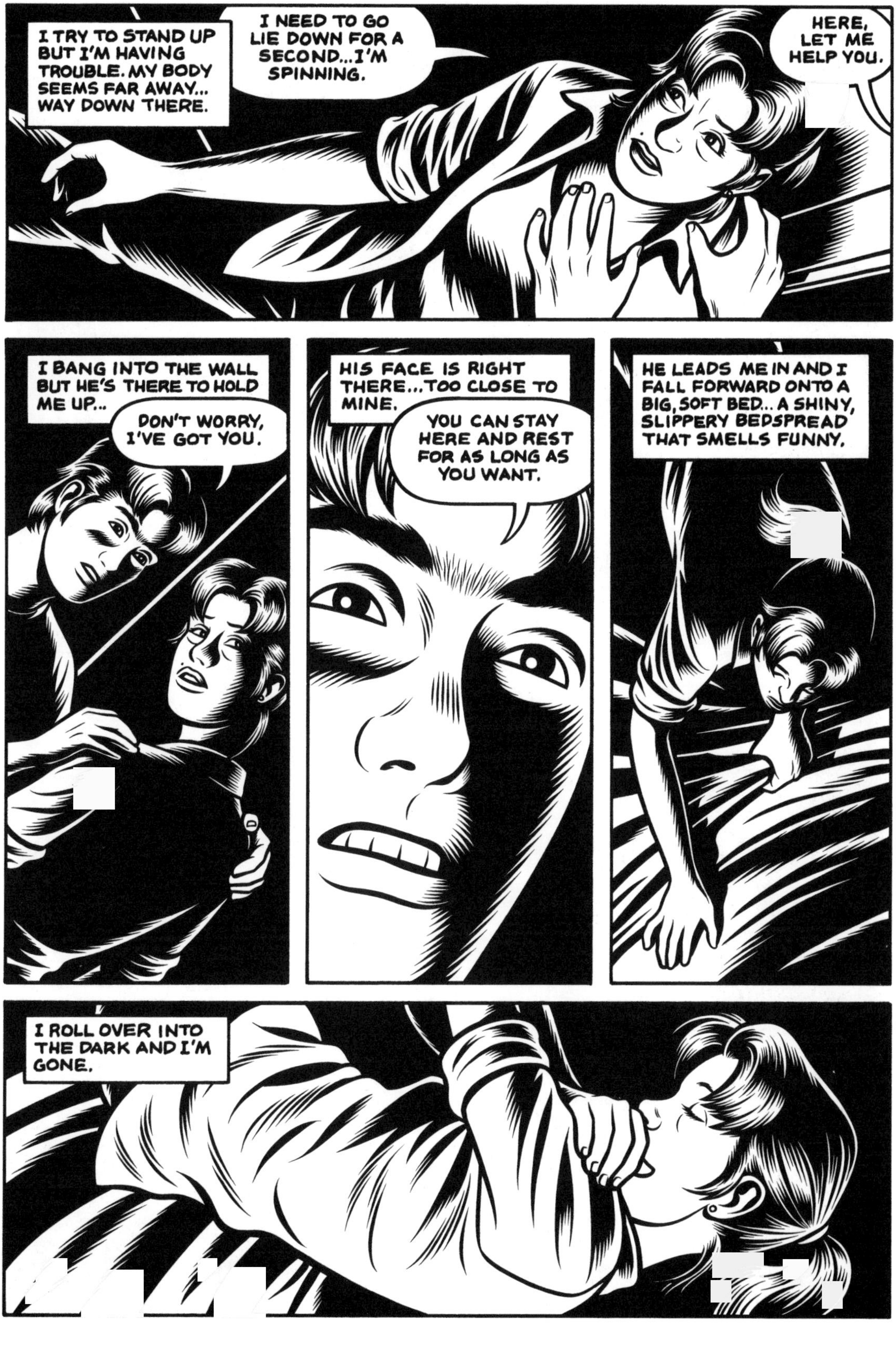
I TRY TO STAND UP BUT I'M HAVING TROUBLE. MY BODY SEEMS FAR AWAY... WAY DOWN THERE.
I NEED TO GO LIE DOWN FOR A SECOND...I'M SPINNING.
HERE, LET ME HELP YOU.
I BANG INTO THE WALL BUT HE'S THERE TO HOLD ME UP...
DON'T WORRY, I'VE GOT YOU.
HIS FACE IS RIGHT THERE...TOO CLOSE TO MINE.
YOU CAN STAY HERE AND REST FOR AS LONG AS YOU WANT.
HE LEADS ME IN AND I FALL FORWARD ONTO A BIG, SOFT BED... A SHINY, SLIPPERY BEDSPREAD THAT SMELLS FUNNY.
I ROLL OVER INTO THE DARK AND I'M GONE.

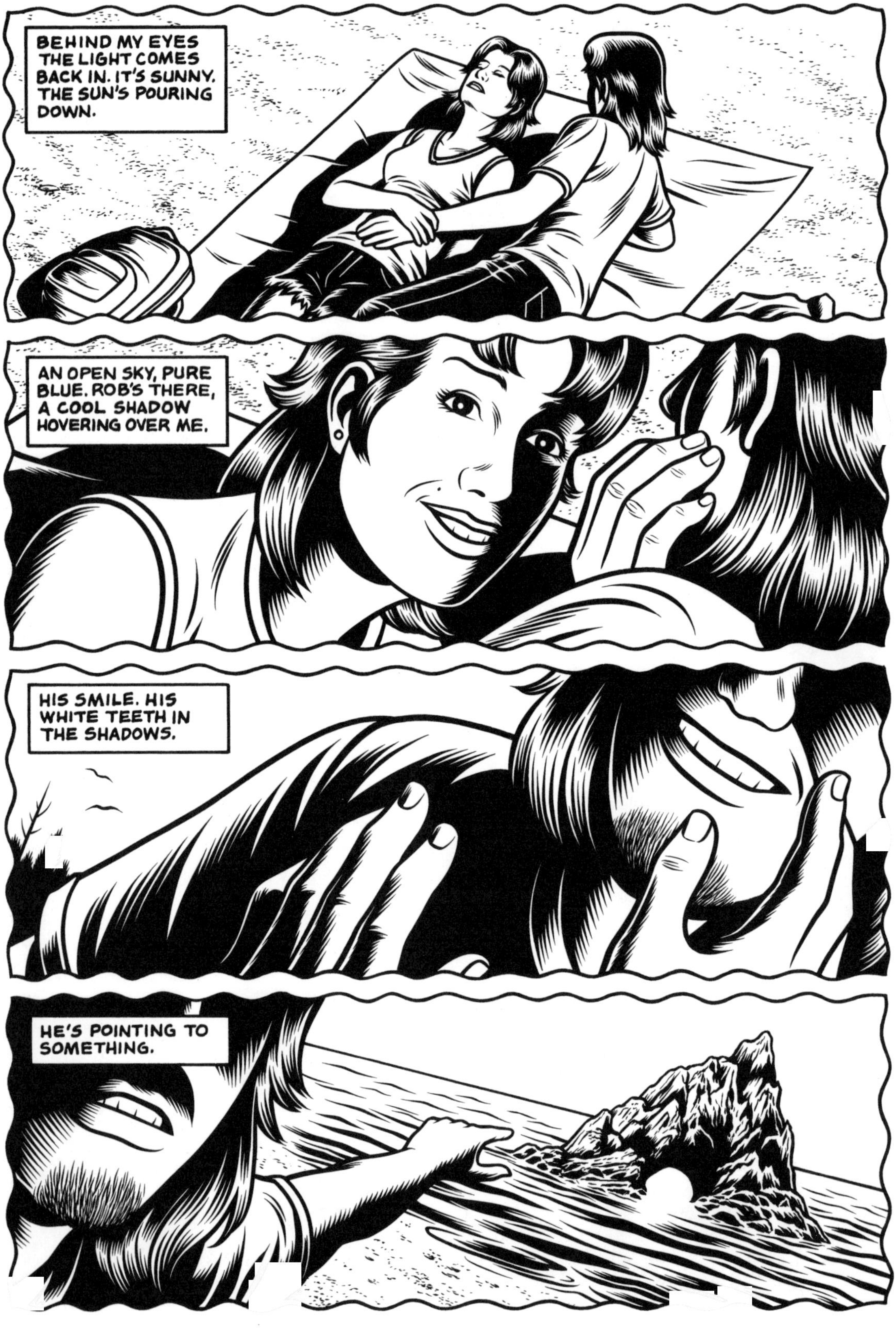
BEHIND MY EYES THE LIGHT COMES BACK IN. IT'S SUNNY. THE SUN'S POURING DOWN.
AN OPEN SKY, PURE BLUE. ROB'S THERE, A COOL SHADOW HOVERING OVER ME.
HIS SMILE. HIS WHITE TEETH IN THE SHADOWS.
HE'S POINTING TO SOMETHING.

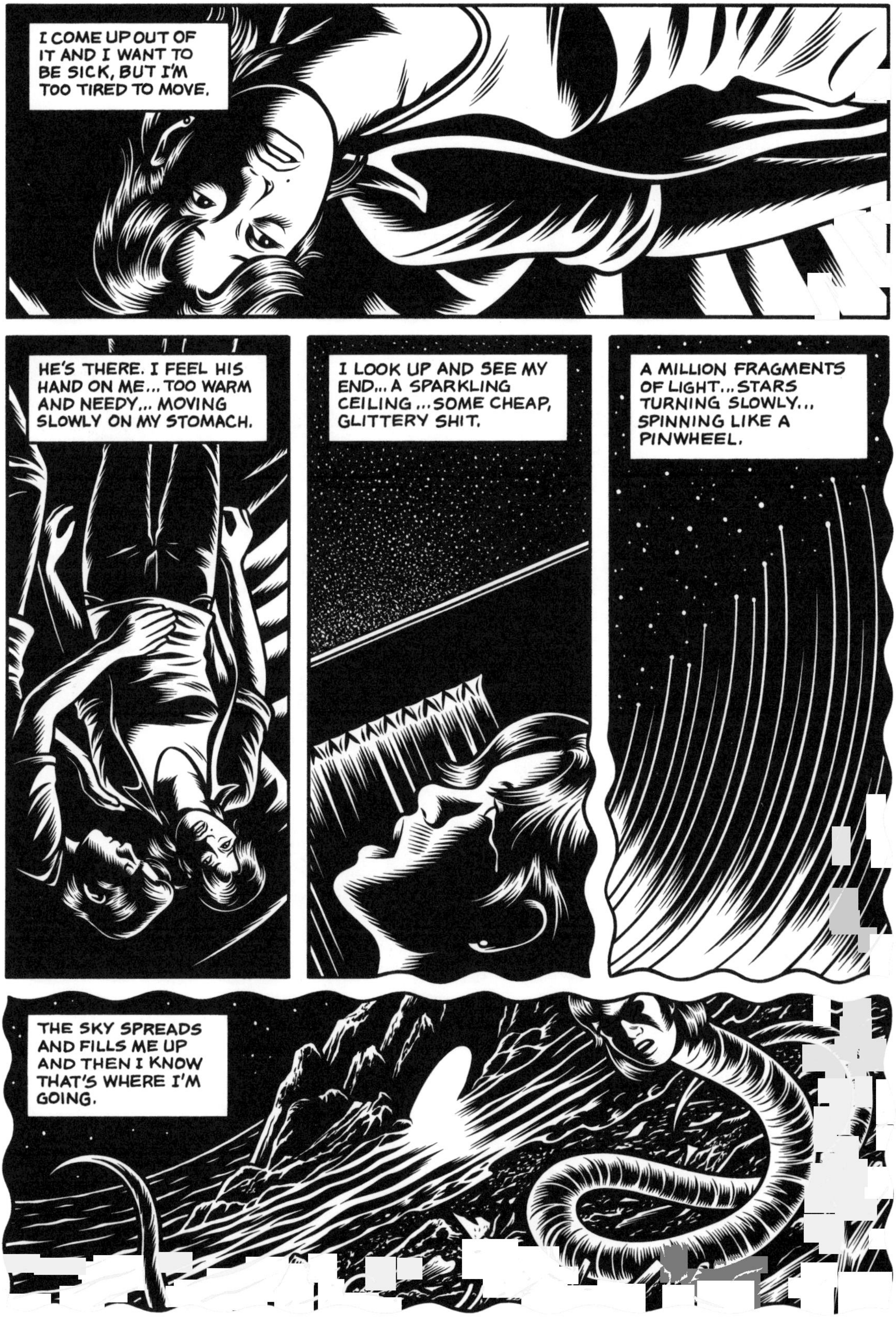
I COME UP OUT OF IT AND I WANT TO BE SICK, BUT I'M TOO TIRED TO MOVE.
HE'S THERE. I FEEL HIS HAND ON ME... TOO WARM AND NEEDY... MOVING SLOWLY ON MY STOMACH.
I LOOK UP AND SEE MY END... A SPARKLING CEILING... SOME CHEAP, GLITTERY SHIT.
A MILLION FRAGMENTS OF LIGHT... STARS TURNING SLOWLY... SPINNING LIKE A PINWHEEL.
THE SKY SPREADS AND FILLS ME UP AND THEN I KNOW THAT'S WHERE I'M GOING.

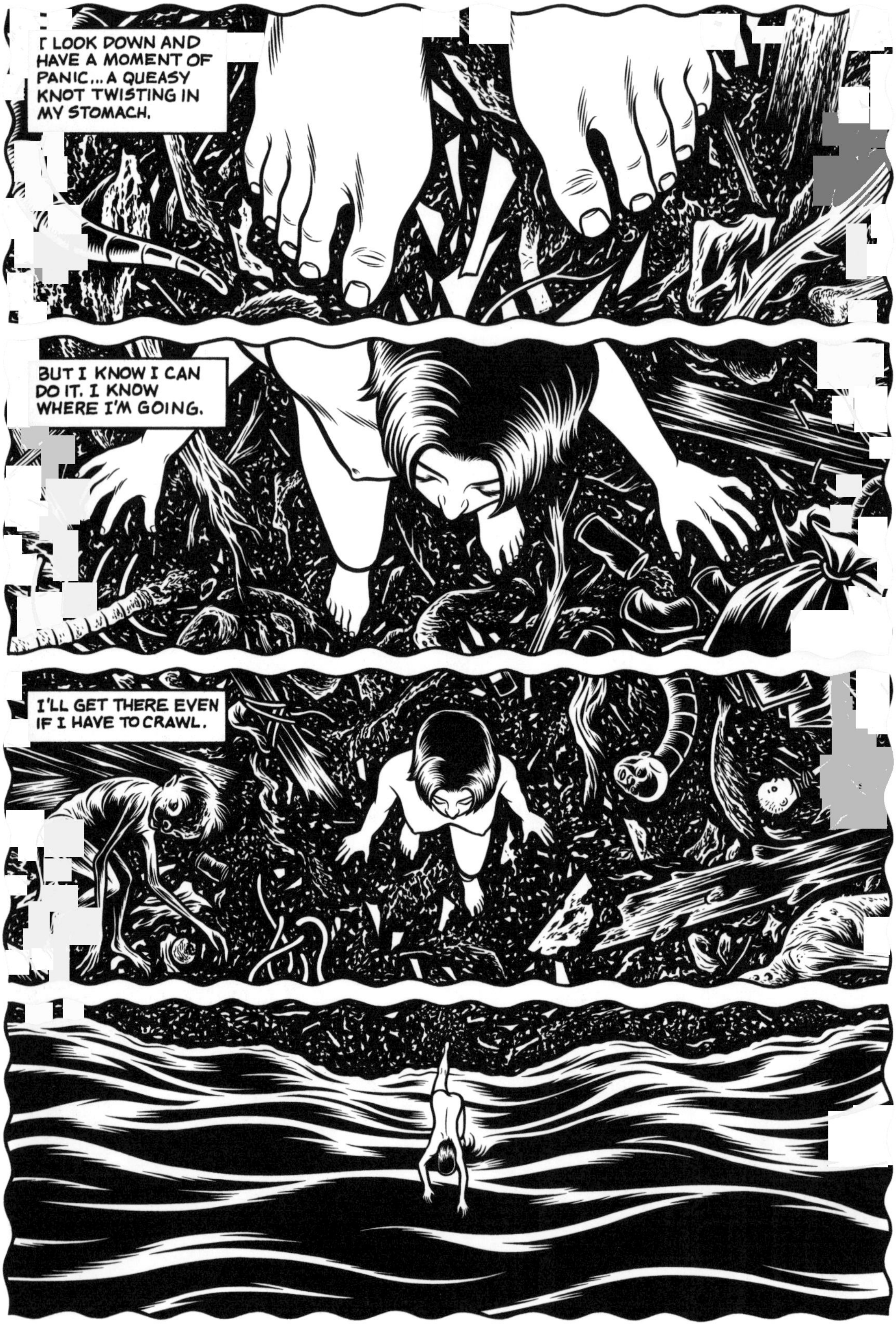
I LOOK DOWN AND HAVE A MOMENT OF PANIC... A QUEASY KNOT TWISTING IN MY STOMACH.
BUT I KNOW I CAN DO IT. I KNOW WHERE I'M GOING.
I'LL GET THERE EVEN IF I HAVE TO CRAWL.

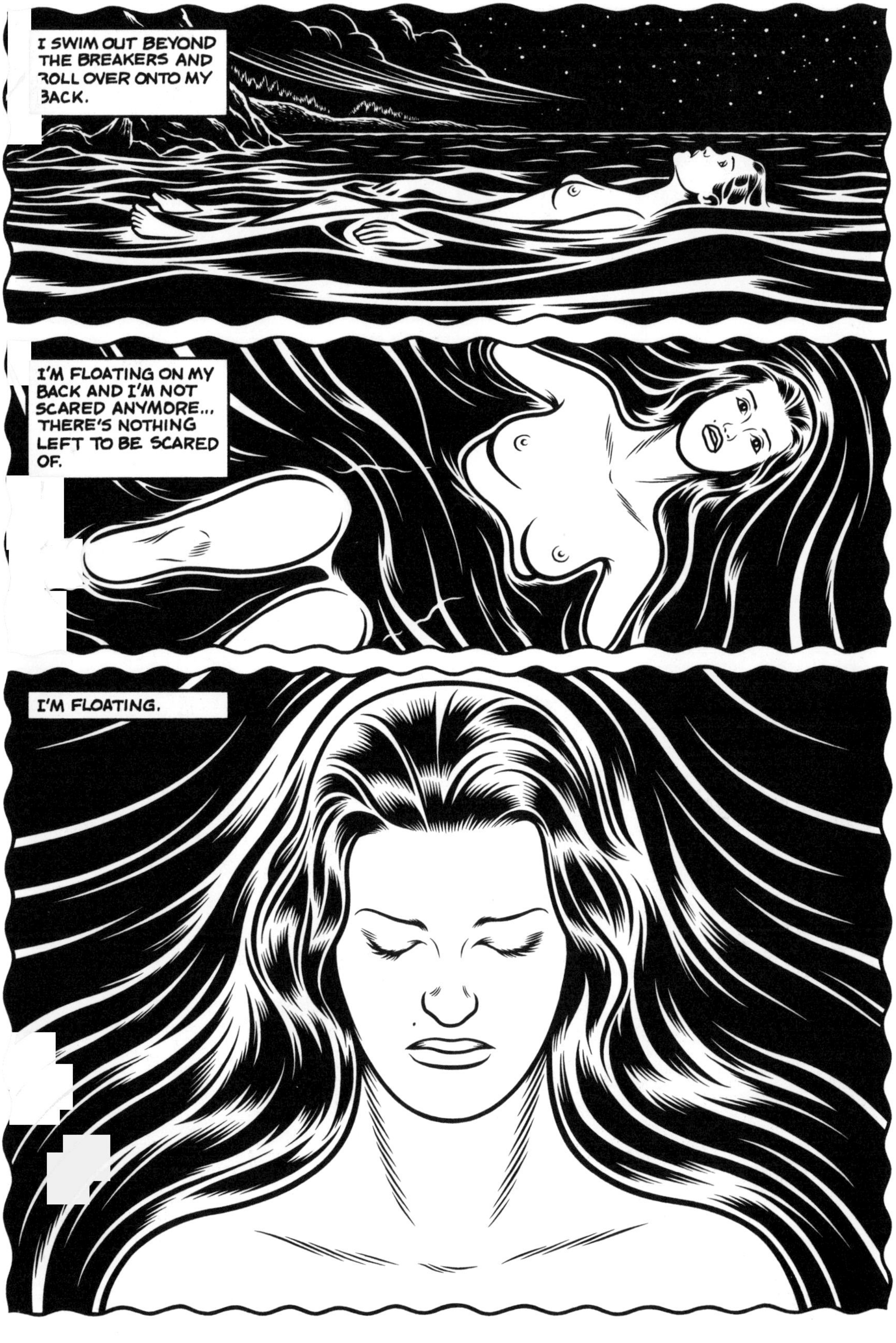
I SWIM OUT BEYOND THE BREAKERS AND ROLL OVER ONTO MY BACK.
I'M FLOATING ON MY BACK AND I'M NOT SCARED ANYMORE... THERE'S NOTHING LEFT TO BE SCARED OF.
I'M FLOATING.

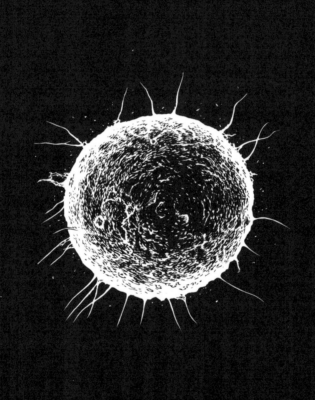

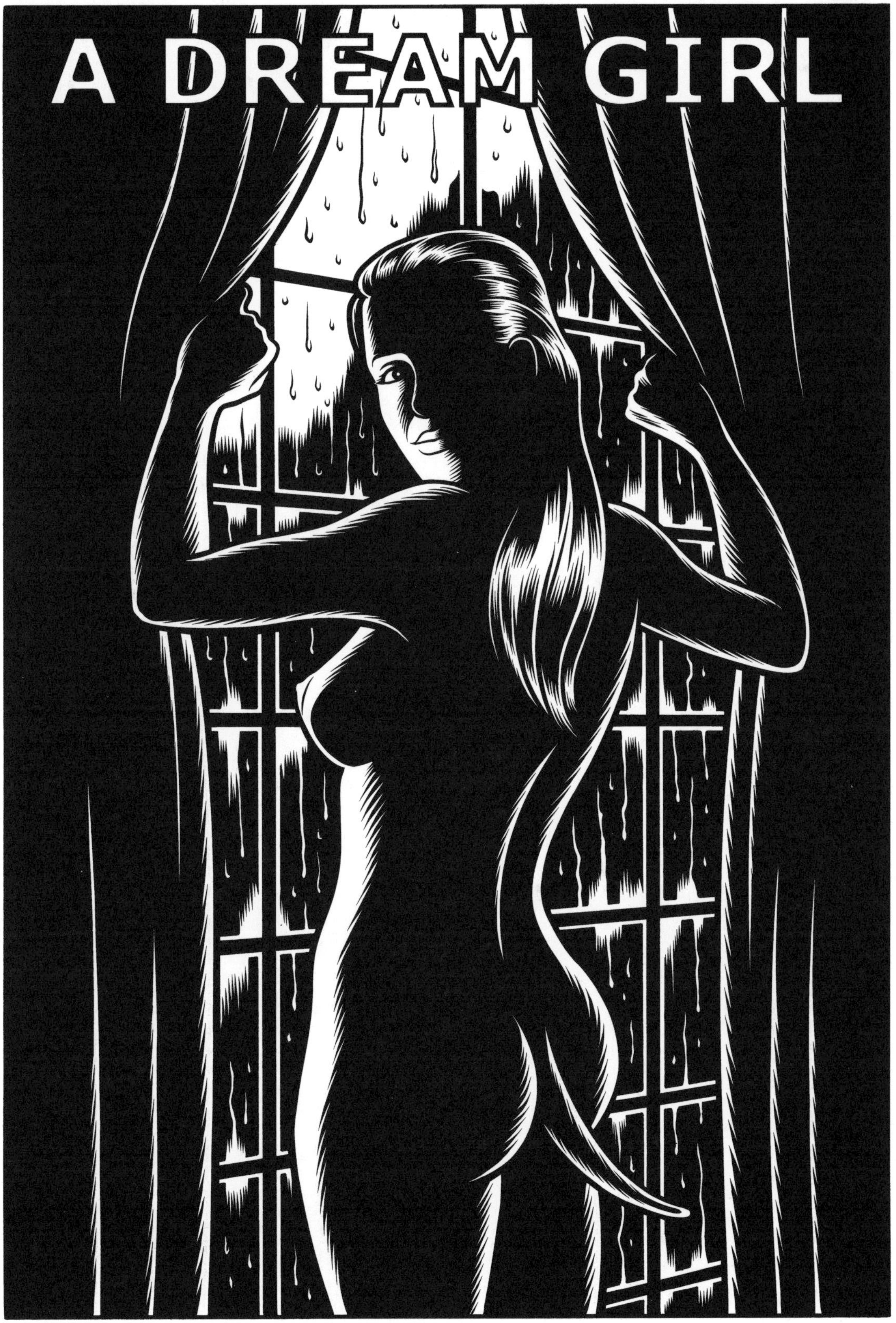
A DREAM GIRL

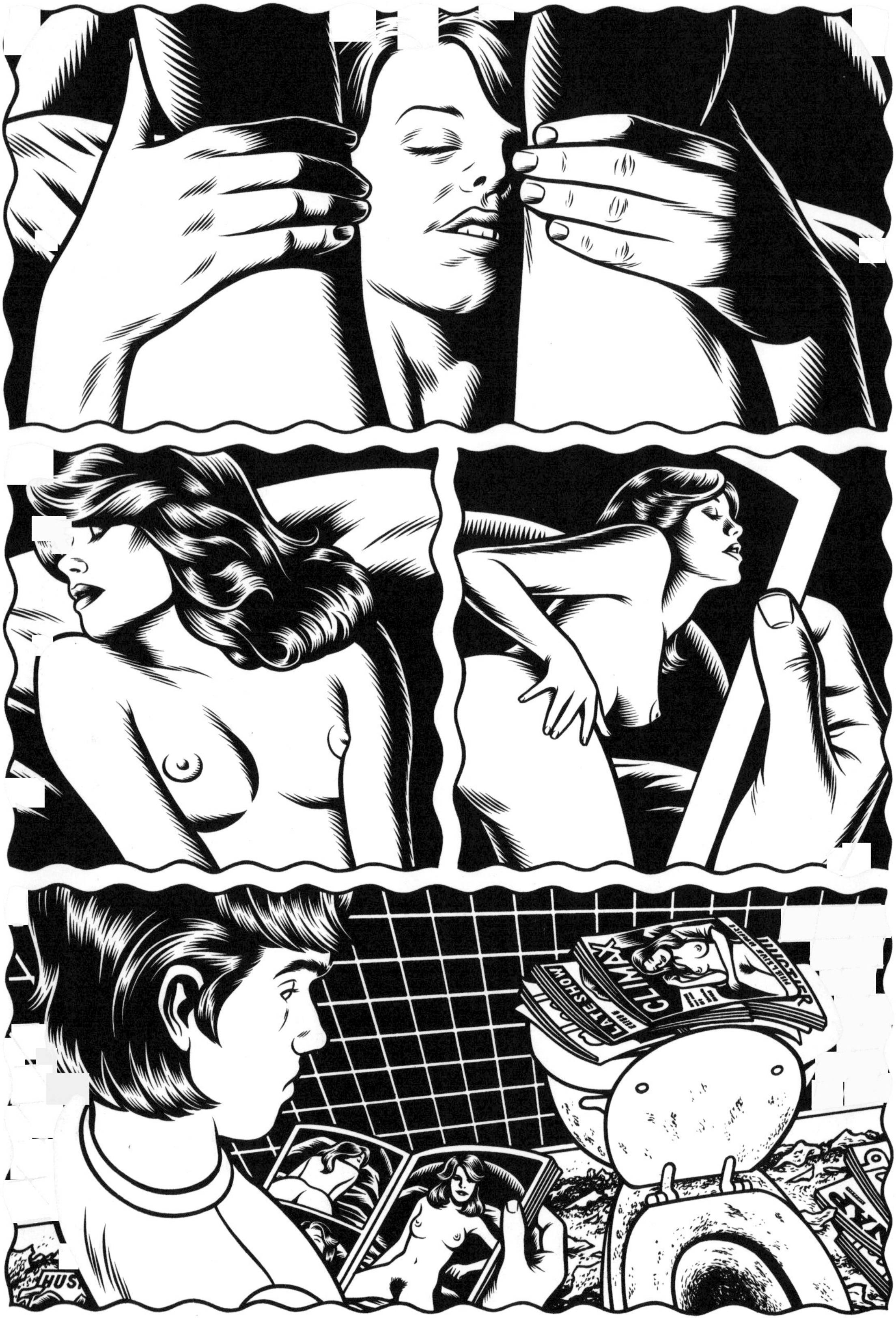
CLIMAX
LATE SHOW

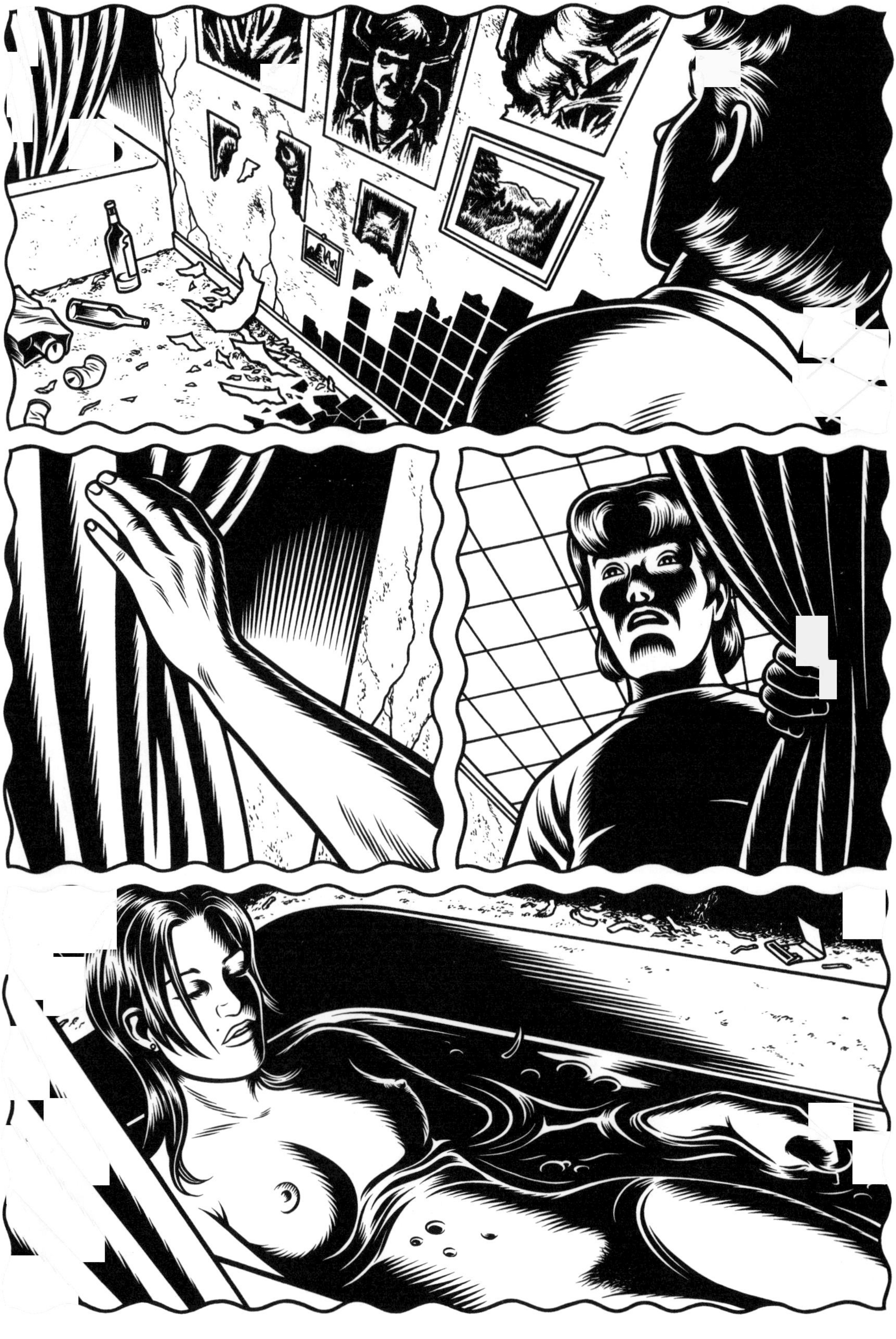

GOWAH OHHWAH...

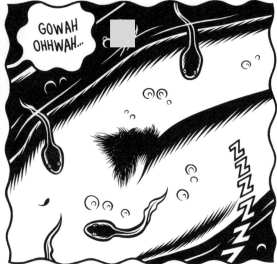

GOWAH OHHWAH...

AHHH... AW, GOD...

GOD, SIX O'CLOCK ALREADY. I STAYED UP *WAY* TOO LATE LAST NIGHT.

...AND IT'S STILL RAINING. WHAT'S THE DEAL ANYWAY? THIS IS SUPPOSED TO BE SUMMER.

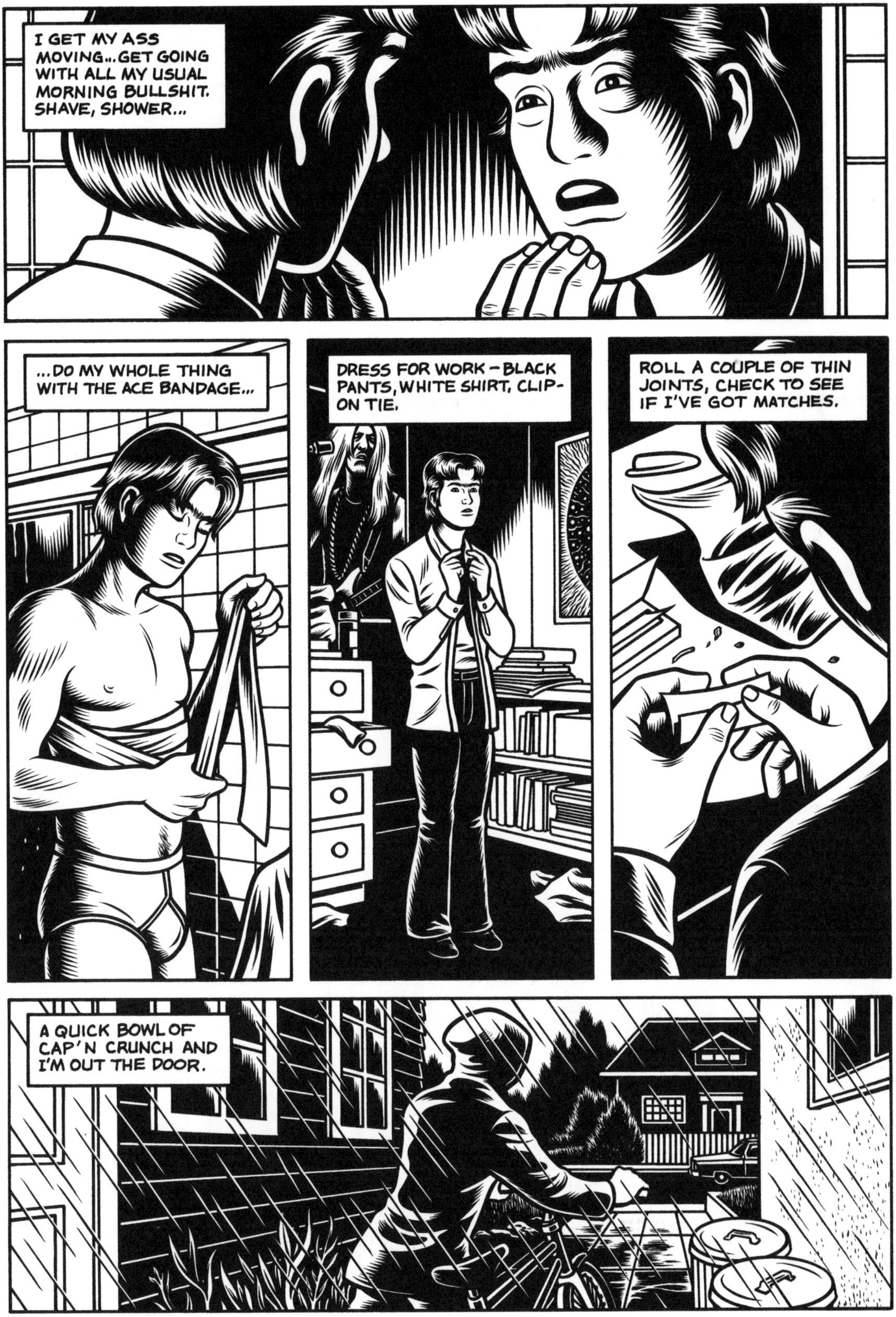
I GET MY ASS MOVING... GET GOING WITH ALL MY USUAL MORNING BULLSHIT. SHAVE, SHOWER...
...DO MY WHOLE THING WITH THE ACE BANDAGE...
DRESS FOR WORK — BLACK PANTS, WHITE SHIRT, CLIP-ON TIE.
ROLL A COUPLE OF THIN JOINTS, CHECK TO SEE IF I'VE GOT MATCHES.
A QUICK BOWL OF CAP'N CRUNCH AND I'M OUT THE DOOR.

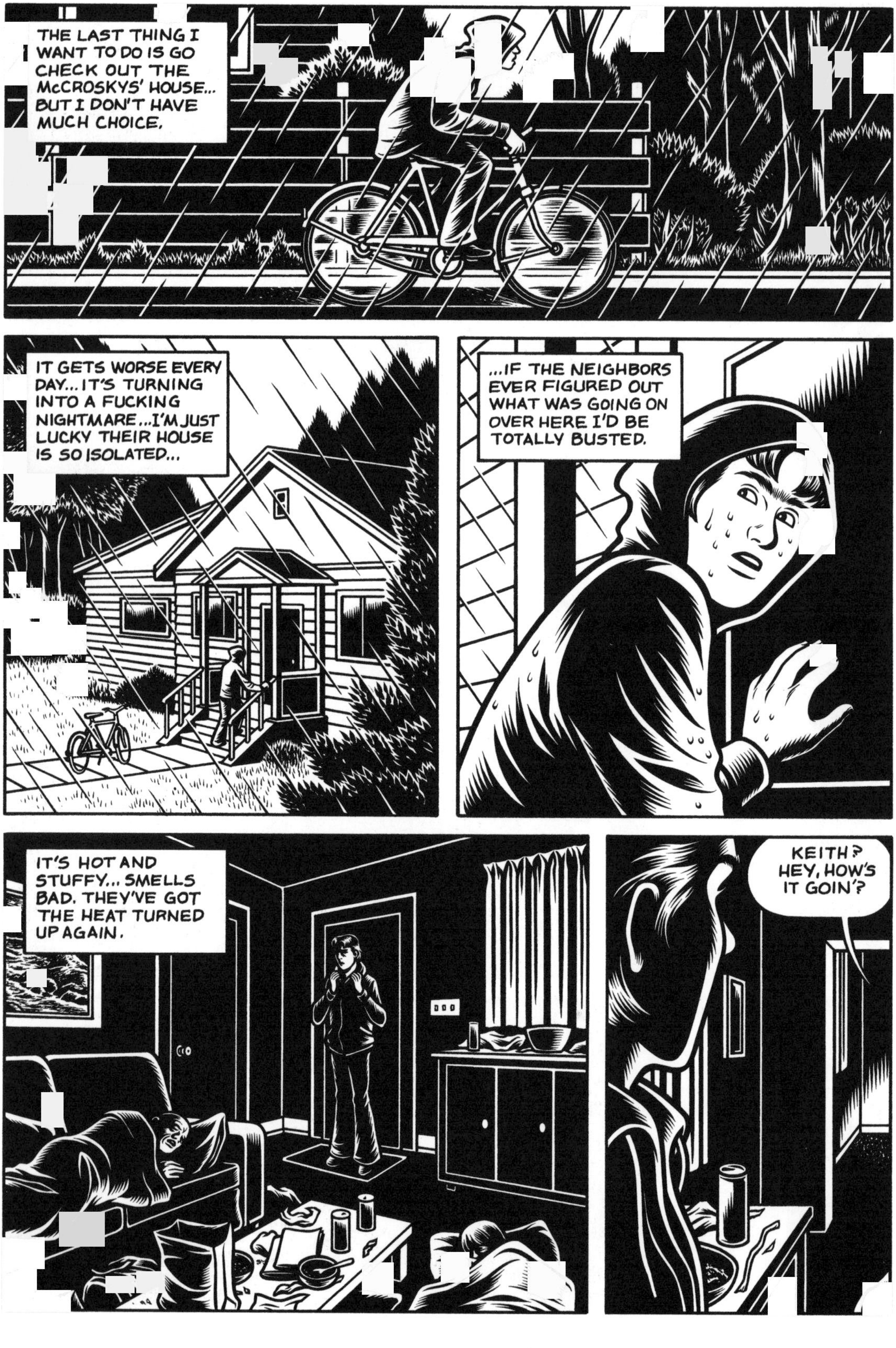
THE LAST THING I WANT TO DO IS GO CHECK OUT THE McCROSKYS' HOUSE... BUT I DON'T HAVE MUCH CHOICE.
IT GETS WORSE EVERY DAY... IT'S TURNING INTO A FUCKING NIGHTMARE... I'M JUST LUCKY THEIR HOUSE IS SO ISOLATED...
...IF THE NEIGHBORS EVER FIGURED OUT WHAT WAS GOING ON OVER HERE I'D BE TOTALLY BUSTED.
IT'S HOT AND STUFFY... SMELLS BAD. THEY'VE GOT THE HEAT TURNED UP AGAIN.
KEITH? HEY, HOW'S IT GOIN'?

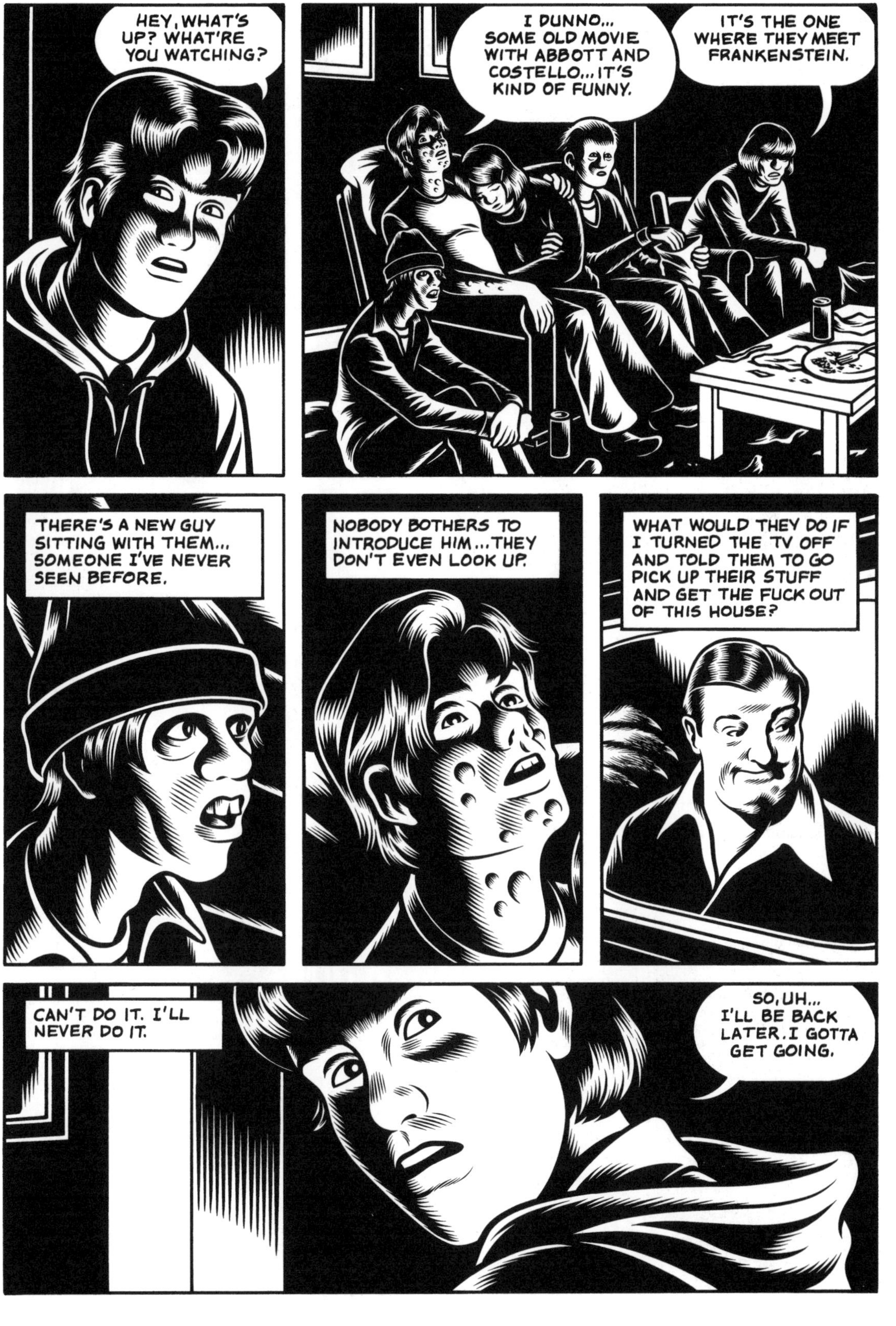
HEY, WHAT'S UP? WHAT'RE YOU WATCHING?
I DUNNO... SOME OLD MOVIE WITH ABBOTT AND COSTELLO... IT'S KIND OF FUNNY.
IT'S THE ONE WHERE THEY MEET FRANKENSTEIN.
THERE'S A NEW GUY SITTING WITH THEM... SOMEONE I'VE NEVER SEEN BEFORE.
NOBODY BOTHERS TO INTRODUCE HIM... THEY DON'T EVEN LOOK UP.
WHAT WOULD THEY DO IF I TURNED THE TV OFF AND TOLD THEM TO GO PICK UP THEIR STUFF AND GET THE FUCK OUT OF THIS HOUSE?
CAN'T DO IT. I'LL NEVER DO IT.
SO, UH... I'LL BE BACK LATER. I GOTTA GET GOING.

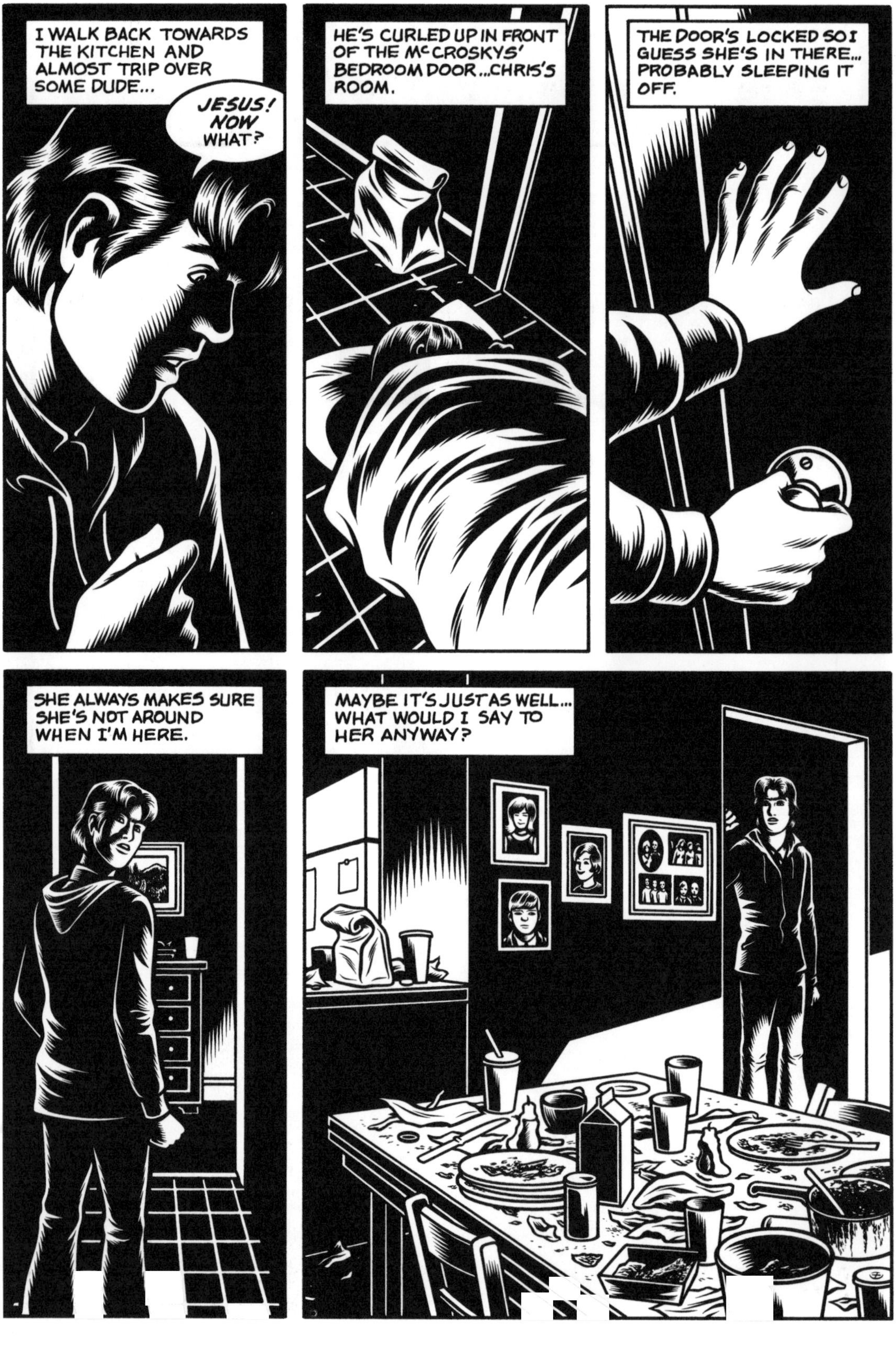
I WALK BACK TOWARDS THE KITCHEN AND ALMOST TRIP OVER SOME DUDE...
JESUS! NOW WHAT?
HE'S CURLED UP IN FRONT OF THE McCROSKYS' BEDROOM DOOR...CHRIS'S ROOM.
THE DOOR'S LOCKED SO I GUESS SHE'S IN THERE... PROBABLY SLEEPING IT OFF.
SHE ALWAYS MAKES SURE SHE'S NOT AROUND WHEN I'M HERE.
MAYBE IT'S JUST AS WELL... WHAT WOULD I SAY TO HER ANYWAY?

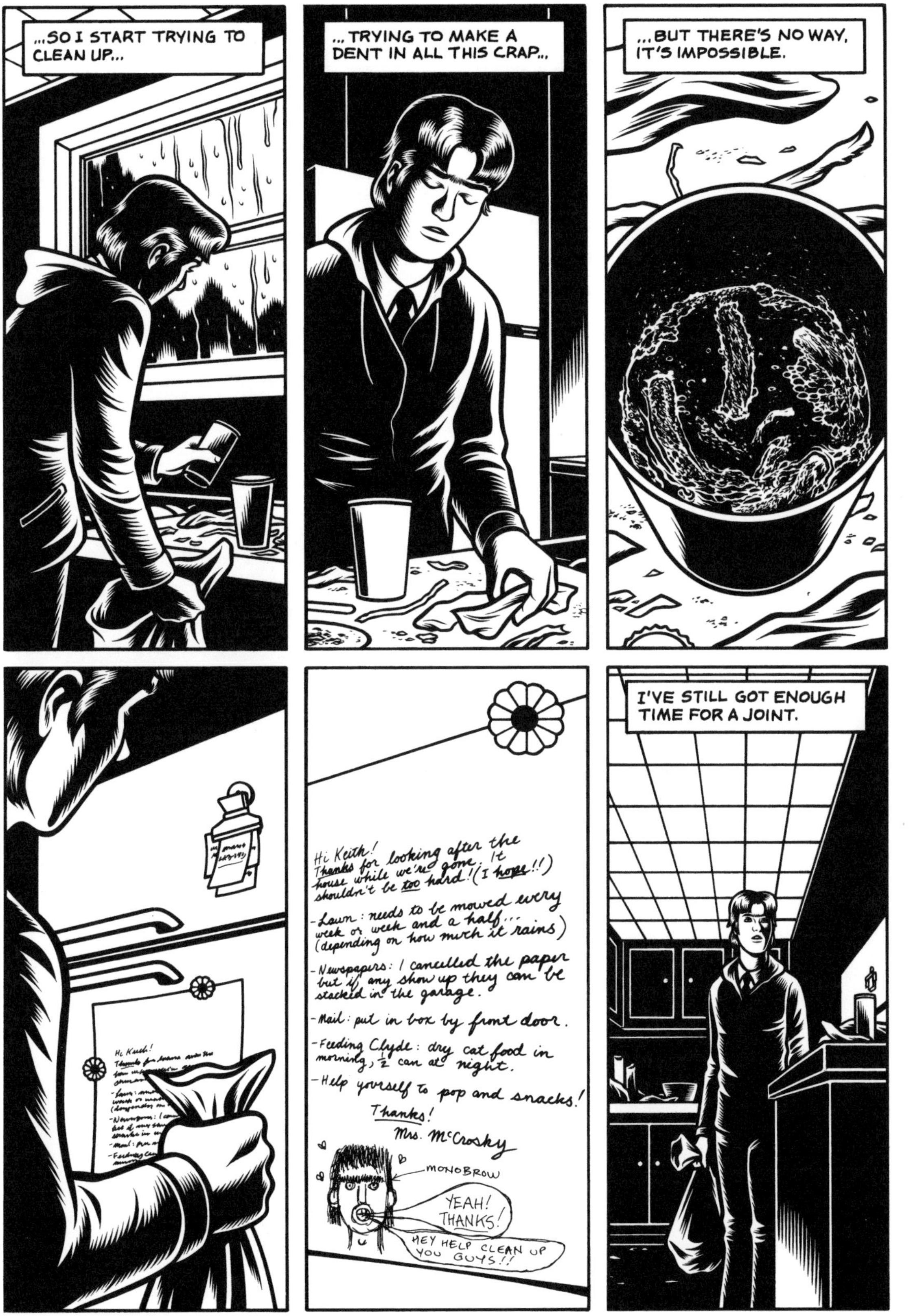
...SO I START TRYING TO CLEAN UP...
...TRYING TO MAKE A DENT IN ALL THIS CRAP...
...BUT THERE'S NO WAY, IT'S IMPOSSIBLE.
Hi Keith! Thanks for looking after the house while we're gone. It shouldn't be too hard! (I hope!!)
-Lawn: needs to be mowed every week or week and a half... (depending on how much it rains)
-Newspapers: I cancelled the paper but if any show up they can be stacked in the garage.
-Mail: put in box by front door.
-Feeding Clyde: dry cat food in morning, ½ can at night.
-Help yourself to pop and snacks!
Thanks!
Mrs. McCrosky
MONOBROW
YEAH! THANKS!
HEY HELP CLEAN UP YOU GUYS!!
I'VE STILL GOT ENOUGH TIME FOR A JOINT.

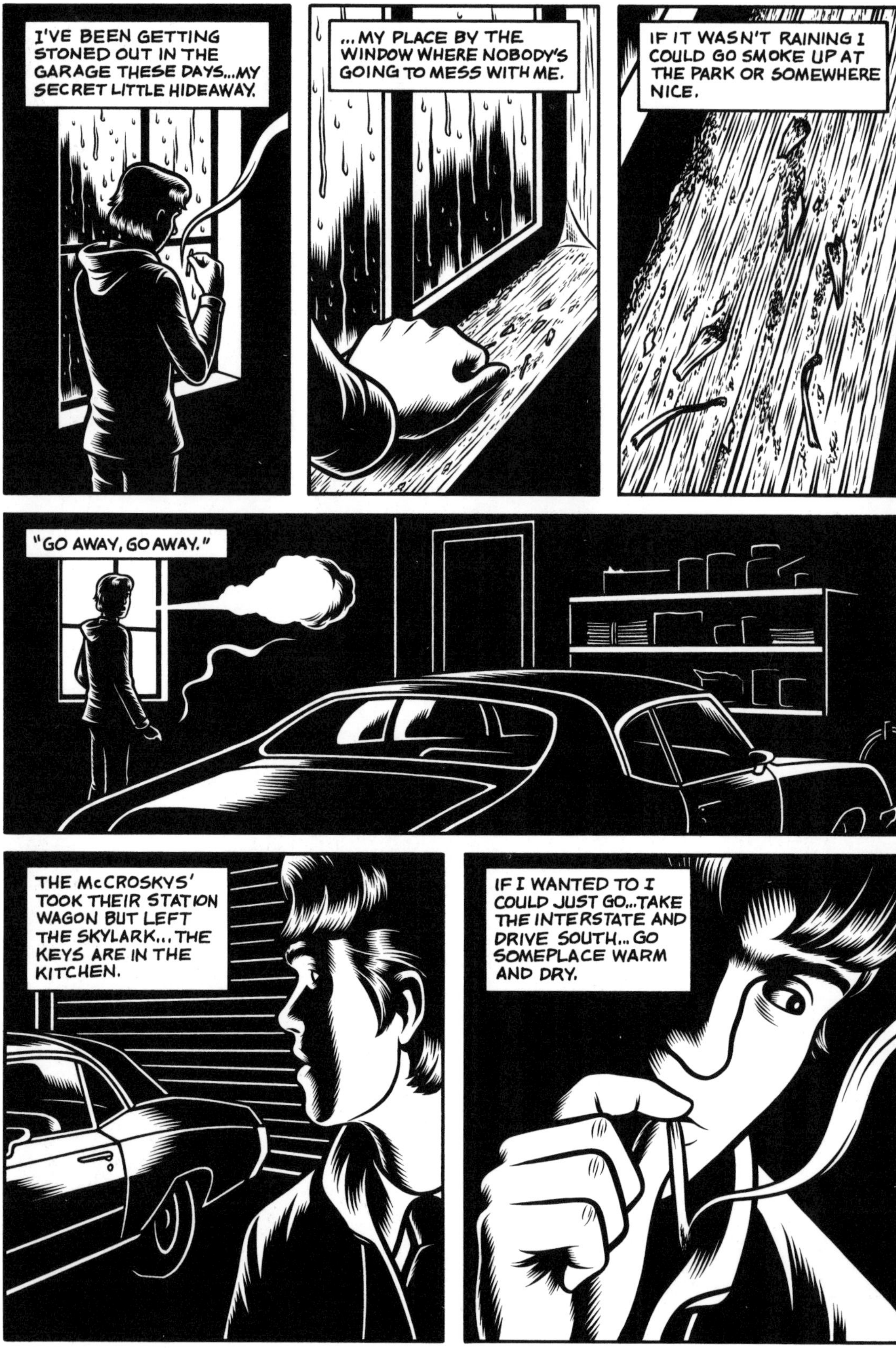
I'VE BEEN GETTING STONED OUT IN THE GARAGE THESE DAYS...MY SECRET LITTLE HIDEAWAY.
...MY PLACE BY THE WINDOW WHERE NOBODY'S GOING TO MESS WITH ME.
IF IT WASN'T RAINING I COULD GO SMOKE UP AT THE PARK OR SOMEWHERE NICE.
"GO AWAY, GO AWAY."
THE McCROSKYS' TOOK THEIR STATION WAGON BUT LEFT THE SKYLARK... THE KEYS ARE IN THE KITCHEN.
IF I WANTED TO I COULD JUST GO...TAKE THE INTERSTATE AND DRIVE SOUTH... GO SOMEPLACE WARM AND DRY.

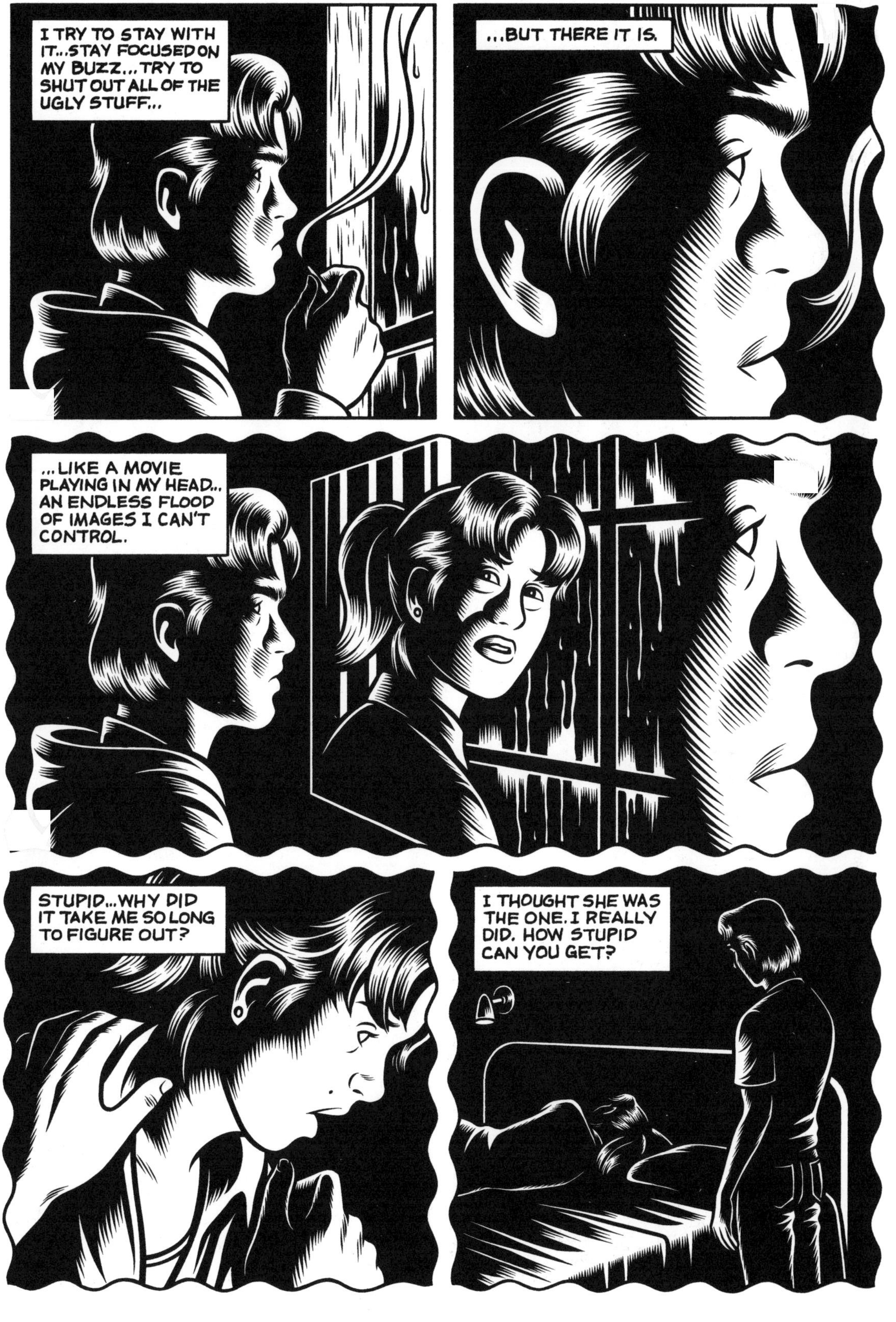
I TRY TO STAY WITH IT...STAY FOCUSED ON MY BUZZ...TRY TO SHUT OUT ALL OF THE UGLY STUFF...
...BUT THERE IT IS.
...LIKE A MOVIE PLAYING IN MY HEAD... AN ENDLESS FLOOD OF IMAGES I CAN'T CONTROL.
STUPID...WHY DID IT TAKE ME SO LONG TO FIGURE OUT?
I THOUGHT SHE WAS THE ONE. I REALLY DID. HOW STUPID CAN YOU GET?

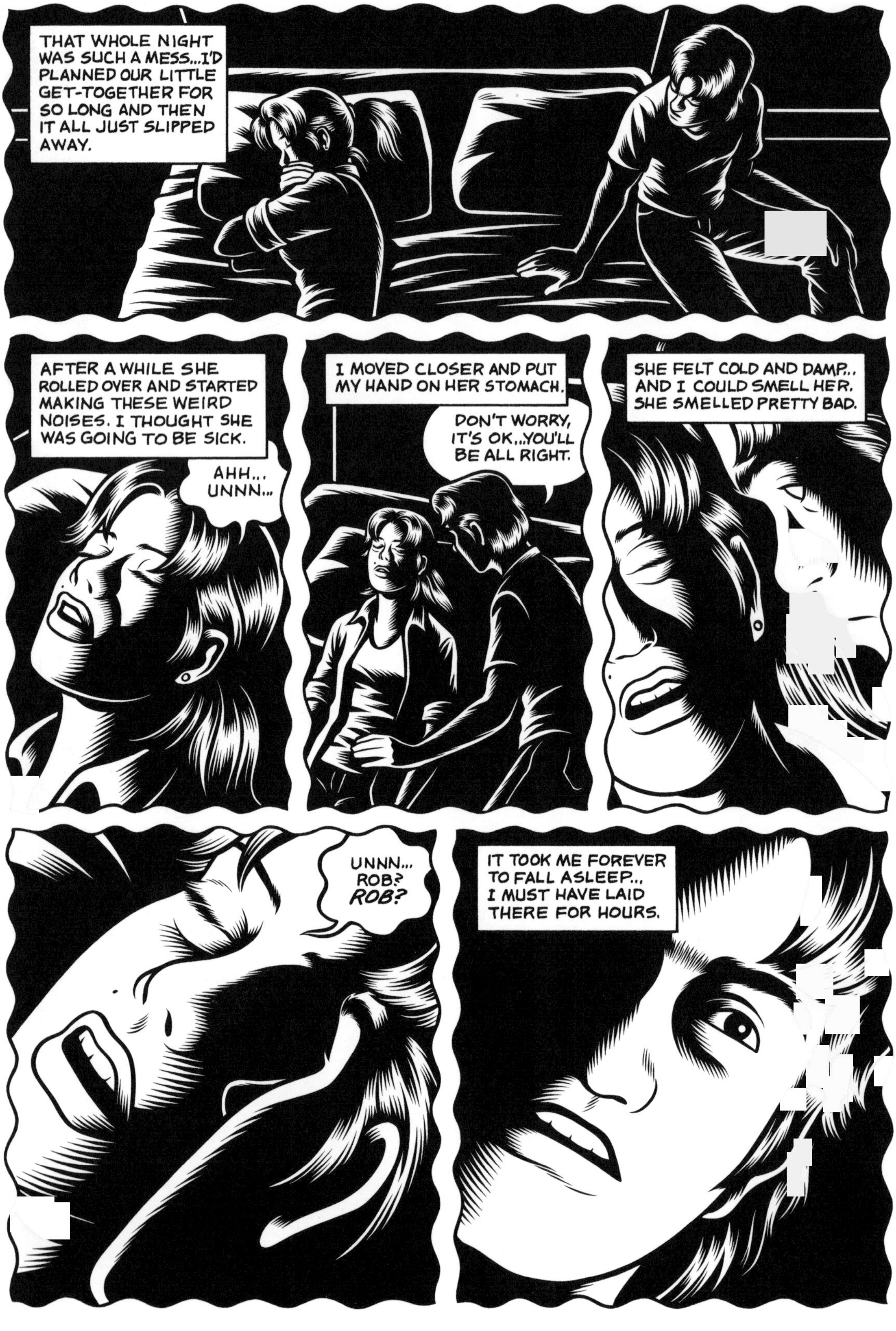
THAT WHOLE NIGHT WAS SUCH A MESS...I'D PLANNED OUR LITTLE GET-TOGETHER FOR SO LONG AND THEN IT ALL JUST SLIPPED AWAY.
AFTER A WHILE SHE ROLLED OVER AND STARTED MAKING THESE WEIRD NOISES. I THOUGHT SHE WAS GOING TO BE SICK.
AHH... UNNN...
I MOVED CLOSER AND PUT MY HAND ON HER STOMACH.
DON'T WORRY, IT'S OK...YOU'LL BE ALL RIGHT.
SHE FELT COLD AND DAMP.. AND I COULD SMELL HER. SHE SMELLED PRETTY BAD.
UNNN... ROB? *ROB?*
IT TOOK ME FOREVER TO FALL ASLEEP.., I MUST HAVE LAID THERE FOR HOURS.

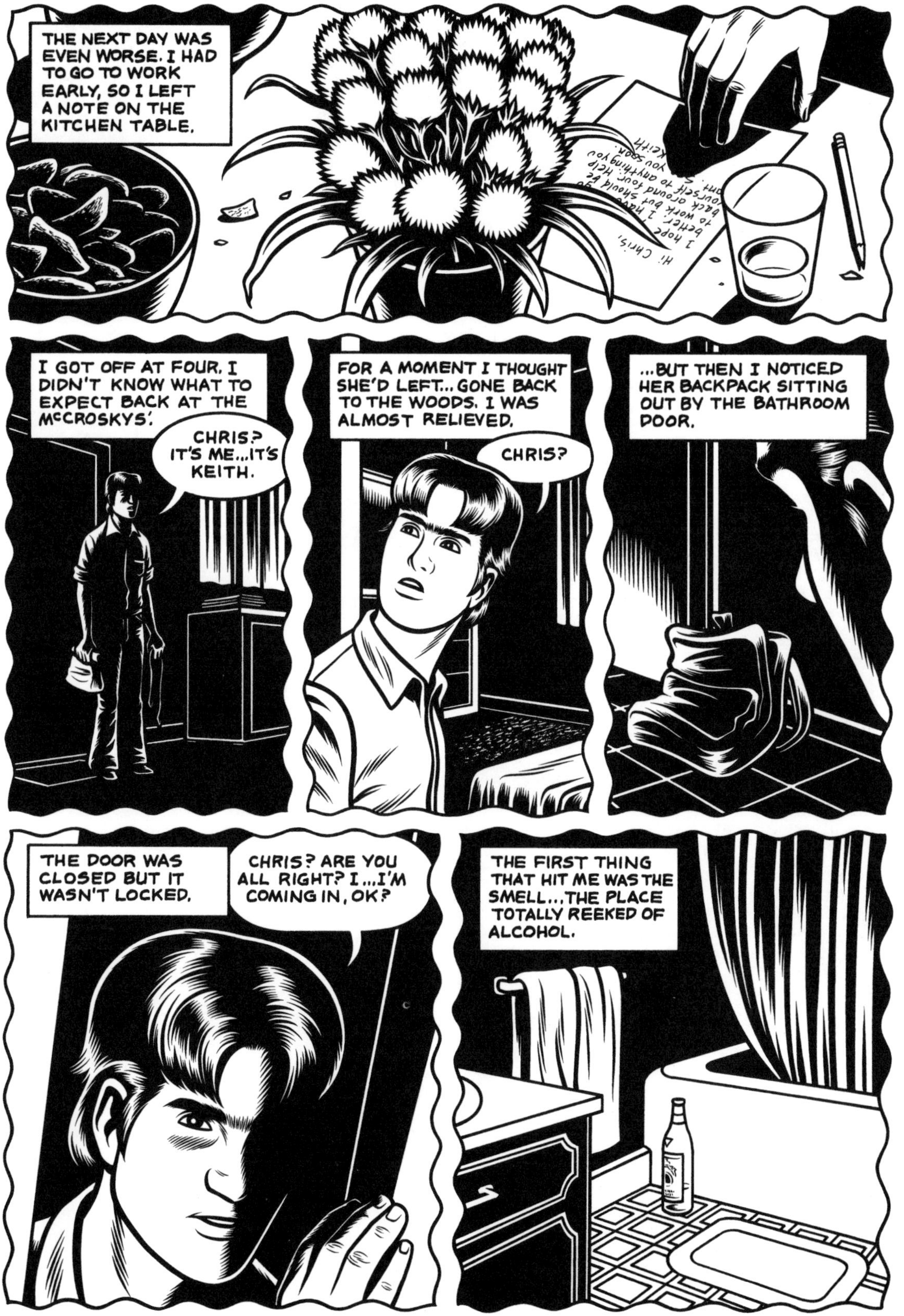
THE NEXT DAY WAS EVEN WORSE. I HAD TO GO TO WORK EARLY, SO I LEFT A NOTE ON THE KITCHEN TABLE.
I GOT OFF AT FOUR. I DIDN'T KNOW WHAT TO EXPECT BACK AT THE McCROSKYS'.
CHRIS? IT'S ME...IT'S KEITH.
FOR A MOMENT I THOUGHT SHE'D LEFT... GONE BACK TO THE WOODS. I WAS ALMOST RELIEVED.
CHRIS?
...BUT THEN I NOTICED HER BACKPACK SITTING OUT BY THE BATHROOM DOOR.
THE DOOR WAS CLOSED BUT IT WASN'T LOCKED.
CHRIS? ARE YOU ALL RIGHT? I...I'M COMING IN, OK?
THE FIRST THING THAT HIT ME WAS THE SMELL... THE PLACE TOTALLY REEKED OF ALCOHOL.

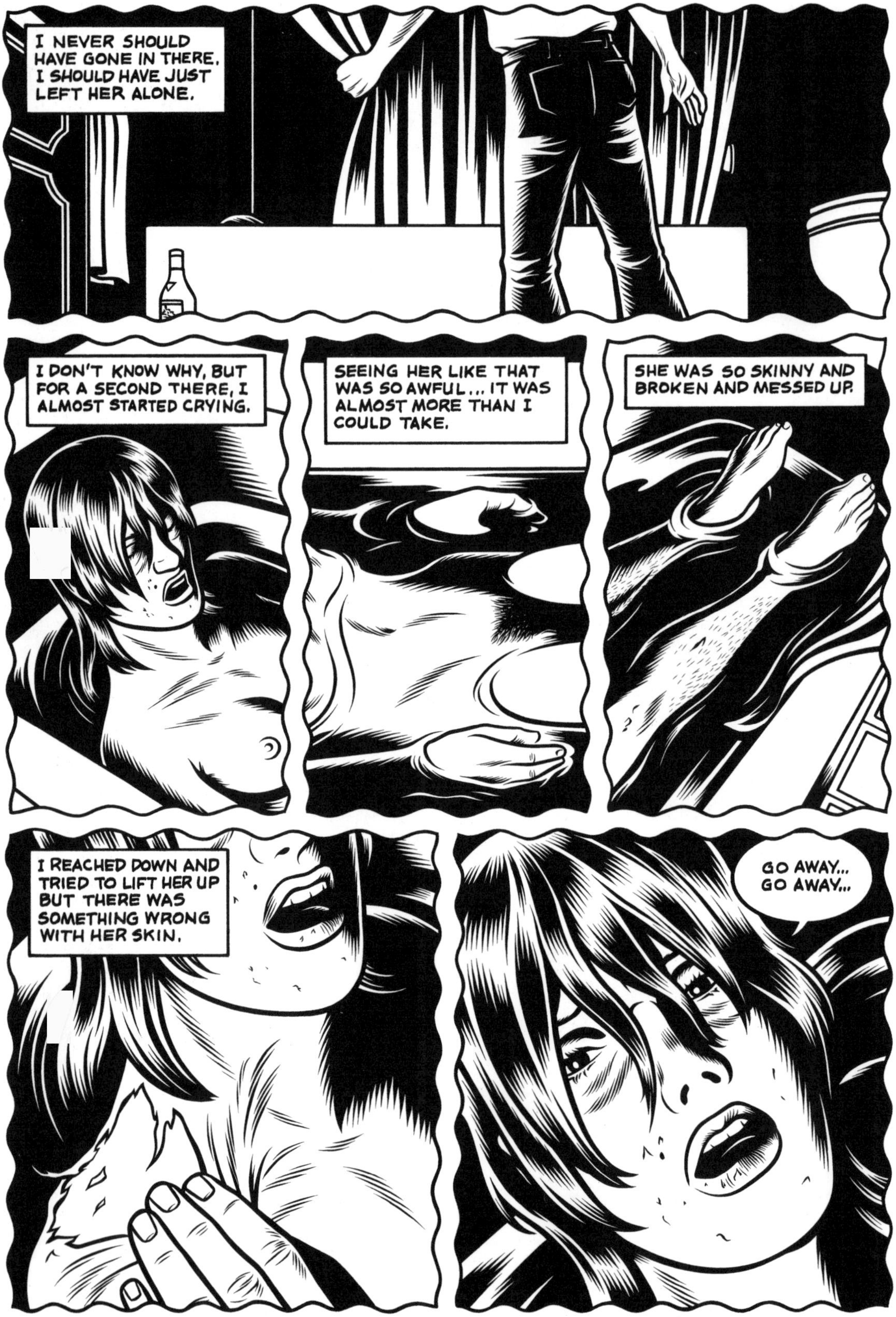
I NEVER SHOULD HAVE GONE IN THERE. I SHOULD HAVE JUST LEFT HER ALONE.
I DON'T KNOW WHY, BUT FOR A SECOND THERE, I ALMOST STARTED CRYING.
SEEING HER LIKE THAT WAS SO AWFUL... IT WAS ALMOST MORE THAN I COULD TAKE.
SHE WAS SO SKINNY AND BROKEN AND MESSED UP.
I REACHED DOWN AND TRIED TO LIFT HER UP BUT THERE WAS SOMETHING WRONG WITH HER SKIN.
GO AWAY... GO AWAY...

THIRD PERIOD. BIOLOGY CLASS...THAT USED TO BE ONE OF THE HIGHLIGHTS OF MY DAY.

SHE WAS SO SWEET AND PERFECT BACK THEN.

WE HAD TO WATCH ALL THESE LAME MOVIES ABOUT HUMAN REPRODUCTION, BUT I DIDN'T MIND...I COULD SIT AND STARE AT CHRIS FOR AS LONG AS I WANTED.

THOSE MOVIES WERE ALWAYS SO SAFE AND CLEAN...EVERYTHING SIMPLIFIED DOWN TO DIAGRAMS AND ANIMATED CARTOONS..

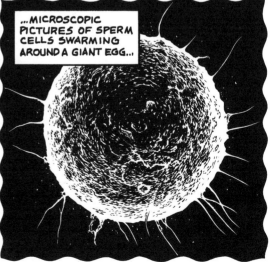

...MICROSCOPIC PICTURES OF SPERM CELLS SWARMING AROUND A GIANT EGG...

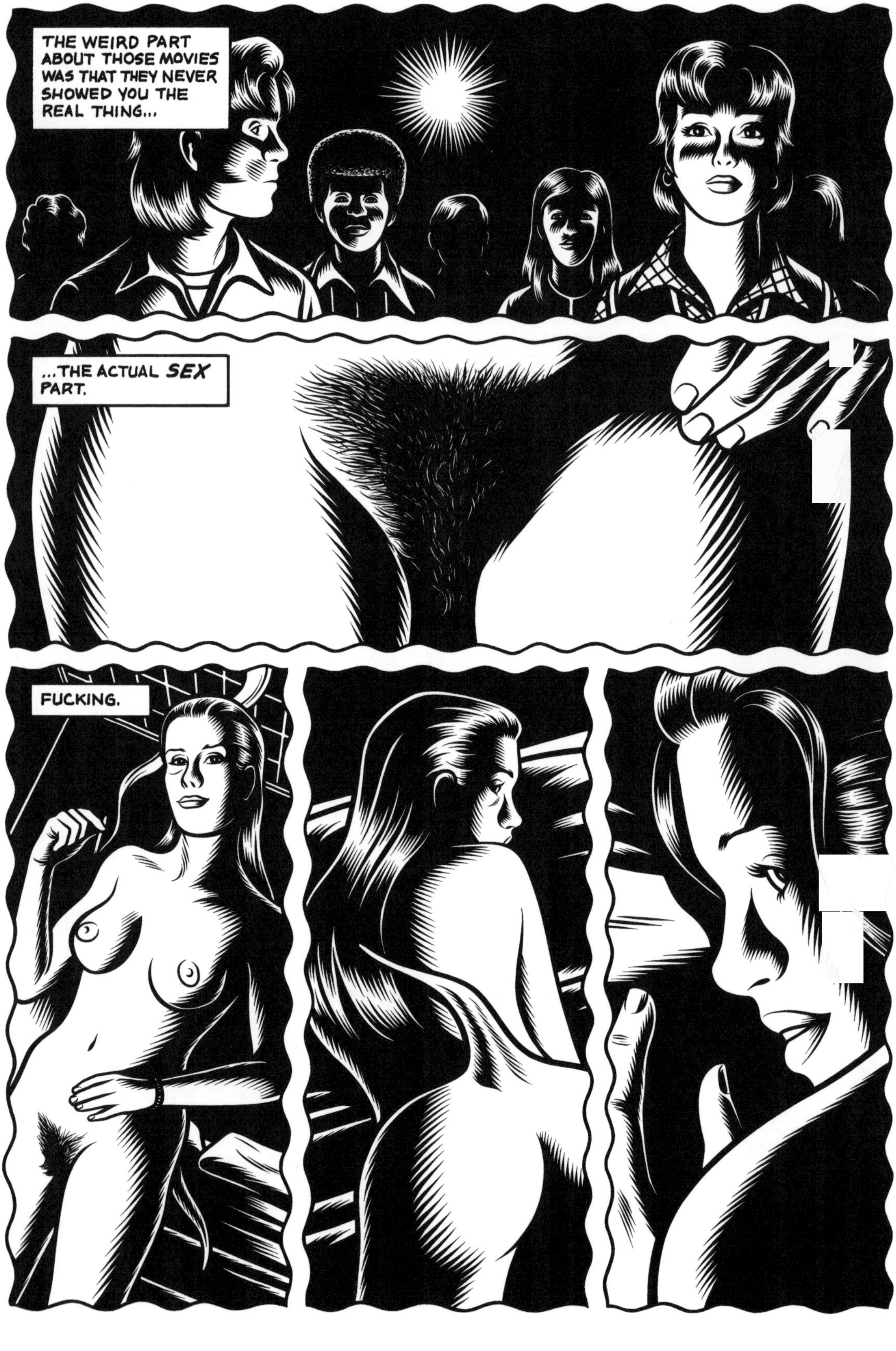
THE WEIRD PART ABOUT THOSE MOVIES WAS THAT THEY NEVER SHOWED YOU THE REAL THING...
...THE ACTUAL SEX PART.
FUCKING.

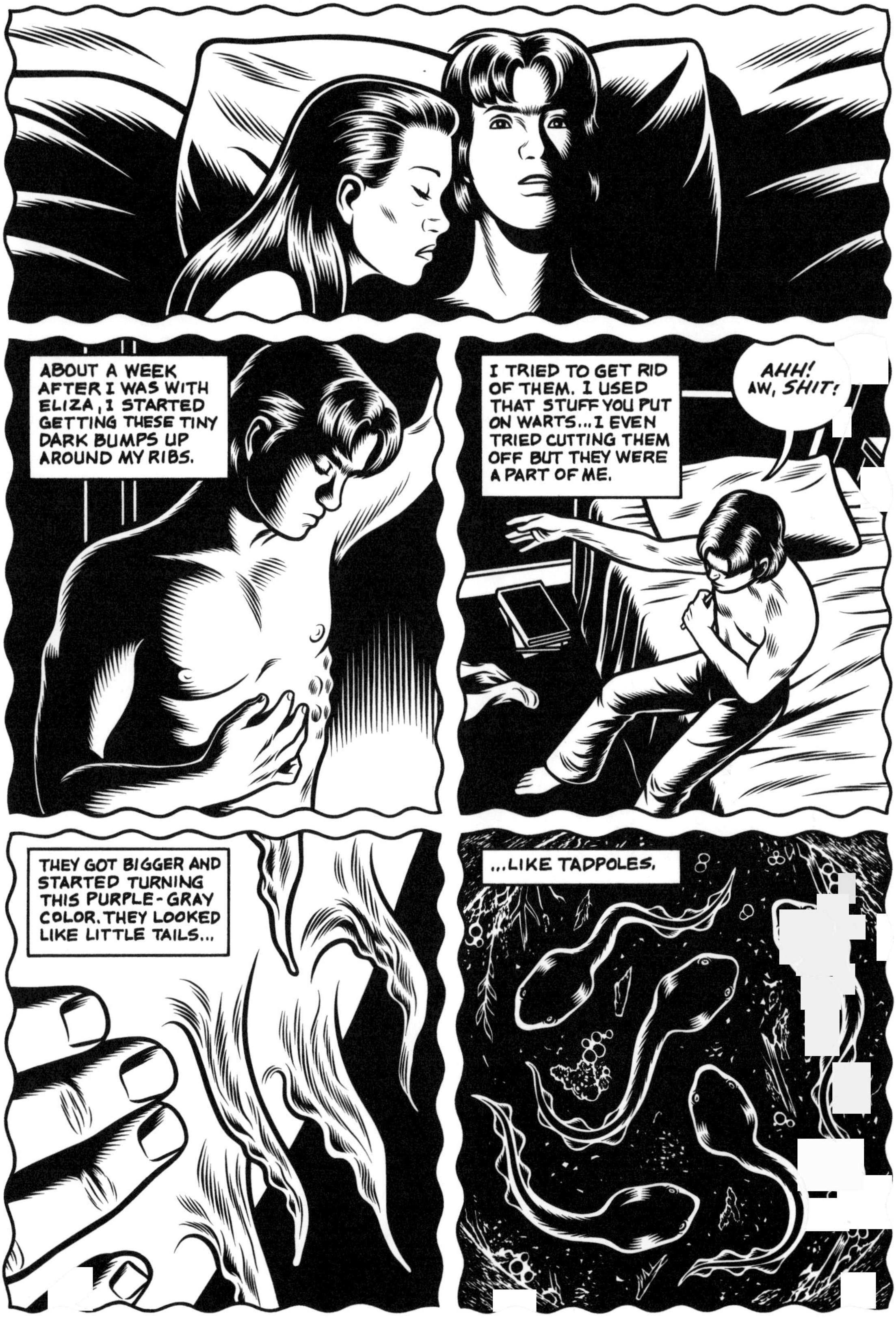
ABOUT A WEEK AFTER I WAS WITH ELIZA, I STARTED GETTING THESE TINY DARK BUMPS UP AROUND MY RIBS.
I TRIED TO GET RID OF THEM. I USED THAT STUFF YOU PUT ON WARTS... I EVEN TRIED CUTTING THEM OFF BUT THEY WERE A PART OF ME.
AHH! AW, SHIT!
THEY GOT BIGGER AND STARTED TURNING THIS PURPLE-GRAY COLOR. THEY LOOKED LIKE LITTLE TAILS...
...LIKE TADPOLES.

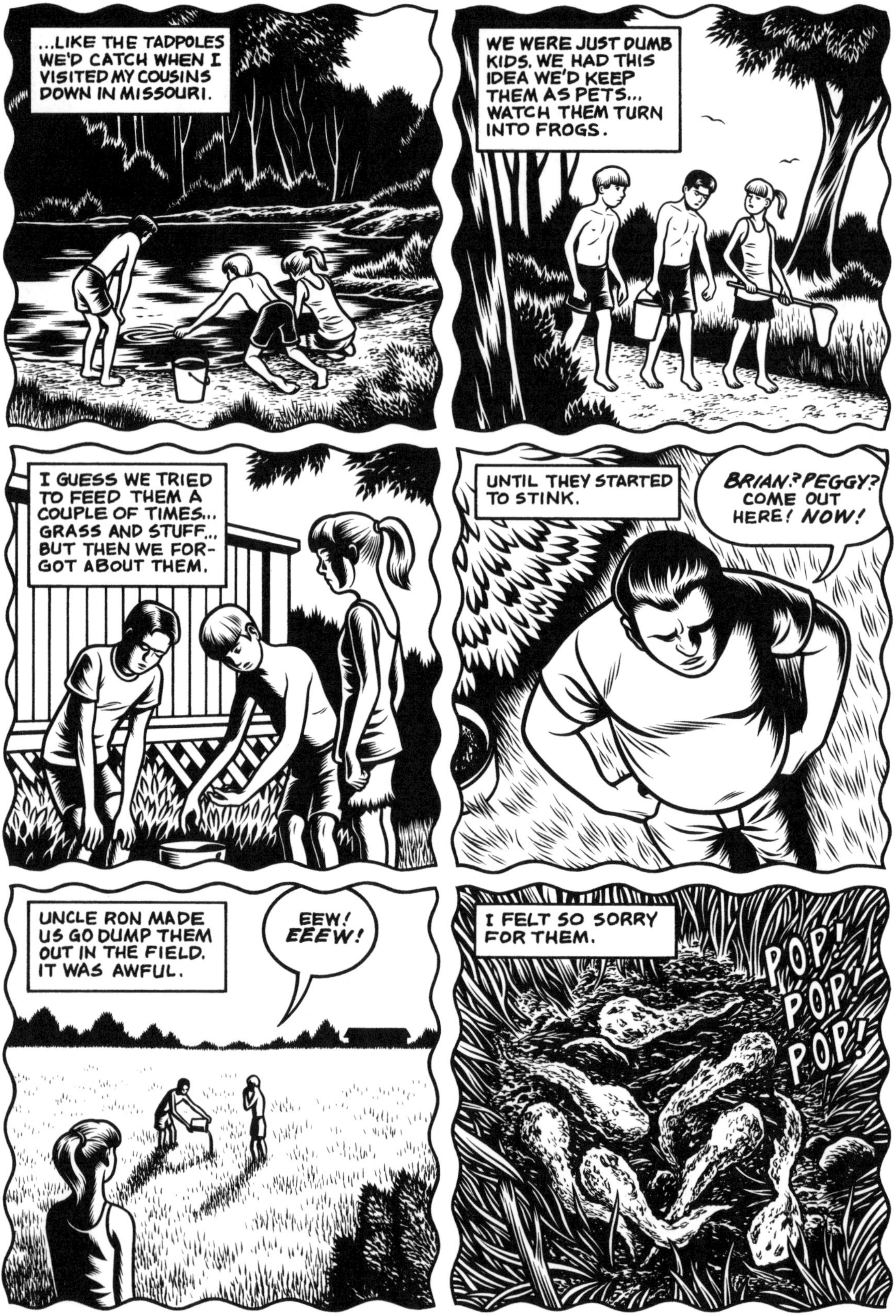
...LIKE THE TADPOLES WE'D CATCH WHEN I VISITED MY COUSINS DOWN IN MISSOURI.
WE WERE JUST DUMB KIDS. WE HAD THIS IDEA WE'D KEEP THEM AS PETS... WATCH THEM TURN INTO FROGS.
I GUESS WE TRIED TO FEED THEM A COUPLE OF TIMES... GRASS AND STUFF... BUT THEN WE FORGOT ABOUT THEM.
UNTIL THEY STARTED TO STINK.
BRIAN? PEGGY? COME OUT HERE! NOW!
UNCLE RON MADE US GO DUMP THEM OUT IN THE FIELD. IT WAS AWFUL.
EEW! EEEW!
I FELT SO SORRY FOR THEM.
POP! POP! POP!

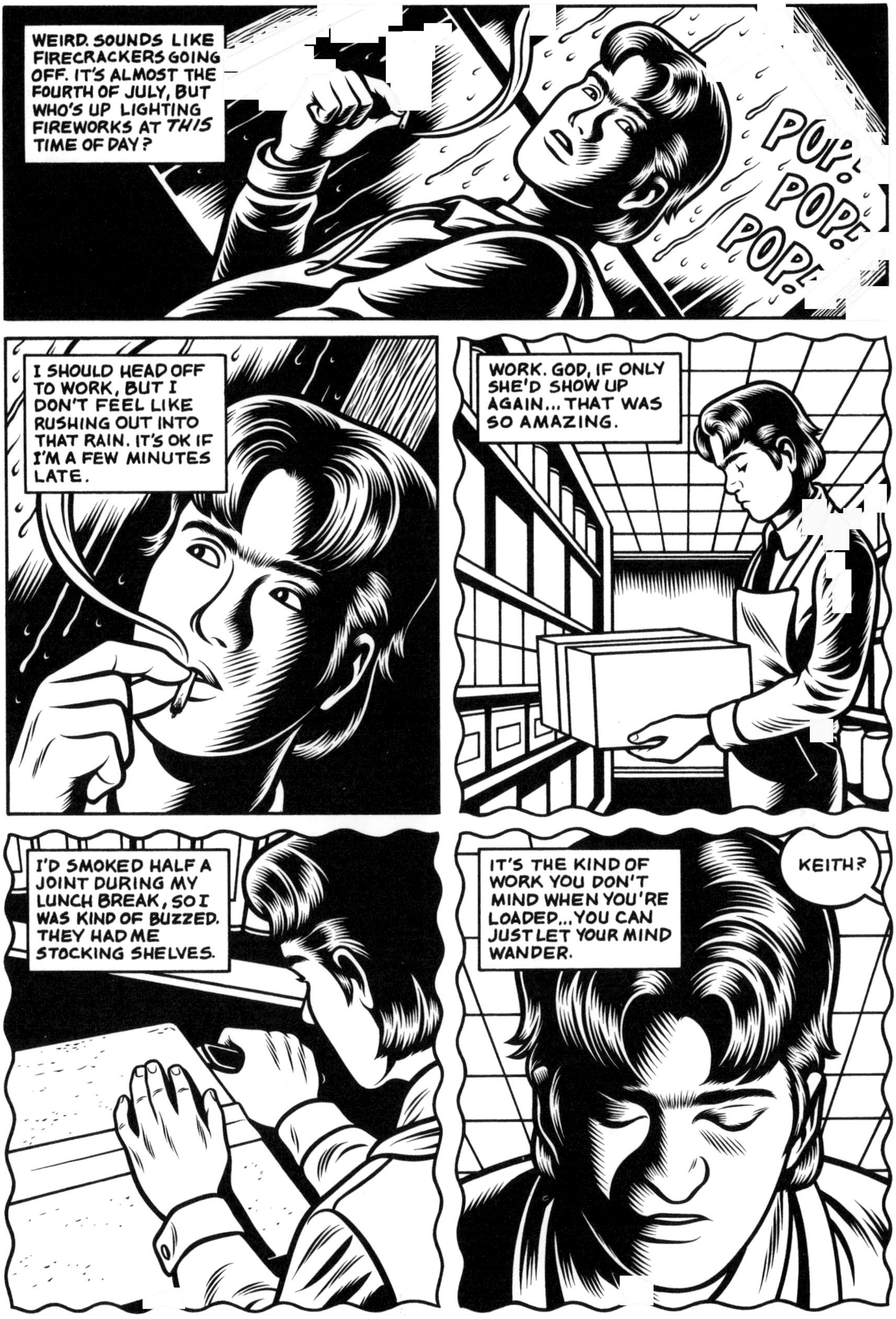
WEIRD. SOUNDS LIKE FIRECRACKERS GOING OFF. IT'S ALMOST THE FOURTH OF JULY, BUT WHO'S UP LIGHTING FIREWORKS AT *THIS* TIME OF DAY?
POP! POP! POP!
I SHOULD HEAD OFF TO WORK, BUT I DON'T FEEL LIKE RUSHING OUT INTO THAT RAIN. IT'S OK IF I'M A FEW MINUTES LATE.
WORK. GOD, IF ONLY SHE'D SHOW UP AGAIN... THAT WAS SO AMAZING.
I'D SMOKED HALF A JOINT DURING MY LUNCH BREAK, SO I WAS KIND OF BUZZED. THEY HAD ME STOCKING SHELVES.
IT'S THE KIND OF WORK YOU DON'T MIND WHEN YOU'RE LOADED... YOU CAN JUST LET YOUR MIND WANDER.
KEITH?

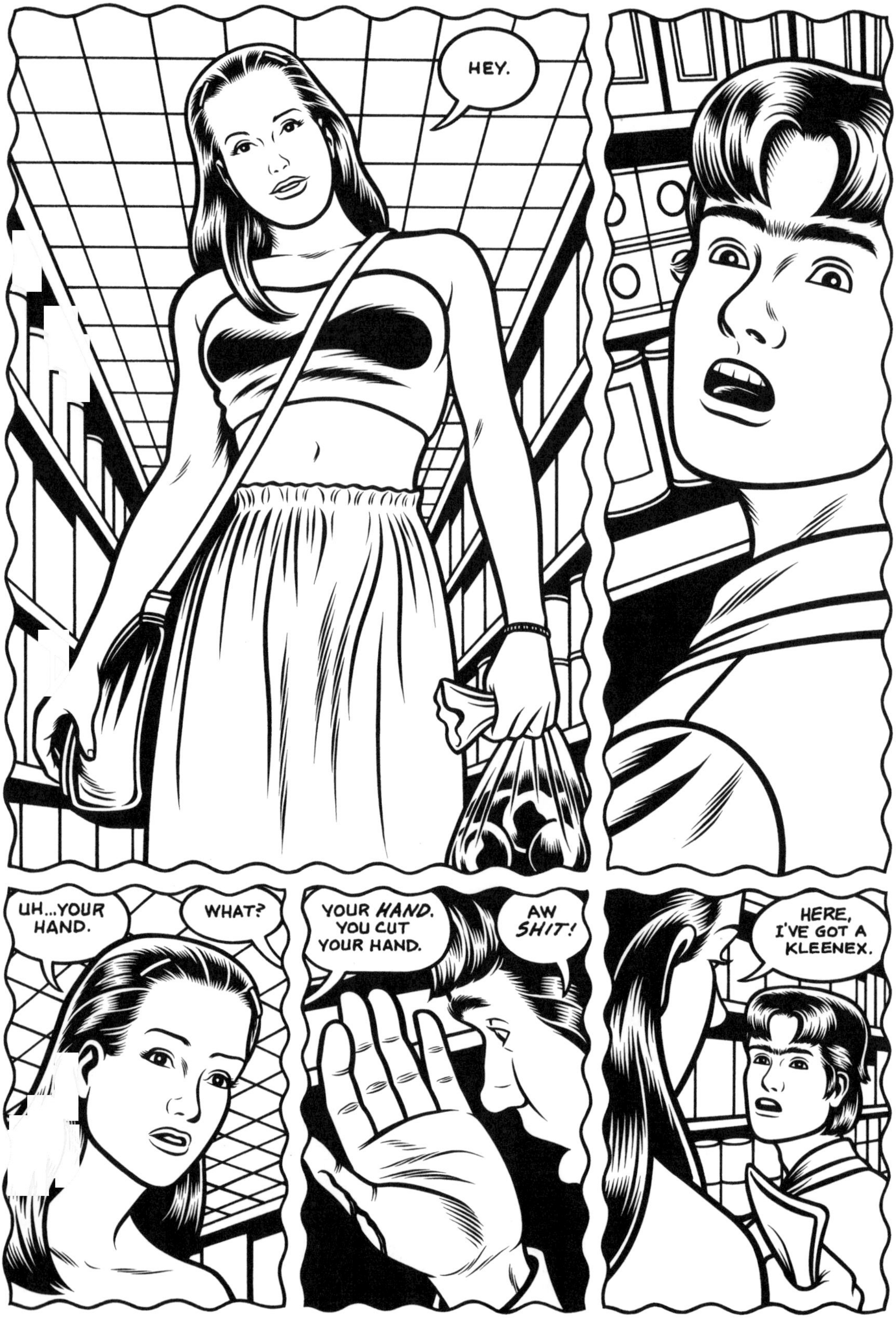
HEY.
UH...YOUR HAND.
WHAT?
YOUR HAND. YOU CUT YOUR HAND.
AW SHIT!
HERE, I'VE GOT A KLEENEX.

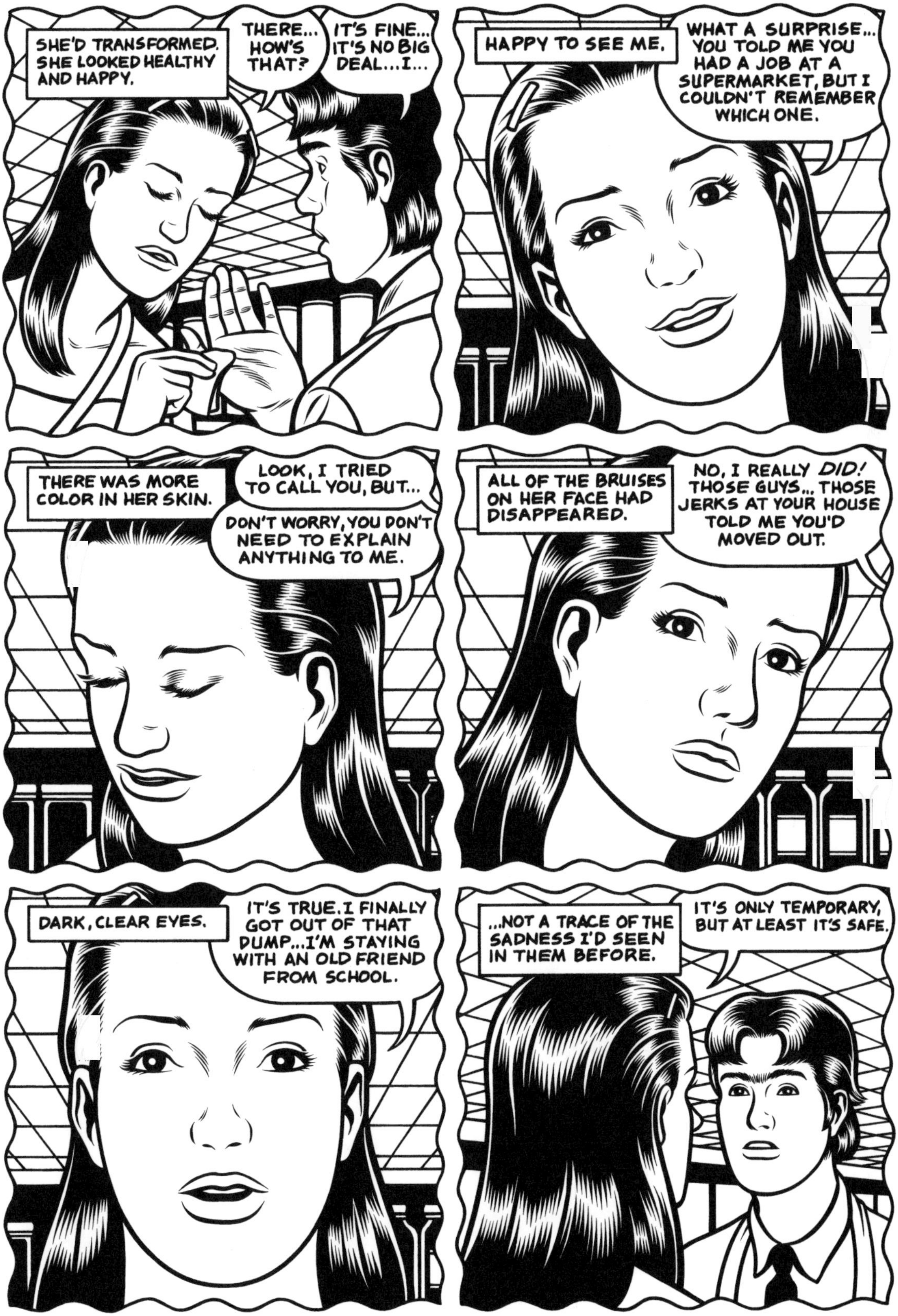
SHE'D TRANSFORMED. SHE LOOKED HEALTHY AND HAPPY.
THERE... HOW'S THAT?
IT'S FINE... IT'S NO BIG DEAL... I...
HAPPY TO SEE ME.
WHAT A SURPRISE... YOU TOLD ME YOU HAD A JOB AT A SUPERMARKET, BUT I COULDN'T REMEMBER WHICH ONE.
THERE WAS MORE COLOR IN HER SKIN.
LOOK, I TRIED TO CALL YOU, BUT...
DON'T WORRY, YOU DON'T NEED TO EXPLAIN ANYTHING TO ME.
ALL OF THE BRUISES ON HER FACE HAD DISAPPEARED.
NO, I REALLY DID! THOSE GUYS... THOSE JERKS AT YOUR HOUSE TOLD ME YOU'D MOVED OUT.
DARK, CLEAR EYES.
IT'S TRUE. I FINALLY GOT OUT OF THAT DUMP... I'M STAYING WITH AN OLD FRIEND FROM SCHOOL.
...NOT A TRACE OF THE SADNESS I'D SEEN IN THEM BEFORE.
IT'S ONLY TEMPORARY, BUT AT LEAST IT'S SAFE.

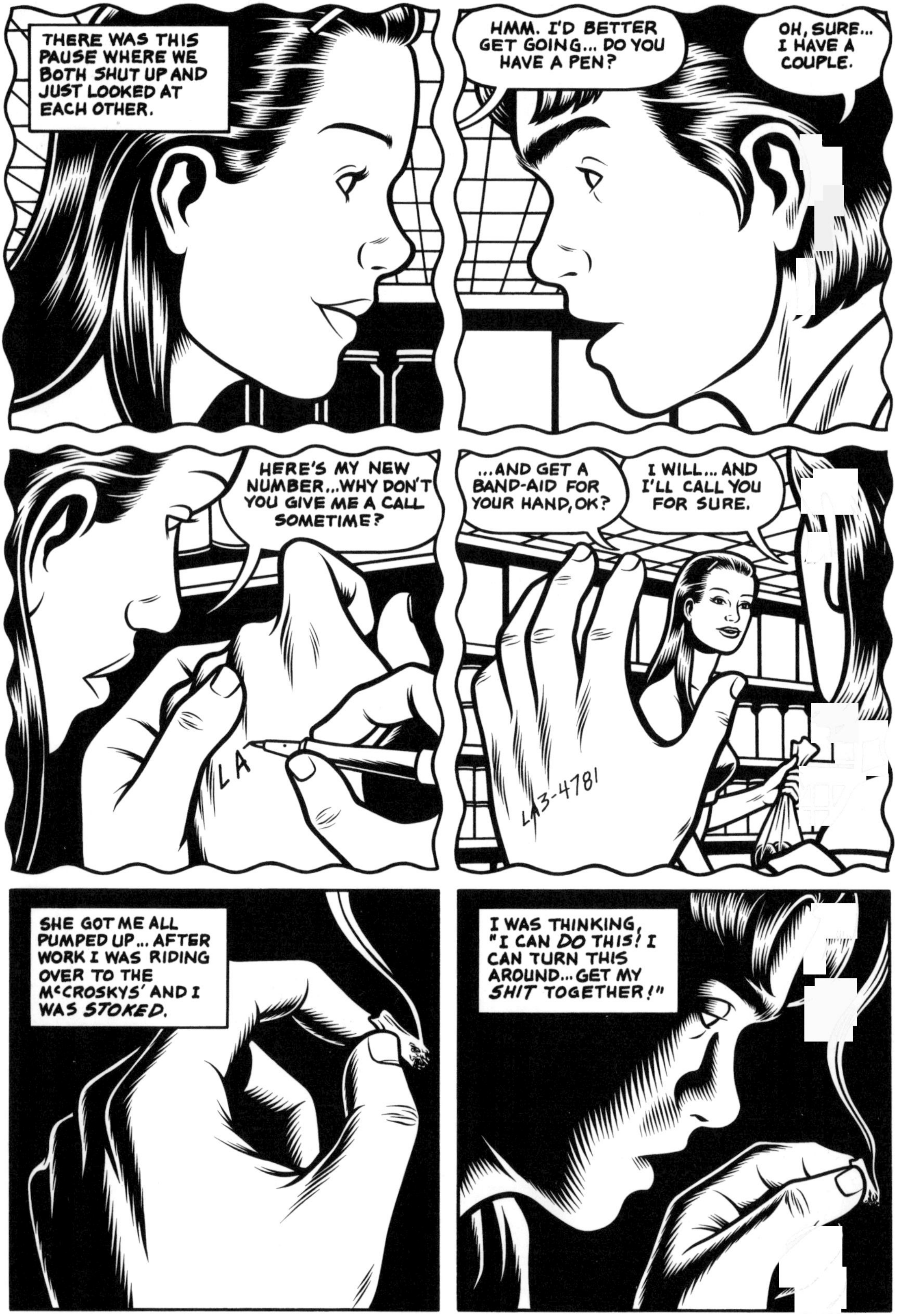
THERE WAS THIS PAUSE WHERE WE BOTH SHUT UP AND JUST LOOKED AT EACH OTHER.
HMM. I'D BETTER GET GOING... DO YOU HAVE A PEN?
OH, SURE... I HAVE A COUPLE.
HERE'S MY NEW NUMBER...WHY DON'T YOU GIVE ME A CALL SOMETIME?
LA
...AND GET A BAND-AID FOR YOUR HAND, OK?
I WILL... AND I'LL CALL YOU FOR SURE.
LA3-4781
SHE GOT ME ALL PUMPED UP... AFTER WORK I WAS RIDING OVER TO THE McCROSKYS' AND I WAS *STOKED*.
I WAS THINKING, "I CAN *DO* THIS! I CAN TURN THIS AROUND... GET MY *SHIT* TOGETHER!"

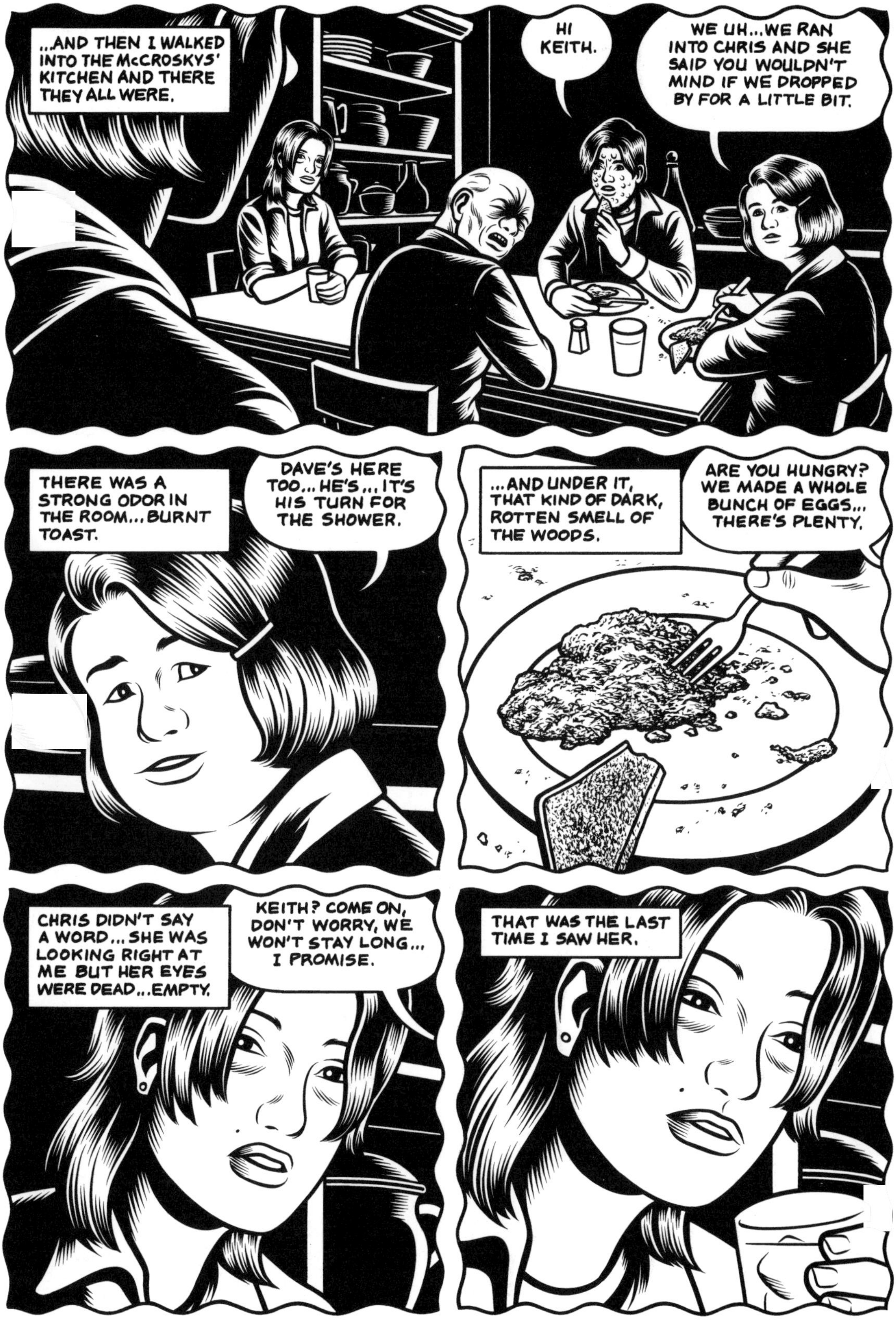
...AND THEN I WALKED INTO THE McCROSKYS' KITCHEN AND THERE THEY ALL WERE.
HI KEITH.
WE UH...WE RAN INTO CHRIS AND SHE SAID YOU WOULDN'T MIND IF WE DROPPED BY FOR A LITTLE BIT.
THERE WAS A STRONG ODOR IN THE ROOM...BURNT TOAST.
DAVE'S HERE TOO...HE'S...IT'S HIS TURN FOR THE SHOWER.
...AND UNDER IT, THAT KIND OF DARK, ROTTEN SMELL OF THE WOODS.
ARE YOU HUNGRY? WE MADE A WHOLE BUNCH OF EGGS... THERE'S PLENTY.
CHRIS DIDN'T SAY A WORD... SHE WAS LOOKING RIGHT AT ME BUT HER EYES WERE DEAD...EMPTY.
KEITH? COME ON, DON'T WORRY, WE WON'T STAY LONG... I PROMISE.
THAT WAS THE LAST TIME I SAW HER.

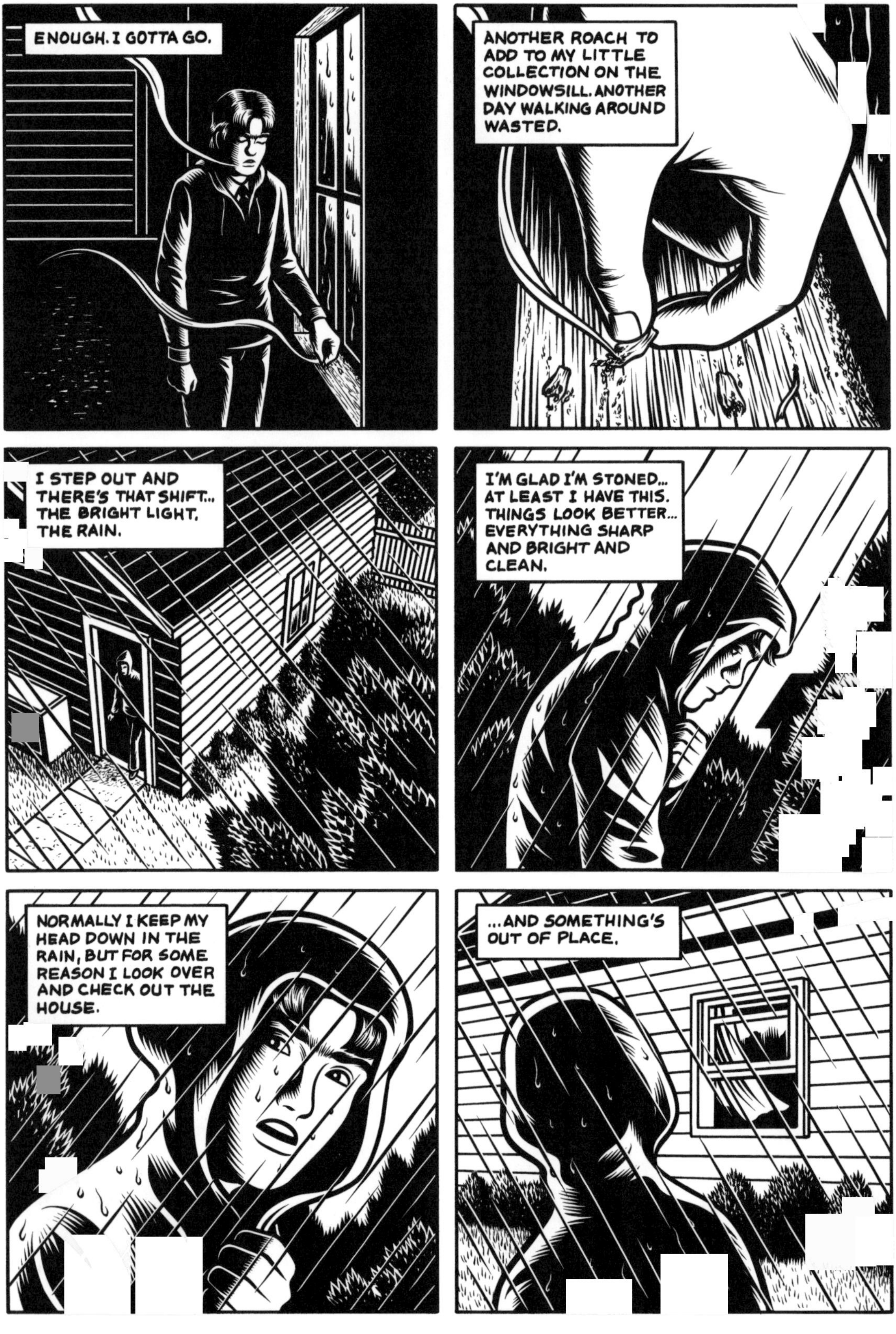
ENOUGH. I GOTTA GO.
ANOTHER ROACH TO ADD TO MY LITTLE COLLECTION ON THE WINDOWSILL. ANOTHER DAY WALKING AROUND WASTED.
I STEP OUT AND THERE'S THAT SHIFT... THE BRIGHT LIGHT, THE RAIN.
I'M GLAD I'M STONED... AT LEAST I HAVE THIS. THINGS LOOK BETTER... EVERYTHING SHARP AND BRIGHT AND CLEAN.
NORMALLY I KEEP MY HEAD DOWN IN THE RAIN, BUT FOR SOME REASON I LOOK OVER AND CHECK OUT THE HOUSE.
...AND SOMETHING'S OUT OF PLACE.

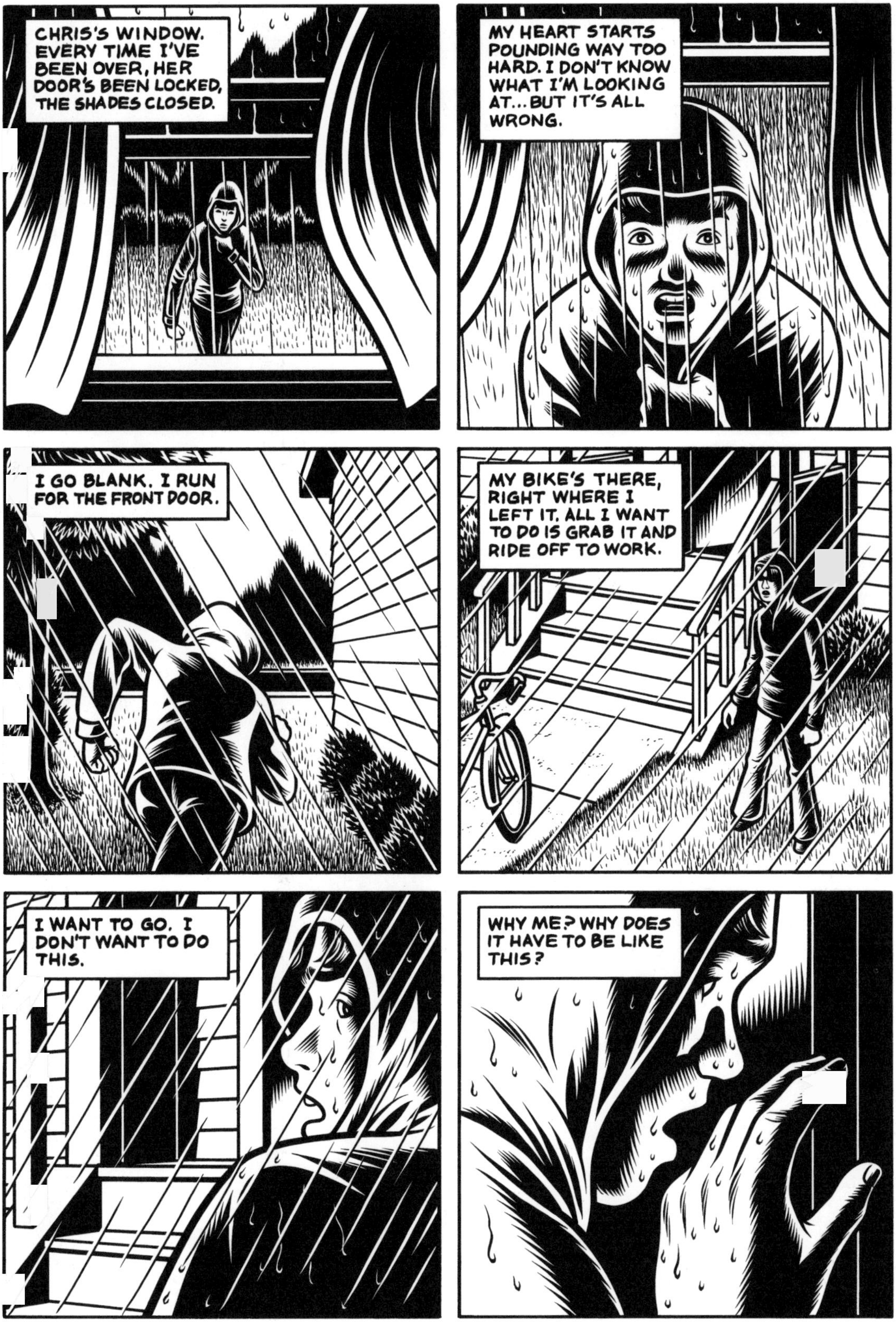
CHRIS'S WINDOW. EVERY TIME I'VE BEEN OVER, HER DOOR'S BEEN LOCKED, THE SHADES CLOSED.
MY HEART STARTS POUNDING WAY TOO HARD. I DON'T KNOW WHAT I'M LOOKING AT... BUT IT'S ALL WRONG.
I GO BLANK. I RUN FOR THE FRONT DOOR.
MY BIKE'S THERE, RIGHT WHERE I LEFT IT. ALL I WANT TO DO IS GRAB IT AND RIDE OFF TO WORK.
I WANT TO GO. I DON'T WANT TO DO THIS.
WHY ME? WHY DOES IT HAVE TO BE LIKE THIS?

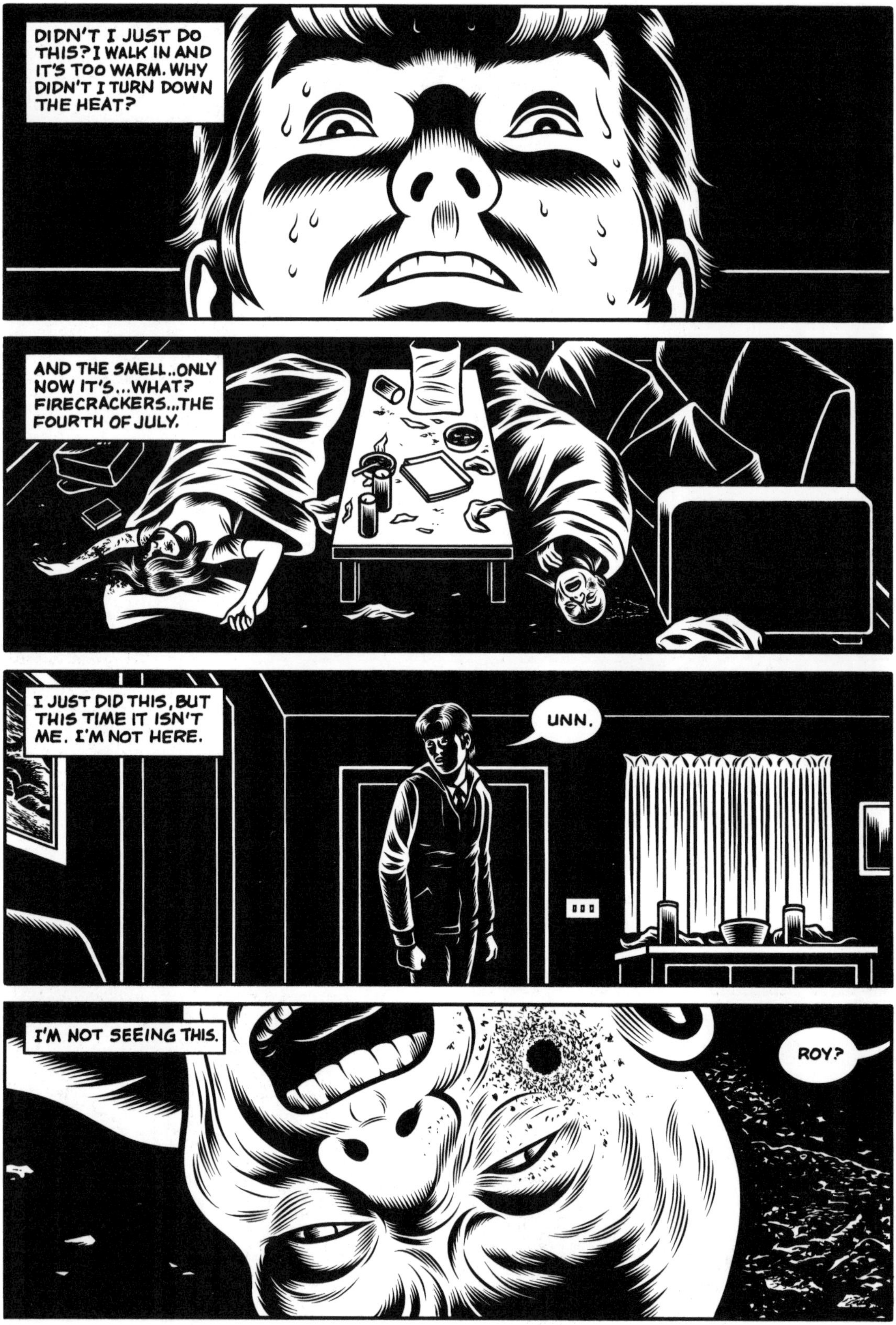
DIDN'T I JUST DO THIS? I WALK IN AND IT'S TOO WARM. WHY DIDN'T I TURN DOWN THE HEAT?
AND THE SMELL..ONLY NOW IT'S...WHAT? FIRECRACKERS...THE FOURTH OF JULY.
I JUST DID THIS, BUT THIS TIME IT ISN'T ME. I'M NOT HERE.
UNN.
I'M NOT SEEING THIS.
ROY?

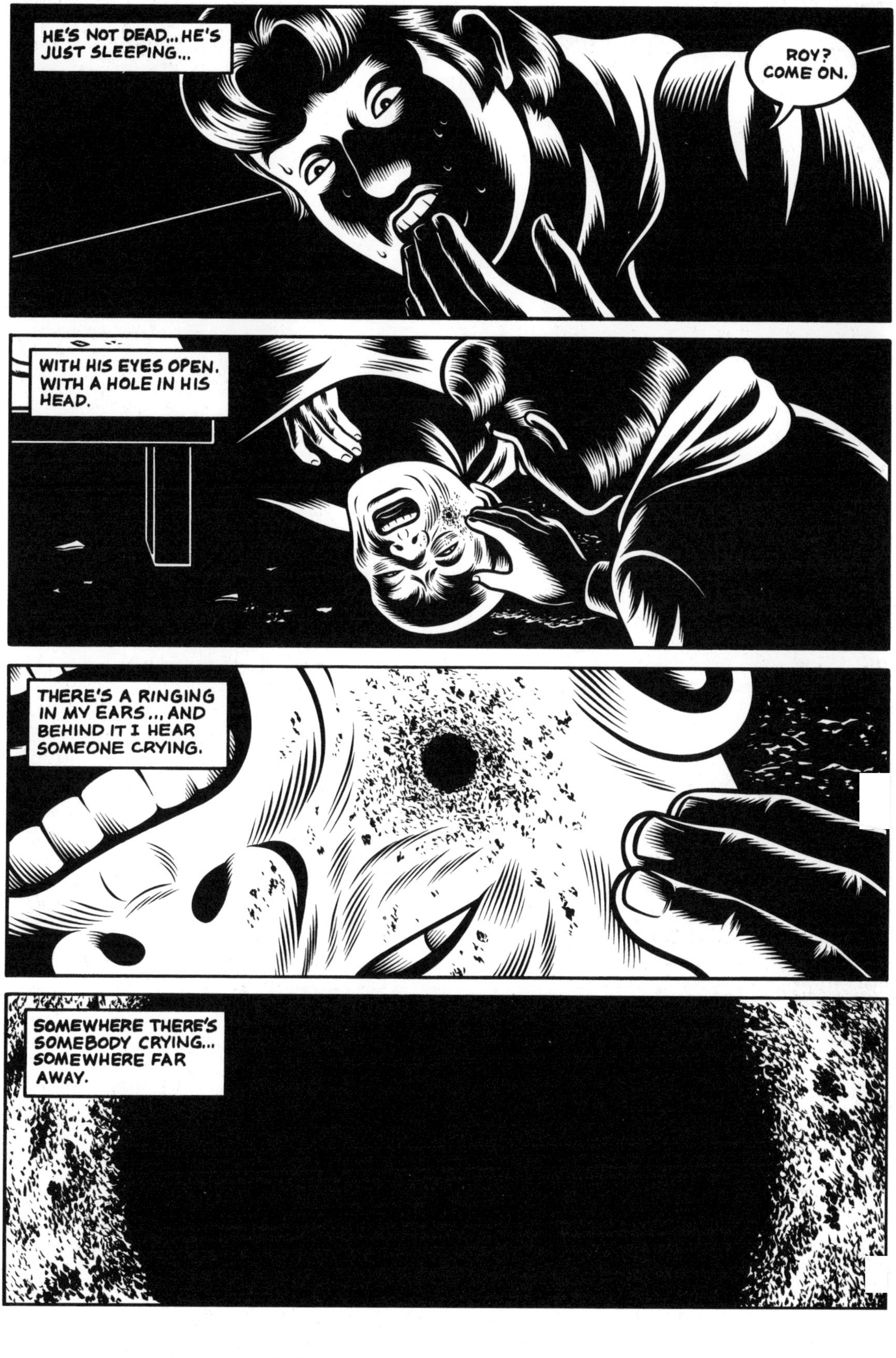
HE'S NOT DEAD... HE'S JUST SLEEPING...
ROY? COME ON.
WITH HIS EYES OPEN. WITH A HOLE IN HIS HEAD.
THERE'S A RINGING IN MY EARS..., AND BEHIND IT I HEAR SOMEONE CRYING.
SOMEWHERE THERE'S SOMEBODY CRYING... SOMEWHERE FAR AWAY.

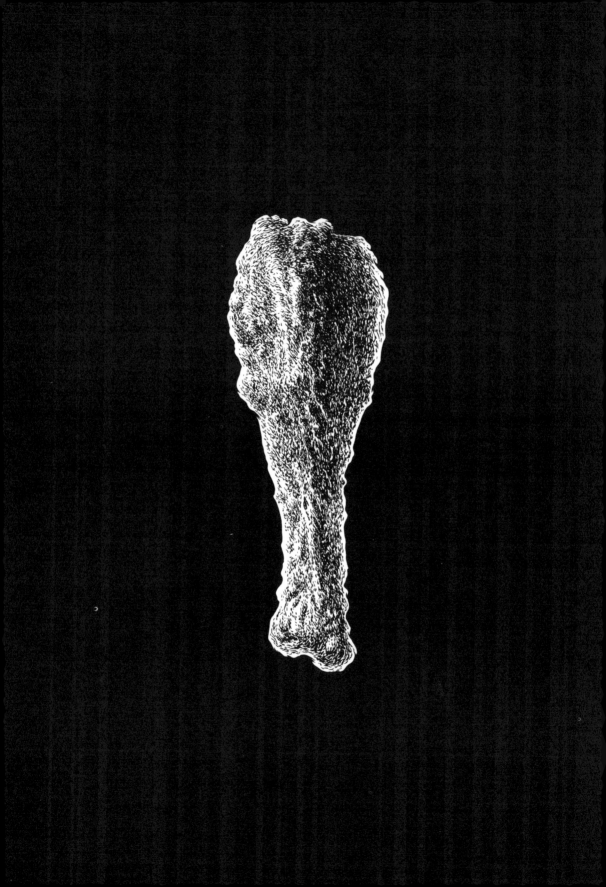

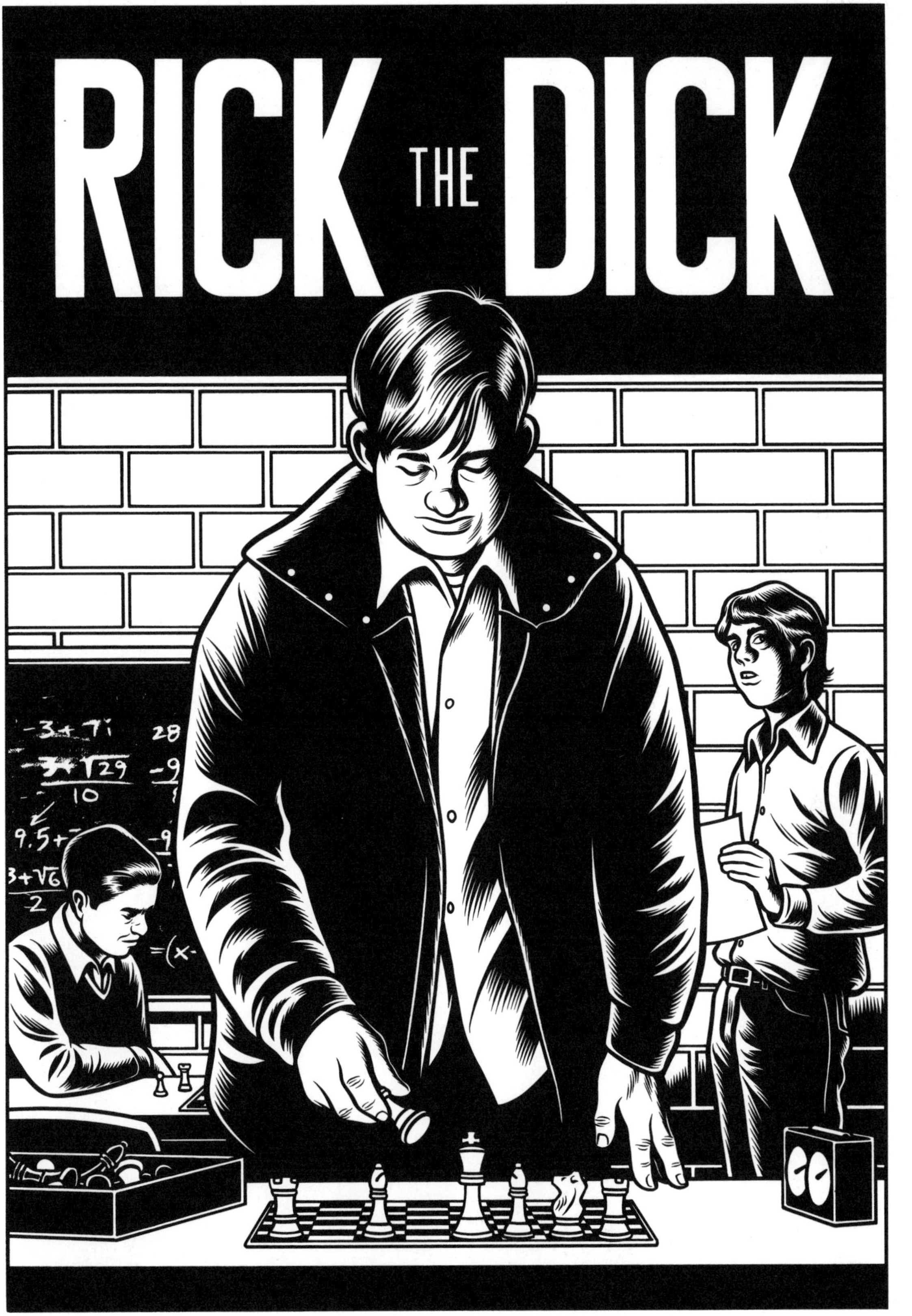
RICK THE DICK

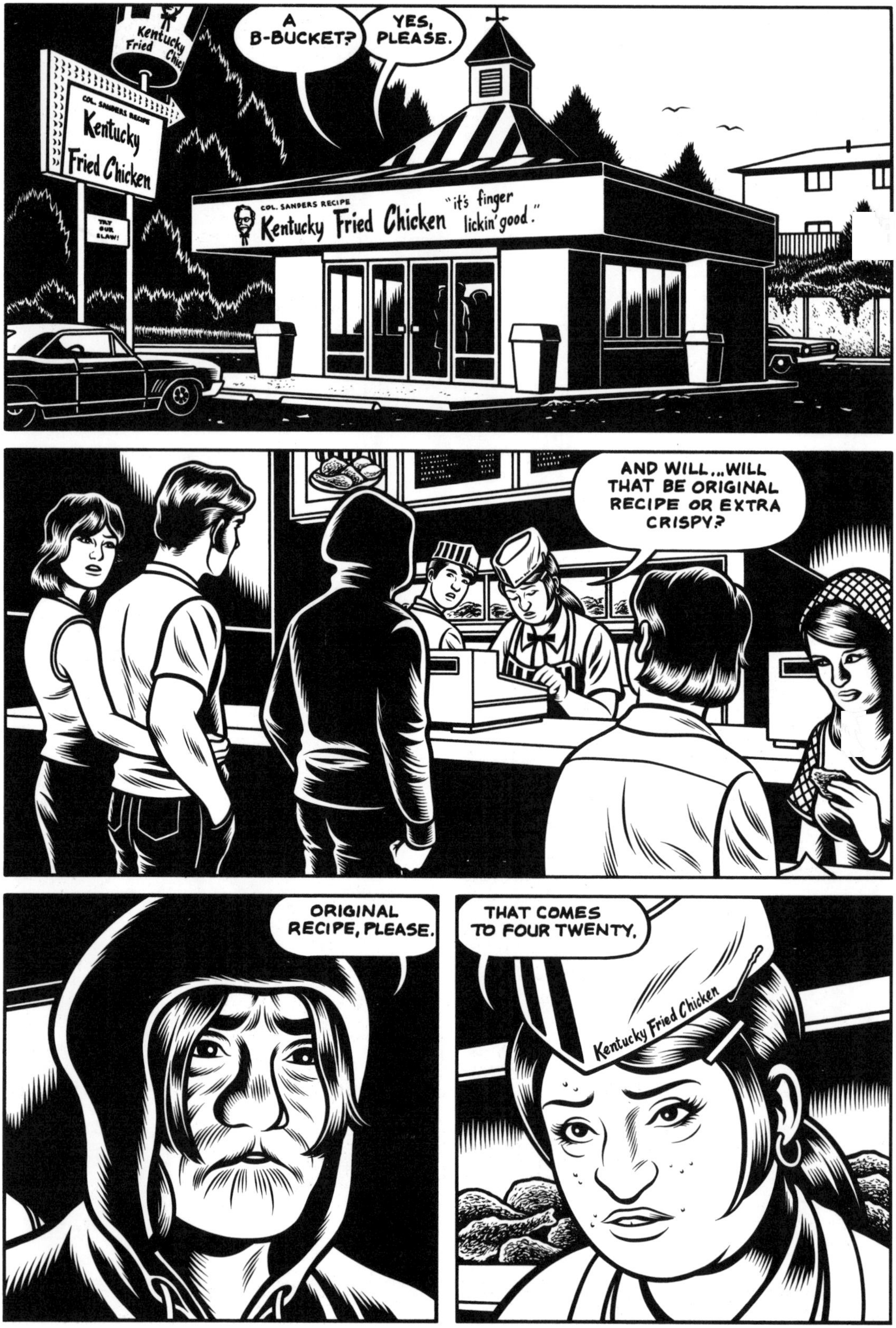
Kentucky Fried Chic
COL. SANDERS RECIPE Kentucky Fried Chicken
TRY OUR SLAW!
A B-BUCKET?
YES, PLEASE.
COL. SANDERS RECIPE Kentucky Fried Chicken "it's finger lickin' good."
AND WILL... WILL THAT BE ORIGINAL RECIPE OR EXTRA CRISPY?
ORIGINAL RECIPE, PLEASE.
THAT COMES TO FOUR TWENTY.
Kentucky Fried Chicken

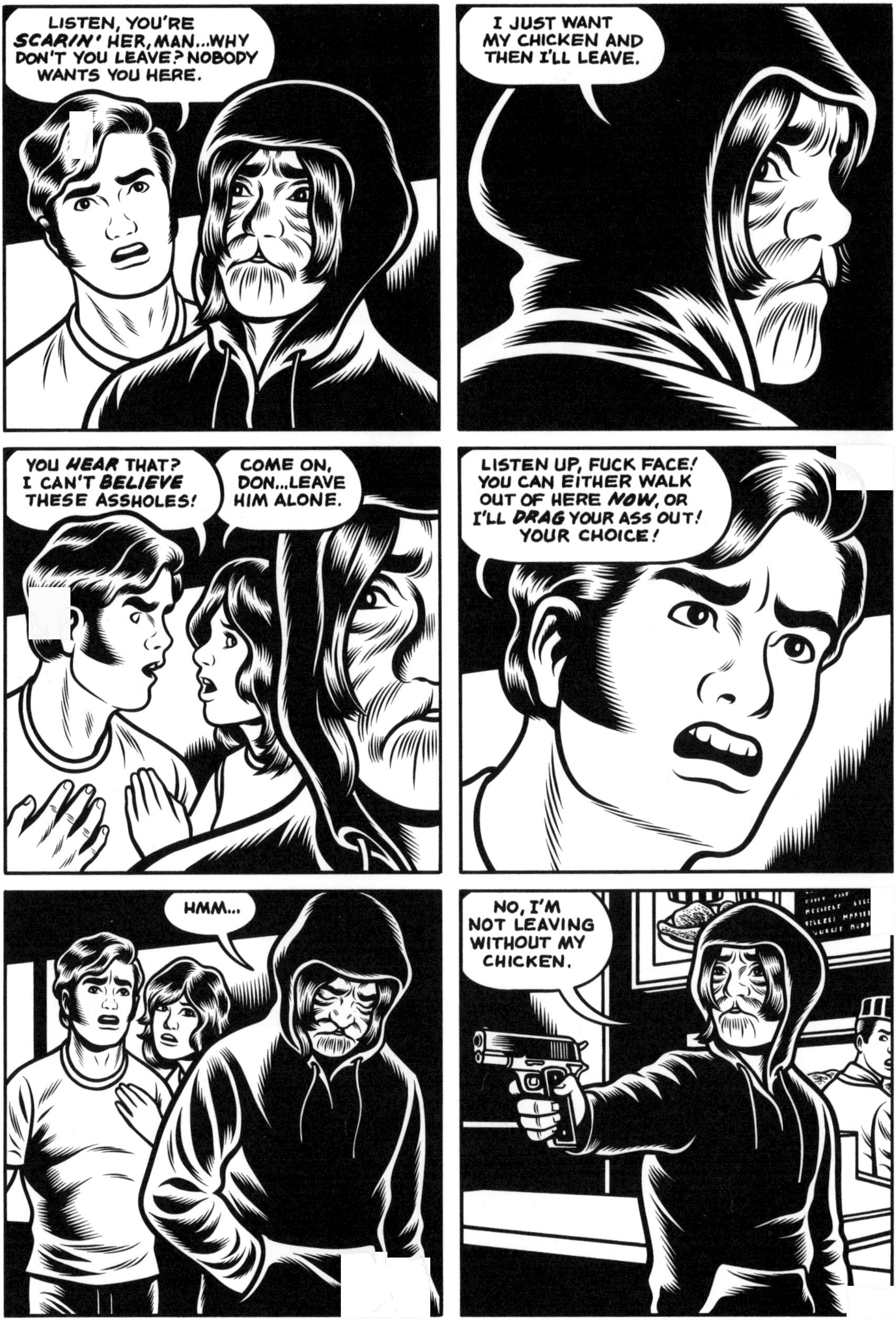
LISTEN, YOU'RE SCARIN' HER, MAN...WHY DON'T YOU LEAVE? NOBODY WANTS YOU HERE.
I JUST WANT MY CHICKEN AND THEN I'LL LEAVE.
YOU HEAR THAT? I CAN'T BELIEVE THESE ASSHOLES!
COME ON, DON...LEAVE HIM ALONE.
LISTEN UP, FUCK FACE! YOU CAN EITHER WALK OUT OF HERE NOW, OR I'LL DRAG YOUR ASS OUT! YOUR CHOICE!
HMM...
NO, I'M NOT LEAVING WITHOUT MY CHICKEN.

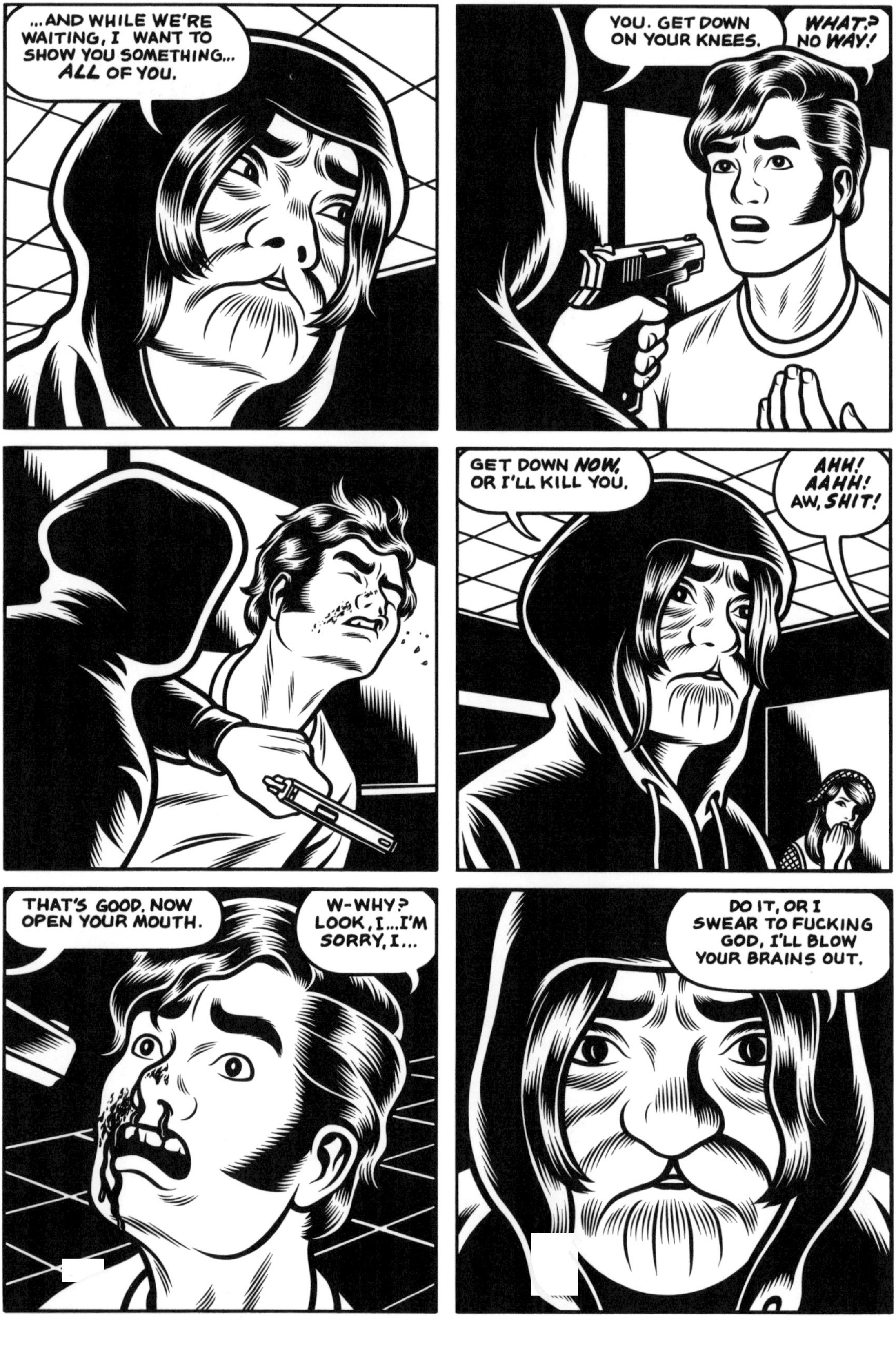
...AND WHILE WE'RE WAITING, I WANT TO SHOW YOU SOMETHING... ALL OF YOU.
YOU. GET DOWN ON YOUR KNEES.
WHAT? NO WAY!
GET DOWN NOW, OR I'LL KILL YOU.
AHH! AAHH! AW, SHIT!
THAT'S GOOD. NOW OPEN YOUR MOUTH.
W-WHY? LOOK, I...I'M SORRY, I...
DO IT, OR I SWEAR TO FUCKING GOD, I'LL BLOW YOUR BRAINS OUT.

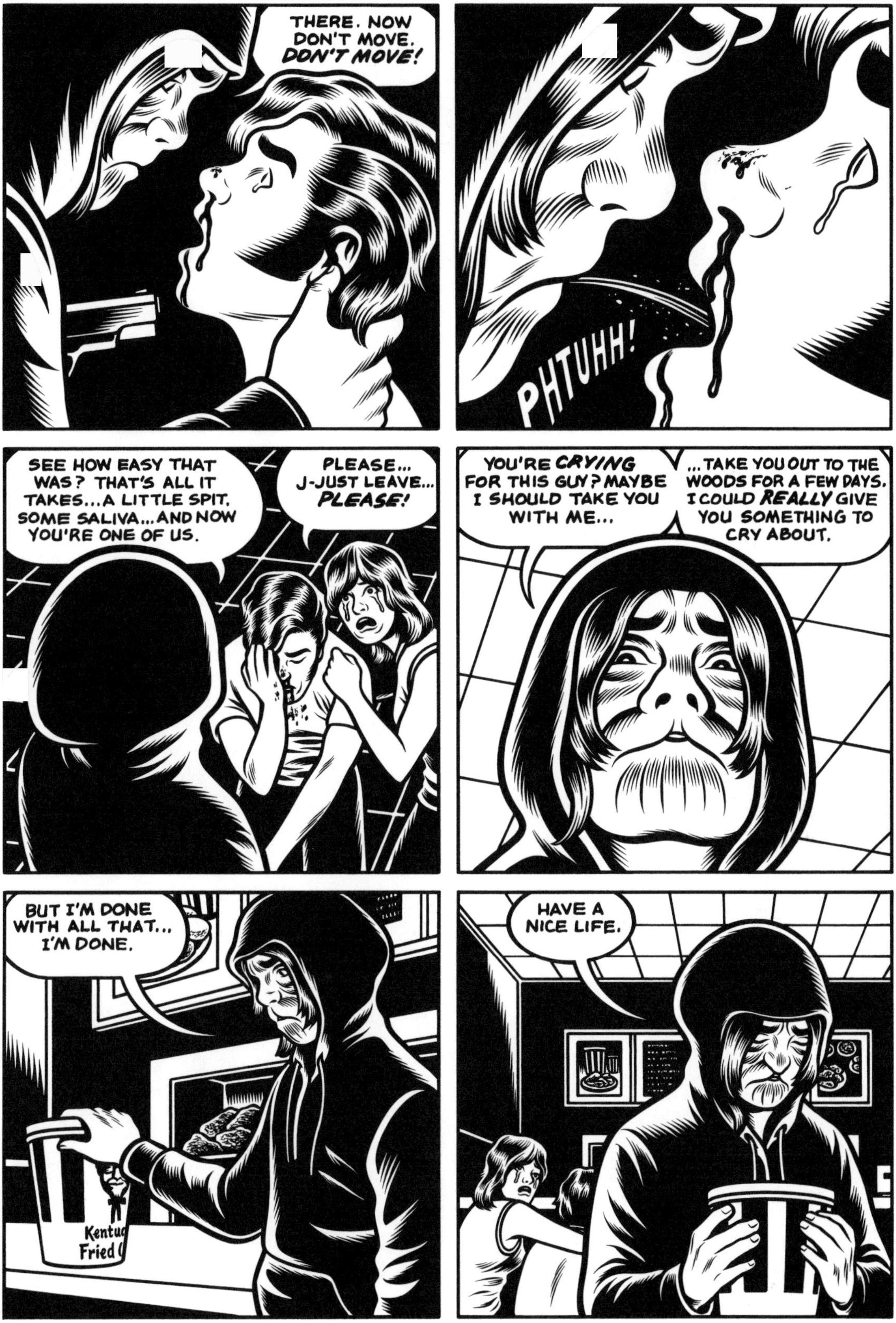
THERE. NOW DON'T MOVE. *DON'T MOVE!*
PHTUHH!
SEE HOW EASY THAT WAS? THAT'S ALL IT TAKES...A LITTLE SPIT, SOME SALIVA...AND NOW YOU'RE ONE OF US.
PLEASE... J-JUST LEAVE... *PLEASE!*
YOU'RE *CRYING* FOR THIS GUY? MAYBE I SHOULD TAKE YOU WITH ME...
...TAKE YOU OUT TO THE WOODS FOR A FEW DAYS. I COULD *REALLY* GIVE YOU SOMETHING TO CRY ABOUT.
BUT I'M DONE WITH ALL THAT... I'M DONE.
HAVE A NICE LIFE.

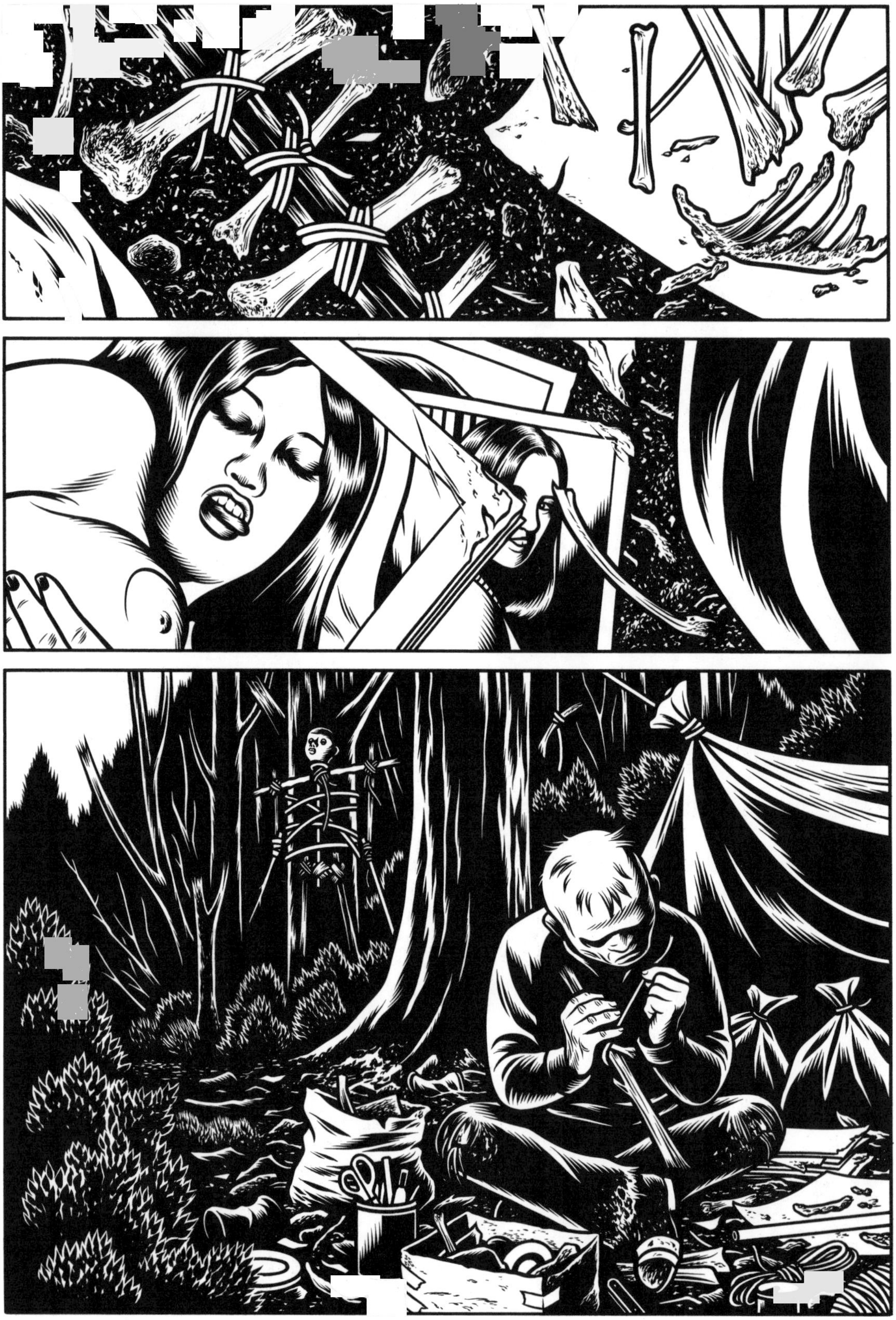

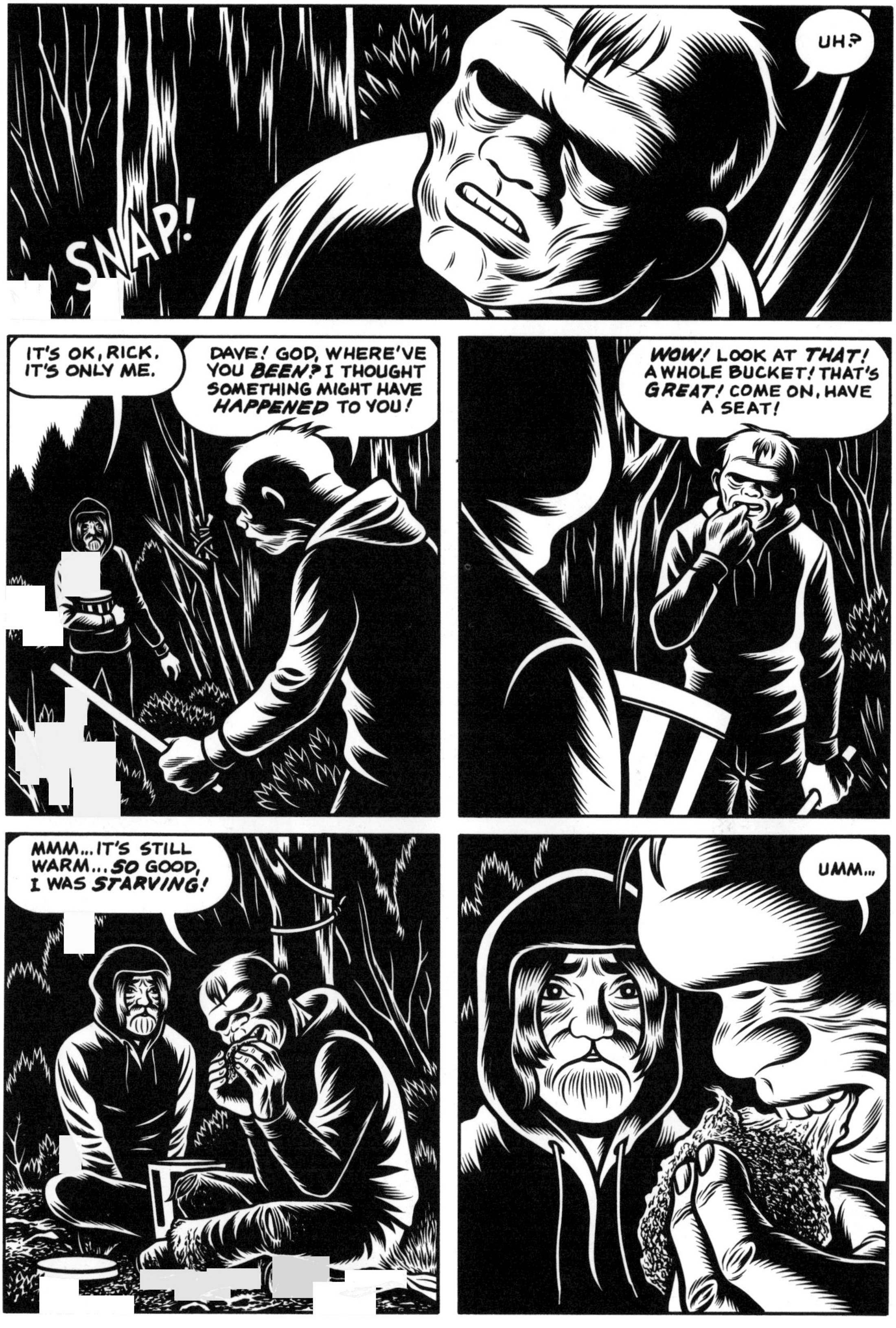
UH?
SNAP!
IT'S OK, RICK. IT'S ONLY ME.
DAVE! GOD, WHERE'VE YOU BEEN? I THOUGHT SOMETHING MIGHT HAVE HAPPENED TO YOU!
WOW! LOOK AT THAT! A WHOLE BUCKET! THAT'S GREAT! COME ON, HAVE A SEAT!
MMM... IT'S STILL WARM... SO GOOD, I WAS STARVING!
UMM...

HEY, WHAT'S THE MATTER? WHY AREN'T YOU EATING? THIS IS *SO* GOOD!

YOU GO AHEAD, I'M NOT HUNGRY.

BOY, I...I GOTTA TELL YOU, I WAS GETTING WORRIED... YOU DIDN'T SHOW UP FOR A FEW DAYS AND...I DIDN'T KNOW *WHAT* TO THINK.

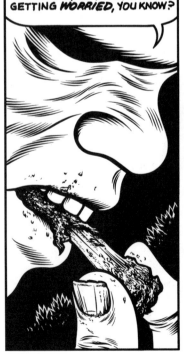

I'M RUNNING OUT OF FOOD AGAIN. I'VE GOT A COUPLE OF SNICKERS BARS AND SOME SALTINES, BUT I WAS REALLY GETTING *WORRIED*, YOU KNOW?

I GUESS YOU'VE BEEN BUSY HANGING AROUND WITH YOUR FRIENDS AND ALL...BUT FOR A WHILE THERE, I THOUGHT MAYBE YOU'D LEFT FOR GOOD.

I'M SORRY I HAVEN'T BEEN AROUND. I REALLY AM. I'LL MAKE IT UP TO YOU.

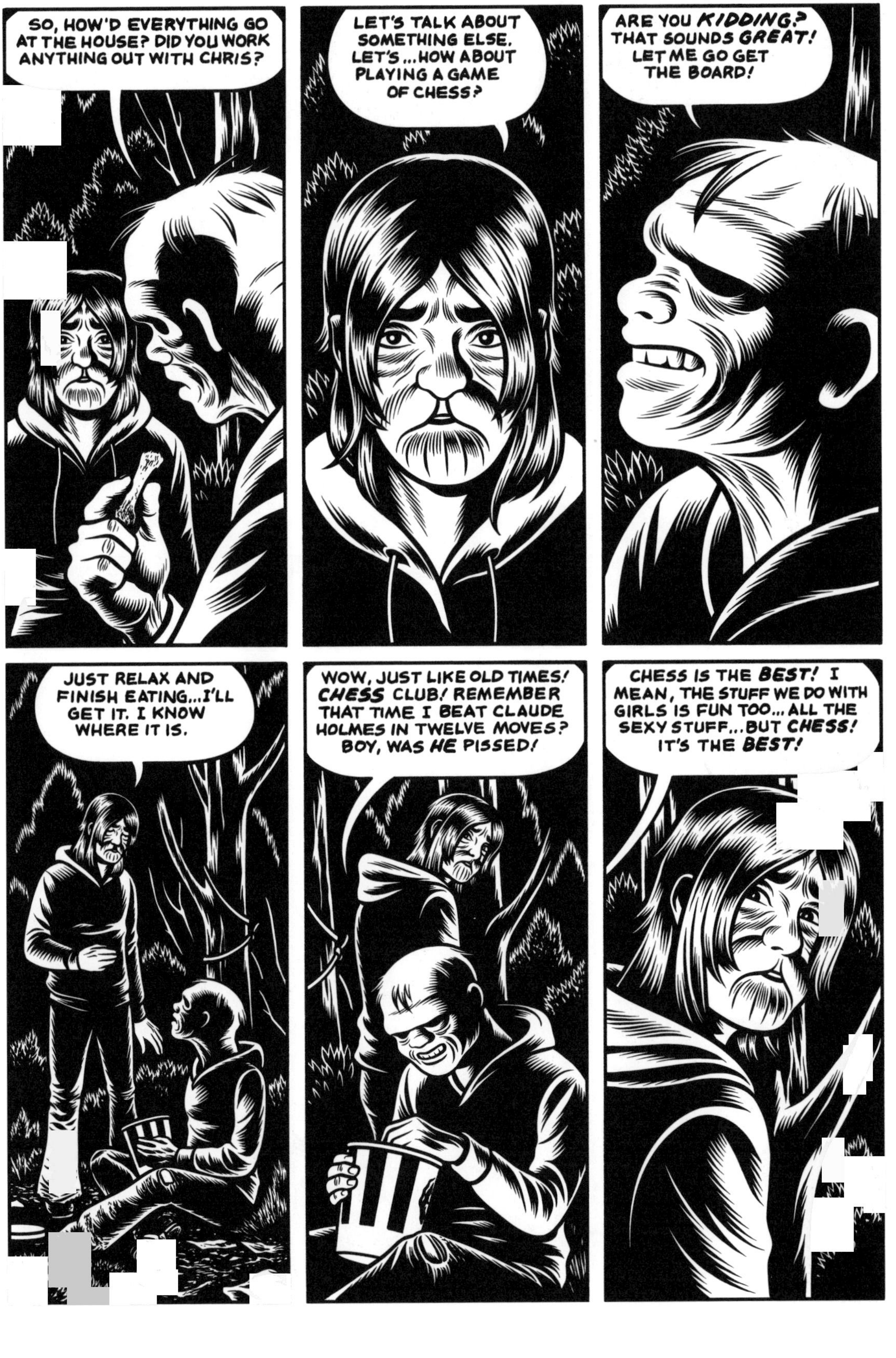
SO, HOW'D EVERYTHING GO AT THE HOUSE? DID YOU WORK ANYTHING OUT WITH CHRIS?
LET'S TALK ABOUT SOMETHING ELSE. LET'S ... HOW ABOUT PLAYING A GAME OF CHESS?
ARE YOU *KIDDING*? THAT SOUNDS *GREAT*! LET ME GO GET THE BOARD!
JUST RELAX AND FINISH EATING...I'LL GET IT. I KNOW WHERE IT IS.
WOW, JUST LIKE OLD TIMES! *CHESS* CLUB! REMEMBER THAT TIME I BEAT CLAUDE HOLMES IN TWELVE MOVES? BOY, WAS *HE* PISSED!
CHESS IS THE *BEST*! I MEAN, THE STUFF WE DO WITH GIRLS IS FUN TOO... ALL THE SEXY STUFF... BUT *CHESS*! IT'S THE *BEST*!

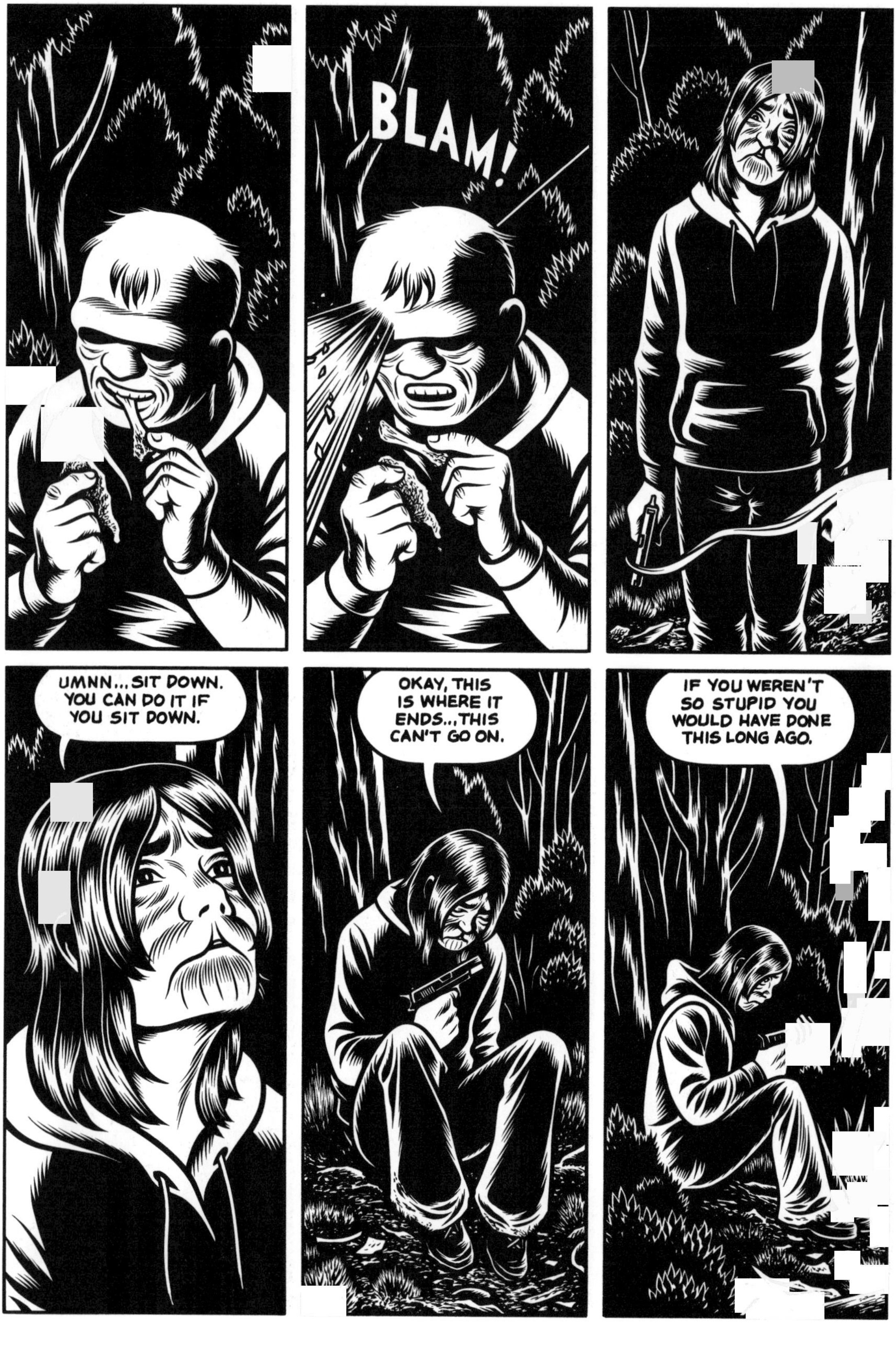
BLAM!
UMNN...SIT DOWN. YOU CAN DO IT IF YOU SIT DOWN.
OKAY, THIS IS WHERE IT ENDS...THIS CAN'T GO ON.
IF YOU WEREN'T SO STUPID YOU WOULD HAVE DONE THIS LONG AGO.

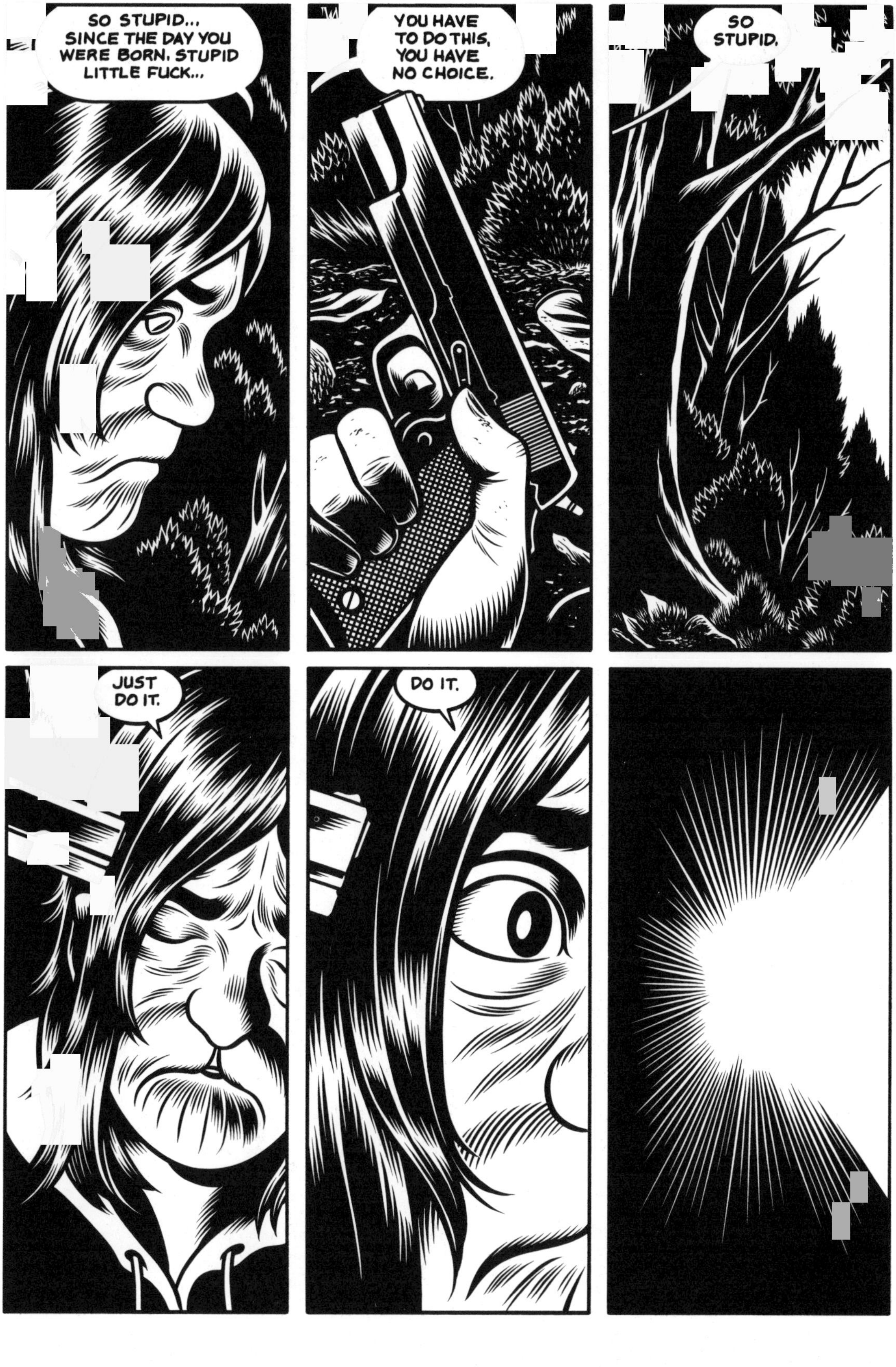
SO STUPID... SINCE THE DAY YOU WERE BORN. STUPID LITTLE FUCK...
YOU HAVE TO DO THIS, YOU HAVE NO CHOICE.
SO STUPID.
JUST DO IT.
DO IT.

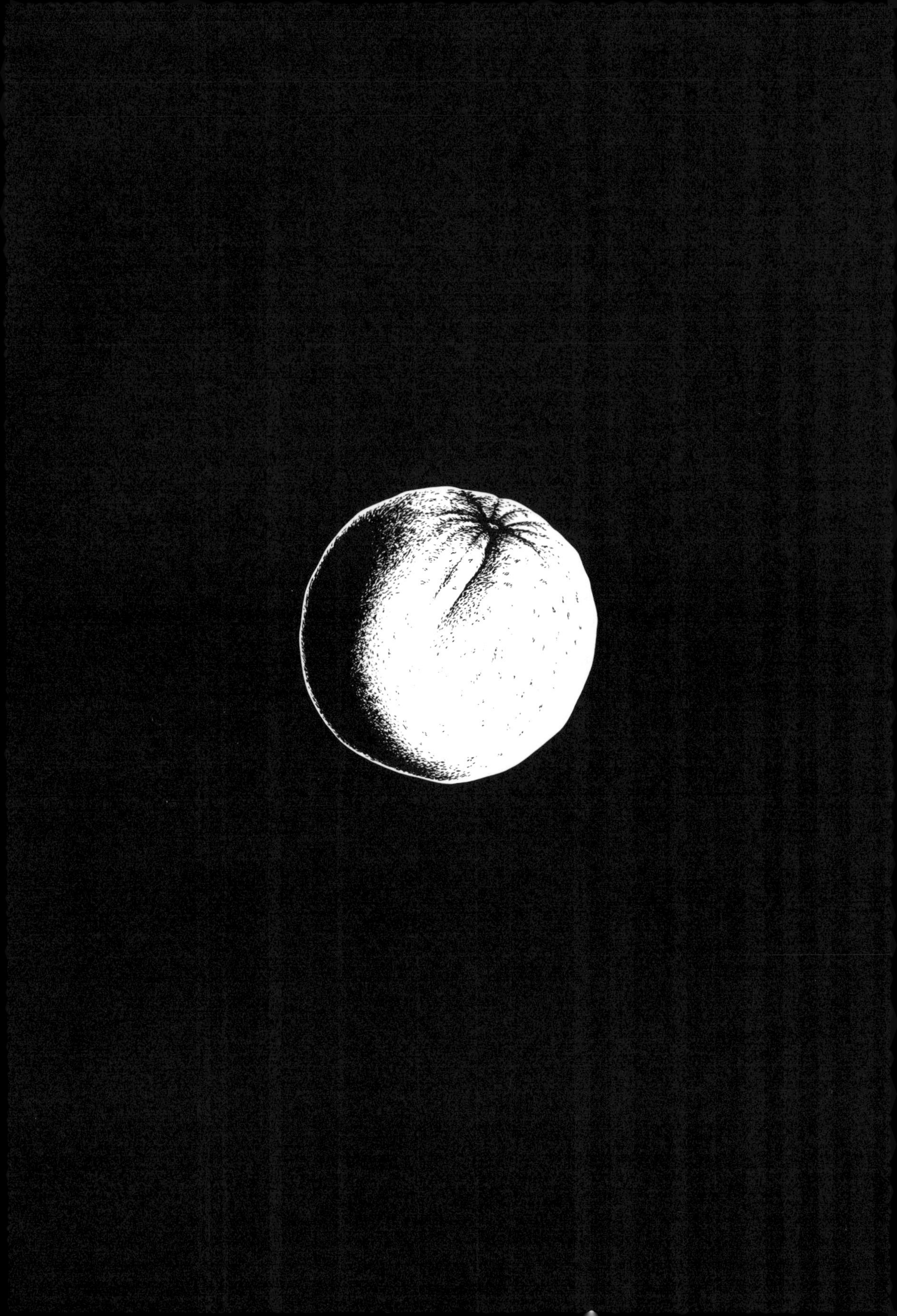

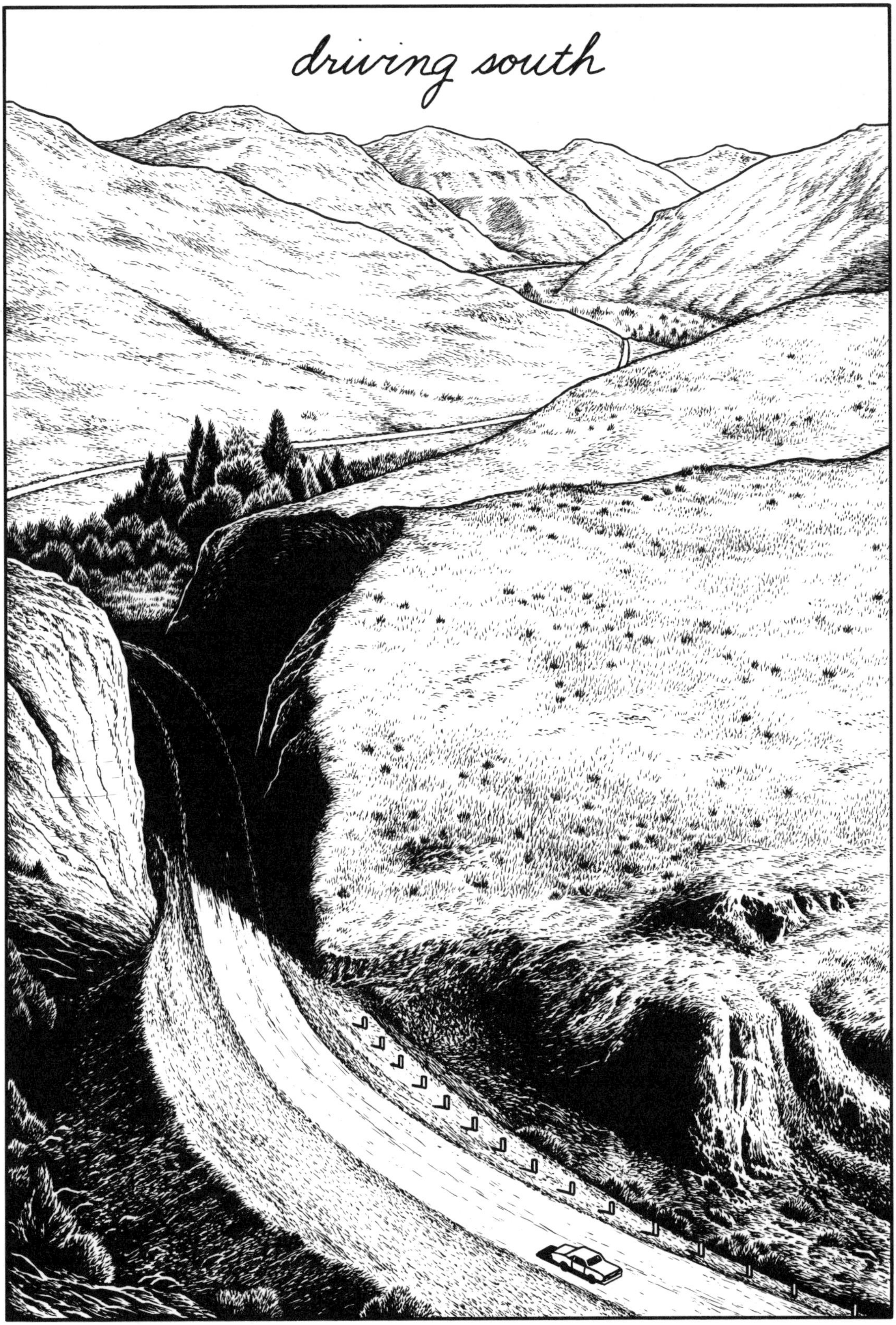
driving south

ELIZA SITTING NAKED ON A PINK TOWEL. SO BEAUTIFUL I COULD DIE.

CONCENTRATING, ALL FOCUSED IN ON HER SKETCHBOOK, BUT AW, GOD... HER TAIL.

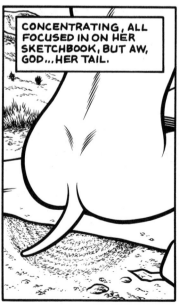

HER CUTE LITTLE TAIL MOVING SLOWLY BACK AND FORTH, MAKING A FAN SHAPE IN THE DIRT.

SHE'S THE ONE, SHE REALLY IS. I KNOW THAT NOW.

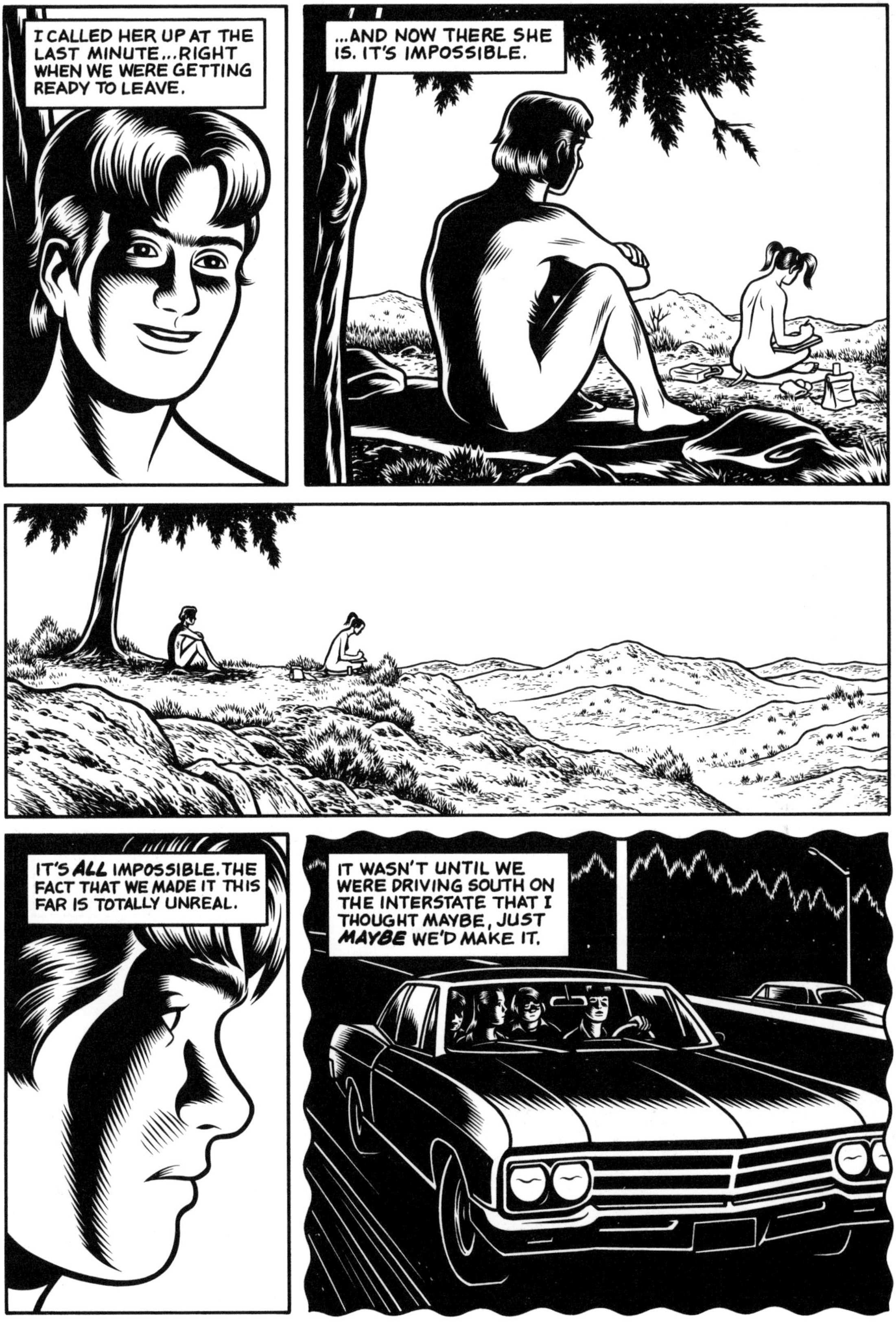
I CALLED HER UP AT THE LAST MINUTE...RIGHT WHEN WE WERE GETTING READY TO LEAVE.
...AND NOW THERE SHE IS. IT'S IMPOSSIBLE.
IT'S ALL IMPOSSIBLE. THE FACT THAT WE MADE IT THIS FAR IS TOTALLY UNREAL.
IT WASN'T UNTIL WE WERE DRIVING SOUTH ON THE INTERSTATE THAT I THOUGHT MAYBE, JUST MAYBE WE'D MAKE IT.

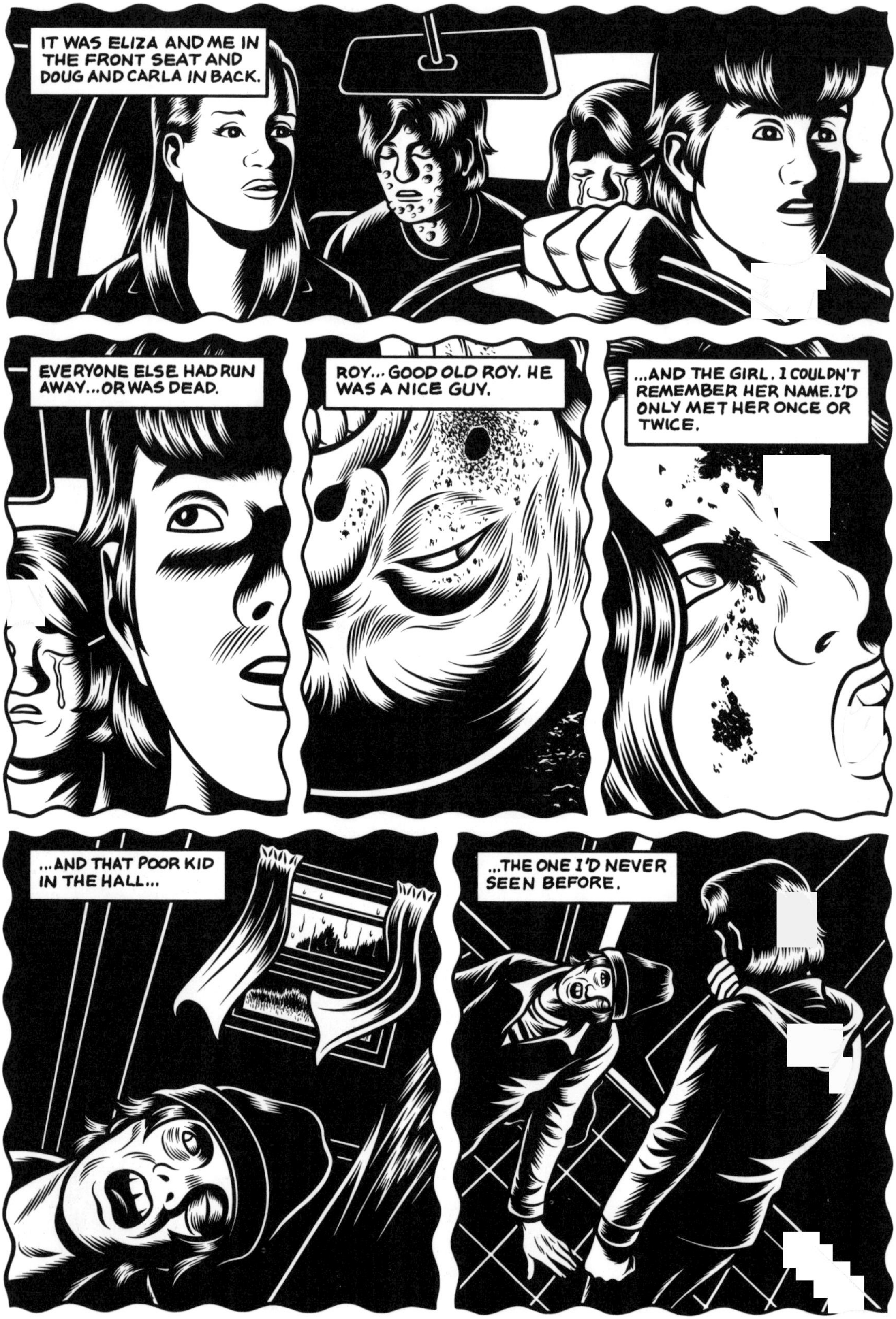
IT WAS ELIZA AND ME IN THE FRONT SEAT AND DOUG AND CARLA IN BACK.
EVERYONE ELSE HAD RUN AWAY...OR WAS DEAD.
ROY... GOOD OLD ROY. HE WAS A NICE GUY.
...AND THE GIRL. I COULDN'T REMEMBER HER NAME. I'D ONLY MET HER ONCE OR TWICE.
...AND THAT POOR KID IN THE HALL...
...THE ONE I'D NEVER SEEN BEFORE.

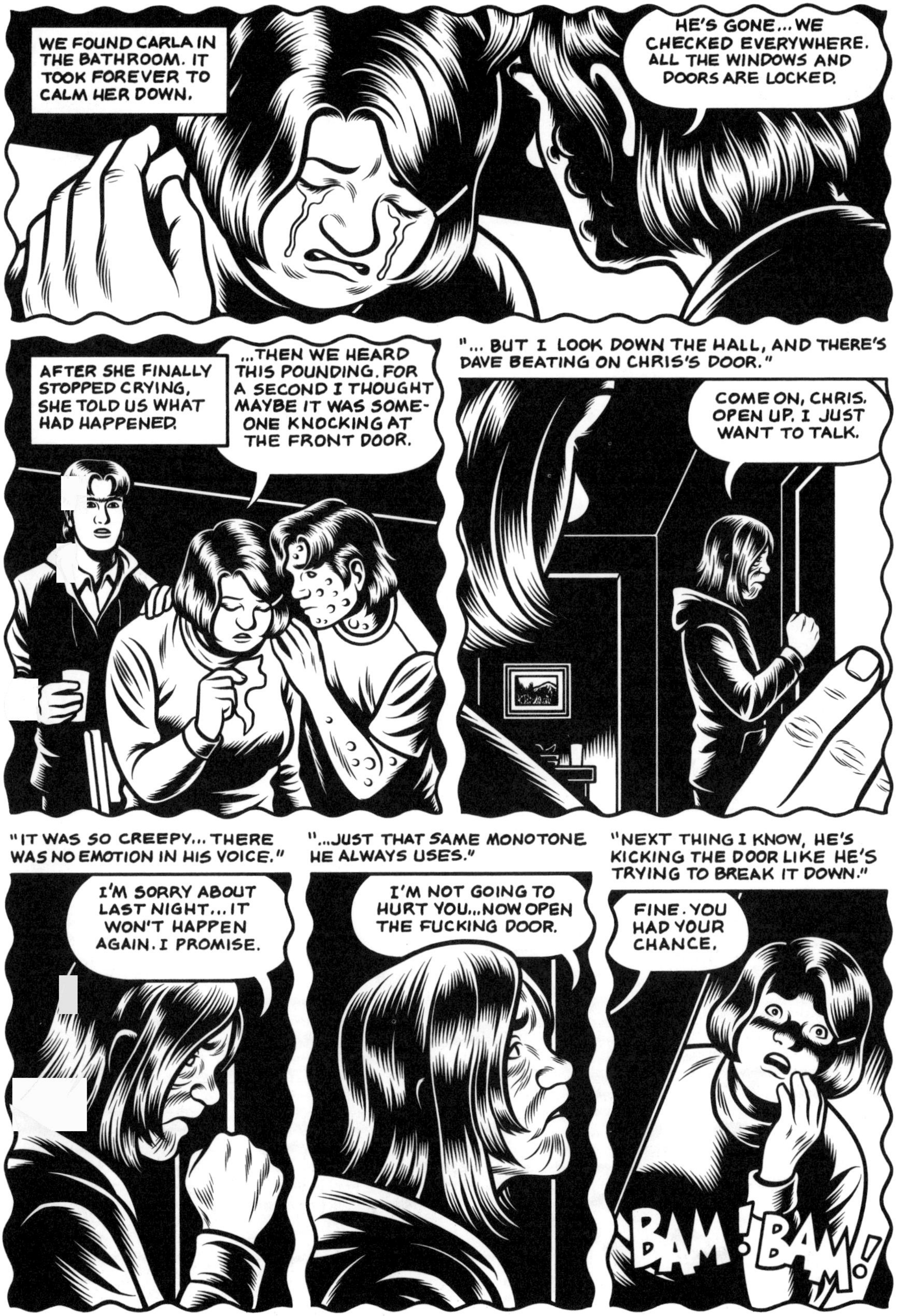
WE FOUND CARLA IN THE BATHROOM. IT TOOK FOREVER TO CALM HER DOWN.
HE'S GONE... WE CHECKED EVERYWHERE. ALL THE WINDOWS AND DOORS ARE LOCKED.
AFTER SHE FINALLY STOPPED CRYING, SHE TOLD US WHAT HAD HAPPENED.
...THEN WE HEARD THIS POUNDING. FOR A SECOND I THOUGHT MAYBE IT WAS SOME-ONE KNOCKING AT THE FRONT DOOR.
"... BUT I LOOK DOWN THE HALL, AND THERE'S DAVE BEATING ON CHRIS'S DOOR."
COME ON, CHRIS. OPEN UP. I JUST WANT TO TALK.
"IT WAS SO CREEPY... THERE WAS NO EMOTION IN HIS VOICE."
I'M SORRY ABOUT LAST NIGHT... IT WON'T HAPPEN AGAIN. I PROMISE.
"...JUST THAT SAME MONOTONE HE ALWAYS USES."
I'M NOT GOING TO HURT YOU...NOW OPEN THE FUCKING DOOR.
"NEXT THING I KNOW, HE'S KICKING THE DOOR LIKE HE'S TRYING TO BREAK IT DOWN."
FINE. YOU HAD YOUR CHANCE.
BAM! BAM!

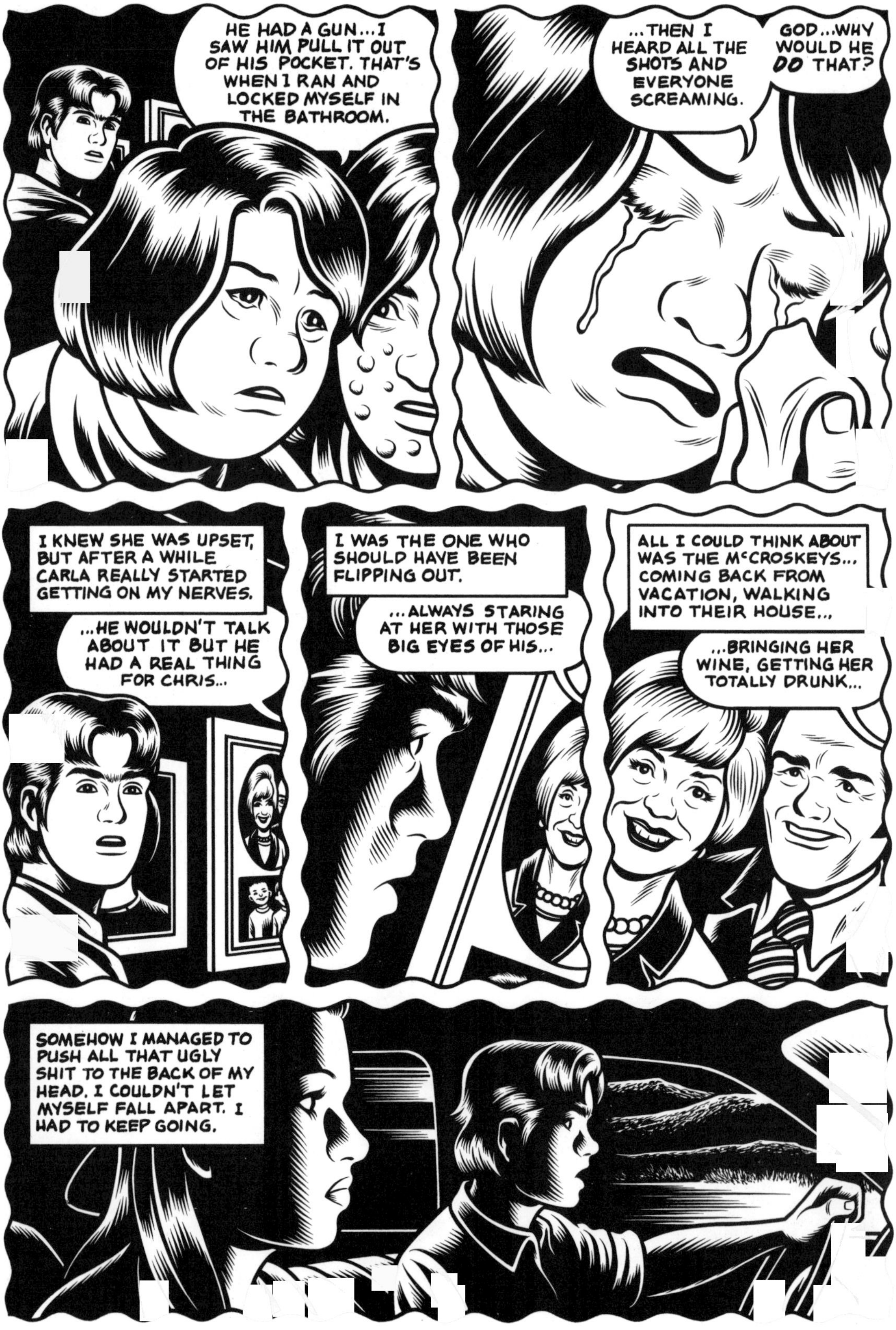
HE HAD A GUN...I SAW HIM PULL IT OUT OF HIS POCKET. THAT'S WHEN I RAN AND LOCKED MYSELF IN THE BATHROOM.
...THEN I HEARD ALL THE SHOTS AND EVERYONE SCREAMING.
GOD...WHY WOULD HE DO THAT?
I KNEW SHE WAS UPSET, BUT AFTER A WHILE CARLA REALLY STARTED GETTING ON MY NERVES.
...HE WOULDN'T TALK ABOUT IT BUT HE HAD A REAL THING FOR CHRIS...
I WAS THE ONE WHO SHOULD HAVE BEEN FLIPPING OUT.
...ALWAYS STARING AT HER WITH THOSE BIG EYES OF HIS...
ALL I COULD THINK ABOUT WAS THE McCROSKEYS... COMING BACK FROM VACATION, WALKING INTO THEIR HOUSE...
...BRINGING HER WINE, GETTING HER TOTALLY DRUNK...
SOMEHOW I MANAGED TO PUSH ALL THAT UGLY SHIT TO THE BACK OF MY HEAD. I COULDN'T LET MYSELF FALL APART. I HAD TO KEEP GOING.

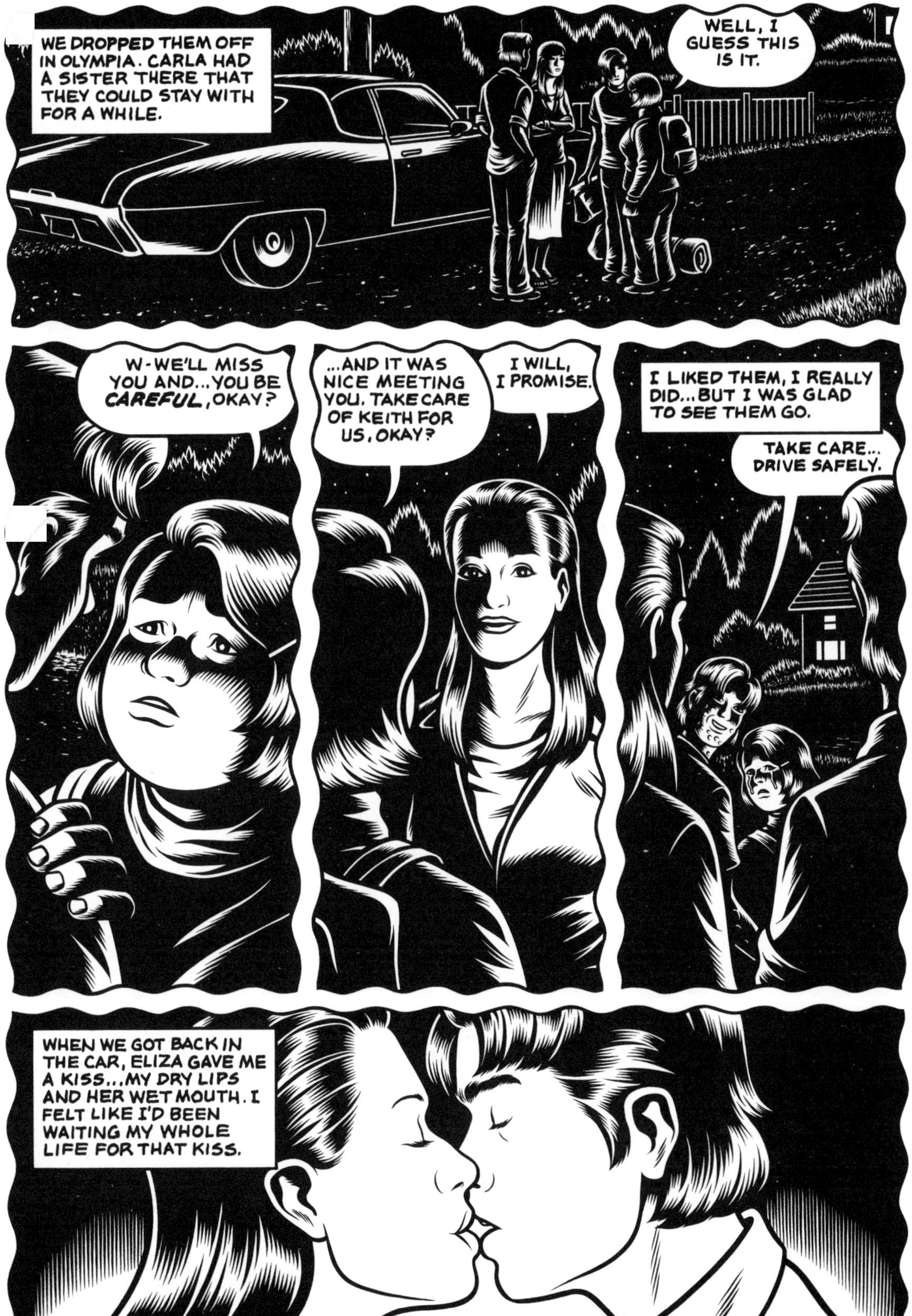
WE DROPPED THEM OFF IN OLYMPIA. CARLA HAD A SISTER THERE THAT THEY COULD STAY WITH FOR A WHILE.
WELL, I GUESS THIS IS IT.
W-WE'LL MISS YOU AND... YOU BE *CAREFUL*, OKAY?
...AND IT WAS NICE MEETING YOU. TAKE CARE OF KEITH FOR US, OKAY?
I WILL, I PROMISE.
I LIKED THEM, I REALLY DID... BUT I WAS GLAD TO SEE THEM GO.
TAKE CARE... DRIVE SAFELY.
WHEN WE GOT BACK IN THE CAR, ELIZA GAVE ME A KISS... MY DRY LIPS AND HER WET MOUTH. I FELT LIKE I'D BEEN WAITING MY WHOLE LIFE FOR THAT KISS.

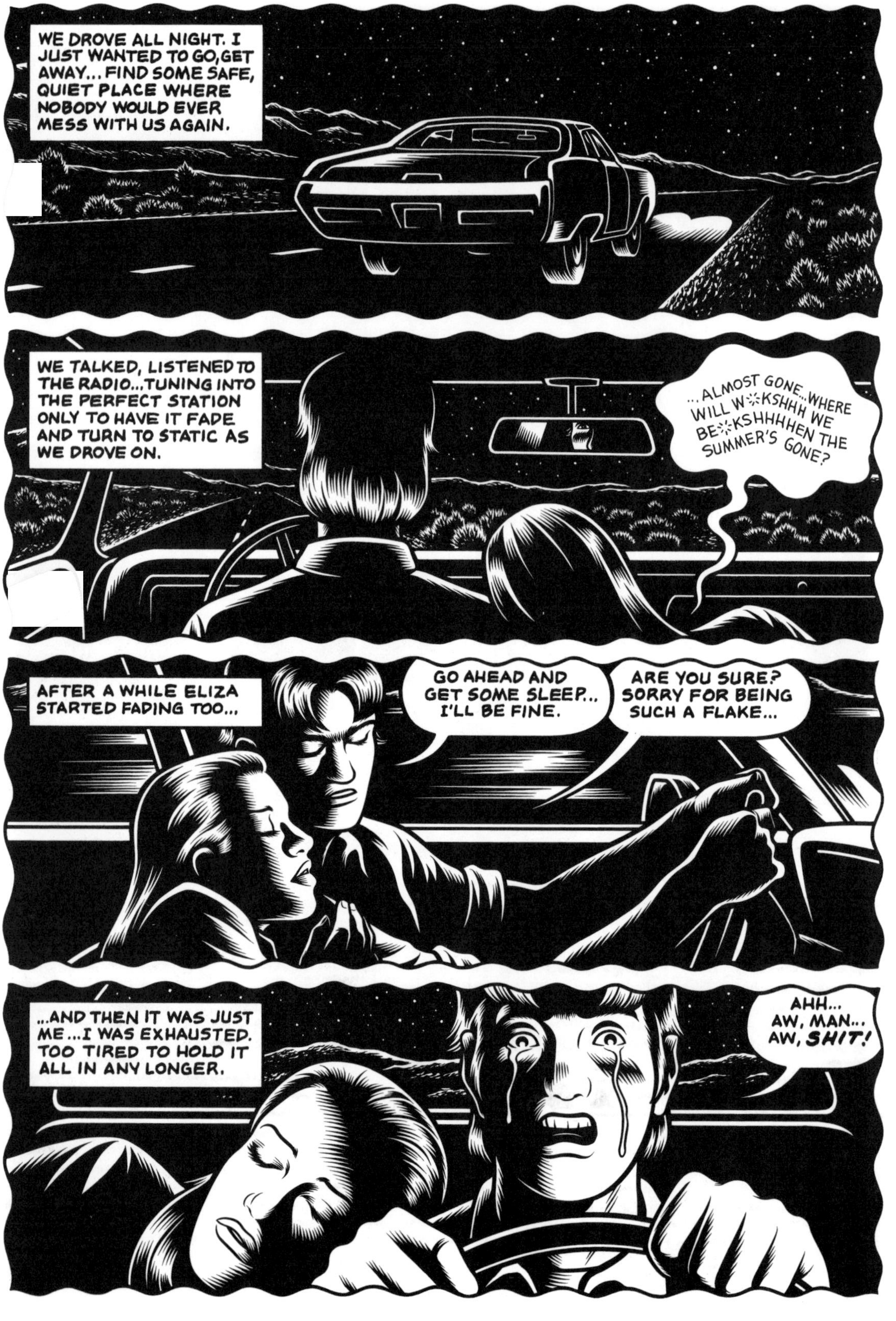
WE DROVE ALL NIGHT. I JUST WANTED TO GO, GET AWAY... FIND SOME SAFE, QUIET PLACE WHERE NOBODY WOULD EVER MESS WITH US AGAIN.
WE TALKED, LISTENED TO THE RADIO... TUNING INTO THE PERFECT STATION ONLY TO HAVE IT FADE AND TURN TO STATIC AS WE DROVE ON.
...ALMOST GONE...WHERE WILL W✲KSHHH WE BE✲KSHHHHHEN THE SUMMER'S GONE?
AFTER A WHILE ELIZA STARTED FADING TOO...
GO AHEAD AND GET SOME SLEEP... I'LL BE FINE.
ARE YOU SURE? SORRY FOR BEING SUCH A FLAKE...
...AND THEN IT WAS JUST ME... I WAS EXHAUSTED. TOO TIRED TO HOLD IT ALL IN ANY LONGER.
AHH... AW, MAN... AW, *SHIT!*

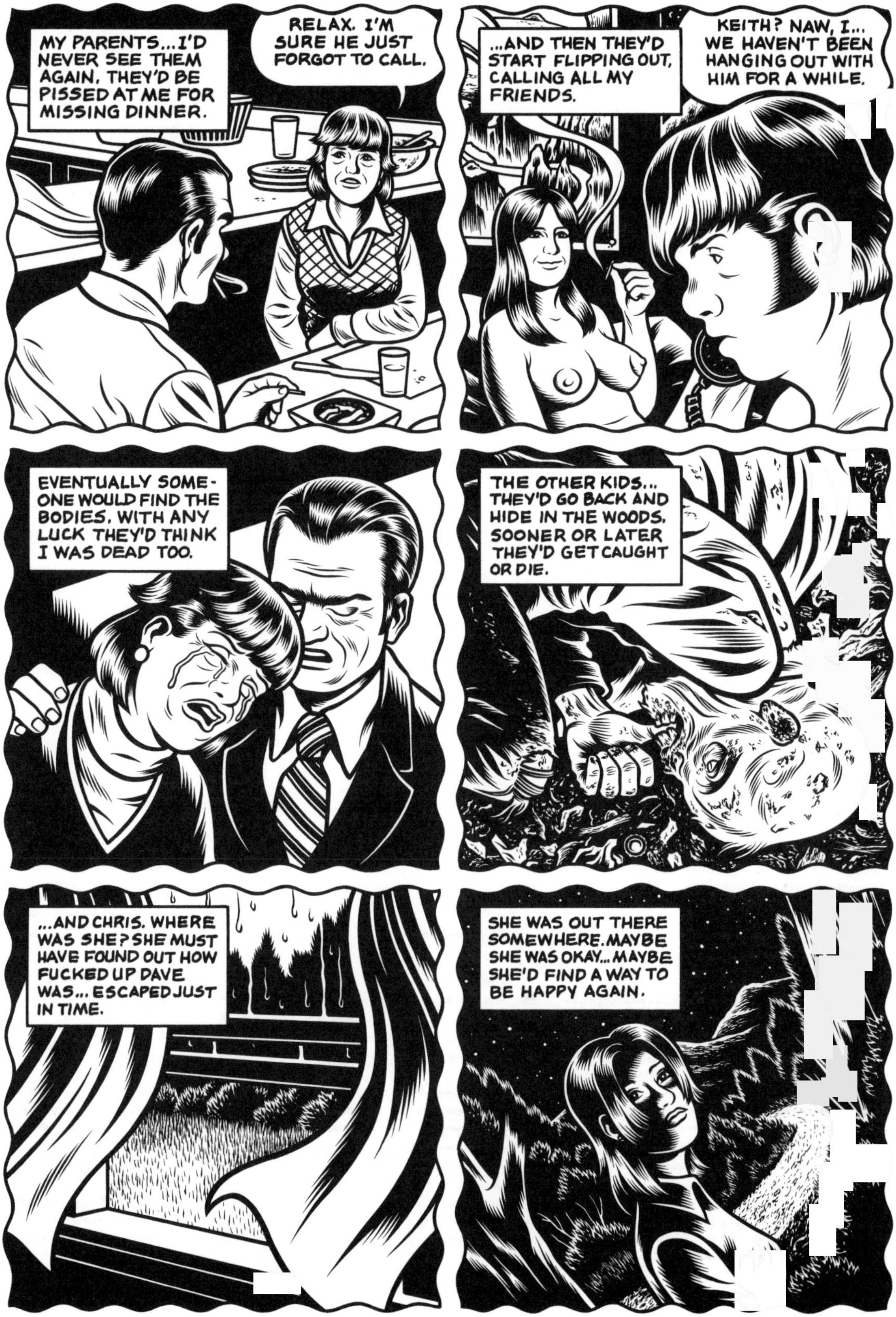
MY PARENTS... I'D NEVER SEE THEM AGAIN, THEY'D BE PISSED AT ME FOR MISSING DINNER.
RELAX. I'M SURE HE JUST FORGOT TO CALL.
...AND THEN THEY'D START FLIPPING OUT, CALLING ALL MY FRIENDS.
KEITH? NAW, I... WE HAVEN'T BEEN HANGING OUT WITH HIM FOR A WHILE.
EVENTUALLY SOME-ONE WOULD FIND THE BODIES. WITH ANY LUCK THEY'D THINK I WAS DEAD TOO.
THE OTHER KIDS... THEY'D GO BACK AND HIDE IN THE WOODS. SOONER OR LATER THEY'D GET CAUGHT OR DIE.
...AND CHRIS. WHERE WAS SHE? SHE MUST HAVE FOUND OUT HOW FUCKED UP DAVE WAS... ESCAPED JUST IN TIME.
SHE WAS OUT THERE SOMEWHERE. MAYBE SHE WAS OKAY... MAYBE SHE'D FIND A WAY TO BE HAPPY AGAIN.

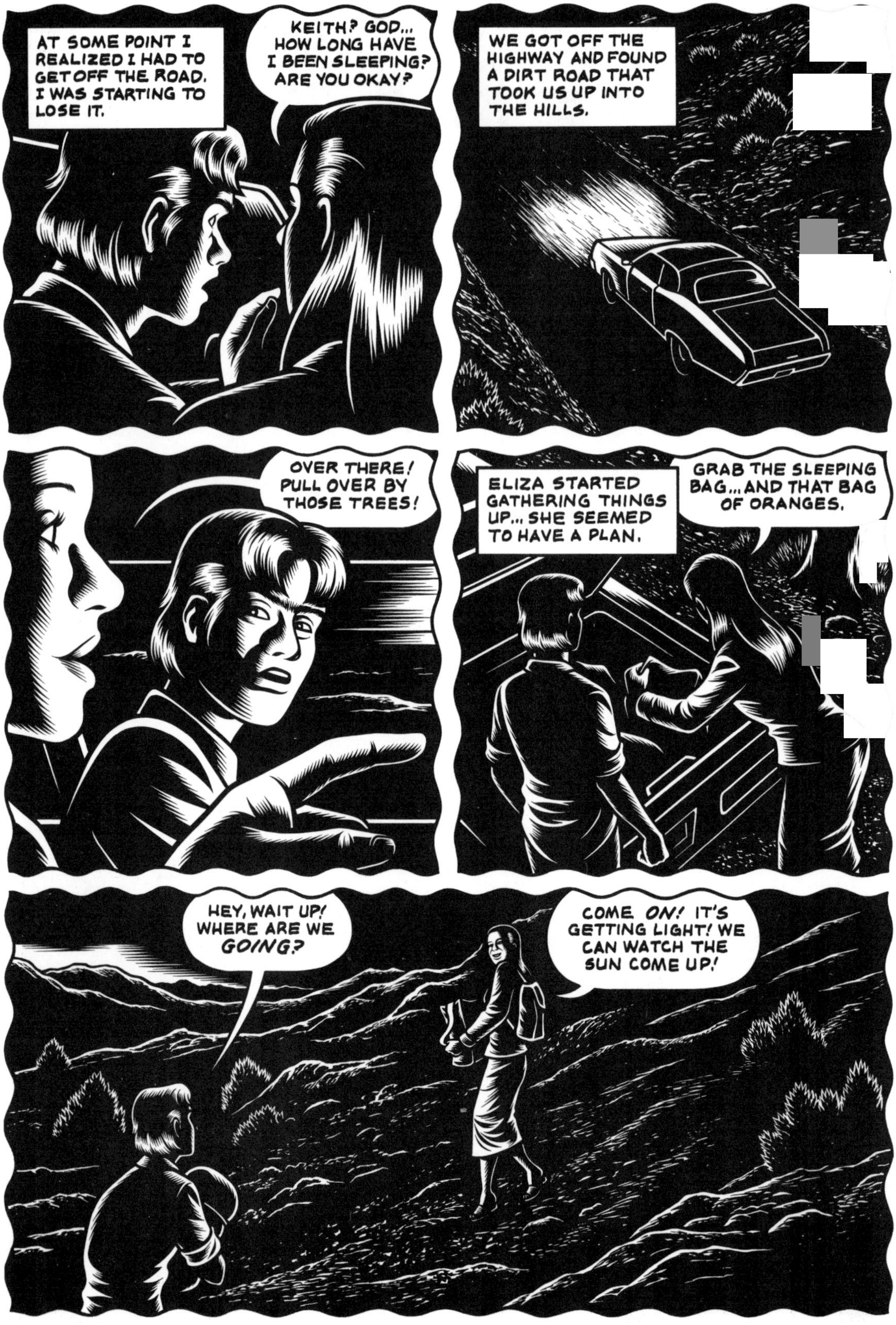

AT SOME POINT I REALIZED I HAD TO GET OFF THE ROAD. I WAS STARTING TO LOSE IT.
KEITH? GOD... HOW LONG HAVE I BEEN SLEEPING? ARE YOU OKAY?
WE GOT OFF THE HIGHWAY AND FOUND A DIRT ROAD THAT TOOK US UP INTO THE HILLS.
OVER THERE! PULL OVER BY THOSE TREES!
ELIZA STARTED GATHERING THINGS UP... SHE SEEMED TO HAVE A PLAN.
GRAB THE SLEEPING BAG... AND THAT BAG OF ORANGES.
HEY, WAIT UP! WHERE ARE WE *GOING*?
COME *ON!* IT'S GETTING LIGHT! WE CAN WATCH THE SUN COME UP!

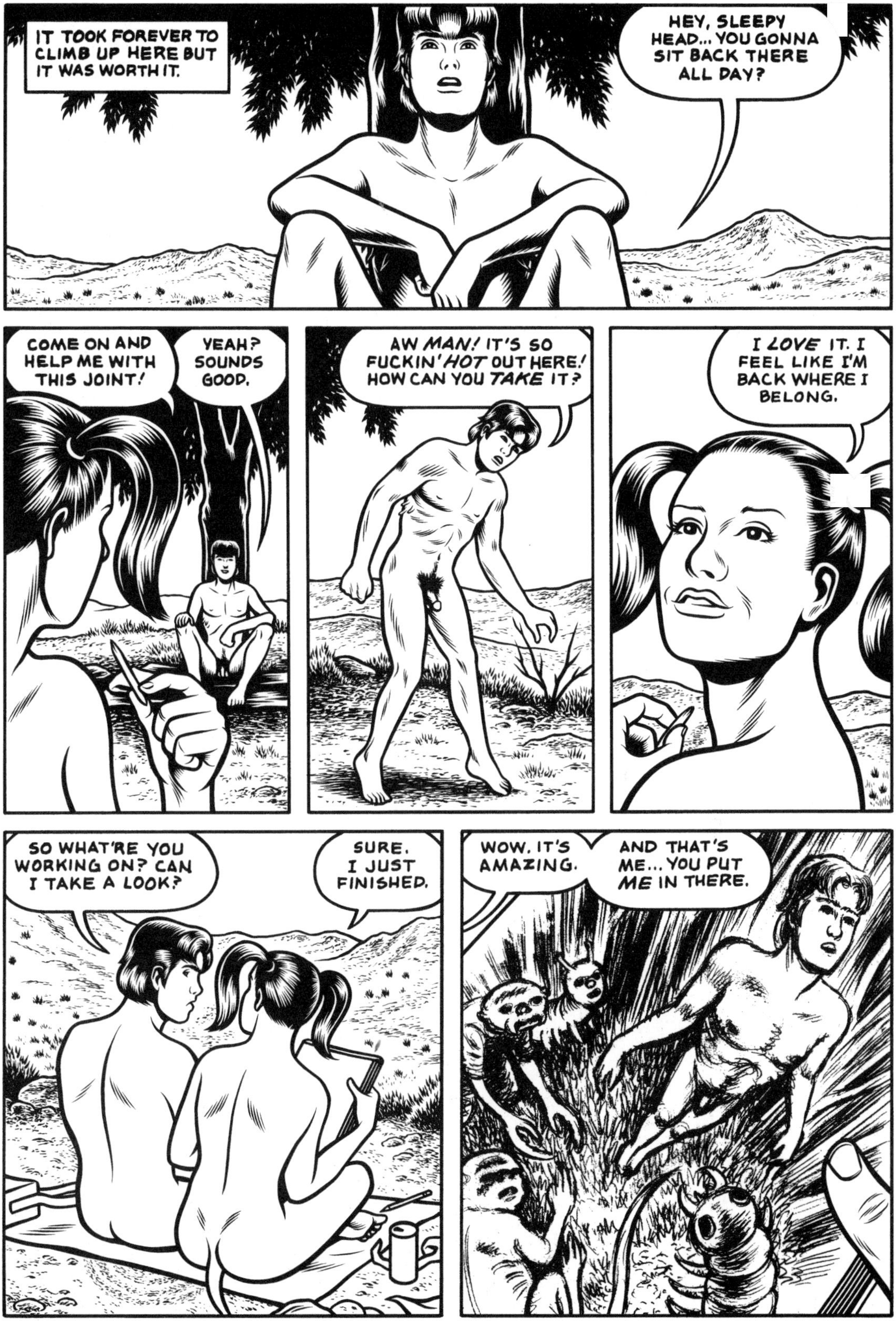
IT TOOK FOREVER TO CLIMB UP HERE BUT IT WAS WORTH IT.
HEY, SLEEPY HEAD... YOU GONNA SIT BACK THERE ALL DAY?
COME ON AND HELP ME WITH THIS JOINT!
YEAH? SOUNDS GOOD.
AW MAN! IT'S SO FUCKIN' HOT OUT HERE! HOW CAN YOU TAKE IT?
I LOVE IT. I FEEL LIKE I'M BACK WHERE I BELONG.
SO WHAT'RE YOU WORKING ON? CAN I TAKE A LOOK?
SURE. I JUST FINISHED.
WOW. IT'S AMAZING.
AND THAT'S ME... YOU PUT ME IN THERE.

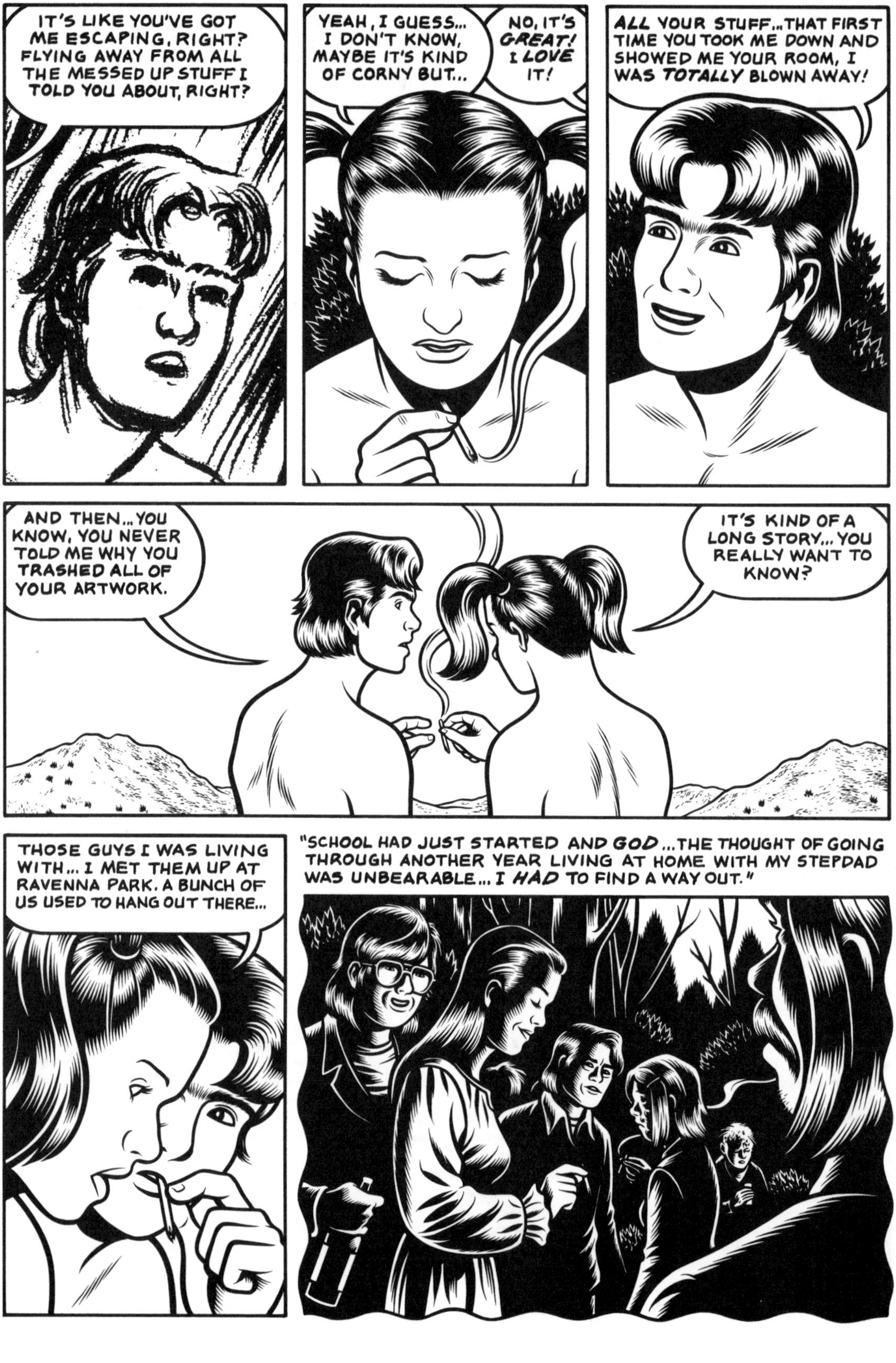
IT'S LIKE YOU'VE GOT ME ESCAPING, RIGHT? FLYING AWAY FROM ALL THE MESSED UP STUFF I TOLD YOU ABOUT, RIGHT?
YEAH, I GUESS... I DON'T KNOW, MAYBE IT'S KIND OF CORNY BUT...
NO, IT'S GREAT! I LOVE IT!
ALL YOUR STUFF... THAT FIRST TIME YOU TOOK ME DOWN AND SHOWED ME YOUR ROOM, I WAS TOTALLY BLOWN AWAY!
AND THEN... YOU KNOW, YOU NEVER TOLD ME WHY YOU TRASHED ALL OF YOUR ARTWORK.
IT'S KIND OF A LONG STORY... YOU REALLY WANT TO KNOW?
THOSE GUYS I WAS LIVING WITH... I MET THEM UP AT RAVENNA PARK. A BUNCH OF US USED TO HANG OUT THERE...
"SCHOOL HAD JUST STARTED AND GOD... THE THOUGHT OF GOING THROUGH ANOTHER YEAR LIVING AT HOME WITH MY STEPDAD WAS UNBEARABLE... I HAD TO FIND A WAY OUT."

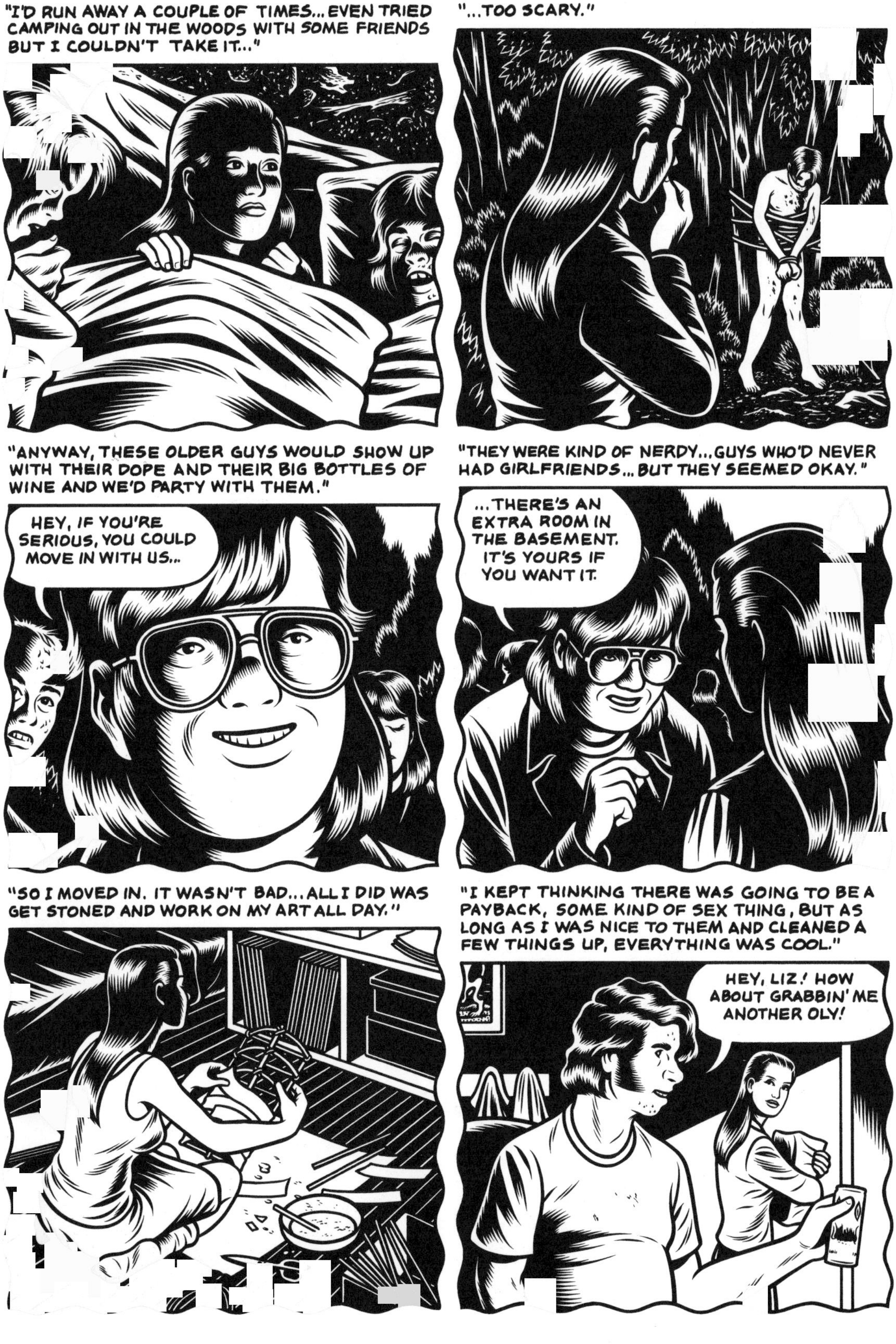
"I'D RUN AWAY A COUPLE OF TIMES... EVEN TRIED CAMPING OUT IN THE WOODS WITH SOME FRIENDS BUT I COULDN'T TAKE IT..."
"...TOO SCARY."
"ANYWAY, THESE OLDER GUYS WOULD SHOW UP WITH THEIR DOPE AND THEIR BIG BOTTLES OF WINE AND WE'D PARTY WITH THEM."
HEY, IF YOU'RE SERIOUS, YOU COULD MOVE IN WITH US...
"THEY WERE KIND OF NERDY... GUYS WHO'D NEVER HAD GIRLFRIENDS... BUT THEY SEEMED OKAY."
...THERE'S AN EXTRA ROOM IN THE BASEMENT. IT'S YOURS IF YOU WANT IT.
"SO I MOVED IN. IT WASN'T BAD... ALL I DID WAS GET STONED AND WORK ON MY ART ALL DAY."
"I KEPT THINKING THERE WAS GOING TO BE A PAYBACK, SOME KIND OF SEX THING, BUT AS LONG AS I WAS NICE TO THEM AND CLEANED A FEW THINGS UP, EVERYTHING WAS COOL."
HEY, LIZ! HOW ABOUT GRABBIN' ME ANOTHER OLY!

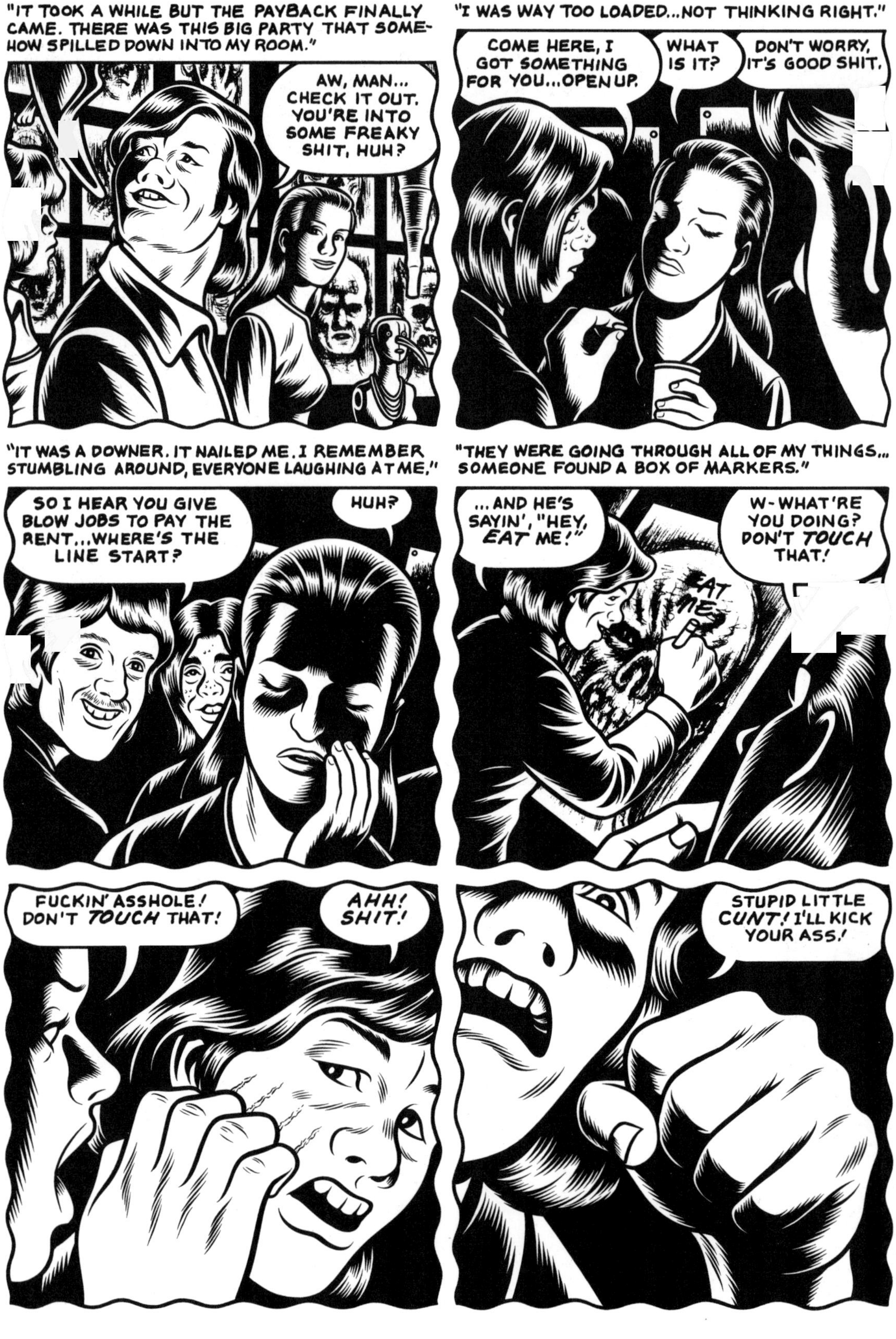
"IT TOOK A WHILE BUT THE PAYBACK FINALLY CAME. THERE WAS THIS BIG PARTY THAT SOMEHOW SPILLED DOWN INTO MY ROOM."
AW, MAN... CHECK IT OUT. YOU'RE INTO SOME FREAKY SHIT, HUH?
"I WAS WAY TOO LOADED...NOT THINKING RIGHT."
COME HERE, I GOT SOMETHING FOR YOU...OPEN UP.
WHAT IS IT?
DON'T WORRY, IT'S GOOD SHIT.
"IT WAS A DOWNER. IT NAILED ME. I REMEMBER STUMBLING AROUND, EVERYONE LAUGHING AT ME."
SO I HEAR YOU GIVE BLOW JOBS TO PAY THE RENT...WHERE'S THE LINE START?
HUH?
"THEY WERE GOING THROUGH ALL OF MY THINGS... SOMEONE FOUND A BOX OF MARKERS."
...AND HE'S SAYIN', "HEY, *EAT* ME!"
EAT ME
W-WHAT'RE YOU DOING? DON'T *TOUCH* THAT!
FUCKIN' ASSHOLE! DON'T *TOUCH* THAT!
AHH! SHIT!
STUPID LITTLE *CUNT*! I'LL KICK YOUR ASS!

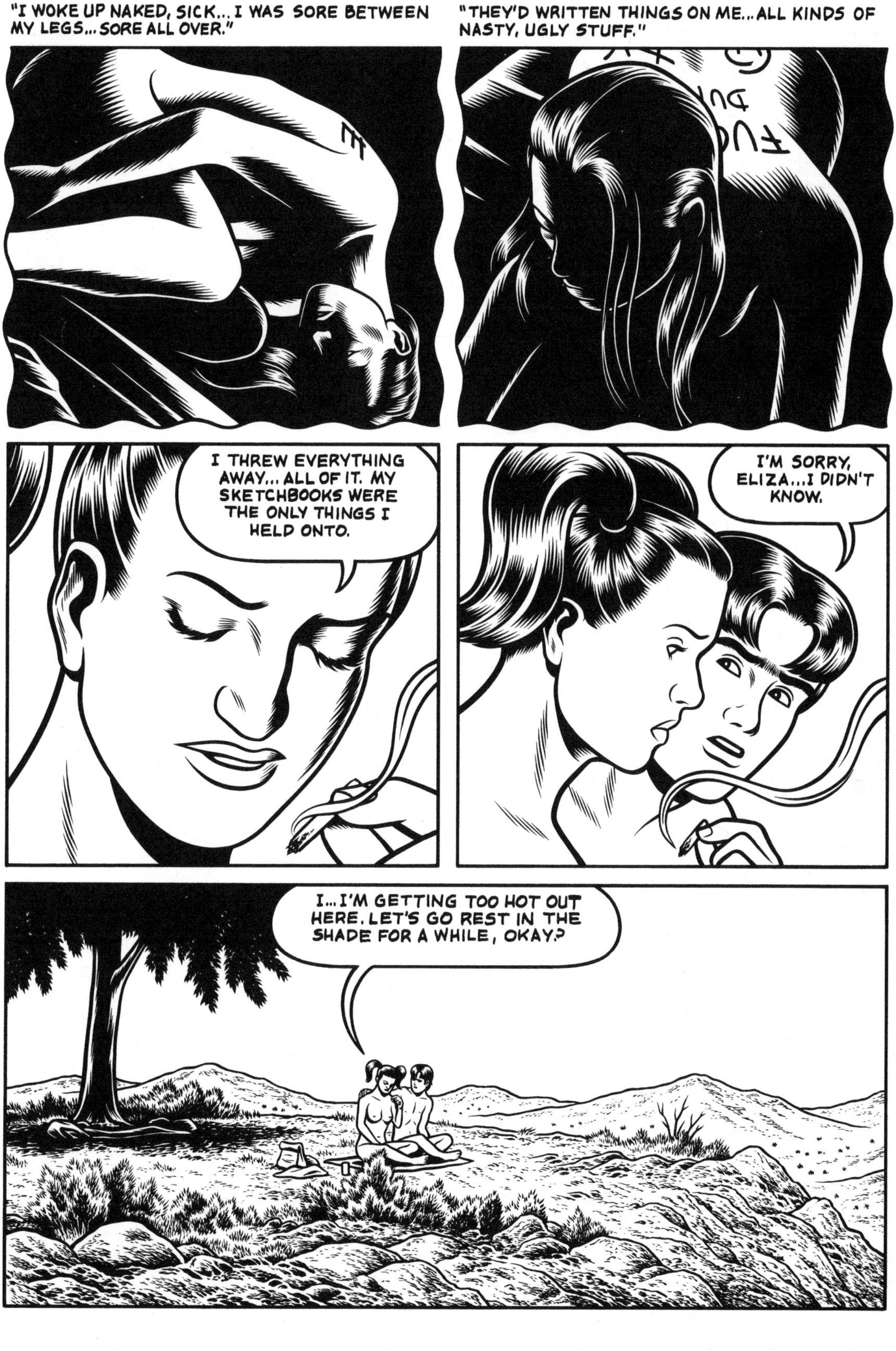
"I WOKE UP NAKED, SICK... I WAS SORE BETWEEN MY LEGS... SORE ALL OVER."
"THEY'D WRITTEN THINGS ON ME... ALL KINDS OF NASTY, UGLY STUFF."
I THREW EVERYTHING AWAY... ALL OF IT. MY SKETCHBOOKS WERE THE ONLY THINGS I HELD ONTO.
I'M SORRY, ELIZA... I DIDN'T KNOW.
I... I'M GETTING TOO HOT OUT HERE. LET'S GO REST IN THE SHADE FOR A WHILE, OKAY?

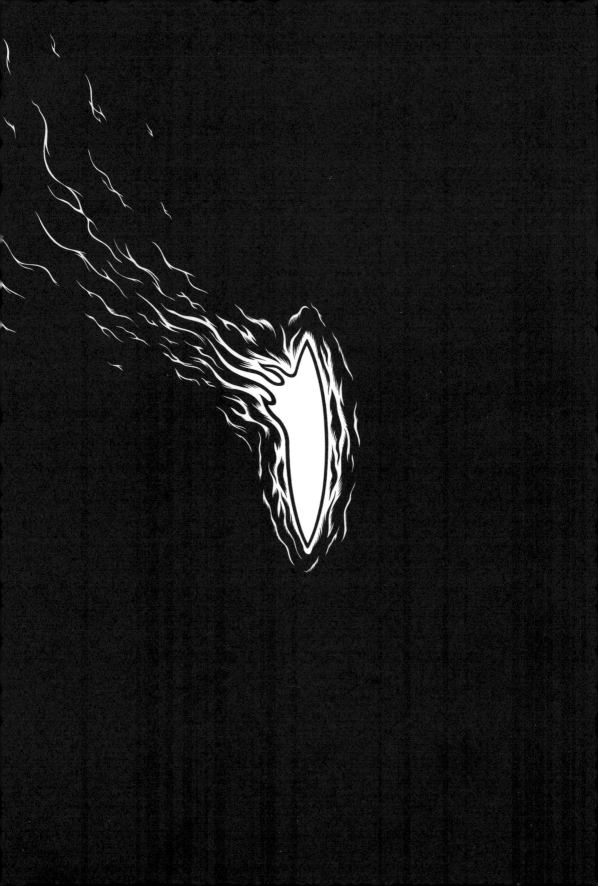

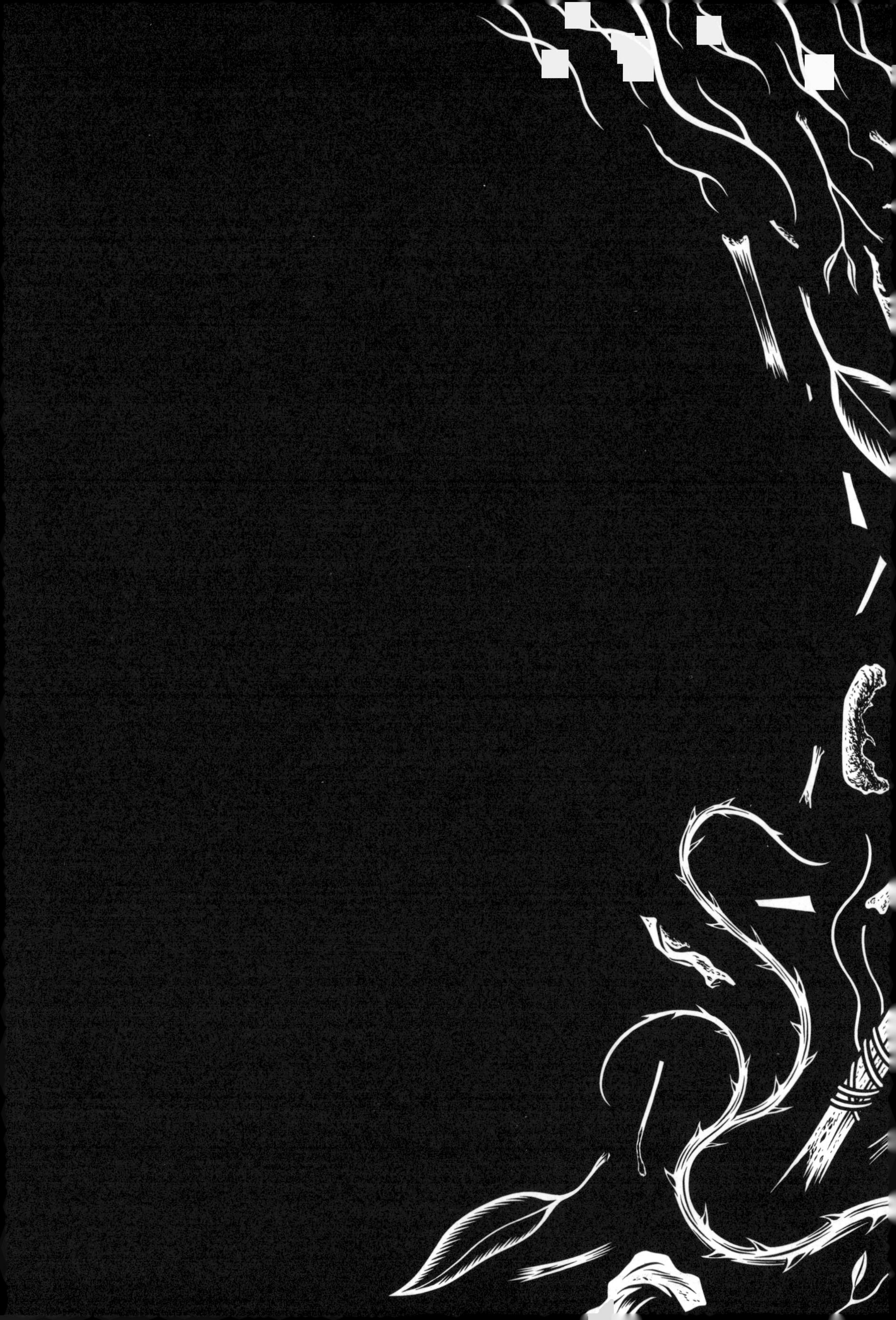

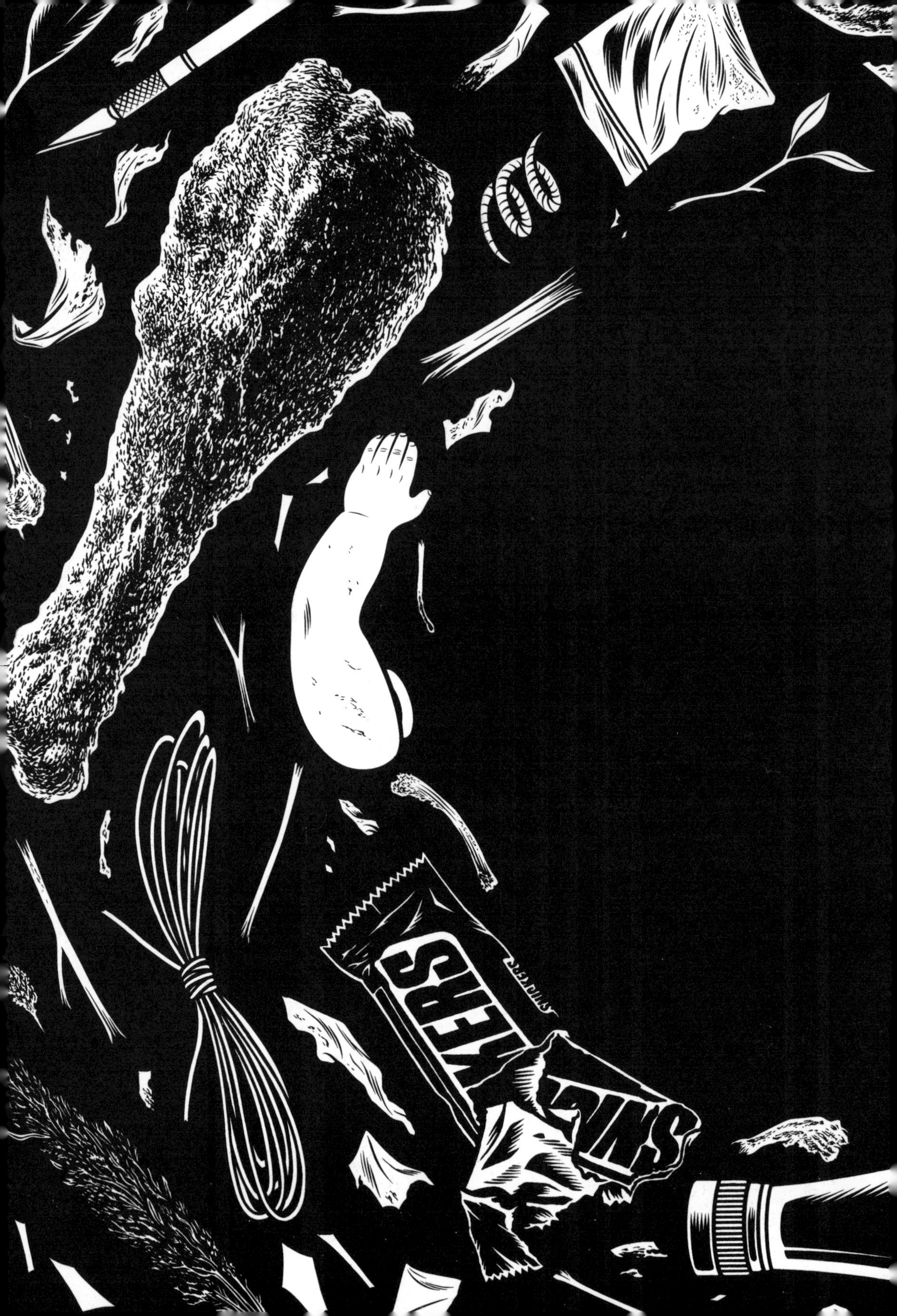
SNICKERS

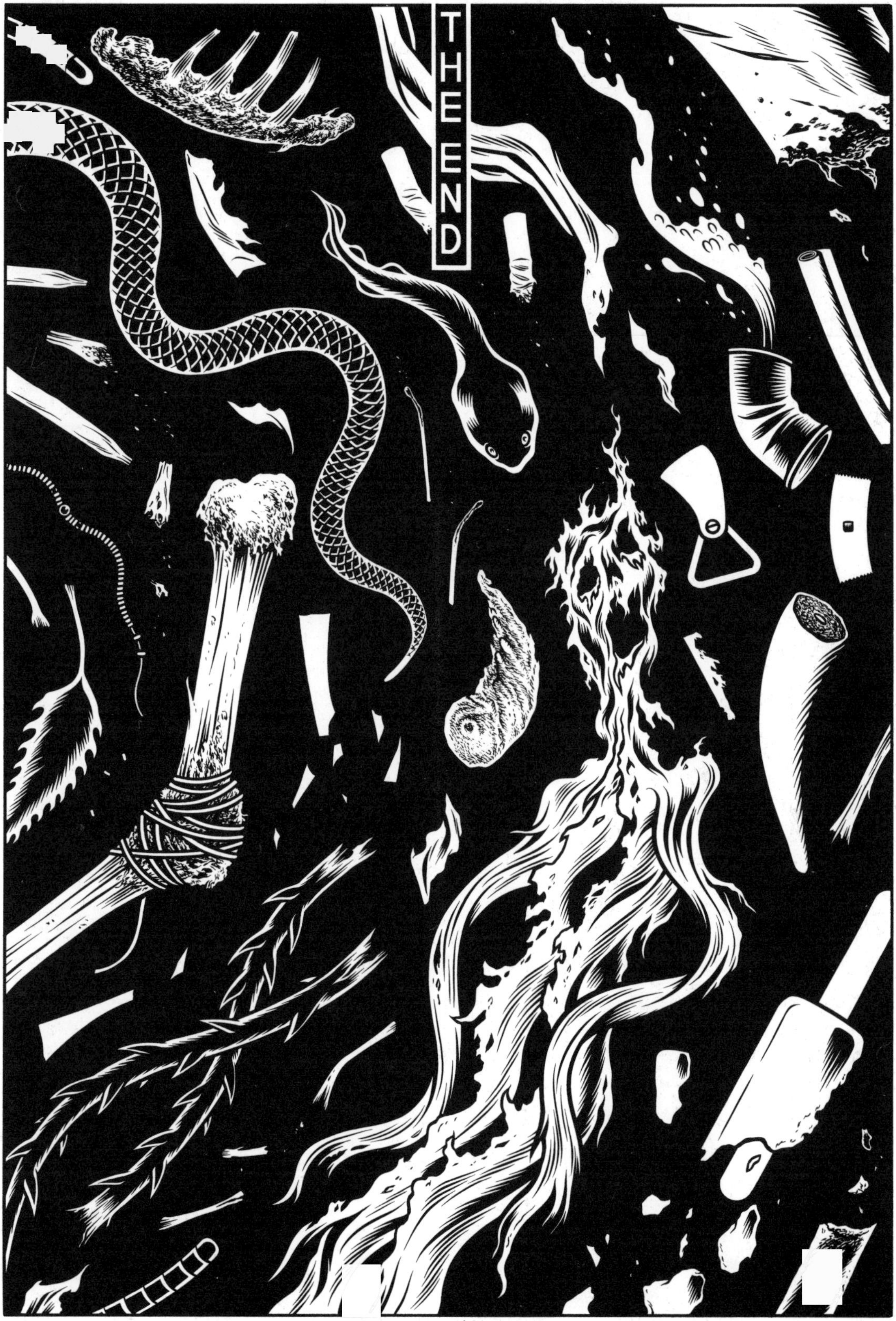
THE END

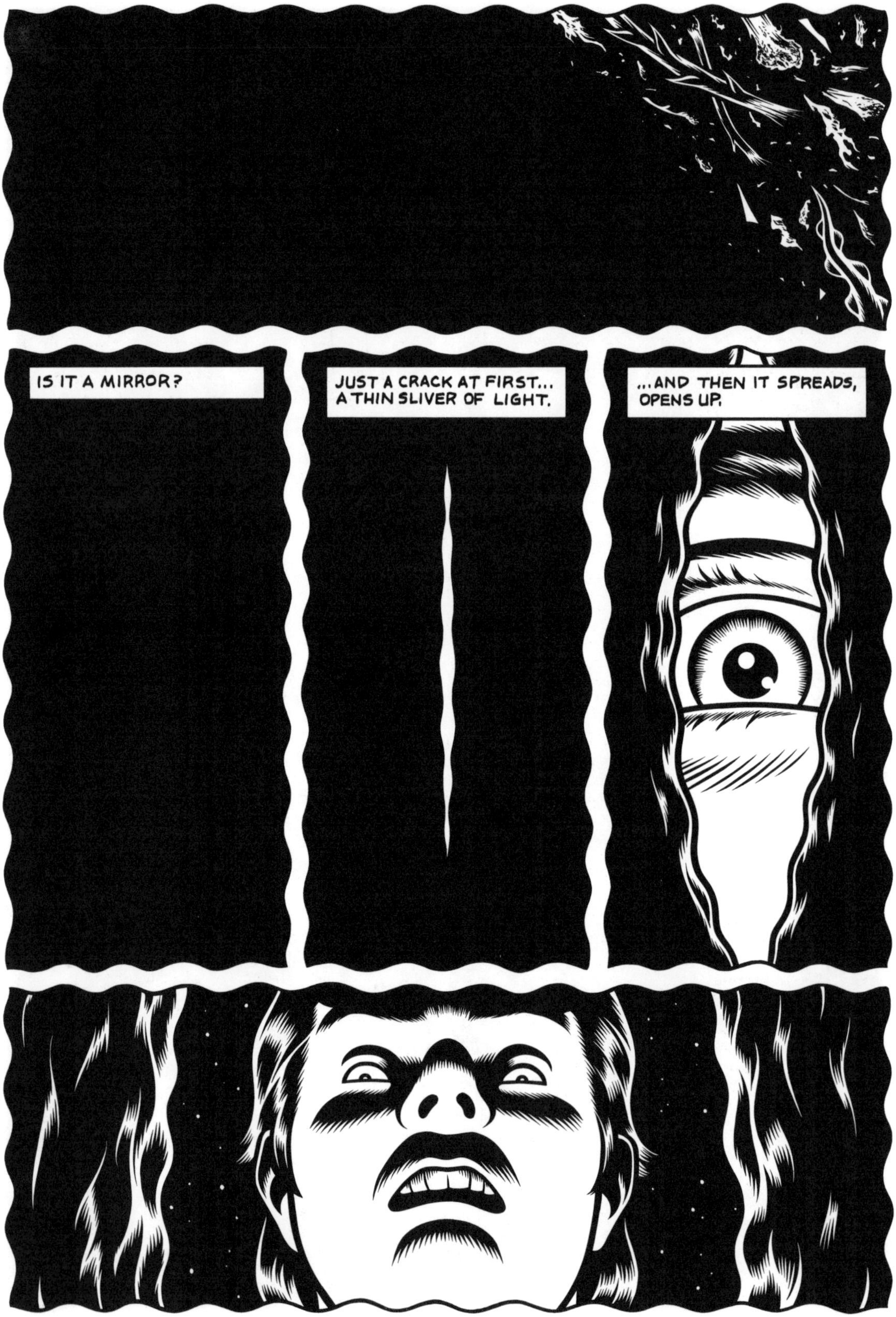
IS IT A MIRROR?
JUST A CRACK AT FIRST... A THIN SLIVER OF LIGHT.
...AND THEN IT SPREADS, OPENS UP.

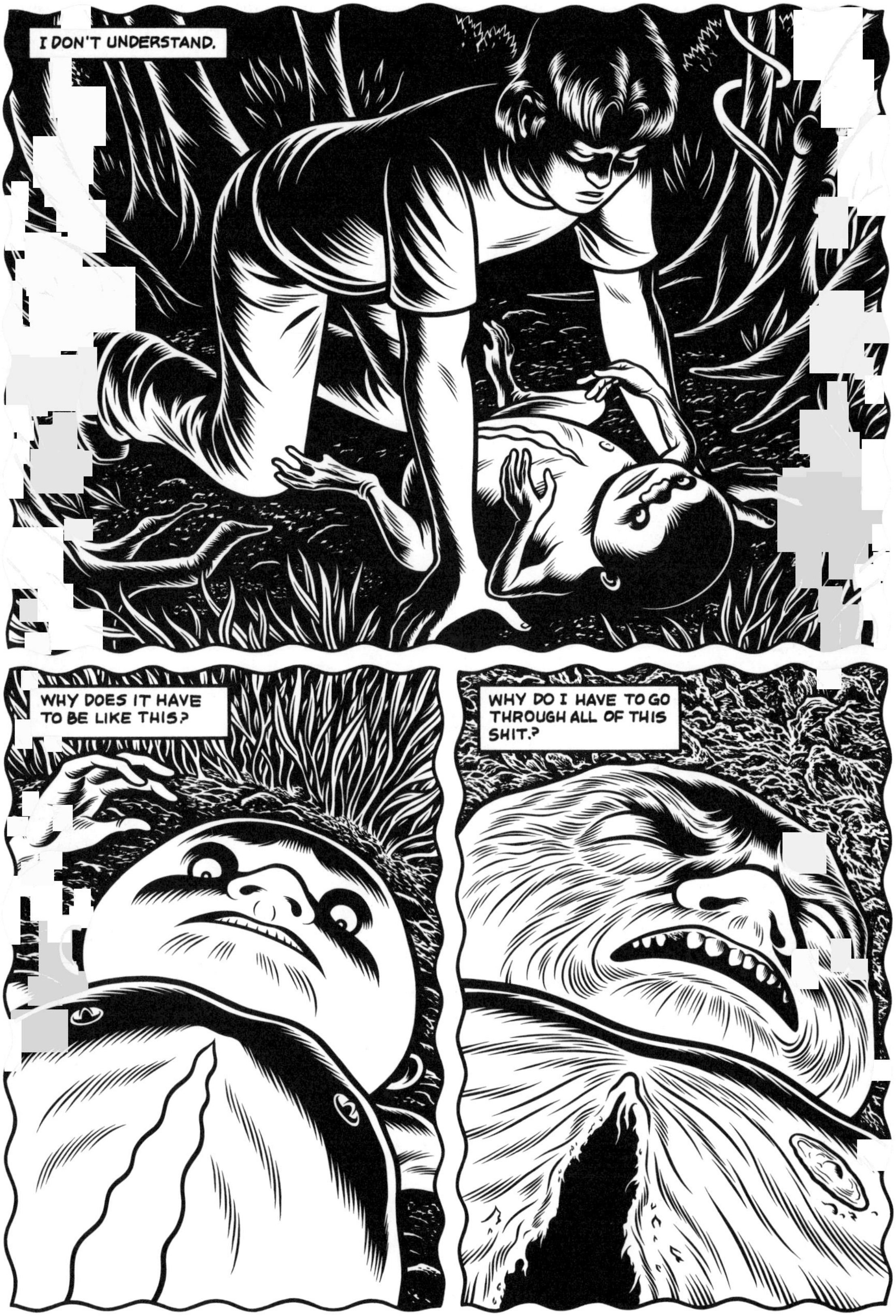
I DON'T UNDERSTAND.
WHY DOES IT HAVE TO BE LIKE THIS?
WHY DO I HAVE TO GO THROUGH ALL OF THIS SHIT.?

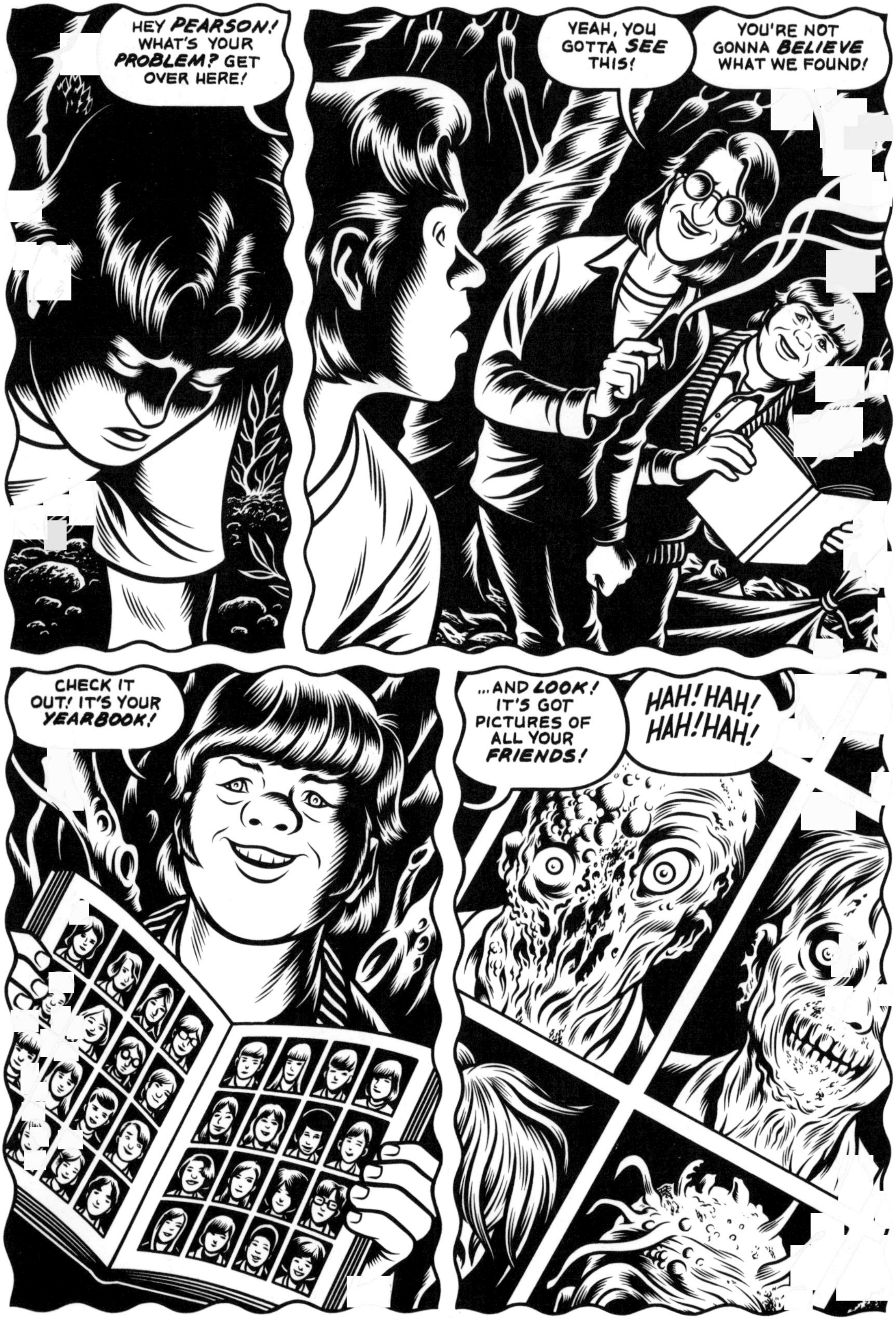
HEY PEARSON! WHAT'S YOUR PROBLEM? GET OVER HERE!
YEAH, YOU GOTTA SEE THIS!
YOU'RE NOT GONNA BELIEVE WHAT WE FOUND!
CHECK IT OUT! IT'S YOUR YEARBOOK!
...AND LOOK! IT'S GOT PICTURES OF ALL YOUR FRIENDS!
HAH! HAH! HAH! HAH!

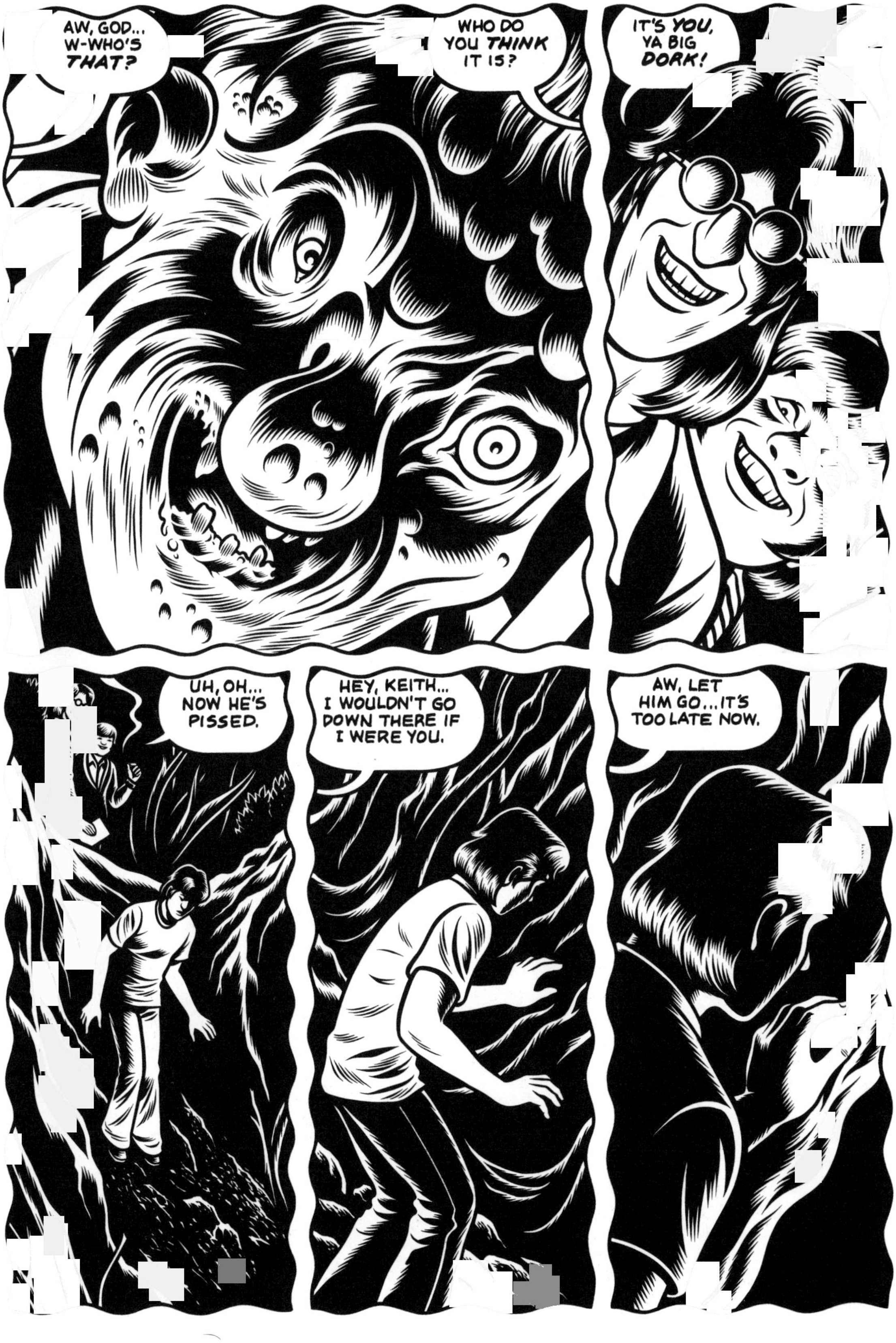
AW, GOD... W-WHO'S *THAT?*
WHO DO YOU *THINK* IT IS?
IT'S *YOU*, YA BIG *DORK!*
UH, OH... NOW HE'S PISSED.
HEY, KEITH... I WOULDN'T GO DOWN THERE IF I WERE YOU.
AW, LET HIM GO... IT'S TOO LATE NOW.

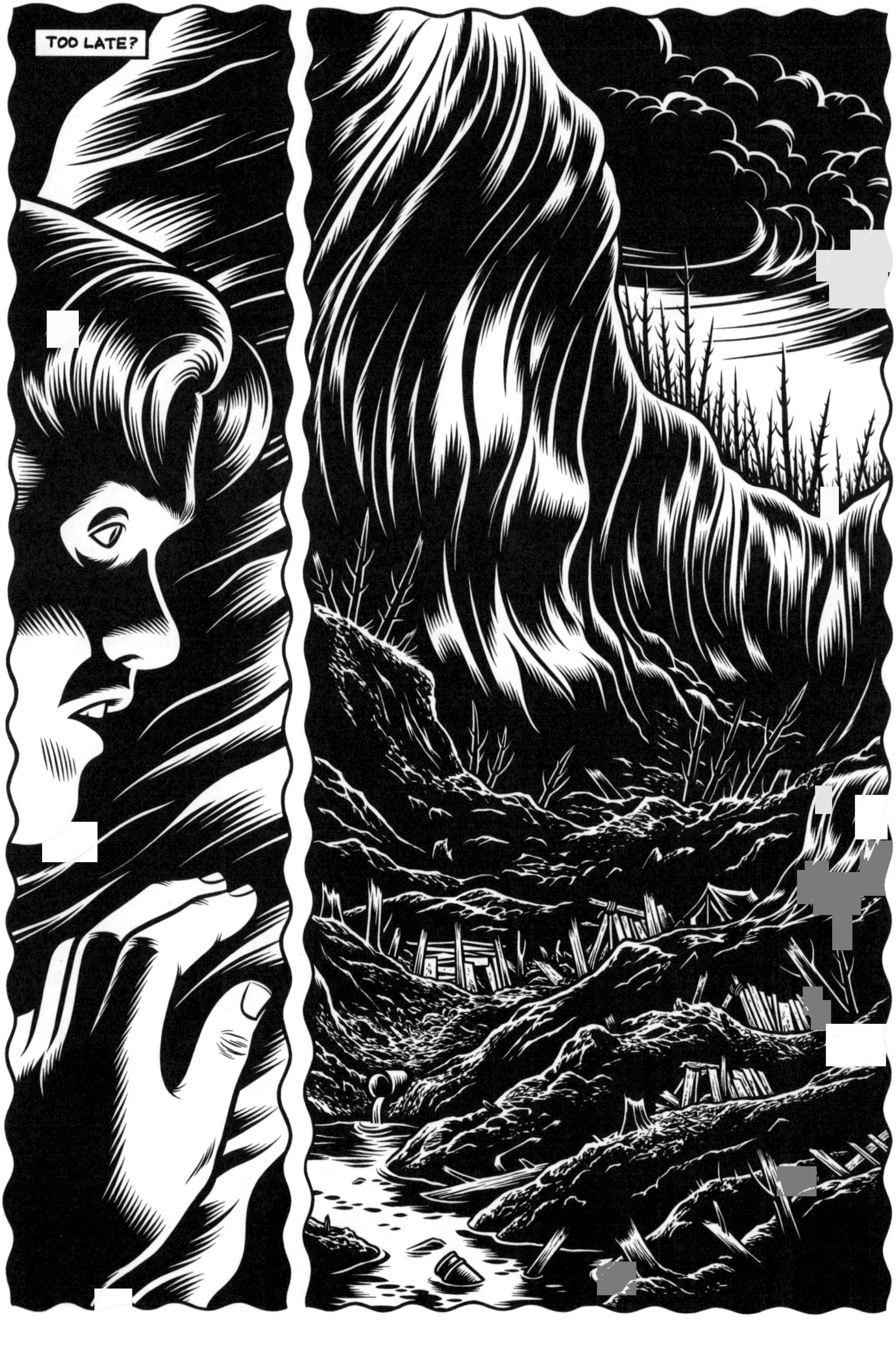
TOO LATE?

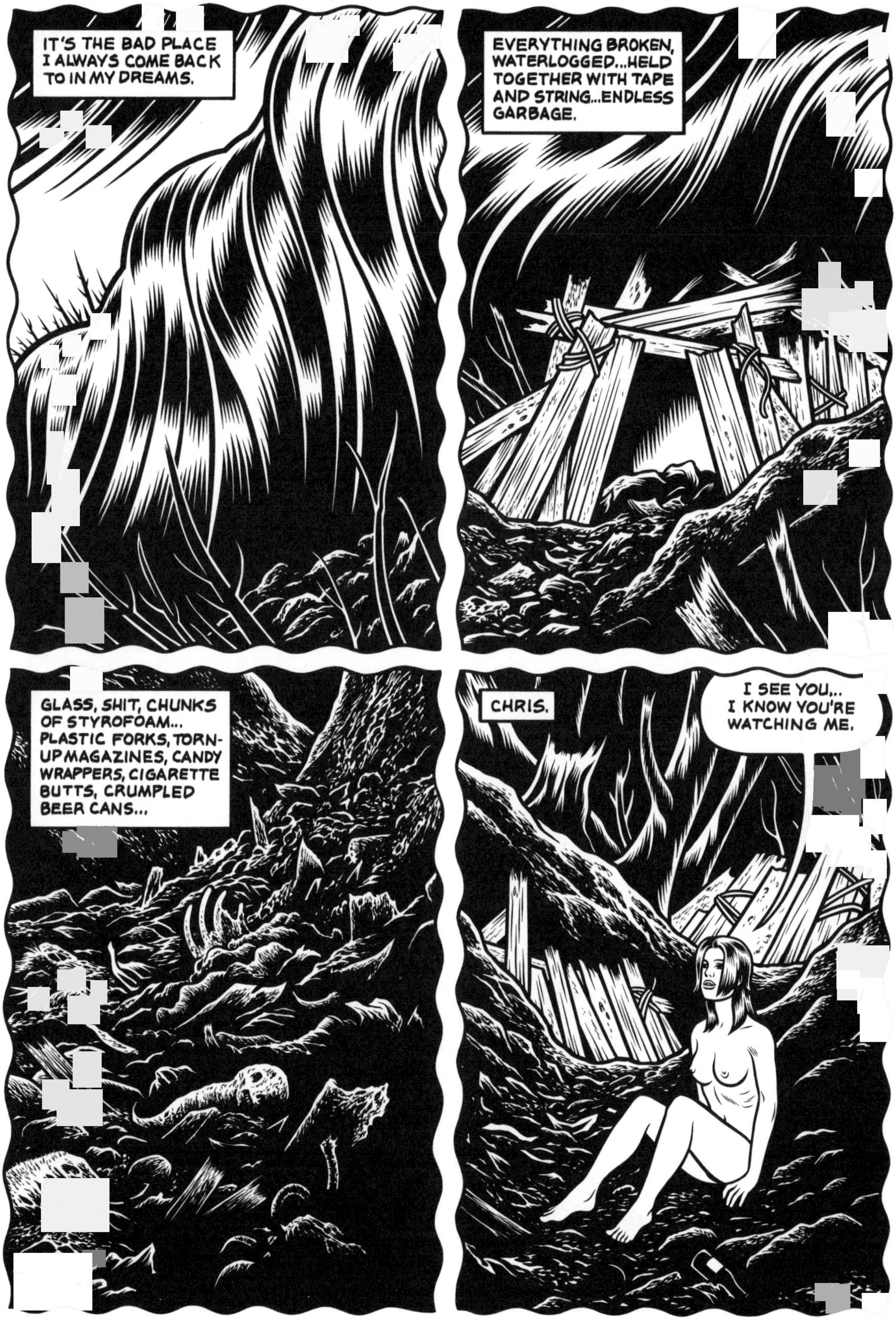
IT'S THE BAD PLACE I ALWAYS COME BACK TO IN MY DREAMS.
EVERYTHING BROKEN, WATERLOGGED...HELD TOGETHER WITH TAPE AND STRING...ENDLESS GARBAGE.
GLASS, SHIT, CHUNKS OF STYROFOAM... PLASTIC FORKS, TORN-UP MAGAZINES, CANDY WRAPPERS, CIGARETTE BUTTS, CRUMPLED BEER CANS...
CHRIS.
I SEE YOU... I KNOW YOU'RE WATCHING ME.

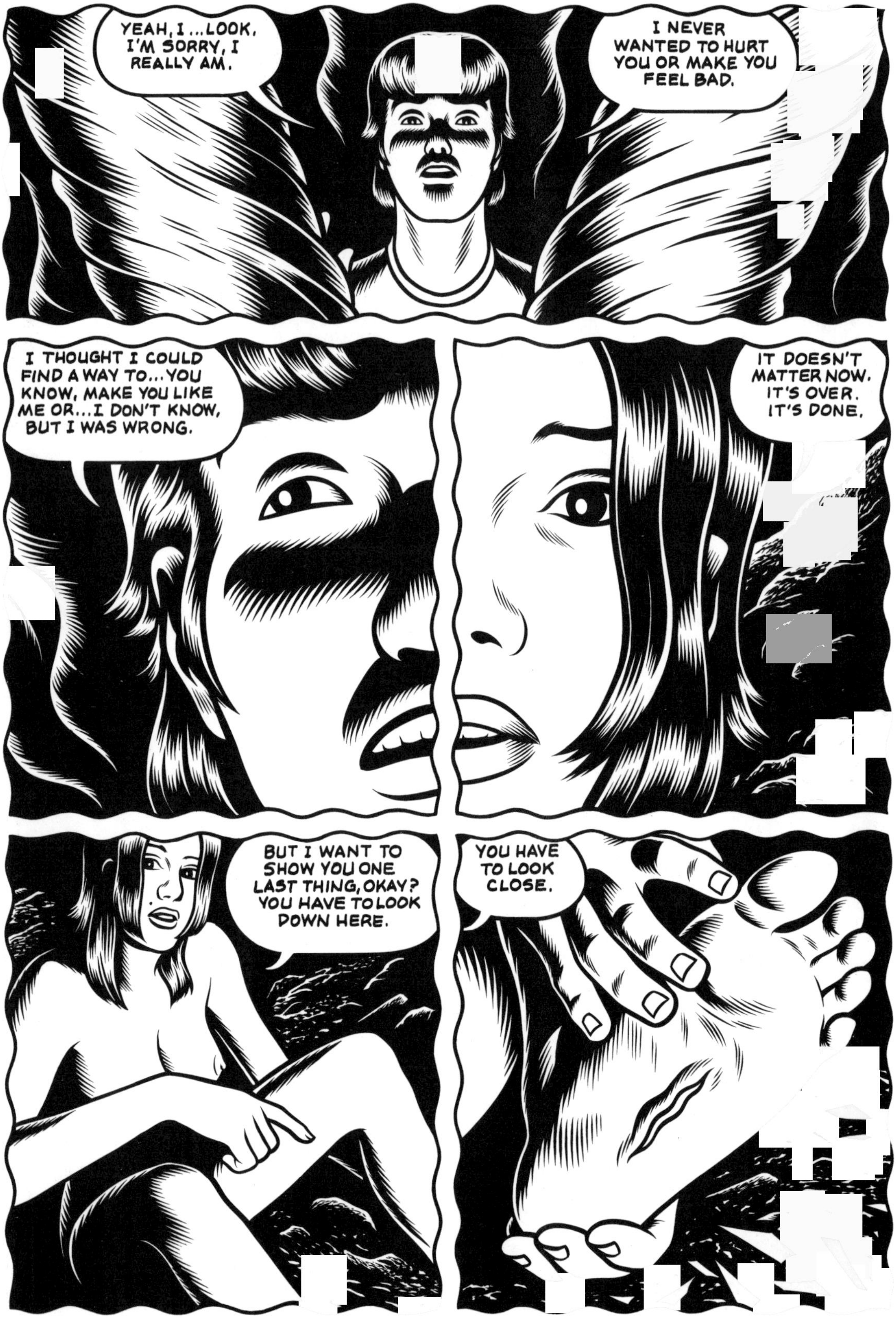
YEAH, I ...LOOK, I'M SORRY, I REALLY AM.
I NEVER WANTED TO HURT YOU OR MAKE YOU FEEL BAD.
I THOUGHT I COULD FIND A WAY TO... YOU KNOW, MAKE YOU LIKE ME OR...I DON'T KNOW, BUT I WAS WRONG.
IT DOESN'T MATTER NOW. IT'S OVER. IT'S DONE.
BUT I WANT TO SHOW YOU ONE LAST THING, OKAY? YOU HAVE TO LOOK DOWN HERE.
YOU HAVE TO LOOK CLOSE.

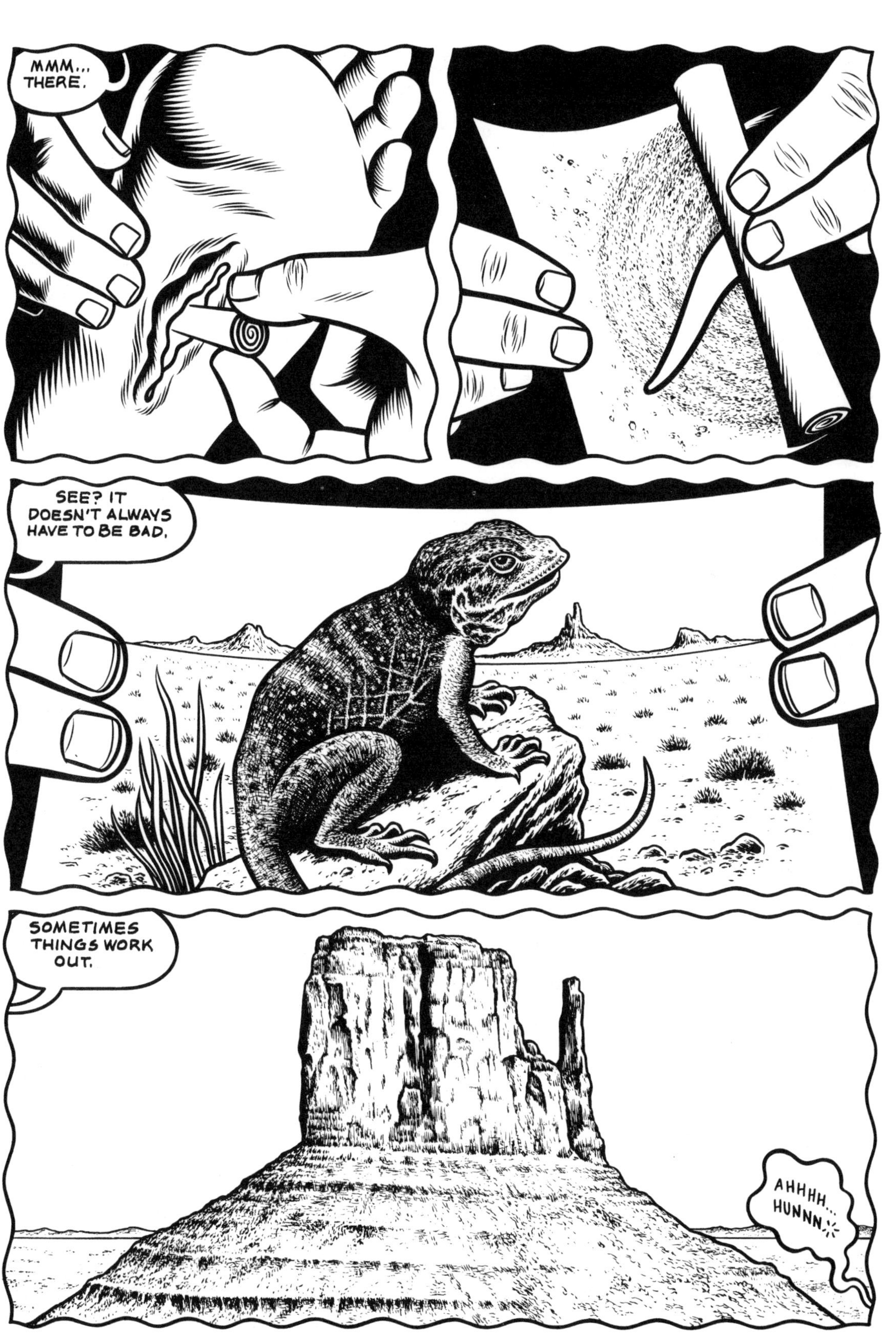
MMM... THERE.
SEE? IT DOESN'T ALWAYS HAVE TO BE BAD.
SOMETIMES THINGS WORK OUT.
AHHHH... HUNNN.

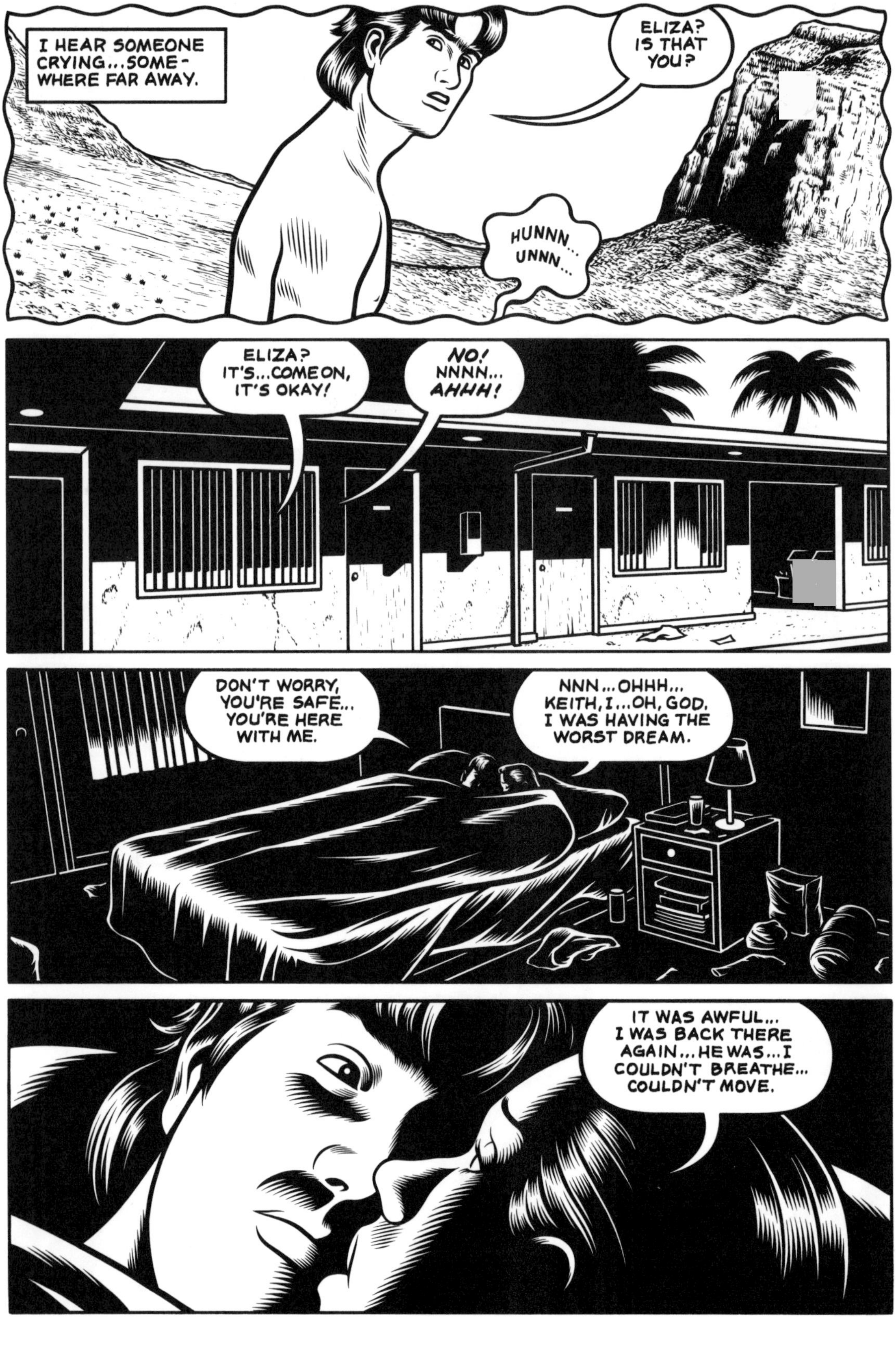
I HEAR SOMEONE CRYING... SOME-WHERE FAR AWAY.
ELIZA? IS THAT YOU?
HUNNN... UNNN...
ELIZA? IT'S... COMEON, IT'S OKAY!
NO! NNNN... AHHH!
DON'T WORRY, YOU'RE SAFE... YOU'RE HERE WITH ME.
NNN... OHHH... KEITH, I... OH, GOD, I WAS HAVING THE WORST DREAM.
IT WAS AWFUL... I WAS BACK THERE AGAIN... HE WAS... I COULDN'T BREATHE... COULDN'T MOVE.

IT TAKES ME A FEW MOMENTS TO FIGURE OUT WHERE WE ARE.

THE RATTLING HUM OF AN AIR CONDITIONER, A BIG, SOFT BED...

KEITH?

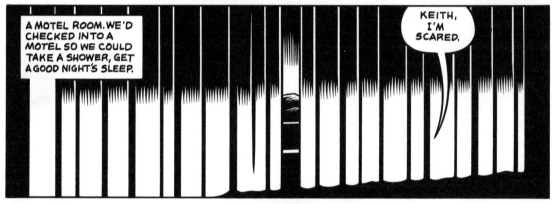

A MOTEL ROOM. WE'D CHECKED INTO A MOTEL SO WE COULD TAKE A SHOWER, GET A GOOD NIGHT'S SLEEP.

KEITH, I'M SCARED.

TELL ME SOMETHING NICE... TELL ME EVERYTHING'S GOING TO BE OKAY.

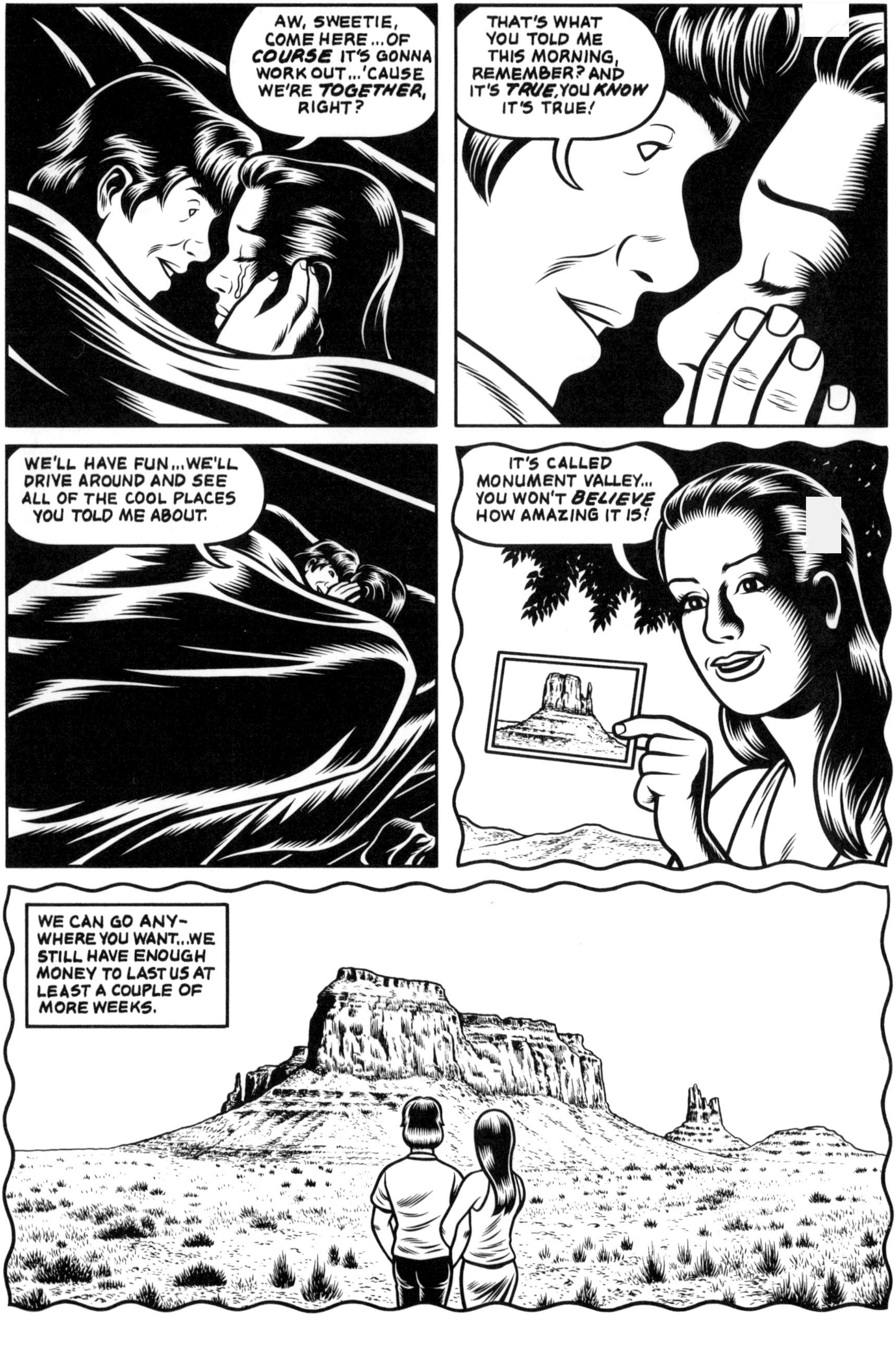
AW, SWEETIE, COME HERE...OF COURSE IT'S GONNA WORK OUT...'CAUSE WE'RE TOGETHER, RIGHT?
THAT'S WHAT YOU TOLD ME THIS MORNING, REMEMBER? AND IT'S TRUE, YOU KNOW IT'S TRUE!
WE'LL HAVE FUN...WE'LL DRIVE AROUND AND SEE ALL OF THE COOL PLACES YOU TOLD ME ABOUT.
IT'S CALLED MONUMENT VALLEY... YOU WON'T BELIEVE HOW AMAZING IT IS!
WE CAN GO ANY-WHERE YOU WANT...WE STILL HAVE ENOUGH MONEY TO LAST US AT LEAST A COUPLE OF MORE WEEKS.

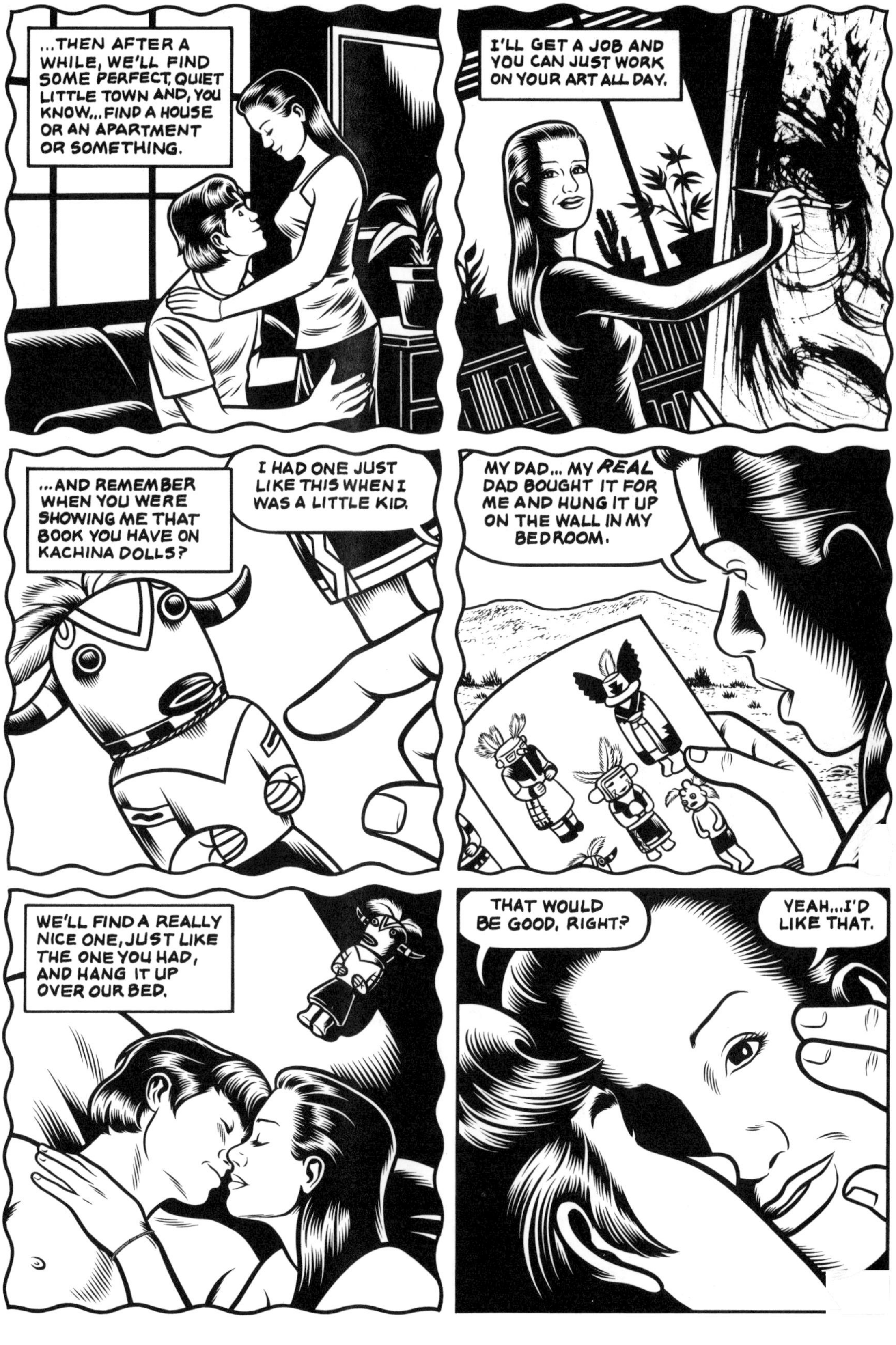
...THEN AFTER A WHILE, WE'LL FIND SOME PERFECT, QUIET LITTLE TOWN AND, YOU KNOW,...FIND A HOUSE OR AN APARTMENT OR SOMETHING.
I'LL GET A JOB AND YOU CAN JUST WORK ON YOUR ART ALL DAY.
...AND REMEMBER WHEN YOU WERE SHOWING ME THAT BOOK YOU HAVE ON KACHINA DOLLS?
I HAD ONE JUST LIKE THIS WHEN I WAS A LITTLE KID.
MY DAD... MY *REAL* DAD BOUGHT IT FOR ME AND HUNG IT UP ON THE WALL IN MY BEDROOM.
WE'LL FIND A REALLY NICE ONE, JUST LIKE THE ONE YOU HAD, AND HANG IT UP OVER OUR BED.
THAT WOULD BE GOOD, RIGHT?
YEAH...I'D LIKE THAT.

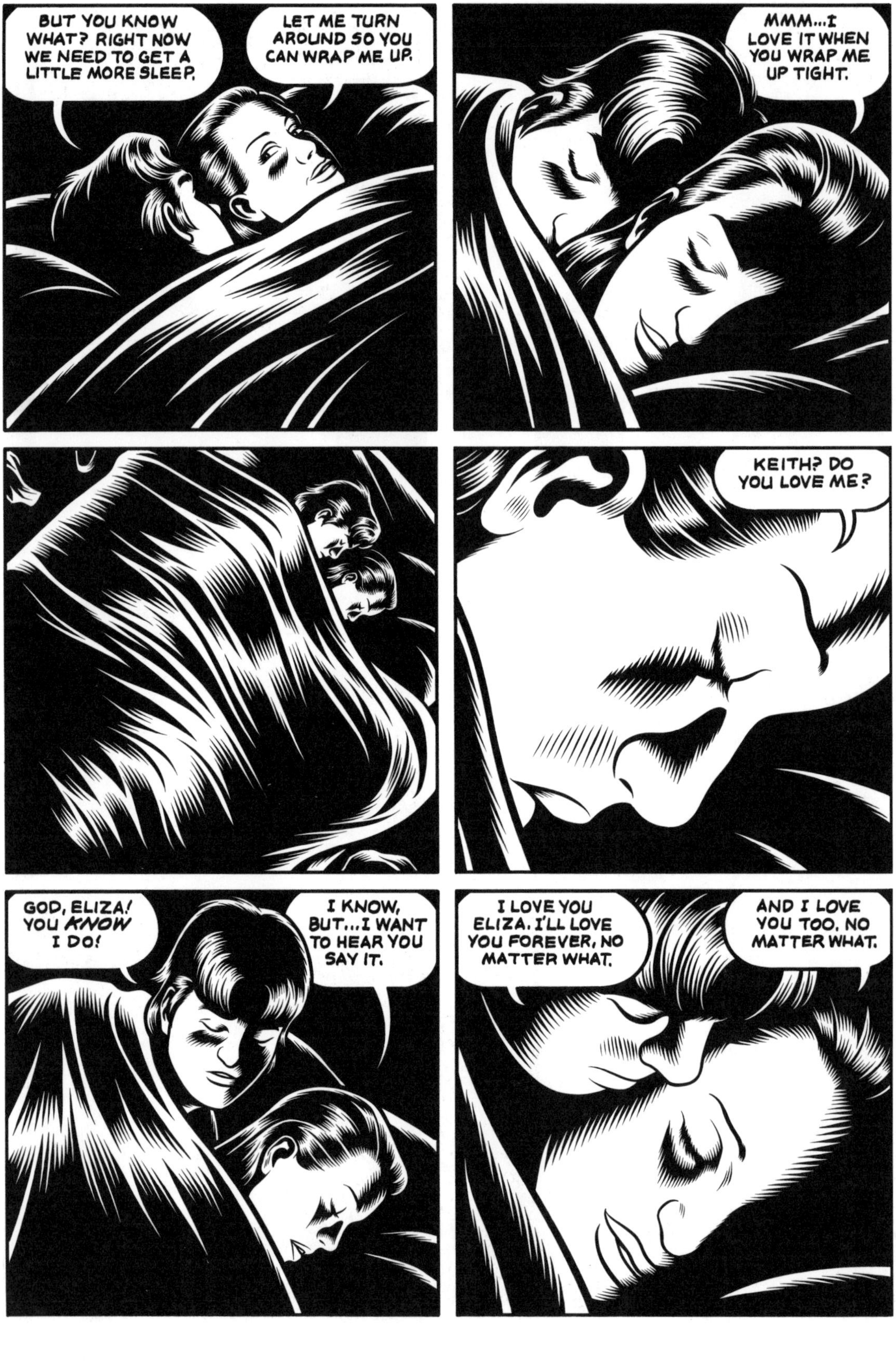
BUT YOU KNOW WHAT? RIGHT NOW WE NEED TO GET A LITTLE MORE SLEEP.
LET ME TURN AROUND SO YOU CAN WRAP ME UP.
MMM...I LOVE IT WHEN YOU WRAP ME UP TIGHT.
KEITH? DO YOU LOVE ME?
GOD, ELIZA! YOU *KNOW* I DO!
I KNOW, BUT...I WANT TO HEAR YOU SAY IT.
I LOVE YOU ELIZA. I'LL LOVE YOU FOREVER, NO MATTER WHAT.
AND I LOVE YOU TOO, NO MATTER WHAT.

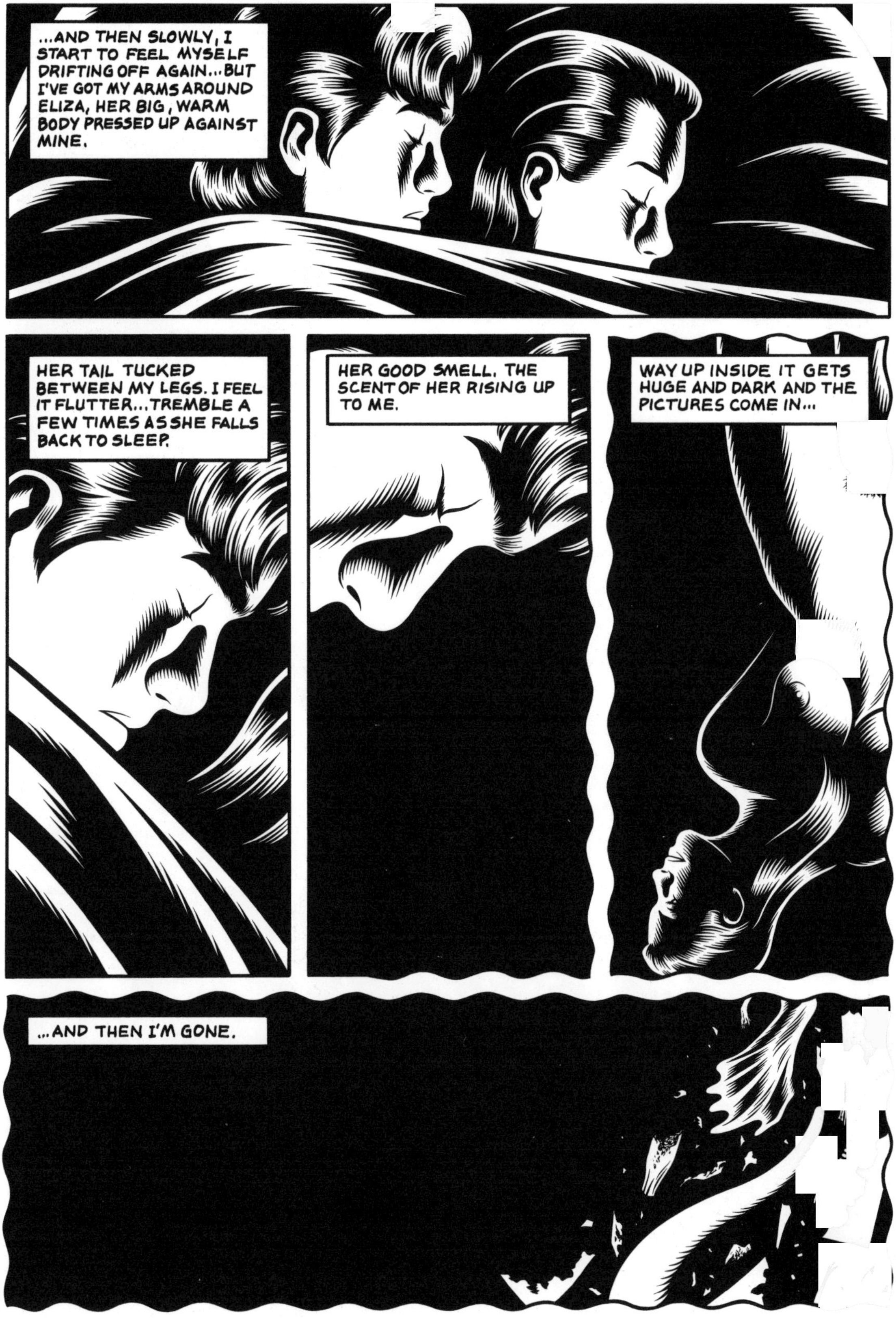
...AND THEN SLOWLY, I START TO FEEL MYSELF DRIFTING OFF AGAIN... BUT I'VE GOT MY ARMS AROUND ELIZA, HER BIG, WARM BODY PRESSED UP AGAINST MINE.
HER TAIL TUCKED BETWEEN MY LEGS. I FEEL IT FLUTTER... TREMBLE A FEW TIMES AS SHE FALLS BACK TO SLEEP.
HER GOOD SMELL. THE SCENT OF HER RISING UP TO ME.
WAY UP INSIDE IT GETS HUGE AND DARK AND THE PICTURES COME IN...
...AND THEN I'M GONE.

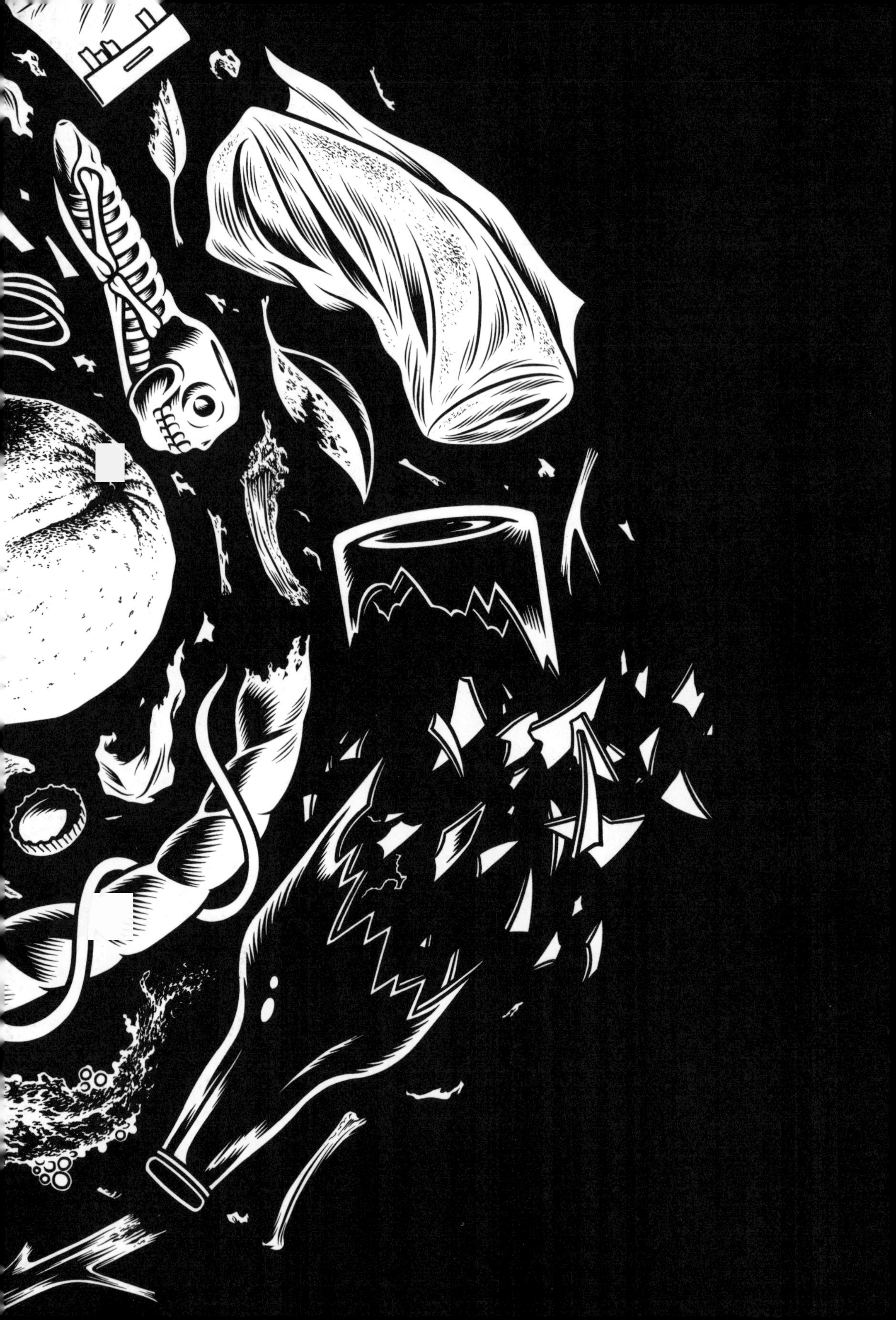

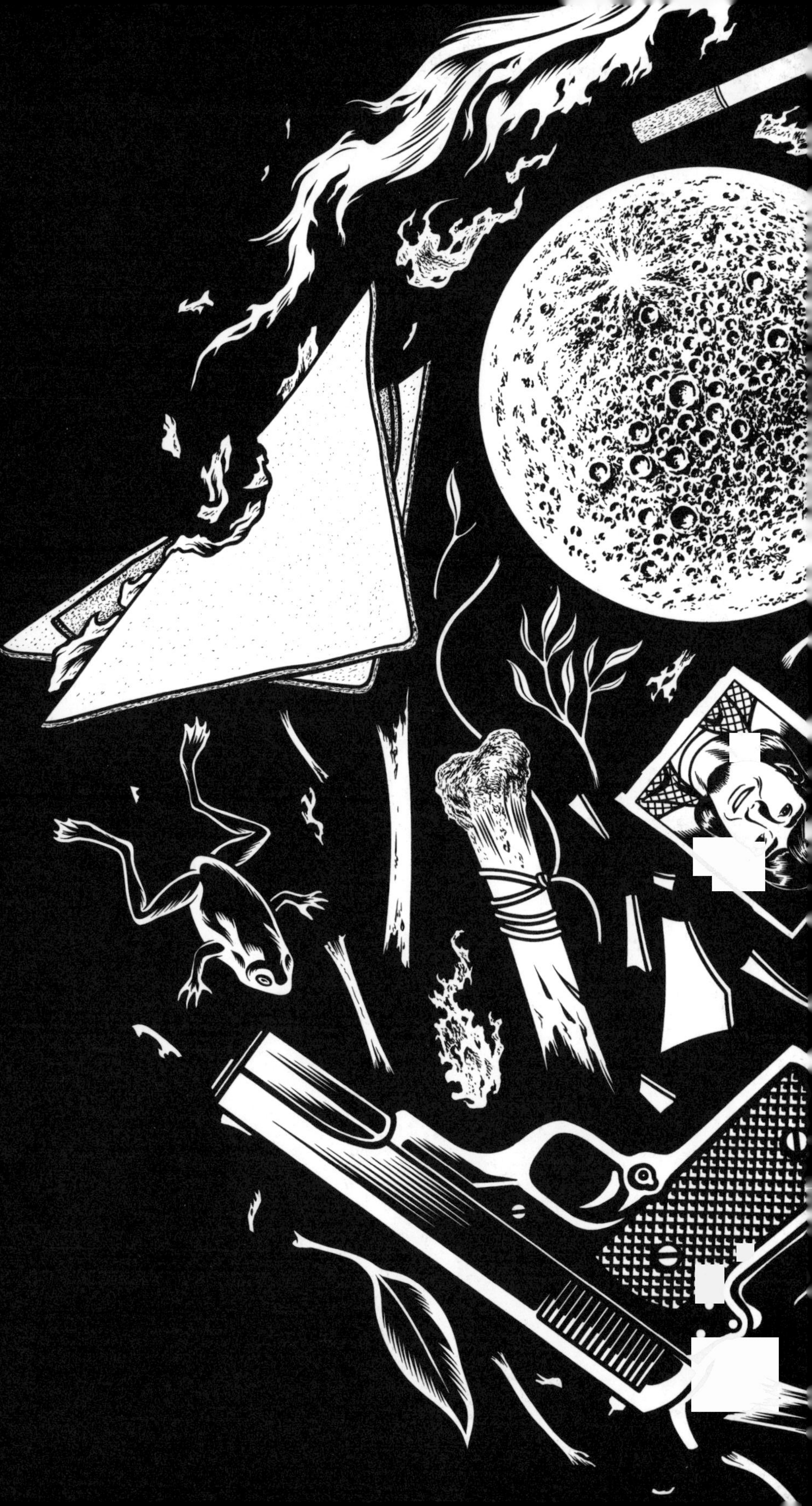

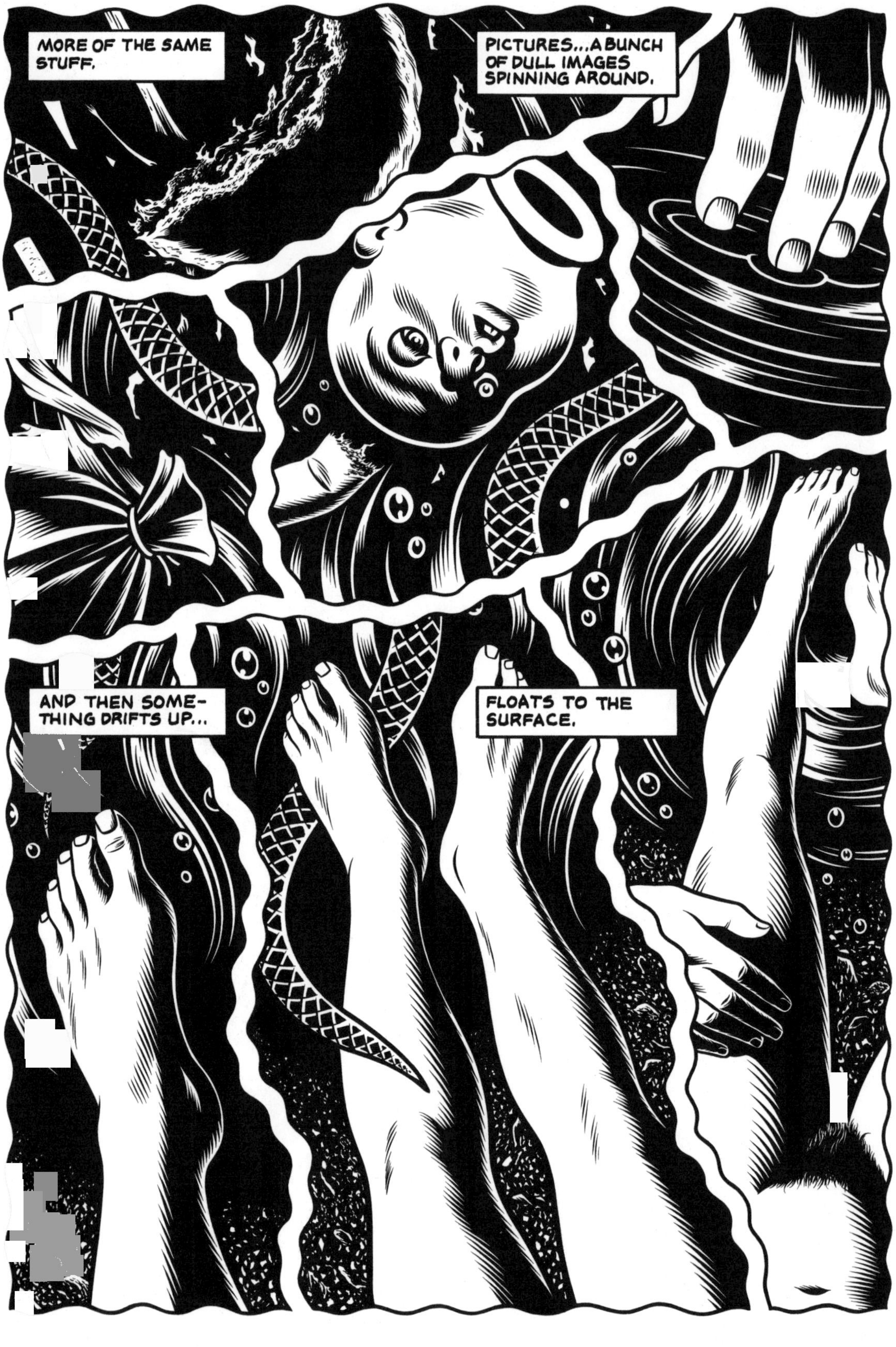
MORE OF THE SAME STUFF.
PICTURES...A BUNCH OF DULL IMAGES SPINNING AROUND.
AND THEN SOME-THING DRIFTS UP...
FLOATS TO THE SURFACE.

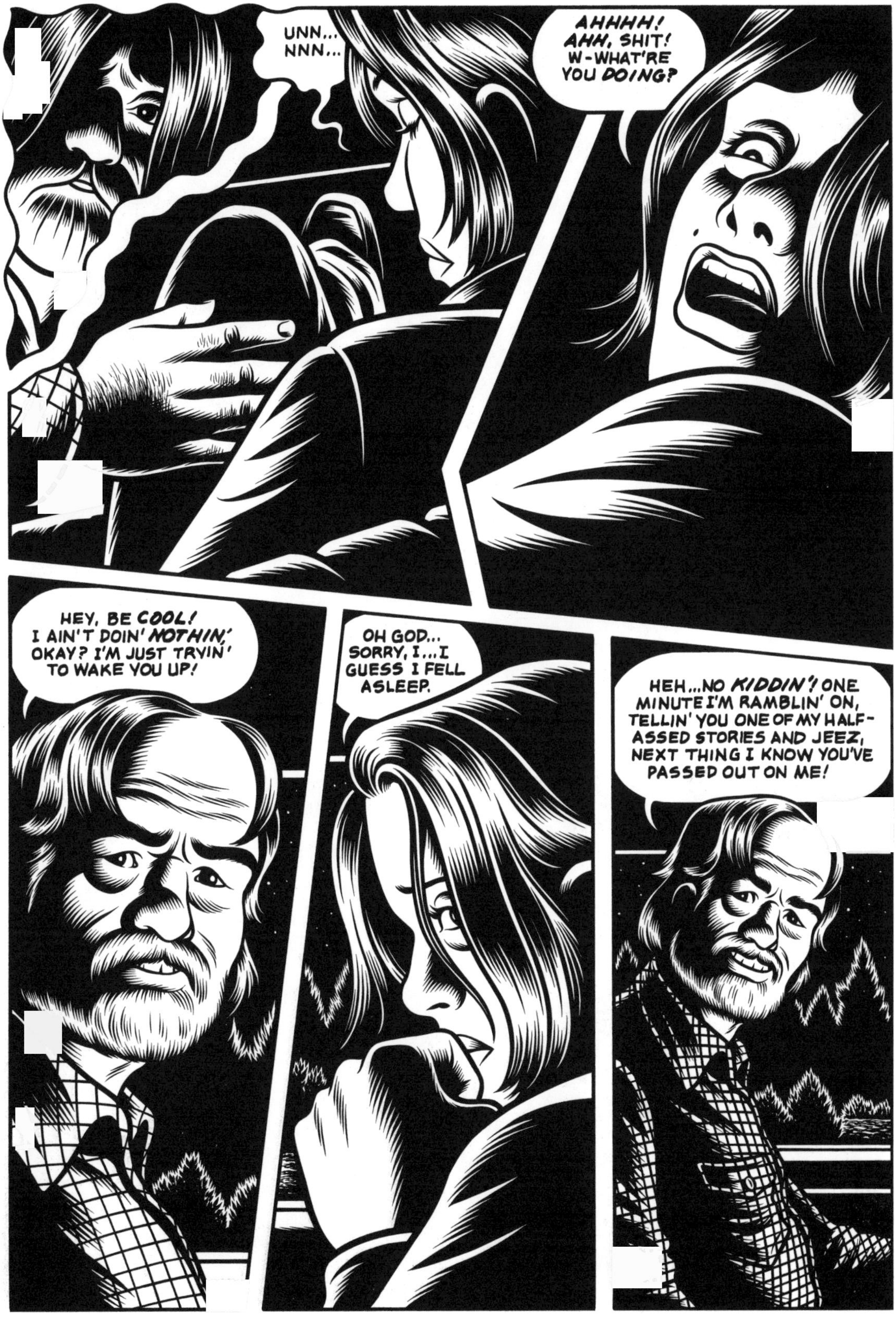
UNN... NNN...
AHHHH! AHH, SHIT! W-WHAT'RE YOU DOING?
HEY, BE COOL! I AIN'T DOIN' NOTHIN,' OKAY? I'M JUST TRYIN' TO WAKE YOU UP!
OH GOD... SORRY, I...I GUESS I FELL ASLEEP.
HEH...NO KIDDIN'! ONE MINUTE I'M RAMBLIN' ON, TELLIN' YOU ONE OF MY HALF-ASSED STORIES AND JEEZ, NEXT THING I KNOW YOU'VE PASSED OUT ON ME!

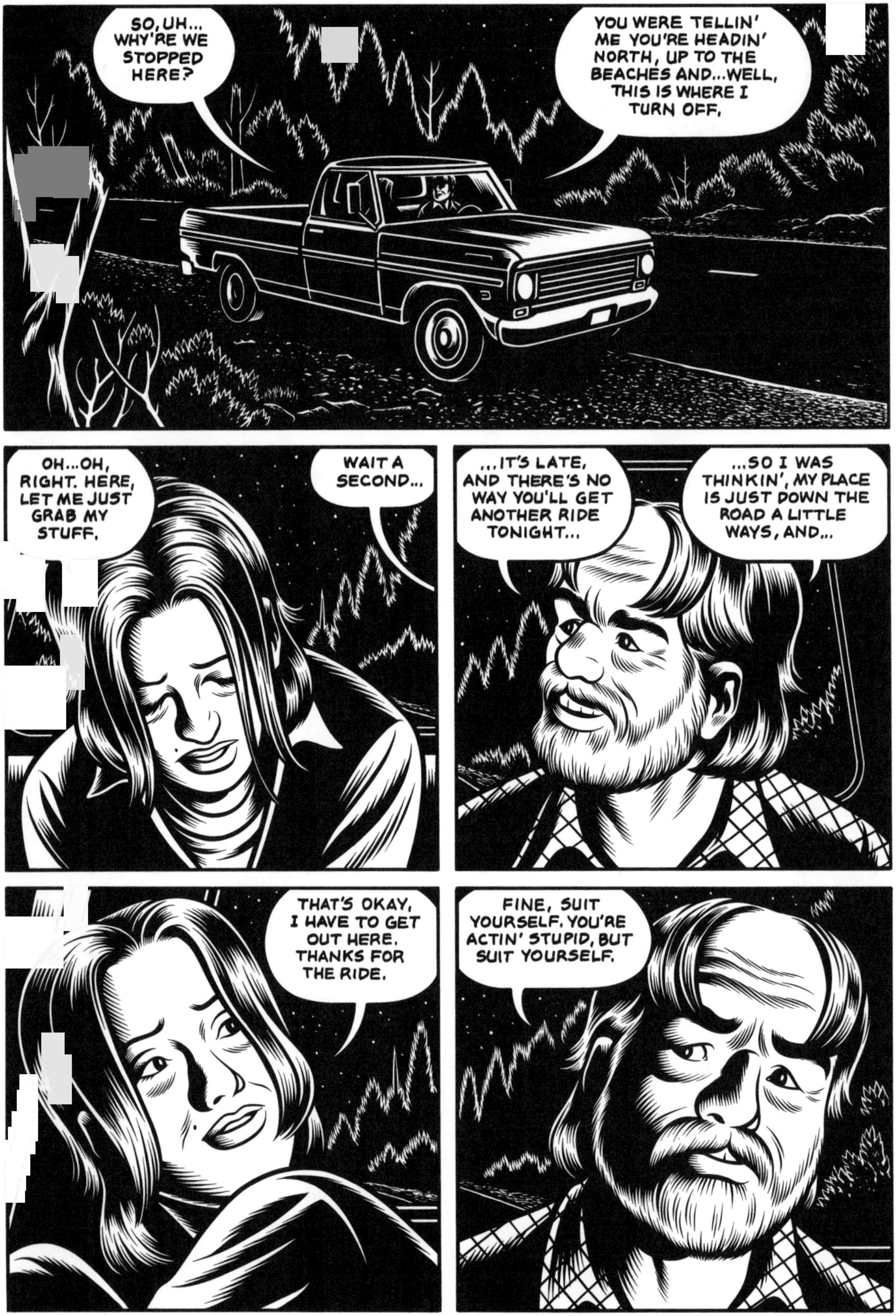
SO, UH... WHY'RE WE STOPPED HERE?
YOU WERE TELLIN' ME YOU'RE HEADIN' NORTH, UP TO THE BEACHES AND...WELL, THIS IS WHERE I TURN OFF.
OH...OH, RIGHT. HERE, LET ME JUST GRAB MY STUFF.
WAIT A SECOND...
...IT'S LATE, AND THERE'S NO WAY YOU'LL GET ANOTHER RIDE TONIGHT...
...SO I WAS THINKIN', MY PLACE IS JUST DOWN THE ROAD A LITTLE WAYS, AND...
THAT'S OKAY, I HAVE TO GET OUT HERE. THANKS FOR THE RIDE.
FINE, SUIT YOURSELF. YOU'RE ACTIN' STUPID, BUT SUIT YOURSELF.

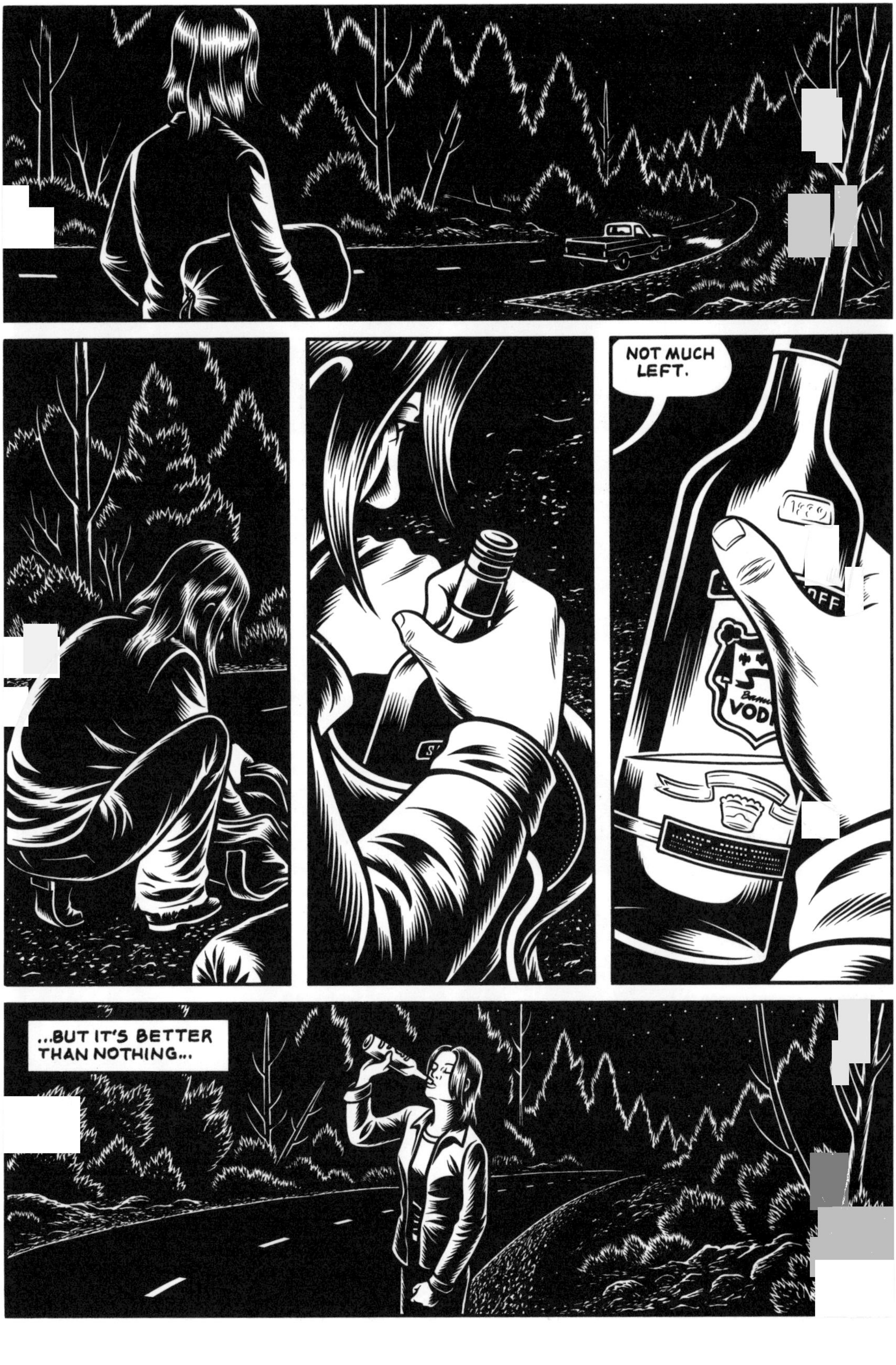
NOT MUCH LEFT.
...BUT IT'S BETTER THAN NOTHING...

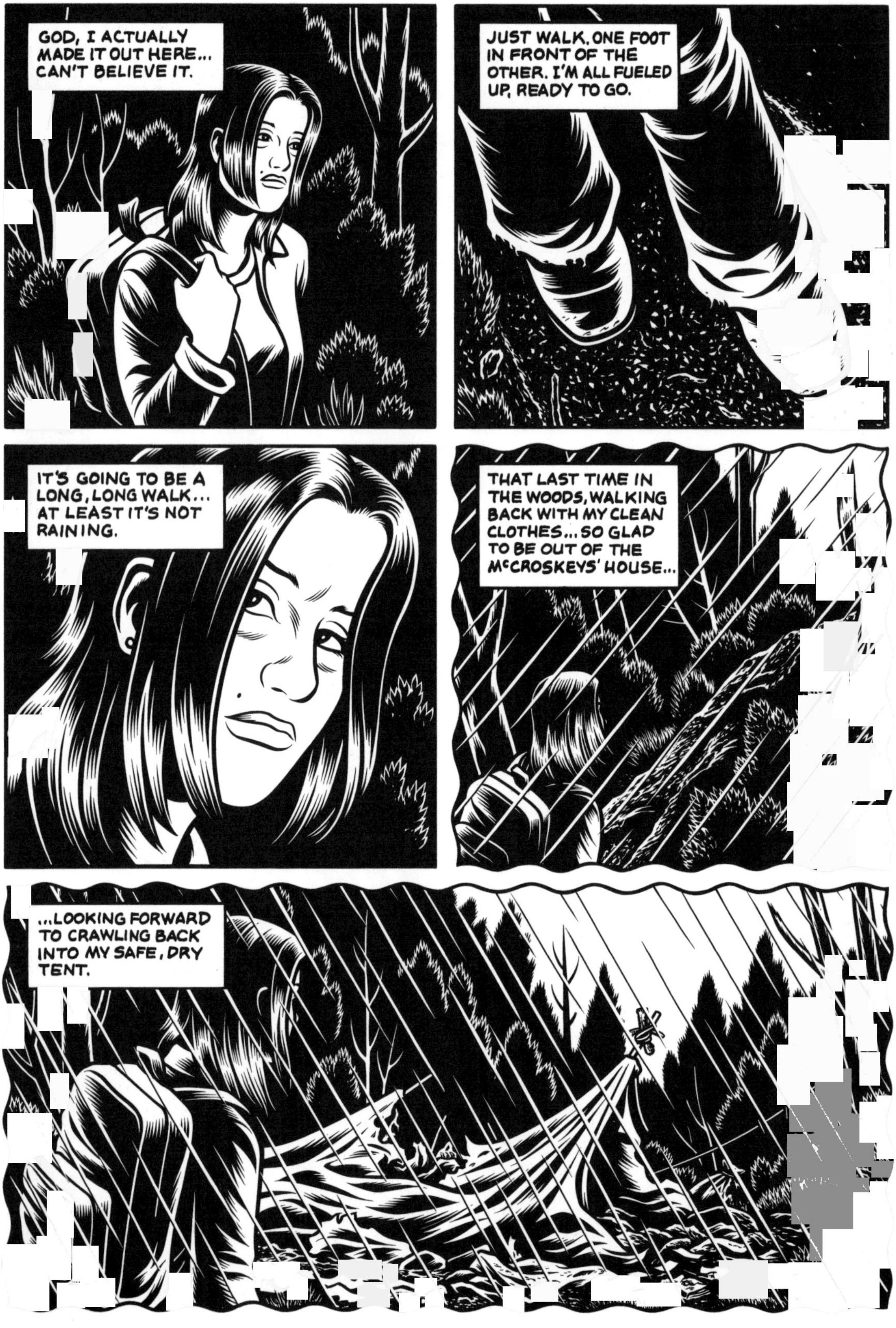
GOD, I ACTUALLY MADE IT OUT HERE... CAN'T BELIEVE IT.
JUST WALK, ONE FOOT IN FRONT OF THE OTHER. I'M ALL FUELED UP, READY TO GO.
IT'S GOING TO BE A LONG, LONG WALK... AT LEAST IT'S NOT RAINING.
THAT LAST TIME IN THE WOODS, WALKING BACK WITH MY CLEAN CLOTHES... SO GLAD TO BE OUT OF THE McCROSKEYS' HOUSE...
...LOOKING FORWARD TO CRAWLING BACK INTO MY SAFE, DRY TENT.

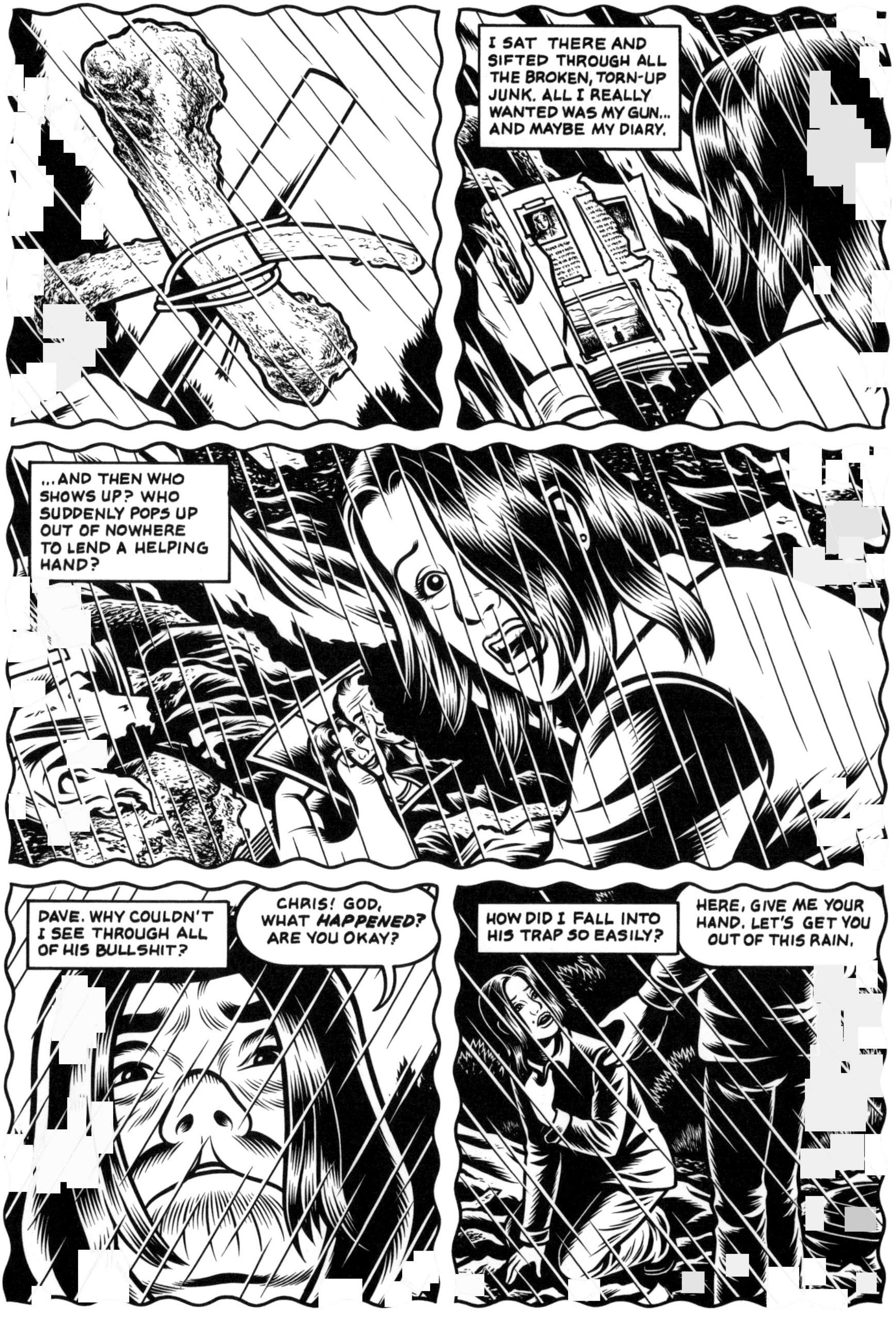

I SAT THERE AND SIFTED THROUGH ALL THE BROKEN, TORN-UP JUNK. ALL I REALLY WANTED WAS MY GUN... AND MAYBE MY DIARY.
...AND THEN WHO SHOWS UP? WHO SUDDENLY POPS UP OUT OF NOWHERE TO LEND A HELPING HAND?
DAVE. WHY COULDN'T I SEE THROUGH ALL OF HIS BULLSHIT?
CHRIS! GOD, WHAT *HAPPENED*? ARE YOU OKAY?
HOW DID I FALL INTO HIS TRAP SO EASILY?
HERE, GIVE ME YOUR HAND. LET'S GET YOU OUT OF THIS RAIN.

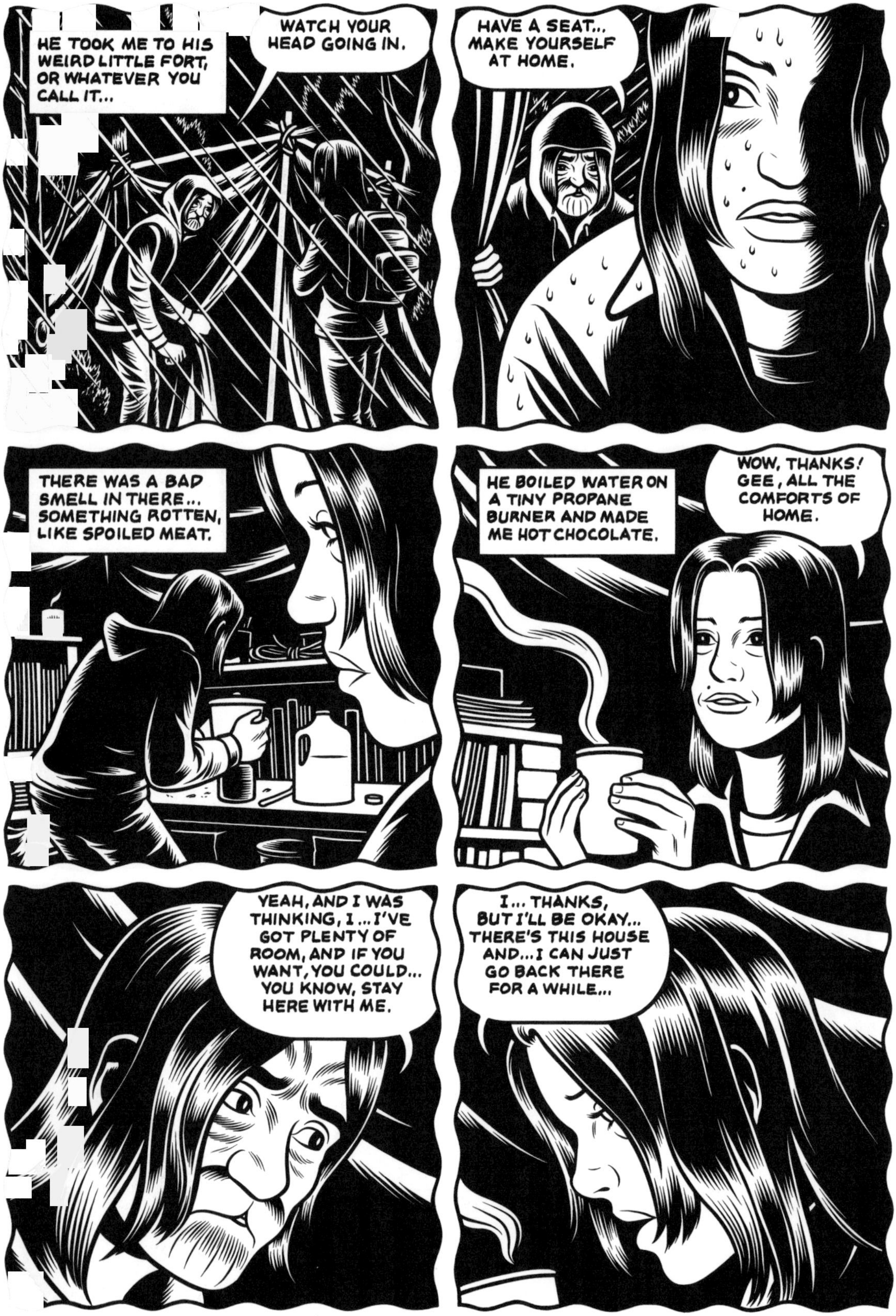
HE TOOK ME TO HIS WEIRD LITTLE FORT, OR WHATEVER YOU CALL IT...
WATCH YOUR HEAD GOING IN.
HAVE A SEAT... MAKE YOURSELF AT HOME.
THERE WAS A BAD SMELL IN THERE... SOMETHING ROTTEN, LIKE SPOILED MEAT.
HE BOILED WATER ON A TINY PROPANE BURNER AND MADE ME HOT CHOCOLATE.
WOW, THANKS! GEE, ALL THE COMFORTS OF HOME.
YEAH, AND I WAS THINKING, I... I'VE GOT PLENTY OF ROOM, AND IF YOU WANT, YOU COULD... YOU KNOW, STAY HERE WITH ME.
I... THANKS, BUT I'LL BE OKAY... THERE'S THIS HOUSE AND... I CAN JUST GO BACK THERE FOR A WHILE...

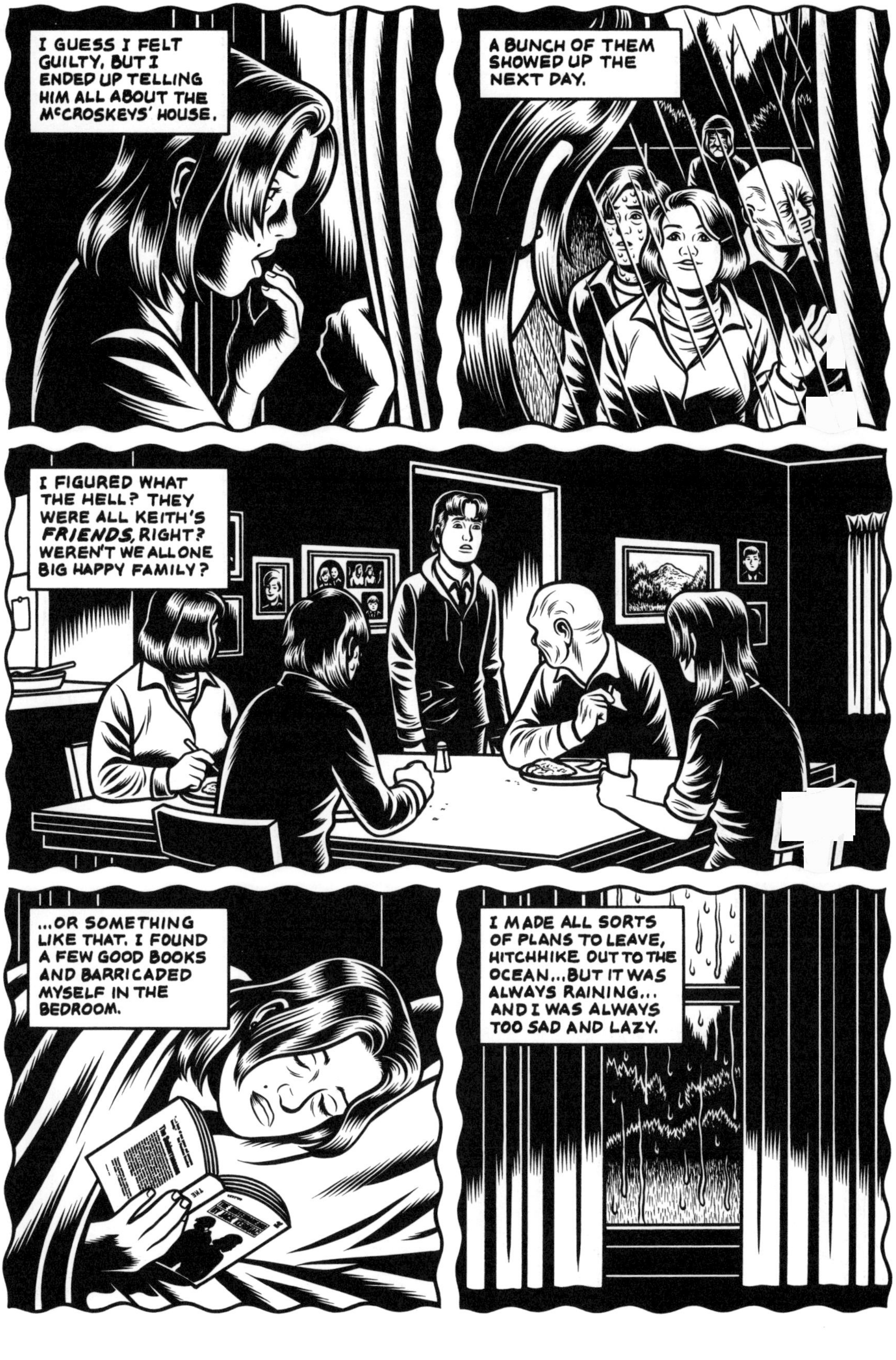

I GUESS I FELT GUILTY, BUT I ENDED UP TELLING HIM ALL ABOUT THE McCROSKEYS' HOUSE.
A BUNCH OF THEM SHOWED UP THE NEXT DAY.
I FIGURED WHAT THE HELL? THEY WERE ALL KEITH'S *FRIENDS*, RIGHT? WEREN'T WE ALL ONE BIG HAPPY FAMILY?
...OR SOMETHING LIKE THAT. I FOUND A FEW GOOD BOOKS AND BARRICADED MYSELF IN THE BEDROOM.
I MADE ALL SORTS OF PLANS TO LEAVE, HITCHHIKE OUT TO THE OCEAN...BUT IT WAS ALWAYS RAINING... AND I WAS ALWAYS TOO SAD AND LAZY.

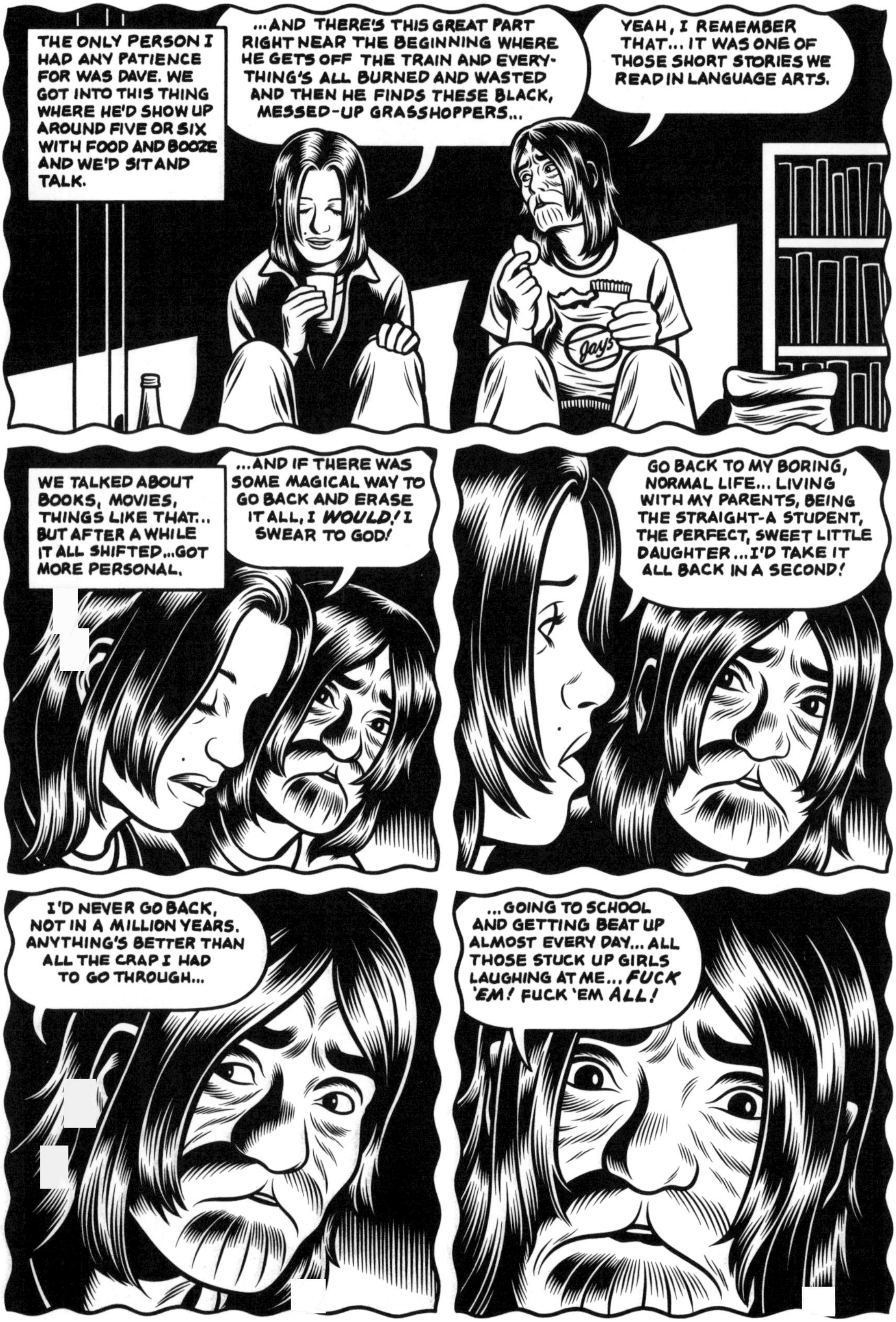
THE ONLY PERSON I HAD ANY PATIENCE FOR WAS DAVE. WE GOT INTO THIS THING WHERE HE'D SHOW UP AROUND FIVE OR SIX WITH FOOD AND BOOZE AND WE'D SIT AND TALK.
...AND THERE'S THIS GREAT PART RIGHT NEAR THE BEGINNING WHERE HE GETS OFF THE TRAIN AND EVERY-THING'S ALL BURNED AND WASTED AND THEN HE FINDS THESE BLACK, MESSED-UP GRASSHOPPERS...
YEAH, I REMEMBER THAT... IT WAS ONE OF THOSE SHORT STORIES WE READ IN LANGUAGE ARTS.
Jays
WE TALKED ABOUT BOOKS, MOVIES, THINGS LIKE THAT... BUT AFTER A WHILE IT ALL SHIFTED...GOT MORE PERSONAL.
...AND IF THERE WAS SOME MAGICAL WAY TO GO BACK AND ERASE IT ALL, I *WOULD!* I SWEAR TO GOD!
GO BACK TO MY BORING, NORMAL LIFE... LIVING WITH MY PARENTS, BEING THE STRAIGHT-A STUDENT, THE PERFECT, SWEET LITTLE DAUGHTER ...I'D TAKE IT ALL BACK IN A SECOND!
I'D NEVER GO BACK, NOT IN A MILLION YEARS. ANYTHING'S BETTER THAN ALL THE CRAP I HAD TO GO THROUGH...
...GOING TO SCHOOL AND GETTING BEAT UP ALMOST EVERY DAY... ALL THOSE STUCK UP GIRLS LAUGHING AT ME... *FUCK 'EM!* FUCK 'EM *ALL!*

YOU TOLD ME YOU DON'T REMEMBER ME FROM FRENCH CLASS BUT I REMEMBER YOU... AND YOU WEREN'T LIKE ALL THE REST OF THEM.

YOU WERE BEAUTIFUL AND POPULAR BUT YOU WERE NICE...YOU TREATED ME LIKE A NORMAL HUMAN BEING.

OH, I REMEMBERED HIM ALRIGHT...HIM AND HIS FRIENDS. GEEKS...LOSERS. THE SHY, UGLY KIDS WHO LAUGHED TOO LOUD, WORE THE WRONG CLOTHES.

NICE? I MAY HAVE BEEN NICE TO HIM BUT I WAS AS GUILTY AS EVERYONE ELSE... I THOUGHT HE WAS CREEPY. I DIDN'T WANT TO HAVE ANYTHING TO DO WITH HIM.

AT LEAST HE HAD FRIENDS. YOU'D SEE THEM IN THE LUNCHROOM, PLAYING CHESS, READING COMICS... GETTING FOOD THROWN AT THEM.

...AND THE GIRLS...SOME OF THEM EVEN HAD GIRLFRIENDS.

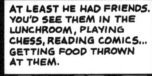

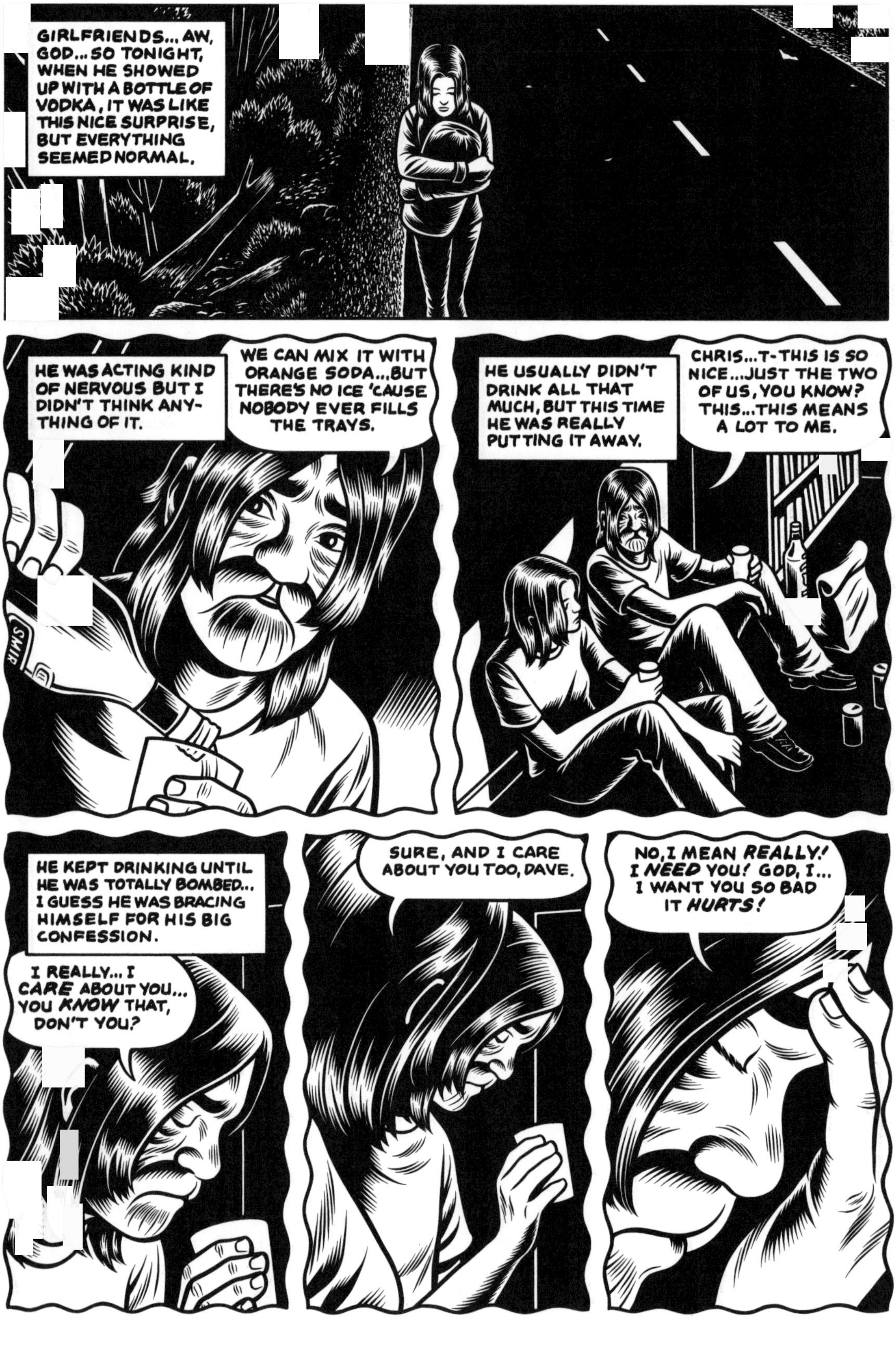
GIRLFRIENDS... AW, GOD... SO TONIGHT, WHEN HE SHOWED UP WITH A BOTTLE OF VODKA, IT WAS LIKE THIS NICE SURPRISE, BUT EVERYTHING SEEMED NORMAL.
HE WAS ACTING KIND OF NERVOUS BUT I DIDN'T THINK ANY-THING OF IT.
WE CAN MIX IT WITH ORANGE SODA...BUT THERE'S NO ICE 'CAUSE NOBODY EVER FILLS THE TRAYS.
HE USUALLY DIDN'T DRINK ALL THAT MUCH, BUT THIS TIME HE WAS REALLY PUTTING IT AWAY.
CHRIS...T-THIS IS SO NICE...JUST THE TWO OF US, YOU KNOW? THIS...THIS MEANS A LOT TO ME.
HE KEPT DRINKING UNTIL HE WAS TOTALLY BOMBED... I GUESS HE WAS BRACING HIMSELF FOR HIS BIG CONFESSION.
I REALLY... I *CARE* ABOUT YOU... YOU *KNOW* THAT, DON'T YOU?
SURE, AND I CARE ABOUT YOU TOO, DAVE.
NO, I MEAN *REALLY!* I *NEED* YOU! GOD, I... I WANT YOU SO BAD IT *HURTS!*

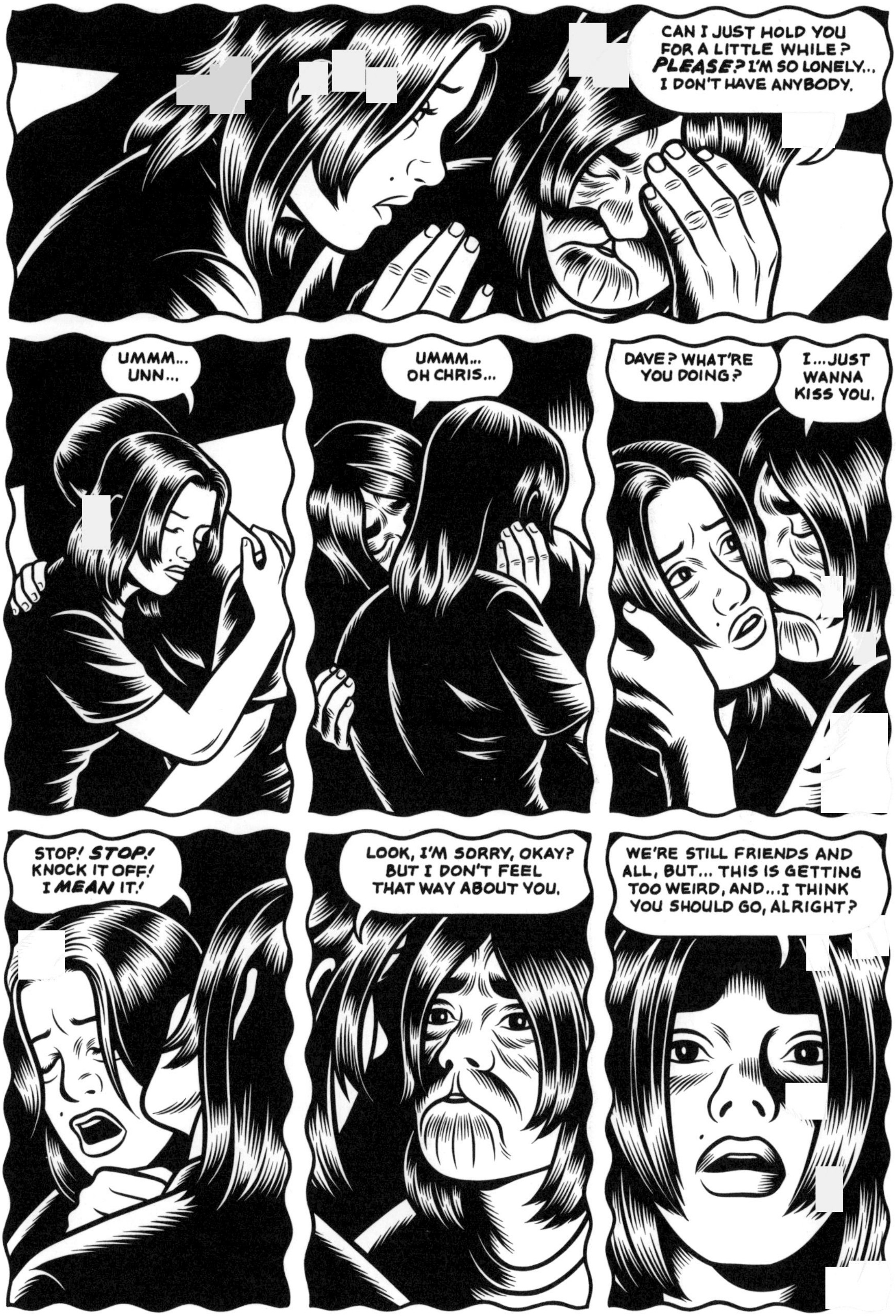
CAN I JUST HOLD YOU FOR A LITTLE WHILE? PLEASE? I'M SO LONELY... I DON'T HAVE ANYBODY.
UMMM... UNN...
UMMM... OH CHRIS...
DAVE? WHAT'RE YOU DOING?
I...JUST WANNA KISS YOU.
STOP! STOP! KNOCK IT OFF! I MEAN IT!
LOOK, I'M SORRY, OKAY? BUT I DON'T FEEL THAT WAY ABOUT YOU.
WE'RE STILL FRIENDS AND ALL, BUT... THIS IS GETTING TOO WEIRD, AND...I THINK YOU SHOULD GO, ALRIGHT?

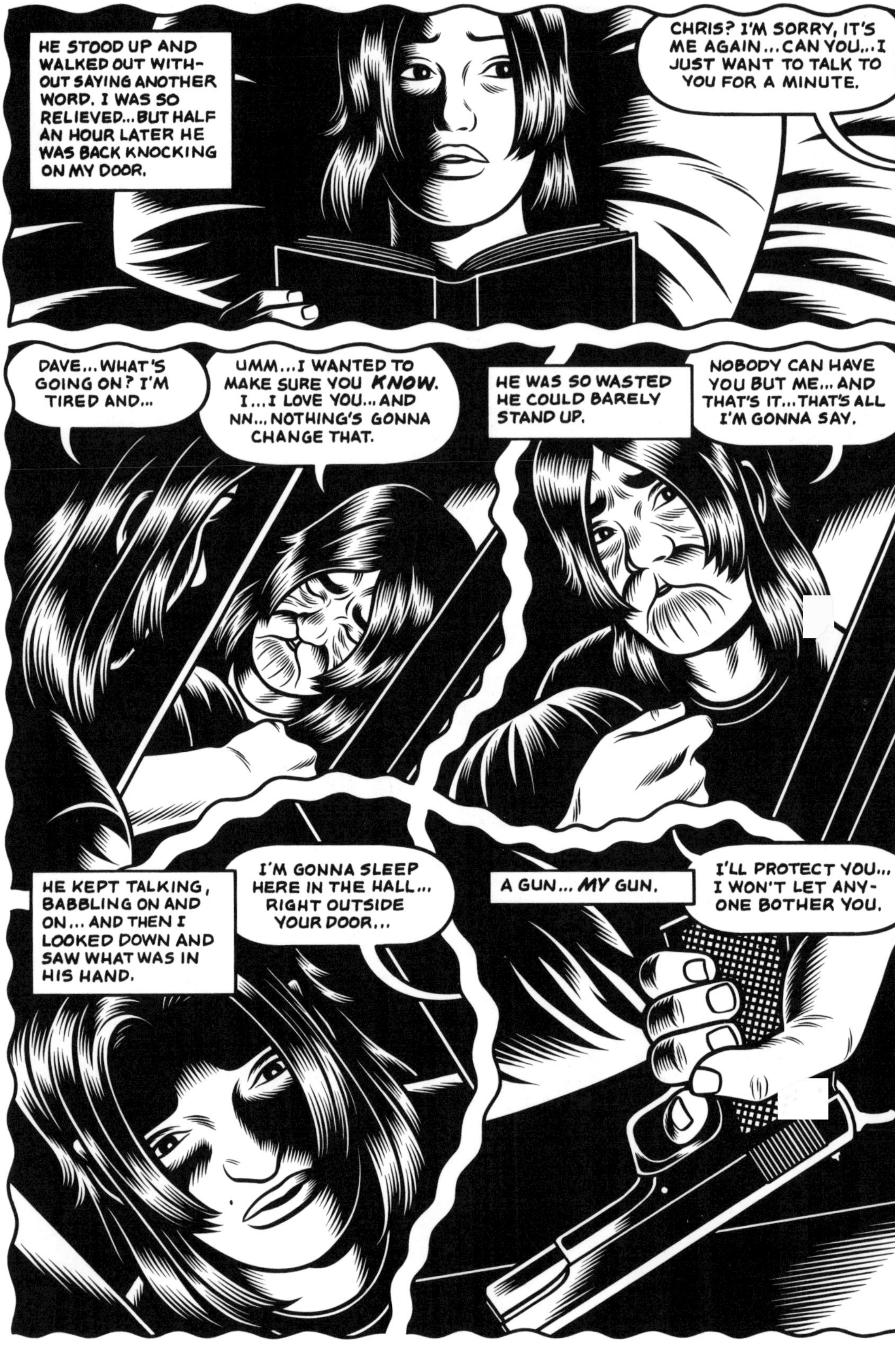

HE STOOD UP AND WALKED OUT WITHOUT SAYING ANOTHER WORD. I WAS SO RELIEVED... BUT HALF AN HOUR LATER HE WAS BACK KNOCKING ON MY DOOR.
CHRIS? I'M SORRY, IT'S ME AGAIN... CAN YOU... I JUST WANT TO TALK TO YOU FOR A MINUTE.
DAVE... WHAT'S GOING ON? I'M TIRED AND...
UMM... I WANTED TO MAKE SURE YOU *KNOW*. I... I LOVE YOU... AND NN... NOTHING'S GONNA CHANGE THAT.
HE WAS SO WASTED HE COULD BARELY STAND UP.
NOBODY CAN HAVE YOU BUT ME... AND THAT'S IT... THAT'S ALL I'M GONNA SAY.
HE KEPT TALKING, BABBLING ON AND ON... AND THEN I LOOKED DOWN AND SAW WHAT WAS IN HIS HAND.
I'M GONNA SLEEP HERE IN THE HALL... RIGHT OUTSIDE YOUR DOOR...
A GUN... *MY* GUN.
I'LL PROTECT YOU... I WON'T LET ANYONE BOTHER YOU.

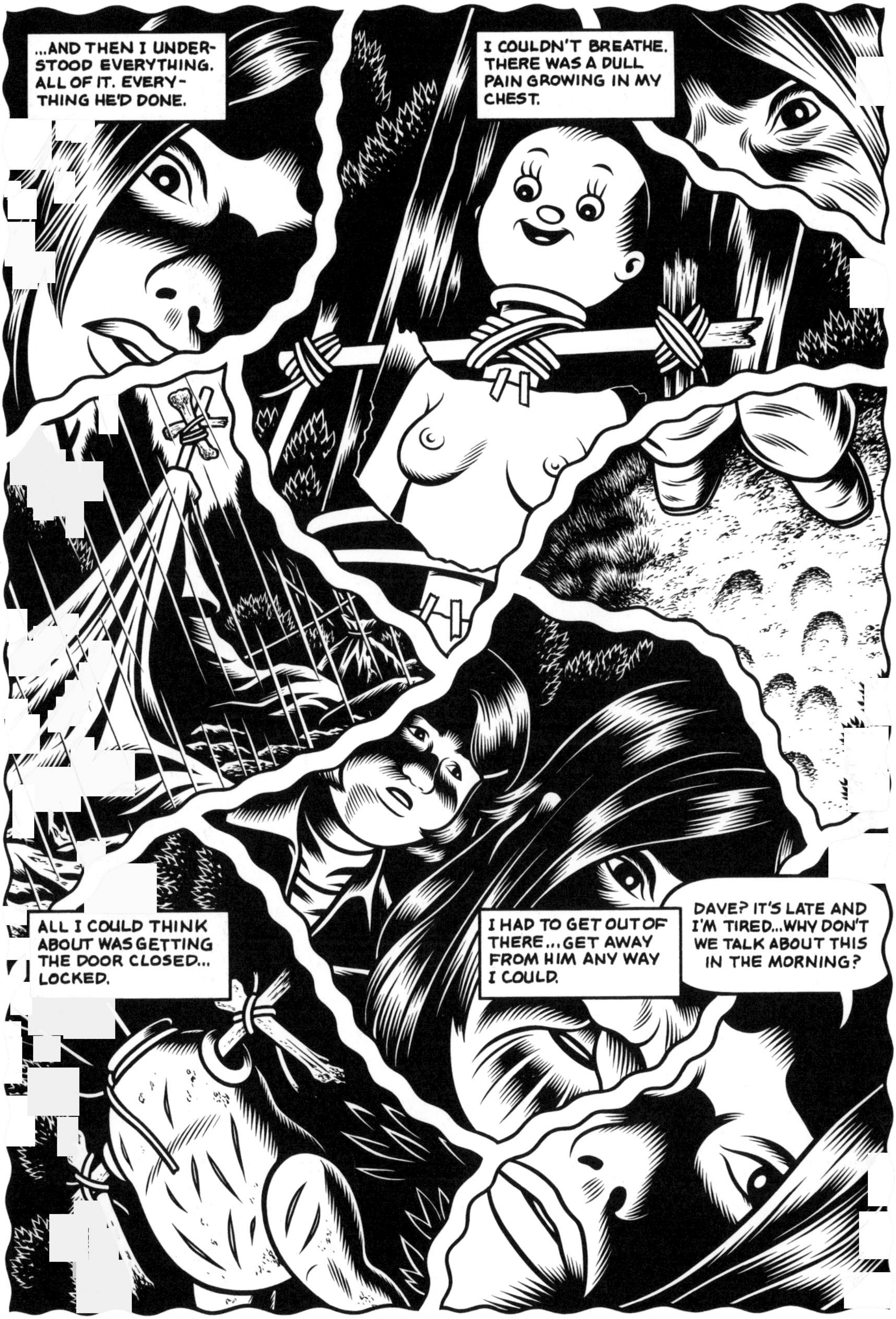
...AND THEN I UNDERSTOOD EVERYTHING. ALL OF IT. EVERYTHING HE'D DONE.
I COULDN'T BREATHE. THERE WAS A DULL PAIN GROWING IN MY CHEST.
ALL I COULD THINK ABOUT WAS GETTING THE DOOR CLOSED... LOCKED.
I HAD TO GET OUT OF THERE... GET AWAY FROM HIM ANY WAY I COULD.
DAVE? IT'S LATE AND I'M TIRED... WHY DON'T WE TALK ABOUT THIS IN THE MORNING?

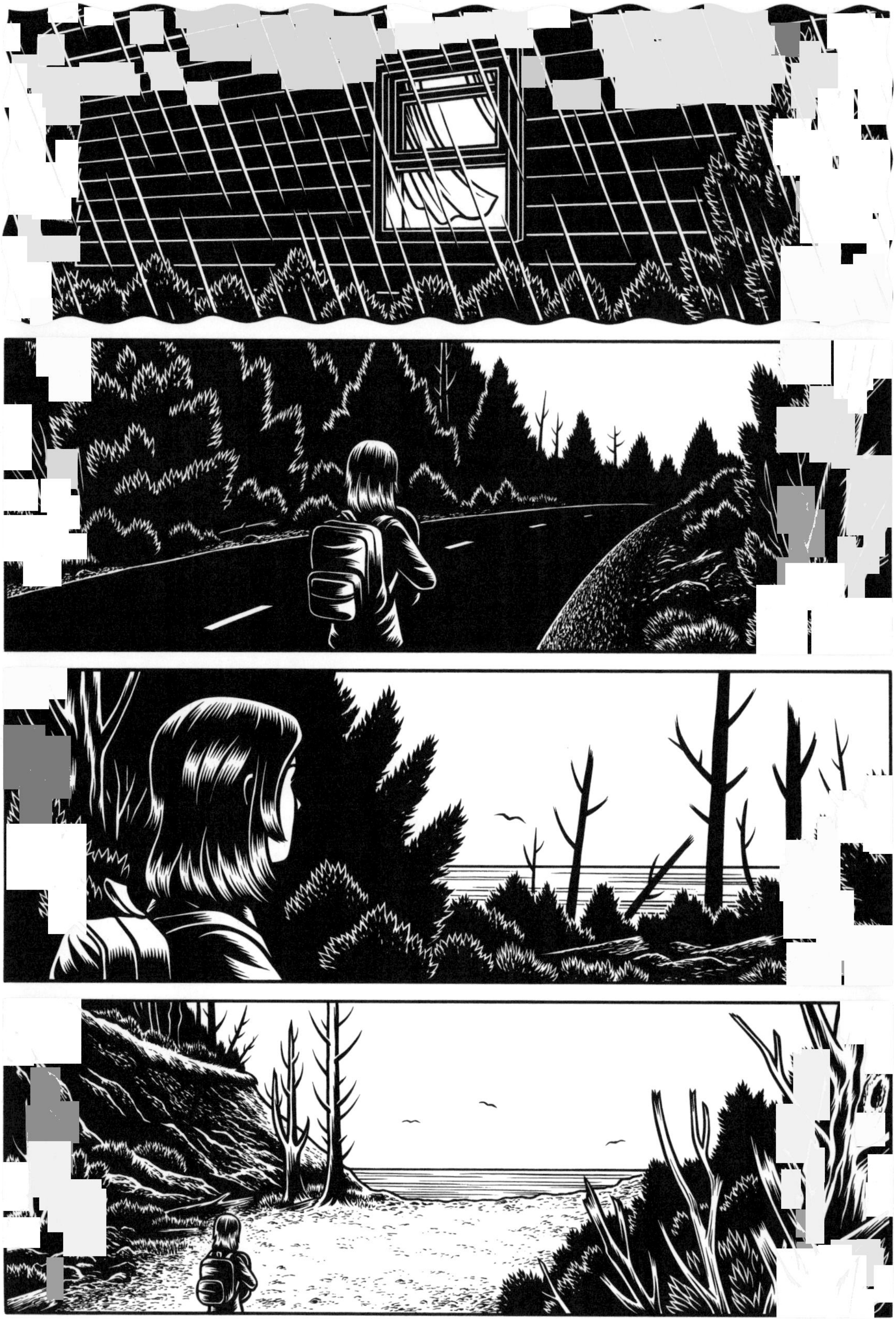

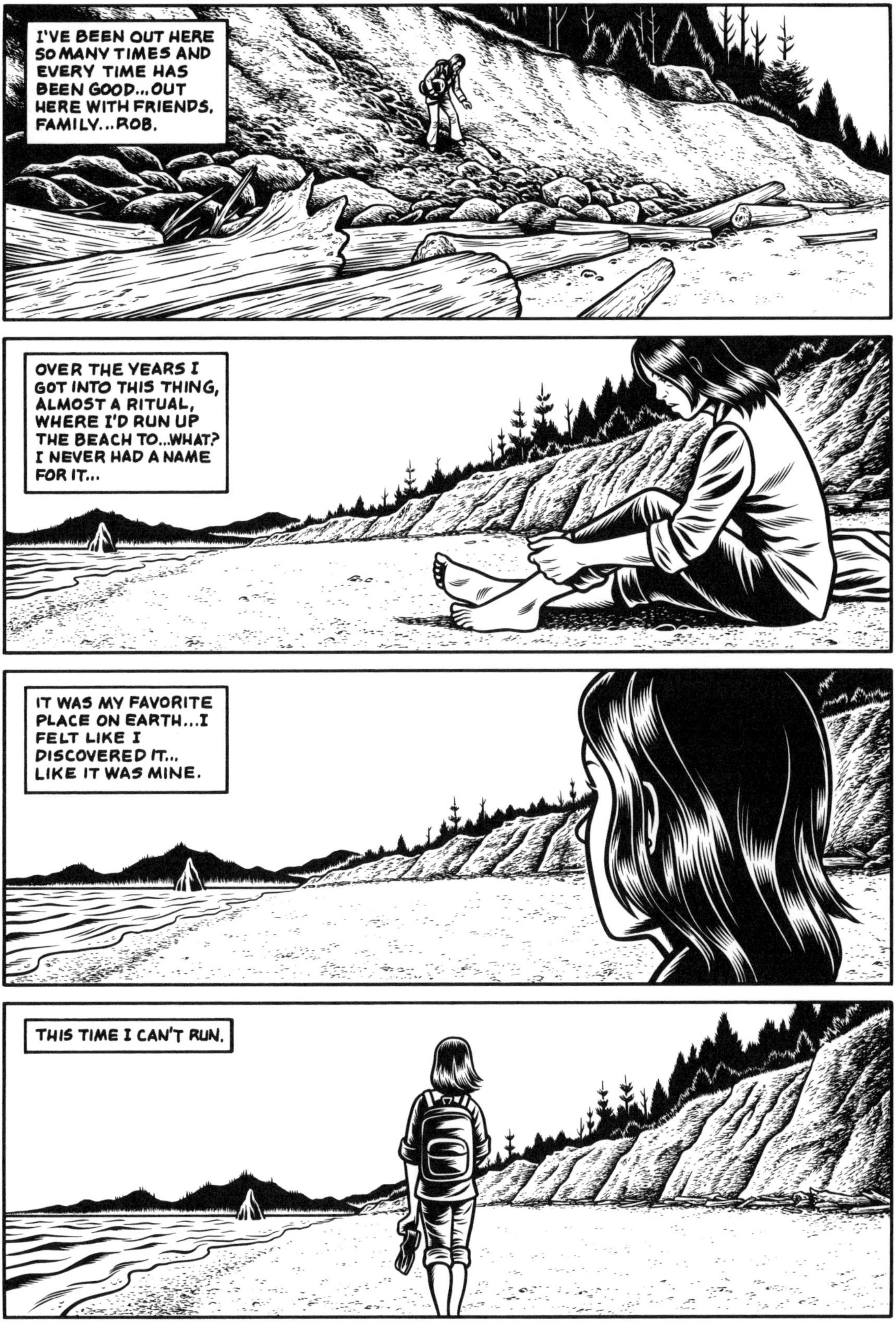
I'VE BEEN OUT HERE SO MANY TIMES AND EVERY TIME HAS BEEN GOOD... OUT HERE WITH FRIENDS, FAMILY... ROB.
OVER THE YEARS I GOT INTO THIS THING, ALMOST A RITUAL, WHERE I'D RUN UP THE BEACH TO... WHAT? I NEVER HAD A NAME FOR IT...
IT WAS MY FAVORITE PLACE ON EARTH... I FELT LIKE I DISCOVERED IT... LIKE IT WAS MINE.
THIS TIME I CAN'T RUN.

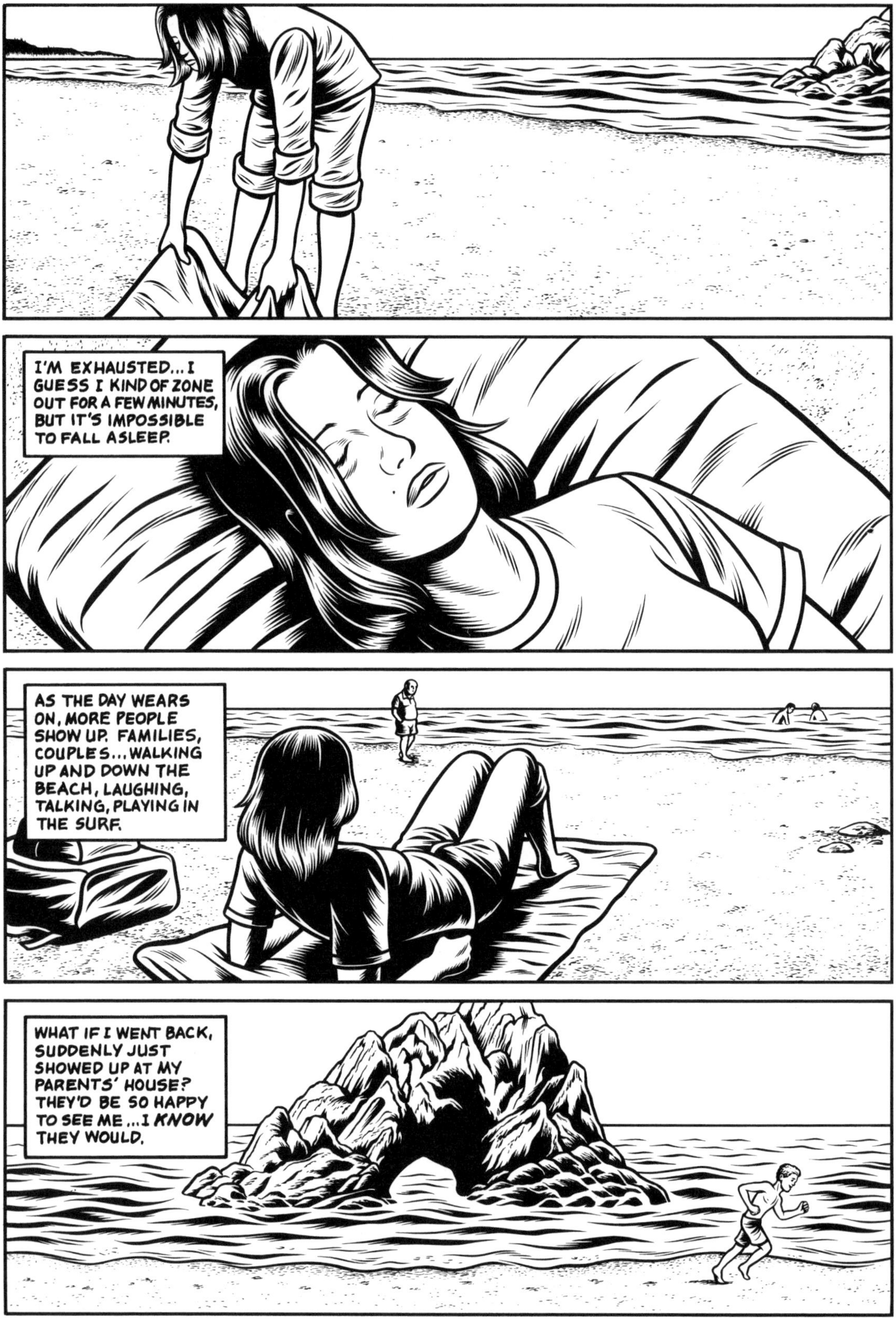
I'M EXHAUSTED... I GUESS I KIND OF ZONE OUT FOR A FEW MINUTES, BUT IT'S IMPOSSIBLE TO FALL ASLEEP.
AS THE DAY WEARS ON, MORE PEOPLE SHOW UP. FAMILIES, COUPLES... WALKING UP AND DOWN THE BEACH, LAUGHING, TALKING, PLAYING IN THE SURF.
WHAT IF I WENT BACK, SUDDENLY JUST SHOWED UP AT MY PARENTS' HOUSE? THEY'D BE SO HAPPY TO SEE ME... I *KNOW* THEY WOULD.

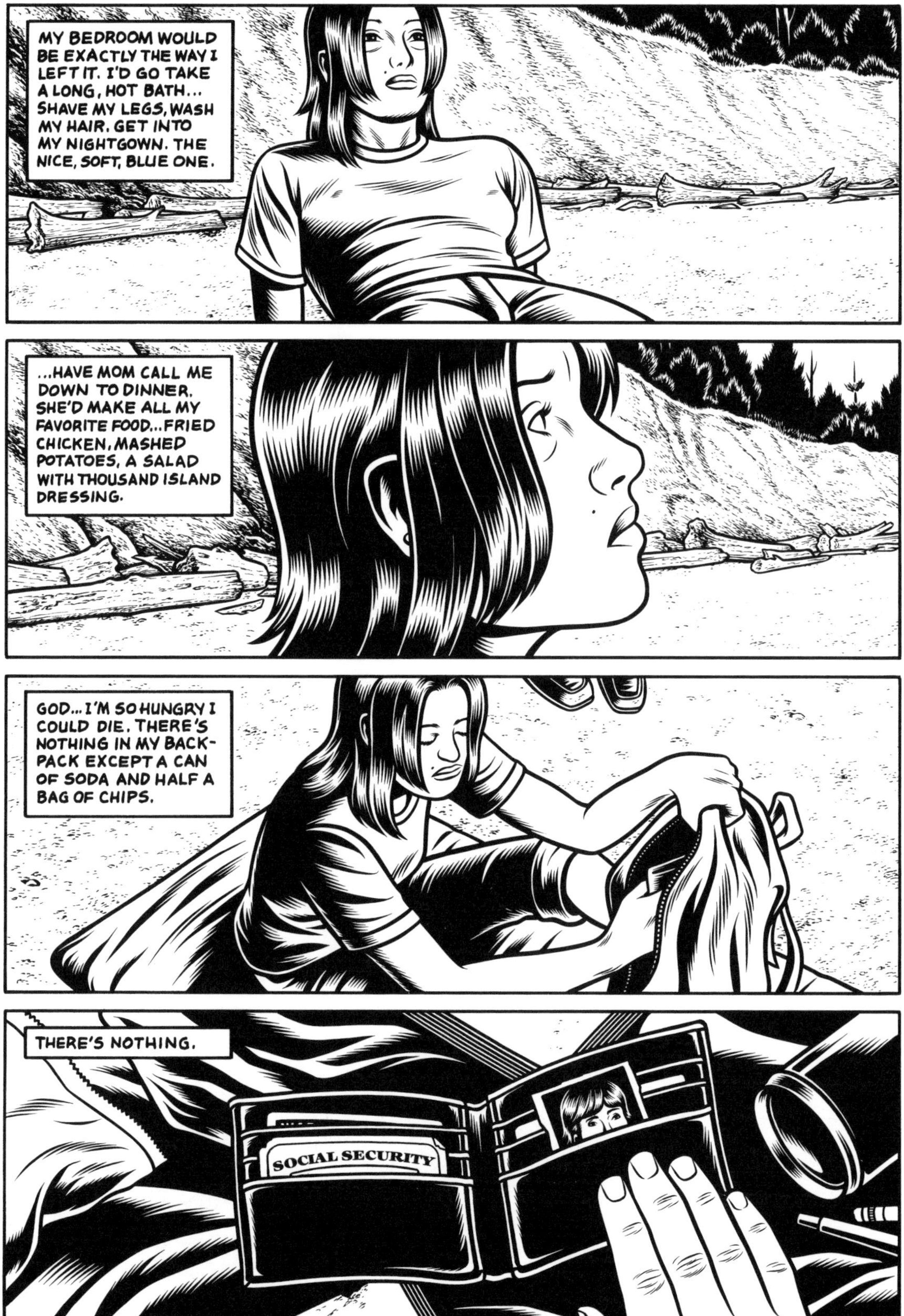
MY BEDROOM WOULD BE EXACTLY THE WAY I LEFT IT. I'D GO TAKE A LONG, HOT BATH... SHAVE MY LEGS, WASH MY HAIR. GET INTO MY NIGHTGOWN. THE NICE, SOFT, BLUE ONE.
...HAVE MOM CALL ME DOWN TO DINNER. SHE'D MAKE ALL MY FAVORITE FOOD... FRIED CHICKEN, MASHED POTATOES, A SALAD WITH THOUSAND ISLAND DRESSING.
GOD... I'M SO HUNGRY I COULD DIE. THERE'S NOTHING IN MY BACK-PACK EXCEPT A CAN OF SODA AND HALF A BAG OF CHIPS.
THERE'S NOTHING.
SOCIAL SECURITY

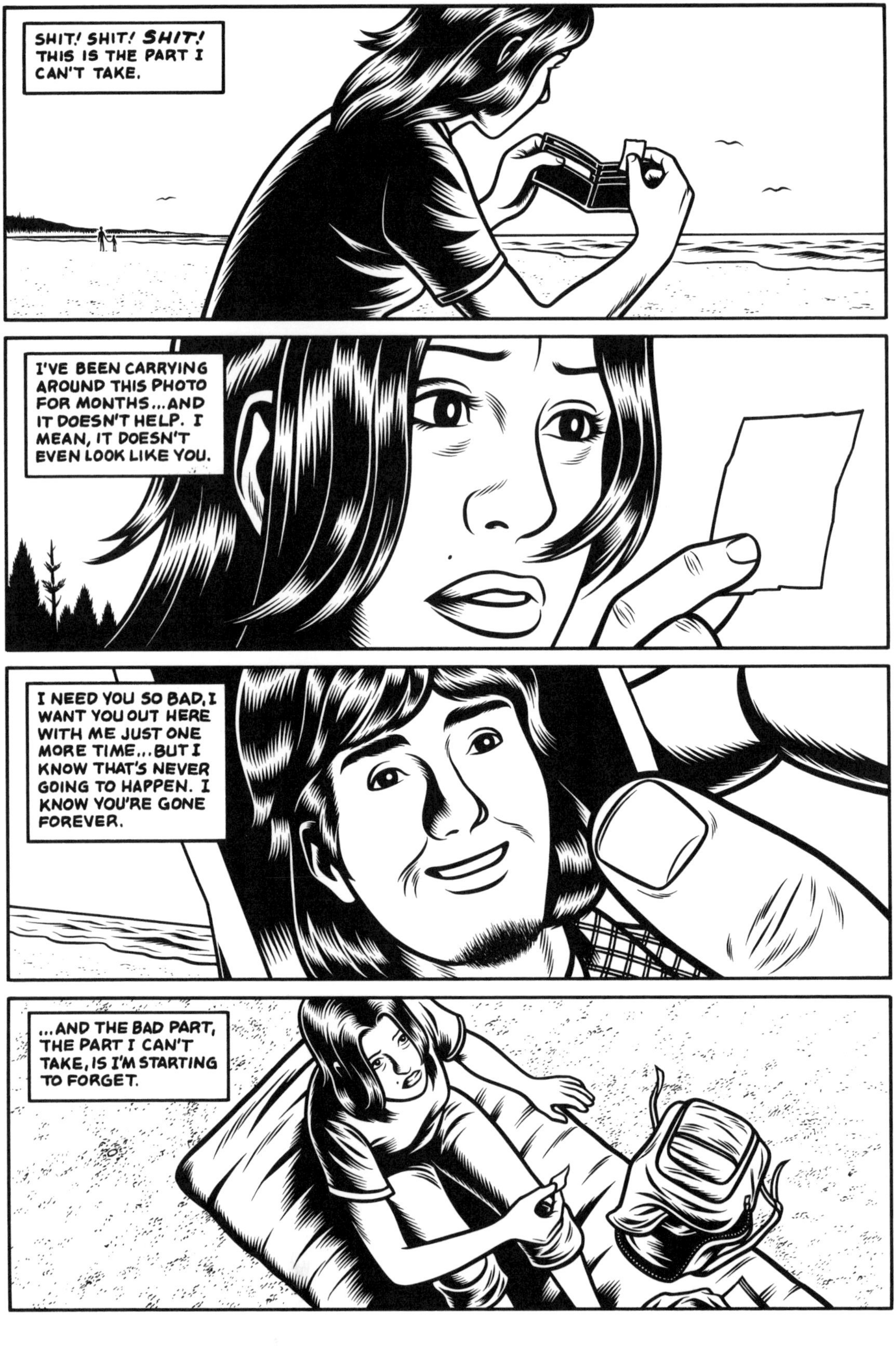
SHIT! SHIT! SHIT!
THIS IS THE PART I CAN'T TAKE.
I'VE BEEN CARRYING AROUND THIS PHOTO FOR MONTHS... AND IT DOESN'T HELP. I MEAN, IT DOESN'T EVEN LOOK LIKE YOU.
I NEED YOU SO BAD, I WANT YOU OUT HERE WITH ME JUST ONE MORE TIME... BUT I KNOW THAT'S NEVER GOING TO HAPPEN. I KNOW YOU'RE GONE FOREVER.
...AND THE BAD PART, THE PART I CAN'T TAKE, IS I'M STARTING TO FORGET.

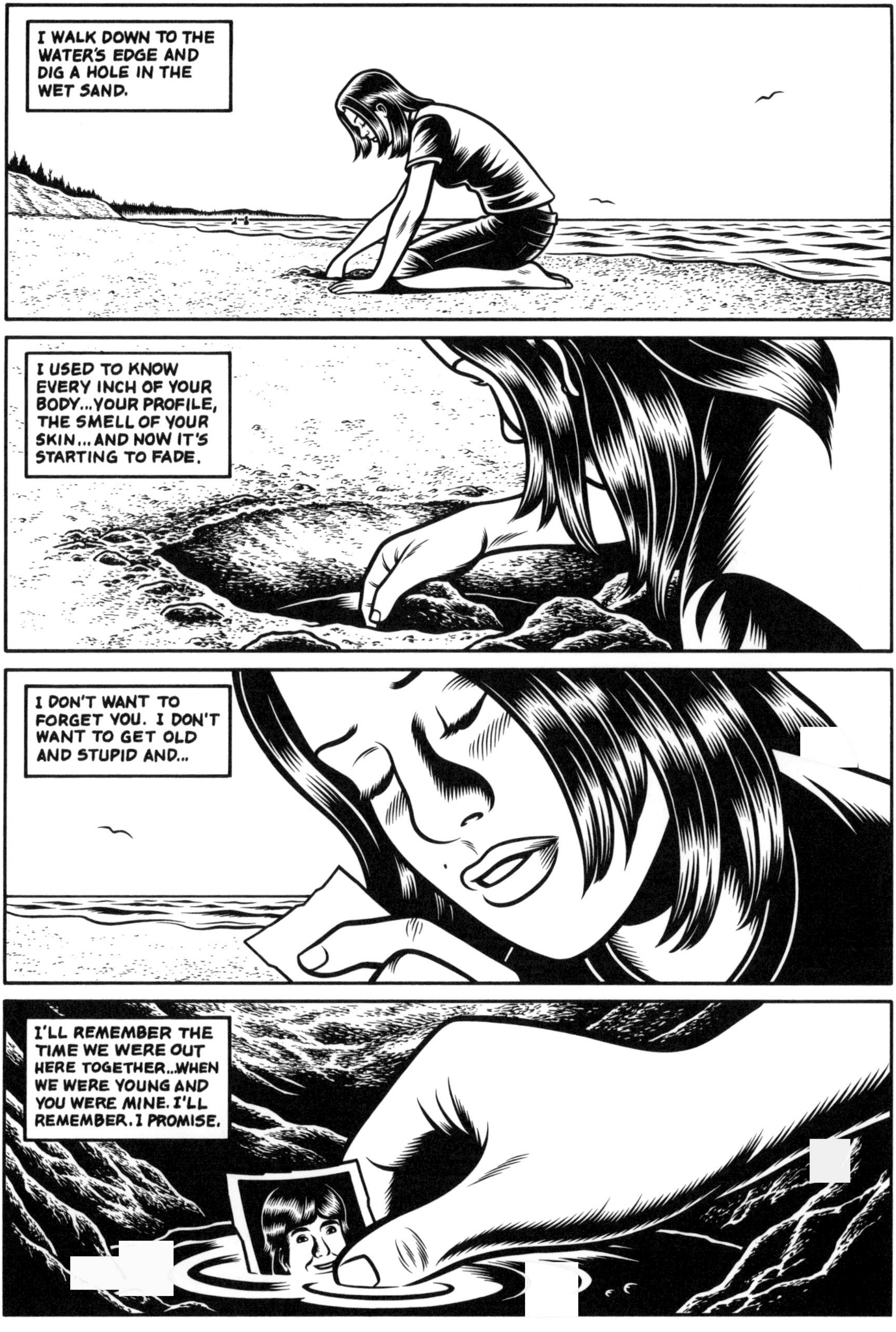
I WALK DOWN TO THE WATER'S EDGE AND DIG A HOLE IN THE WET SAND.
I USED TO KNOW EVERY INCH OF YOUR BODY...YOUR PROFILE, THE SMELL OF YOUR SKIN... AND NOW IT'S STARTING TO FADE.
I DON'T WANT TO FORGET YOU. I DON'T WANT TO GET OLD AND STUPID AND...
I'LL REMEMBER THE TIME WE WERE OUT HERE TOGETHER...WHEN WE WERE YOUNG AND YOU WERE MINE. I'LL REMEMBER. I PROMISE.

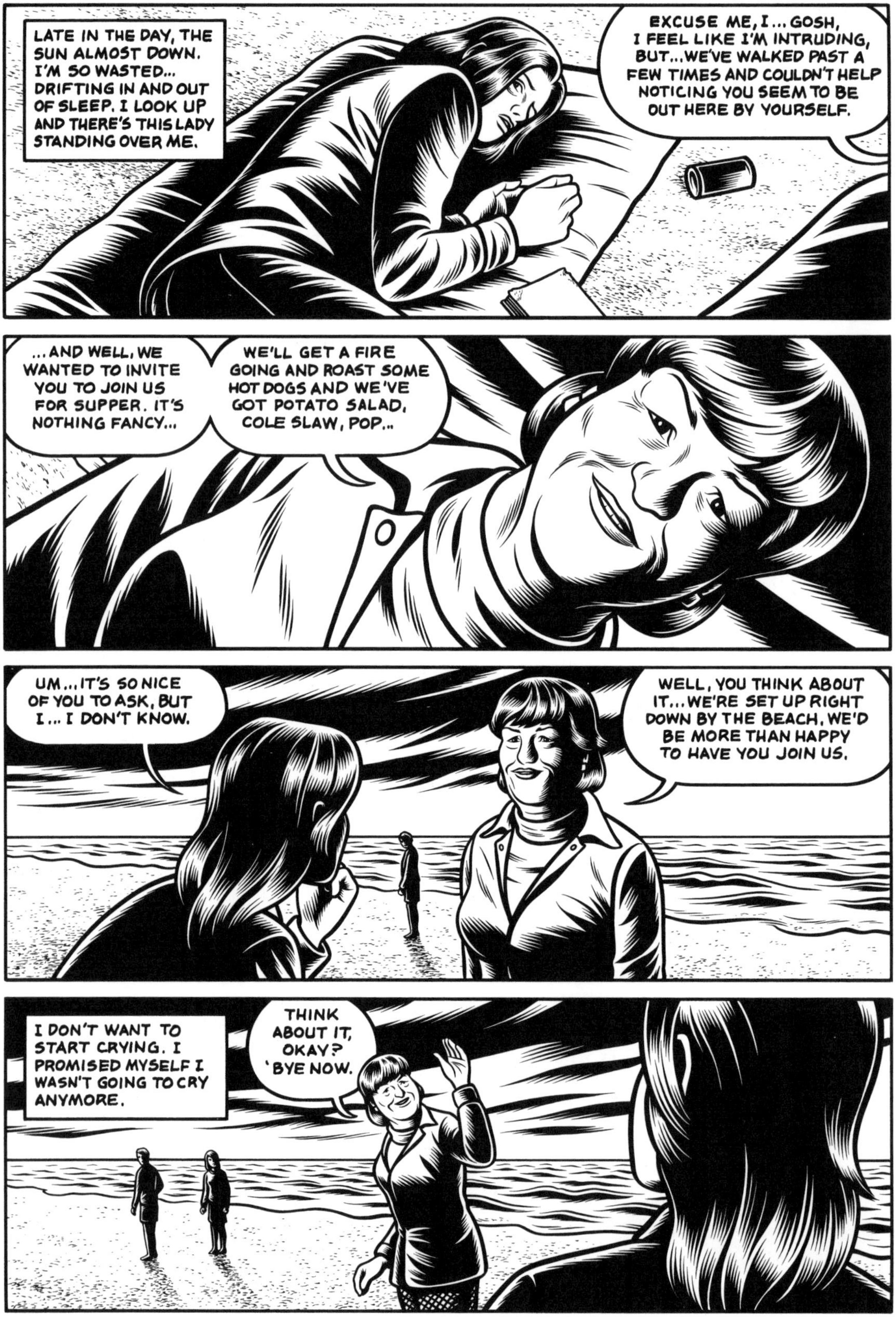
LATE IN THE DAY, THE SUN ALMOST DOWN. I'M SO WASTED... DRIFTING IN AND OUT OF SLEEP. I LOOK UP AND THERE'S THIS LADY STANDING OVER ME.
EXCUSE ME, I... GOSH, I FEEL LIKE I'M INTRUDING, BUT... WE'VE WALKED PAST A FEW TIMES AND COULDN'T HELP NOTICING YOU SEEM TO BE OUT HERE BY YOURSELF.
...AND WELL, WE WANTED TO INVITE YOU TO JOIN US FOR SUPPER. IT'S NOTHING FANCY...
WE'LL GET A FIRE GOING AND ROAST SOME HOT DOGS AND WE'VE GOT POTATO SALAD, COLE SLAW, POP..
UM... IT'S SO NICE OF YOU TO ASK, BUT I... I DON'T KNOW.
WELL, YOU THINK ABOUT IT... WE'RE SET UP RIGHT DOWN BY THE BEACH. WE'D BE MORE THAN HAPPY TO HAVE YOU JOIN US.
I DON'T WANT TO START CRYING. I PROMISED MYSELF I WASN'T GOING TO CRY ANYMORE.
THINK ABOUT IT, OKAY? 'BYE NOW.

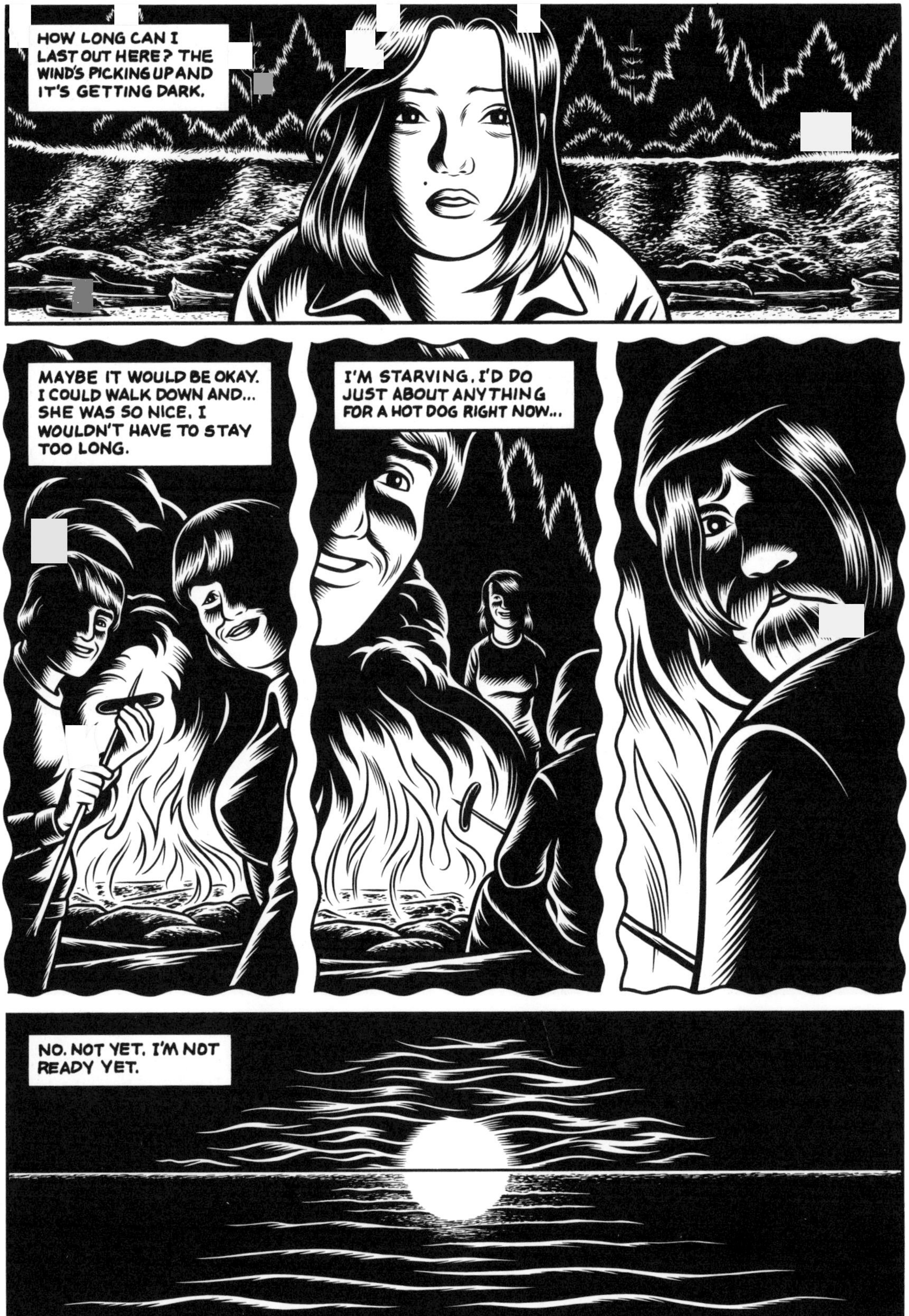
HOW LONG CAN I LAST OUT HERE? THE WIND'S PICKING UP AND IT'S GETTING DARK.
MAYBE IT WOULD BE OKAY. I COULD WALK DOWN AND... SHE WAS SO NICE. I WOULDN'T HAVE TO STAY TOO LONG.
I'M STARVING. I'D DO JUST ABOUT ANYTHING FOR A HOT DOG RIGHT NOW...
NO. NOT YET. I'M NOT READY YET.

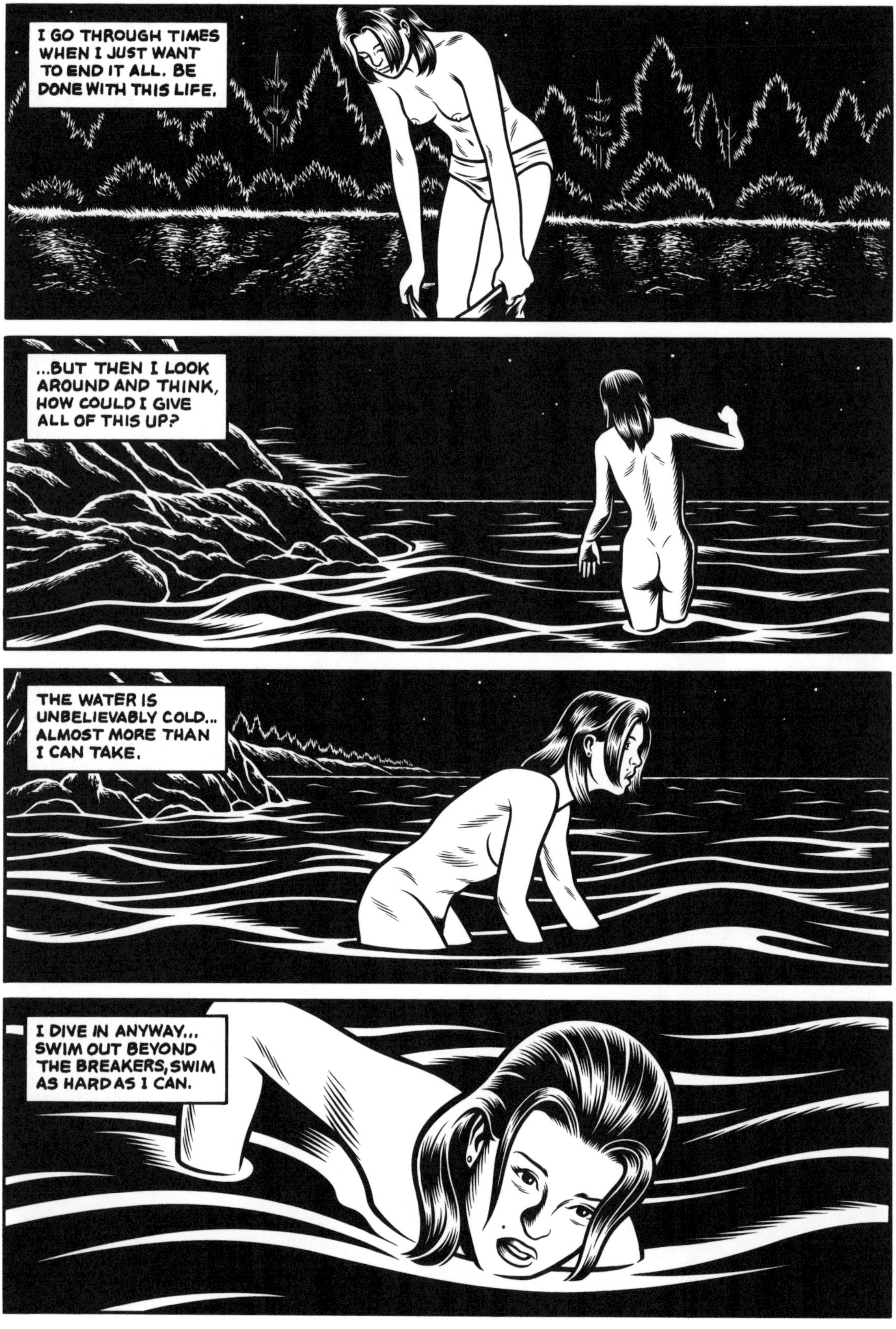
I GO THROUGH TIMES WHEN I JUST WANT TO END IT ALL. BE DONE WITH THIS LIFE.
...BUT THEN I LOOK AROUND AND THINK, HOW COULD I GIVE ALL OF THIS UP?
THE WATER IS UNBELIEVABLY COLD... ALMOST MORE THAN I CAN TAKE.
I DIVE IN ANYWAY... SWIM OUT BEYOND THE BREAKERS, SWIM AS HARD AS I CAN.

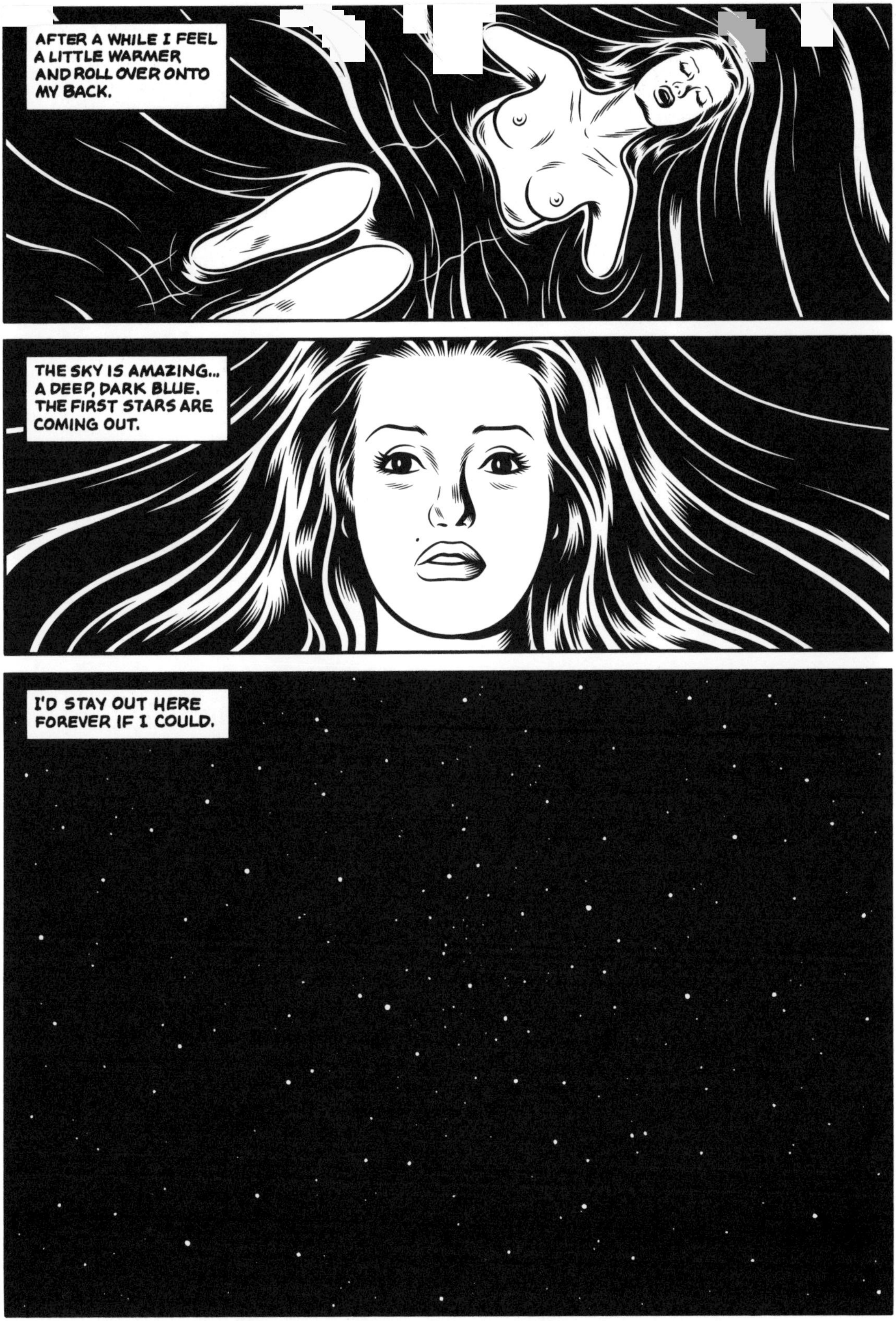

AFTER A WHILE I FEEL A LITTLE WARMER AND ROLL OVER ONTO MY BACK.
THE SKY IS AMAZING... A DEEP, DARK BLUE. THE FIRST STARS ARE COMING OUT.
I'D STAY OUT HERE FOREVER IF I COULD.

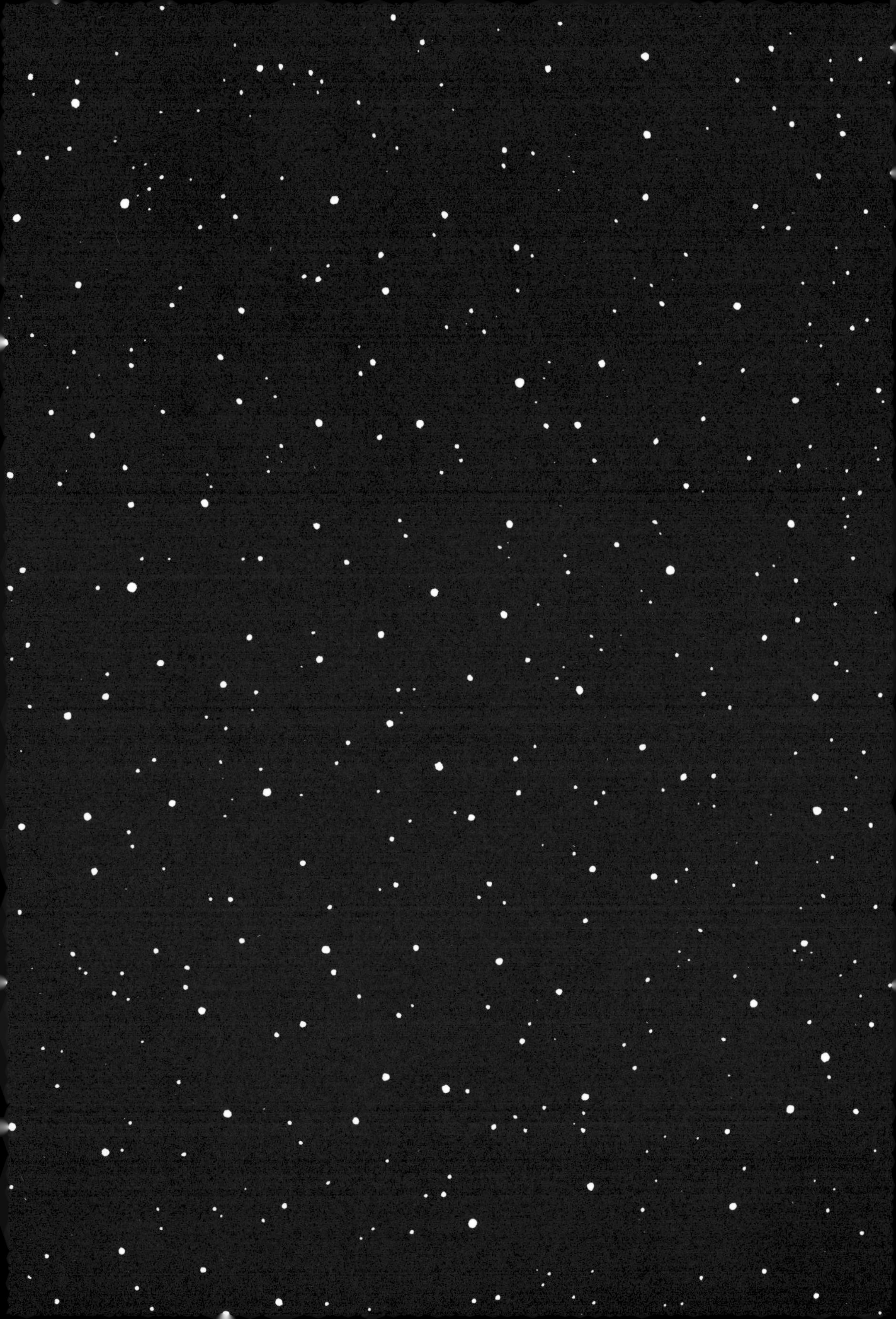

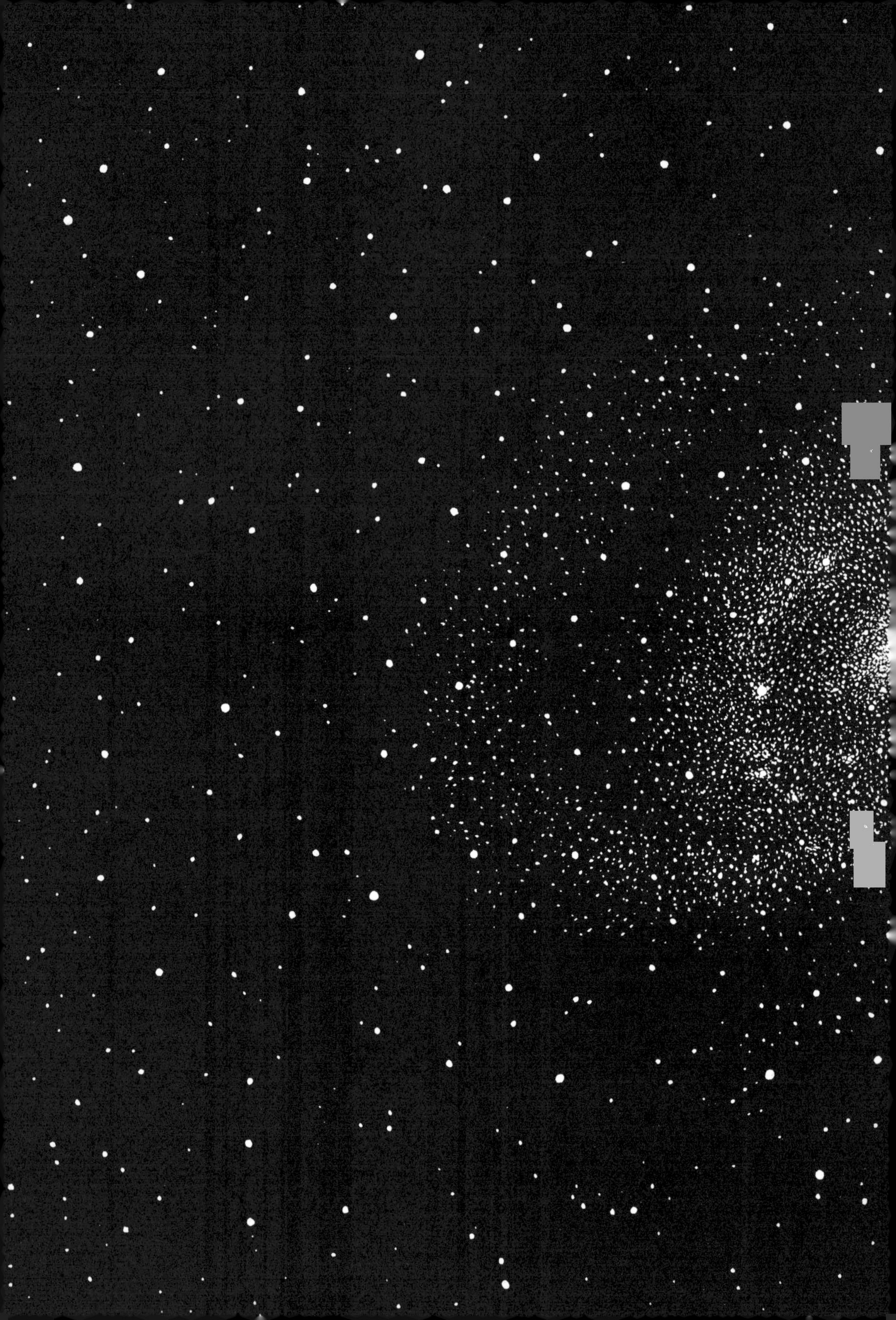